PRAISE FOR
CLIVE BARKER

"Barker's extravagantly unconventional inventions are ingenious refractions of our common quest to experience and understand the mysterious world around us and the mysteries within ourselves."
—*New York Times Book Review*

"A powerful and fascinating writer with a brilliant imagination . . . an outstanding storyteller."
—J. G. Ballard

"I think Clive Barker is so good I am almost literally tongue-tied."
—Stephen King

"Barker has an unparalleled talent for envisioning other worlds."
—*Washington Post Book World*

"[An] artist's eye for detail . . . a writer of stunning imagination."
—*Atlanta Journal & Constitution*

"Barker's work reads like a cross between Stephen King and Gabriel Garcia Marquez. He creates a world where our biggest fears appear to be our own dreams."
—*Boston Herald*

"Clive Barker hits a nerve dead-center and makes the brain squeal."
—*San Francisco Chronicle*

"Barker has been an amazing writer from his first appearance, with the great gifts of invention and commitment to his visions stamped on every page."
—Peter Straub

"[Clive Barker is] sexier than King and more inventive than Anne Rice."
—*Dallas Morning Star Telegram*

"Mr. Barker extends one's appreciation of the possible. He's a fine writer."
—*Wall Street Journal*

"Refreshing creativity and imagination."
—*Baltimore Sun*

ALSO BY CLIVE BARKER

The Books of Blood

The Damnation Game

Weaveworld

Cabal

The Hellbound Heart

Imajica

The Thief of Always

Everville

Incarnations

Forms of Heaven

Sacrament

Galilee

The Essential Clive Barker

THE GREAT AND SECRET SHOW

THE FIRST BOOK OF THE ART

CLIVE BARKER

HarperPerennial

A Division of HarperCollins*Publishers*

A hardcover edition of this book was published in 1989 by Harper & Row, Publishers, Inc. A mass market paperback edition was published in 1990 by HarperPaperbacks.

HarperCollins books may be purchased for educational, business, or sales promotional use. For information please write: Special Markets Department, HarperCollins Publishers Inc., 10 East 53rd Street, New York, NY 10022.

First HarperPerennial edition published 1999

Designed by Elliott Beard

The Library of Congress has catalogued the hardcover edition as follows:

Barker, Clive, 1952–
    The great and secret show : the first book of the art / Clive Barker. — 1st U.S. ed.
        p.   cm.
    "First published in Great Britain in 1989 by Williams Collins Sons & Co. Ltd." — T.p. verso
ISBN 0-06-016276-7
I. Title
PR6052.A6475G7 1989
823'.914—dc20   89-45787

ISBN 0-06-093316-X (pbk.)

05 06 ❖/RRD 10 9 8 7 6 5

CONTENTS

PART ONE   THE MESSENGER   1

PART TWO   THE LEAGUE OF VIRGINS   59

PART THREE   FREE SPIRITS   103

PART FOUR   PRIMAL SCENES   169

PART FIVE   SLAVES AND LOVERS   295

PART SIX   IN SECRETS, MOST REVEALED   381

PART SEVEN   SOULS AT ZERO   505

Memory, prophecy and fantasy—
the past, the future and
the dreaming moment between—
are all one country,
living one immortal day.

To know that is Wisdom.

To use it is the Art.

INTRODUCTION

I learned early in my short academic life that I have very little capacity for abstract thinking. At that time I was a student of philosophy, and I'd entered the field out of a passion for metaphysics, only to discover that much modern philosophical debate sounds more like a discussion between two mathematicians than it does an exchange on what I then considered (indeed *still* consider) the essential issues of our lives: the intricacies of belief, the function of our imaginations, the nature of mind.

Faced with the challenge of "philosophical equations" I found myself adrift. My head simply refused to connect with these abstractions. I could talk about God; numbers left me speechless.

I began to realize that I was a literalist, and a fairly extreme one. There's divine revelation to be discovered in the rarifications of mathematics, no doubt, but that would always be beyond my grasp. There was, however, a strange compensation. If I was deficient in my skills as an abstract thinker, I was blessed with an extra helping of the ability to bring concrete images into my mind's eye. A perfectly useless skill if you're learning logic, of course, but useful when it comes to turning ideas into literary reality.

Paradoxically I first encountered the idea that lies at the heart of *The Great and Secret Show* in my philosophy classes. One of the lecturers made a brief and somewhat disparaging reference to Carl Jung's theory of the collective unconscious, and it instantly piqued my interest. Jung's psychoanalytical writings offer a variety of descriptions of the collective unconscious, and they're not always consistent. But it comes down to this: he suggests that despite the fact that we seem—as nations, as tribes, as individuals—very different from one another, there is a pool of ancient and archetypal images that lies beneath our myriad variations, and these images recur with uncanny frequency in dreams and visions, in mythology and folklore and urban myth. Breaking with Freud—whose theories often use mythological models to present a reductionist, even mechanistic, picture of our interior lives—Jung was clearly drawn to the idea that the collective unconscious offers us some glimpse of how we might interact with the divine. These images are globally recognized, he suggested, because they are part of something greater than the individual mind, but of which the individual still partakes in certain states.

The notion appealed to me for many reasons, not least that I could immediately conjure up its physical analogue. It was a sea. A place where we swim—in sleep, or some other altered state—and there encounter forms that we then bring back with us into the waking world. Sometimes we encounter one another there. Sometimes, we encounter the divine. We also, inevitably, meet forces that mean us harm. In short, the collective unconscious is another world; a world both strange to us—filled with images remote from our domestic lives—and closer than the concrete reality in which we live, because the door that leads into it lies *inside* us.

This idea stayed with me for several years before I found an adequate way to express it. I called the sea Quiddity, and slowly developed a mythology around it. Human beings would enter Quiddity, the dream-sea, three times, I decided. Once when they were born, once when they slept beside the person they would love most in their lives, and once before they died. Three life-changing immersions in the sea of the unconscious. Three confrontations with the secret show of our dreams.

When I sat down to write the book, it flowed easily enough. I wasn't living in California at the time, but I came here regularly for meetings related to my film projects, and felt confident enough to write a novel set here. I visited the Simi Valley, and spent a few days in various towns out there, getting a sense of the way they were designed. I researched the Mormon material, and dug deeply into the history of Trinity, which is the location for the penultimate scene of the novel. (If I sound oblique here, that's because I don't want to spoil the surprise in the narrative for new readers). I also made maps of Quiddity, for my own reference, though I suspected when I began the book that I wouldn't be staying in the dream-sea for very long. There would be other books, I knew, to follow this, in which I would investigate the place more fully. But I wanted to have some gazetteer for my reference at the beginning of the process, so that I could do some planning of later voyages.

There's no question that much of my enthusiasm for the idea was fueled by a romantic feeling for the sea. I was born in a city on a river, which in my childhood was filled with ships. My godfather was a ship's captain; my paternal grandfather, a ship's cook; my father, a navy man during the war, and later a dock worker; my brother, a ship's engineer. I, the black sheep artist of the family, was here returning to my own roots, exploring a dream of the sea in the form of a sea of dreams.

The other part of the book's metaphysical life is theater. It's there in the title. The Show is Mind; the endless parade of consciousness, which is—the book(s) will argue—evolution's pride and joy. Again, I surrounded the metaphor with pieces of invented mythology, postulating a poetic synthesis of alchemy and modern science as the means by which the Show becomes manifest. Its advocate is a substance I dubbed the *Nuncio*—the Messenger—which speeds up the process of evolution a thousandfold, advancing the physical and mental capacities of those it touches.

The idea that occult forces may make themselves visible in public ways, that the unconscious is on constant display in the world—the Ultimate Show—intrigues me because it refers back to the very process of making art. The subtitle of *The Great and Secret Show* is, not coincidentally, *The First Book of the Art*; and that Art (the final form of which will not become apparent until the third book of the trilogy) is described thus:

*Memory, prophecy and fantasy—the past, the future
and the dreaming moment between—are all one
country, living one immortal day.
To know that is Wisdom.
To use it is the Art.*

Sophistry, of course; literary sleight of hand. But that, too, is the point. The Show is both at the end of the journey to some long-hidden revelation and at the beginning of a new phase of inquiry. Beyond Showing comes the question of how and why the Show was even created. The mystery is solved, only to uncover, in its solving, what is hopefully a more profound mystery. In this book, the question of good and evil is the main consideration: two forces, the Jaff and Fletcher, representing darkness and light, are at war, and the lovers of the book, one from each side, like Romeo and Juliet, must battle the pernicious influence of their own parents to see their love fulfilled. By the end of the novel, they are united. But in the process of the struggle they have seen more than human eyes were intended to see. They've bathed in Quiddity, in a state of full consciousness; they know that another world, another state of being, lies just a veil away.

What does their union mean in light of that revelation? Certainly they've earned a happier ending than the one accorded most star-crossed lovers. But a larger scheme has been revealed, in which the uniting of lovers is a relatively inconsequential event. The stage is set, as it were, for another show, another series of spectacles and revelations. By the time I'd finished this book, I knew, at least vaguely, what form that show would take. It would be a book in which I unpicked some of the knots I'd tied at the close of this novel, in order to demonstrate something central to the Books of the Art: the uncertainty of things, especially of finality. Nothing, I had come to believe by the end, was more illusory than the idea of ending.

—*Clive Barker*
August 12, 1999

PART ONE

THE MESSENGER

ONE

Homer opened the door.

"Come on in, Randolph."

Jaffe hated the way he said *Randolph*, with the faintest trace of contempt in the word, as though he knew every damn crime Jaffe had ever committed, right from the first, the littlest.

"What are you waiting for?" Homer said, seeing Jaffe linger. "You've got work to do. The sooner it's started, the sooner I can find you more."

Randolph stepped into the room. It was large, painted the same bilious yellow and battleship gray as every other office and corridor in the Omaha Central Post Office. Not that much of the walls was visible. Piled higher than head-height on every side was mail. Sacks, satchels, boxes and carts of it, spilling out onto the cold concrete floor.

"Dead letters," Homer said. "Stuff even the good ol' U.S. Post Office can't deliver. Quite a sight, huh?"

Jaffe was agog, but he made sure not to show it. He made sure to show nothing, especially to wise guys like Homer.

"This is all yours, Randolph," his superior said. "Your little corner of heaven."

"What am I supposed to do with it?" Jaffe said.

"Sort it. Open it, look for any important stuff so we don't end up putting good money in the furnace."

"There's money in them?"

"Some of 'em," Homer said with a smirk. "Maybe. But most of it's just junk-mail. Stuff people don't want and just put back in the system. Some of it's had the wrong address put on and it's been flying backwards and forwards till it ends up in Nebraska. Don't ask me why, but whenever they don't know what to do with this shit they send it to Omaha."

"It's the middle of the country," Jaffe observed. "Gateway to the West. Or East. Depending on which way you're facing."

"Ain't the dead center," Homer countered. "But we still end up with all the crap. And it's all got to get sorted. By hand. By *you.*"

"All of it?" Jaffe said. What was in front of him was two weeks', three weeks', four weeks' work.

"All of it," said Homer, and didn't make any attempt to conceal his satisfaction. "All yours. You'll soon get the hang of it. If the envelope's got some kind of government marking, put it in the burn pile. Don't even bother to open it. Fuck 'em, right? But the rest, open. You never know what we're going to find." He grinned conspiratorially. "And what we find, we *share,*" he said.

Jaffe had been working for the U.S. Post Office only nine days, but that was long enough, easily long enough, to know that a lot of mail was intercepted by its hired deliverers. Packets were razored open and their contents filched, checks were cashed, love-letters were laughed over.

"I'm going to be coming back in here on a regular basis," Homer warned. "So don't you try hiding anything from me. I got a nose for stuff. I know when there's bills in an envelope, and I know when there's a thief on the team. Hear me? I got a sixth sense. So don't you try anything clever, bud, 'cause me and the boys don't take kindly to that. And you want to be one of the team, don't you?" He put a wide, heavy hand on Jaffe's shoulder. "Share and share alike, right?"

"I hear," Jaffe said.

"Good," Homer replied. "So—" He opened his arms to the spectacle of piled sacks. "It's all yours." He sniffed, grinned and took his leave.

One of the team, Jaffe thought as the door clicked closed, was what he'd never be. Not that he was about to tell Homer that. He'd let the man patronize him; play the willing slave. But in his heart? In his heart, he had other plans, other ambitions. Problem was, he wasn't any closer to realizing those ambitions than he'd been at twenty. Now he was thirty-seven, going on thirty-eight. Not the kind of man women looked at more than once. Not the kind of character folks found exactly charismatic. Losing his hair the way his father had. Bald at forty, most likely. Bald, and wifeless, and not more than beer-change in his pocket because he'd never been able to hold down a job for more than a year, eighteen months at the outside, so he'd never risen higher than private in the ranks.

He tried not to think about it too hard, because when he did he began to get really itchy to do some harm, and a lot of the time it was harm done to himself. It would be so easy. A gun in the mouth, tickling the back of his throat. Over and done with. No note. No explanation. What would he write anyway? *I'm killing myself because I didn't get to be King of the World?* Ridiculous.

But . . . that was what he wanted to be. He'd never known how, he'd never even had a sniff of the way, but that was the ambition that had nagged him from the first. Other men rose from nothing, didn't they? Messiahs, presidents, movie stars. They pulled themselves up out of the mud the way the fishes had when they'd decided to go for a walk. Grown legs, breathed air, become more than what they'd been. If fucking fishes could do it, why couldn't he? But it had to be soon. Before he was forty. Before he was bald. Before he was dead, and gone, and no one to even remember him, except maybe as a nameless asshole who'd spent three weeks in the winter of 1969 in a room full of dead letters, opening orphaned mail looking for dollar bills. Some epitaph.

He sat down and looked at the task heaped before him.

"Fuck you," he said. Meaning Homer. Meaning the sheer volume of crap in front of him. But most of all, meaning himself.

———

At first, it was drudgery. Pure hell, day after day, going through the sacks.

The piles didn't seem to diminish. Indeed they were several times fed by a leering Homer, who led a trail of peons in with further satchels to swell the number.

First Jaffe sorted the interesting envelopes (bulky; rattling; perfumed) from dull; then the private correspondence from official, and the scrawl from the Palmer method. Those decisions made, he began opening the envelopes, in the first week with his fingers, till his fingers became calloused, thereafter with a short-bladed knife he bought especially for the purpose, digging out the contents like a pearl-fisher in search of a pearl, most of the time finding nothing, sometimes, as Homer had promised, finding money or a check, which he dutifully declared to his boss.

"You're good at this," Homer said after the second week. "You're really good. Maybe I should put you on this full time."

Randolph wanted to say fuck you, but he'd said that too many times to bosses who'd fired him the minute after, and he couldn't afford to lose this job: not with the rent to pay and heating his one-room apartment costing a damn fortune while the snow continued to fall. Besides, something was happening to him while he passed the solitary hours in the Dead Letter Room, something it took him to the end of the third week to begin to enjoy, and the end of the fifth to comprehend.

He was sitting at the crossroads of America.

Homer had been right. Omaha, Nebraska, wasn't the geographical center of the USA, but as far as the Post Office was concerned, it may as well have been.

The lines of communication crossed, and recrossed, and finally dropped their orphans here, because nobody in any other state wanted them. These letters had been sent from coast to coast looking for someone to open them, and had found no takers. Finally they'd ended with him: with Randolph Emest Jaffe, a balding nobody with ambitions never spoken and rage not expressed, whose little knife slit them,

and little eyes scanned them, and who—sitting at his crossroads—
began to see the private face of the nation.

There were love-letters, hate-letters, ransom notes, pleadings, sheets
on which men had drawn round their hard-ons, valentines of pubic
hair, blackmail by wives, journalists, hustlers, lawyers and senators,
junk-mail and suicide notes, lost novels, chain letters, résumés, unde-
livered gifts, rejected gifts, letters sent out into the wilderness like bottles from an island, in the hope of finding help, poems, threats and
recipes. So much. But these many were the least of it. Though sometimes the love-letters got him sweaty, and the ransom notes made him
wonder if, having gone unanswered, their senders had murdered their
hostages, the stories of love and death they told touched him only
fleetingly. Far more persuasive, far more moving, was another story,
which could not be articulated so easily.

Sitting at the crossroads he began to understand that America had a
secret life; one which he'd never even glimpsed before. Love and
death he knew about. Love and death were the great clichés; the twin
obsessions of songs and soap operas. But there was another life, which
every fortieth letter, or fiftieth, or hundredth, hinted at, and every
thousandth stated with a lunatic plainness. When they said it plain, it
was not the whole truth, but it was a beginning, and each of the writers
had their own mad way of stating something close to unstateable.

What it came down to was this: the world was not as it seemed. Not
remotely as it seemed. Forces conspired (governmental, religious,
medical) to conceal and silence those who had more than a passing
grasp of that fact, but they couldn't gag or incarcerate every one of
them. There were men and women who slipped the nets, however
widely flung; who found back-roads to travel where their pursuers got
lost, and safe houses along the way where they'd be fed and watered by
like visionaries, ready to misdirect the dogs when they came sniffing.
These people didn't trust Ma Bell, so they didn't use telephones. They
didn't dare assemble in groups of more than two for fear of attracting
attention to themselves. But they *wrote*. Sometimes it was as if they
had to, as if the secrets they kept sealed up were too hot, and burned
their way out. Sometimes it was because they knew the hunters were

on their heels and they'd have no other chance to describe the world
to itself before they were caught, drugged and locked up. Sometimes
there was even a subversive glee in the scrawlings, sent out with deliberately indistinct addresses in the hope that the letter would blow the
mind of some innocent who'd received it by chance. Some of the mis-
sives were stream-of-consciousness rantings, others precise, even clini-
cal, descriptions of how to turn the world inside out by sex-magic or
mushroom-eating. Some used the nonsense imagery of *National
Enquirer* stories to veil another message. They spoke of UFO sightings
and zombie cults; news from Venusian evangelists and psychics who
tuned in to the dead on the TV. But after a few weeks of studying these
letters (and *study* it was; he was like a man locked in the ultimate
library) Jaffe began to see beyond the nonsenses to the hidden story.
He broke the code; or enough of it to be tantalized. Instead of being
irritated each day when Homer opened the door and had another half
dozen satchels of letters brought in, he welcomed the addition. The
more letters, the more clues; the more clues the more hope he had of
a solution to the mystery. It was, he became more certain as the weeks
turned into months and the winter mellowed, not several mysteries
but *one*. The writers whose letters were about the Veil, and how to
draw it aside, were finding their own way forward towards revelation;
each had his own particular method and metaphor; but somewhere in
the cacophony a single hymn was striving to be sung.

It was not about love. At least not as the sentimentalists knew it.
Nor about death, as a literalist would have understood the term. It
was—in no particular order—something to do with fishes, and the sea
(sometimes the Sea of Seas); and three ways to swim there; and
dreams (a lot about dreams); and an island which Plato had called
Atlantis, but had known all along was some other place. It was about
the end of the World, which was in turn about its beginning. And it
was about Art.

Or rather, *the* Art.

That, of all the codes, was the one he beat his head hardest against,
and broke only his brow. The Art was talked about in many ways. As
The Final Great Work. As *The Forbidden Fruit*. As *da Vinci's Despair* or

The Finger in the Pie or *The Butt-Digger's Glee*. There were many ways to describe it, but only one Art. And (here was a mystery) no *Artist*.

"So, are you happy here?" Homer said to him one May day.

Jaffe looked up from his work. There were letters strewn all around him. His skin, which had never been too healthy, was as pale and etched upon as the pages in his hand.

"Sure," he said to Homer, scarcely bothering to focus on the man. "Have you got some more for me?"

Homer didn't answer at first. Then he said: "What are you hiding, Jaffe?"

"Hiding? I'm not hiding anything."

"You're stashing stuff away you should be sharing with the rest of us."

"No I'm not," Jaffe said. He'd been meticulous in obeying Homer's first edict, that anything found among the dead letters be shared. The money, the skin magazines, the cheap jewelry he'd come across once in a while; it all went to Homer, to be divided up. "You get everything," he said. "I swear."

Homer looked at him with plain disbelief. "You spend every fucking hour of the day down here," he said. "You don't talk with the other guys. You don't drink with 'em. Don't you like the smell of us, Randolph? Is that it?" He didn't wait for an answer. "Or are you just a *thief?*"

"I'm no thief," Jaffe said. "You can look for yourself." He stood up, raising his hands, a letter in each. "Search me."

"I don't want to fucking touch you," came Homer's response. "What do you think I am, a fucking fag?" He kept staring at Jaffe. After a pause he said: "I'm going to have somebody else come down here and take over. You've done five months. It's long enough. I'm going to move you."

"I don't want—"

"What?"

"I mean . . . what I mean to say is, I'm quite happy down here. Really. It's work I like doing."

"Yeah," said Homer, clearly still suspicious. "Well from Monday you're out."

"Why?"

"Because I say so! If you don't like it find yourself another job."

"I'm doing good work, aren't I?" Jaffe said.

Homer was already turning his back.

"It smells in here," he said as he exited. "Smells real bad."

There was a word Randolph had learned from his reading which he'd never known before: synchronicity. He'd had to go buy a dictionary to look it up, and found it meant that sometimes events coincided. The way the letter writers used the word it usually meant that there was something significant, mysterious, maybe even miraculous in the way one circumstance collided with another, as though a pattern existed that was just out of human sight.

Such a collision occurred the day Homer dropped his bombshell, an intersecting of events that would change everything. No more than an hour after Homer had left, Jaffe took his short-bladed knife, which was getting blunt, to an envelope that felt heavier than most. He slit it open, and out fell a small medallion. It hit the concrete floor: a sweet ringing sound. He picked it up, with fingers that had been trembling since Homer's exit. There was no chain attached to the medallion, nor did it have a loop for that purpose. Indeed it wasn't attractive enough to be hung around a woman's neck as a piece of jewelry, and though it was in the form of a cross closer inspection proved it not to be of Christian design. Its four arms were of equal length, the full span no more than an inch and a half. At the intersection was a human figure, neither male nor female, arms outstretched as in a crucifixion, but not nailed. Spreading out along the four routes were abstract designs, each of which ended in a circle. The face was very simply rendered. It bore, he thought, the subtlest of *smiles*.

He was no expert on metallurgy, but it was apparent the thing was not gold or silver. Even if the dirt had been cleaned from it he doubted it would ever gleam. But there was something deeply attractive about it nevertheless. Looking at it he had the sense he'd sometimes had waking in the morning from an intense dream but unable to remember the details. This was a significant object, but he didn't know why. Were the sigils spreading from the figure vaguely familiar from one of the letters he'd read, perhaps? He'd scanned thousands upon thousands in the last twenty weeks, and many of them had carried little sketches, obscene sometimes, often indecipherable. Those he'd judged the most interesting he'd smuggled out of the Post Office, to study at night. They were bundled up beneath the bed in his room. Perhaps he'd break the dream-code on the medallion by careful examination of those.

He decided to take lunch that day with the rest of the workers, figuring it'd be best to do as little as possible to irritate Homer any further. It was a mistake. In the company of the good ol' boys talking about news he'd not listened to in months, and the quality of last night's steak, and the fuck they'd had, or failed to have, after the steak, and what the summer was going to bring, he felt himself a total stranger. They knew it too. They talked with their backs half-turned to him, dropping their voices at times to whisper about his weird look, his wild eyes. The more they shunned him the more he felt happy to be shunned, because they *knew*, even fuckwits like these *knew*, he was different from them. Maybe they were even a little afraid.

He couldn't bring himself to go back to the Dead Letter Room at one-thirty. The medallion and its mysterious signs was burning a hole in his pocket. He had to go back to his lodgings and start the search through his private library of letters *now*. Without even wasting breath telling Homer, he did just that.

It was a brilliant, sunny day. He drew the curtains against the invasion of light, turned on the lamp with the yellow shade, and there, in a jaundiced fever, began his study, taping the letters with any trace of illustration to the bare walls, and when the walls were full spreading them on the table, bed, chair and floor. Then he went from sheet to sheet, sign to sign, looking for anything that even faintly resembled the medallion in his hand. And as he went, the same thought kept creeping back into his head: that he knew there was an Art, but no Artist, a practice but no practitioner, and that maybe *he* was that man.

The thought didn't have to creep for long. Within an hour of perusing the letters it had pride of place in his skull. The medallion hadn't fallen into his hands by accident. It had come to him as a reward for his patient study, and as a way to draw together the threads of his investigation and finally begin to make some sense of it. Most of the symbols and sketches on the pages were irrelevant, but there were many, too many to be a coincidence, that echoed images on the cross. No more than two ever appeared on the same sheet, and most of these were crude renderings, because none of the writers had the complete solution in their hands the way he did, but they'd all comprehended some part of the jigsaw, and their observations about the part they had, whether haiku, dirty talk or alchemical formulas, gave him a better grasp of the system behind the symbols.

A term that had cropped up regularly in the most perceptive of the letters was the *Shoal*. He'd passed over it several times in his reading, and never thought much about it. There was a good deal of evolutionary talk in the letters, and he'd assumed the term to be a part of that. Now he understood his error. The Shoal was a cult, or a church of some kind, and its symbol was the object he held in the palm of his hand. What it and the Art had to do with each other was by no means clear, but his long-held suspicion that this was *one* mystery, *one* journey, was here confirmed, and he knew that with the medallion as a map he'd find his way from Shoal to Art eventually.

In the meantime there was a more urgent concern. When he thought back to the tribe of co-workers, with Homer at its head, he shuddered to think that any of them might ever share the secret he'd uncovered. Not that they had any chance of making any real progress decoding it: they were too witless. But Homer was suspicious enough to at least sniff along the trail a little way, and the idea of anybody— but especially the boorish Homer—tainting this sacred ground was unbearable. There was only one way to prevent such a disaster. He had to act quickly to destroy any evidence that might put Homer on the right track. The medallion he'd keep, of course: he'd been entrusted with it by higher powers, whose faces he'd one day get to see. He'd also keep the twenty or thirty letters that had proffered the best information on the Shoal; the rest (three hundred or so) had to be burned. As to the collection in the Dead Letter Room, they had to go into the furnace too. All of them. It would take time, but it had to be done, and the sooner the better. He made a selection of the letters in his room, parcelled up those he didn't need to keep, and headed off back to the Sorting Office.

It was late afternoon now, and he travelled against the flow of human traffic, entering the Office by the back door to avoid Homer, though he knew the man's routine well enough to suspect he'd punched out at five-thirty to the second, and was already guzzling beer somewhere. The furnace was a sweaty rattling antique, tended by another sweaty rattling antique, called Miller, with whom Jaffe had never exchanged a single word, Miller being stone-deaf. It took some time for Jaffe to explain that he was going to be feeding the furnace for an hour or two, beginning with the parcel he'd brought from home, which he immediately tossed into the flames. Then he went up to the Dead Letter Room.

Homer had not gone guzzling beer. He was waiting, sitting in Jaffe's chair under a bare bulb, going through the piles around him.

"So what's the scam?" he said as soon as Jaffe stepped through the door.

It was useless trying to pretend innocence, Jaffe knew. His months of study had carved knowledge into his face. He couldn't pass for a naïf any longer. Nor—now that it came to it—did he want to.

"No *scam*," he said to Homer, making his contempt for the man's puerile suspicions plain. "I'm not taking anything you'd want. Or could use."

"I'll be the judge of that, asshole," Homer said, throwing the letters he was examining down among the rest of the litter. "I want to know what you've been up to down here. 'Sides jerking off."

Jaffe closed the door. He'd never realized it before, but the reverberations of the furnace carried through the walls into the room. Everything here trembled minutely. The sacks, the envelopes, the words on the pages tucked inside. And the chair on which Homer was sitting. And the knife, the short-bladed knife, lying on the floor beside the chair on which Homer was sitting. The whole place was moving, ever so slightly, like there was a rumble in the ground. Like the world was about to be flipped.

Maybe it was. Why not? No use pretending the *status* was still *quo*. He was a man on his way to some throne or other. He didn't know which and he didn't know where, but he needed to silence any pretender quickly. Nobody was going to find him. Nobody was going to blame him, or judge him, or put him on Death Row. He was his own law now.

"I should explain . . ." he said to Homer, finding a tone that was almost flippant, ". . . what the *scam* really is."

"Yeah," Homer said, his lip curling. "Why don't you do that?"

"Well it's real simple . . ."

He started to walk towards Homer, and the chair, and the knife beside the chair. The speed of his approach made Homer nervous, but he kept his seat.

". . . I've found a secret," Jaffe went on.

"Huh?"

"You want to know what it is?"

Now Homer stood up, his gaze trembling the way everything else was. Everything except Jaffe. All the tremors had gone out of his hands, his guts and his head. He was steady in an unsteady world.

"I don't know what the fuck you're doing," Homer said. "But I don't like it."

"I don't blame you," Jaffe said. He didn't have his eyes on the knife. He didn't need to. He could sense it. "But it's your job to know, isn't it?" Jaffe went on, "what's been going on down here."

Homer took several steps away from the chair. The loutish gait he liked to affect had gone. He was stumbling, as though the floor was tilting.

"I've been sitting at the center of the world," Jaffe said. "This little room . . . this is where it's all happening."

"Is that right?"

"Damn right."

Homer made a nervous little grin. He threw a glance towards the door.

"You want to go?" Jaffe said.

"Yeah." He looked at his watch, not seeing it. "Got to run. Only came down here—"

"You're afraid of me," Jaffe said. "And you should be. I'm not the man I was."

"Is that right?"

"You said that already."

Again, Homer looked towards the door. It was five paces away; four if he ran. He'd covered half the distance when Jaffe picked up the knife. He had the door handle clasped when he heard the man approaching behind him.

He glanced round, and the knife came straight at his eye. It wasn't an accidental stab. It was synchronicity. His eye glinted, the knife glinted. Glints collided, and the next moment he was screaming as he fell back against the door, Randolph following him to claim the letter-opener from the man's head.

The roar of the furnace got louder. With his back to the sacks Jaffe could feel the envelopes nestling against each other, the words being shaken on the pages, till they became a glorious poetry. Blood, it said; like a sea; his thoughts like clots in that sea, dark, congealed, hotter than hot.

He reached for the handle of the knife, and clenched it. Never before in his life had he shed blood; not even squashed a bug, at least intentionally. But now his fist on the hot wet handle seemed wonderful. A prophecy; a proof.

Grinning, he pulled the knife out of Homer's socket, and before his victim could slide down the door stuck it into Homer's throat to the hilt. This time he didn't let it lie. He pulled it out as soon as he'd stopped Homer's screams, and he stabbed the middle of the man's chest. There was bone there, and he had to drive hard, but he was suddenly very strong. Homer gagged, and blood came out of his mouth, and from the wound in his throat. Jaffe pulled the knife out. He didn't stab again. Instead he wiped the blade on his handkerchief and turned from the body to think about his next move. If he tried to lug the sacks of mail to the furnace he risked being discovered, and sublime as he felt, high on the boorslob's demise, he was still aware that there was danger in being found out. It would be better to bring the furnace *here*. After all, fire was a moveable feast. All it required was a light, and Homer had those. He turned back to the slumped corpse and searched in the pockets for a box of matches. Finding one, he pulled it out, and went over to the satchels.

Sadness surprised him as he prepared to put a flame to the dead letters. He'd spent so many weeks here, lost in a kind of delirium, drunk with mysteries. This was good-bye to all that. After this—Homer dead, the letters burnt—he was a fugitive, a man without a history, beckoned by an Art he knew nothing about, but which he wished more than anything to practice.

He began to screw up a few of the pages, to provide some initial fodder for the flame. Once begun, he didn't doubt that the fire would sustain itself: there was nothing in the room—paper, fabric, flesh—that wasn't combustible. With three heaps of paper made, he struck a match. The flame was bright, and looking at it he realized how much he hated brightness. The dark was so much more interesting; full of secrets, full of threats. He put the flame to the piles of paper and watched while the fires gained strength. Then he retreated to the door.

Homer was slumped against it, of course, bleeding from three places, and his bulk wasn't that easy to move, but Jaffe put his back into the task, his shadow thrown up against the wall by the burgeoning bonfire behind him. Even in the half minute it took him to move the corpse aside the heat grew exponentially, so that by the time he glanced back at the room it was ablaze from side to side, the heat stirring up its own wind, which in turn fanned the flames.

It was only when he was clearing out his room of any sign of himself—eradicating every trace of Randolph Ernest Jaffe—that he regretted doing what he'd done. Not the burning—that had been altogether wise—but leaving Homer's body in the room to be consumed along with the dead letters. He should have taken a more elaborate revenge, he realized. He should have backed the body into pieces, packaged it up, tongue, eyes, testicles, guts, skin, skull, divided piece from piece—

and sent the pieces out into the system with scrawled addresses that made no real sense, so that chance (or synchronicity) was allowed to elect the doorstep on which Homer's flesh would land. The mailman mailed. He promised himself not to miss such ironic possibilities in the future.

The task of clearing his room didn't take long. He had very few belongings, and most of what he had meant little to him. When it came down to basics, he barely existed. He was the sum of a few dollars, a few photographs, a few clothes. Nothing that couldn't be put in a small suitcase and still leave room alongside them for a set of encyclopedias.

By midnight, with that same small suitcase in hand, he was on his way out of Omaha, and ready for a journey that might lead in any direction. Gateway to the East, Gateway to the West. He didn't care which way he went, as long as the route led to the Art.

TWO

J affe had lived a small life. Born within fifty miles of Omaha, he'd been educated there, he'd buried his parents there, he'd courted and failed to persuade to the altar two women of that city. He'd left the state a few times, and even thought (after the second of his failed courtships) of retreating to Orlando, where his sister lived, but she'd persuaded him against it, saying he wouldn't get on with the people, or the incessant sun. So he'd stayed in Omaha, losing jobs and getting others, never committing himself to anything or anybody for very long, and in turn not being committed to.

But in the solitary confinement of the Dead Letter Room he'd had a taste of horizons he'd never known existed, and it had given him an appetite for the open road. When there'd only been sun, suburbs and Mickey Mouse out there he'd not given a damn. Why bother to go looking for such banalities? But now he knew better. There were mysteries to be unveiled, and powers to be seized, and when he was King of the World he'd pull down the suburbs (and the sun if he could) and make the world over in a hot darkness where a man might finally get to know the secrets of his own soul.

There'd been much talk in the letters about *crossroads*, and for a long time he'd taken the image literally, thinking that in Omaha he was probably *at* that crossroads, and that knowledge of the Art would come to him there. But once out of the city, and away, he saw the error of such literalism. When the writers had spoken of crossroads they hadn't meant one highway intersecting with another. They'd meant places where states of being crossed, where the human system met the alien, and both moved on, changed. In the flow and flurry of such places there was hope of finding revelation.

He had very little money, of course, but that didn't seem to matter. In the weeks that followed his escape from the scene of his crime, all that he wanted simply came to him. He had only to stick out his thumb and a car squealed to a halt. When a driver asked him where he was headed, and he said he was headed as far as *he*, Jaffe, wanted to go, that was exactly as far as the driver took him. It was as if he was blessed. When he stumbled, there was someone to pick him up. When he got hungry, there was someone to feed him.

It was a woman in Illinois, who'd given him a lift then asked him if he wanted to stay the night with her, who confirmed his blessedness.

"You've seen something extraordinary, haven't you?" she whispered to him in the middle of the night. "It's in your eyes. It was your eyes made me offer you the lift."

"And offer me this?" he said, fingering between her legs.

"Yes. That too," she said. "What have you seen?"

"Not enough," he replied.

"Will you make love to me again?"

"No."

Every now and then, moving from state to state, he got a glimpse of what the letters had schooled him in. He saw the secrets peeping out, only daring to show themselves because *he* was passing through and they knew him as a coming man of power. In Kentucky he chanced to witness the corpse of an adolescent being hauled from a river, the body left sprawled on the grass, arms spread, fingers spread, while a woman howled and sobbed beside it. The boy's eyes were open; so were the buttons of his trousers. Watching from a short distance, the only witness not to be ordered away by the cops (the eyes, again) he took a moment to savor the way the boy was arrayed, like the figure on the medallion, and half wanted to throw himself into the river just for the thrill of drowning. In Idaho, he met a man who'd lost an arm in an automobile accident and while they sat and drank together he explained that he still had feeling in the lost limb, which the doctors said was just a phantom in his nervous system, but which he knew was his astral body, still complete on another plane of being. He said he jerked off with his lost hand regularly, and offered to demonstrate. It was true. Later, the man said:

"You can see in the dark, can't you?"

Jaffe hadn't thought about it, but now that his attention was drawn to the fact it seemed he could.

"How'd you learn to do that?"

"I didn't."

"Astral eyes, maybe."

"Maybe."

"You want me to suck your cock again?"

"No."

He was gathering up experiences, one of each, passing through people's lives and out the other side leaving them obsessed or dead or weeping. He indulged his every whim, going wherever instinct pointed, the secret life coming to find him the moment he arrived in town.

There was no sign of pursuit from the forces of law. Perhaps Homer's body had never been found in the gutted building, or if it had the police had assumed he was simply a victim of the fire. For whatever reason, nobody came sniffing after him. He went wherever he wanted and did whatever he desired, until he'd had a surfeit of desires satisfied and wants supplied, and it came time for him to push himself over the brink.

He came to rest in a roach-ridden motel in Los Alamos, New Mexico, locked himself in with two bottles of vodka, stripped, closed the curtains against the day, and let his mind go. He hadn't eaten in forty-eight hours, not because he didn't have money, he did, but because he enjoyed the light-headedness. Starved of sustenance, and whipped up by vodka, his thoughts ran riot, devouring themselves and shitting each other out, barbaric and baroque by turns. The roaches came out in the darkness, and ran over his body as he lay on the floor. He let them come and go, pouring vodka on his groin when they got too busy there, and made him hard, which was a distraction. He wanted only to think. To float and think.

He'd had all he needed of the physical; felt hot and cold, sexy and sexless; fucked and fucker. He wanted none of that again: at least not as Randolph Jaffe. There was another way to be, another place to feel from, where sex and murder and grief and hunger and all of it might be interesting again, but that would not be until he'd got beyond his present condition; become an Artist; remade the world.

Just before dawn, with even the roaches sluggish, he felt the invitation.

A great calm was in him. His heart was slow and steady. His bladder emptied of its own accord, like a baby's. He was neither too hot nor too cold. Neither too sleepy nor too awake. And at that crossroads—which was not the first, nor would be the last—something tugged on his gut, and summoned him.

He got up immediately, dressed, took the full bottle of vodka that remained, and went out walking. The invitation didn't leave his innards. It kept tugging as the cold night lifted and the sun began to rise. He'd come barefoot. His feet bled, but his body wasn't of great interest to him, and he kept the discomfort at bay with further helpings of vodka. By noon, the last of the drink gone, he was in the middle of the desert, just walking in the direction he was called, barely aware of one foot moving ahead of the other. There were no thoughts in his head now, except the Art and its getting, and even that ambition came and went.

So, finally, did the desert itself. Somewhere towards evening, he came to a place where even the simplest facts—the ground beneath him, the darkening sky above his head—were in doubt. He wasn't even sure if he was walking. The absence of everything was pleasant, but it didn't last. The summons must have pulled him on without his even being aware of its call, because the night he'd left became a sudden day, and he found himself standing—alive, again; Randolph Ernest Jaffe again—in a desert barer even than the one he'd left. It was early morning here. The sun not yet high, but beginning to warm the air, the sky perfectly clear.

Now he felt pain, and sickness, but the pull in his gut was irresistible. He had to stagger on though his whole body was wreckage. Later, he remembered passing through a town, and seeing a steel tower standing in the middle of the wilderness. But that was only when the journey had ended, at a simple stone hut, the door of which opened to him as the last vestiges of his strength left him, and he fell across its threshold.

THREE

The door was closed when he came round, but his mind wide open. On the other side of a guttering fire sat an old man with doleful, slightly stupid features, like those of a clown who'd worn and wiped off fifty years of makeup, his pores enlarged and greasy, his hair, what was left of it, long and gray. He was sitting cross-legged. Occasionally, while Jaffe worked up the energy to speak, the old man raised a buttock and loudly passed wind.

"You found your way through," he said, after a time. "I thought you were going to die before you made it. A lot of people have. It takes real will."

"Through to *where?*" Jaffe managed to ask.

"We're in a Loop. A loop in time, encompassing a few minutes. I tied it, as a refuge. It's the only place I'm safe."

"Who are you?"

"My name's Kissoon."

"Are you one of the Shoal?"

The face beyond the fire registered surprise.

"You know a great deal."

"No. Not really. Just bits and pieces."

"Very few people know about the Shoal."

"I know of several," said Jaffe.

"Really?" said Kissoon, his tone toughening. "I'd like their names."

"I had letters from them . . ." Jaffe said, but faltered when he realized he no longer knew where he'd left them, those precious clues that had brought him through so much hell and heaven.

"Letters from whom?" Kissoon said.

"People who know . . . who *guess* . . . about the Art."

"Do they? And what do they say about it?"

Jaffe shook his head. "I've not made sense of it yet," he said. "But I think there's a sea—"

"There is," said Kissoon. "And you'd like to know where to find it, and how to be there, and how to have power from it."

"Yes. I would."

"And in return for this education?" Kissoon said. "What are you offering?"

"I don't have anything."

"Let me be the judge of that," Kissoon said, turning his eyes up to the roof of the hut as though he saw something in the smoke that roiled there.

"OK," Jaffe said. "Whatever I've got that you want. You can have it."

"That sounds fair."

"I need to know. I want the Art."

"Of course. Of course."

"I've had all the living I need," Jaffe said.

Kissoon's eyes came back to rest on him.

"Really? I doubt that."

"I want to get . . . I want to get . . ." (What? he thought. What do you want?) "*Explanations*," he said.

"Well, where to begin?"

"The sea," Jaffe said.

"Ah, the sea."

"Where is it?"

"Have you ever been in love?" Kissoon replied.

"Yes. I think so."

"Then you've been to Quiddity twice. Once the first night you slept out of the womb. The second occasion the night you lay beside that woman you loved. Or man, was it?" He laughed. "Whichever."

"Quiddity is the sea."

"Quiddity is the sea. And in it are islands, called the Ephemeris."

"I want to go there," Jaffe breathed.

"You will. One more time, you will."

"When?"

"The last night of your life. That's all we ever get. Three dips in the dream-sea. Any less, and we'd be insane. Any more—"

"And?"

"And we wouldn't be human."

"And the Art?"

"Ah, well . . . opinions differ about that."

"Do you have it?"

"*Have it?*"

"This Art. Do you have it? Can you do it? Can you teach me?"

"Maybe."

"You're one of the Shoal," Jaffe said. "You've got to have it, right?"

"*One?*" came the reply. "I'm the last. I'm the only."

"So share it with me. I want to be able to change the world."

"Just a *little* ambition."

"Don't fuck with me!" Jaffe said, the suspicion growing in him that he was being taken for a fool.

"I'm not going to leave empty-handed, Kissoon. If I get the Art I can enter Quiddity, right? That's the way it works."

"Where'd you get your information?"

"*Isn't it?*"

"Yes. And I say again: where'd you get your information?"

"I can put the clues together. I'm still doing it." He grinned as the pieces fitted in his head. "Quiddity's somehow *behind* the world, isn't it? And the Art lets you step through, so you can be there any time you like. The Finger in the Pie."

"Huh?"

"That's what somebody called it. The Finger in the Pie."

"Why stop with a finger?" Kissoon remarked.

"Right! Why not my whole fucking arm?"

Kissoon's expression was almost admiring. "What a pity," he said, "you couldn't be more *evolved*. Then maybe I could have shared all this with you."

"What are you saying?"

"I'm saying you're too much of an ape. I couldn't give you the secrets in my head. They're too powerful, too dangerous. You'd not know what to do with them. You'd end up tainting Quiddity with your puerile ambition. And Quiddity must be preserved."

"I told you . . . I'm not leaving here empty-handed. You can have whatever you want from me. Whatever I've got. Only teach me."

"You'd give me your body?" Kissoon said. "Would you?"

"What?"

"That's all you've got to bargain with. Do you want to give me that?"

The reply flummoxed Jaffe.

"You want sex?" he said.

"Christ, no."

"What then? I don't understand."

"The flesh and blood. The vessel. I want to occupy your body."

Jaffe watched Kissoon watching him.

"Well?" the old man said.

"You can't just climb into my skin," Jaffe said.

"Oh but I can, as soon as it's vacated."

"I don't believe you."

"Jaffe, you of *all* people should never say *I don't believe*. The extra-ordinary's the norm. There are loops in time. We're in one now. There are armies in our minds, waiting to march. And suns in our groins and cunts in the sky. Suits being wrought in every state—"

"Suits?"

"Petitions! Conjurations! *Magic, magic!* It's everywhere. And you're right, Quiddity *is* the source, and the Art its lock and key. And you think it's tough for me to climb inside your skin. Have you learned *nothing*?"

"Suppose I agree."

"Suppose you do."

"What happens to me, if I was to vacate my body?"

"You'd stay here. As spirit. It's not much but it's home. I'll be back, after a while. And the flesh and blood's yours again."

"Why do you even want my body?" Jaffe said. "It's utterly fucked up."

"That's *my* business," Kissoon replied.

"I need to know."

"And I choose not to tell you. If you want the Art then you damn well do as I say. You've got no choice."

The old man's manner—his arrogant little smile, his shrugs, the way he half closed his lids as though using all his gaze on his guest would be a waste of eyesight—all of this made Jaffe think of Homer. They could have been two halves of a double-act; the lumpen boor and the wily old goat. When he thought of Homer he inevitably thought of the knife in his pocket. How many times would he need to slice Kissoon's stringy carcass before the agonies made him speak? Would he have to take off the old man's fingers, joint by joint? If so, he was ready. Maybe cut off his ears. Perhaps scoop out his eyes. Whatever it took, he'd do. It was too late now for squeamishness, much too late.

He slid his hand into his pocket, and around the knife.

Kissoon saw the motion.

"You understand nothing, do you?" he said, his eyes suddenly roving violently to and fro, as though speed-reading the air between him and Jaffe.

"I understand a lot more than you think," Jaffe said. "I understand I'm not *pure* enough for you. I'm not—how did you say it?—*evolved*. Yeah, evolved."

"I said you were an ape."

"Yeah, you did."

"I insulted the ape."

Jaffe's hold on the knife tightened. He started to get to his feet.

"Don't you *dare*," Kissoon said.

"Red rag to a bull," Jaffe said, his head spinning from the effort of rising, "—saying *dare* to me. I've seen stuff . . . done stuff . . ." He started to take the knife out of his pocket ". . . I'm not afraid of you."

Kissoon's eyes stopped their speed-reading and settled on the blade. There was no surprise on his face, the way there'd been on Homer's; but there was fear. A small thrill of pleasure coursed through Jaffe, seeing that expression.

Kissoon began to get to his feet. He was a good deal shorter than Jaffe, almost stunted, and every angle slightly askew, as though all his bones and joints had once been broken, and reset in haste.

"You shouldn't spill blood," he said hurriedly. "Not in a Loop. It's one of the rules of the looping suit, not to spill blood."

"Feeble," said Jaffe, beginning to step around the fire towards his victim.

"That's the truth," Kissoon said, and he gave Jaffe the strangest, most misbegotten smile, "I make it a point of honor not to lie."

"I had a year working in a slaughterhouse," Jaffe said. "In Omaha, Nebraska. Gateway to the West. I worked for a whole year, just cutting up meat. I know the business."

Kissoon was very frightened now. He'd backed against the wall of the hut, his arms spread out to either side of him for support, looking, Jaffe thought, like a silent-movie heroine. His eyes weren't half-open now, but huge and wet. So was his mouth, huge and wet. He couldn't even bring himself to make threats; he just shook.

Jaffe reached out and put his hand around the man's turkey throat. He gripped hard, fingers and thumb digging into the sinew. Then he brought his other hand, bearing the blunt knife, up to the corner of Kissoon's left eye. The old man's breath smelled like a sick man's fart. Jaffe didn't want to inhale it, but he had no choice, and the moment he did he realized he'd been fucked. The breath was more than sour air. There was something else in it, being expelled from Kissoon's body and snaking its way into him—or at least attempting to. Jaffe took his hand from the scrawn of the neck, and stepped away.

"*Fucker!*" he said, spitting and coughing out the breath before it occupied him.

Kissoon didn't concede the pretense.

"Aren't you going to kill me?" he said. "Am I reprieved?"

It was he who advanced now; Jaffe the one retreating.

"Keep away from me!" Jaffe said.

"I'm just an old man!"

"I felt the breath!" Jaffe yelled, slamming his fist against his chest. "You're trying to get inside me!"

"No," Kissoon protested.

"Don't fucking lie to me. I felt it!"

He still could. A weight in his lungs where there'd not been weight before. He backed towards the door, knowing that if he stayed the fucker would have the better of him.

"Don't leave," Kissoon said. "Don't open the door."

"There's other ways to the Art," Jaffe said.

"No," Kissoon said. "Only me. The rest are dead. There's nobody can help you but me."

He tried that little smile of his, bowing his wretched body, but the humility was as much a sham as the fear had been. All tricks to keep his victim near, so as to have his flesh and blood. Jaffe wasn't buying the routine a second time. He tried to block out Kissoon's seductions with memories. Pleasures taken, that he'd take again if he could only get out of this trap alive. The woman in Illinois, the one-armed man in Idaho, the caress of roaches. The recollections kept Kissoon from getting any further hold on him. He reached behind him and grabbed the door handle.

"Don't open that," Kissoon said.

"I'm getting out of here."

"I made a mistake. I'm sorry. I underestimated you. We can come to some arrangement surely? I'll tell you all you want to know. I'll teach you the Art. I don't have the skill myself. Not in the Loop. But *you* could have it. You could take it with you. Out there. Back into the world. Arm in the pie! Only *stay*. *Stay*, Jaffe. I've been alone here a long time. I need company. Someone to explain it all to. Share it with."

Jaffe turned the handle. As he did so he felt the earth beneath his feet shudder, and a brightness seemed to appear momentarily beyond the door. It seemed too livid to be mere daylight, but it must have been, because there was only sun awaiting him on the step outside.

"Don't leave me!" he heard Kissoon yelling, and with the yell felt the man clutching at his innards the way he had bringing him here. But the hold was nowhere near as strong as it had been. Either Kissoon had burned up too much of his energy in attempting to breathe his spirit into Jaffe, or his fury was weakening him. Whichever, the hold was resistible, and the farther Jaffe ran the weaker it became.

A hundred yards from the hut he glanced back, and thought he saw a patch of darkness moving across the ground towards him, like dark rope uncurling. He didn't linger to discover what new trick the old bastard was mounting, but ran and ran, following his own trail across the ground, until the steel tower came in sight. Its presence suggested some attempt to populate this wasteland, long abandoned. Beyond it, an aching hour later, was further proof of that endeavor. The town he half-remembered staggering through on his way here, its street empty not only of people and vehicles but of any distinguishing marks whatsoever, like a film-set yet to be dressed for shooting.

Half a mile beyond it an agitation in the air signalled that he had reached the perimeters of the Loop. He braved its confusions willingly, passing through a place of sickening disorientation in which he was not certain he was even walking, and suddenly he was out the other side, and back in a calm, starlit night.

Forty-eight hours later, drunk in an alleyway in Santa Fe, he made two momentous decisions. One, that he'd keep the beard he'd grown in the last few weeks, as a reminder of his search. Two, that every wit he possessed, every hint of knowledge he'd gained about the occult life of America, every iota of power his astral eyes lent him, would go to the possessing of the Art (Fuck Kissoon; Fuck the Shoal), and that only when he'd got it would he once again show his face unshaven.

FOUR

Holding to the promises he'd made himself was not easy. Not when there were so many simple pleasures to be had from the power he'd gained; pleasures he made himself forfeit for fear of depleting his little strength before he stole his way to greater.

His first priority was to locate a fellow quester; someone who could aid him in his search. It was two months before his enquiries threw up the name and reputation of a man perfectly suited to that role. That man was Richard Wesley Fletcher, who'd been—until his recent fall from grace—one of the most lauded and revolutionary minds in the field of evolutionary studies; the head of several research programs in Boston and Washington; a theorist whose every remark was scrutinized by his peers for clues to his next breakthrough. But his genius had been flawed by addiction. Mescaline and its derivatives had brought him low, much to the satisfaction of many of his colleagues, who made no bones about their contempt for the man once his guilty secret came out. In article after article Jaffe found the same smug tone, as the academic community rounded on the deposed *Wunderkind*, condemning his theories as ludicrous and his morals as reprehensible. Jaffe couldn't have cared less about Fletcher's moral standing. It was the man's theories that intrigued him, dovetailing as they did with his own ambition. Fletcher's researches had been aimed at isolating, and synthesizing in a laboratory, the force in living organisms that drove them to evolve. Like Jaffe, he believed heaven could be stolen.

It took persistence to find the man, but Jaffe had that in abundance, and found him in Maine. The genius was much the worse for despair, teetering on the brink of complete mental breakdown. Jaffe was cautious. He didn't press his suit at first, but instead ingratiated himself by supplying drugs of a quality Fletcher had long since been too poor to afford. Only when he'd gained the addict's trust did he begin to make oblique reference to Fletcher's studies. Fletcher was less than lucid on the subject at first, but Jaffe gently fanned the embers of his obsession, and in time the fire flared. Once burning, Fletcher had much to tell. He believed he'd twice come close to isolating what he called the Nuncio, the messenger. But the final processes had always eluded him. Jaffe offered a few observations of his own on the subject, garnered from his readings in the occult. The two of them, he gently suggested, were fellow seekers. Though he, Jaffe, used the vocabulary of the ancients—of alchemists and magicians—and Fletcher the language of science, they had the same desire to nudge evolution's elbow; to advance the flesh, and perhaps the spirit, by artificial means. Fletcher poured scorn on these observations at the outset, but slowly came to value them, finally accepting Jaffe's offer of facilities in which to begin his researches afresh. This time, Jaffe promised, Fletcher wouldn't have to work in an academic hothouse, constantly required to justify his work to hold on to his funding. He guaranteed his dope-fiend genius a place to work that would be well hidden from prying eyes. When the Nuncio had been isolated, and its miracle reproduced, Fletcher would reappear from the wilderness and put his vilifiers to flight. It was an offer no obsessive could have resisted.

Eleven months later, Richard Wesley Fletcher stood on a granite headland on the Pacific Coast of the Baja and cursed himself for succumbing to Jaffe's temptations. Behind him, in the Misión de Santa Catrina where he'd labored for the best part of a year, the Great Work (as

Jaffe liked to call it) had been achieved. The Nuncio was a reality. There were surely few less likely places for labors most of the world would have judged ungodly than an abandoned Jesuit Mission, but then from the outset this endeavor had been shot through with paradox.

For one, the liaison between Jaffe and himself. For another, the intermingling of disciplines that had made the Great Work possible. And for a third the fact that now, in what should have been his moment of triumph, he was minutes away from destroying the Nuncio before it fell into the hands of the very man who'd funded its creation.

As in its making, so in its unmaking: system, obsession and pain. Fletcher was too well versed in the ambiguities of matter to believe that the total destruction of anything was possible. Things couldn't be *un*discovered. But if the change that he and Raul wrought on the evidence was thorough enough it was his belief that nobody would easily reconstruct the experiment he'd conducted here in the wilds of Baja California. He and the boy (it was still difficult to think of Raul as a boy) had to be like perfect thieves, rifling their own house to remove every last trace of themselves. When they'd burned all the research notes and trashed all the equipment it had to be as though the Nuncio had never been made. Only then could he take the boy, who was still busy feeding the fires in front of the Mission, to this cliff edge, so that hand in hand they could fling themselves off. The fall was steep, and the rocks below plenty sharp enough to kill them. The tide would wash their blood and bodies out into the Pacific. Then, between fire and water, the job would have been done.

None of which would prevent some future investigator from finding the Nuncio all over again; but the combination of disciplines and circumstances which had made that possible were very particular. For humanity's sake Fletcher hoped they would not occur again for many years. There was good reason for such hope. Without Jaffe's strange, half-intuitive grasp of occult principles to marry with his own scientific methodology, the miracle would not have been made, and how often did men of science sit down with men of magic (the suit-mongers, as Jaffe called them) and attempt a mingling of crafts? It was good they didn't. There was too much dangerous stuff to discover. The occultists whose codes Jaffe had broken knew more about the nature of things than Fletcher would ever have suspected. Beneath their metaphors, their talk of the Bath of Rebirth, and of golden Progeny begotten by fathers of lead, they were ambitious for the same solutions he'd sought all his life. Artificial ways to advance the evolutionary urge: to take the human beyond itself. *Obscurum per obscurius, ignotum per ignotius,* they advised. Let the obscure be explained by the more obscure, the unknown by the more unknown. They knew whereof they wrote. Between his science and theirs Fletcher had solved the problem. Synthesized a fluid that would carry evolution's glad tidings through any living system, pressing (so he believed) the humblest cell towards a higher condition. *Nuncio* he'd called it: the Messenger. Now he knew he'd misnamed it. It was not a messenger of the gods, but the god itself. It had a life of its own. It had energy, and ambition. He *had* to destroy it, before it began to rewrite Genesis, beginning with Randolph Jaffe as Adam.

"Father?"

Raul had appeared behind him. Once again the boy had stripped off his clothes. After years of going naked, he was still unable to get used to their constrictions. And once again he used that damn word.

"I'm not your father," Fletcher reminded him. "I never was and never will be. Can't you get that into your head?"

As ever, Raul listened. His eyes lacked whites, and were difficult to read, but his steady gaze never failed to mellow Fletcher.

"What do you want?" he said more softly.

"The fires," the boy replied.

"What about them?"

"The wind, father—" he began.

It had got up in the last few minutes, coming straight off the ocean. When Fletcher followed Raul round to the front of the Mission, in the lee of which they'd built the Nuncio's pyres, he found the notes being scattered, many of them far from consumed.

"*Damn you,*" Fletcher said, as much irritated by his own lack of attention to the task as the boy's. "I told you: don't put too much paper on at the same time."

He took hold of Raul's arm, which was covered in silky hair, as was his entire body. There was a distinct smell of singeing, where the flames had risen suddenly and caught the boy by surprise. It took, he knew, considerable courage on Raul's part to overcome his primal fear of fire. He was doing it for his *father's* sake. He'd have done it for no other. Contrite, Fletcher put his arm around Raul's shoulder. The boy clung, the way he'd clung in his previous incarnation, burying his face in the smell of the human.

"We'd better just let them go," Fletcher said, watching as another gust of wind took leaves off the fire and scattered them like pages from a calendar, day after day of pain and inspiration. Even if one or two of them were to be found, and that was unlikely along such a barren stretch of coast, nobody would be able to make any sense of them. It was only his obsessiveness that made him want to wipe the slate completely clean, and shouldn't he know better, when that very obsessiveness had been one of the qualities that had brought this waste and tragedy about?

The boy detached himself from around Fletcher and turned back to the fires.

"No Raul . . ." he said, ". . . forget them . . . let them go . . ."

The boy chose not to hear; a trick he'd always had, even before the changes the Nuncio's touch had brought about. How many times had Fletcher summoned the ape Raul had been only to have the wretched animal willfully ignore him? It was in no small measure that very perversity which had encouraged Fletcher to test the Great Work on him: a whisper of the human in the simian which the Nuncio turned into a shout.

Raul wasn't making an attempt to collect the dispersed papers, however. His small, wide body was tensed, his head tilted up. He was sniffing the air.

"What is it?" Fletcher said. "You can smell somebody?"

"Yes."

"Where?"

"Coming up the hill."

Fletcher knew better than to question Raul's observation. The fact that he, Fletcher, could hear and smell nothing was simply a testament to the decadence of his senses. Nor did he need to ask from which direction their visitor was coming. There was only one route up to the Mission. Forging a single road through such inhospitable terrain, then up a steep hill, must have taxed even the masochism of Jesuits. They'd built one road, and the Mission, and then, perhaps failing to find God up here, vacated the place. If their ghosts ever drifted through, they'd find a deity now, Fletcher thought, in three vials of blue fluid. So would the man coming up the hill. It could only be Jaffe. Nobody else knew of their presence here.

"Damn him," Fletcher said. "Why now? Why now?"

It was a foolish question. Jaffe had chosen to come now because he knew his Great Work was being conspired against. He had a way of maintaining a presence in a place where he wasn't; a spying echo of himself. Fletcher didn't know how. One of Jaffe's *suits*, no doubt. The kind of minor mind-tricks Fletcher would have dismissed as trickery once, as he would have dismissed so much else. It would take Jaffe several more minutes to get all the way up the hill, but that wasn't enough time, by any means, for Fletcher and the boy to finish their labors.

There were two tasks only he might yet complete if he was efficient. Both were vital. First, the killing and disposal of Raul, from whose transformed system an educated enquirer might glean the nature of the Nuncio. Second, the destruction of the three vials inside the Mission.

It was there he returned now, through the chaos he had gladly wreaked on the place. Raul followed, walking barefoot through the smashed instrumentation and splintered furniture, to the inner sanctum. This was the only room that had not been invaded by the clutter of the Great Work. A plain cell that boasted only a desk, a chair, and an antiquated stereo. The chair was set in front of the window which overlooked the ocean. Here, in the first days following Raul's successful transmutation, before the full realization of the Nuncio's purpose and consequence had soiled Fletcher's triumph, man and boy had sat, and watched the sky, and listened to Mozart together. All the mysteries, Fletcher had said, in one of his first lessons, were footnotes to music. Before everything, music.

Now there'd be no more sublime Mozart; no more sky-watching; no more loving education. There was only time for a shot. Fletcher took the gun from beside his mescaline in the desk drawer.

"We're going to die?" Raul said.

He'd known this was coming. But not so soon.

"Yes."

"We should go outside," the boy said. "To the edge."

"No. There isn't time. I've . . . I've got some work to do before I join you."

"But you said together."

"I know."

"You *promised* together."

"*Jesus, Raul!* I said: *I know!* But it can't be helped. He's coming. And if he takes you from me, alive or dead, he'll use you. He'll cut you up. Find out how the Nuncio works in you!"

His words were intended to scare, and they succeeded. Raul let out a sob, his face knotted up with terror. He took a step backwards as Fletcher raised the gun.

"I'll be with you soon," Fletcher said. "I swear it. Just as soon as I can."

"Please, father . . ."

"*I'm not your father! Once and for all, I'm nobody's father!*"

His outburst broke any hold he had on Raul. Before Fletcher could take a bead on him the boy was away through the door. He still fired wildly, the bullet striking the wall, then he gave chase, firing a second time. But the boy had simian agility in him. He was across the laboratory and out into the sunlight before a third shot could be fired. Out, and away.

Fletcher threw the gun aside. It was a waste of what little time remained to follow Raul. Better to use those minutes to dispose of the Nuncio. There was precious little of the stuff, but enough to wreak evolutionary havoc in any system that it tainted. He'd plotted against it for days and nights now, working out the safest way to be rid of it. He knew it couldn't simply be poured away. What might it do if it got into the earth? His best hope, he'd decided—indeed his *only* hope—

was to throw it into the Pacific. There was a pleasing neatness about that. The long climb to his species' present rung had begun in the ocean, and it was there—in the myriad configurations of certain marine animals—that he'd first observed the urge things had to become something other than themselves. Clues to which the three vials of Nuncio were the solution. Now he'd give that answer back to the element that had inspired it. The Nuncio would literally become drops in the ocean, its powers so diluted as to be negligible.

He crossed to the bench where the vials still stood in their rack. God in three bottles, milky blue, like a della Francesca sky. There was movement in the distillation, as though it was stirring up its own internal tides. And if it knew he was approaching, did it also know his intention? He had so little idea of what he'd created. Perhaps it could read his mind.

He stopped in his tracks, still too much the man of science not to be fascinated by this phenomenon. He'd known the liquor was powerful, but that it possessed the talent for self-fermentation it was now displaying—even a primitive propulsion, it seemed; *it was climbing the walls of the vials*—astonished him. His conviction faltered. Did he really have the right to put this miracle out of the world's sight? Was its appetite really so unhealthy? All it wanted to do was speed the ascent of things. Make fur of scales. Make flesh of fur. Make spirit, perhaps, of flesh. A pretty thought.

Then he remembered Randolph Jaffe, of Omaha, Nebraska, sometime butcher and opener of Dead Letters; collector of other people's secrets. Would such a man use the Nuncio well? In the hands of someone sweet-natured and loving, the Great Work might begin a universal papacy, every living being in touch with the meaning of its Creation. But Jaffe wasn't loving, nor sweet-natured. He was a thief of revelations, a magician who didn't care to understand the principles of his craft, only to rise by it.

Given that fact the question was not *did he have the right to dispose of the miracle*, but rather, *how dare he hesitate?*

He stepped towards the vials, charged with fresh conviction. The Nuncio knew he meant it harm. It responded with a frenzy of activity, climbing the glass walls as best it could, churning against its confines.

As Fletcher reached out to snatch the rack up, he realized its true intention. It didn't simply desire escape. It wanted to work its wonders on the very flesh that was plotting its harm.

It wanted to recreate its Creator.

The realization came too late to be acted upon. Before he could withdraw his outstretched hand, or shield himself, one of the vials shattered. Fletcher felt the glass cut his palm, and the Nuncio splash against him. He staggered away from it, raising his hand in front of his face. There were several cuts there, but one particularly large, in the middle of his palm, for all the world as though someone had driven a nail through it. The pain made him giddy, but it lasted only a moment, giddiness and pain. Coming after was another sensation entirely. Not even sensation. That was too trivial a description. It was like mainlining on Mozart; a music that bypassed the ears and went straight to the soul. Hearing it, he would never be the same again.

FIVE

Randolph had seen the smoke rising from the fires outside the Mission as he rounded the first bend in the long haul up the hill, and had confirmed, in that sight, the suspicion that had been gnawing in him for days: that his hired genius was in revolt. He revved the jeep's engine, cursing the dirt that slid away in powder clouds behind his wheels, slowing his ascent to a laboring crawl. Until today it had suited both him and Fletcher that the Great Work be accomplished so far from civilization, though it had required a good deal of persuasion on his part to get equipped a laboratory of the sophistication Fletcher had demanded in a setting so remote. But then persuasion was easy nowadays. The trip into the Loop had stoked the fires in Jaffe's eyes. What the woman in Illinois, whose name he'd never known, had said: *You've seen something extraordinary, haven't you?* was true now as never before. He'd seen a place out of time, and himself in it, driven beyond sanity by his hunger for the Art. People knew all that though they could never have put words to the thought. They saw it in his look, and either out of fear or awe simply did as he asked.

But Fletcher had been an exception to that rule from the outset. His peccadilloes, and his desperation, had made him pliable, but the man still had a will of his own. Four times he'd refused Jaffe's offer to come out of hiding and recommence his experiments, though Jaffe had reminded him on each occasion how difficult it had been to trace the lost genius, and how much he desired that they work together. He'd sweetened each of the four offers by bringing mescaline in modest supply, always promising more, and promising too that any and every facility Fletcher required would be provided if he could only be persuaded back to his studies. Jaffe had known from first reading about Fletcher's radical theories that here was the way to cheat the system that stood between him and the Art. He didn't doubt that the route to Quiddity was thronged with tests and trials, designed by high-minded gurus or lunatic shamans like Kissoon to keep what they judged lower-class minds from approaching the Holy of Holies. Nothing new about that. But with Fletcher's help he could trip the gurus; get to power over their backs. The Great Work would evolve him beyond the condition of any of the self-elected wise men, and the Art would sing in his fingers.

At first, having set up the laboratory to Fletcher's specifications, and offered the man some thoughts on the problem he'd gleaned from the Dead Letters, Jaffe left the maestro alone, dispatching supplies (starfish, sea urchins; mescaline; an ape) as and when they were requested, but visiting only once a month. On each occasion he'd spent twenty-four hours with Fletcher, drinking and sharing gossip which Jaffe had plucked from the academic grapevine to feed Fletcher's curiosity. After eleven such visits, sensing that the researches at the Mission were beginning to move towards some conclusion, he began to make the journey more regularly. He was less welcome each time. On one occasion Fletcher had even attempted to keep Jaffe out of the Mission altogether, and there'd been a short, mismatched struggle. Fletcher was no fighter. His stooping, undernourished body was that of a man who'd been bent at his studies since adolescence. Beaten, he'd been obliged to allow access. Inside, Jaffe had found the ape, transformed by Fletcher's distillation, the Nuncio, into an ugly but undeniably human child. Even then, in the midst of this triumph, there'd been hints of the breakdown which Jaffe couldn't doubt Fletcher had finally succumbed to. The man had been uneasy about what they'd achieved. But Jaffe had been too damned pleased to take the warning signs seriously. He'd even suggested he try the Nuncio for himself, there and then. Fletcher had counselled against it; suggested several months of further study to be undertaken before Jaffe risk such a step. The Nuncio was still too volatile, he argued. He wanted to examine the way it worked on the boy's system before any further tests. Suppose it simply proved fatal to the child in a week? Or a day? That argument was enough to cool Jaffe's ardor for a while. He left Fletcher to undertake the proposed tests, returning on a weekly basis now, becoming more aware of Fletcher's disintegration with each visit, but assuming the man's pride in his own masterwork would prevent him trying to undo it.

Now, as flocks of scorched notes flew across the ground towards him, he cursed his trust. He stepped from the jeep and began to make his way through the scattered fires towards the Mission. There had always been an apocalyptic air about this spot. The earth so dry and sandy it could sustain little more than a few stunted yucca; the Mission, perched so close to the cliff-edge that one winter the Pacific would inevitably claim it, the boobies and tropic birds making din overhead.

Today there were only words on the wing. The Mission's walls were stained with smoke where fires had been built close to them. The earth was dusted with ash, even less fertile than sand.

Nothing was as it had been.

He called Fletcher's name as he stepped through the open door, the anxiety he'd felt coming up the hill now close to fear, not for himself but for the Great Work. He was glad he'd come armed. If Fletcher's grasp on sanity had finally slipped he might be obliged to coerce the formula for the Nuncio from him. It would not be the first time he'd gone seeking knowledge with a weapon in his pocket. It was sometimes necessary.

The interior was all ruin; several hundred thousand dollars' worth of instrumentation—coaxed, bullied or seduced from academics who'd given him what he asked for just to get Jaffe's eyes off them—destroyed; table-tops cleared with the sweep of an arm. The windows had all been thrown open and the Pacific wind blew through the place, hot and salty. Jaffe navigated the wreckage and made his way through to Fletcher's favorite room, the cell he'd once (high on mescaline) called the plug in the hole in his heart.

He was there, alive, sitting in his chair in front of the flung window, staring up at the sun: the very act that had blinded him in his right eye. He was dressed in the same shabby shirt and overlarge trousers he always wore; his face presented the same pinched, unshaven profile; the pony-tail of graying hair (his only concession to vanity), was in place. Even his posture—hands at his lap, the body sagging—was one Jaffe had seen innumerable times. And yet there was something subtly wrong with the scene, enough to hold Jaffe at the door, refusing to step into the cell. It was as if Fletcher was *too much* himself. This was too perfect an image of him: the contemplative, staring at the sun, his every pore and pucker demanding the attention of Jaffe's aching retina, as if his portrait had been painted by a thousand miniaturists, all of whom had been granted an inch of their subject and with brushes bearing a single hair rendered their portion in nauseating detail. The rest of the room—the walls, the window, even the chair on which Fletcher sat—swam out of focus, unable to compete with the too-thorough *reality* of this man.

Jaffe closed his eyes against the portrait. It overloaded his senses. Made him nauseous. In the darkness, he heard Fletcher's voice, as unmusical as ever.

"Bad news," he said, very quietly.

"Why?" Jaffe said, not opening his eyes. Even with them closed he knew damn well the prodigy was speaking to him without use of tongue or lips.

"Just leave," Fletcher said. "And *yes*."

"Yes what?"

"You're right. I don't need my throat any longer."

"I didn't say—"

"You don't need to, Jaffe. I'm in your head. It's in there, Jaffe. Worse than I thought. You must leave . . ."

The volume faded, though the words still came. Jaffe tried to catch them, but most slipped by. Something about *do we become sky?*, was it? Yes, that's what he said:

". . . *do we become sky?*"

"What are you talking about?" Jaffe said.

"Open your eyes," Fletcher replied.

"It makes me sick to look at you."

"The feeling's mutual. But still . . . you should open your eyes. See the miracle at work."

"What miracle?"

"Just look."

He did as Fletcher urged. The scene was exactly as it had been when he'd closed them. The wide window; the man sitting before it. The same exactly.

"The Nuncio's in me," Fletcher announced in Jaffe's head. His face didn't move at all. Not a twitch of the lips. Not a flicker of an eyelash. Just the same terrible *finishedness*.

"You mean you tested it on yourself?" Jaffe said. "After all you told me?"

"It changes everything, Jaffe. It's the whip to the back of the world."

"You took it! It was supposed to be me!"

"I didn't take it. It took me. It's got a life of its own, Jaffe. I wanted to destroy it, but it wouldn't let me."

"Why destroy it in the first place? It's the Great Work."

"Because it doesn't operate the way I thought it would. It's not interested in the flesh, Jaffe, except as an afterthought. It's the mind it plays with. It takes thought for its inspiration, and runs with that. Makes us what we'd hope to be, or fear we are. Or both. Maybe both."

"You haven't changed," Jaffe observed. "Still sound the same."

"But I'm talking in your head," Fletcher reminded him. "Did I ever do that before?"

"So, telepathy's in the future of the species," Jaffe replied. "No surprise there. You've just accelerated the process. Leap-frogged a few thousand years."

"Will I be sky?" Fletcher said again. "That's what I want to be."

"Then be it," Jaffe said. "I've got more ambition than that."

"Yes. Yes, you have, more's the pity. That was why I tried to keep it out of your hands. Stop it using you. But it distracted me. I saw the window open and I couldn't keep away. The Nuncio made me so dreamy. Made me sit, and wonder: will I . . . will I be sky?"

"It stopped you cheating me," Jaffe said. "It wants to be used, that's all."

"Mmmm."

"So where's the rest? You didn't take it all."

"No," Fletcher said. The power to deceive had been sluiced from him. "But please, *don't* . . ."

"Where?" Jaffe said, advancing into the room now. "You've got it on you?"

He felt myriad tiny brushes against his skin as he stepped forward, as though he'd walked into a dense cloud of invisible gnats. The sensation should have warned him against tackling Fletcher, but he was too eager for the Nuncio to take notice. He put his fingers on the man's shoulder. Upon contact the figure seemed to fly apart, a cloud of motes—gray, white and red—breaking against him like a pollen storm.

In his head he heard the genius begin to laugh, not, Jaffe knew, at his expense but at the sheer liberation of shrugging off this skin of dulling dust, which had begun to gather upon him at birth, accruing steadily until all but the brightest hints of brightness were stopped. Now, when the dust blew away, Fletcher was still sitting in the chair as he had been. But now he was incandescent.

"I am too bright?" he said. "I'm sorry."

He turned down his flame.

"I want this too!" Jaffe said. "I want it now."

"I know," Fletcher replied. "I can taste your need. Messy, Jaffe, messy. You're dangerous. I don't think I ever really knew till now how dangerous you are. I can see you inside out. Read your past." He stopped for a moment, then let out a long, pained moan. "You killed a man," he said.

"He deserved it."

"Stood in your way. And this other I'm seeing . . . *Kissoon* is it? Did he die too?"

"No."

"But you'd like to have done it? I can taste hatred in you."

"Yes, I'd have killed him if I'd had the chance." He smiled.

"And me as well, I think," Fletcher said. "Is that a knife in your pocket," he asked, "or are you just pleased to see me?"

"I want the Nuncio," Jaffe said. "I want it, and *it* wants *me* . . ."

He turned away. Fletcher called after him.

"It works on the mind, Jaffe. Maybe on the soul. Don't you understand? Nothing *outside* that doesn't begin *inside*. Nothing real that isn't dreamed first. Me? I never wanted my body except as a vehicle. Never really wanted anything at all, except to be sky. But *you*, Jaffe. *You!* Your mind's full of shit. Think of that. Think what the Nuncio's going to *magnify*. I beg you—"

The entreaty, breathed in his skull, made Jaffe halt a moment, and look back at the portrait. It had risen from its chair, though by the expression on Fletcher's face it was a torment to tear himself away from the view.

"I beg you," he said again. "Don't let it use you."

Fletcher extended a hand towards Jaffe's shoulder, but he retreated out of touching range, stepping through into the laboratory. His eyes almost instantly came to rest on the bench and the two vials left in the rack, their contents boiling up against the glass.

"Beautiful," Jaffe said, and stepped towards them, the Nuncio leaping up in the vials at his approach, like a dog wanting to lick its master's face. Its fawning made a lie of Fletcher's fears. He, Randolph Jaffe, was the user in this exchange. The Nuncio, the used.

In his head, Fletcher continued to issue his warning:

"Every cruelty in you, Jaffe, every fear, every stupidity, every cowardice. All making you over. Are you prepared for that? I don't think so. It'll show you too much."

"No such thing as *too much*," Jaffe said, tuning the protests out and reaching for the nearest of the vials. The Nuncio couldn't wait. It broke the glass, its contents jumping to meet his skin. His knowledge (and his terror) were instantaneous, the Nuncio communicating its message on contact. The moment Jaffe realized Fletcher was right was the same moment he became powerless to correct the error.

The Nuncio had little or no interest in changing the order of his cells. If that happened it would only be as a consequence of a profounder alteration. It viewed his anatomy as a cul-de-sac. What minor improvements it could make in the system were beneath its notice. It wasn't going to waste time sophisticating finger-joints or taking the kinks out of the lower bowel. It was an evangelist not a beautician. Mind was its target. Mind which used body for its gratification, even when that gratification harmed the vehicle. Mind which was the source of the hunger for transformation and its most ardent and creative agent.

Jaffe wanted to beg for help, but the Nuncio had already taken control of his cortex, and he was prevented from uttering a word. Prayer was no more plausible. The Nuncio was God. Once in a bottle; now in his body. He couldn't even die, though his system shook so violently it seemed ready to throw itself apart. The Nuncio forbade everything but its work. Its awesome, perfecting work.

Its first act was to throw his memory into reverse, shooting him back through his life from the moment it touched him, piercing each event until he struck the waters of his mother's womb. He was granted a moment of agonizing nostalgia for that place—its calm, its safety—before his life came to drag him out again, and began the return journey, revisiting his little life in Omaha. From the beginning of his conscious life there'd been so much rage. Against the petty and the politic; against the achievers and the seducers, the ones who made the girls and the grades. He felt it all over again, but intensified: like a cancer cell getting fat in the flick of an eye, distorting him. He saw his parents fading away, and him unable to hold on to them, or—when they'd gone—to mourn them, but raged nevertheless, not knowing why they'd lived, or bothered to bring him into the world. He fell in love again, twice. Was rejected again, twice. Nurtured the hurt, decorated the scars, let the rage grow fatter and fatter. And between those notable lows the perpetual grind of jobs that he couldn't hold, and people who forgot his name day after day, and Christmases coming on Christmases, and only age to mark them. Never getting closer to understanding *why* he'd been made — why *anyone* was made, when everything was a cheat and a sham and went to nothing anyway.

Then, the room at the crossroads, filled with Dead Letters, and suddenly his rage had echoes from coast to coast, wild, bewildered people like him stabbing at their confusion and hoping to see sense when it bled. Some of them had. They'd tumbled mysteries, albeit fleetingly. And he had the evidence. Signs and codes; the Medallion of the Shoal, falling into his hands. A moment later he had his knife buried in Homer's head, and he was away, with only a parcel of clues, on a trip that had taken him, growing more powerful with every step, to Los Alamos, and the Loop, and finally to the Misión de Santa Catrina.

And still he didn't know why he'd been made, but he'd accrued enough in his four decades for the Nuncio to give him a temporary answer. For rage's sake. For revenge's sake. For the having of power and the using of power.

Momentarily he hovered over the scene, and saw himself on the floor below, curled round in a litter of glass, clutching at his skull as though to keep it from splitting. Fletcher moved into view. He seemed to be haranguing the body, but Jaffe couldn't hear the words. Some self-righteous speech, no doubt, on the frailty of human endeavor. Suddenly he rushed at the body, his arms raised, and brought his fists down upon it. It came apart, like the portrait at the window. Jaffe howled as his dislocated spirit was claimed for the substance on the floor, drawn down into his Nunciate anatomy.

He opened his eyes and looked up at the man who'd struck off his crust, seeing Fletcher with new comprehension.

From the beginning they'd been an uneasy partnership, the fundamental principles of which had confounded both. But now Jaffe saw the mechanism clearly. Each was the other's nemesis. No two entities on earth were so perfectly opposed. Fletcher loving light as only a man in terror of ignorance could; one eye gone from looking at the sun's face. He was no longer Randolph Jaffe, but the *Jaff,* the one and only, in love with the dark where his rage had found its sustenance and its expression. The dark where sleep came, and the trip to the dream-sea beyond sleep began. Painful as the Nuncio's education had been, it was good to be reminded of what he was. More than reminded, *magnified* through the glass of his own history. Not *in* the dark now, but *of* it, capable of using the Art. His hand already itched to do so. And with the itch came a grasp of how to snatch the veil aside and enter Quiddity. He didn't need ritual. He didn't need suits or sacrifices. He was an evolved soul. His need could not be denied, and he had need in abundance.

But in reaching this new self he had accidentally created a force that would, if he didn't stop here and now, oppose him every step of the way. He got to his feet, not needing to hear a challenge from Fletcher's lips to know that the enmity between them was perfectly understood. He read the revulsion in the flame that flared behind his enemy's eye. The genius *sauvage*, the dope-fiend and Pollyanna Fletcher had been dissolved and reconstructed: joyless, dreamy and bright. Minutes ago he'd been ready to sit by the window, longing to be sky, until longing or death did its work. But not now.

"I see the whole thing," he announced, choosing to use his voice-box now that they were equal and opposite. "You tempted me to raise you up, so you could steal your way to revelation."

"And I *will*," the Jaff replied. "I'm halfway there already."

"Quiddity won't open to the likes of you."

"It'll have no choice," the Jaff replied. "I'm inevitable now." He raised his hand. Beads of power, like tiny ball-bearings, came sweating from it. "You see?" he said, "I'm an Artist."

"Not till you use the Art you're not."

"And who's going to stop me? *You?*"

"I've got no choice. I'm responsible."

"How? I beat you to a pulp once. I'll do it again."

"I'll raise visions to oppose you."

"You can try." A question came into the Jaff mind as he spoke, which Fletcher had begun to answer before the other had even voiced it.

"Why did I touch your body? I don't know. It demanded I did. I kept trying to shout it down, but it called."

He paused, then said:

"Maybe opposites attract, even in our condition."

"Then the sooner you're dead, the better," the Jaff said, and reached to tear out his enemy's throat.

In the darkness that was creeping over the Mission from the Pacific, Raul heard the first din of battle begin. He knew from echoes in his own Nunciate system that the distillation had been at work behind the walls. His father, Fletcher, had gone out of his own life and into something new. So had the other man, the one he'd always distrusted, even when words like evil were just sounds from a human palate. He understood them now; or at least put them together with his animal response to Jaffe: revulsion. The man was sick to his core, like fruit full of rot. To judge by the sound of violence from inside, Fletcher had decided to fight that corruption. The brief, sweet time he'd had with his father was over. There'd be no more lessons in civility; no more sitting together by the window, listening to "the sublime Mozart" and watching the clouds change shape.

As the first stars appeared, the sounds from the Mission ceased. Raul waited, hoping that Jaffe had been destroyed, but fearing his father had gone too. After an hour in the cold he decided to venture inside. Wherever they'd gone—Heaven or Hell—he couldn't follow. The best he could do was put on his clothes, which he'd always despised wearing (they chafed and caged) but which were now a reminder of his master's tuition. He'd wear them always, so as not to forget the Good Man Fletcher.

Reaching the door, he realized that the Mission had not been vacated. Fletcher was still there. So was his enemy. Both men still possessed bodies that resembled their former selves, but there was a change in them. Shapes hovered over each: a huge-headed infant, the color of smoke, over Jaffe; a cloud, with the sun somewhere in its cushion, over Fletcher. The men had their hands at each other's throats and eyes. Their subtle bodies were similarly intertwined. Perfectly matched, neither could gain victory.

Raul's entrance broke the impasse. Fletcher turned, his one good eye focusing on the boy, and in that instant the Jaff took his advantage, flinging his enemy back across the room.

"*Out!*" Fletcher yelled to Raul. "*Get out!*"

Raul did as he was ordered, darting between the dying fires as he raced from the Mission, the ground trembling beneath his bare soles as new furies were unleashed behind him. He had three seconds' grace to fling himself a little way down the slope before the leeway side of the Mission—walls which had been built to survive until the end of faith—shattered before an eruption of energy. He didn't cover his eyes against it. Instead he watched, glimpsing the forms of Jaffe and the Good Man Fletcher, twin powers locked together in the same wind, fly out from the center of the blast over his head, and away into the night.

The force of the explosion had scattered the bonfires. Hundreds of smaller fires now burned around the Mission. The roof had been almost entirely blown off. The walls bore gaping wounds.

Lonely already, Raul limped back towards his only refuge.

SIX

There was a war waged in America that year, perhaps the bitterest and certainly the strangest ever fought on, in or above its soil. For the most part it went unreported, because it went unnoticed. Or rather its consequences (which were many, and often traumatic) seemed so unlike the effects of battle they were consistently misinterpreted. But then this was a war without precedent. Even the most crackpot prophets, the kind who annually predicted Armageddon, didn't know how to interpret the shaking of America's entrails. They knew something of consequence was afoot, and had Jaffe still been in the Dead Letter Room in the Omaha Post Office he would have discovered countless letters flying back and forth, filled with theories and suppositions. None, however—even from correspondents who'd known in some oblique fashion about the Shoal and the Art—came close to the truth.

Not only was the combat without precedent, but its nature developed as the weeks went by. The combatants had left the Misión de Santa Catrina with only a rudimentary understanding of their new condition and the powers that went with it. They soon explored and learned to exploit those powers, however, as the necessity of conflict threw their invention into overdrive. As he'd sworn, Fletcher willed an army from the fantasy lives of the ordinary men and women he met as he pursued Jaffe across the country, never giving him time to concentrate his will and use the Art he had access to. He dubbed these visionary soldiers *hallucigenia*, after an enigmatic species whose fossil remains recorded their existence five hundred and thirty million years previously. A family which, like the fantasies now named for them, bore no antecedents. These soldiers had lives barely longer than that of butterflies. They soon lost their particularity, becoming smoky and vague. But gossamer as they were, they several times carried the day against the Jaff and his legions, the *terata*, primal fears which Randolph now had the power to call forth from his victims, and make solid for a time. The terata were no less fleeting than the battalions shaped against them. In that, as in everything else, the Jaff and Good Man Fletcher were equally matched.

So it proceeded, in feints and counterfeints, pincer movements and sweeps, the intention of each army to slaughter the leader of the other. It was not a war the natural world took kindly to. Fears and fantasies were not supposed to take physical form. Their arena was the mind. Now they were *solid*, their combat raging across Arizona and Colorado, and into Kansas and Illinois, the order of things undone in countless ways by its passage. Crops were slow to show their shoots, preferring to stay in the earth rather than risk their tender heads when creatures in defiance of all natural law were abroad. Flocks of migrating birds, avoiding the paths of haunted thunderheads, came late to their resting grounds, or lost their way entirely and perished. There was in every state a trail of stampedes and gorings, the panicked response of animals who sensed the scale of the conflict being waged to extinction around them. Stallions set their sights on cattle and boulders, and gutted themselves mounting cars. Dogs and cats turned savage overnight, and were shot or gassed for the crime. Fish in quiet rivers tried to take to the land, knowing there was ambition in the air, and perished aspiring.

Fear in front and bedlam behind, the conflict ground to a halt in

Wyoming, where the armies, too equally matched for anything but a war of attrition, fought each other to a complete standstill. It was the end of the beginning, or near it. The sheer scale of the energies required by Good Man Fletcher and the Jaff to create and lead these armies (no warlords these, by any stretch of the definition; they were merely men in hate with each other) had taken a terrible toll. Weakened to the point of near collapse they punched on like boxers who'd been battered into a stupor, but who fought because they knew no other sport. Neither would be satisfied until the other was dead.

On the night of July 16th the Jaff broke from the field of battle, shedding the remnants of his army as he made a dash for the southwest. His intended destination was the Baja. Knowing that the war against Fletcher could not be won under present conditions, he wanted access to the third vial of the Nuncio, with which he might re-invest his much diminished power.

Ravaged as he was, Fletcher gave chase. Two nights later, with a spurt of agility that would have impressed his much-missed Raul, he overtook the Jaff in Utah.

There they met, in a confrontation as brutal as it was inconclusive. Fuelled by a passion for each other's destruction which had long ago escalated beyond the issue of the Art and its possessing, and was now as devoted and as intimate as love, they fought for five nights. Again, neither triumphed. They beat and tore at each other, dark matched with bright, until they were barely coherent. When the Wind took them they lacked all power to resist it. What little strength remained they used to prevent one another from making a break for the Mission, and the sustenance there. The Wind carried them over the border into California, dropping them closer to the earth with every mile they covered. South-southeast over Fresno, and towards Bakersfield they travelled, until—on Friday, July 27th, 1971, their powers so depleted they could no longer keep themselves aloft—they fell in Ventura County, on the wooded edge of a town called Palomo Grove, during a minor electrical storm which brought not so much as a flicker to the roving searchlights and illuminated billboards of nearby Hollywood.

PART TWO

THE LEAGUE OF VIRGINS

ONE

I

The girls went down to the water twice. The first time was the day after the rainstorm that had broken over Ventura County, shedding more water on the small town of Palomo Grove in a single night than its inhabitants might have reasonably expected in a year. The downpour, however monsoonal, had not mellowed the heat. With what little wind there was coming off the desert, the town baked in the high nineties. Children who'd exhausted themselves playing in the heat through the morning wailed away the afternoon indoors. Dogs cursed their coats; birds declined to make music. Old folks took to their beds. Adulterers did the same, dressed in sweat. Those unfortunates with tasks to perform that couldn't be delayed until evening, when (God willing) the temperature dropped, went about their labors with their eyes to the shimmering sidewalks, every step a trial, every breath sticky in their lungs.

But the four girls were used to heat; it was at their age the condition of the blood. Between them, they had seventy years' life on the planet, though when Arleen turned nineteen the following Tuesday, it would be seventy-one. Today she felt her age; that vital few months that separated her from her closest friend, Joyce, and even further from Carolyn and Trudi, whose mere seventeen was an age away for a mature woman like herself. She had much to tell on the subject of experience that day, as they sauntered through the empty streets of Palomo Grove. It was good to be out on a day like this, without being ogled by the men in the town—they knew them all by name—whose wives had taken to sleeping in the spare room; or their sexual banter being overheard by one of their mothers' friends. They wandered, like Amazons in shorts, through a town taken by some invisible fire which blistered the air and turned brick into mirage but did not kill. It merely laid the inhabitants stricken beside their open fridges.

"Is it love?" Joyce asked Arleen.

The older girl had a swift answer.

"Hell no," she said. "You are so *dumb* sometimes."

"I just thought . . . with you talking about him that way."

"What do you mean: *that way?*"

"Talking about his eyes and stuff."

"Randy's got nice eyes," Arleen conceded. "But so's Marty, and Jim, and Adam—"

"Oh *stop*," said Trudi, with more than a trace of irritation. "You're such a slut."

"I am not."

"So stop it with the names. We all know that boys like you. And we all know why."

Arleen threw her a look which went unread given that all but Carolyn were wearing sunglasses. They walked on a few yards in silence.

"Anyone want a Coke?" Carolyn said. "Or ice cream?" They'd come to the bottom of the hill. The Mall was ahead, its air-conditioned stores tempting.

"Sure," said Trudi, "I'll come with you." She turned to Arleen. "You want something?"

"Nope."

"Are you sulking?"

"Nope."

"Good," said Trudi. "'Cause it's too hot to argue." The two girls headed into Marvin's Food and Drug, leaving Arleen and Joyce on the street corner.

"I'm sorry . . ." Joyce said.

"What about?"

"Asking you about Randy. I thought maybe you . . . you know . . . maybe it was serious."

"There's no one in the Grove that's worth two cents," Arleen murmured. "I can't wait to get out."

"Where will you go? Los Angeles?"

Arleen pulled her sunglasses down her nose and peered at Joyce.

"Why would I want to do that?" she said. "I've got more sense than to join the line there. No, I'm going to New York. It's better to study there. Then work on Broadway. If they want me they can come and get me."

"Who can?"

"*Joyce*," Arleen said, mock-exasperated. "Hollywood."

"Oh. Yeah. Hollywood."

She nodded appreciatively at the completedness of Arleen's plan. She had nothing in her own head anywhere near so coherent. But it was easy for Arleen. She was California Beautiful, blonde, blue-eyed and the envied possessor of a smile that brought the opposite sex to their knees. If that weren't advantage enough she had a mother who'd been an actress, and already treated her daughter like a Star.

Joyce had no such blessings. No mother to pave the way, no glamour to get her through the bad times. She couldn't even drink a Coke without getting acne. Sensitive skin, Doctor Briskman kept saying, you'll grow out of it. But the promised transformation was like the end of the world that the Reverend talked about on a Sunday; delayed and delayed. With my luck, Joyce thought, the day I lose my zits and get my tits is the day the Reverend's right. I'll wake up perfect, open the curtains, and the Grove will be gone. I'll never get to kiss Randy Krentzman.

There, of course, lay the real reason behind her close questioning of Arleen. Randy was in Joyce's every thought, or every other, though she'd only met him three times and spoken to him twice. She'd been with Arleen during the first encounter, and Randy had scarcely looked her way when she was introduced, so she'd said nothing. The second occasion she'd not had any competition, but her friendly hello had been greeted with an off-hand: "Who are you?" She'd persisted; reminded him; even told him where she lived. On the third meeting ("Hello again," she'd said. "Do I know you?" he'd replied), she'd recited all her personal details shamelessly; even asked him, in a sudden rush of optimism, if he was a Mormon. That, she'd later decided, had been a tactical error. Next time she'd use Arleen's approach, and treat the boy as though his presence was barely endurable; never look at him; only smile if it was absolutely necessary. Then, when you were about to saunter away look straight into his eyes, and purr something vaguely dirty. The law of mixed messages. It worked for Arleen, why not for her? And now that the great beauty had publicly announced her indifference to Joyce's idol she had some sliver of hope. If Arleen had been seriously interested in Randy's affections then Joyce might have gone right around to the Reverend Meuse and asked him if he could hurry the Apocalypse up a little.

She took off her glasses and squinted up at the white hot sky, vaguely wondering if it was already on its way. The day was strange.

"Shouldn't do that," Carolyn said, emerging from Marvin's Food and Drug with Trudi following, "the sun'll burn out your eyes."

"It will not."

"It will so," Carolyn, ever the source of unwanted information, replied, "your retina's a lens. Like in a camera. It focuses—"

"All right," Joyce said, returning her gaze to solid ground. "I believe you." Colors cavorted behind her eyes for a few moments, disorienting her.

"Where now?" said Trudi.

"I'm going back home," Arleen said. "I'm tired."

"I'm not," Trudi said brightly. "I'm not going home, either. It's boring."

"Well it's no use standing in the middle of the Mall," Carolyn said. "That's as boring as being at home. And we'll cook in the sun."

She looked roasted already. The heaviest of the four by twenty pounds or more, and a redhead, the combination of her weight, and skin that never tanned, should have driven her indoors. But she seemed indifferent to the discomfort, as she was to every other physical stimulus but that of taste. The previous November the entire Hotchkiss family had been involved in a freeway pile-up. Carolyn had crawled free of the wreckage, slightly concussed, and had subsequently been found by the police some way down the freeway, with half-chewed Hershey bars in both hands. There was more chocolate on her face than blood, and she'd screamed blue murder—or so rumor went—when one of the cops attempted to dissuade her from her snack. Only later was it discovered that she'd sustained half a dozen cracked ribs.

"So where?" said Trudi, returning to the burning issue of the day. "In this heat: *where?*"

"We'll just walk," said Joyce. "Maybe down to the woods. It'll be cooler there." She glanced at Arleen. "Are you coming?"

Arleen made her companions hang on her silence for ten seconds. Finally she agreed.

"Nowhere better to go," she said.

II

Most towns, however small, make themselves after the pattern of a city. That is, they divide. White from black, straight from gay, wealthy from less wealthy, less wealthy from poor. Palomo Grove, the population of which was in that year, 1971, a mere one thousand two hundred, was no exception. Built on the flanks of a gently sloping hillside, the town had been designed as an embodiment of democratic principles, in which every occupant was intended to have equal access to the center of power in the town, the Mall. It lay at the bottom of Sunrise Hill, known simply as the Hill, with four villages—Stillbrook, Deerdell, Laureltree and Windbluff—radiating from its hub, their feed thoroughfares aligned with the compass points. But that was as far as the planners' idealism went. Thereafter the subtle differences in the geography of the villages made each quite different in character.

Windbluff, which lay on the southwest flank of the hill, commanded the best views, and its properties the highest prices. The top third of the Hill was dominated by half a dozen grand residences, their roofs barely visible behind lush foliage. On the lower slopes of this Olympus were the Five Crescents, streets bowed upon themselves, which were—if you couldn't afford a house at the very top—the next most desirable places to live.

By contrast, Deerdell. Built on flat ground, and flanked on two sides by undeveloped woodland, this quadrant of the Grove had rapidly gone downhill. Here the houses lacked pools and needed paint. For some, the locale was a hip retreat. There were, even in 1971, a few artists living in Deerdell; that community would steadily grow. But if there was anywhere in the Grove where people went in fear for their automobiles' paintwork, it was here.

Between these two extremes, socially and geographically, lay Stillbrook and Laureltree, the latter thought marginally more upscale because several of its streets were built on the second flank of the Hill, their scale and their prices less modest with every bend the streets took as they climbed.

None of the quartet were residents of Deerdell. Arleen lived on Emerson, the second highest of the Crescents, Joyce and Carolyn within a block of each other on Steeple Chase Drive in Stillbrook Village, and Trudi in Laureltree. So there was a certain adventure in treading the streets of the East Grove, where their parents had seldom, if ever, ventured. Even if they had strayed down here, they'd certainly never gone where the girls now went: into the woods.

"It's no cooler," Arleen complained when they'd been wandering a few minutes. "In fact, it's worse."

She was right. Though the foliage kept the stare of the sun off their heads, the heat still found its way between the branches. Trapped, it made the damp air steamy.

"I haven't been here for years," Trudi said, whipping a switch of stripped twig back and forth through a cloud of gnats. "I used to come with my brother."

"How is he?" Joyce enquired.

"Still in the hospital. He's never going to come out. All the family knows that but nobody ever says it. Makes me sick."

Sam Katz had been drafted and gone to Vietnam fit in mind and body. In the third month of his tour of duty all that had been undone by a land mine, which had killed two of his comrades and badly injured him. There'd been a squirmingly uneasy homecoming, the Grove's little mighty lined up to greet the crippled hero. What followed was much talk of heroism and sacrifice; much drinking; some hidden tears. Through it all Sam Katz had sat stony featured, not setting his face against the celebrations but detached from them, as though his mind were still rehearsing the moment when his youth had been blown to smithereens. A few weeks later he'd been taken back to the hospital. Though his mother had told enquirers it was for corrective surgery to his spine the months dragged on until they became years, and Sam didn't reappear. Everyone guessed the reason, though it went unadmitted. Sam's physical wounds had healed adequately well. But his mind had not proved so resilient. The detachment he'd evidenced at his homecoming party had deepened into catatonia.

All the other girls had known Sam, though the age difference between Joyce and her brother had been sufficient for them to have looked upon him almost as another species. Not simply *male*, which was strange enough, but old, too. Once past puberty, however, the roller-coaster ride began to speed. They could see twenty-five up ahead: a little way yet, but visible. And the waste of Sam's life began to make sense to them the way it could never have made sense to an eleven-year-old. Fond, sad memories of him silenced them for a while. They walked on through the heat, their bodies side by side, arms occasionally brushing arms, their minds diverging. Trudi's thoughts were of those childhood games, played with Sam in these thickets. He'd been an indulgent older brother, allowing her to tag along when she was seven or eight, and he thirteen. A year later, when his juices started telling him girls and sisters weren't the same animal, the invitations to play war had ceased. She'd mourned the loss of him; a rehearsal for the mourning she'd felt more acutely later. She saw his face in her mind now, a weird melding of the boy he'd been and the man he was; of the life he'd had and the death he lived. It made her hurt.

For Carolyn, there were few hurts, at least in her waking life. And today—barring her wishing she'd bought a second ice cream—none. Night was quite a different matter. She had bad dreams; of earth-quakes. In them Palomo Grove would fold up like a canvas chair and disappear into the earth. That was the penalty for knowing too much, her father had told her. She'd inherited his fierce curiosity, and had applied it—from first hearing of the San Andreas Fault—to a study of the earth they walked upon. Its solidity could not be trusted. Beneath their feet, she knew, the ground was riddled with fissures, which might at any moment gape, as they would gape beneath Santa Barbara and Los Angeles, all the way up and down the West Coast, swallowing the lot. She kept her anxieties at bay with swallowings of her own: a sort of sympathetic magic. She was fat because the earth's crust was thin; an irrefutable excuse for gluttony.

Arleen cast a glance over at the Fat Girl. It never hurt, her mother had once instructed her, to keep the company of the less attractive. Though no longer in the public eye, the sometime star Kate Farrell still surrounded herself with dowdy women, in whose company her looks were twice as compelling. But for Arleen, especially on days like today, it seemed too high a price. Though they flattered her looks she didn't really like her companions. Once she'd have counted them her dearest friends. Now they were reminders of a life from which she could not escape quickly enough. But how else was she going to spend the time till her parole came through? Even the joys of sitting in front of the mirror palled after a time. The sooner I'm out of here, she thought, the sooner I'm happy.

Had she been able to read Arleen's mind Joyce would have applauded the urgency. But she was lost in thoughts of how best to arrange an accidental encounter with Randy. If she made a casual enquiry about his routines Arleen would guess her purpose, and she might be selfish enough to spike Joyce's chances even though she had no interest in the boy herself. Joyce was a fine reader of character, and knew it was quite within Arleen's capabilities to be so perverse. But then who was she to condemn perversity? She was pursuing a male who'd three times made his indifference to her perfectly plain. Why couldn't she just forget him and save herself the grief of rejection? Because love wasn't like that. It made you fly in the face of the evidence, however compelling.

She sighed audibly.

"Something wrong?" Carolyn wanted to know.

"Just . . . hot," Joyce replied.

"Anyone we know?" Trudi said. Before Joyce could muster an adequately disparaging reply she caught sight of something glittering through the trees ahead.

"Water," she said.

Carolyn had seen it too. Its brightness made her squint.

"Lots of it," she said.

"I didn't know there was a lake down here," Joyce remarked, turning to Trudi.

"There wasn't," came the reply. "Not that I remember."

"Well there is now," said Carolyn.

She was already forging ahead through the foliage, not caring to take the less thronged route. Her blundering passage cleared a way for the others.

"Looks like we're going to get cool after all," Trudi said, and went after her at a run.

It was indeed a lake, maybe fifty feet wide, its placid surface broken by half-submerged trees, and islands of shrubbery.

"Flood water," Carolyn said. "We're right at the bottom of the hill here. It must have gathered after the storm."

"That's a lot of water," Joyce said. "Did this all fall last night?"

"If it didn't where did it come from?" Carolyn said.

"Who cares?" said Trudi. "It looks cool."

She moved past Carolyn to the very edge of the water. The ground became more swampy underfoot with every step, mud rising up over her sandals. But the water, when she reached it, was as good as its promise: refreshingly cold. She crouched down, and put her hand in the lake, bringing a palmful of it up to splash her face.

"I wouldn't do that," Carolyn cautioned. "It's probably full of chemicals."

"It's only rainwater," Trudi replied. "What's cleaner than that?"

Carolyn shrugged. "Please yourself," she said.

"I wonder how deep it is?" Joyce mused. "Deep enough to swim, do you think?"

"Shouldn't have thought so," Carolyn commented.

"Don't know till we try," Trudi said, and began to wade out into the lake. She could see grass and flowers beneath her feet; drowned now. The earth itself was soft, and her steps stirred up clouds of mud, but she advanced until she was in deep enough for the hem of her shorts to be soaked.

The water was cold. It brought gooseflesh. But that was preferable to the sweat that had stuck her blouse to her breasts and spine. She looked back towards the shore.

"Feels great," she said. "I'm going in."

"Like that?" Arleen said.

"Of course not." Trudi waded back towards the trio, pulling her blouse out of her shorts as she went. The air rising from the water tingled against her skin, its *frisson* welcome. She wore nothing beneath, and would normally have been more modest, even in front of her friends, but the lake's invitation was not to be postponed.

"Anybody going to join me?" she asked as she stepped back among the others.

"I am," Joyce said, already unknotting her sneakers.

"I think we should keep our shoes on," Trudi said. "We don't know what's underfoot."

"It's only grass," said Joyce. She sat down and worked on the knots, grinning. "This is great," she said.

Arleen was watching her whooping enthusiasm with disdain.

"You two not joining us?" Trudi said.

"No," Arleen said.

"Afraid your mascara'll run?" Joyce replied, her grin widening.

"Nobody's going to see," said Trudi, before a rift developed. "Carolyn? What about you?"

The girl shrugged. "Can't swim," she said.

"It's not deep enough to swim in."

"You don't know that," Carolyn observed. "You only waded out a few yards."

"So stay close to the shore. You'll be safe there."

"Maybe," Carolyn said, far from convinced.

"Trudi's right," Joyce said, sensing Carolyn's reluctance was as much to do with uncovering her fat as with swimming. "Who's going to see us?"

As she stripped off her shorts it occurred to her that any number of peepers might be hidden among the trees, but what the heck? Wasn't the Reverend forever saying life was short? Best not to waste it then. She stepped out of her underwear and started into the water.

William Witt knew each one of the bathers' names. In fact he knew the names of every woman in the Grove under forty, and where they lived, and which was their bedroom window; a feat of memory which he declined to boast of to any of his schoolmates for fear they spread it around. Though he could see nothing wrong with looking through windows he knew enough to know it was frowned upon. And yet he'd been born with eyes, hadn't he? Why shouldn't he use them? Where was the harm in *watching*? It wasn't like stealing, or lying, or killing people. It was just doing what God had created eyes to do, and he couldn't see what was criminal in that.

He crouched, hidden by trees, half a dozen yards from the edge of the water, and twice that distance from the girls, watching them undress. Arleen Farrell was hanging back, he saw, which frustrated him. To see her naked would be an achievement even he'd not be able to keep to himself. She was the most beautiful girl in Palomo Grove: sleek and blonde and snooty, the way movie stars were supposed to be. The other two, Trudi Katz and Joyce McGuire, were already in the water, so he turned his attentions to Carolyn Hotchkiss, who was even now taking off her bra. Her breasts were heavy, and pink, and the sight of them made him hard in his trousers. Though she stripped off her shorts and panties he kept staring at her breasts. He couldn't under-

stand the fascination some of the other boys—he was ten—had with
that lower part; it seemed so much less exciting than the bosom, which
was as different from girl to girl as her nose or hips. The other, the part
he didn't like any of the words for, seemed to him quite uninteresting:
a patch of hair with a slit buried in the middle. What was the big deal
about that?

He watched as Carolyn stepped into the water, only just suppress-
ing a giggle of pleasure when she responded to the cold water with a
half step backwards which set her flesh jiggling like jello.

"Come on! It's wonderful!" the Katz girl was coaxing her.

Plucking up her courage, Carolyn advanced a few more steps.

And now—William could scarcely believe his luck—Arleen was
taking off her hat and unbuttoning her halter top. She was joining
them after all. He forgot the others and fixed his gaze on Miss Sleek.
As soon as he'd realized what the girls—whom he'd been following for
an hour, unsuspected—were planning to do, his heart had started
thumping so hard he thought he'd be ill. Now that thump redoubled,
as the prospect of Arleen's breasts came before him. Nothing—not
even fear of death—would have made him look away. He set himself
the challenge of memorizing every tiny motion, so as to add veracity to
his account when he told it to disbelievers.

She went slowly about it. If he'd not known better he'd have suspected she knew she had an audience, the way she teased and
paraded. Her bosom was a disappointment. Not as large as Carolyn's,
nor boasting large, dark nipples like Joyce's. But the overall impression, when she stepped from her cut-off jeans and slid down her
panties, was wonderful. It made him feel almost panicky to see her.
His teeth chattered like he had the flu. His face got hot, his innards
seemed to rattle. Later in life William would tell his analyst that this
was the first moment he realized that he was going to die. In fact that
was hindsight speaking. Death was very far from his mind now. And
yet the sight of Arleen's nakedness, and his invisibility as he witnessed
it, did mark this moment as one which he would never quite outgrow.
Events were about to occur that would temporarily make him wish
he'd never come peeping (he'd live in fear of the memory, in fact), but

when, after several years, the terror mellowed, he returned to the image of Arleen Farrell stepping into the waters of this sudden lake, as to an icon.

It was not the moment that he first knew he was going to die; but it was perhaps the first time he understood that ceasing would not be so bad, if beauty was there to escort him on his way.

The lake was seductive, its embrace cool but reassuring. There was no undertow, as at the beach. No surf beating against your back nor salt stinging your eyes. It was like a swimming pool created for the four of them only; an idyll that no one else in the Grove had access to.

Trudi was the strongest swimmer of the quartet, and it was she who headed from the shore with the greatest vigor, discovering, as she went, that contrary to expectation the water was getting deeper all the time. It must have gathered where the ground dipped naturally, she reasoned, perhaps even in a place where there'd once been a small lake, though she could remember no such spot from her ramblings with Sam. The grass had now gone from beneath her toes, which brushed instead bare rock.

"Don't go too far," Joyce called to her.

She turned. The shore was further than she'd estimated, the glaze of water in her eyes reducing her friends to three pink blurs, one blonde, two brunettes, half submerged in the same sweet-tasting element as she. It would be impossible to keep this fragment of Eden to themselves unfortunately. Arleen would be bound to talk about it. By evening the secret would be out. By tomorrow, thronged. They'd better make the most of their privacy. So thinking, she struck out for the middle of the lake.

Ten yards closer to shore, sculling along on her back in water no more than navel-deep, Joyce watched Arleen at the lake's edge, stooping to splash her belly and breasts. A spasm of envy for her friend's beauty went through her. No wonder the Randy Krentzmans of the world went gaga at the sight of her. She found herself wondering what it would be like to stroke Arleen's hair, the way a boy would, or kiss her breasts, or her lips. The idea possessed her so suddenly and so forcibly she lost her balance in the water, and swallowed a mouthful as she tried to right herself. Once she had, she turned her back on Arleen, and with a splashing stroke headed into deeper waters.

Up ahead Trudi was shouting something to her.

"What did you say?" Joyce yelled back, subduing her stroke so as to hear better.

Trudi was laughing. "Warm!" she said, splashing around, "it's *warm* out here!"

"Are you kidding?"

"Come and feel!" Trudi replied.

Joyce began to swim out to where Trudi was treading water, but her friend was already turning from her to follow the call of the warmth. Joyce could not resist glancing back at Arleen. She had finally deigned to join the swimming party, immersing herself till her long hair spread around her neck like a golden collar, then starting an even-paced stroke towards the center of the lake. Joyce felt something close to fear at the thought of Arleen's proximity. She wanted some leavening company.

"Carolyn!" she called. "Are you coming?"

Carolyn shook her head.

"It's warmer out here," Joyce promised.

"I don't believe you."

"Really it is!" Trudi shouted. "It's beautiful!"

Carolyn seemed to relent, and began to splash her way in Trudi's wake.

Trudi swam on a few more yards. The water was not getting any warmer, but it *was* becoming more agitated, bubbling up around her like a jacuzzi. Suddenly unnerved she tried to touch bottom, but the ground had gone from beneath her. Mere yards behind her the water had been at most four and a half feet deep; now her toes didn't even graze solid earth. The ground must have slid away violently, at almost the same spot that the warm current had appeared. Taking courage from the fact that three strokes would take her back to safety she ducked her head below the water.

Though her eyes were bad at a distance her short-range sight was good, and the water was clear. She could see down the length of her body to her pedalling feet. Beyond them, solid darkness. The ground had simply vanished. Shock made her gasp. She breathed water in through her nose. Spluttering and flailing she threw her head up to snatch some air.

Joyce was yelling to her.

"Trudi? What's wrong? Trudi?"

She tried to form some words of warning, but a primal terror had seized her: all she could do was throw herself in the direction of the shore, her panic merely churning the water to fresh and choking frenzy. *Darkness below, and something warm there, waiting to pull me down.*

In his hiding place on the shore William Witt saw the girl struggling. Her panic made him lose his erection. Something odd was happening out on the lake. He could see darts on the water's surface, circling Trudi Katz, like fish that were only just submerged. Some were breaking off and sliding towards the other girls. He didn't dare cry out. If he did they'd know he'd been spying on them. All he could do was watch with mounting trepidation as the events in the lake unfolded.

Joyce felt the warmth next. It ran over her skin and inside her too, like a swallow of Christmas brandy, coating her innards. The sensation distracted her from Trudi's splashing, and indeed from her own jeopardy. She watched the darting water, and the bubbles breaking the surface all around her, popping like lava, slow and thick, with an odd detachment. Even when she tried to touch bottom, and couldn't, the thought that she might drown was a casual one. There were more important feelings. One, that the air breaking from the bubbles around her was the lake's breath, and breathing it was like kissing the lake. Two, that Arleen would be swimming this way very soon, the golden collar of hair floating in the water behind her. Seduced by the pleasure of the warm water, she didn't forbid herself the thoughts she'd turned her back on mere moments before. Here they were, she and Arleen, buoyed up in the same body of sweet water, getting closer and closer to each other, while the element between them carried the echoes of their every motion back and forth. Perhaps they would dissolve in the water, their bodies become fluid, until they mingled in the lake. She and Arleen, one mixture, released from any need for shame; beyond sex into blissful singularity.

The possibility was too exquisite to be postponed a moment longer. She threw her arms above her head and let herself sink. The spell of the lake, however, powerful as it was, couldn't quite discipline the animal panic that rose in her as the water closed over her head. Without her willing it, her body began to resist the pact she'd made with the water. She began to struggle wildly, reaching up to the surface as if to snatch a handhold of air.

Both Arleen and Trudi saw Joyce go under. Arleen instantly went to her aid, shouting as she swam. Her agitation was matched by the water around her. Bubbles rose on all sides. She felt their passage, like hands brushing her belly, her breasts and between her legs. At their caress the same dreaminess that had caught Joyce, and had now subdued Trudi's panic, took hold of her. There was no specific object of desire to carry her under, however. Joyce was conjuring the image of Randy Krentzman (who else?) but for Arleen her seducer was a crazy quilt of famous faces. Dean's cheekbones, Sinatra's eyes, Brando's sneer. She succumbed to this patchwork the same way Joyce and, a few yards from her Trudi, had. She threw up her arms and let the waters take her.

From the safety of the shallows Carolyn watched the behavior of her friends, appalled. Seeing Joyce go under she'd assumed there was something in the water, dragging her down. But the behavior of Arleen and Trudi gave the lie to that. She witnessed them plainly *giving up*. Nor was this simple suicide. She'd been close enough to Arleen to observe a look of pleasure crossing that beautiful face before it sank. She'd even *smiled!* Smiled, then let herself go.

These three girls were Carolyn's only friends in the world. She could not simply watch them drown. Though the water where they'd disappeared was becoming more frenzied by the moment she struck out for the place using the only stroke she was faintly proficient in: an ungainly mixture of doggy-paddle and crawl. Natural laws, she knew, were on her side. Fat floated. But that was little comfort as she saw the ground falling away beneath her feet. The bottom of the lake had vanished. She was swimming over a fissure, which was somehow claiming the other girls.

Ahead of her, an arm broke the surface. In desperation she reached for it. Reached; snatched; connected. As she took hold, however, the water around her began to churn with fresh fury. She made a cry of horror. Then the hand she'd grasped took fierce hold of her, and dragged her down.

The world went out like a pinched flame. Her senses deserted her. If she was still holding somebody's fingers she couldn't feel them. Nor, though her eyes were open, could she see anything in the murk. Vaguely, distantly, she was aware that her body was drowning; that her lungs were filling with water through her gaping mouth, her last breath leaving her. But her mind had forsaken its casing and was drifting away from the flesh it had been hostage to. She saw that flesh now: not with her physical eyes (they were still in her head, rolling wildly) but with her mind's sight. A barrel of fat; rolling and pitching as it sank. She felt nothing for its demise, except perhaps disgust at the rolls of blubber, and the absurd inelegance of her distress. In the water beyond her body the other girls still resisted. Their thrashings were also, she presumed, merely instinctual. Their minds, like hers, had probably floated out of their heads, and were watching the spectacle with the same dispassion. True, their bodies were more attractive than hers, and thus perhaps more painful in the losing. But resistance was, in the end, a waste of effort. They were all going to die very soon, here in the middle of this midsummer lake. Why?

As she asked the question her eyeless gaze offered the answer. There was something in the darkness below her floating mind. She could not see it, but she felt it. A power—no, *two powers*—whose breaths were the bubbles that had broken around them and whose arms the eddies that beckoned them to be corpses. She looked back at her body, which still struggled for air. Her legs were pedalling the water madly. Between them, her virgin cunt. Momentarily she felt a pang for pleasures that she'd never risked pursuing, and would never now have. Damn fool that she was, to have valued pride over sensation. Mere ego seemed a nonsense now. She should have asked for the act from every man who'd looked at her twice, and not been content till one had said yes. All that system of nerves and tubes and eggs, going to death unused. The waste of it was the only thing here that smacked of tragedy.

Her gaze returned to the darkness of the fissure. The twin forces she'd sensed there were still approaching. She could see them now; vague forms, like stains in the water. One was bright; or at least brighter than the other. But that was the only distinction she could make. If either had features they were too blurred to be seen, and the rest—limbs and torso—were lost in the shoals of dark bubbles that rose with them. They could not disguise their purpose, however. Her mind grasped that all too easily. They were emerging from the fissure to claim the flesh from which her thoughts were now mercifully disconnected. Let them have their bounty, she thought. It had been a burden, that body, and she was glad to be rid of it. The rising powers had no jurisdiction over her thoughts; nor sought any. Flesh was their ambition; and they each wanted the entire quartet. Why else were they struggling with each other, stains light and dark interwoven like a barber's pole as they rose to snatch the bodies down?

She had assumed herself free prematurely. As the first tendrils of mingled spirit touched her foot the precious moments of liberation ceased. She was called back into her cranium, the door of her skull slamming behind her with a crack. Eyesight replaced mindsight; pain and panic, that sweet detachment. She saw the warring spirits wrap themselves around her. She was a morsel, pulled back and forth between them as they each fought to possess her. The why of it beyond her. She would be dead in seconds. It mattered not at all to her which claimed the corpse, the bright or the less than bright. Both, if they wanted her sex (she felt their investigations there, even at the last), would have no joy back from her, nor from any of them. They were gone; the four of them.

Even as she relinquished the last bubble of breath from her throat, a gleam of sunlight hit her eyes. Could it be she was rising again? Had they dismissed her body as redundant to their purpose, and let the fat float? She snatched the chance, however small it was, pushing up towards the surface. A new shoal of bubbles rose with her, that almost seemed to bear her up towards the air. It was closer by the instant. If she could hold on to consciousness a heartbeat longer she might yet survive.

God loved her! She broke the surface face-first, puking water then drinking air. Her limbs were numb, but the very forces that had been so intent on drowning her now kept her afloat. After three or four breaths she realized the others had also been released. They choked and splashed around her. Joyce was already making towards the shore, pulling Trudi after her. Arleen now began to follow. Solid ground was only a few yards away. Even with legs and arms barely functional Carolyn covered the distance, until all four of them could stand up. Bodies racked with sobs they staggered towards dry land. Even now they cast backward glances, for fear whatever had assaulted them decided to pursue them into the shallows. But the spot in the middle of the lake was completely placid.

Before they'd reached the shore, hysteria took hold of Arleen. She began to wail, and shudder. Nobody went to comfort her. They had barely sufficient energy to advance one foot in front of the other, never mind waste breath in trying to calm the girl. She overtook Trudi and Joyce to reach the grass first, dropping down on the ground where she'd left her clothes and attempting to drag on her blouse, her sobs redoubling as she struggled, failing to find the armholes. A yard from the shore Trudi fell to her knees and threw up. Carolyn trudged down-wind of her, knowing that if she caught a whiff of vomit she'd end up doing the same. It was a wasted maneuver. The gagging sound was sufficient cue. She felt her stomach flip; then she was painting the grass in bile and ice cream.

Even now, though the scene he was watching had moved from the erotic to the terrifying to the nauseating, William Witt could not take his eyes off it. To the end of his life he'd remember the sight of the girls rising from the depths where he was certain they must have drowned, their efforts, or pressure from below, shoving them up into the air so high he saw their breasts bob.

Now the waters that had almost claimed them were still. Not a ripple moved; not a bubble broke. And yet, could he doubt that something other than an accident had occurred in front of him? There was something *alive* in the lake. The fact that he'd seen only its consequences—the flailings, the screams—rather than the thing itself, shook him to the gut. Nor would he ever be able to quiz the girls as to their assailants' nature. He was alone with what he'd seen.

For the first time in his life his self-elected role as voyeur weighed heavily upon him. He swore to himself he'd never spy on anyone again. It was an oath he kept for a day before breaking.

As to this event, he'd had enough of it. All he could see of the girls now were the outlines of their hips and buttocks as they lay in the grass. All he could hear, with the vomiting over, was weeping.

As quietly as he could, he slipped away.

Joyce heard him go. She sat up in the grass.

"Somebody's watching us," she said.

She studied the patch of sunlit foliage, and again it moved. Just the wind, catching the leaves.

Arleen had finally found her way into her blouse. She sat with her arms wrapped around her. "I want to die," she said.

"No you don't," Trudi told her. "We just escaped that."

Joyce put her hands back to her face. The tears she thought she'd bettered came again, in a wave.

"What in Christ's name happened?" she said. "I thought it was just . . . flood water."

It was Carolyn who supplied the answer, her voice without inflection, but shaking.

"There are caves under the whole town," she said. "They must have filled with water during the storm. We swam out over the mouth of one of them."

"It was so dark," Trudi said. "Did you look down?"

"There was something else," Arleen said. "Besides the darkness. Something in the water."

Joyce's sobs intensified in response to this.

"I didn't *see* anything," Carolyn said. "But I felt it." She looked at Trudi. "We all felt the same, didn't we?"

"No," Trudi replied, shaking her head. "It was currents out of the caves."

"It tried to drown me," Arleen said.

"Just currents," Trudi reiterated. "It's happened to me before, at the beach. Undertow. Pulled the legs from under me."

"You don't believe that," Arleen said flatly. "Why bother to lie? We all know what we felt."

Trudi stared hard at her.

"And what was that?" she said. "Exactly."

Arleen shook her head. With her hair plastered to her scalp and mascara smeared across her cheeks, she looked anything but the Prom Queen beauty of ten minutes before.

"All I know is it wasn't undertow," she said. "I saw shapes. Two shapes. Not fishes. Nothing like fishes." She looked away from Trudi, down between her legs. "I felt them touch me," she said, shuddering. "Touch me *inside*."

"Shut up!" Joyce suddenly erupted. "Don't say it."

"It's true, isn't it?" Arleen replied. "*Isn't it?*" She looked up again. First at Joyce, then at Carolyn; finally at Trudi, who nodded.

"Whatever's out there wanted us because we're women."

Joyce's sobs climbed to a fresh plateau.

"Keep quiet," Trudi snapped. "We've got to think about this."

"What's to think?" Carolyn said.

"What we're going to say for one thing," Trudi replied.

"We say we went swimming—" Carolyn began.

"Then what?"

"—we went swimming and—"

"Something attacked us? Tried to get inside us? Something not human?"

"Yes," said Carolyn. "It's the truth."

"Don't be so stupid," Trudi said. "They'll laugh at us."

"But it's still *true*," Carolyn insisted.

"You think that makes any difference? They'll say we were idiots to go swimming in the first place. Then they'll say we got the cramps or something."

"She's right," said Arleen.

But Carolyn clung to her convictions. "Suppose somebody else comes here?" she said. "And the same thing happens. Or they drown. Suppose they drown. Then we'd be responsible."

"If this is just flood water it'll be gone in a few days," Arleen said. "If we say anything everyone in town will talk about us. We'll never live it down. It'll spoil the rest of our lives."

"Don't be such an actress," Trudi said. "We're none of us going to do anything we don't all agree on. Right? Right, Joyce?" There was a stifled sob of acknowledgment from Joyce. "Carolyn?"

"I suppose so," came the reply.

"We just have to agree on a story."

"We say nothing," Arleen replied.

"Nothing?" said Joyce. "Look at us."

"Never explain. Never apologize," Trudi murmured.

"Huh?"

"It's what my daddy says all the time." The thought of this being a family philosophy seemed to brighten her. "Never explain . . ."

"We heard," said Carolyn.

"So it's agreed," Arleen went on. She stood up, gathering the rest of her clothes from the ground.

"We all keep quiet about it."

There was no further sound of argument from any source. Taking their cue from Arleen, they all proceeded to dress then headed back towards the road, leaving the lake to its secrets and its silences.

TWO

I

At first, nothing happened. There were not even nightmares. Only a pleasant languor, affecting all four of them, which was perhaps the after glow of coming so close to death and walking away from it. They concealed their bruises from view, and went about being themselves, and keeping their secret.

In a sense it kept itself. Even Arleen, who had been the first to voice her horror at the intimate assault they'd all suffered, rapidly came to take a strange *pleasure* in the memory, which she didn't dare confess, even to the other three. In fact they spoke to each other scarcely at all. They didn't need to. The same strange conviction moved in all of them: that they were, in some extraordinary fashion, the *chosen*. Only Trudi, who'd always had a love of the Messianic, would have put such a word to what she felt. For Arleen, the feeling was simply a reinforcing of what she'd always known about herself: that she was a uniquely glamorous creature, for whom the rules by which the rest of the world was run did not apply. For Carolyn, it meant a new confidence in herself which was a dim echo of that revelation she'd had when death had seemed imminent: that every hour without appetites fulfilled was wasted. For Joyce, the feeling was simpler still. She had been saved from death for Randy Krentzman.

She wasted no time in making her passion known. The very day after the events at the lake she went directly to the Krentzman house in Stillbrook and told him in the plainest possible terms that she loved him and intended to sleep with him. He didn't laugh. He simply looked at her with bewilderment, then asked her, somewhat shame-faced, whether they knew each other. On previous occasions his for-getting her had practically broken her heart. But something had changed in her. She was no longer so fragile. Yes, she told him, you *do* know me. We've met several times before. But I don't care if you remember me or not. I love you and I want you to make love to me. He went on staring at her through this speech, then said: this is some joke, right? To which she replied that it absolutely was *not* a joke, that she meant every word she said, and given that the day was warm and the house empty but for the two of them was there any time better than the present?

Bewilderment had not undone the Krentzman libido. Though he didn't understand why this girl was offering herself *gratis*, an opportu-nity like this came along too infrequently to be despised. Thus, attempting the tone of one to whom such proposals come daily, he accepted. They spent the afternoon together, performing the act not once but three times. She left the house around six-fifteen and wended her way home through the Grove with a sense of some imper-ative satisfied. It was not love. He was dim, self-centered, and a sloppy lover. But he had perhaps put life into her that afternoon, or at least offered his teaspoonful of stuff to the alchemy, and that was all she'd really wanted from him. This change of priorities went unquestioned. Her mind was crystal clear on the need for fecundity. On the rest of life, past, future and present, it was a blur.

Early the next morning, having slept more deeply than she had for years, she called him up, and suggested a second liaison, that very afternoon. Was I that good? he enquired. She told him he was better than good; he was a bull; his dick the world's eighth wonder. He read-ily agreed, both to the flattery and the liaison.

Of the quartet she turned out to be perhaps the luckiest in her choice of mates. Vain and empty-headed though Krentzman was, he was also harmless, and in his inept way, tender. The urge that took Joyce to his bed, working with equal vigor upon Arleen, Trudi and Carolyn, drove the others into less conventional embraces.

Carolyn made overtures to one Edgar Lott, a man in his mid-fifties who had moved down the street from her parents' house the year before. None of the neighbors had become friendly with him. He was a loner; his only company two dachshunds. These, the absence of female visitors, and most particularly his penchant for color coordination in his dress (handkerchief, neck-tie and socks always in matching pastel) led all to assume he was homosexual. But naive as Carolyn was in the particularities of intercourse she knew Lott better than her elders. She'd caught his eye several times, and hindsight told her his looks had meant more than hello. Intercepting him as he took the dachshunds for their morning constitutional she got to talking with him, then asked—when the dogs had marked their territory for the day—if maybe she could come home with him. Later, he would tell her that his intentions had been perfectly honorable, and if she hadn't thrown herself upon him, demanding his devotion on the kitchen table, he would not have laid a finger on her. But with the offer there, how could he refuse?

Mismatched in years and anatomy they nevertheless coupled with a rare fury, the dachshunds sent into a frenzy of jealousy as they did so, yapping and chasing their tails till they exhausted themselves. After the first bout he told her he hadn't touched a woman in the six years since his wife's death, which had driven him to alcohol. She too, he said, had been a substantial creature. Talk of her girth made him hard again. They set to. This time the dogs just slept.

At first, the match worked well. Neither was the least judgmental when it came to the removal of clothes; neither wasted time with declarations on the other's beauty, which would have sounded ridiculous; neither pretended this was forever. They were together to do what nature had designed their bodies to do, careless of the frills. Not for them the candlelit romance. Day in, day out she went visiting Mr.

Lott, as she referred to him in her parents' company, only to have his face between her breasts seconds after the door was closed.

Edgar could hardly believe his luck. That she'd seduced him was extraordinary enough (even in his youth no woman had ever paid him that compliment); that she came back, and back again, unable to keep her hands off him until the act was thoroughly performed, verged on the miraculous. He was not surprised therefore when, after two weeks and four days, she stopped visiting. A little saddened, but not surprised. After a week of her absence he saw her on the street and he asked her politely if—quote, unquote—we could resume our hanky-panky? She looked at him strangely, then told him no. He hadn't sought an explanation, but she offered one anyway. I don't need you any more, she told him lightly, and tapped her stomach. Only later, sitting in his stale house with his third bourbon in his hand, did he realize what the words and the gesture meant. It drove him to a fourth and a fifth. A return to his old ways all too rapidly followed. Though he had tried very hard to keep sentiment out of the exchange, now—with the fat girl gone—he realized she had broken his heart.

Arleen had no such problems. The path she chose, pressed by the same unspoken dictate as the rest, took her into the kind of company which wore their hearts not on their sleeves, but on their forearms, in Prussian blue ink. It had begun for her, as it had for Joyce, the day after their neardrowning. She'd dressed up in her finest clothes, got in her mother's car, and taken herself off down to Eclipse Point, a small stretch of beach north of Zuma, notorious for its bars and its bikers. The occupants of the area were not all that surprised to see a rich girl in their midst. Such types regularly drove down from their fancy houses to taste the low-life, or have the low-life taste them. A couple of hours was usually enough, before they beat a retreat, back to where the closest they got to rough trade was the chauffeur.

In its time the Point had seen some famous faces come, incognito, looking to suck on its underbelly a while. Jimmy Dean had been a regular in his wildest times, seeking a smoker who wanted a human ash-tray. One of the bars had a pool table sacred to the memory of Jayne Mansfield, who had reputedly performed on it an act even now spoken of only in reverential whispers. Another had carved in the boards of its floor the outline of a woman who had claimed to be Veronica Lake, and had passed out dead drunk on that spot. Arleen, therefore, followed a well-trodden path from luxury's lap to the squalor of a bar she chose for no better reason than its name: The Slick. Unlike many who had preceded her; however, she didn't need a drink to give her an excuse for licentiousness. She simply offered herself. There were any number of takers, among whom she made no distinction whatsoever. Nobody who came seeking failed to find.

The next night she came back for more, and for more the night after, her eyes fixing on her paramours as though she were addicted to them. Not all took advantage. Some, after that first night, viewed her warily, suspecting that such largesse was only offered by the mad or the diseased. Others found a streak of gallantry in them they'd not suspected, and tried to coax her up off the floor before the line had reached the runts of the pack. But she protested loudly and ripely at any such intervention; told them to leave her be. They withdrew. Some even joined the line again.

While Carolyn and Joyce were able to keep their affairs to themselves, Arleen's behavior could not go unnoticed indefinitely. After a week of her disappearing from the house in the middle of the evening and returning as dawn came up—a week in which her only reply to questions about where she was going was a quizzical look, almost as though she herself wasn't sure—her father, Lawrence Farrell, decided to follow her. He considered himself a liberal parent, but if his princess was falling in with a bad crowd—footballers, maybe, or hippies—then he might be obliged to give her some advice. Once out of the Grove she drove like one demented, and he had to put his foot down just to keep a discreet distance. A mile or two shy of the beach he lost her. It took him an hour of scouring the parking lots before he found the car, parked outside The Slick. The bar's reputation had reached even his liberally plugged ears. He entered, fearing for his jacket and his wallet. There was great commotion inside; a howling ring of men, beer-gutted animals with hair to the middle of their backs, gathered around some floor show at the far end of the bar.

There was no sign of Arleen. Satisfied that he'd made a mistake (she was probably simply walking the beach, watching the surf) he was about to leave when somebody began chanting his princess's name.

"Arleen! Arleen!"

He turned back. Was she watching the floor show too? He dug through the crowd of onlookers. There, at the center, he found his beautiful child. Somebody was pouring beer into her mouth, while another performed with her that deed he, like all fathers, hated to think of his daughter performing, except—in dreams—with him. She looked like her mother, lying beneath this man; or rather, as her mother had looked that long ago when she'd still been capable of arousal. Thrashing and grinning, mad for the man on top of her. Lawrence yelled Arleen's name, and stepped forward to pull the brute from his labor. Somebody told him to wait his turn. He hit the man on the jaw, a blow which sent the slob staggering back into the crowd, many of whom were already unzipped and primed. The fellow spat out a wad of blood, and launched himself at Lawrence, who complained as he was beaten to his knees that this was his daughter, his daughter . . . *my God, his daughter.* He didn't give up his protests till his mouth was no longer capable of making the words. Even then he tried to crawl to where Arleen was lying, and slap her into recognition of what she was doing. But her admirers simply dragged him out and dumped him on the edge of the highway. There he lay for a while, until he could muster the energy to get to his feet. He staggered back to the car, and waited several hours, crying sometimes, until Arleen emerged.

She seemed quite unmoved by his bruises and his bloody shirt. When he told her he'd seen what she'd done she cocked her head slightly, as though she wasn't entirely certain what he was talking about. He ordered her into his car. She went without protest. They drove home in silence.

Nothing was said that day. She stayed in her room, and played the radio, while Lawrence spoke to his lawyer about closing down The Slick, to the cops about bringing his assailants to justice, and his analyst about where he'd failed. That night she left again, in the early

evening, or at least tried to. He intercepted her in the driveway however, and the round of recriminations postponed from the previous
night erupted. All the time, she just stared at him, glassy-eyed. Her
indifference inflamed him. She wouldn't come inside when he asked
her, nor would she tell why she was doing what she was doing. His
concern became fury, his voice rising in decibels and his vocabulary in
venom until he was calling her a whore at the top of his voice, and
there were drapes being twitched aside all around the Crescent. Eventually, blinded by tears of sheer incomprehension, he struck her, and
might have done further damage had Kate not intervened. Arleen
didn't wait. With her raging father in her mother's custody she ran off,
and found herself a ride down to the beach.

The Slick was raided that night. There were twenty-one arrests,
mostly for minor drug offenses, and the bar was closed down. When
the officers arrived Lawrence Farrell's princess was performing the
same bump and grind number she'd been performing nightly for over
a week. It was a story not even Lawrence's crude attempts at bribery
could keep out of the newspapers. It became prime reading material
up and down the coast. Arleen was put into the hospital for a full medical check-up. She was found to have two sexually transmitted dis-
eases, plus an infestation of crabs, and was suffering the kind of wear
and tear her exploits had been bound to induce. But at least she wasn't
pregnant. Lawrence and Kathleen Farrell thanked the Lord for that
small mercy.

The revelations about Arleen's forays to The Slick brought a severe
tightening of parental controls around the town. Even in the East
Grove there were noticeably fewer kids wandering the streets after
dark. Illicit romance became tough to come by. Even Trudi, the last of
the four, would soon be obliged to give up her partner, though she'd
found a near-perfect cover for her activities: religion. She'd had the wit
to seduce one Ralph Contreras, a man of mixed blood who worked as
a gardener for the Prince of Peace Lutheran Church in Laureltree,
and had a stammer of such proportions it to all intents and purposes
left him speechless. She liked him that way. He provided the service
she required, and kept his mouth shut about it. All in all, the perfect

lover. Not that she cared much about his technique, as he valiantly played the male for her. He was simply a functionary. When he had completed his duties—and her body would tell her when that moment came—she would not think of him again. At least, so she told herself.

As it was, the affairs they were all having (Trudi's included) were—because of Arleen's indiscretions—quickly to become public knowledge. Though *she* might have found it easy to forget her trysts with Ralph the Silent, Palomo Grove would not.

II

The newspaper reports about the scandalous secret life of small-town beauty Arleen Farrell were as explicit as the legal departments of those journals would permit, but the details had to be left for rumor to supply. A small black market in what were claimed to be photographs of the orgy proved lucrative, though the pictures were so dingy it was difficult to be sure they were of the real thing. The family itself—Lawrence, Kate, sister Jocelyn and brother Craig—had a brighter light thrown upon them. Folks living on the other side of the Grove rerouted their shopping trips so as to come along the Crescent past the house of infamy. Craig had to be taken out of school because his peers bullied him unmercifully for the dirt on his big sister; Kate upped her tranquilizer intake until she was slurring any word of more than two syllables. But there was worse to come. Three days after Arleen had been snatched back from the bikers' den an interview purporting to be with one of Arleen's nurses appeared in the *Chronicle*. It said that the Farrell girl spent most of her time in a sexual frenzy, her talk one obscenity after another, interrupted only by tears of frustration. This in itself was newsworthy enough. But, the report went on, the patient's sickness went beyond that of an overheated libido. Arleen Farrell believed herself possessed.

The tale she told was elaborate, and bizarre. She, plus three of her friends, had gone swimming in a lake close to Palomo Grove, and been attacked by something that had entered them all. What this occupying entity had demanded of Arleen, and—presumably—of her fellow bathers, was that she get herself with child by whomever was available to provide the service. Hence her adventures at The Slick. The Devil in her womb had simply been looking for a surrogate father amid that rank company.

The article was presented with no trace of irony; the text of Arleen's so-called confession was quite absurd enough without requiring editorial gilding. Only those in the Grove blind or illiterate failed to read the revelations brought on by drugs and beauty. No one considered there to be an iota of truth in her claims, of course, except the families of the friends Arleen had been out with on Saturday, July 28th. Though she didn't name Joyce, Carolyn or Trudi the quartet were known to be fast friends. There could be no doubt in the minds of any who had a passing acquaintance with Arleen whom she'd written into her Satanic fantasies.

It rapidly became apparent that the girls would have to be shielded from the fallout following Arleen's preposterous claims. In the McGuire, Katz and Hotchkiss households the same exchange, give or take an endearment, took place.

The parent asked: "Do you want to leave the Grove for a while, until the worst of this blows over?" To which the child replied; "No, I'm fine. Never better."

"Are you sure it's not upsetting you, sweetheart?"

"Do I look upset?"

"No."

"Then I'm not upset."

Such well-balanced children, the parents thought, to face the tragedy of a friend's lunacy with this show of calm; aren't they a credit to us?

For a few weeks they were just that: model daughters, bearing the stress of their situation with admirable aplomb. Then the perfect picture began to deteriorate, as oddities in their behavior patterns made themselves apparent. It was a subtle process; one which might well have gone unnoticed for longer had the parents not been watching over their babies with such fastidiousness. First, the parents noticed their offspring keeping odd hours: sleeping at noon, and pacing at midnight. Food-fads appeared. Even Carolyn, who had never been known to refuse the edible, took a near pathological dislike to certain items: seafood in particular. The girls' air of serenity disappeared. In its place came moods that swung from the monosyllabic to the garrulous, the glacial to the crazed. It was Betty Katz who first suggested her daughter see the family doctor. Trudi didn't object. Nor did she seem in the slightest surprised when Doctor Gottlieb pronounced her healthy in every respect; and pregnant.

Carolyn's parents were the next to fear that the mystery of their off-spring's behavior merited medical investigation. The news was the same, with the added rider that if their daughter intended to carry her child to full-term then it would be advisable if the mother-to-be lost thirty pounds.

If there had been any hope of denying a pattern in these diagnoses that hope was undone by the third and final proof. Joyce McGuire's parents had been the most reluctant to concede their child's complicity in this scandal, but finally they too sought examination of their daughter. She, like Carolyn and Trudi, was in good health. She too was pregnant. The news called for a reassessment of Arleen Farrell's story. Was it possible that lurking beneath her insane ramblings was a shred of truth?

The parents met, and talked together. Between them they beat out the only scenario that made any sense. There had clearly been a pact of some kind made between the girls. They'd decided—for some reason known only to them—to become pregnant. Three of them had succeeded. Arleen had failed, and it had pitched what had always been a highly strung girl into the throes of a nervous breakdown. The problems that now had to be addressed were threefold. First, to locate the would-be fathers and then prosecute them for their sexual opportunism. Second, to terminate the pregnancies as quickly and safely as possible. Thirdly, to keep the whole business quiet so that the reputations of the three families would not suffer the same fate as that of the

Farrells, whom the righteous inhabitants of the Grove now treated as pariahs.

In all three they failed. In the matter of the fathers simply because none of the girls, even under parental duress, would name the culprits. In the issue of aborting the babies, because again the children steadfastly refused to be browbeaten into giving up what they'd wasted no little sweat procuring. And finally, in their attempts to keep the whole sorry business under wraps, because scandal likes the light, and it only took one indiscreet doctor's receptionist to begin the journalists sniffing after fresh evidence of delinquency.

The story broke two days after the parents' meeting, and Palomo Grove—which had been rocked by Arleen's disclosures, but not overturned—sustained an almost mortal blow. The Mad Girl's Tale had made interesting reading for the UFO sighting and Cancer Cure crowd, but it was essentially a bust. These new developments, however, touched a much more sensitive nerve. Here were four families whose solid, well-heeled lives had been shattered by a pact made by their own daughters. Was there some kind of cult involved, the press demanded to know? Was the anonymous father conceivably the *same man*, a seducer of young women whose very namelessness left endless room for speculation. And what of the Farrell child, who'd first blown the whistle on what was being called the *League of Virgins?* Had she been driven to more extreme behavior than her friends because, as the *Chronicle* was the first to report, she was actually infertile? Or had the others yet to unburden themselves of their true excesses? This was a story that would run and run. It had everything: sex, possession, families in chaos, small-town bitchery, sex, insanity and sex. What was more, it could only get better from here.

As the pregnancies advanced the press could follow the progress. And with luck there'd be some startling payoff. The children would be all triplets, or black, or born dead.

Oh, the possibilities!

THREE

It was hushed at the center of the storm; hushed and still. The girls heard the howls and accusations heaped on them from parents, press and peers alike, but weren't much touched by them. The process that had begun in the lake continued on its own inevitable way, and they let it shape their minds as it had, and did, their bodies. They were calm as the lake was calm; their surface so placid the most violent attack upon it left not so much as a ripple.

Nor did they seek each other out during this time. Their interest in each other, and indeed in the outside world, dwindled to zero. All they cared to do was sit at home growing fuller, while controversy raged around them. That too, despite its early promise, dwindled as the months went by, and new scandals claimed the public's attention. But the damage to the Grove's equilibrium had been done. The League of Virgins had put the town on the Ventura County map in a fashion it would never have wished upon itself, but, given the fact, was determined to profit by. The Grove had more visitors that autumn than it had enjoyed since its creation, people determined to be able to boast that they'd visited *that* place; Crazyville; the place where girls made eyes at anything that moved if the Devil told them to.

There were other changes in the town, which were not so observable as the full bars and the bustling Mall. Behind closed doors the children of the Grove had to fight more vehemently for their privileges, as their parents, particularly the fathers of daughters, withdrew freedoms previously taken for granted. These domestic frays cracked several families, and broke some entirely. The alcohol intakes went up correspondingly; Marvin's Food and Drug did exceptional business in hard liquor during October and November, the demand taking off into the stratosphere over the Christmas period, when, in addition to the usual festivities, incidents of drunkenness, adultery, wife-beating and exhibitionism turned Palomo Grove into a sinners' paradise.

With the public holidays, and their private woundings, over, several families decided to move out of the Grove altogether, and a subtle reorganization of the town's social structure began, as properties thought desirable—such as those in the Crescents (now marred by the Farrells' presence)—fell in value, and were bought up by individuals who could never have dreamt of living in that neighborhood the summer before.

So many consequences, from a battle in troubled waters.

That battle had not gone unwitnessed, of course. What William Witt had learned of secrecy in his short life as a voyeur proved invaluable as subsequent events unfolded. More than once he came close to telling somebody what he'd seen at the lake, but he resisted the temptation, knowing that the brief stardom he'd earn from it would have to be set against suspicion and possible punishment. Not only that; there was every chance he'd not even be believed. He kept the memory alive in his own head, however, by going back to where it had happened on a regular basis. In fact he'd returned there the day after it had all happened, to see if he could spot the occupants of the lake. But the water was already retreating. It had shrunk by perhaps a third overnight. After a week it had gone entirely, revealing a fissure in the ground which was evidently a point of access to the caves that ran beneath the town.

He wasn't the only visitor to the spot. Once Arleen had unburdened herself of what had happened there that afternoon, countless sightseers came looking for the spot. The more perceptive among them quickly recognized it: the water had left the grass yellowed and dusted with dried silt. One or two even attempted to gain access to the caves, but the fissure presented a virtually straight drop with no ready means of descent. After a few days of fame the spot was left to itself and to William's solitary visits. It gave him a strange satisfaction, going there, despite the fear he felt. A sense of complicity with the caves and their secret, not to mention the erotic *frisson* that came when he stood where he'd stood that day, and imagined again the nakedness of the bathers.

The fate of the girls didn't much interest him. He read about them once in a while, and heard them talked about, but out of sight for William was pretty much out of mind. There were better things to watch. With the town in disarray he had much to spy on: casual seductions and abject slavery; furies; beatings; bloody-nosed farewells. One day, he thought, I'll write all of this down. It'll be called *Witt's Book*, and everyone in it will know, when it's published, that their secrets all belong to me.

When, on the infrequent occasions he did think of the girls' present condition, it was thoughts of Arleen he favored, simply because she was in a hospital where he couldn't see her even if he wanted to, and his powerlessness, as for every voyeur, was a spur. She was sick in the head, he'd heard, and nobody quite knew why. She wanted men to come to her all the time, she wanted babies the way the others had babies, but she couldn't and that was why she was sick. His curiosity concerning her died, however, when he overheard somebody report that the girl had lost all trace of her glamour.

"She looks half dead" was the way he'd heard it put. "Drugged and dead."

After that, it was as if Arleen Farrell no longer existed, except as a beautiful vision, shedding her clothes on the edge of a silver lake. Of what that lake had done to her he cleansed his mind thoroughly.

Unfortunately the wombs of the quartet's remaining members could *not* cast the experience and its consequence out except as a bawling reality, which new stage in the humiliation of Palomo Grove began on April 2nd, when the first of the League of Virgins gave birth.

Howard Ralph Katz was born to his eighteen-year-old mother Trudi at 3:46 A.M., by cesarean section. He was frail, weighing a mere four pounds and two ounces when he first saw the light of the delivery room. A child, it was agreed, who resembled his mother, for which his grandparents were duly grateful given that they had no clue as to the father. Howard had Trudi's dark, deep-set eyes, and a spiral skull cap of brown hair, even at birth. Like his mother, who had also been premature, he had to fight for every breath during the first six days of his life, after which he strengthened quickly. On April 19th Trudi brought her son back to Palomo Grove, to nurse him in the place she knew best.

Two weeks after Howard Katz saw the light, the second of the League of Virgins gave birth. This time there was something more for the press to elaborate on than the production of a sickly baby boy. Joyce McGuire gave birth to twins, one of each, born within a minute of each other in a perfectly uncomplicated fashion. She named them Jo-Beth and Tommy-Ray, names she'd chosen (though she would never admit this, not to the end of her days) because they had two fathers: one in Randy Krentzman, one in the lake. Three, if she counted their Father in Heaven, though she feared he'd long passed her over in favor of more compatible souls.

Just over a week after the birth of the McGuire twins Carolyn also produced twins, boy and girl, but the boy was delivered dead. The girl, who was big-boned and strong, was named Linda. With her birth the saga of the League of Virgins seemed to have reached its natural conclusion. The funeral of Carolyn's other child drew a small audience, but otherwise the four families were left alone. Too much alone in fact. Friends ceased to call; acquaintances denied ever having known them. The story of the League of Virgins had besmirched Palomo Grove's good name, and despite the profit the town had earned from the scandal there was now a general desire to forget that the incident had ever occurred.

Pained by the rejection they sensed from every side the Katz family made plans to leave the Grove and return to Alan Katz's home city, Chicago. They sold their home in late June to an out-of-towner who got a bargain, a fine property and a reputation in one fell swoop. The Katz family were gone two weeks later.

It proved to be good timing. Had they delayed their departure by a few more days they would have been caught up in the last tragedy of the League's story. On the evening of July 26th the Hotchkiss family went out for a short while, leaving Carolyn at home with baby Linda. They stayed out longer than they intended, and it was well after midnight, and therefore the 27th, when they got back. Carolyn had celebrated the anniversary of her swim by smothering her daughter and taking her own life. She had left a suicide note, which explained, with the same chilling detachment the girl had used to talk of the San Andreas Fault, that Arleen Farrell's story had been true all along. They *had* gone swimming. They *had* been attacked. To this day she did not know what by, but she had sensed its presence in her, and in the child, ever since, and it was *evil*. That was why she had smothered Linda. That was why she was now going to slit her wrists. *Don't judge me too harshly*, she asked. *I never wanted to hurt anybody in my life.*

The letter was interpreted by the parents thus: that the girls had indeed been attacked and raped by somebody, and for reasons of their own had kept the identity of the culprit or culprits to themselves. With Carolyn dead, Arleen insane and Trudi gone to Chicago, it fell upon Joyce McGuire to tell the whole truth, without excision or addition, and to lay the story of the League of Virgins to rest.

At first, she refused. She couldn't remember anything about that day, she claimed. The trauma had wiped the memory from her mind. Neither Hotchkiss or Farrell were content with that, however. They kept applying the pressure, through Joyce's father. Dick McGuire was not a strong man, either in spirit or body, and his Church was wholly unsupportive in the matter, siding with the non-Mormons against the girl. The truth had to be told.

At last, to keep the browbeaters from doing any more damage to her father than they already had, Joyce told. It made a strange scene. The six parents, plus Pastor John, who was the spiritual leader of the Mor-

mon community in the Grove and its surroundings, were sitting in the
McGuires' dining room listening to the pale, thin girl whose hands
went first to one cradle then to the other as she rocked her children to
sleep telling, as she rocked, of their conception. First she warned her
audience that they weren't going to like what she was about to tell.
Then she justified her warning with the telling. She gave them the
whole story. The walk; the lake; the swim; the things that had fought
over their bodies in the water; their escape; her passion for Randy
Krentzman—whose family had been one of those to leave the Grove
months before, presumably because he'd made a quiet confession of
his own; the desire she'd shared with all the girls to get pregnant as effi-
ciently as possible—

"So Randy Krentzman was responsible for them all?" Carolyn's
father said.

"Him?" she said. "He wasn't capable."

"So who was?"

"You promised to tell the whole story," the Pastor reminded her.

"So I am," she replied. "As far as I know it. Randy Krentzman was
my choice. We all know how Arleen went about it. I'm sure Carolyn
found somebody different. And Trudi too. The fathers weren't important, you see. They were just men."

"Are you saying the Devil is in you, child?" the Pastor asked.

"No."

"The children, then?"

"No. No." She rocked both cradles now, one with each hand.
"Jo-Beth and Tommy-Ray aren't possessed. At least not the way you
mean. They just aren't Randy's children. Maybe they've got some of
his good looks . . ." she allowed herself a tiny smile. ". . . I'd like that,"
she said. "Because he was so very handsome. But the spirit that made
them is in the lake."

"There is no lake," Arleen's father pointed out.

"There was that day. And maybe there will be again, if it rains hard
enough."

"Not if I can help it."

———

Whether he entirely believed Joyce's story or not Farrell was as good as his word. He and Hotchkiss rapidly raised sufficient donations from around town to have the entrance to the caves sealed up. Most of the contributors signed a check simply to get Farrell off their doorstep. Since his princess had lost her mind he had all the conversational skill of a ticking bomb.

In October, a few days short of fifteen months after the girls had first gone down to the water, the fissure was blocked with concrete. They would go there again, but not for many years.

Until then, the children of Palomo Grove could play in peace.

PART THREE

FREE SPIRITS

ONE

O f the hundreds of erotic magazines and films which William
Witt purchased as he grew to manhood over the next seventeen years, first by mail order then later taking trips into Los Angeles
for that express purpose, his favorites were always those in which he
was able to glimpse a life behind the camera. Sometimes the photographer—equipment and all—could be seen reflected in a mirror
behind the performers. Sometimes the hand of a technician, or a
fluffer—someone hired to keep the stars aroused between shots—
would be caught on the edge of the frame, like the limb of a lover just
exiled from the bed.

Such obvious errors were relatively rare. More frequent—and to
William's mind far more telling—were subtler signs of the reality
behind the scene he was witnessing. The times when a performer,
offered a multitude of sins and not certain which hole to pleasure
next, glanced off camera for instruction; or when a leg was speedily
shifted because the power behind the lens had yelled that it obscured
the field of action.

At such times, when the fiction he was aroused by—which was not
quite a fiction, because hard was hard, and could not be faked—

William felt he understood Palomo Grove better. Something lived behind the life of the town, directing its daily processes with such self-lessness no one but he knew it was there. And even he would forget. Months would go by, and he'd go about his business, which was real estate, forgetting the hidden hand. Then, like in the porno, he'd *glimpse* something. Maybe a look in the eye of one of the older resi-dents, or a crack in the street, or water running down the Hill from an oversprinkled lawn. Any of these were enough to make him remem-ber the lake, and the League, and know that all the town seemed to be was a fiction (not quite a fiction, because flesh was flesh and could not be faked), and he was one of the performers in its strange story.

That story had proceeded without a drama to equal that of the League in the years since the sealing of the caves. Marked town though it was, the Grove prospered, and Witt with it. As Los Angeles grew in size and affluence towns out in the Simi Valley, the Grove among them, became dormitories for the metropolis. The price of the town's real estate rose steeply in the late seventies, just about the time when William entered the business. It rose again, particularly in Windbluff, when several minor stars elected to take houses on the Hill, conferring on the locale a chic it had hitherto lacked. The biggest of the houses, a palatial residence with a panoramic view of the town, and the valley beyond, was bought by the comedian Buddy Vance, who at the time had the highest-rated TV show on any of the networks. A little lower down the hill the cowboy actor Raymond Cobb demolished a house and built on the spot his own sprawling ranch, complete with a pool in the shape of a sheriff's badge. Between Vance's house and Cobb's lay a house entirely concealed by trees occupied by the silent star Helena Davis, who in her day had been the most gossiped-about actress in Hollywood. Now in her late seventies she was a complete recluse, which only fuelled rumors in the Grove whenever a young man appeared in town—always six foot, always blond—and declared himself a friend of Miss Davis. Their presence earned the house its nickname: Iniquity's Den.

There were other imports from Los Angeles. A Health Club opened up in the Mall, and was quickly oversubscribed. The craze for Szechuan restaurants brought two such establishments, both sufficiently patronized to survive the competition. Style stores flourished, offering Deco, American Naive and simple kitsch. The demand for space was so heavy the Mall gained a second floor. Businesses which the Grove would never have supported in its early days were now indispensable. The pool supply store, the nail sculpture and tanning service, the karate school.

Once in a while, sitting waiting for a pedicure, or in the pet shop while the kids chose between three kinds of chinchilla, a newcomer might mention a rumor they'd heard about the town. Hadn't something happened here, way back when? If there was a long-standing Grover in the vicinity the conversation would very quickly be steered into less controversial territory. Although a generation had grown up in the intervening years there was still a sense among the natives, as they liked to call themselves, that the League of Virgins was better forgotten.

There were some in the town, however, who would never be able to forget. William was one, of course. The others he still followed as they went about their lives. Joyce McGuire, a quiet, intensely religious woman who had brought up Tommy-Ray and Jo-Beth without the benefit of a husband. Her folks had moved to Florida some years back, leaving the house to their daughter and grandchildren. She was now virtually unseen beyond its walls. Hotchkiss, who had lost his wife to a lawyer from San Diego seventeen years her senior, and seemed never quite to have recovered from her desertion. The Farrell family, who had moved out of town to Thousand Oaks, only to find that their reputations had followed them. They'd eventually relocated to Louisiana, taking Arleen with them. She had never fully recovered. It was—William had heard—a good week if she strung more than ten words together. Jocelyn Farrell, her younger sister, had married and come back to live in Blue Spruce. He saw her on occasion, when she came to visit friends in town. The families were still very much part of the Grove's history; yet though William was on nodding acquaintance with them all—the McGuires, Jim Hotchkiss, even Jocelyn Farrell—there was never a word exchanged between them.

There didn't need to be. They all knew what they knew.

And knowing, lived in expectation.

TWO

I

The young man was virtually monochrome, his shoulder-length hair, which curled at his neck, black, his eyes as dark behind his round spectacles, his skin too white to be that of a Californian. His teeth were whiter still, though he seldom smiled. Didn't do much speaking either, come to that. In company, he stammered.

Even the Pontiac convertible he parked in the Mall was white, though its bodywork had been rusted by snow and salt from a dozen Chicago winters. It had got him across country, but there'd been a few close calls along the way. The time was coming when he was going to have to take it out into a field and shoot it. Meanwhile, if anyone needed evidence of a stranger in Palomo Grove they only had to cast their eye along the row of automobiles.

Or indeed, over him. He felt hopelessly out of place in his corduroys and his shabby jacket—(too long in the arms, too tight across the chest, like every jacket he'd ever bought). This was a town where they measured your worth by the name on your sneakers. He didn't wear sneakers; he wore black leather high-tops that he'd use day in, day out until they fell apart, whereupon he'd buy an identical pair.

Out of place or not, he was here for a good reason, and the sooner he got started the better he'd start feeling.

First, he needed directions. He selected a Frozen Yoghurt store as the emptiest along the row, and sauntered in. The welcome that met him from the other side of the counter was so warm he almost thought he'd been recognized.

"Hi! How can I help you?"

"I'm . . . new," he said. Dumb remark, he thought. "What I mean is, is there any place . . . any place I can buy a map?"

"You mean of California?"

"No. Palomo Grove," he said, keeping the sentences short. That way he stammered less.

The grin on the far side of the counter broadened.

"Don't need a map," it said. "The town's not that big."

"OK. How about a hotel?"

"Sure. Easy. There's one real close. Or else there's a new place, up in Stillbrook Village."

"Which is the cheapest?"

"The Terrace. It's just two minutes' drive, round the back of the Mall."

"Sounds perfect."

The smile he got in return said: *everything's* perfect here. He could almost believe it too. The polished cars shone in the lot; the signs pointing him round to the back of the shopping center gleamed; the motel facade—with another sign—Welcome to Palomo Grove, The Prosperous Haven—was as brightly painted as a Saturday morning cartoon. He was glad, when he'd secured a room, to pull down the blind against the daylight, and lurk a little.

The last stretch of the drive had left him weary, so he decided to perk his system up with some exercises and a shower. The machine, as he referred to his body, had been in a driver's seat too long; it needed a working over. He warmed up with ten minutes of shadow sparrings, a combination of kicks and punches, followed by a favorite cocktail of specialized kicks: axe, jump crescent, spinning hook and jump spinning back kicks. As usual, what warmed up his muscles heated his mind. By the time he got to his leg-lifts and sit-ups he was ready to take on half of Palomo Grove to get an answer to the question he'd come here asking.

Which was: who is Howard Katz? *Me* wasn't a good enough answer any more. *Me* was just the machine. He needed more information than that.

It was Wendy who'd asked the question, in that long night of debate which had ended in her leaving him.

"I like you, Howie," she'd said. "But I can't love you. And you know why? Because I don't know you."

"You know what I am?" Howie had replied. "A man with a hole in his middle."

"That's a weird way to put it."

"It's a weird way to feel."

Weird, but true. Where others had some sense of themselves as peo-ple—ambition, opinion, religion—he just had this pitiful unfixedness. Those who liked him—Wendy, Richie, Lem—were patient with him. They waited through his stumblings and stammerings to hear what he had to say, and seemed to find some value in his comments. (You're my holy fool, Lem had once told Howie; a remark which Howie was still pondering.) But to the rest of the world he was Katz the klutz. They didn't bait him openly—he was too fit to be taken on hand to hand, even by heavyweights—but he knew what they said behind his back, and it always amounted to the same thing: Katz had a piece missing.

That Wendy had finally given up on him was too much to bear. Too hurt to show his face he'd brooded on the conversation for the best part of a week. Suddenly, the solution came clear. If there was any place on earth he'd understand the how and why of himself it was surely the town where he'd been born.

He raised the blind and looked out at the light. It was pearly; the air sweet-smelling. He couldn't imagine why his mother would ever have left this pretty place for the bitter winter winds and smothering summers of Chicago. Now that she was dead (suddenly, in her sleep) he would have to solve that mystery for himself; and perhaps, in its solving, fill the hole that haunted the machine.

Just as she reached the front room, Momma called down from her room, her timing as faultless as ever.

"Jo-Beth? Are you there? Jo-Beth?"

Always the same falling note in the voice, that seemed to warn: be loving to me now because I may not be here tomorrow. Perhaps not even the next hour.

"Honey, are you still there?"

"You know I am, Momma."

"Can I have a word?"

"I'm late for work."

"Just a minute. Please. What's minute?"

"I'm coming. Don't get upset. I'm coming."

Jo-Beth started upstairs. How many times a day did she cover this route? Her life was being counted out in stairs climbed and descended, climbed and descended.

"What is it, Momma?"

Joyce McGuire lay in her usual position: on the sofa beside the open window, a pillow beneath her head. She didn't look sick; but most of the time she was. The specialists came, and looked, and charged their fees, and left again shrugging. Nothing wrong physically, they said. Sound heart, sound lungs, sound spine. It's between her ears she's not so well. But that was news Momma didn't want to hear. Momma had once known a girl who'd gone mad, and been hospitalized, and never come out again. That made her more afraid of madness than of anything. She wouldn't have the word spoken in the house.

"Will you have the Pastor call me?" Joyce said. "Maybe he'll come over tonight."

"He's a very busy man, Momma."

"Not too busy for me," Joyce said. She was in her thirty-ninth year but she behaved like a woman twice that age. The slow way she raised her head from the pillow as if every inch was a triumph over gravity; the fluttering hands and eyelids; that perpetual sigh in her voice. She had cast herself as a movie consumptive, and would not be dissuaded from the role by mere medical opinion. She dressed for the role, in sickroom pastels; she let her hair, which was a rich brunette, grow long, not caring to fashion it or pin it up. She wore no trace of make-up, which further enhanced the impression of a woman tottering on the tip of the abyss. All in all, Jo-Beth was glad Momma no longer went out in public. People would talk. But that left her here, in the house, calling her daughter up and down the stairs. Up and down, up and down.

When, as now, Jo-Beth's irritation reached screaming pitch she reminded herself that her mother had her reasons for this withdrawal. Life hadn't been easy for an unmarried woman bringing up her children in a town as judgmental as the Grove. She'd earned her malady in censure and humiliation.

"I'll get Pastor John to call," Jo-Beth said. "Now listen, Momma, I've got to go."

"I know, honey, I know."

Jo-Beth returned to the door, but Joyce called after her.

"No kiss?" she said.

"Momma—"

"You never miss kissing me."

Dutifully Jo-Beth went back to the window, and kissed her mother on the cheek.

"You take care," Joyce said.

"I'm fine."

"I don't like you working late."

"This is not New York, Momma."

Joyce's eyes flickered towards the window, from which she watched the world go by.

"Makes no difference," she said, the lightness going from her voice. "There's no place safe."

It was a familiar speech. Jo-Beth had been hearing it, in one version or another, since childhood. Talk of the world as a Valley of Death, haunted by faces capable of unspeakable malice. That was the chief comfort Pastor John gave Momma. They agreed on the presence of the Devil in the world; in Palomo Grove.

"I'll see you in the morning," Jo-Beth said.

"I love you, honey."

"I love you too, Momma."

Jo-Beth closed the door and started downstairs.

"Is she asleep?"

Tommy-Ray was at the foot of the flight.

"No. She's not."

"Damn."

"You should go in and see her."

"I know I should. Only she's going to give me a hard time about Wednesday."

"You were drunk," she said. "Hard liquor, she kept saying. True?"

"What do you think? If we'd been brought up like normal kids, with liquor around the house, it wouldn't go to my head."

"So it's her fault you got drunk?"

"*You've* got something against me, too, haven't you? Shit. Everybody's got something against me."

Jo-Beth smiled, and put her arms around her brother. "No, Tommy, they haven't. They all think you're wonderful and you know it."

"You too?"

"Me too."

She kissed him, lightly, then went to the mirror to check her appearance.

"Pretty as a picture," he said, coming to stand beside her. "Both of us."

"Your ego," she said. "It's getting worse."

"That's why you love me," he said, gazing at their twin reflections. "Am I growing more like you or you like me?"

"Neither."

"Ever seen two faces more alike?"

She smiled. There was an extraordinary resemblance between them. A delicacy in Tommy-Ray's bones matched by clarity in hers which had both of them idolized. She liked nothing better than to walk out hand in hand with her brother, knowing she had beside her a companion as attractive as any girl could wish, and knowing he felt the same. Even among the forced beauties of the Venice boardwalk they turned heads.

But in the last few months they hadn't gone out together. She'd been working long hours at the Steak House, and he'd been out with his pals among the beach crowd: Sean, Andy and the rest. She missed the contact.

"Have you been feeling weird these last couple of days?" he asked, out of nowhere.

"What kind of funny?"

"I don't know. Probably just me. Only I feel like everything's coming to an end."

"It's almost summer. Everything's just beginning."

"Yeah, I know . . . but Andy's gone off to college, so fuck him. Sean's got this girl in L.A., and he's real private with her. I don't know. I'm left here waiting, and I don't know what for."

"So don't."

"Don't what?"

"Wait. Take off somewhere."

"I want to. But . . ." He studied her face in the mirror. "Is it true? You don't feel . . . strange?"

She returned his look, not certain she wanted to admit to the dreams she'd been having, in which she was being carried by the tide, and all her life was waving to her from the shore. But if not to Tommy, whom she loved and trusted more than any creature alive, to whom?

"OK. I admit it," she said, "I do feel something."

"What?"

She shrugged. "I don't know. Maybe I'm waiting too."

"Do you know what for?"

"Nope."

"Neither do I."

"Don't *we* make a pair?"

She reran the conversation with Tommy as she drove down to the Mall. He had, as usual, articulated their shared feelings. The last few weeks had been charged with anticipation. Something was going to

happen soon. Her dreams knew it. Her bones knew it. She only hoped
it was not delayed, because she was coming to the point, with
Momma and the Grove, and the job at the Steak House, when she
would lose her cool completely. It was a race now, between the fuse
on her patience and the something on the horizon. If it hadn't come
by summer, she thought (whatever it was, however unlikely), then
she'd up and go looking for it.

II

N obody seemed to walk much in this town, Howie noticed. On
his three-quarter-hour stroll up and back down the Hill he
encountered only five pedestrians, and they all had children or dogs
in tow to justify their waywardness. Short though this initial journey
was it took him to a fair vantage point from which to grasp something
of the town's lay-out. It also sharpened his appetite.

Beef for the desperado, he thought, and selected Butrick's Steak
House from the eating places available in the Mall. It was not large,
and not more than half full. He took a table at the window, opened
the tattered copy of Hesse's *Siddhartha*, and continued his struggle
with the text, which was in the original German. The book had
belonged to his mother, who had read and re-read it many times—
though he could not remember her so much as uttering a word of the
language she was apparently fluent in. He was not. Reading the book
was like an interior stuttering; he fought for the sense, catching it only
to lose it again.

"Something to drink?" the waitress asked him.

He was about to say "Coke" when his life changed.

Jo-Beth stepped over the threshold of Butrick's the way she had
three nights a week for the last seven months, but tonight it was as if
every other time had been a rehearsal for this stepping; this turning;
this meeting of eyes with the young man sitting at table five. She took
him in with a glance. His mouth was half open. He wore gold-

rimmed spectacles. There was a book in his hand. Its owner's name she didn't know, *couldn't* know. She'd never set eyes on him before. Yet he watched her with the same recognition she knew was on her own face.

It was like being born, he thought, seeing this face. Like coming out of a safe place into an adventure that would take his breath away. There was nothing more beautiful in all the world than the soft curve of her lips as she smiled at him.

And smiling now, like a perfect flirt. Stop it, she told herself, look away! He'll think you're out of your mind staring. But then he's staring too, isn't he?

I'll keep looking—as long as *she* keeps looking

—as long as he keeps looking—

"Jo-Beth!"

The summons came from the kitchen. She blinked.

"Did you say a Coke?" the waitress asked him.

Jo-Beth glanced towards the kitchen—Murray was calling her, she had to go—then back at the boy with the book. He still had his eyes fixed on her.

"Yes," she saw him say.

The word was for her, she knew. *Yes, go*, he said, *I'll still be here.*

She nodded, and went.

The whole encounter occupied maybe five seconds, but it left them both trembling.

In the kitchen Murray was his usual martyred self.

"Where have you been?"

"Two minutes late, Murray."

"I make it ten. There's a party of three in the corner. It's your table."

"I'm putting my apron on."

"Hurry."

Howie watched the kitchen door for her re-emergence, *Siddhartha* forgotten. When she appeared she didn't look his way but went to serve a table on the far side of the restaurant. He wasn't distressed that she failed to look. An understanding had been reached between them in that first exchange of gazes. He would wait all night if need be, and all through tomorrow if that was what it took, until she had finished her work and looked at him again.

In the darkness below Palomo Grove the inspirers of these children still held on to each other as they had when they'd first fallen to earth, neither willing to risk the other's freedom. Even when they'd risen to touch the bathers, they'd gone together, like twins joined at the hip. Fletcher had been slow comprehending the Jaff's intention that day. He'd thought the man planned to draw his wretched *terata* out of the girls. But his mischief had been more ambitious than that. It was the making of children he was about, and, squalid as it was, Fletcher had been obliged to do the same. He was not proud of his assault. As news of its consequences had reached them his shame had deepened. Once, sitting by a window with Raul, he had dreamed of being sky. Instead his war with the Jaff had reduced him to a spoiler of innocents, whose futures they had blighted with touch. The Jaff had taken no little pleasure in Fletcher's distress. Many times, as the years in darkness passed, Fletcher would sense his enemy's thoughts turning to the children they'd made, and wondering which would come first to save their true father.

Time did not mean to them what it had meant before the Nuncio. They didn't hunger, nor did they sleep. Buried together like lovers, they waited in the rock. Sometimes they could hear voices from the overground, echoing down passages opened by the subtle but perpetual grinding of the earth. But these snatches offered no clue to the progress of their children, with whom their mental links were at best tenuous. Or at least had been, until tonight.

Tonight their offspring had met, and contact was suddenly clear, as though their children had understood something of their own natures, seeing their perfect opposites, and had unwittingly opened their minds to the creators. Fletcher found himself in the head of a youth called Howard, the son of Trudi Katz. Through the boy's eyes he saw his enemy's child just as the Jaff saw Howie from his daughter's head.

This was the moment they'd waited for. The war they'd fought halfway across America had exhausted them both. But their children were in the world to fight for them now; to finish the battle that had been left unresolved for two decades. This time, it would be to the death.

Or so they'd expected. Now, for the first time in their lives, Fletcher and the Jaff shared the same pain—like a single spike thrust through both their souls.

This was not war, damn it. This was nothing like war.

"Lost your appetite?" the waitress wanted to know.

"Guess I have," Howie replied.

"You want me to take it away?"

"Yeah."

"You want coffee? Dessert?"

"Another Coke."

"One Coke."

Jo-Beth was in the kitchen when Beverly came through with the plate.

"Waste of good steak," Beverly said.

"What's his name?" Jo-Beth wanted to know.

"What am I, a dating service? I didn't ask."

"Go ask."

"You ask. He wants another Coke."

"Thanks. Will you look after my table?"

"Just call me Cupid."

Jo-Beth had managed to keep her mind on her job and her eyes off the boy for half an hour: enough was enough. She poured a Coke, and took it out. To her horror, the table was empty. She almost dropped the glass; the sight of the empty chair made her feel physically sick. Then, out of the corner of her eye, the sight of him emerging from the restroom, and returning to the table. He saw her, and smiled. She crossed to the table, ignoring two calls for service en route. She already knew the question she was going to ask first: it had been on her mind from the start. But he was there with the same enquiry before her.

"Do we know each other?"

And of course she knew the answer.

"No," she said.

"Only when you . . . you . . . you . . ." He was stumbling over the word, the muscles in his jaw working like he was chewing gum. ". . . You . . ." he kept saying, ". . . you . . ."

"I thought the same," she said, hoping her finishing his thought wouldn't offend. It seemed not to. He gave a smile, his face relaxing.

"It's strange," she said. "You're not from the Grove, are you?"

"No. Chicago."

"That's a ways to come."

"I was born here, though."

"You were?"

"My name's Howard Katz. Howie."

"I'm Jo-Beth . . ."

"What time do you finish here?"

"Around eleven. It's good you came in tonight. I'm only here Mondays, Wednesdays and Fridays. If you'd come in tomorrow you would have missed me."

"We'd have found each other," he said, and the certainty in his statement made her want to cry.

"I have to go back to work," she told him.

"I'll wait," he replied.

At eleven-ten they stepped out of Butrick's together. The night was warm. Not a pleasant, breezy warmth, but humid.

"Why did you come to the Grove?" she asked him as they walked to her car.

"To meet you."

She laughed.

"Why not?" he said.

"All right. So why did you leave in the first place?"

"My mother moved us to Chicago when I was only a few weeks old. She never really spoke much about the ol' home town. When she did it was like she was talking about hell. I suppose I wanted to see for myself. Maybe understand her and me a bit better."

"Is she still in Chicago?"

"She's dead. Died two years ago."

"That's sad. What about your father?"

"I don't have one. Well . . . I mean . . . is . . . is—" He started to stumble, fought it, and won. "I never knew him," he said.

"This gets weirder."

"Why?"

"It's the same for me. I don't know who my father is either."

"Doesn't matter much, does it?"

"It used to. Less now. I've got a twin, see? Tommy-Ray. He's always been there for me. You must meet Tommy. You'll love him. Everybody does."

"And you. I bet every . . . every . . . everybody loves you too."

"Meaning?"

"You're beautiful. I'm going to be competing with half the guys in Ventura County, right?"

"Nope."

"Don't believe you."

"Oh they look. But they don't touch."

"Me included?"

She stopped walking. "I don't know you, Howie. At least, I do and I don't. Like when I saw you in the Steak House, I recognized you from somewhere. Except that I've never been to Chicago and you've not been in the Grove since—" She suddenly frowned. "How old are you?" she said.

"Eighteen last April."

Her frown deepened.

"What?" he said.

"Me too."

"Huh?"

"Eighteen last April. The fourteenth."

"I'm on the second."

"This is getting very strange, don't you think? Me thinking I knew you. You thinking the same."

"It makes you uneasy."

"Am I that obvious?"

"Yes. I never saw . . . saw . . . I never saw a face so . . . transparent. Makes me want to kiss it."

In the rock, the spirits writhed. Every word of seduction they'd heard had been a twisting of the blade. But they were powerless to prevent the exchange. All they could do was sit in their children's heads and listen.

"Kiss me," she said.

They shuddered.

Howie put his hand on her face.

—They shuddered till the ground around them shook.—

She took a half step towards him and put her smiling lips on his.

—Till cracks opened up in the concrete that eighteen years before had sealed them up. Enough! they screamed in their children's ears, enough! Enough!

"Did you feel something?" he said.

She laughed. "Yes," she said. "I think the earth moved."

THREE

I

The girls went down to the water twice.

The second time was the morning after the night on which Howard Ralph Katz met Jo-Beth McGuire. A bright morning, the muggy air of the evening before blown away on a wind that promised cool gusts to mellow the heat of the afternoon.

Buddy Vance had slept alone again, up in that bed he'd had built for three. Three in a bed—he'd said (and unfortunately been quoted saying)—was hog-heaven. Two was marriage; and hell. He'd had enough of that to be certain it didn't suit him but it would have made a morning as fine as this finer still to have known there was a woman waiting at the end of it, even if she was a wife. His affair with Ellen had proved too perverse to last; he would have to dismiss her from his employ very soon. Meanwhile his empty bed made this new early morning regime a little easier. With nothing to seduce him back to the mattress it wasn't so difficult to put on his jogging gear and take the road down the Hill.

Buddy was fifty-four. Jogging made him feel twice that. But too many of his contemporaries had died on him of late, his sometime agent Stanley Goldhammer being the most recent departure, and they'd all died of the same excesses that he was still thoroughly addicted to. The cigars, the booze, the dope. Of all his vices women were the healthiest, but even they were a pleasure to be taken in moderation these days. He couldn't make love through the night the way he'd been able to in his thirties. On a few traumatic occasions recently he hadn't been able to perform at all. It had been that failure which had sent him to his doctor, demanding a panacea, whatever the price.

"There isn't one," Tharp had said. He'd been treating Buddy since the TV years, when *The Buddy Vance Show* had topped the ratings every week, and a joke he told at eight at night would be on the lips of every American the following morning. Tharp knew the man once billed as the funniest man in the world inside out.

"You're doing your body harm, Buddy, every damn day. And you say you don't want to die. You still want to be playing Vegas at a hundred."

"Right."

"On present progress, I give you another ten years. That's if you're lucky. You're overweight, you're overstressed. I've seen healthier corpses."

"I do the gags, Lou."

"Yeah, and I fill in the death certificates. So start taking care of yourself, for Christ's sake, or you're going to go the way Stanley went."

"You think I don't think about that?"

"I know you do, Bud. I know."

Tharp stood up and walked round to Buddy's side of the desk. On the wall were signed photographs of the stars whom he'd advised and treated. So many great names. Most of them dead; too many of them prematurely. Fame had its price.

"I'm glad you're coming to your senses. If you're really serious about this . . ."

"I'm here aren't I? How much more fucking serious do I have to get? You know how I hate talking about this shit. I never did a death gag in my life, Lou. You know that? Not once. Anything else. *Anything*. But not that!"

"It's got to be faced sooner or later."

"I'll take later."

"OK, so I'll have a health plan drawn up for you. Diet; exercise; the works. But I'm telling you now, Buddy, it won't make pleasant reading!"

"I heard somewhere: laughter makes you live longer."

"Show me where it says comedians live forever, I'll show you a tomb with a quip on it."

"Yeah. So when do I begin?"

"Start today. Throw out the malts and the nose-candy, and try using that pool of yours once in a while."

"It needs cleaning."

"So get it cleaned."

That was the easy part. Buddy had Ellen call the Pool Service as soon as he got home and they sent somebody up the following day. The health plan, as Tharp had warned, was a tougher call, but whenever his will faltered he thought of the way he looked in the mirror some mornings, and the fact that his dick was only visible if he held his gut in so hard it ached. When vanity failed he thought of death, but only as a last resort.

He'd always been an early riser, so getting up for a morning run wasn't a great chore. The sidewalks were empty, and often—as today—he'd make his way down the Hill and through the East Grove to the woods, where the ground didn't bruise the soles the same way the concrete did, and his panting was set to birdsong. On such days the run was strictly a one-way journey; he'd have Jose Luis bring the limo down the Hill and meet him when he emerged from the woods, the car stocked with towels and iced tea. Then they'd head back up to Coney Eye, as he'd dubbed the estate, the easy way: on wheels. Health was one thing; masochism, at least in public, quite another.

The run had other benefits besides firming up his belly. He had an hour or so alone to get to grips with anything that was troubling him. Today, inevitably, his thoughts were of Rochelle. The divorce settlement would be finalized this week, and his sixth marriage would be history. It would be the second shortest of the six. His forty-two days with Shashi had been the fastest, ending with a shot that had come so close to blowing off his balls his sweat ran cold whenever he thought of it. Not that he'd spent more than a month with Rochelle in the year they'd been married. After the honeymoon, and its little surprises, she'd taken herself back to Fort Worth to calculate her alimony. It had been a mismatch from the beginning. He should have realized that, the first time she failed to laugh at his routine, which was, coincidentally, the first time she *heard* his routine. But of all his wives, including Elizabeth, she was the most physically alluring. Stonefaced she'd been, but the sculptor had genius.

He was thinking of her face as he came off the sidewalk and hit the woods. Maybe he should call her; ask her to come back to Coney for one final try. He'd done it before, with Diane, and they'd had the best two months of their years together, before the old resentments had set in afresh. But that had been Diane, this was Rochelle. It was useless attempting to project behavior patterns from one woman to the next. They were all so gloriously different. Men were a dull bunch by comparison: dowdy and mono-minded. Next time around he wanted to be born a lesbian.

Off in the distance, he heard laughter; the unmistakable giggling of young girls. A strange sound to hear so early in the morning. He stopped running and listened for it again, but the air was suddenly empty of all other sounds, even birdsong. The only noises he could hear were internal: the laborings of his system. Had he imagined the laughter? It was perfectly possible, his thoughts being as full of women as they were. But as he prepared to about-face and leave the thicket to its songlessness, the giggling came again, and with it an odd, almost hallucinatory, change in the scene around him. The sound seemed to animate the entire wood. It brought movement to the leaves, it brightened the sunlight. More than that: it changed the very *direction* of the sun. In the silence, the light had been pallid, its source still low in the east. On the cue of laughter it became noon-day bright, pouring down on the upturned faces of the leaves.

Buddy neither believed nor disbelieved his eyes: he simply stood before the experience as before feminine beauty, mesmerized. Only when the third round of laughter began did he grasp its direction, and start off at a run towards it, the light still vacillating.

A few yards on he saw a movement ahead of him through the trees. Bare skin. A girl stripping off her underwear. Beyond her was another girl, this one blonde, and strikingly attractive, beginning to do the same. He knew instinctively they weren't quite real, but he still advanced cautiously, for fear of startling them. Could illusions *be* startled? He didn't want to risk it; not with such pretty sights to see. The blonde girl was the last one undressed. There were three others, he counted, already wading out into a lake that flickered on the rim of solidity. Its ripples threw light up on to the blonde's face—*Arleen*, they named her, as they shouted back to the shore. Advancing from tree to tree, he got to within ten feet of the lake's edge. Arleen was in up to her thighs now. Though she bent to cup water in her hands and splash it on her body it was virtually invisible. The girls who were in deeper than she, and swimming, seemed to be floating in midair.

Ghosts, he half-thought; these are ghosts. I'm spying on the past, being rerun in front of me. The thought propelled him from hiding. If his assumption was correct then they might vanish at any moment and he wanted to drink their glory down in gulps before they did.

There was no trace of the clothes they'd shed in the grass where he stood, nor any sign—when one or the other of them glanced back towards the shore—that they saw him there.

"Don't go too far," one of the quartet yelled to her companion. The advice was ignored. The girl was moving further from the shore, her legs spreading and closing, spreading and closing as she swam. Not since the first wet dreams of his adolescence could he remember an experience as erotic as this, watching these creatures suspended in the gleaming air, their lower bodies subtly blurred by the element that bore them up, but not so much he could not enjoy their every detail.

"Warm!" yelled the adventurer, who was treading water a good distance from him, "it's *warm* out here."

"Are you kidding?"

"Come and feel!"

Her words inspired further ambition in Buddy. He'd *seen* so much.

Dare he now *touch?* If they couldn't see him—and they plainly couldn't—where was the harm in getting so close he could run his fingertips along their spines?

The water made no sound as he stepped into the lake; nor did he feel so much as a touch against his ankles and shins as he waded deeper. It buoyed Arleen up well enough however. She was floating on the lake's surface, her hair spread around her head, her gentle strokes taking her further from him. He hurried in pursuit, the water no brake upon him, halving the distance between himself and the girl in seconds. His arms were extended, his eyes fixed upon the pinkness of her labia as she kicked away from him.

The adventurer had begun to shout something, but he ignored her agitation. To touch Arleen was all he could think about. To put his hand upon her and she not protest, but go on swimming, while he had his way. In his haste his foot snagged on something. Arms still reaching for the girl he fell, face down. The jolt brought him to his senses enough to interpret the shouts from the deeper water. They were no longer cries of pleasure, but of alarm. He raised his head from the ground. The two furthest swimmers were struggling in midair, turning their faces up to the sky.

"Oh my Lord," he said.

They were drowning. Ghosts, he'd called them moments ago, not really thinking about what that name implied. Here was the sickening truth. The swimming party had come to grief in these phantom waters. He'd been ogling the dead.

Revolted with himself, he wanted to retreat, but a perverse obligation to this tragedy kept him watching.

All four of them were caught up in the same turmoil now, thrashing in the air, their faces darkening as they fought for breath. How was it possible? They looked to be drowning in four or five feet of water. Had some current taken hold of them? It seemed unlikely, in water so shallow and so apparently placid.

"Help them . . ." he found himself saying. "Why doesn't somebody help them?"

As though he might lend aid himself he started towards them.

Arleen was closest to him. All the beauty had gone from her face. It was contorted by desperation and terror. Suddenly her wide eyes seemed to see something in the water beneath her feet. Her struggling ceased, and a look of utter surrender took its place. She was giving up life.

"*Don't,*" Buddy murmured, reaching for her as if his arms might lift her up out of the past and carry her back to life. At the very moment his flesh met that of the girl, he knew this was fatal business for them both. He was too late in his regrets, however. The ground beneath them trembled. He looked down. There was only a thin cover of earth there, he saw, sustaining a meager crop of grass. Beneath the earth, gray rock; or was it concrete? Yes! Concrete! A hole in the ground had been plugged here, but the seal was fracturing in front of him, cracks widening in the concrete.

He looked back towards the edge of the lake, and solid ground, but a rift had already opened between him and safety, a slab of concrete sliding into it a yard from his toes. Icy air rose from underground.

He looked back towards the swimmers, but the mirage was receding. As it went he caught the same look on all the four faces, eyes rolled up so they showed solid white, mouths open to drink death down. They hadn't perished in shallow water, he now understood. This had been a pit when they'd come swimming here, and it had claimed them as it was now claiming him: them with water, him with wraiths.

He started to howl for help, as the violence in the ground mounted, the concrete grinding itself to dust between his feet. Perhaps some other early-morning jogger would hear him, and come to his aid. But quickly; it had to be quickly.

Who was he kidding? And he, a kidder. Nobody was going to come. He was going to die. For fuck's sake, he was going to die.

The rift between him and good ground had widened considerably, but leaping it was his only hope for salvation. He had to be fast, before the concrete beneath him slid into the pit, taking him with it. It was now or never.

He jumped. It was a good jump too. Another few inches and he'd have made it to safety. But a few were everything. He snatched at the air, short of his target, and fell.

One moment the sun was still shining on the top of his head. The next, darkness, icy darkness, and he was plummeting through it with cobs of concrete hurtling past him on the same downward journey. He heard them crack against the face of the rock as they went; then realized it was *he* who was making the noise. It was the breaking of his bones and back he could hear as he fell. And fell and fell.

II

The day began earlier for Howie than he'd ordinarily have welcomed after sleeping so little, but once he was up and exercising he felt good about being awake. It was a crime to lie in bed on a morning so fine. He bought himself a soda from the machine and sat at the window, gazing at the sky and musing on what the day might bring.

Liar; not of the day at all. Of Jo-Beth; only of Jo-Beth. Her eyes, her smile, her voice, her skin, her scent, her secrets. He watched the sky, and saw her, and was obsessed.

This was a first for him. He'd never felt an emotion as strong as that possessing him now. Twice in the night he'd woken in a sudden sweat. He couldn't remember the dreams that had brought it on, but she was in them, for certain. How could she not be? He had to go find her. Every hour he spent out of her company was a wasted hour; every moment not seeing her he was blind; every moment not touching her, numb.

She'd told him, as they'd parted the previous night, that she worked at Butrick's during the evening, and at a book store during the day. Given the size of the Mall, it wouldn't be too difficult to locate her work place. He picked up a bag of doughnuts to fill the hole not eating the previous night had left. That other hole, the one he'd come here to heal, was very far from his thoughts. He wandered along the rows of businesses, looking for *her* store. He found it, between a dog-grooming service and a real estate office. Like many of the stores, it was still closed, opening time, according to the sign on the door, still three quarters of an hour off. He sat down in the steadily warming sun, and ate, and waited.

Her instinct, from the moment she'd opened her eyes, was to forget about work today, and go find Howie. The events of the previous night had run and re-run in her dreams, changed each time in some subtle way, as though they might be alternative realities, a few of an infinite selection born from the same encounter. But among such possibilities she could conceive of none that did not contain him. He had been there, waiting for her, from her first breath; her cells were certain of it. In some imponderable way she and Howie belonged together.

She knew very well that if any of her friends had confessed such sentiments she'd have politely dismissed them as ludicrous. That was not to say she'd not moped over a few faces, of course; turned up the radio when a particular love song was played. But even as she'd listened she'd known it was all a distraction from an unmelodious reality. She saw a perfect victim of that reality every day of her life. Her mother, living like a prisoner—both of the house, and of the past—talking, on those days when she could muster the will to talk, of hopes she'd had, and the friends she'd shared them with. Until now that sad sight had kept Jo-Beth's romantic ambitions, indeed any ambition, in check.

But what had happened between herself and the Chicago boy would not end the way her mother's one great affair had ended, with her deserted, and the man in question so despised she could not bring herself to name him. If all the Sunday teachings she'd dutifully attended had instructed her in anything, it was that revelation came when and where least expected. To Joseph Smith, on a farm in Palmyra, New York; news of the Book of Mormon, revealed to him by an angel. Why not to her then, in circumstances no more promising? Stepping into Butrick's Steak House; standing in a parking lot with a man she knew from everywhere and nowhere?

Tommy-Ray was in the kitchen, his perusal as sharp as the scent of the coffee he was brewing. He looked like he'd slept in his clothes.

"Late night?" she said.

"For both of us."

"Not particularly," she said. "I was home before midnight."

"You didn't sleep though."

"On and off."

"You stayed awake. I heard you."

That was unlikely, she knew. Their bedrooms were at opposite ends of the house, and his route to the bathroom didn't take him within earshot of her.

"So?" he said.

"So what?"

"Talk to me."

"Tommy?" There was an agitation in his demeanor that unnerved her. "What's wrong with you?"

"I heard you," he said again. "I kept hearing you, all through the night. Something happened to you last night. Didn't it?"

He couldn't know about Howie. Only Beverly had any clue as to what had gone on at the Steak House, and she wouldn't have had time to spread rumors, even if she'd had a mind to, which was doubtful. She had enough secrets of her own to keep from the vine. Besides, what was there to tell? That she'd made eyes at a diner? Kissed him in the parking lot? What did any of that matter to Tommy-Ray?

"Something happened last night," he was still saying. "I felt some kind of *change*. But whatever we were waiting for . . . it didn't come to me. So it must have come to you, Jo-Beth. Whatever it is, it came to you."

"Want to pour me some of that coffee?"

"Answer me."

"What's to answer?"

"What happened?"

"Nothing."

"You're lying," he remarked, with more bafflement than accusation. "Why are you lying to me?"

It was a reasonable question. She wasn't ashamed of Howie, or what she felt for him. She'd shared every victory and defeat of her eighteen years with Tommy-Ray. He wouldn't go blabbing this secret to Momma or Pastor John. But the looks he kept giving her were odd; she couldn't read them. And there was that talk of hearing her through the night. Had he been listening at her door?

"I have to get down to the store," she said. "Or I'll be real late."

"I'll come with you," he said.

"What for?"

"The ride."

"Tommy . . ."

He smiled at her. "What's wrong with giving your brother a ride?" he said. She was almost taken in by the performance, until she nodded her acquiescence and caught the smile dropping from his lips.

"We have to trust each other," he said, once they were in the car and moving. "Like we always have."

"I know that."

"Because we're *strong* together, right?" He was staring through the window, glassy-eyed. "And right now I need to feel strong."

"You need to get some sleep. Why don't you let me drive you back? It doesn't matter if I'm late."

He shook his head. "Hate that house," he said.

"What a thing to say."

"It's true. We both hate it. It gives me bad dreams."

"It's not the house, Tommy."

"Yes, it is. The house, and Momma, and being in this fucking town! Look at it!" Suddenly, out of nowhere, he was raging. "Look at this shit! Don't you want to tear the whole fucking place apart?" His volume was nerve-shredding in the confines of the car. "I know you do," he said, staring at her, eyes now wild and wide. "Don't lie to me, little sister."

"I'm not your little sister, Tommy," she said.

"I'm thirty-five seconds older," he said. This had always been a joke between them. Suddenly it was power-play. "Thirty-five seconds more in this shit-hole."

"Stop talking stupid," she said, bringing the car to a sudden halt. "I'm not listening to this. You can get out and walk."

"You want me shouting in the street?" he said. "I'll do it. Don't think I won't. I'll scream till their fucking houses fall down!"

"You're behaving like an asshole," she said.

"Well, *there's* a word I don't hear from my little sister's lips too often," he said, with smug satisfaction. "Something's got into *both* of us this morning."

He was right. She found his rage igniting her in a way she'd never allowed it to before. Twins they were, and in so many ways similar, but he had always been the more openly rebellious of the two. She had played the quiescent daughter, concealing the contempt she'd felt for the Grove's hypocrisies because Momma, so much its victim, still needed its approval. But there were times when she'd envied Tommy-Ray's open contempt, and longed to spit in the eye of propriety the way he had, knowing he'd be forgiven his trespasses upon payment of a smile. He'd had it easy, all those years. His tirade against the town was narcissism; he was in love with himself as rebel. And it was spoiling a morning she'd wanted to luxuriate in.

"We'll talk tonight, Tommy," she said.

"Will we?"

"I just said we would."

"We have to help each other."

"I know."

"Especially now."

He was suddenly hushed, as though all the rage had gone from him in a single breath, and with it all his energy.

"I'm afraid," he said, very quietly.

"There's nothing to be afraid of, Tommy. You're just tired. You should go home and sleep."

"Yeah."

They were at the Mall. She didn't bother to park the car. "Take it home," she said. "Lois will run me back this evening."

As she went to get out of the car he took hold of her arm, his fingers gripping her so hard it hurt.

"Tommy—" she said.

"You really mean it?" he said. "There's nothing to be afraid of?"

"No," she said.

He leaned over to kiss her.

"I trust you," he said, his lips very close to hers. His face filled her sight; his hand held her arm as though he possessed her.

"Enough, Tommy," she said, pulling her arm free. "Go home."

She got out, slamming rather than closing the car door, deliberately not looking back at him.

"Jo-Beth."

Ahead of her, Howie. Her stomach flipped at the sight of him. Behind her, she heard a car-horn blare, and glanced back to see that Tommy-Ray had not taken the wheel of the car, which was blocking access for several other vehicles. He was staring at her; reaching for the handle of the door; getting out. The horns multiplied. Somebody began to shout at him to get out of the way, but he ignored them. His attention was fixed upon Jo-Beth. It was too late for her to signal Howie away. The look on Tommy-Ray's face made it plain he'd understood the whole story from the smile of welcome on Howie's face.

She looked back at Howie, feeling an ashen despair.

"Well lookee here," she heard Tommy-Ray say behind her.

It was more than despair; it was fear.

"Howie—" she began.

"Christ, was I dumb," Tommy-Ray went on.

She tried a smile as she turned back to him. "Tommy," she said, "I want you to meet Howie."

She'd never seen a look on Tommy-Ray's face like the look she was witnessing now; hadn't known those idolized features capable of such malice.

"Howie?" he said. "As in *Howard?"*

She nodded, glancing back at Howie. "I'd like you to meet my brother," she said. "My twin brother. Howie, this is Tommy-Ray."

Both men stepped forward to shake hands, bringing them into her vision at the same time. The sun shone with equal strength on both, but it didn't flatter Tommy-Ray, despite his tan. He looked sickly beneath the veneer of health he wore; his eyes sunk without a gleam, his skin too tightly drawn over his cheeks and temples. He looks dead, she found herself thinking. Tommy-Ray looks dead.

Though Howie extended his hand to be shaken Tommy-Ray ignored it, suddenly turning to his sister.

"Later," he said, so softly.

His murmur was almost drowned out by the din of complaints from behind him but she caught its menace clearly enough. Having spoken he turned his back and returned to the car. She couldn't see the mollifying smile he was putting on, but she could imagine it. Mr. Golden, raising his arms in mock-surrender, knowing his captors didn't have a hope.

"What was that about?" Howie said.

"I don't exactly know. He's been odd since—"

She was going to say since yesterday, but she'd seen a canker in his beauty moments ago that must have been there always, except that she—like the rest of the world—had been too dazzled to recognize it.

"Does he need help?" Howie asked.

"I think it's better we let him go."

"Jo-Beth!" somebody called. A middle-aged woman was striding towards them, both dress and features plain to the point of severity.

"Was that Tommy-Ray?" she said as she approached.

"Yes it was."

"He never stops by any longer." She had come to a halt a yard from Howie, staring at him with a look of mild puzzlement on her face. "Are you coming to the store, Jo-Beth?" she said, not looking away from Howie. "We're already late opening."

"I'm coming."

"Is your *friend* coming too?" the woman asked pointedly.

"Oh yes . . . I'm sorry . . . Howie . . . this is Lois Knapp."

"*Mrs.*," the woman put in, as though her marital status were a talisman against strange young men.

"Lois . . . this is Howie Katz."

"Katz?" Mrs. Knapp replied. "Katz?" She removed her gaze from Howie, and studied her watch. "Five minutes late," she said.

"It's no problem," Jo-Beth said. "We never get anyone in before noon."

Mrs. Knapp looked shocked at this indiscretion.

"The Lord's work is not to be taken lightly," she remarked. "Please be quick." Then she stalked off.

"Fun lady," Howie commented.

"She's not as bad as she looks."

"That'd be difficult."

"I'd better go."

"Why?" Howie said. "It's a beautiful day. We could go someplace. Make the most of the weather."

"It'll be a beautiful day tomorrow, and the day after, and the day after that. This is California, Howie."

"Come with me anyway."

"Let me try to make my peace with Lois first. I don't want to be on everyone's shit list. It'll upset Momma."

"So when?"

"When what?"

"When will you be free?"

"You don't give up, do you?"

"Nope."

"I'll tell Lois I'm going back home to look after Tommy-Ray this afternoon. Tell her he's sick. It's only half a lie. Then I'll come by the motel. How's that?"

"Promise?"

"Promise." She began to move away, then said: "What's wrong?"

"Don't want to . . . kiss . . . kiss me in public, huh?"

"Certainly not."

"How about in private?"

She half-heartedly shushed him as she backed away.

"Just say yes."

"Howie."

"Just say yes."

"Yes."

"See? It's real easy."

In the late morning, as she and Lois sat sipping ice water in the otherwise deserted store, the older woman said:

"Howard Katz."

"What about him?" Jo-Beth said, preparing herself for a lecture on behavior with the opposite sex.

"I couldn't think where I knew the name from."

"And now you remember?"

"A woman who lived in the Grove. 'Way back," she said, then turned her attention to wiping a ring of water from the counter with her napkin. Her silence, and the effort she gave to this minor mopping, suggested she was happy to let the subject drop if Jo-Beth chose not to pursue it. Yet she'd felt obliged to raise the issue. Why?

"Was she a friend of yours?" Jo-Beth asked.

"Not of mine."

"Of Momma's?"

"Yes," Lois said, still mopping, though the counter was dry. "Yes. She was one of your momma's friends."

Suddenly, it came clear.

"One of the four," Jo-Beth said. "She was one of the four."

"I believe she was."

"And she had children?"

"You know, I don't remember."

This was the closest a woman of Lois's scrupulousness came to lying. Jo-Beth called her on it.

"You remember," she said. "Please tell me."

"Yes. I guess I do remember. She had a boy."

"Howard."

Lois nodded.

"You're sure?" Jo-Beth said.

"Yes. I'm sure."

Now it was Jo-Beth who kept her silence, while in her head she'd tried to re-evaluate the events of recent days in the light of this discovery. What did her dreams, and Howie's appearance, and Tommy-Ray's sickness have to do with each other, and with the story she'd heard in ten different versions of the bathing party that had ended in death, insanity and children?

Perhaps Momma knew.

III

B uddy Vance's driver Jose Luis waited at their agreed rendezvous for fifty minutes before deciding that his boss must have made his way up the Hill under his own power. He called Coney on the car phone. Ellen was at the house but the boss wasn't. They debated what was best to do, and agreed he'd wait with the car the full hour then drive back via the route the boss would be likeliest to take.

He was nowhere along that route. Nor had he got home ahead of his ride. Again they debated the options, Jose Luis tactfully avoiding mention of the likeliest: that somewhere along the way he'd encountered female company. After sixteen years in Mr. Vance's employ he knew his boss's skill with the ladies verged on the supernatural. He would come home when he'd performed his magic.

For Buddy, there was no pain. He was thankful for the fact, but not so self-deceiving as to ignore its significance. His body was surely so messed up his brain had simply overloaded on agony, and pulled the plugs.

The darkness that enclosed him was without qualification; expert only in blinding him. Or perhaps his eyes were out; dashed from his head on the way down. Whatever the reason, detached from sight and feeling, he floated, and while he floated he calculated. First, the time it would take for Jose Luis to realize his boss wasn't coming home: two hours at the outside. His route through the woods would not be difficult to follow; and once they reached the fissure his peril would be self-evident. They'd be down after him by noon. On the surface and having his bones mended by the middle of the afternoon.

Perhaps it was almost midday already.

The only means he had of calculating time's passing was his heartbeat, which he could hear in his head. He began to count. If he could get some sense of how long a minute lasted he'd be able to hold on to that span of time, and after sixty, know he'd lived an hour. But no sooner had he started counting than his head started a different calculation altogether.

How long have I lived, he thought. Not breathed, not existed, but actually *lived?* Fifty-four years since birth: how many weeks was that? How many hours? Better think of it year by year; it was easier. One year was three hundred and sixty days, give or take a few. Say he slept a third of that. One hundred and twenty days in slumberland. Oh Lord, already the moments dwindled. Half an hour a day on the john, or emptying his bladder. That was another seven and a half days a year, just doing the dirt. And shaving and showering, another ten days; and eating another thirty or forty; and all of this multiplied by fifty-four years . . .

He began to sob. Get me out of here, he murmured, please God get me out of here, and I'll live like I never lived, I'll make every hour, every *minute* (even sleeping, even shitting) a minute spent trying to understand, so that when the next darkness comes along I won't be so lost.

At eleven Jose Luis got in the car and drove back down the Hill to see if he could spot the boss somewhere on the street. Drawing a blank there he called in at the Food Stop in the Mall, where they'd named a sandwich in honor of Mr. Vance's patronage (flatteringly, it was mostly meat), then at the record store, where the boss would frequently purchase a thousand dollars' worth of stock. While quizzing Ryder, who owned the place, a customer came and announced to any who were interested that there was some serious shit going down in the East Grove, and did somebody get shot?

The road down to the woods was closed by the time Jose Luis arrived, a solitary cop directing traffic to turn around.

"No way through," he told Jose Luis. "The road's closed."

"What happened? Who got shot?"

"Nobody got shot. It's just a crack in the road."

Jose Luis was out of the car now, staring past the cop to the woods.

"My boss," he said, knowing he needn't name the owner of the limo, "he was running down here this morning."

"So?"

"He hasn't come back yet."

"Oh shit. You'd better follow me."

They made their way through the trees in a silence broken only by barely coherent messages coming through on the cop's radio, all of which he ignored, until the thicket opened into a clearing. Several uniformed police were setting up barriers at its fringes to prevent anyone straying where Jose Luis was now led. The ground beneath his feet was cracked, and the cracks widened as the cop led him to where his Chief was standing, staring at the earth. Long before he came near the spot Jose Luis knew what lay ahead. The crack in the street and those he'd stepped over to reach this place were the consequence of a larger disturbance: a crevice fully ten feet across, opening into a devouring darkness.

"What's he want?" the Chief demanded, jabbing his finger in Jose Luis's direction. "We're keeping this under wraps."

"Buddy Vance," the cop said.

"What about him?"

"He's missing," Jose Luis said.

"He went running—" the cop explained.

"Let *him* tell it," the Chief said.

"This is where he goes running every morning. Only today he hasn't come back."

"Buddy Vance?" the Chief said. "The comedian?"

"Yeah."

The Chief's gaze left Jose Luis and returned to the hole.

"Oh my Lord," he said.

"How deep is it?" Jose Luis asked.

"Huh?"

"The crack."

"It's not a crack. It's a fucking abyss. I dropped a stone down a minute ago. I'm still waiting for it to hit bottom."

The realization that he was alone came to Buddy slowly, like a memory stirred up from the silt at the bottom of his brain. Indeed at first he thought it *was* a memory, of a sand storm he'd been caught in once, on his third honeymoon, in Egypt. But he was lost and guideless in this maelstrom as he'd not been then. And it was not sand that stung his eyes back into sight, nor wind that beat his ears into hearing. It was another power entirely, less natural than a storm, and trapped as no storm had ever been here in a chimney of stone. He saw the hole he'd fallen down for the first time, stretching above him to a sunlit sky so far from him no hint of its reassurance touched him. Whatever ghosts haunted this place, spinning themselves into creation in front of him, they surely came from a time before his species was a gleam in evolution's eye. Things awesomely simple; powers of fire and ice.

He was not so wrong; and yet completely. The forms emerging from the darkness a short distance from where he lay seemed in one moment to resemble men like himself, and in the next unalloyed energies, wrapped around each other like champions in a war of snakes, sent from their tribes to strangle the life from each other. The vision ignited his nerves as well as his senses. The pain he'd been spared seeped into his consciousness, the trickle becoming first a stream and then a flood. He felt as though he was laid on knives, their points slicing between his vertebrae, puncturing his innards.

Too weak even to moan, all he could be was a mute, suffering witness of the spectacle in front of him, and hope that salvation or death came quickly, to put him out of this agony. Best death, he thought. A godless sonofabitch like him had no hope of redemption, unless the holy books were wrong and fornicators, drunkards and blasphemers were fit for paradise. Better death, and be done with it. The joke ended here.

I want to die, he thought.

As he formed the intention, one of the entities battling in front of him turned his way. He saw a face in the storm. It was bearded, its flesh so swelled with emotion it seemed to dwarf the body it was set upon, like that of a fetus: skull domed, eyes vast. The terror he felt when it laid its gaze on him was nothing to that which he felt when its arms reached for him. He wanted to crawl away into some niche and escape the touch of the spirit's fingers, but his body was beyond coaxing or bullying.

"*I am the Jaff,*" he heard the bearded spirit say. "*Give me your mind, I want terata.*"

As the fingertips grazed Buddy's face he felt a spurt of power, white like lightning, cocaine, or semen, run through his head and down into his anatomy. With it, the recognition that he'd made an error. The split flesh and broken bone was not all he was. Despite his immoralities, there was something in him the Jaff coveted; a corner of his being which this occupying force could profit by. He'd called it *terata*. Buddy had no idea what that word meant. But he understood all too clearly the terror when the spirit entered him. The touch *was* lightning, burning a path into his essential self. And a drug too, making images of that invasion cavort in his mind's eye. And jism? That as well, or else why did a life he'd never had before, a creature born in his pith from the Jaff's rape, leap out of him now?

He glimpsed it as it went. It was pale and primitive. No face, but legs by the scrabbling dozen. No mind, either, except to do the Jaff's will. The bearded face laughed to see it. Withdrawing his fingers from Buddy, the spirit let his other arm drop from the neck of his enemy and, riding the terata headed up the rock chimney towards the sun.

The remaining combatant fell back against the cavern wall. From where he lay Buddy caught a glimpse of the man. He looked much less the warrior than his opponent, and consequently more brutalized by their exchange. His body was wasted, his expression one of weary distraction. He stared up the rock chimney.

"*Jaffe!*" he called, his shout shaking dust from the shelves Buddy had struck on his way down. There was no answer from the shaft. The man looked down towards Buddy, narrowing his eyes.

"I'm Fletcher," he said, his voice mellifluous. He moved towards Buddy, trailing a subtle light. "Forget your pain."

Buddy tried his damnedest to say: help me, but he didn't need to. Fletcher's very proximity soothed the agonies he felt.

"Imagine with me," Fletcher said. "Your fondest wish."

To die, Buddy thought.

The spirit heard the unspoken reply.

"No," he said. "Don't imagine death. Please don't imagine death. I can't arm myself with that."

Arm yourself? Buddy thought.

"Against the Jaff."

Who are you?

"Men once. Spirits now. Enemies forever. You have to help me. I need the last squeezings of your mind, or I go to war with him naked."

Sorry, I already gave, Buddy thought. You saw him do the taking. And by the way, what *was* that thing?

"The terata? Your primal fears made solid. He's riding to the world on it." Fletcher looked up the chimney again. "But he won't break surface yet. The day's too bright for him."

Is it still day?

"Yes."

How do you know?

"The process of the sun still moves me, even here. I wanted to be sky, Vance. Instead, two decades I've lived in darkness, with the Jaff at my throat. Now he's taking the war overground, and I need arms against him, plucked out of your head."

There's nothing left, Buddy said. I'm finished.

"Quiddity must be preserved," Fletcher said.

Quiddity?

"The dream-sea. You might even see its island, as you die. It's wonderful; I envy you the freedom to leave this world . . ."

Heaven you mean? Buddy thought. Is it Heaven you mean? If so, I haven't got a chance.

"Heaven's only one of many stories, told on the shores of Ephemeris. There are hundreds, and you'll know them all. So don't be afraid. Only give me a little of your mind, so that Quiddity may be preserved."

Who from?

"The Jaff, who else?"

Buddy had never been much of a dreamer. His sleep, when it wasn't drugged or drunk, was that of a man who lived himself to exhaustion daily. After a gig, or a fuck, or both, he would give himself to sleep as to a rehearsal for the final oblivion that called him now. With the fear of nullity a rod to his broken back he scrabbled to make sense of Fletcher's words. A sea; a shore; a place of stories, in which Heaven was just one of many possibilities? How could he have lived his life and never known this place?

"You've known it," Fletcher told him. "You've swum Quiddity twice in your life. The night you were born, and the night you first slept beside the one you loved most in your life. Who was that, Buddy? There've been so many women, right? Which one of them meant most to you? Oh . . . but of course. In the end, there was only one. Am I right? Your mother."

How the hell did you know that?

"Put it down to a lucky guess . . ."

Liar!

"OK, so I'm digging around in your thoughts a little. Forgive me the trespass. I need help, Buddy, or the Jaff has me beaten. You don't want that."

No, I don't.

"Imagine for me. Give me something more than regret to make an ally of. Who are your heroes?"

Heroes?

"Picture them for me."

Comedians! All of them.

"An army of comedians? Why not?"

The thought of it made Buddy smile. Why not indeed? Hadn't there been a time when he'd thought his art could cleanse the world of malice? Perhaps an army of holy fools could succeed with laughter where bombs had failed. A sweet, ridiculous vision. Comedians on the battlefields, baring their asses to the guns, and beating the generals over the head with rubber chickens; grinning cannon fodder, confounding the politicians with puns and signing the peace treaties in polkadotted ink.

His smile became laughter.

"Hold that thought," Fletcher said, reaching into Buddy's mind.

The laughter hurt. Even Fletcher's touch could not mellow the fresh spasms it initiated in Buddy's system.

"Don't die!" he heard Fletcher say. "Not yet! For Quiddity's sake, not yet!"

But it was no use his hollering. The laughter and the pain had hold of Buddy head to toe. He looked at the hovering spirit with tears pouring down his face.

Sorry, he thought. Can't seem to hold on. Don't want to—

Laughter racked him.

—You shouldn't have asked to remember.

"A moment!" said Fletcher. "That's all I need."

Too late. The life went out of him, leaving Fletcher with vapors in his hands too frail to be set against the Jaff.

"Damn you!" Fletcher said, yelling at the corpse as he'd once (so long ago) stood and shouted at Jaffe as he lay on the floor of the Misión de Santa Catrina. This time there was no life to be bullied from the corpse. Buddy was gone. On his face sat an expression both tragic and comical, which was only right. He'd lived his life that way. And in dying he'd assured Palomo Grove of a future burgeoning with such contradictions.

IV

Time in the Grove would play countless tricks in the next few days, but none surely as frustrating to its victim as the stretch between Howie's parting from Jo-Beth and the time when he would see her again. The minutes lengthened to the scale of hours; the hours seemed long enough to produce a generation. He distracted himself as best he could by going to look for his mother's house. That had after all been his ambition here: to learn his nature better by grasping his family tree closer to the root. So far, of course, he'd merely succeeded in adding confusion to confusion. He'd not known himself capable of what he'd felt last night—and felt now even more strongly. This soaring, unreasoning belief that all was well with the world, and could never be made unwell again. The fact of time unravelling the way it was could not best his optimism; it was just a game reality was playing with him, to confirm the absolute authority of what he was feeling.

And to that trick was added another, more subtle still. When he came to the house where his mother had lived it was almost supernaturally unchanged, exactly as in the photographs he'd seen of the place. He stood in the middle of the street and stared at it. There was no traffic in either direction; nor any pedestrians. This corner of the Grove floated in midmorning languor, and he felt almost as though his mother might appear at the window, a child again, and gaze out at him. That notion would not have occurred to him but for the events of the previous night. The miraculous recognition in that locking of eyes—the sense he'd had (still had) that his encounter with Jo-Beth had been a joy *in waiting* somewhere—led his mind to make patterns it had never dared before, and this possibility (a place from which a deeper self had drawn knowledge of Jo-Beth and known her imminence) would have been beyond him twenty-four hours before. Again, a loop. The mysteries of their meeting had taken him into realms of supposition which led from love to physics to philosophy and back to love again in such a way that art and science could no longer be distinguished.

Nor indeed, could the sense of mystery he felt, standing here in front of his mother's house, be separated from the mystery of the girl. House, mother, and meeting were one whole extraordinary story. He, the common factor.

He decided against knocking on the door (after all, how much more could he learn from the place?) and was about to retrace his steps when some instinct checked him and instead he continued up the gentle gradient of the street to its summit. There he was startled to find himself presented with a panoramic view of the Grove, looking east over the Mall to where the far fringes of the town gave way to solid foliage. Or nearly solid; here and there the canopy broke, and in one of the gaps quite a crowd appeared to have gathered. Arc-lamps had been erected in a ring, bearing down on some sight too far off for him to see. Were they making a movie down there? He'd spent so much of the morning in a daze he'd noticed almost nothing on his way up here; he could have passed all the stars who'd ever won an Oscar walking these streets and not registered the fact.

While he stood watching, he heard something whisper to him. He looked around. The street behind him was empty. There was no breeze, even here on the brow of his mother's hill, to carry the sound to him. Yet it came again; a sound so close to his ear it was almost inside his head. The voice was soft. It spoke two syllables only, joined into a necklace of sound.

—*ardhowardhowardhow*—

It didn't take a degree in logic to associate this mystery with whatever was going on in the woods below. He couldn't pretend to understand the processes at work upon and around him. The Grove was clearly a law unto itself, and he'd profited by its enigmas too much to turn his back on future adventures. If pursuit of a steak could bring him the love of his life what might following a whisper bring?

It wasn't difficult to find his way down to the trees. He had the oddest sense, making the descent, that the whole town *led* that way; that the hillside was a tipped plate, the contents of which might at any moment slide away into the maw of the earth. That image was reinforced when he finally reached the woods and asked what was going on. Nobody seemed much interested in telling him until a kid piped up:

"There's a hole in the ground, an' it swallowed him whole."

"Swallowed who?" Howie wanted to know. It wasn't the boy who replied but the woman with him.

"Buddy Vance," she said. Howie was none the wiser, and his ignorance must have registered, because the woman offered supplementary information. "He used to be a TV star," she said. "Funny guy. My husband loves him."

"Have they brought him up?" he asked.

"Not yet."

"Doesn't matter," the boy chipped in. "He's dead anyhow."

"Is that right?" Howie said.

"Sure," came the woman's reply.

The scene suddenly took on a fresh perspective. This crowd wasn't here to watch a man being snatched from death's door. They were here to claim a glimpse of the body as it was put in the back of an ambulance. All they wanted was to say: I was there, when they brought him up. I saw him, under a sheet. Their morbidity, especially on a day so full of possibilities, revolted him. Whoever had called his name was calling it no longer; or if he was the crowd's lowering presence blocked it. There was no purpose in his staying, when he had eyes to gaze into and lips to kiss. Turning his back on the trees, and his summoner, he headed back to the motel to wait for Jo-Beth's arrival.

FOUR

Only Abernethy ever called Grillo by his first name. To Saralyn, from the day they'd met to the night they'd parted, he was always Grillo; to every one of his colleagues and friends, the same. To his enemies (and what journalist, particularly a disgraced one, did not court enemies?) he was sometimes That Fuckhead Grillo, or Grillo the Righteous, but always Grillo.

Only Abernethy ever dared: "Nathan?"

"What do you want?"

Grillo had just stepped out of a shower, but the very sound of Abernethy's voice and he was ready to scrub himself down again.

"What are you doing at home?"

"I'm working," Grillo lied. It had been a late night. "The pollution piece, remember?"

"Forget it. Something's come up and I want you there. Buddy Vance—the comedian?—he turned up missing."

"When?"

"This morning."

"Where?"

"Palomo Grove. You know it?"

151

"It's a name on a freeway sign."

"They're trying to dig him out. It's noon now. How long before you can get there?"

"An hour. Maybe ninety minutes. What's the big interest?"

"You're too young to remember *The Buddy Vance Show.*"

"I caught the reruns."

"Let me tell you something, Nathan my boy—" Of all Abernethy's modes Grillo hated the avuncular most. "—there was a time *The Buddy Vance Show* emptied the bars. He was a great man and a great American."

"So you want a sob piece?"

"Shit, no. I want the news on his wives, the alcohol, and how come he ended up in Ventura County when he used to swan around Burbank in a limo three fucking blocks long."

"The dirt, in other words."

"There were drugs involved, Nathan," Abernethy said. Grillo could picture the look of mock-sincerity on the man's face. "And our readers need to know."

"They want the dirt, and so do you," Grillo said.

"So sue me," Abernethy said. "Just get your ass out there."

"So we don't even know where he is? Suppose he just took off somewhere?"

"Oh they know where he is," Abernethy said. "They're trying to bring the body up in the next few hours."

"Bring it up? You mean he drowned?"

"I mean he fell down a hole."

Comedians, Grillo thought. Anything for a laugh.

Except that it wasn't funny. When he'd first joined Abernethy's happy band, after the debacle in Boston, it had been a vacation from the heavy-duty investigative journalism in which he'd made his name, and *at* which, finally, he'd been out-maneuvered. The notion of working for a small-circulation scandal sheet like the *County Reporter* had seemed light relief. Abernethy was a hypocritical buffoon, a born-again Christian to whom forgiveness was a four-letter word. The stories he told Grillo to cover were easy in the gathering and easier still in the telling, given that the *Reporter*'s readers liked their news to perform one function only: the ameliorating of envy. They wanted tales of pain among the high rollers; the flipside of fame. Abernethy knew his congregation well. He'd even brought his biography into the act, making much in his editorials of his conversion from alcoholic to Fundamentalist. Dry and High on the Lord, was how he liked to describe himself. This holy sanction allowed him to peddle the muck he edited with a beatific smile, and allowed his readers to wallow in it without guilt. They were reading stories of the wages of sin. What could be more Christian?

For Grillo the joke had long since soured. If he'd thought of telling Abernethy to fuck off once he'd thought of it a hundred times, but where was he going to get a job, hot-shot reporter turned dupe that he was, except with a small operation like the *Reporter?* He'd contemplated other professions, but he had neither the desire nor aptitude to pursue any other. He had wanted to report the world to itself for as long as he could remember. There was something *essential* about that function. He could imagine himself performing no other. The world knew itself indifferently well. It needed people to tell it the story of its life, daily, or else how could it learn by its mistakes? He had been making headlines of one such mistake—an act of corruption in the Senate—when he discovered (his gut still turned, recalling that moment) that he had been set up by his target's opponents, his position as press prosecutor used to besmirch innocent parties. He had apologized, grovelled and resigned. The matter had been forgotten quickly, as a fresh slew of headlines replaced those that he'd created. Politicians, like scorpions and cockroaches, would be there when the warheads had levelled civilization. But journalists were frail. One miscalculation and their credibility was dust. He had fled West until he met the Pacific. He'd considered throwing himself in, but had instead chosen to work for Abernethy. More and more that seemed like an error.

Look on the bright side, he told himself every day, there's no direction from here but up.

The Grove surprised him. It had all the distinguishing marks of a town created on paper—the central Mall, the cardinal point villages, the sheer *order* of the streets—but there was a welcome diversity in the styles of the houses, and—perhaps because it was in part built on a hill—a sense that it might have secret reaches.

If the woods had any secrets of their own, they'd been trampled down by the sightseers who'd come to see the exhumation. Grillo flashed his credentials and asked a few questions of one of the cops at the barrier. No, there was no likelihood that the corpse would be raised soon; it had yet to be located. Nor could Grillo speak with any of those in charge of the operation. Come back later, was the suggestion. It looked like good advice. There was very little activity around the fissure. Despite there being tackle of various kinds on the ground nobody seemed to be putting it to use. He decided to risk leaving the scene to make a few calls. He found his way to the Mall and to a public telephone. His first call was to Abernethy, to report that he'd arrived and to enquire whether a photographer had been sent down. Abernethy was away from his desk. Grillo left a message. He had more luck with his second call. The answering machine began playing its familiar message—

"Hi. This is Tesla and Butch. If you want to speak to the dog, I'm out. If it's Butch you need—" only to be interrupted by Tesla.

"Hello?"

"It's Grillo."

"Grillo? Shut the fuck up, Butch! Sorry, Grillo, he's trying to—" the phone was dropped, and there was a good deal of commotion, followed by Tesla's breathless return to the receiver. "That animal. Why did I take him, Grillo?"

"He was the only male who'd live with you."

"Fuck you."

"Your words."

"I said that?"

"You said that."

"Out of my mind! I got good news, Grillo. I got a development deal for one of the screenplays. That castaway picture I wrote last year? They want it rewritten. In space."

"You're going to do it?"

"Why not? I need something produced. Nobody's going to do any of the heavy-duty stuff till I have a hit. So fuck Art, I'm going to be so crass they'll be coming in their pants. And before you say it, don't give me any of that artistic integrity shit. A girl's got to feed herself."

"I know, I know."

"So," she said, "what's new?"

There were a lot of answers to that: a litany. He could tell her about how his hairdresser, with a palmful of straw-blond clippings, had smilingly informed Grillo that he had a bald patch at his crown. Or how this morning, meeting himself in the mirror, he'd decided his long, anemic features, which he'd always hoped would mature into an heroic melancholia, were simply looking doleful. Or that he kept having those damn elevator dreams, trapped between floors with Abernethy and a goat Abernethy kept wanting Grillo to kiss. But he kept the biography to himself; and just said:

"I need help."

"It figures."

"What do you know about Buddy Vance?"

"He's down a hole. It's been on the TV."

"What's his life-story?"

"This is for Abernethy, right?"

"Right."

"So it's just the dirt."

"Got it in one."

"Well, comedians aren't my strongest point. I majored in Sex Goddesses. But I looked him up when I heard the news. Married six times; once to a seventeen-year-old. That lasted forty-two days. His second wife died of an overdose . . ."

As Grillo had hoped, Tesla had chapter and verse on the Life and Sordid Times of Buddy Vance (neé, of all things, Valentino). The addictions to women, controlled substances and fame; the TV series; the films; the fall from grace.

"You can write about that with feeling, Grillo."

"Thanks for nothing."

"I only love you because I hurt you. Or do I mean the other way around?"

"Very funny. Speaking of which: was he?"

"Was he what?"

"Funny."

"Vance? I suppose, in his way. You never saw him?"

"I must have, I suppose. I don't remember the act."

"He had this rubber-face. You looked at him, you laughed. And this weird persona. Half idiot, half slimeball."

"So how come he was so successful with women?"

"The dirt?"

"Of course."

"The enormous appendage."

"Are you kidding me?"

"The biggest dick in television. I got that from an unimpeachable source."

"Who was that?"

"*Please*, Grillo," Tesla said, aghast. "Do I sound like a girl who'd gossip?"

Grillo laughed. "Thanks for the information. I owe you dinner."

"Sold. Tonight."

"I'll still be here, looks like."

"So I'll come find you."

"Maybe tomorrow, if I'm still here. I'll call you."

"If you don't, you're dead."

"I said I'll call; I'll call. Go back to Castaways in Space."

"Don't do anything I wouldn't do. And Grillo—"

"What?"

Before answering she put the phone down, winning for the third consecutive time the game of who hangs up first they'd been playing since Grillo, in a maudlin stupor one night, had confessed he'd hated goodbyes.

FIVE

I

M omma?"
   She was sitting by the window as usual.

"Pastor John didn't come last night, Jo-Beth. You did call him like you promised?" She read the look on her daughter's face. "You did-n't," she said. "How could you forget a thing like that?"

"I'm sorry, Momma."

"You know how I rely upon him. I've got good reason, Jo-Beth. I know you don't think so, but I do."

"No. I believe you. I'll call him later. First . . . I have to speak to you."

"Shouldn't you be at the store?" Joyce said. "Did you come home sick? I heard Tommy-Ray . . ."

"Momma, listen to me. I have to ask you something very impor-tant."

Joyce looked troubled already. "I can't talk now," she said. "I want the Pastor."

"He'll come later. First: I have to know about a friend of yours."

Joyce said nothing, but her face was all frailty. Jo-Beth had seen her turn that expression on too often to be cowed by it.

"I met a man last night, Momma," she said, determined to be plain in her telling. "His name is Howard Katz. His mother was Trudi Katz."

Joyce's face lost its mask of delicacy. Beneath, was a look eerily like satisfaction. "Didn't I say?" she murmured to herself, turning her head back towards the window.

"Didn't you say what?"

"How could it be over? How could it ever be over?"

"Momma, explain."

"It wasn't an accident. We all knew it wasn't an accident. They had reasons."

"Who had reasons?"

"I need the Pastor."

"Momma: *who* had reasons?"

Without replying Joyce stood up.

"Where is he?" she said, her voice suddenly loud. She started towards the door. "I have to see him."

"All right, Momma! All right! Calm down."

At the door, she turned back to Jo-Beth. Tears welled in her eyes.

"You mustn't go near Trudi's boy," she said. "You hear me? You mustn't see him, speak to him, even *think* of him. Promise me."

"I can't promise that. It's stupid."

"You haven't *done* anything with him, have you?"

"What do you mean?"

"Oh my Lord, you have."

"I've done nothing."

"Don't lie to me!" Momma demanded, her hands clutched into bony fists. "You must pray, Jo-Beth!"

"I don't want to pray. I came wanting help from you, that's all. I don't need prayers."

"He's got into you already. You never spoke this way before."

"I never *felt* this way before!" she replied. Tears were perilously close; anger and fear all muddled up. It was no use listening to Momma, she wasn't going to provide anything but calls to prayer. Jo-Beth crossed to the door, her momentum enough to warn Momma that she wouldn't be prevented from leaving. There was no resistance. Momma stepped aside and let her go, but as she headed down the stairs called after her:

"Jo-Beth, come back! I'm sick, Jo-Beth! Jo-Beth! Jo-Beth!"

Howie opened the door to his beauty in tears.

"What's wrong?" he said ushering her in.

She put her hands to her face and sobbed. He wrapped his arms around her. "It's OK," he said. "Nothing's that bad." The sobs diminished steadily, until she disengaged herself from him and stood forlornly in the middle of the room, wiping the tears from her cheeks with the back of her hand.

"I'm sorry," she said.

"What happened?"

"It's a long story. It goes way back. To your mother and mine."

"They knew each other?"

She nodded. "They were best friends."

"So this was in the stars," he said, smiling.

"I don't think that's the way Momma sees it."

"Why not? Son of her best friend—"

"Did your mother ever tell you why she left the Grove?"

"She was unmarried."

"So's Momma."

"Maybe she's tougher than my—"

"No, what I mean is: maybe that's more than a coincidence. All my life there's been rumors about what happened before I was born. About Momma and her friends."

"I know nothing about this."

"I only know bits and pieces. There were four of them. Your mother; mine; a girl called Carolyn Hotchkiss, whose father still lives in the Grove, and another. I forget her name. Arleen something. They were attacked. Raped, I think."

Howie's smile had long since disappeared.

"Mother?" he said softly. "Why did she never say anything?"

"Who's going to tell their kid they were conceived that way?"

"Oh my God," Howie said. "Raped . . ."

"Maybe I'm wrong," Jo-Beth said, looking up at Howie. His face was knotted up, as though he'd just been slapped.

"I've lived with these rumors all my life, Howie. I've seen Momma driven half-mad by them. Talking about the Devil all the time. It used to scare me so much, when she started talking about Satan having his eye on me. I used to pray to be invisible, so he couldn't see me."

Howie took his spectacles off and threw them on to the bed.

"I never really told you why I came here, did I?" he said. "I think . . . think . . . think it's time I did. I came because I don't have the first clue as to who or what I am. I wanted to find out about the Grove and why it drove my mother out."

"Now you wish you'd never come."

"No. If I hadn't come I wouldn't have met you. Wouldn't have — have . . . have . . . fallen in love — "

"With someone who's probably your own *sister?*"

The slapped look slackened. "No," he said. "I can't believe that."

"I recognized you the moment I stepped into Butrick's. You recognized me. Why?"

"Love at first sight."

"I wish."

"That's what I feel. It's what you feel too. I know it is. You said it is."

"That was before."

"I love you, Jo-Beth."

"You can't. You don't know me."

"I do! And I'm not going to give up on that because of gossip. We don't even know if any of this is true." In his vehemence, all trace of his stammer had disappeared. "This could be all lies, right?"

"It could," she conceded. "But why would anybody invent a story like that? Why did neither your mother nor mine ever tell us who our fathers were?"

"We'll find out."

"Who from?"

"Ask your momma."

"I already tried."

"And?"

"She told me not to go near you. Not to even think of you . . ."

Her tears had dried as she'd told the story. Now, thinking of Momma again, they began to flow. "But I can't stop that, can I?" she said, appealing for help from the very source she'd been forbidden.

Watching her, Howie longed to be the holy fool Lem had always called him. To have the freedom from censure only idiots, animals and babes-in-arms were granted; to lick and lap at her, and not be slapped away. There was no denying the possibility that she was indeed his sister, but his libido vaulted taboo.

"I think maybe I should go," she said, as though sensing his heat. "Momma wants the Pastor."

"Say a few prayers and maybe I'll go away, you mean?"

"That's not fair."

"Stay awhile, please," he coaxed. "We don't have to talk. We don't have to do anything. Just stay."

"I'm tired."

"So we'll sleep."

He reached and touched her face, very lightly.

"Neither of us got enough sleep last night," he said.

She sighed, and nodded.

"Maybe it'll all come clear if we just let it be."

"I hope."

He excused himself and went through to the bathroom to empty his bladder. By the time he got back she had taken off her shoes and was lying on the bed.

"Room for two?" he said.

She murmured yes. He lay down beside her, trying not to think about what he'd hoped they'd be doing between these sheets.

Again, she sighed.

"It'll be all right," he said. "Sleep."

II

M ost of the audience gathered for Buddy Vance's final show had drifted away by the time Grillo got back to the woods. They'd decided, apparently, that he wasn't worth the wait. With the onlookers dispersed the barrier-guards had become lax. Grillo stepped over the rope and approached the policeman who looked to be in charge of the operation. He introduced himself, and his function.

"Can't tell you much," the man replied, in answer to Grillo's questions. "We've got four climbers going down now, but God knows how long it'll take to raise the body. We haven't found it yet. And Hotchkiss tells us there's all kinds of rivers under there. The corpse could be in the Pacific for all we know."

"Will you work through the night?"

"Looks like we'll have to." He looked at his watch. "We've got maybe four hours of daylight left. Then we'll be relying on the lamps."

"Has anybody investigated these caves before?" Grillo asked. "Are they mapped?"

"Not that I know of. You'd better ask Hotchkiss. He's the guy in black over there."

Again, Grillo made his introductions. Hotchkiss was a tall, grim individual, with the baggy look of a man who'd lost substantial amounts of weight.

"I understand you're the cave expert," Grillo said.

"Only by default," Hotchkiss replied. "It's just that nobody knows any better." His eyes didn't settle on Grillo for a moment, but roved and roved in search of some place to rest. "What's below us . . . people don't think much about."

"And you do?"

"Yeah."

"You've made some kind of study of it?"

"In a strictly amateur capacity," Hotchkiss explained. "There's some subjects just take hold of you. This did me."

"So have you been down there yourself?"

Hotchkiss broke his rule, holding his gaze on Grillo's face for a full two seconds before saying: "Until this morning these caves were *sealed*, Mr. Grillo. I had them sealed myself, many years ago. They were—they *are*—a danger to innocents."

Innocents, Grillo noted. A strange word to use.

"The policeman I was talking to—"

"Spilmont."

"Right. He said there's rivers down there."

"There's a whole *world* down there, Mr. Grillo, about which we know next to nothing. And it's changing all the time. Sure, there's rivers, but there's a good deal else besides. Whole species that never see the sun."

"Doesn't sound like much fun."

"They accommodate," Hotchkiss said. "As we all do. They live with their limitations. We're all of us living on a fault line, after all, which could open up at any moment. We accommodate that."

"I try not to think about it."

"That's your way."

"And yours?"

Hotchkiss made a tight, tiny smile, his eyes half-closing as he did so.

"A few years ago I thought about leaving the Grove. It had . . . bad associations for me."

"But you stayed."

"I discovered I was a sum of my . . . *accommodations*," he replied. "When the town goes, so will I."

"*When?*"

"Palomo Grove is built on bad land. The earth beneath our feet feels solid enough but it's on the move."

"So the whole town could go the way of Buddy Vance? Is that what you're saying?"

"You can quote me as long as you don't name me."

"That's fine by me."

"Got what you need?"

"More than enough."

"No such thing," Hotchkiss observed. "Not with bad news. Excuse me, would you?"

There had been a sudden galvanizing of forces around the fissure. Leaving Grillo with a punchline for his story any comedian would have envied, Hotchkiss strode off to oversee the raising of Buddy Vance.

In his bedroom Tommy-Ray lay and sweated. He'd come out of the sunlight and closed the windows, then drawn the curtains. Sealing the room thus had made it into an oven, but the heat and the gloom soothed him. In their embrace he didn't feel so alone, and exposed, as he'd felt in the bright, clean air of the Grove. Here he could smell his own juices as they oozed from his pores; his own stale breath as it rose from his throat and dropped back down over his face. If Jo-Beth had cheated on him then he would have to seek out new company, and where better to begin than with himself?

He'd heard her come back to the house in the early afternoon, and argue with Momma, but he didn't try to catch the words between them. If her pathetic romance was already falling apart—and why else would she be sobbing on the stairs?—then that was her own damn fault. He had more important business.

Lying in the heat, the strangest pictures came haunting his head. They all rose from a darkness which his curtained room couldn't hope to match. Was that, perhaps, why they were incomplete as yet? Fragments of a scheme he wanted passionately to grasp but that kept slipping from him. In them, there was blood; there was rock; there was a pale, flickering creature his gut turned at seeing. And there was a man he could not make out but who would, if he sweated enough, come clear in front of him.

When he did, the waiting would be over.

First, there was a shout of alarm from the fissure. Men around the hole, Spilmont and Hotchkiss included, set to work to haul the men up, but whatever was taking place underground was too violent to be controlled from the surface. The cop closest to the crevice cried out as the rope he was holding suddenly tightened around his gloved hand and he was jerked towards the lip like a hooked fish. It was Spilmont who saved him, taking hold of the man from behind long enough for him to pull his fingers free of the gloves. As both fell backwards on to the ground the shouts from below multiplied, supplemented by warnings from above.

"*It's opening!*" somebody yelled. "*Jesus Christ, it's opening!*"

Grillo was a physical coward until he sniffed news; then he was ready to stand face to face with anything. He pushed past Hotchkiss and a cop to get a better view of what was happening. Nobody stopped him; not with their own safety to consider. Dust was rising from the widening fissure, blinding the anchor men who were holding the ropes on which the retrieval party's life depended. Even as he watched, one of the men was hauled towards the crevice, from which shrieks that suggested massacre were rising. He added his as the earth went to dust beneath his heels. Somebody threw himself past Grillo in the confusion and attempted to snatch at the man but too late. The rope tightened. He was pulled out of sight, leaving his failed savior face down at the edge of the crack. Grillo took three steps towards the survivor, barely able to see either the ground or its absence beneath his feet. He felt its tremors, however, rising through his legs and up his spine, throwing his thoughts into chaos. Instinct sufficed. Legs spread to keep his balance, he reached down for the fallen man. It was Hotchkiss, face bloodied when he'd hit the earth, a dazed look in his eyes. Grillo yelled his name. The man responded by grabbing at Grillo's proffered arm, as the ground around them both split open.

Side by side on the motel bed, neither Jo-Beth nor Howie woke, though both gasped and shuddered like lovers saved from drowning. There had been dreams of water for them both. Of a dark sea which was carrying them towards some wonderful place. But their journey had been interrupted. Something below their dreaming selves had snatched at them, dragging them out of that lulling tide and down into a shaft of rock and pain. Men were screaming all around them as they fell to their deaths, ropes following like obedient snakes.

Somewhere in the confusion they heard each other, each sobbing the other's name, but there wasn't time for reunion before their downward motion was checked and an upward surge caught them. It was icy cold; a torrent of water from a river that had never seen the sun but mounted the chasm now, bearing dead men, dreamers and whatever else occupied this nightmare, before it. The walls became a blur as they rose to meet the sky.

Grillo and Hotchkiss were four yards from the fissure when the waters broke, the violence of the breakage enough to throw them off their feet as a freezing rain fell. It stung Hotchkiss from his daze. He grabbed hold of Grillo's arm, hollering:

"Look at that!"

There was something *alive* in the flood. Grillo saw it for the briefest of moments—a form, or *forms*—that seemed human as he glimpsed them but left on his inner eye another impression entirely, like the after-burn of fireworks. He shook the image off and looked again. But whatever he'd seen had gone.

"We got to get out!" he heard Hotchkiss yell. The ground was still cracking. They hauled themselves upright, their feet scrabbling in the mud for purchase, and ran blindly through rain and dust, only knowing they'd reached the perimeter when they tripped over the rope. One of the retrieval team, his hand half gone, lay where the first spurt had dropped him. Beyond rope and body, in the cover of the trees, were Spilmont and a number of cops. The rain came down lightly here, tapping on the canopy like a midsummer shower, while behind the storm from the earth roared itself out.

Soaking with his own sweat, Tommy-Ray stared at the ceiling and laughed. He hadn't had a ride like that since the summer before last, out at Topanga, when a freak tide had thrown up a magnificent swell. He, Andy and Sean had ridden it for hours, high on speed.

"I'm ready," he said, wiping salt-water from his eyes. "Ready and willing. Just come get me, whoever the fuck you are."

———

Howie looked dead, lying on the bed all bundled up, his teeth clenched, his eyes closed. Jo-Beth backed away, hand to her mouth to block the panic, her words—*Dear God forgive me*—coming in muffled sobs. They'd done wrong, even lying together on the same bed. It was a crime against the laws of the Lord to dream the way she'd dreamt (of him naked beside her on a warm sea, their hair intertwined the way she'd wanted their bodies to be) and what had that dream brought? Cataclysm! Blood, rock and a terrible rain which had killed him in his sleep.

Dear God, forgive me—

He opened his eyes so suddenly her prayer deserted her. In its place, his name.

"Howie? You're alive."

He unknotted himself, reaching out to claim his spectacles from beside the bed. He put them on. Her shock came into focus.

"You dreamed it too," he said.

"It wasn't like a dream. It was real." She was shaking from head to foot. "What have we done, Howie?"

"Nothing," he said, coughing the growl from his throat. "We've done nothing."

"Momma was right. I shouldn't have—"

"Stop it," he said, swinging his legs over the edge of the bed and standing up. "We've done nothing wrong."

"What was that then?" she said.

"A bad dream."

"In both our heads?"

"Maybe it wasn't the same," he said, hoping to calm her.

"I was floating, with you beside me. Then I was underground. Men were screaming—"

"All right—" he said.

"It *was* the same."

"Yes."

"See?" she said. "Whatever's between us . . . it's wrong. Maybe it's the Devil's work."

"You don't believe that."

"I don't know what I believe," she said. He moved towards her, but she kept him at bay with a gesture. "Don't, Howie. It's not right. We shouldn't touch each other." She started towards the door. "I have to go."

"This is . . . is . . . is . . . absurd," he said, but no stumbling words of his were going to stop her leaving. She was already fumbling with the security bolt he'd put on when she'd entered.

"I'll get it," he said, leaning past her to open the door. In lieu of any comforting words he kept a silence which she only broke with:

"Goodbye."

"You're not giving us time to think this through."

"I'm afraid, Howie," she said. "You're right, I don't believe the Devil's in this. But if he isn't, who is? Have you got any answers for that?"

She was barely able to keep her emotions in check; she kept gulping air as if trying to swallow, and failing. The sight of her distress made him long to hug her, but what had been invited last night was now forbidden.

"No," he told her. "No answers."

She took the cue of his reply to leave him at the door. He watched her for a count of five, defying himself to stand and let her go, knowing what had happened between them was more significant than anything he'd experienced in eighteen years of breathing the air of the planet. At five, he closed the door.

PART FOUR

PRIMAL SCENES

ONE

G rillo had never heard Abernethy happier. The man fairly whooped when Grillo told him the Buddy Vance story had taken a turn for the cataclysmic, and that he'd been there to witness it all.

"Start writing!" he said. "Take a room in town—charge it to me—and start writing! I'll hold the front page." If Abernethy sought to excite Grillo with B-movie clichés he failed. What had happened at the caves had left him numb. But the suggestion that he take a room was welcome. Though he'd dried off at the bar where he and Hotchkiss had given their account to Spilmont, he felt dirty and exhausted.

"What about this Hotchkiss guy?" Abernethy said. "What's his story?"

"I don't know."

"Find out. And get some more background on Vance. Have you been up to the house yet?"

"Give me time."

"You're on the spot," Abernethy said. "It's your story. Get to it."

He revenged himself on Abernethy, albeit pettily, by taking the most expensive room on offer at the Hotel Palomo, in Stillbrook Village, ordering up champagne and a rare hamburger, and tipping the waiter so well the man asked him if he hadn't made a mistake. The booze made him light-headed; his favorite condition in which to call Tesla. She wasn't in. He left a message stating his present locale. Then he looked up Hotchkiss in the directory and called him. He had heard the man give his account to Spilmont. No mention had been made of what they'd glimpsed escaping from the fissure. Grillo had similarly kept quiet on the subject, and the absence of any questions on the subject from Spilmont suggested nobody else had been close enough to the fissure to witness the sight. He wanted to compare notes with Hotchkiss, but he drew a blank. Either he wasn't in or he'd decided not to answer the telephone.

With that route of enquiry blocked, he turned his attention to the Vance mansion. It was almost nine in the evening, but there was no harm in his wandering up the Hill to have a look at the dead man's estate. He might even talk his way inside if the champagne hadn't got the better of his tongue. In some regards the timing was advantageous. This morning Vance had been the focal point of events in the Grove. His relatives, if they had a taste for the limelight—and few didn't—could bide their time before choosing between suitors for their story. But now Vance's demise had been superseded by a larger, and fresher, tragedy. Grillo might therefore find the contingent more eager to talk than he would have done at noon.

He regretted deciding to walk. The Hill was steeper than it had seemed from below, and badly lit. But there were compensations. He had the street to himself, and so could leave the sidewalk and wander up the center, admiring the stars as they appeared overhead. Vance's residence wasn't hard to locate. The road stopped at its gates. After Coney Eye, there was only sky.

The main gate was unguarded but locked. A side gate, however, gave him access to a path which wound through a colonnade of undisciplined evergreens, which were alternately flooded with green, yellow and red light, to the front of the house. It was vast, and utterly idiosyncratic; a palace which defied the aesthetic of the Grove in every way. There was no trace here of the pseudo-Mediterranean, or the ranch style, or the Spanish style, or the mock-Tudor, or the modern colonial. The whole mansion looked like a funfair ride, its facade painted in the same primaries that had lit the trees, its windows ringed with lights which were presently turned off. Coney Eye, Grillo now understood, was a little piece of the Island: Vance's homage to Carnival. There were lights burning inside. He knocked, aware that he was being scrutinized by cameras above the door. A woman of oriental extraction—Vietnamese, perhaps—opened it, and informed him that Mrs. Vance was indeed in residence. If he'd wait in the hallway, she told him, she'd see if the lady of the house was available. Grillo thanked her, and waited while the woman took herself off upstairs.

As outside, so in: a temple to fun. Every inch of the hallway was hung with panels from all manner of Carnival rides: brilliantly colored advertisements for Tunnels of Love, Ghost Train Rides, Carousels, Freak Shows, Wrestling Shows, Gal Shows, Waltzes, Dippers, and Mystic Swings. The renderings were for the most part crude, the work of painters who knew their craft was in the service of commerce, and had no lasting merit. Close scrutiny didn't flatter the displays; their gaudy self-confidence was to be viewed through the crush of a crowd rather than studied under the spotlight. Vance had not been blind to that fact. By hanging the items cheek by jowl on every wall he effectively drew the eye on from one to the next, preventing it from lingering too long on any detail. The display, for all its vulgarity, drew a smile from Grillo, as no doubt Vance had intended, a smile that fell from his face when Rochelle Vance appeared at the top of the stairs and began her descent.

Never in his life had he seen a face more flawless. With every step she took towards him he expected to find a compromise in its perfection, but there was none. She was of Caribbean blood, he guessed, her dark features had that ease about their line. Her hair was drawn back tight, emphasizing the dome of her forehead and the symmetry of her brows. She wore no jewelry, and only the simplest of black dresses.

"Mr. Grillo," she said, "I'm Buddy's widow." The word, despite the color of her dress, couldn't have seemed more inappropriate. This was not a woman who'd risen from a tearsoaked pillow. "How can I help you?" she asked.

"I'm a journalist—"

"So Ellen told me."

"I wanted to ask you about your husband."

"It's a little late."

"I was in the woods most of the afternoon."

"Ah yes," she said. "You're *that* Mr. Grillo."

"I'm sorry?"

"I had one of the policemen . . ." She turned to Ellen. "What was his name?"

"Spilmont."

"Spilmont. He was here, to tell me what happened. He mentioned your great heroism."

"It wasn't so great."

"Enough to deserve a night's rest I would have thought," she said. "Rather than business."

"I'd like to get the story."

"Yes. Well come in."

Ellen opened a door to the left of the hallway. As Rochelle led Grillo in she laid out the ground rules.

"I'll answer your questions as best I can, as long as you limit them to Buddy's professional life." Her speech was devoid of accent. A European education, perhaps? "I know nothing about his other wives so don't bother prying. Nor will I speculate on his addictions. Would you like some coffee?"

"That'd be most welcome," Grillo said, aware that he was doing what he did so often during interviews: catching a tone from his interviewee.

"Coffee for Mr. Grillo, Ellen," Rochelle said, inviting her guest to sit. "And water for me."

The room they'd entered ran the full length of the house, and was two stories high, the second marked by a gallery which ran around all four walls. These, like the hallway walls, were a painted din. Invitations, seductions and warnings fought for his eye. *"The Ride of a Life-*

time!" one modestly promised; *"All the Fun You Can Stand!"* another announced, *"And Then Some!"*

"This is just part of Buddy's collection," Rochelle said. "There's more in New York. I believe it's the biggest in private hands."

"I didn't know anybody collected this stuff."

"Buddy called it the true art of America. It may be that it is, which says something . . ." She trailed off, her distaste for this hollering parade quite plain. The expression, crossing a face so devoid of sculptural error, carried distressing force.

"You'll break the collection up, I suppose," Grillo said.

"That depends on the Will," she said. "It may not be mine to sell."

"You've got no sentimental attachments to it?"

"I think that comes under the heading of private life," she said.

"Yes. I suppose it does."

"But I'm sure Buddy's obsession was harmless enough." She stood up and flipped a switch between two panels from a ghost-train facade. Multicolored lights came on beyond the glass wall at the far end of the room. "Allow me to show you," she said, wandering down the length of the room, and stepping out into the soup of colors. Pieces too big to be fitted into the house were assembled here. A carved face, maybe twelve feet high, the yawning, saw-toothed mouth of which had been the entrance to a ride. A placard advertising The Wall of Death, written out in lights. A full-size, bas-relief locomotive, driven by skeletons, appearing to burst from a tunnel.

"My God," was all Grillo could muster.

"Now you know why I left him," Rochelle said.

"I didn't realize," Grillo replied. "You didn't live here?"

"I tried," she said. "But look at the place. It's like walking into Buddy's mind. He liked to make his mark on everything. Every*body*. There was no room for me here. Not if I wasn't prepared to play things his way."

She stared at the mammoth maw. "Ugly," she said. "Don't you think?"

"I'm no judge," Grillo said.

"It doesn't offend you?"

"It might get to me with a hangover."

"He used to tell me I had no sense of humor," she said. "Because I don't find this . . . stuff of his amusing. The fact is I didn't find *him* very amusing either. As a lover, yes . . . he was wonderful. But funny? No."

"Is all this off the record?" Grillo wondered.

"Does it matter if I say it is? I've had enough bad publicity in my life to know you don't give a fuck for my privacy."

"But you're telling me anyway."

She turned from the mouth to look at him. "Yes I am," she said. There was a pause. Then she said: "I'm cold," and stepped back inside. Ellen was pouring coffee.

"Leave it," Rochelle instructed. "I'll do it."

The Vietnamese woman lingered at the door a fraction of a moment too long for servility before exiting.

"So that's the Buddy Vance story," Rochelle said. "Wives, wealth and Carnival. Nothing terribly new in it I'm afraid."

"Do you know if he had any premonition of this?" Grillo asked as they resumed their seats.

"Of dying? I doubt it. He wasn't exactly attuned to that kind of thinking. Cream?"

"Yes, please. And sugar."

"Help yourself. Is that the kind of news your readers would like to hear? That Buddy had seen his death in a dream?"

"Stranger things have happened," Grillo said, his thoughts inevitably tripping back to the fissure and its escapees.

"I don't think so," Rochelle replied. "I don't see much sign of miracles. Not any more." She extinguished the lights outside. "When I was a child, my grandfather taught me to influence other children."

"How?"

"Just by thinking about it. It was something he'd done all his life, and he passed it on to me. It was easy. I could make kids drop their ice creams. Make them laugh and not know why: I thought nothing of it. There were miracles then. Waiting round the corner. But I lost the knack. We all lose it. Everything changes for the worse."

"Your life can't be that bad," Grillo said. "I know you're grieving at the—"

"Fuck my grief," she said suddenly. "He's dead, and I'm here waiting to see what the last laugh's going to be."

"The Will?"

"The Will. The wives. The bastards who're going to pop up from nowhere. He's finally got me on one of his damn mystery rides." Her words were charged with feeling, but she spoke them calmly enough. "You can go home and turn all this into deathless prose."

"I'm going to stay in town," Grillo said. "Until your husband's body is found."

"It won't be," Rochelle replied. "They've given up the search."

"What?"

"That's what Spilmont came up to explain. They've already lost five men. Apparently the chances of finding him are slim anyhow. It's not worth the risk."

"Does that upset you?"

"Not having a body to bury? No, not really. It's better he be remembered smiling than being brought up out of a hole in the ground. So, you see, your story finishes here. There'll be a memorial service for him in Hollywood, presumably. The rest, as they say, is television history." She stood up, marking an end to the interview. Grillo had unasked questions aplenty, most of them about the one subject she'd pronounced herself willing to talk about yet hadn't touched: his professional life. There were a few loopholes Tesla couldn't plug, he knew. Rather than press the widow Vance beyond her patience he let the questions go. She'd supplied more insights than he'd expected.

"Thank you for seeing me," he said, shaking her hand. Her fingers were as thin as twigs. "You've been most kind."

"Ellen will see you out," she said.

"Thanks."

The girl was waiting in the hallway. As she opened the front door she touched Grillo's arm. He looked at her. She made a hushing face and pressed a scrap of paper into his hand. Without a word being exchanged he was ushered out on to the step and the door was closed behind him.

He waited until he was out of video range before he looked at the scrap. It bore the woman's name—Ellen Nguyen—and an address in Deerdell Village. Buddy Vance might be staying buried but his story, it seemed, was still digging its way out. Stories had a way of doing that, in Grillo's experience. It was his belief that nothing, but *nothing*, could stay secret, however powerful the forces with interests vested in silence. Conspirators might conspire and thugs attempt to gag but the truth, or an approximation of same, would show itself sooner or later, very often in the unlikeliest form. It was seldom hard facts that revealed the life behind the life. It was rumor, graffiti, strip cartoons and love songs. It was what people gabbled about in their cups, or between fucks, or read on a toilet wall.

The art of the underground, like the figures he'd seen in the spurt, rising to change the world.

TWO

J o-Beth lay on her bed in darkness and watched the breeze by turn belly the curtains then draw them out into the night. She had gone to talk to Momma as soon as she returned to the house, and told her that she would not be seeing Howie again. It had been a promise made in haste, but she doubted whether Momma had even heard it. She'd had a distracted air about her, pacing her room, wringing her hands and murmuring prayers to herself. The prayers reminded Jo-Beth that she'd promised to call the Pastor and hadn't. Composing herself as best she could, she went downstairs and called the church. Pastor John was not available, however. He'd gone to comfort Angelie Datlow, whose husband Bruce had been killed in the attempt to raise Buddy Vance's body. This was the first Jo-Beth had heard of the tragedy. She curtailed the conversation, and came off the telephone, trembling. She needed no detailed description of the deaths. She'd seen them, and so had Howie. Their shared dream had been interrupted by a live report from the shaft where Datlow and his colleagues had died.

She sat in the kitchen, the fridge humming, the birds and bugs in the backyard making blithe music, and tried to make sense of the senseless. Maybe she'd been sold an overly optimistic vision of the world, but she'd preceded thus far believing that if she couldn't grasp things personally there were those in her vicinity who could. It gave her comfort to know that. Now she was not sure. If she told anyone from church—who made up most of her circle—what had happened at the motel (the dream of water, the dream of death) they'd take the line Momma had taken: that this was the Devil's doing. When she'd said as much to Howie he'd told her she didn't believe it and he was right. It was nonsense. And if that was nonsense, what else that she'd been taught besides?

Unable to think her way through her confusions, and too tired to bully them, she took herself off to her room to lie down. She had no wish to sleep so soon after the trauma of her last slumber, but fatigue overcame her resistance. A string of scenes, black and white with a pearly sheen, appeared before her as she fell. Howie in Butrick's; Howie at the Mall, face to face with Tommy-Ray; his face on the pillow, when she'd thought him dead. Then the string broke and the pearls flew off. She sank into sleep.

The clock said eight-thirty-five when she woke. The house was completely hushed. She got up, moving as silently as she could to avoid a summons from Momma. Downstairs she fixed herself a sandwich and brought it back up to her room, where now—sandwich consumed—she lay, watching the curtains do the wind's will.

The evening light had been smooth as apricot cream, but it had gone now. Darkness was very close. She could feel its approach—cancelling distance, silencing life—and it distressed her as it never had before. In homes not so far from here families would be in mourning. Husbandless wives, fatherless children, facing their first night of grief. In others, sadnesses which had been put away would be brought out; studied; wept over. She had something of her own now, that made her part of that greater sorrow. Loss had touched her, and the darkness— which took so much away from the world and gave so little back— would never be the same again.

Tommy-Ray was woken by the window rattling. He sat up in bed. The day had passed in a self-created fever. Morning seemed more than a dozen hours away, yet what had he done in the intervening time? Just slept, and sweated, and waited for a sign.

Was that what he was hearing now; the chatter of the window, like a dying man's teeth? He threw off the covers. At some stage he'd stripped to his underwear. The body he caught sight of in the mirror was lean and shiny; like a healthy snake. Distracted by admiration, he stumbled, and in attempting to stand up realized he'd lost all grasp of the room. It was suddenly strange to him—and he to it. The floor sloped as it never had before; the wardrobe had shrunk to the size of a suitcase, or else he'd grown grotesquely large. Nauseated, he reached out for something solid to orient himself. He intended the door but either his hand or the room undid his intention and it was the window frame he grasped. He stood still, clinging to the wood until the queasiness passed. As he waited he felt the all but imperceptible motion of the frame move up through the bones in his fingers into his wrists and arms, and thence across his shoulders to his spine. Its progress was a jittering dance in his marrow, which made no sense until it climbed his last few vertebrae and struck his skull. There the motion, which had been a chatter in the glass, became sound again: a loop of clicks and rattles which spoke a summons to him.

He didn't need to be called twice. Letting the window frame go, he turned giddily towards the door. His feet kicked the clothes he'd discarded in his sleep. He picked up his T-shirt and jeans, vaguely thinking that he should dress before leaving the house but not getting beyond dragging his clothes after him as he went, down the stairs and out into the blackness at the back of the house.

The yard was large, and chaotic, having been neglected over many years. The fencing had fallen into disrepair, and the shrubbery which had been planted to shield the yard from the road had grown into a solid wall of foliage. It was towards that little jungle he went now, drawn by the Geiger counter in his skull, which was getting louder with every step he took.

Jo-Beth rose from her pillow with an ache in her teeth. Tentatively she touched the side of her face. It felt tender; almost as though bruised. She got up and slipped down the hall to the bathroom. Tommy-Ray's bedroom door was open, she noticed, which it hadn't previously been. If he was there, she couldn't see him. The curtains were drawn, the interior pitch black.

A brief perusal of her face in the bathroom mirror reassured her that though her crying had taken its toll she was otherwise unmarked. The ache, however, continued in her jaw, creeping around to the base of her skull. She'd never felt anything like it before. The pressure was not consistent but rhythmic, like a pulse that was not her heart's doing, but had come into her from somewhere other.

"Stop," she murmured, clenching her teeth against the percussion. But it wouldn't be controlled. It simply tightened its hold on her head, as if to squeeze her thoughts out altogether.

In desperation she found herself conjuring Howie; an image of light and laughter to set against this mindless beat that had come out of the dark. It was a forbidden image—one she had promised Momma she'd not dwell on—but she was weaponless otherwise. If she didn't fight back the beat in her head would pulp her thoughts with its insistence; make her move to its rhythm and its alone.

Howie . . .

He smiled at her out of the past. She held on to the brightness of his memory, and bent to the sink to splash cold water on her face. Water and memory subdued the assault. Unsteady on her feet she stepped out of the bathroom and headed towards Tommy-Ray's room. Whatever this sickness was it would surely have afflicted him too. From their earliest childhood they'd caught every virus, and suffered it, together. Perhaps this new, strange affliction had caught him earlier than she, and his behavior at the Mall had been a consequence of it. The thought brought hope. If he was sick then he could be healed. Both of them, healed together.

Her suspicions were confirmed when she stepped through the door. It smelt like a sickroom; unbearably hot, and stale.

"Tommy-Ray? Are you there?"

She pushed the door open to throw a better light inside. The room was empty, the bed heaped with bedclothes, the carpet rucked up as though he'd danced a tarantella upon it. She crossed to the window, intending to open it, but she got no further than drawing the curtains aside. The sight she was presented with was enough to take her down the stairs fast, calling Tommy-Ray's name. By the light from the kitchen door she saw him staggering across the yard, dragging his jeans after him.

The thicket at the end of the garden was moving; and there was more than the wind in it.

"My son," said the man in the trees. *"We meet at last."*

Tommy-Ray could not see his summoner clearly, but there was no doubt that this was the man. The chatter in his head grew softer at the sight of him.

"Come closer," he instructed. There was something of the stranger with candy about his voice, and his half-concealment. That *my son* could not be literally true, could it? Wouldn't it be fine if it were? After giving up all hope of meeting that man, after the childhood taunts and the hours wasted trying to imagine him, to have his lost father here at last, calling him from the house with a code known only to fathers and sons. So fine, so very fine.

"Where's my daughter?" the man said. *"Where's Jo-Beth?"*

"I think she's in the house."

"Go fetch her for me, will you?"

"In a minute."

"Now!"

"I want to see you first. I want to know this isn't a trick."

The stranger laughed.

"Already I hear my voice in you," he said. *"I've had tricks played on me, too. It makes us cautious, yes?"*

"Yes."

"Of course you must see me," he said, stepping out of the trees. *"I am your father. I am the Jaff."*

As Jo-Beth reached the bottom of the stairs she heard Momma call from her room.

"Jo-Beth? What's happening?"

"It's all right, Momma."

"Come here! Something terrible . . . in my sleep . . ."

"A moment, Momma. Stay in bed."

"Terrible—"

"I'll be back in a while. Just stay where you are."

He was here, in the flesh: the father Tommy-Ray had dreamed of in a thousand forms since he'd realized that other boys had a second parent, a parent whose sex they shared, who knew men's stuff, and passed it down to their sons. Sometimes he'd fantasized that he was some movie star's bastard, and that one day a limo would glide up the street and a famous smile step out and say exactly what the Jaff had just said. But this man was better than any movie star. He didn't look like much, but he shared with the faces the world idolized an eerie poise, as though he was beyond needing to demonstrate his power. Where that authority came from Tommy-Ray didn't yet know, but its signs were perfectly visible.

"*I'm your father,*" the Jaff said again. "*Do you believe me?*"

Of course he did. He'd be a fool to deny a father like this.

"Yes," he said, "I believe you."

"*And you'll obey me like a loving son?*"

"Yes, I will."

"*Good,*" the Jaff said, "*so now, please fetch me my daughter. I called her but she refuses to come. You know why . . .*"

"No."

"*Think.*"

Tommy-Ray thought, but no answer immediately sprang to mind.

"*My enemy,*" the Jaff said, "*has touched her.*"

Katz, Tommy-Ray thought: he means that fuckwit Katz.

"*I made you, and Jo-Beth, to be my agents. My enemy did the same. He made a child.*"

"Katz isn't your enemy?" Tommy-Ray said, struggling to put this together, "he's your enemy's son?"

"*And now he's touched your sister. That's what keeps her from me. That taint.*"

"Not for long."

So saying Tommy-Ray turned and ran back to the house, calling Jo-Beth's name in a light, easy voice.

Inside the house, she heard his call and was reassured. It didn't sound like he was suffering. He was at the yard door by the time she stepped into the kitchen, arms spread across its width, leaning in, grinning. Wet with sweat, and almost naked like this, he looked like he'd just run up the beach.

"Something wonderful," he grinned.

"What?"

"Outside. Come with me."

Every vein in his body seemed to be bulging from his skin. In his eyes was a gleam she didn't trust. His smile only deepened her suspicion.

"I'm not going anywhere, Tommy . . ." she said.

"Why are you fighting?" he asked, cocking his head. "Just because he touched you it doesn't mean you belong to him."

"What are you talking about?"

"*Katz*. I know what he did. Don't be ashamed. You're forgiven. But you have to come and apologize in person."

"Forgiven?" she said, her raised voice encouraging the ache in her skull to new mischief. "You've got no right to forgive me, you asshole! You of all—"

"Not me," Tommy-Ray said, the smile unwavering. "Our father."

"What?"

"Who art outside—"

She shook her head. The ache was getting worse.

"Just come with me. He's in the yard." He left off holding the door frame and started across the kitchen towards her. "I know it hurts," he said. "But the Jaff'll make it better."

"Keep away from me!"

"This is *me*, Jo-Beth. This is Tommy-Ray. There's nothing to be afraid of."

"Yes there is! I don't know what, but there is."

"You think that because you've been *tainted* by Katz," he said. "I'm not going to do anything to hurt you, you know that. We feel things together, don't we? What hurts you hurts me. I don't like pain." He laughed. "I'm weird but I'm not *that* weird."

Despite her doubts, he won her over with that argument, because it was the truth. They'd shared a womb for nine months; they were half of the same egg. He meant her no harm.

"Please come," he said, extending his hand.

She took it. Immediately the ache in her head subsided, for which she was grateful. In place of the chatter, her name, whispered.

"*Jo-Beth.*"

"Yes?" she said.

"Not me," said Tommy-Ray. "The Jaff. He's calling you."

"*Jo-Beth.*"

"Where is he?"

Tommy-Ray pointed to the trees. They were suddenly a long way from the house now; almost at the bottom of the yard. She wasn't quite sure how she got so far so quickly, but the wind that had toyed with the curtains now had her in thrall, ushering her forward, it seemed, towards the thicket. Tommy-Ray let his hand slip from hers.

Go on, she heard him say, *this is what we've been waiting for . . .*

She hesitated. There was something about the way the trees moved, their foliage churning, which reminded her of bad sights: a mushroom cloud, perhaps; or blood in water. But the voice that came to coax her was deep and reassuring, and the face that spoke it—visible now—moved her. If she was going to call any man father, this would be a good man to choose. She liked his beard and his heavy brow. She liked the way his lips shaped the words he spoke with a delicious precision.

"*I'm the Jaff,*" he said. "*Your father.*"

"Really?" she said.

"*Really.*"

"Why are you here now? After all this time?"

"*Come closer. I'll tell you.*"

She was about to make another step when she heard a cry from the house.

"Don't let it touch you!"

It was Momma, her voice raised to a volume Jo-Beth would never have believed her capable of. The shout stopped her in her tracks. She turned on her heel. Tommy-Ray was standing directly behind her. Beyond him, coming across the lawn barefoot, her nightgown unbuttoned, was Momma.

"Jo-Beth, come away from it!" she said.

"Momma?"

"Come away!"

It was almost five years since Momma had stepped out of the house; more than once in that time she'd said she'd never leave it again. Yet here she was, her expression all alarm, her cries not requests but commands.

"Come away, both of you!"

Tommy-Ray turned to face his mother. "Go inside," he said. "This is nothing to do with you."

Momma slowed her approach to a walk.

"You don't *know*, son," she said. "You can't begin to understand."

"This is our father," Tommy-Ray replied. "He's come home. You should be grateful."

"For *that*?" Momma said, her eyes huge. "That's what broke my heart. And it'll break yours too if you let it." She stood a yard from Tommy now. "Don't let it," she said softly, reaching out to touch his face. "Don't let it hurt us."

Tommy-Ray dashed Momma's hand away.

"I warned you," he said. "This is nothing to do with you!"

Momma's response was instant. She took a step towards Tommy-Ray and struck him across the face; an openhanded slap which echoed against the house.

"Stupid!" she yelled at him. *"Don't you know evil when you see it?"*

"I know a fucking lunatic when I see one," Tommy-Ray spat back. "All your prayers and talk of the Devil . . . You make me sick! You try and spoil my life. Now you want to spoil this. Well, no way! Poppa's home! So fuck you!"

His display seemed to amuse the man in the trees; Jo-Beth heard

laughter from him. She glanced round. He had apparently not anticipated her glance because he'd let the mask he was wearing slip a little.
The face she'd found so fatherly had swelled; or something behind it
had. His eyes and forehead were enlarged; the bearded chin, and his
mouth, which she'd thought so fine, almost vestigial. Where her
father had been was a monstrous infant. She cried out at the sight of
him.

Instantly the thicket around threw itself into a frenzy. The branches
lashed at themselves like flagellants, stripping bark and shredding
foliage, their motion so violent she was sure they would uproot themselves and come for her.

"Momma!" she said, turning back towards the house.

"Where are you going?" Tommy-Ray said.

"That's not our father!" she said. "It's a trick! Look! It's a terrible
trick!"

Tommy-Ray either knew and didn't care or was so deeply under the
Jaff's influence he only saw what the Jaff wanted him to see.

"You're staying with me!" he said, grabbing hold of Jo-Beth's arm,
"with *us!*"

She struggled to be free of him but his grip was too fierce. It was
Momma who intervened, with a downward stroke of her fist which
broke his hold. Before Tommy-Ray could recapture her, Jo-Beth
made a dash for the house. The storm of foliage followed her across
the grass, as did Momma, whose hand she took as they raced for the
door.

"Lock it! Lock it!" Momma said, as they got inside.

She did so. No sooner had she turned the key than Momma was
calling her to follow.

"Where?" Jo-Beth said.

"My room. I know how to stop it. Hurry!"

The room smelt of Momma's perfume, and stale linen, but for
once its familiarity offered comfort. Whether the room also offered
safety was moot. Jo-Beth could hear the back door kicked open downstairs, then a ruckus that sounded as though the contents of the refrigerator was being pitched around the kitchen. Silence followed.

"Are you looking for the key?" Jo-Beth said, seeing Momma reaching beneath her pillows. "I think it's on the outside."

"Then get it!" Momma said. "And be quick!"

There was a creak on the other side of the door which made Jo-Beth think twice about opening it. But with the door unlocked they had no means of defense whatsoever. Momma talked of stopping the Jaff, but if it wasn't the key she was digging for it was her prayer-book, and prayers weren't going to stop anything. People died all the time with supplication on their lips. She had no choice but to fling the door open.

Her eyes went to the stairs. The Jaff was there, a bearded fetus, his vast eyes fixing her. His tiny mouth grinned. She reached for the key as he climbed. *"We're here,"* he said.

The key wouldn't come out of the lock. She jiggled it, and it suddenly freed itself, slipping from both the lock and her fingers. The Jaff was within three steps of the top of the stairs. He didn't rush. She went down on her haunches to pick up the key, aware for the first time since entering the house that the percussion that had first alerted her to his presence had begun again. Its din confounded her thoughts. Why was she stooping? What was she looking for? The sight of the key reminded her. Snatching it up (the Jaff at the summit) she stood, retreated, slammed the door and locked it.

"He's here!" she said to Momma, glancing her way.

"Of course," said Momma. She'd found what she was looking for. It was not a prayer-book, it was a knife, an eightinch kitchen knife which had gone missing some while ago.

"Momma?"

"I knew it would come. I'm ready."

"You can't fight him with that," she said. "He's not even human. Is he?"

Momma's eyes went to the door.

"Tell me, Momma."

"I don't know what he is," she said. "I've tried to think . . . all these years. Maybe the Devil. Maybe not." She looked back at Jo-Beth. "I've been afraid for so long," she said. "And now he's here and it all seems so simple."

"Then explain it," Jo-Beth said. "Because I don't understand. Who is he? What has he done to Tommy-Ray?"

"He told the truth," Momma said. "After a fashion. He *is* your father. Or rather one of them."

"How many do I need?"

"He made a whore of me. He drove me half mad with desires I didn't want. The man who slept with me is your father; but this—" she pointed the knife in the direction of the door, from the far side of which came the sound of tapping "—this is what really made you."

"*I hear you,*" the Jaff murmured. "*Loud and clear.*"

"Keep away," Momma said, moving towards the door. Jo-Beth tried to shoo her back but she ignored the instruction. And with reason. It wasn't the door she wanted to stand beside but her daughter. She seized Jo-Beth's arm and dragged her close, putting the knife to her throat.

"I'll kill her," she said to the thing on the landing. "So help me as there's a God in Heaven I mean it. Try and come in here and your daughter's dead." Her grip on Jo-Beth was as strong as Tommy-Ray's. Minutes ago he'd called her a lunatic. Either her present performance was a bluff of Oscarwinning skill or else he'd been right. Either way, Jo-Beth was forfeit.

The Jaff was tapping on the door again.

"*Daughter?*" he said.

"Answer him," Momma told her.

"*Daughter?*"

". . . Yes . . ."

"*Do you fear for your life? Honestly now. Tell me honestly. Because I love you and I want no harm to come to you.*"

"She fears," Momma said.

"*Let her answer,*" the Jaff said.

Jo-Beth had no hesitation in replying. "Yes," she said. "Yes. She's got a knife and—"

"*You would be a fool,*" the Jaff said to Momma, "*to kill the only thing that made your life worth living. But you might, mightn't you?*"

"I won't let you have her," Momma said.

There was a silence from the other side of the door. Then the Jaff said:

"Fine by me . . ." He laughed softly. *"There's always tomorrow."*

He rattled the door one last time, as though to be certain that he was indeed locked out. Then the laughter and the rattling ceased, to be replaced by a low, guttural sound that might have been the groan of something being born into pain, knowing with its first breath there was no escape from its condition. The distress in the sound was at least as chilling as the seductions and threats that had gone before. Then it began to fade.

"It's leaving," Jo-Beth said. Momma still held the blade at her neck. "It's leaving, Momma. Let me go."

The fifth stair from the bottom of the flight creaked twice, confirming Jo-Beth's belief that their tormentors were indeed exiting the house. But it was another thirty seconds before Momma relaxed her hold on Jo-Beth's arm, and another minute still before she let her daughter go entirely.

"It's gone from the house," she said. "But stay here a while."

"What about Tommy?" Jo-Beth said. "We have to go and find him."

Momma shook her head. "I was bound to lose him," she said. "No use now."

"We've got to *try*," Jo-Beth said.

She opened the door. Across the landing, leaning against the banister, was what could only be Tommy-Ray's handiwork. When they were children he'd made dolls for Jo-Beth by the dozen, makeshift toys that nevertheless bore the imprint of his disposition. Always, they had smiles. Now he had created a new doll; a father for the family, made from food. A head of hamburger, with thumb-press eyes; legs and arms of vegetables; a torso of a milk carton, the contents of which spilled out between its legs, pooling around the chili pepper and garlic bulbs placed there. Jo-Beth stared at its crudity: the meat-face stared back at her. No smile this time. No mouth even. Just two holes in the hamburger. At its groin the milk of manhood spread, and stained the carpet. Momma was right. They'd lost Tommy-Ray.

"You knew that bastard was coming back," she said.

"I guessed it would come, given time. Not for me. It didn't come for me. I was just a convenient womb, like all of us—"

"The League of Virgins," Jo-Beth said.

"Where did you hear that?"

"Oh, Momma . . . people have been talking since I was a kid . . ."

"I was so ashamed," Momma said. She put her hand to her face; the other, still holding the knife, hung at her side. "So very ashamed. I wanted to kill myself. But the Pastor kept me from it. Said I had to live. For the Lord. And for you and Tommy-Ray."

"You must have been very strong," Jo-Beth said, turning away from the doll to face her. "I love you, Momma. I know I said I was afraid but I know you wouldn't have hurt me."

Momma looked up at her, the tears running steadily from her eyes and dripping from her jaw.

Without thinking she said:

"I would have killed you stone dead."

THREE

M y enemy is still here," said the Jaff.
   Tommy-Ray had led him along a path unknown to any but the children of the Grove, which took them round the back of the Hill to a giddy vantage point. It was too rocky for a trysting place and too unstable to be built upon, but it gave those who troubled to climb so high an unsurpassed view over Laureltree and Windbluff.

There they stood, Tommy-Ray and his father, taking in the sights. There were no stars overhead; and barely any lights burning in the houses below. Clouds dulled the sky; sleep, the town. Untroubled by witnesses, father and son stood and talked.

"Who is your enemy?" Tommy-Ray said. "Tell me and I'll tear his throat out for you."

"I doubt he'd allow that."

"Don't be sarcastic," Tommy-Ray said. "I'm not dumb, you know. I know when you're treating me like a kid. I'm not a kid."

"You'll have to prove that to me."

"I will. I'm not afraid of anything."

"We'll see about that."

"Are you trying to frighten me?"

"No. Merely prepare you."

"For what? Your enemy? Just tell me what he's like."

"His name is Fletcher. He and I were partners, before you were born. But he cheated me. Or at least he tried to."

"What was your business?"

"Ah!" The Jaff laughed, a sound Tommy-Ray had heard many times now, and liked more each time he heard it. The man had a sense of humor, even if Tommy-Ray—as now—didn't quite get the gag. "Our *business?*" said the Jaff. "It was, in essence, the getting of power. More specifically, one particular power. It's called the Art, and with it I will be able to step into the dreams of America."

"Are you kidding me?"

"Not all the dreams. Just the important ones. You see, Tommy-Ray, I'm an explorer."

"Yeah?"

"Yeah. Only what's left to explore outside in the world? Not much. A few pockets of desert; a rain-forest—"

"Space," Tommy-Ray suggested, glancing up.

"More desert, and a lot of nothing between," the Jaff said. "No, the real mystery—the *only* mystery—is inside our heads. And I'm going to get to it."

"You don't mean like a shrink, do you? You mean *being there*, somehow."

"That's right."

"And the Art is the way in?"

"Right again."

"But you said it's just dreams. We all dream. You can get in there any time you like, just by falling asleep."

"Most dreams are just juggling acts. Folks picking up their memories and trying to put them in some kind of order. But there's another kind of dream, Tommy-Ray. It's a dream of what it means to be born, and fall in love, and die. A dream that explains what *being* is for: I know this is confusing . . ."

"Go on. I like to hear anyhow."

"There's a sea of mind. It's called Quiddity," the Jaff said. "And floating in that sea is an island which appears in the dreams of every one of us at least twice in our lives: at the beginning and at the end. It was first discovered by the Greeks. Plato wrote of it in a code. He called it Atlantis . . ." He faltered, distracted from the telling by the substance of his tale.

"You want this place very much, don't you?" Tommy-Ray said.

"Very much," said the Jaff. "I want to swim in that sea when I choose, and go to the shore where the great stories are told."

"Rad."

"Huh?"

"It sounds awesome."

The Jaff laughed. "You're reassuringly crass, son. We're going to get on fine, I can tell. You can be my agent in the field, right?"

"Sure," said Tommy-Ray with a grin. Then: "What's that?"

"I can't show my face to just anybody," the Jaff said. "Nor do I much like the daylight. It's very . . . unmysterious. But you can get out and about for me."

"You're staying then? I thought maybe we'd go off someplace."

"We will, later. But first, my enemy must be killed. He's weak. He won't try to leave the Grove until he has some protection. He'll look for his own child, I'd guess."

"Katz?"

"That's right."

"So I should kill Katz."

"That sounds like a useful thing to do, if the opportunity presents itself."

"I'll make sure it does."

"Though you should thank him."

"Why?"

"Were it not for him I'd still be underground. Still be waiting for you or Jo-Beth to put the pieces together and come and find me. What she and Katz did—"

"What *did* they do? Did they fuck?"

"That matters to you?"

"Sure it does."

"To me too. The thought of Fletcher's child *touching* your sister sickens me. For what it's worth, it sickened Fletcher too. For once, we agreed on something. The question was, which one of us would make it to the surface first, and which would be strongest when we got here?"

"*You.*"

"Yes, me. I have an advantage Fletcher lacks. My army, my *terata*, are best drawn out of dying men. I drew one from Buddy Vance."

"Where is it?"

"When we were coming up here you thought somebody was following us, remember? I told you it was a dog. I lied."

"Show me."

"You may not be so eager when you see it."

"Show me, Poppa. Please!"

The Jaff whistled. At the sound, the trees a little way behind him began to move, identifying the face that had thrashed the thicket to fragments in the yard. This time, however, that face came into view. It was like something the tide had washed up: a deep-sea monster that had died and floated to the surface, been baked by the sun and pecked at by gulls, so that by the time it reached the human world it had fifty eye-holes and a dozen mouths, and its skin was half flayed from it.

"Gross," Tommy-Ray said softly. "You got that from a comedian? Don't look too funny to me."

"It came from a man on the brink of death," the Jaff said. "Frightened and alone. They always produce fine specimens. I'll tell you sometime the places I've gone looking for lost souls to produce terata from. The things I've seen. The scum I've met . . ." He looked out over the town. "But here?" he said. "Where will I find such subjects here?"

"You mean people dying?"

"I mean people vulnerable. People without mythologies to protect them. Frightened people. Lost people. Mad people."

"You could begin with Momma."

"She's not mad. She may wish she were; she may wish she could dismiss all she's seen and suffered as hallucinations, but she knows better. And she's protected herself. She has a faith, however idiot it is. No . . . I need naked people, Tommy-Ray. Folks without deities. Lost folk."

"I know a few."

Tommy-Ray could have taken his father to literally hundreds of households, had he been able to read the minds behind the faces that he passed every day of his life. People shopping in the Mall, loading their carts up with fresh fruit and wholesome cereals, people with good complexions, like his own, and clear eyes, like his own, who seemed in every regard selfpossessed and happy. Maybe they'd see an analyst once in a while, just to keep themselves on an even keel; maybe they'd raise their voices to the children, or cry to themselves when another birthday marked another year, but they considered themselves to all intents and purposes souls at peace. They had more than enough money in the bank; the sun was warm most days, and when it wasn't they lit fires and thought themselves robust to survive the chill. If asked, they would have called themselves believers in something. But nobody asked. Not here; not now. It was too late in the century to talk about faith without a twinge of embarrassment, and embarrassment was a trauma they labored to keep from spoiling their lives. Safer not to speak of faith, then, or the divinities who inspired it, except at weddings, baptisms and funerals, and only then by rote.

So. Behind their eyes the hope in them was sickening, and in many, dead. They lived from event to event with a subtle terror of the gap between, filling up their lives with distractions to avoid the emptiness where curiosity should have been, and breathing a sigh of relief when the children passed the point of asking questions about what life was for.

Not everyone hid their fears so well, however.

At the age of thirteen Ted Elizando's class was told by a forward-thinking teacher that the superpowers held enough missiles between them to destroy civilization many hundreds of times over. The thought had bothered him far more than it seemed to bother his classmates, so he'd kept his nightmares of Armageddon to himself for fear of being laughed at. The deception worked; on Ted as much as the classmates. Through his teens he'd virtually forgotten the fears. At twenty-one, with a good job in Thousand Oaks, he married Loretta. They were parents the following year. One night, a few months after the birth of baby Dawn, the nightmare of the final fire came back. Sweaty and shaking, Ted got up and went to check on his daughter. She was asleep in her cot, sprawled on her stomach, the way she liked to sleep. He watched her slumbers for an hour or more, then went back to bed. The sequence of events repeated itself almost every night thereafter, until it had the predictability of ritual. Sometimes the baby would turn over in her sleep and her longlashed eyes would flicker open. Seeing her daddy there by her cot she would smile. The vigil took its toll on Ted, however. Night after night of broken sleep drained him of strength; he found it steadily more difficult to prevent the horrors that came by the hours of darkness invading those of light. Sitting at his desk in the middle of the working day the terrors would visit him. The spring sun, shining on the papers before him, became the blinding brightness mushrooming in front of him. Every breeze, however balmy, carried distant cries to his ears.

And then, one night, standing guard at Dawn's cot, he heard the missiles coming. Terrified, he picked Dawn up, trying to hush her as she wept. Her complaints woke Loretta, who came after her husband. She found him in the dining room, unable to speak for the terror he felt, staring at his daughter, whom he'd let fall when he'd seen her body carbonized in his arms, her skin blackening, her limbs becoming smoking sticks.

He was hospitalized for a month, then returned to the Grove, the medical consensus being that his best hopes for a return to full health lay in the bosom of his family. A year later, Loretta filed for divorce, citing irreconcilable differences. It was granted, as was the custody of the child.

Very few people visited Ted these days. In the four years since his breakdown he'd worked in the pet store in the Mall, a job which had made mercifully few demands upon him. He was happy among the animals, who were, like him, bad dissemblers. There was about him the air of a man who knew no home now but a razor's edge. Tommy-Ray, forbidden pets by Momma, had been indulged by Ted: allowed free access to the store (even minding it on one or two occasions, when Ted had to run errands), playing with the dogs and the snakes. He'd got to know Ted and his story well, though they'd never been friends. He'd never visited Ted at home, for instance, as he did tonight.

"I brought someone to see you, Teddy. Someone I want you to meet."

"It's late."

"This can't wait. See, it's really good news and I had no one to share it with but you."

"Good news?"

"My dad. He came home."

"He did? Well, I'm really happy for you, Tommy-Ray."

"Don't you want to meet him?"

"Well, I—"

"*Of course he does,*" said the Jaff stepping out of the shadow, and extending his hand to Ted. "*Any friend of my son's is a friend of mine.*"

Seeing the power Tommy-Ray had introduced as his father, Teddy took a frightened step back into his house. This was another species of nightmare altogether. Even in the bad old times they'd never come calling. They'd crept up, stealthily. This one talked and smiled and invited itself in.

"*I want something from you,*" the Jaff said.

"What's going on, Tommy-Ray? This is my house. You can't just come in here and take stuff."

"*This is something you don't want,*" the Jaff said, reaching towards Ted, "*something you'll be much happier without.*"

Tommy-Ray watched, amazed and impressed, as Ted's eyes began to roll up beneath his lids, and he started to make noises that suggested he was about to throw up. But nothing came; at least from his throat. It was out of his pores the prize appeared, the juices of his body bubbling up and thickening, paling, and rising off his skin, soaking through his shirt, through his trousers.

Tommy-Ray danced from side to side, enthralled. It was like some grotesque magic act. The drops of moisture were defying gravity, hanging in the air in front of Ted, touching each other and forming larger drops, those drops in turn meeting and joining, until pieces of solid matter, like a sickly gray cheese, were floating in front of his chest. And still the waters came at the Jaff's call, each mote adding bulk to the body. It had form now, too: the first rough sketches of Ted's private horror. Tommy-Ray grinned to see it: its twitching legs, its mismatched eyes. Poor Ted, to have had this baby inside him and been unable to let it go. Like the Jaff had said, he'd be better off without it.

That was the first of several visits that night, and each time there was some new beast out of the lost soul. All pale, all vaguely reptilian, but in every other regard a personal creation. The Jaff put it best, when the night's adventures were drawing to a close:

"It's an art," he said. "This drawing forth. Don't you think?"

"Yeah. I like it."

"Not *the* Art, of course. But an echo of it. As, I suppose, is every art."

"Where are we going now?"

"I need to rest. Find somewhere shady, and cool."

"I know some places."

"No. You've got to go home."

"Why?"

"Because I want the Grove to wake up tomorrow morning and believe the world is just as it was."

"What do I tell Jo-Beth?"

"Tell her you remember nothing. If she presses you, apologize."

"I don't want to go," Tommy-Ray said.

"I know," the Jaff said, reaching out to put his hand on Tommy-Ray's shoulder. He massaged the muscle as he spoke. "But we don't want a search party out looking for you. They could discover things we only intend to reveal in *our* time!"

Tommy-Ray grinned at this.

"How long will that be?"

"You want to see the Grove turned upside down, don't you?"

"I'm counting the hours."

The Jaff laughed.

"Like father, like son," he said. "Hang loose, boy. I'll be back."

And laughing, he led his beasts off into the dark.

FOUR

The girl of his dreams had been wrong, Howie thought when he woke: the sun doesn't shine in the state of California every day. The dawn was sluggish when he opened the blinds; the sky showing no hint of blue. He dutifully ran through his exercises—the barest minimum his conscience would allow him. They did little or nothing to enliven his system; they simply made him sweat. Having showered and shaved, he dressed and went down to the Mall.

He didn't yet have the words of reclamation he was going to need when he saw Jo-Beth. He knew from past experience that any attempt on his part to plan a speech would only result in a hopeless, stammering tangle when he opened his mouth. It would be better to respond to the moment as it came. If she was dismissive, he'd be forceful. If she was contrite, he'd be forgiving. All that mattered was that he mend the breach of the previous day.

If there was some explanation for whatever had happened to them at the motel, hours of soul-searching on his part hadn't unearthed it. All he could conclude was that somehow their shared dream—the idea of which, given the strength of feeling between them, didn't seem so difficult to understand—had been rerouted by an inept telepathic

switchboard towards a nightmare which they neither understood nor
deserved. It was an astral error of some kind. Nothing to do with them;
best forgotten. With a little will on both sides they could pick up their
relationship where they'd left it outside Butrick's Steak House, when
there'd still been so much promise in the air.

He went straight to the book store. Lois—Mrs. Knapp—was at the
counter. Otherwise, the store was empty. He offered a smile, and a
hello, then asked if Jo-Beth had yet arrived. Mrs. Knapp consulted her
watch before frostily informing him that no, she hadn't, and that she
was late.

"I'll wait then," he said, not about to be dissuaded from his purpose
by the woman's lack of geniality. He wandered over to the bookstack
closest to the window, where he could browse and watch for Jo-Beth's
arrival at the same time.

The books before him were all religious. One in particular caught
his eye: *The Story of the Savior*. Its cover carried a painting of a man on
his knees before a blinding light and the pronouncement that its pages
contained the Greatest Message of the Age. He thumbed through it.
The slim volume—it was scarcely more than a pamphlet—was published by the Church of Jesus Christ of the Latter-Day Saints, and presented in easily assimilated paragraphs and paintings the story of the
Great White God of ancient America. To judge by the pictures whatever incarnation this Lord appeared in—Quetzalcoatl in Mexico,
Tonga-Loa god of the ocean sun in Polynesia, Illa-Tici, Kukulean or
half a dozen other guises—he always looked like the perfect white-
bread hero: tall, aquiline, pale-skinned, blue-eyed. Now, the pamphlet
claimed, he was back in America to celebrate the millennium. This
time he'd be called by his true name: Jesus Christ.

Howie moved on to another shelf, looking for a book more suited to
his mood. Love poetry perhaps; or a sex-manual. But as he scanned
the rows of volumes it became apparent that every single book in the
store was published by the same press or one of its subsidiaries. There
were books of prayers, of inspirational songs for the family, heavy duty
tomes on the building of Zim, the city of God on earth, or on the significance of baptism. Among them, a picture book on the life of

Joseph Smith, with photographs of his homestead, and the sacred grove where he'd apparently seen a vision. The text beside it caught Howie's eye.

I saw two Personages, whose brightness and glory defy all description, standing above me in the air. One of them spake unto me, calling me by name, and said—

"I called Jo-Beth's house. There's no answer there. Something must have called them away."

Howie looked up from the text. "That's a pity," he said, not entirely believing the woman. If she'd made the call, she'd made it very quietly.

"She's probably not going to come in today," Mrs. Knapp went on, avoiding meeting Howie's gaze as she spoke. "I've got a very informal arrangement with her. She works whatever hours suit her best."

He knew this to be a lie. Only the morning before he'd heard her chide Jo-Beth for being unpunctual; there was nothing informal about her working hours. But Mrs. Knapp, good Christian that she was, seemed determined to have him out of the shop. Perhaps she'd caught him smirking as he browsed.

"It's not the least use you waiting," she told him. "You could be here all day."

"I'm not scaring off the customers, am I?" Howie said, defying her to make her objections to him plain.

"No," she said, with a joyless little smile. "I'm not trying to say you are."

He approached the counter. She took an involuntary step backwards, almost as though she was in fear of him.

"Then what exactly *are* you saying?" he asked, barely able to preserve his civility. "What is it about me you don't like? My deodorant? My haircut?"

Again, she tried the little smile, but this time, despite her versing in hypocrisy, she couldn't make it. Instead, her face twitched.

"I'm not the Devil," Howie said. "I haven't come here to do anybody any harm."

She made no answer to this.

"I was . . . b . . . b . . . I was born here," he went on. "In Palomo Grove."

"I know," she said.

Well, well, he thought, here's a revelation.

"What else do you know?" he asked her, gently enough.

Her eyes went to the door, and he knew she was reciting a silent prayer to her Great White God that somebody open it and save her from this damn boy and his questions. Neither God nor customer obliged.

"What do you know about me?" Howie asked again. "It can't be that bad . . . can it?"

Lois Knapp made a small shrug. "I suppose not," she said.

"Well then."

"I knew your mother," she said, stopping there as though that might satisfy him. He didn't reply, but left her to fill the charged silence with further information. "I didn't know her well of course," she continued. "She was slightly younger than me. But everybody knew everybody back then. It's long time ago. Then of course when the accident happened—"

"You can s . . . s . . . say it," Howie told her.

"Say what?"

"You call it an accident but it was . . . was . . . was rape, right?"

By the look on her face she'd thought never to hear that word (or anything remotely so obscene) voiced in her shop.

"I don't remember," she replied, with a kind of defiance. "And even if I could—" She stopped, took a breath, then started on a fresh tack. "Why don't you just go back where you came from?" she said.

"But I *am* back," he told her. "This is my home town."

"That's not what I meant," she said, finally allowing her exasperation to show. "Don't you know how things look? You come back here, just at the same time Mr. Vance is killed."

"What the hell's that got to do with it?" Howie wanted to know. He hadn't taken all that much notice of the news in the last twenty-four hours, but he knew that the retrieval of the comedian's corpse he'd seen in progress the previous day had turned into a major tragedy. What he didn't understand was the connection.

"I didn't kill Buddy Vance. And my mother certainly didn't."

Apparently resigned to her function as messenger, Lois gave up on innuendo and told the rest plainly, and quickly, so as to get the business done with.

"The place where your mother was raped," she said, "is the same place Mr. Vance fell to his death."

"The very same?" Howie said.

"Yes," came the reply, "I'm told the very same. I'm not about to go and look for myself. There's enough evil in the world without going out to find it."

"And you think I'm part of this somehow?"

"I didn't say that."

"No. But th . . . th . . . that's what you think."

"As you ask me: yes it is."

"And you'd like me out of your shop so I'll stop spreading my influence around."

"Yes," she said plainly, "I would."

He nodded. "OK," he said, "I'll go. Just as long as you promise me you'll tell Jo-Beth I was here."

Mrs. Knapp's face was all reluctance. But her fear of him gave him a power over her he couldn't help but relish.

"Not much to ask is it?" he said. "You won't be telling any lies."

"No."

"So you'll tell her?"

"Yes."

"On the Great White God of America?" he said. "What's his name . . . Quetzalcoatl?" She looked confounded. "Never mind," he said, "I'll leave. I'm sorry if I've crippled the morning's trade."

Leaving her looking panicky, he stepped out into the open air. In the twenty minutes he'd spent in the shop the cloud layer had broken, and the sun was coming through, shining on the Hill. In a few minutes it would break through on the mortals in the Mall, like himself. The girl of his dreams had spoken the truth after all.

FIVE

Grillo woke to the sound of the telephone, lashed out, knocked over a half-filled glass of champagne—his last drunken toast of the previous night: *To Buddy, gone but not forgotten*—cursed, claimed the receiver and put it to his ear.

"Hello?" he growled.

"Did I wake you?"

"Tesla?"

"I love a man who remembers my name," she said.

"What time is it?"

"Late. You should be up and working. I want you to be free of your labors for Abernethy by the time I arrive."

"What are you saying? You're coming here?"

"You owe me dinner, for all the gossip on Vance," she said. "So find somewhere expensive."

"What time are you planning to be here?" he asked her.

"Oh I don't know. About—" With her in mid-sentence he put down the receiver, and grinned at the telephone, thinking of her cursing herself at the other end. The smile dropped from his face when he stood up, however. His head throbbed to beat the band: if he'd emptied that last half-glass he doubted he could have even stood up. He punched Suite Service and ordered up coffee.

"Any juice with that, sir?" came the voice in the kitchen.

"No. Just coffee."

"Eggs, croissant—"

"Oh Jesus, no. No eggs. No nothing. Just coffee."

The idea of sitting down to write was almost as repugnant as the thought of breakfast. He decided instead to contact the woman from the Vance house, Ellen Nguyen, whose address, minus a telephone number, was still in his pocket.

His system jazzed by a substantial caffeine intake he got in the car and drove down to Deerdell. The house, when he finally found it, contrasted forcibly with the woman's workplace on the Hill. It was small, unglamorous and badly in need of repair. Grillo already had his suspicions about the conversation that lay ahead: the disgruntled employee dishing the dirt on her paymaster. On occasion in the past such informants had proved fruitful, though just as often they'd been suppliers of malicious fabrications. In this case he doubted that. Was it because Ellen looked at him with such vulnerability in her open features as she welcomed him in and brewed him a further fix of coffee; or because when her child kept calling from the next room—he was sick with the flu, she explained—each time she returned from tending to him and picked up her story afresh the facts remained consistent; or simply that the story she told not only bruised Buddy Vance's reputation but her own as well? The latter fact, perhaps, more than any of the others, convinced him she was a reliable source. The story told spread the blemishes democratically.

"I was his mistress," she explained. "For almost five years. Even when Rochelle was in the house—which wasn't long of course—we used to find ways to be together. Often. I think she knew all along. That's why she got rid of me the first chance she could."

"You're no longer employed up at Coney, then?"

"No. She was just waiting for an excuse to dismiss me, and you provided it."

"Me?" said Grillo. "How?"

"She said I was flirting with you. Typical that she'd use that kind of reason." Not for the first time in their exchanges Grillo heard a depth of feeling—in this instance, contempt—which the woman's passive demeanor scarcely betrayed. "She judges everyone by her standards," she went on. "And you know what those are."

"No," Grillo said frankly, "I don't."

Ellen looked astonished. "Wait here," she told him. "I don't want Philip listening to all this."

She got up and went to her son's bedroom, spoke a few words to him Grillo didn't hear, then closed the door before coming back to continue her story.

"He's already learned too many words I wish he hadn't, just in one year at school. I want him to have a chance to be . . . I don't know, innocent? Yes, innocent, if it's only for a little while. The ugly things come along soon enough, don't they?"

"The ugly things?"

"You know: the people who cheat you and betray you. Sex things. Power things."

"Oh sure," Grillo replied. "They come along."

"So I was telling you about Rochelle, right?"

"Yes, you were."

"Well, it's simple enough. Before she married Buddy she was a hooker."

"She was *what?*"

"You heard right. Why are you so surprised?"

"I don't know. She's so beautiful. There must have been other ways to make a buck."

"She has an expensive habit," Ellen replied. Again, the contempt, mingled with disgust.

"Did Buddy know when he married her?"

"About what? The habits or the hooking?"

"Both."

"I'm sure he did. That's part of why he married her, I guess. See, there's this thick streak of perversity in Buddy. Sorry, I mean there *was*. I can't quite get over the fact that he's dead."

"It must be extremely difficult talking about this so close to losing him. I'm sorry to put you through it."

"I volunteered, didn't I?" she replied. "I want somebody to know all this. In fact I want *everybody* to know. It was *me* he loved, Mr. Grillo. Me he really loved, all those years."

"And I presume you loved him?"

"Oh yes," she said softly. "Very much. He was self-centered, of course, but all men are self-centered, aren't they?" She didn't leave time for Grillo to exclude himself before heading on. "You're all brought up to think the world revolves around you. I make the same mistake with Philip. I can see myself doing it. The difference with Buddy was that for a time at least the world *did* revolve around him. He was one of the best-loved men in America. For a few years. Everybody knew his face, everyone had his routines by heart. And of course they wanted to know all about his private life."

"So he took a real risk, marrying a woman like Rochelle?"

"I'd say so, wouldn't you? Especially when he was trying to clean up his act, and get one of the networks to give him another show. But there was this streak of perversity, like I said. A lot of the time it was plain self-destructiveness."

"He should have married you," Grillo said.

"He could have done worse," she observed. "He could have done a *lot* worse." The thought brought a show of feeling that had been conspicuous by its absence through her account of her own place in this. Tears welled in her eyes. At the same moment the boy called from his bedroom. She put her hand to her mouth to stifle her sobs.

"I'll go," said Grillo, getting up. "His name's Philip?"

"Yes," she said, the word almost incoherent.

"I'll take care of him, don't worry."

He left her wiping the tears from beneath her eyes with the heels of her hands. Opening the door to the boy's room, he said:

"Hi, I'm Grillo."

The boy, in whose face his mother's solemn symmetry was much apparent, was sitting up in bed, surrounded by a chaos of toys, crayons and scrawled-upon sheets of paper. The TV was playing in the corner of the room, its cartoon show silent.

"You're Philip, right?"

"Where's Mommy?" the boy wanted to know. He made no bones about being suspicious of Grillo, peering past him for a glimpse of his mother.

"She'll be here in a moment," Grillo reassured him, approaching the bed. The drawings, many of which had slipped from the comforter and were scattered underfoot, all seemed to picture the same bulbous character. Grillo went down on his haunches and picked one of them up. "Who's this?" he asked.

"Balloon Man," Philip replied, gravely.

"Does he have a name?"

"Balloon Man," came the response, with an edge of impatience.

"Is he from the TV?" Grillo asked, studying the multicolored nonsense creature on the page.

"Nope."

"Where's he from then?"

"Out of my head," Philip replied.

"Is he friendly?"

The boy shook his head.

"He bites does he?"

"Only you," came the response.

"That's not very polite," Grillo heard Ellen say. He glanced over his shoulder. She'd made an attempt to conceal her tears but it clearly didn't convince her son, who gave Grillo an accusing look.

"You shouldn't get too close to him," Ellen told Grillo. "He's been really sick, haven't you?"

"I'm OK now."

"No you're not. You're to stay in bed while I take Mr. Grillo to the door."

Grillo stood up, laying the picture on the bed among the other portraits.

"Thank you for showing me the Balloon Man," he said.

Philip made no reply, but returned to his handiwork, coloring another drawing scarlet.

"What I was telling you . . ." Ellen said, once they were out of the child's earshot, ". . . that's not all the story. There's a lot more, believe me. But I'm not quite ready to tell it yet."

"When you are, I'm ready to hear," Grillo said. "You can find me at the hotel."

"Maybe I'll call. Maybe I won't. Anything I tell you is only part of the truth, isn't it? The most important piece is Buddy, and you'll never be able to write him down. Never."

This parting thought went with Grillo as he drove back through the Grove to the hotel. It was a simple enough observation, but one that carried much weight. Buddy Vance was indeed at the center of this story. His death had been both enigmatic and tragic; but more enigmatic still, surely, was the life that had preceded it. He had enough clues to that life to intrigue him mightily. The Carnival collection crowding the walls of Coney Eye (the True Art of America); the moral mistress who still loved him, the hooker wife who most likely did not, nor ever had. Even without that singularly absurd death as a punchline it was one hell of a story. The question was not *whether* to tell it but *how*.

Abernethy's view on the subject would be unequivocal. He should favor supposition over fact, and dirt over dignity. But there were mysteries here in the Grove. Grillo had seen them, breaking out of Buddy Vance's grave, no less; taking to the sky. It was important to tell this story honestly and well, or he'd simply be adding to the sum of confusions here, which would do nobody any favors.

First things first; he had to set the facts down as he'd learned them in the last twenty-four hours: from Tesla, from Hotchkiss, from Rochelle and now from Ellen. This he set to doing as soon as he got back to the hotel, producing an initial draft of the Buddy Vance Story in longhand, poring over the tiny desk in his room. His back began to ache as he labored, and the first signs of a fever brought sweat to his brow. He didn't notice, however—at least not until he'd generated twenty odd pages of cross-referenced notes. Only then, stretching as he rose from his work, did he realize that even if the Balloon Man hadn't bitten him, its creator's flu had.

SIX

I

On the trek up from the Mall to Jo-Beth's house it became very clear to Howie why she'd made so much of events between them—particularly that shared terror in the motel—being the Devil's doing. It was little wonder, given that she worked alongside a highly devout woman in a store stocked from floor to ceiling with Mormon literature. Difficult as his exchange with Lois Knapp had been it had given him a better sense of the challenge that lay before him than he would have had without it. Somehow he had to convince Jo-Beth that there was no crime against God or man in their affection for each other; and nothing demonic lurking in him. As pitches went, he could envisage easier.

As it was, he didn't get much of a chance at persuasion. At first even his attempts to get the door opened to him failed. He rapped and rang for fully five minutes, knowing instinctively that there was somebody in the house to answer. It was only when he stood back in the street and started to holler up at the blinded windows that he heard the sound of the safety chains being taken off the door and returned to the step to request from the woman who peered through the sliver at him, Joyce McGuire presumably, a word with her daughter. He'd usually been successful with mothers. His stammer and his spectacles gave him the air of a diligent and somewhat introspective student; quite safe company. But Mrs. McGuire knew appearances deceived. Her advice was a re-run of Lois Knapp's.

"You're not wanted here," she told him. "Go back home. Leave us alone."

"I just need a few moments with Jo-Beth," he said. "She's here, isn't she?"

"Yes, she's here. But she doesn't want to see you."

"I'd like to hear that from her if you don't mind."

"Oh would you?" said Mrs. McGuire, and, much to his surprise, opened the door.

It was dark inside the house, and bright on the step, but he could see Jo-Beth standing in the gloom, at the far end of the hall. She was dressed in dark clothes, as though a funeral was in the offing. It made her look even more ashen than she was. Only her eyes caught any light from the step.

"Tell him," her mother instructed.

"Jo-Beth?" Howie said. "Could we talk?"

"You mustn't come here," Jo-Beth said softly. Her voice barely carried from the interior. The air between them was dead. "It's dangerous for us all. You mustn't come here ever again."

"But I have to talk to you."

"It's no use, Howie. Terrible things are going to happen to us if you don't go."

"What things?" he wanted to know.

It wasn't she who answered, however, but her mother.

"You're not to blame," the woman said, the fierceness he'd been greeted with all gone from her now. "Nobody blames you. But you must understand, Howard, what happened to your mother, and to me, isn't over."

"No, I'm afraid I don't understand that," he returned. "I don't understand that at all."

"Maybe it's better you don't," came the reply. "Better you just leave. Now." She started to close the door.

"W . . . w . . . w . . ." Howie began. Before he could say *wait* he was looking at wood panelling, two inches from his nose.

"Shit," he managed, without a slip.

He stood like a fool staring at the closed door for several seconds, while the bolts and chains were put back in place on the opposite side. A more comprehensive defeat was scarcely imaginable. Not only had Mrs. McGuire sent him packing, Jo-Beth had added her voice to the chorus. Rather than make another attempt, and fail, he let the problem be.

His next port of call was already planned, even before he turned from the step and started off down the street.

Somewhere in the woods, at the far side of the Grove, was the spot where Mrs. McGuire, and his mother, and the comedian had all come to their various griefs. Rape, death and disaster marked the spot. Perhaps somewhere there was a door that would not be so readily closed.

"It's for the best," said Momma, when the sound of Howard Katz's footsteps had finally faded.

"I know," Jo-Beth said, still staring at the bolted door.

Momma was right. If the events of the previous night—the Jaff's appearance at the house, and his claiming of Tommy-Ray—proved anything it was that nobody could be trusted. A brother she'd thought she'd known and known she'd loved had been taken from her, body and soul, by a power that had come out of the past. Howie too had come out of the past; from Momma's past. Whatever was now happening in the Grove, he was a part of it. Perhaps its victim, perhaps its invoker. But whether innocent or guilty, to invite him over the threshold of their house was to put at risk the small hope for salvation they'd won from the previous night's assault.

None of which made it any easier to see the door closed against him. Even now her fingers itched to pull back the bolts and haul the door open; to call him back and hug him to her; tell him things could be made good between them. What was *good* now? Their being together, living the adventure her heart had been aching for all her life, to claim and kiss this boy who was perhaps her own brother? Or to hold on to the old virtues in this flood, though with every wave another was swept away.

Momma had an answer; the answer she always offered when adversity presented itself.

"We must pray, Jo-Beth. Pray for delivery from our oppressors. *And then shall that Wicked be revealed, whom the Lord shall consume with the spirit of His mouth, and shall destroy with the brightness of His coming—*"

"I don't see any brightness, Momma. I don't think I ever did."

"It'll come," Momma insisted. "Everything will be made clear."

"I don't think so," Jo-Beth said. She pictured Tommy-Ray, who'd returned to the house late last night and smiled his innocent smile when she'd asked him about the Jaff, as though nothing had happened. Was he one of the Wicked whose destruction Momma was now praying so fervently for? Would the Lord consume *him* with the spirit of His mouth? She hoped not. Indeed she prayed not, when she and Momma knelt to speak with God; prayed that the Lord not judge Tommy-Ray too harshly. Nor her, for wanting to follow the face on the step out into the sun, and off wherever he had gone.

II

Though the day beat hard on the woods, the atmosphere beneath its canopy was that of a place under the spell of night. Whatever animals and birds made their dwelling here they were keeping to their nests and dens. Light, or something that lived in light, had silenced them. Howie felt their scrutiny however. They observed his every step, as though he were a hunter coming among them under a too-bright moon. He was not welcome here. And yet the urge to go forward increased with every yard he covered. A whisper had brought him down here the day before; a whisper he'd later dismissed as his dizzied mind playing tricks. But now no cell in his system doubted that the call had been genuine. There was somebody here who wanted to see him; to meet him; to know him. Yesterday he'd rejected the summons. Today he would not.

Some impulse, not entirely his own, made him throw back his head as he walked, so that the sun piercing the foliage struck his upturned face like a blow. He didn't flinch from its glare, but rather opened his eyes wider to it. The brightness, and the rhythmic way it struck his retina, seemed to mesmerize him. In most circumstances he hated to relinquish control of his mental processes. He drank only when brow-beaten by his peers, stopping the moment he felt his hold over the machine slipping; drugs were unthinkable. But here he was welcoming this intoxication; inviting the sun to burn out the real.

It worked. When he looked back at the scene around him he was half-blinded with colors no blade of grass could have laid claim to. His mind's eye was quick to seize the space vacated by the palpable. Suddenly his sight was filling up, brimming and spilling over with images he must have dredged up from some uncharted place in his cortex, because he had no memory of having lived them.

He saw a window in front of him, as solid—no, *more* solid—than the trees he was wandering between. It was open, this window, and it let on to a view of sea and sky.

That vision gave way to another; this less peaceful. Fires sprang up around him, in which pages of books seemed to be burning. He walked through the fires fearlessly, knowing these visions could do him no harm; only wanting them more.

He was granted a third far stranger than its predecessors. Even as the fires dimmed fishes appeared out of the colors in his eyes, darting ahead of him in rainbow shoals.

He laughed out loud at the sheer incongruity of the sight, and his laughter inspired another wonder, as the three hallucinations synthe-sized, drawing into their pattern the very woods he was walking, until fires, fishes, sky, sea and trees became one brilliant mosaic.

The fishes swam with fire for fins. The sky grew green and threw down starfish blossom. The grass rippled like a tide beneath his feet; or rather beneath the mind that saw the feet, because feet were suddenly nothing to him; nor legs, not any part of the machine. In the mosaic he was *mind*: a pebble skipped from its place, and roving.

In this joy, a question came to trouble him. If he was only mind, what was the machine? Nothing at all? Something to be cast off? To be drowned with the fishes, burned with the words?

Somewhere in him, a tick of panic began.

I'm out of control, he told himself, I've lost my body and I'm out of control. My God. My God. My God!

Hush, somebody murmured in his head. There's nothing wrong.

He stopped walking; or hoped he had.

"Who's there?" he said; or hoped he'd said.

The mosaic was still in place all around him, inventing new paradoxes by the moment. He tried to shatter it with a shout; to be out of this place into somewhere simpler.

"I want to see!" he yelled.

"I'm here!" came the answer. *"Howard, I'm here."*

"Make it stop," he begged.

"Make what stop?"

"The pictures. Make the pictures stop!"

"Don't be afraid. It's the real world."

"No!" he yelled back. "It isn't! It isn't!"

He put his hands up to his face in the hope of blotting the confusion out, but they—his own *hands*—were conspiring with the enemy.

There, in the middle of his palms, were his eyes, looking back at him. It was too much. He unleashed a howl of horror, and started to fall forward. The fish brightened; the fires flared; he felt them ready to consume him.

As he struck the ground they disappeared, as though somebody had flipped a switch.

He lay still a moment to be certain this wasn't another trick, then, turning his hands palm upwards to confirm they were sightless, hauled himself to his feet. Even then he clung on to a low-hanging branch, to keep himself in touch with the world.

"You disappoint me, Howard," said his summoner.

For the first time since he'd heard the voice it had a clear point of origin: a spot some ten yards from him, where the trees made a glade within a glade, at its center a pool of light. Bathing there, a man with a pony-tail and one dead eye. Its living twin studied Howie with great intensity.

"*Can you see me clearly enough?*" he asked.

"Yes," said Howie. "I see you fine. Who are you?"

"*My name is Fletcher,*" came the reply. "*And you're my son.*"

Howie took even firmer hold of the branch.

"*I'm what?*" he said.

There was no smile on Fletcher's wasted face. Clearly what he'd said, however preposterous, was not intended as a joke. He stepped out of the ring of trees.

"*I hate to hide,*" he said. "*Especially from you. But there's been so many people back and forth—*" He gestured wildly with his arms. "*Back and forth! All to watch an exhumation. Can you imagine? What a waste of a day!*"

"Did you say *son?*" said Howie.

"*I did,*" said Fletcher. "*My favorite word! As above, so below, isn't that right? One ball in the sky. Two between the legs.*"

"It *is* a joke," Howie said.

"*You know better than that,*" Fletcher replied, deadly serious. "*I've been calling you for a long time: father to son.*"

"How did you get in my head?" Howie wanted to know.

Fletcher didn't bother to reply to the question.

"*I needed you down here, to help me,*" he said. "*But you kept resisting me. I suppose I would have done the same in your situation. Turned my back on the burning bush. We're the same in that. Family resemblance.*"

"I don't believe you."

"*You should have let the visions run awhile. We were tripping there, weren't we? Haven't done that in a long while. I always favored mescaline, though that's out of fashion by now I suppose.*"

"I wouldn't know," Howie replied.

"*You don't approve.*"

"No."

"*Well, that's a bad start, but I suppose it can only get better from here on in. Your father, you see, was addicted to mescaline. I wanted the visions so badly. You like them too. Or at least you did for a while.*"

"They made me sick."

"*Too much too soon, that's all. You'll get used to it.*"

"No way."

"*But you'll have to learn, Howard. That wasn't an indulgence; it was a lesson.*"

"In what?"

"*In the science of being and becoming. Alchemy, biology and metaphysics in one discipline. It took me a long time to grasp it, but it made me the man I am*"—Fletcher tapped at his lips with his forefinger—"*which is, I realize, a somewhat pathetic sight. There are better ways to meet your progenitor, but I did my best to give you a taste of the miracle before you saw its maker in the flesh.*"

"This is just a dream," Howie said. "I stared too much at the sun and it's cooked my brains."

"*I like to look at the sun too,*" said Fletcher. "*And no—this isn't a dream. We're both here in the same moment, sharing our thoughts like civilized beings. This is as real as life gets.*" He opened his arms. "*Come closer, Howard. Embrace me.*"

"No way."

"*What are you afraid of?*"

"You're not my father."

"*All right,*" said Fletcher. "*I'm just one of them. There was another. But believe me, Howard, I'm the important one.*"

"You talk shit, you know that?"

"*Why are you so angry?*" Fletcher wanted to know. "*Is it your desperate affair with the Jaff's child? Forget her, Howard.*"

Howie pulled his spectacles from his face and narrowed his eyes at Fletcher. "How do you know about Jo-Beth?" he said.

"*Whatever's in your mind, son, is in mine. At least since you fell in love. Let me tell you, I don't like it any better than you do.*"

"Who said I don't like it?"

"*I never fell in love in my life, but I'm getting a taste of it through you, and it's not too sweet.*"

"If you've got some hold on Jo-Beth—"

"*She's not my daughter, she's the Jaff's. He's in her head the way I'm in yours.*"

"This *is* a dream," Howie said again. "It's got to be. It's all a fucking dream."

"*So try waking,*" said Fletcher.

"Huh?"

"*If it's a dream, boy, try waking. Then we can get the skepticism over with and get down to some work.*"

Howie put his spectacles on again, bringing Fletcher's face back into focus. There was no smile on it.

"*Go on,*" Fletcher said. "*Get your doubts sorted through, because we haven't much time. This isn't a game. This isn't a dream. This is the world. And if you don't help me then there's more than your dime-store romance in jeopardy.*"

"Fuck you!" said Howie, making a fist. "I can wake up. Watch!"

Mustering all his strength he delivered a punch to the tree beside him that shook the foliage overhead.

A few leaves dropped around him. Again he punched the coarse bark. The second blow hurt, as had the first. So did the third and the fourth. There was no wavering in Fletcher's image, however: he remained solid in the sunlight. Howie punched the tree again, feeling the skin on his knuckles break, and begin to bleed. Though the pain he felt mounted with each successive blow the scene around him offered no sign of capitulation. Determined to defy its hold he beat at the trunk again and again, as though this were some new exercise, designed not to strengthen the machine but to wound it. No pain, no gain.

"Just a dream," he said to himself.

"*You're not going to wake,*" Fletcher warned him. "*Stop it now before you break something. Fingers aren't easy to come by. Took a few eons to get fingers—*"

"It's just a dream," Howie said. "Just a dream."

"*Stop, will you?*"

There was more than an urge to break the dream fuelling Howie, however. Half a dozen other furies had risen to give momentum to these blows. Rage against Jo-Beth, and her mother, and *his* mother too come to that; against himself for his ignorance, for being a holy fool when the rest of the world was so damn wise, running rings around him. If he could shatter this illusion's hold on him he'd never be a fool again.

"You're going to break your hand, Howard—"

"I'm going to wake."

"Then what will you do?"

"I'm going to wake."

"But with a broken hand, what will you do when she wants you to touch her?"

He stopped, and looked round at Fletcher. The pain was suddenly excruciating. From the corner of his eye he could see that the bark of the tree was bright scarlet. He felt nauseous.

"She doesn't . . . want . . . me to touch her," he murmured. "She . . . locked me out . . ."

He let his wounded hand fall to his side. Blood was dripping from it, he knew, but he couldn't bear to look. The sweat on his face had suddenly turned to prickles of icy water. His joints had gone to water too. Giddily, he swung his throbbing hand away from Fletcher's eyes (dark, like his own; even the dead one) and up towards the sun.

A beam found him, shot between the leaves on to his face.

"It's . . . not . . . a dream," he murmured.

"There are easier proofs," he heard Fletcher remark through the whine that was filling his head.

"I'm . . . going to throw up . . . " he said. "I hate the sight . . ."

"Can't hear you, son."

"I hate the sight . . . of my . . . own . . ."

"Blood?" said Fletcher.

Howie nodded. It was an error. His brain spun in his skull, the connections confounded. His tongue gained sight, his ears tasted wax, his eyes felt the wet touch of his lids as they closed.

"I'm out of here," he thought, and collapsed.

Such a long time, son, waiting in the rock for a glimpse of the light.

And now I'm here, I won't have a chance to enjoy it. Or you. No time to have fun with you, the way fathers should enjoy the company of their sons.

Howie moaned. The world was just out of sight. If he wanted to open his eyes it would be there, waiting for him. But Fletcher told him not to try too hard.

I've got you, he said.

It was true. Howie felt his father's arms surrounding him in the dark, wrapping him up. They felt huge. Or perhaps he'd shrunk; become a babe again.

I never had plans to be a father, Fletcher was saying. *It was pretty much forced upon me by circumstance. The Jaff decided to make some children, you see, to have his agents in flesh. I was obliged to do the same.*

"Jo-Beth?" Howie muttered.

Yes?

"Is she his or yours?"

His, of course. His.

"So we're not . . . brother and sister?"

No, of course not. She and her brother are of his making, you're of mine. That's why you have to help me, Howie. I'm weaker than he is. A dreamer. I always was. A drugged dreamer. He's already out there, raising his damn terata—

"His what?"

His creatures. His army. That's what he got from the comedian: something to carry him away. Me? I got nothing. Dying people don't have many fantasies. It's all fear. He loves fear.

"Who is he?"

The Jaff? My enemy.

"And who are you?"

His enemy.

"That's not an answer. I want a better answer than that."

It'd take too much time. We don't have time, Howie.

"Just the bones."

Howie felt Fletcher smile inside his head.

Oh . . . bones I can give you, his father said. *Bones of birds and fishes. Things buried in the ground. Like memories. Back to the first cause.*

"Am I stupid, or are you talking nonsense?"

I've so much to tell you, and so little time. Best I show you, maybe.

His voice had taken on a strained quality; Howie felt anxiety in it.

"What are you going to do?" he said.

I'm going to open up my mind, son.

"You're afraid . . ."

It'll be quite a ride. But I don't know any other way.

"I don't think I want to."

Too late, said Fletcher.

Howie felt the arms encircling him loosen their grip; felt himself falling from his parent's hold. This was the first of all nightmares surely; to be dropped. But gravity was askew in this thought-world. Instead of his father's face receding from him as he was released it appeared—vast, and growing vaster—as he toppled into it.

There were no words now, to reduce thought: only thoughts themselves, and those in abundance. Too much to understand. It was all Howie could do not to drown.

Don't fight, he heard his father instruct. *Don't even try to swim. Let go. Sink into me. Be in me.*

I won't be myself any longer, he returned. If I drown I won't be me. I'll be you. I don't want to be you.

Take the risk. There's no other way.

I won't! I can't! I have to . . . control.

He started to struggle against the element that surrounded him. Ideas and images kept breaking through his mind however. Thoughts fixed in his mind by another mind, that were beyond his present comprehension.

—Between this world, called the Cosm—also called the Clay, also called the Helter Incendo—between this world and the Metacosm, also called the Alibi, also called the Exordium and the Lonely Place, is a sea called Quiddity—

An image of that sea appeared in Howie's head, and amid the confusion was a sight he knew. He'd floated here, during the brief dream he'd shared with Jo-Beth. They'd been carried on a gentle tide, their hair tangled, their bodies brushing against each other. Recognition calmed his fears. He listened to Fletcher's instruction more closely now.

—and on that sea, there's an island—

He glimpsed it, albeit distantly.

It's called Ephemeris—

A beautiful word, and a beautiful place. Its head was couched in cloud, but there was light on its lower slopes. Not sunlight; the light of spirit.

I want to be there, Howie thought, I want to be there with Jo-Beth.

Forget her.

Tell me what's there. What's on Ephemeris?

The Great and Secret Show, his father's thoughts returned, *which we see three times. At birth, at death and for one night when we sleep beside the love of our lives.*

Jo-Beth.

I told you, forget her.

I went with Jo-Beth! We were floating there, together.

No.

Yes. That means she's the love of my life. You just said so.

I told you to forget her.

It does! My God! It does!

Something that the Jaff fathered is too tainted to be loved. Too corrupt.

She's the most beautiful thing I ever saw.

She rejected you, Fletcher reminded him.

Then I'll win her back.

His image of her was clear in his head; clearer than the island now, or the dream-sea it floated upon. He reached for her memory and by it hauled himself out of the grip of his father's mind. Back came the nausea, and then the light, splashing through the foliage above his head.

He opened his eyes. Fletcher was not holding him, if indeed he ever had. Howie was lying on his back on the grass. His arm was numb from elbow to wrist, but the hand beyond felt twice its proper size.

The pain in it was the first proof that he wasn't dreaming. The second, that he had just woken from a dream. The man with the pony-tail was real; no doubt of it. Which meant that the news he brought could be true. This *was* his father, for better or worse. He raised his head from the grass as Fletcher spoke:

"*You don't understand how desperate our situation is,*" he said. "*Quiddity will be invaded by the Jaff if I don't stop him.*"

"I don't want to know," Howie said.

"*You have a responsibility,*" Fletcher stated. "*I wouldn't have fathered you if I didn't think you could help me.*"

"Oh that's very touching," said Howie. "That really makes me feel wanted."

He started to get to his feet, avoiding the sight of his injured hand. "You shouldn't have shown me the island, Fletcher—" he said. "Now I know what's between Jo-Beth and me's the real thing. She's not tainted. And she's not my sister. That means I can get her back."

"*Obey me!*" Fletcher said. "*You're my child. You're supposed to obey!*"

"You want a slave, go find one," Howie said. "I've got better things to do."

He turned his back on Fletcher, or at least believed he had, until the man appeared in front of him.

"How the hell did you do that?"

"*There's a lot I can do. Little stuff. I'll teach you. Only don't leave me alone, Howard.*"

"Nobody calls me Howard," Howie said, raising his hand to push Fletcher away. He'd momentarily forgotten his injury: now it came into sight. His knuckles were puffed up, the back of his hand and his fingers gummy with blood. Blades of grass had stuck to it, bright green on bright red. Fletcher took a step back, repulsed.

"Don't like the sight of blood, either, huh?" Howie said.

As he retreated something about Fletcher's appearance altered, too subtle for Howie to quite grasp. Was it that he'd backed away into a patch of sunlight, and that it somehow pierced him? Or that a piece of sky locked in his belly came undone and floated up into his eyes? Whatever, it was there and gone.

"I'll make a deal," Howie said.

"*What's that?*"

"You leave me alone; I'll leave you—"

"*There's only us, son. Against the whole world.*"

"You're fucking crazy, you know that?" Howie said. He took his eyes off Fletcher and set them on the route he'd come. "That's where I got it from. This holy fool shit! Well, not me! No more. I've got people who love me!"

"*I love you!*" Fletcher said.

"Liar."

"*All right, then I'll learn.*"

Howie started away from him, his bloody arm outstretched.

"*I can learn!*" he heard his father call from behind him. "*Howard, listen to me! I can learn!*"

He didn't run. He didn't have the strength. But he reached the road without falling down, which was a victory of mind over matter, given how weak his legs felt. There he rested for a short time, content that Fletcher wouldn't follow him into such open territory. The man had secrets he didn't want mere human eyes to see. While resting, he planned. First he'd return to the motel, and tend to his hand. Then? Back to Jo-Beth's house. He had good news to impart, and he'd find a way to tell it if he had to wait all night for the opportunity.

The sun was hot and bright. It threw his shadow in front of him as he went. He fixed his eyes on the sidewalk, and followed his pattern there, step for step, back towards sanity.

In the woods behind him, Fletcher cursed his inadequacy. He'd never been much good at persuasion, leaping from banality to visions with no proper grasp of the middle ground between: the simple social skills which most people were proficient in by the age of ten. He had failed to win his son over by straightforward argument, and Howard in his turn had resisted the revelations which might have made him comprehend his father's jeopardy. Not just his; the world's. Not for an instant did Fletcher doubt that the Jaff was as dangerous now as he'd

been back in the Misión de Santa Catrina, when the Nuncio had first
rarefied him. More so. He had his agents in the Cosm; children who
would obey him because he had a way with words. Howard was heading back into the embrace of one of those agents even now. As good as
lost. Which left him with no alternative but to go into the Grove on
his own, and look for people from whom he might raise hallucigenia.

There was no value in putting off the moment. He had a few hours
before dusk, when the day turned towards darkness, and the Jaff would
have an even greater advantage than he had already. Even though he
didn't much like the idea of walking the streets of the Grove for all to
see and study, what choice did he have? Maybe there would be a few
he could catch dreaming, even in the light of day.

He looked up at the sky, and thought of his room in the Mission, in
which he'd sat with Raul for so many blissful hours, listening to
Mozart and watching the clouds change as they came off the ocean.
Changing, always changing. A flux of forms in which they'd find
echoes of earthly things: a tree, a dog, a human face. One day, he
would join those clouds, when his war with the Jaff was over. Then the
sadness of parting he felt now—Raul gone, Howard gone, everything
sliding away from him—would be extinguished.

Only the fixed felt pain. The protean lived in everything, always.
One country, living one immortal day.

Oh, to be there!

SEVEN

For William Witt, Palomo Grove's Boswell, the morning had seen his worst nightmare become reality. He'd stepped out of his attractive, one-story residence in Stillbrook, which he boasted to clients had appreciated by thirty thousand dollars in the five years since he'd purchased, to do a normal day's real estate business in his favorite town on earth. But things were different this morning. Had he been asked to say *what* exactly, he couldn't have offered a cogent answer, but he knew by instinct that his beloved Grove was sickening. He spent most of the morning standing at the window of his offices, which looked directly across at the supermarket. Almost everybody in the Grove used the market at least once a week; it had for many the double function of suppliers and meeting place. William prided himself on the fact that he could name fully ninety-eight percent of the people who entered its doors. He'd been instrumental in finding houses for a good number of them; rehousing them when their families outgrew their first purchase as newlyweds; often rehousing those in middle-age when the children left; finally selling houses on when the occupants died. And he in turn was known by most of them. They called him by his first name, they commented on his bow ties (which were his trademark; he owned one hundred and eleven), they introduced him to visiting friends.

But today, as he watched from his window, he took no joy in the ritual. Was it simply the fact of Buddy Vance's death, and the tragedy that had come as its consequence, that subdued folks so mightily; that kept them from greeting each other as they passed on the parking lot? Or was it that they, like he, had woken with a strange expectation, as though some event was in the offing that they'd neglected to write in their diaries, but at which they'd be sorely missed were they not to attend.

Simply standing and watching, unable to interpret what he saw or felt, dragged his spirits to their knees. He decided to go on a round of appraisals. There were three houses—two in Deerdell, one in Windbluff—that needed looking over, and prices determined. His anxiety didn't diminish as he drove over to Deerdell. The sun that beat on the sidewalks and the lawns beat to bruise; the air above shimmered as if to dissolve brick and slate: to take his precious Grove away entirely.

The two properties in Deerdell were in very different states of repair; both required his full attention as he went through them, totting up their merits and demerits. By the time he'd finished with them, and begun towards the Wind-bluff house, he'd been long enough distracted from his fears to think that maybe he'd been over-reacting. The task ahead, he knew, would afford him considerable pleasure. The house on Wild Cherry Glade, just below the Crescents, was large and desirable. He was already creating the Better Homes Bulletin pitch as he stepped from the car:

Be King of the Hill! The perfect family home is waiting for you!

He selected the front door key from the two on the ring, and opened up. Legal wrangles had kept the property empty and off the market since the spring; the air inside was dusty and stale. He liked the smell. There was something about empty places that touched him. He liked to think of them as homes in waiting; blank canvases upon which buyers would paint their own particular paradise. He wandered through the house, making meticulous notes in each room, turning seductive phrases over in his head as he went:

Spacious and Immaculate. A Home to Delight even the Choosiest Buyer. 3 Bedrooms, 2 1/2 baths, with Terrazzo floors, Birch panelling in formal living room, kitchen fully equipped, covered patio . . .

Given its size and location the house would, he knew, command a good price. Having made a circuit of the lower floor he unlocked the yard door and stepped outside. The houses, even on the lower parts of the Hill, were well spread. The yard was not overlooked by either of the neighbors' houses. Had it been, they might well have complained of its condition. The lawn was shin-high, patchy and sere; the trees needed cutting back. He walked across the sun-baked ground to measure the pool. It had not been drained after Mrs. Lloyd, who'd owned the property, had died. The water was low, its surface encrusted with an algae greener than the grass which sprang between the tiling at the pool's edge. It smelt rank. Rather than linger to measure the pool, he guessed its dimensions, knowing his practiced eye was virtually as accurate as his tape. He was jotting the figures down when a ripple started in the center of the pool, crawling over the sluggish surface towards him. He stepped away from the edge, making a note to get the Pool Services up here *soonest*. Whatever was breeding in the filth—fungus or fish—could count their teeming tenancy in hours.

The water moved again; darting motions that put him in mind of another day entirely, and of another body of haunted water. He put the memory from his head—or at least tried to—and, turning his back on the pool, began towards the house. But the memory had been too long alone; it insisted on going with him. He could see the four girls—Carolyn, Trudi, Joyce and Arleen, lovely Arleen—as clearly as if it were just yesterday he'd spied on them. He watched them in his mind's eyes, stripping off their clothes. He heard their chatter; their laughter.

He stopped walking, and glanced back at the pool. The soup was once more still. Whatever it had bred or was a bed for had gone back to sleep. He glanced at his watch. He'd been away from the office only an hour and three quarters. If he picked up his pace and finished here quickly, he could slip back home for a while, and watch a video from his collection. The notion, fuelled in part by the erotic recollections the pool had stirred, took him back into the house with renewed zeal. He locked up the back, and started upstairs.

Halfway up, a noise from above brought him to a halt.

"Who's there?" he demanded.

There was no reply, but the noise came again. He made his demand a second time; a dialogue of question and sound, question and sound. Were there children in the house, perhaps? Breaking into empty properties, which had been a fad some years before, was once again on the increase. This was the first time he'd had the opportunity to catch a culprit in the act of trespass however.

"Are you coming down?" he said, giving as much *basso profundo* to his question as he could muster. "Or am I coming up to bring you down?"

The only reply was the same skittering sound he'd heard twice already, like a small dog with unclipped nails running over a hardwood floor.

So be it, William thought. He began up the stairs again, making his steps as heavy as possible to intimidate the trespassers. He knew most of the Grove's children by their names and nicknames. Those that he didn't he could readily point out in the schoolyard. He'd make an example of them, and so dissuade further offenders.

By the time he reached the top of the stairs all was silent. The afternoon sun poured through the window, its warmth calming what small anxiety ticked in him. There was no danger here. Danger was a midnight street in L.A., and the sound of a knife scraping brick as someone came in pursuit. This was the Grove, on a sunny Friday afternoon.

As if to confirm that thought a wind-up toy came scuttling through the green door of the master bedroom; a foot-and-a-half-long white centipede, its plastic feet tapping the floor in rhythm. He smiled at the gesture. The child was sending his toy out to signal surrender. Smiling indulgently, William stooped to pick it up, his eyes on the floor through the door.

His gaze flickered back to the toy as his fingers made contact, however, his touch confirming what sight comprehended too late to act upon: that the thing he was picking up was not a toy at all. Its shell was soft, hot and damp beneath his hand, its peristaltic motion repulsive. He tried to let it go but its body adhered to his hand, working against his palm. Dropping notebook and pencil, he snatched the creature from one hand with the other, and threw it down. It fell on its segmented back, its dozen legs pedalling like an overturned shrimp. Gasping, he staggered back against the wall, until a voice from beyond the door said:

"Don't stand on ceremony. You're welcome inside."

The speaker was no child, William realized, but then he'd decided several seconds ago that his first scenario had been optimistic.

"Mr. Witt," said a second voice. It was lighter than the first; and recognizable.

"Tommy-Ray?" William said, unable to disguise the relief he felt. "Is that you, Tommy-Ray?"

"Sure is. Come on in. Meet the gang."

"What's going on here?" William said, stepping clear of the struggling beast and pushing open the door. Mrs. Lloyd's chintz drapes had been drawn against the sun, and after the blaze of light outside the room seemed doubly dark. But he could make out Tommy-Ray McGuire, standing in the middle of the room, and behind him, sitting in the darkest corner, another presence. One of them had been dipping in the rank water of the pool, it seemed; the sickly smell pricked William's sinuses.

"You shouldn't be in here," he chided Tommy-Ray. "Do you realize you're trespassing? This house—"

"You're not going to tell on us, are you?" said Tommy-Ray. He took a step towards William, eclipsing his colleague entirely.

"It's not that simple—" William began.

"Yes it is," said Tommy-Ray flatly. He took another step, and another, suddenly moving past William to the door, and slamming it. The sound excited Tommy-Ray's companion—or rather, his companion's companions—for William's eyes were now sufficiently accustomed to the murk to see that the bearded man slumped in the corner was swarming with creatures that bore a family resemblance to the centipede outside. They covered him like a living armor. They crawled over his face, lingering at his lips and eyes; they gathered around his groin, massaging him. They drank at his armpits, they cavorted on his stomach. There were so many of them his bulk was swelled to twice human size.

"Jesus Lord," said William.

"Unreal, huh?" said Tommy-Ray.

"You and Tommy-Ray know each other from way back, I hear," said the Jaff. "Tell all. Was he a considerate child?"

"What the hell is this?" William said, glancing back at Tommy-Ray. The youth's eyes gleamed as they roved.

"This is my father," came his reply. "This is the Jaff."

"We'd like you to show us the secret of your soul," said the Jaff.

Instantly, William thought of his private collection, locked up back at home. How did this obscenity know about that? Had Tommy-Ray spied on him? The peeper peeped upon?

William shook his head. "I don't have any secrets," he said softly.

"Probably right," said Tommy-Ray. "Boring little shit."

"Unkind," said the Jaff.

"Everybody says it," said Tommy-Ray. "Look at him, with his fucking bow ties and his little nods at everyone."

Tommy-Ray's words stung William. It was they as much as the sight of the Jaff which brought a tremor to his cheek.

"Most boring little shit in the whole fucking town," Tommy-Ray said.

In response the Jaff snatched one of the beasts from his belly and lobbed it at Tommy-Ray. His aim was true. The creature, which had tails like whips, and a minuscule head, fixed itself to Tommy-Ray's face, pressing its belly against his mouth. He lost his balance, toppling sideways as he clawed at the parasite. It came away from his face with a comical kissing sound, revealing Tommy-Ray's grin, which was echoed with laughter from the Jaff. Tommy-Ray tossed the creature back in its master's direction, a half-hearted throw which left the thing a foot from where William stood. He retreated from it, bringing a fresh sound of laughter from father and son.

"It won't harm you," the Jaff said. "Unless I want it to."

He called to the creature that he and the boy had made a game of; it skulked back to the comfort of the Jaff's belly.

"You probably know most of these folks," the Jaff said.

"Yeah," Tommy-Ray murmured. "And they know him."

"This one, for instance," the Jaff said, hauling a cat-sized beast from behind him. "This one came from that woman . . . what was her name, Tommy?"

"I don't remember."

The Jaff slid the creature, which resembled a vast bleached scorpion, around to his feet. The thing seemed almost shy; it wanted to retreat back to its hiding place.

"The woman with the dogs, Tommy—" the Jaff said. "Mildred something."

"Duffin," said William.

"Good! Good!" the Jaff said, jabbing a thick thumb in his direction. "Duffin! How easily we forget! Duffin!"

William knew Mildred. He'd seen her that very morning—minus the poodle pack—standing in the lot staring ahead of her as though she'd driven down here only to forget why she'd come. What she and the scorpion had in common was beyond him.

"I can see you're flummoxed, Witt," the Jaff said. "You're wondering: is this Mildred's new pet? The answer is no. The answer is, this is Mildred's deepest secret, made flesh. And that's what I want from you, William. The deep stuff. The secret stuff."

Red-blooded heterosexual voyeur that he was, William grasped instantly the cocksucking sub-text of the Jaff's request. He and Tommy-Ray weren't father and son, they were fucking each other. All this talk of the deep stuff, the secret stuff, was a veil over that.

"I don't want any part of this," William said. "Tommy-Ray'll tell you, I don't do any weird stuff."

"Nothing weird about fear," the Jaff said.

"Everybody's got it," Tommy-Ray put in.

"Some more than others. You . . . I suspect . . . more than most. 'Fess up, William. You've got some bad stuff in your head. I just want to take it out and make it mine."

More innuendo. William heard Tommy-Ray make a step in his direction.

"Keep your distance," William warned. It was pure bluff, and by the grin on Tommy-Ray's face he knew it.

"You'll feel better afterwards," said the Jaff.

"Much," said Tommy-Ray.

"It doesn't hurt. Well . . . maybe a little, at the start. But once you get the bad stuff out into the open you'll be a different person."

"Mildred was just one," said Tommy-Ray. "He visited a whole bunch last night."

"Sure I did."

"I pointed the way, and he went."

"I get a scent off some people, you know? I get a real strong scent."

"Louise Doyle . . . Chris Seapara . . . Harry O'Connor . . ."

William knew them all.

". . . Gunther Rothbery . . . Martine Nesbitt . . ."

"Martine had some really impressive sights to show," the Jaff said. "One of them's outside. Keeping cool."

"The pool?" William murmured.

"You saw it?"

William shook his head.

"You really must. It's important to know what people have been hiding from you all these years." That touched a nerve, though William guessed the Jaff was ignorant of the fact. "You think you know these people," he went on, "but they've all got fears they never confess; dark places they cover up with smiles. These . . ." he raised his arm, to which a creature resembling a furless monkey clung, ". . . are what live in those places. I just call them forth."

"Martine, too?" William said, the vaguest glint of escape showing itself.

"Oh sure," said Tommy-Ray. "She had one of the best."

"I call them terata," the Jaff said. "Which means a monstrous birth; a prodigy. How do you like that?"

"I'd . . . I'd like to see what Martine produced," William replied.

"A pretty lady," said the Jaff, "with an ugly fuck in her head. Go show him, Tommy-Ray. Then bring him back up."

"Sure."

Tommy-Ray turned the handle but hesitated before opening the door, as though he'd read the thoughts going through William's head.

"You really want to see?" the youth said.

"I want to see," said Witt. "Martine and I . . ." He let the line trial a little. The Jaff bit.

"You and that woman, William? Together?"

"Once or twice," he lied. He'd not so much as touched Martine, nor indeed ever wanted to, but he hoped it gave motive to his curiosity.

The Jaff seemed persuaded.

"All the more reason to see what she was keeping from you," he said. "Take him, Tommy-Ray! Take him!"

The McGuire boy did as ordered, leading William downstairs. He whistled tunelessly as he went, his easy gait and his casual manner all belying the hellish company he was keeping. More than once William was tempted to ask the kid *why*, just so he could better understand what was happening to the Grove. How could it be that evil was so happy-go-lucky? How could souls so plainly corrupted as Tommy-Ray saunter, and sing, and exchange repartee like ordinary folks?

"Freaky, huh?" Tommy-Ray said, as he took the rear door key from William. He's read my mind, Witt thought, but Tommy-Ray's next remark gave the lie to that.

"Empty houses. Freaky places. 'Cept for you, I guess. You're used to 'em, right?"

"I've got that way."

"The Jaff doesn't much like the sun, so I found him this place. Somewhere he could hide away."

Tommy-Ray squinted against the bright sky as they headed outside. "Guess I must be getting like him," he commented. "Used to love the beach, y'know. Topanga; Malibu. Now it kinda makes me sick to think about all that . . . brightness."

He started to lead the way to the pool, keeping his head down and the chatter up.

"So you and Martine had a thing goin', huh? She's no Miss World, you know what I'm saying? And she sure had some freaky stuff inside

her. You should see the way it comes out . . . Boy oh boy. That's a
sight. They kinda sweat it out. Right out through the little holes—"

"Pores."

"Huh?"

"The little holes. Pores."

"Yeah. Neat."

They had reached the pool. Tommy-Ray approached, saying:

"The Jaff's got this way of calling them, you know? With his mind. I
just call 'em by their names; or the names of the people they belonged
to." He glanced back at William, catching him in the act of scanning
the fencing around the yard, looking for a break in it. "Getting bored?"
Tommy-Ray said.

"No. No . . . I just . . . no, I'm not bored."

The youth looked back towards the pool. "Martine?" he called.
There was a disturbance on the surface of the water. "Here she
comes," said Tommy-Ray. "You're going to be real impressed."

"I bet I am," said William, taking a step towards the edge. As whatever
it was in the water began to break surface he threw out his arms and
pushed Tommy-Ray in the small of the back. The boy yelled, and lost his
balance. William got a glimpse of the terata in the pool—like a man o'
war with legs. Then Tommy-Ray was falling on top of it, boy and beast
thrashing around. William didn't linger to see who bit whom. He was
racing for the weakest place in the fence, and clambering over, and away.

"You let him slip," said the Jaff, when, after a time, Tommy-Ray
returned to the nest upstairs. "I'm not going to be able to rely upon
you, I can see that."

"He tricked me."

"You shouldn't sound so damn surprised. Haven't you learned yet?
Folk have secret faces. That's what makes them interesting."

"I tried to chase him, but he'd got away already. You want me to go
to his home? Kill him, maybe?"

"Easy, easy," said the Jaff. "We can live with him spreading rumors
for a day or two. Who's going to believe him, anyhow? We'll just have
to vacate this place after dark."

"There's other empty houses."

"We won't need to look," said the Jaff. "I found us a permanent residence last night."

"Where?"

"She's not quite ready for us, but she will be."

"Who?"

"You'll see. Meanwhile, I'm going to need you to take a little journey for me."

"Sure."

"You won't have to be away long. But there's a place down the coast where I left something important to me, a long time ago. I want you to get it back for me, while I dispatch Fletcher."

"I want to be here for that."

"You like the idea of death, don't you?"

Tommy-Ray grinned. "Yeah. I do. My friend Andy, he had this neat tattoo, of a skull, right there." Tommy-Ray pointed to his chest. "Right over his heart. He used to say he'd die young. He said he'd go down to Bombora, the peaks are real dangerous there—waves just drop away, you know?—and he'd wait for one last wave, and when he was really travelling he'd just throw himself off the board. Just do it. Like that. Ride and die."

"Did he?" asked the Jaff. "Die, I mean?"

"Did he fuck," said Tommy-Ray contemptuously. "Didn't have the balls."

"But you could."

"Right now? Sure as shit."

"Well, don't be in too much of a hurry. There's going to be a party."

"Yeah?"

"Oh yeah. A major party. This town never saw the likes of this party."

"Who's invited?"

"Half of Hollywood. And the other half'll wish it had been."

"And us?"

"Oh yes, we'll be there. You can be sure of that. We'll be there, ready and waiting."

———

At last, William thought as he stood on Spilmont's doorstep on Peaseblossom Drive, at last a story I can tell. He'd escaped the horrors of the Jaff's court with a tale he could unburden himself of, and be dubbed a hero for the warning.

Spilmont was one of the many William had guided through a house purchase; two, in fact. They knew each other well enough to be on first name terms.

"Billy?" Spilmont said, looking William up and down. "You don't look too good."

"I'm not."

"Come on in."

"Something terrible's happened, Oscar," William said, allowing himself to be ushered inside. "I never saw anything worse."

"Sit. Sit," said Spilmont. "Judith? It's Bill Witt. What do you need, Billy? Something to drink? Jeeze, you're shaking like a leaf."

Judith Spilmont was a perfect earth mother, broadhipped and big-breasted. She appeared from the kitchen, and repeated her husband's observations. William requested a glass of ice water, but couldn't hold off starting his story before it was in his hands. He knew even as he began how ludicrous it would sound. It was a campfire tale, not meant to be told in broad daylight while the listener's kids yelled as they danced in and out of the lawn sprinklers, just beyond the window. But Spilmont listened dutifully, shooing his wife away once she'd supplied the water. William persevered through his account, even remembering the names of those whom the Jaff had touched the night before, explaining once in a while that he knew all this sounded preposterous but it had really happened. It was with that observation he finished the telling:

"I know how this must sound," he said.

"Can't say it's not some story," Spilmont replied. "If it came from anyone but you I think I'd be less willing to listen. But shit, Bill . . . Tommy-Ray McGuire? He's a nice kid."

"I'll take you back up there," William said. "As long as we go armed."

"No, you're in no state for that."

"You mustn't go alone," William said.

"Hey, neighbor, you're looking at a man who loves his kids. Think I'd leave 'em orphans?" Spilmont laughed. "Listen, you go back home. Stay there. I'll call you when I've got some news. Deal?"

"Deal."

"You sure you're fit to drive? I could get somebody—"

"I got this far."

"Right."

"I'll be OK."

"Meanwhile, keep it to yourself, Bill, OK? I don't want anyone getting trigger-happy."

"No. Sure. I understand."

Spilmont watched while William downed the rest of his ice water then escorted him to the door, shook his hand, and waved him off. William did as instructed. He drove straight home, called in to Valerie and told her he wouldn't be coming back to the office, locked all the doors and windows, undressed, threw up, showered and waited by the telephone for further news of the depravity that had come to Palomo Grove.

EIGHT

Suddenly dog-tired, Grillo had taken to his bed around three-fifteen, instructing the switchboard to hold all calls through to his suite until further notice. It was therefore a rapping on the door that woke him. He sat up, his head so light it almost floated off.

"Room Service," a woman said.

"I didn't order anything," he replied. Then he realized: "Tesla?"

Tesla it was, looking good in her usual defiant fashion. Grillo had long ago concluded that it took a kind of genius to transform, in the wearing of certain clothes and items of jewelry, the tacky into the glamorous, and the tasteful into the kitsch. Tesla managed the transition in both directions without seeming to try. Today, she wore a man's white shirt, too big for her small, slim frame, with a cheap Mexican bola at the neck, bearing an image of the Madonna, slinky blue trousers, high heels (which still only brought her up to shoulder height on him), and silver snake earrings that lurked in red hair she'd had streaked with blonde, but only streaked because, as she'd explained, blondes did indeed have more fun but a whole head's worth was sheer indulgence.

"You were asleep," she said.

"Yep."

"Sorry."

"I have to take a piss."

"Take it. Take it."

"Will you check my calls?" he yelled back to her as he met his reflection in the mirror. He looked wretched, he thought: like the undernourished poet he'd given up trying to be the first time he went hungry. It was only as he swayed at the bowl, one hand on his dick—which had never looked so far from him, or so small—the other holding on to the door frame to keep himself from keeling over, that he admitted to himself just how sick he was feeling.

"You'd better stay away from me," he told Tesla as he staggered back. "I think I got flu."

"Then go back to bed. Who gave you flu?"

"Some kid."

"Abernethy called," Tesla informed him. "So did a woman called Ellen."

"Her kid."

"Who she?"

"She nice lady. What's the message?"

"Needs to talk to you urgently. No number."

"Don't think she's got a phone," Grillo said. "I should find out what she wants. She used to work for Vance."

"Scandal?"

"Yeah." His teeth had begun to chatter. "Shit," he said. "I feel like I'm burning up."

"Maybe I should take you back to L.A."

"No way. There's a story here, Tesla."

"There's stories every place. Abernethy can put somebody on this."

"This one's *strange*," Grillo said. "Something's going on here I don't understand." He sat down, his head thumping. "You know I was there when the men who were looking for Vance's body got killed?"

"No. What happened?"

"Whatever they said on the news, it wasn't some underground dam burst. Or at least it wasn't *just* that. For one thing I heard shouts long before the water. I think they were yelling *prayers* down there, Tesla. Prayers. And then there was this fucking geyser. Water, smoke, dirt. Bodies. And something else. No: *two* something elses. Coming out of the ground, under cover."

"Climbing?"

"Flying."

Tesla gave him a long, hard look.

"I swear, Tesla," Grillo said. "Maybe they were human . . . maybe not. They seemed more like . . . I don't know . . . more like *energies* maybe. And before you ask, I was clean and sober."

"Were you the only one who saw this?"

"No, there was a guy called Hotchkiss with me. I think he saw most of it too. Only he won't answer his phone to corroborate."

"You realize you sound certifiable?"

"Well that just confirms what you've always thought, right? Working for Abernethy digging up dirt on the rich and famous—"

"Not falling in love with me."

"Not falling in love with you."

"Lunatic."

"Insane."

"Listen, Grillo, I'm a lousy nurse, so don't expect sympathy. But if you want more practical help while you're sick, just point me in the right direction."

"You could look in on Ellen. Tell her the kid gave me the flu. Get her feeling guilty. There's a story there, and I've only got a piece of it so far."

"That's my Grillo. Sick but never shamed."

It was late afternoon by the time Tesla set out for Ellen Nguyen's house, refusing to take the car even though Grillo warned her she'd have quite a walk. A breeze had mustered itself, and escorted her through the town. It was the kind of community she rather fancied setting a thriller in; something about a man with an atom bomb in his suitcase, maybe. It had been done before, of course, but she had a twist on the tale. Rather than telling it as a parable of evil she'd tell it of apathy. People simply choosing not to believe what they were told; just going about their daily business with expressions of blithe indifference. And the heroine would try to galvanize these people into a recognition of their own danger, and fail, and at the end she'd be dumped outside the town limits by a mob who resented her stirring up the mud, just as the ground rocked and the bomb went off. Fade out. The End. Of course it would never get made that way, but then she was a past mistress at writing screenplays that never saw celluloid. The stories kept coming, however. She couldn't walk in a new place or meet new faces without dramatizing them. She didn't analyze too closely the stories her mind created for each cast and setting, unless—as now—it was so obvious as to be unavoidable. Presumably her gut told her that Palomo Grove was a town that would one day go bang.

Her sense of direction was unfailingly good. She found her way to the Nguyen residence without need of backtracking. The woman who answered the door looked so delicate Tesla feared to speak above a whisper, much less try to pry some evidence of indiscretion from her. She just stated the facts simply: that she'd come at Grillo's request because he had caught the flu.

"Don't worry, he'll survive," she said, when Ellen looked distressed. "I just came over to explain why he wouldn't be coming over to see you."

"Come in, please," Ellen said.

Tesla resisted. She was in no mood for a fragile soul. But the woman would not be denied.

"I can't talk here," she said as she closed the door. "And I can't leave Philip for too long. I don't have a phone any longer. I had to use my neighbor's to call Mr. Grillo. Will you take a message to him?"

"Sure," Tesla said, thinking: if it's a love letter I'm trashing it. The Nguyen woman was Grillo's type, she knew. Sweetly feminine, soft-spoken. In sum, utterly unlike her.

The contagious child was sitting on the sofa.

"Mr. Grillo has flu," his mother told him. "Why don't you send him one of your drawings, so he gets better?"

The boy padded through to his bedroom, giving Ellen an opportunity to pass her message along.

"Will you tell him that things have changed at Coney?" Ellen said.

"Changed at Coney," Tesla repeated. "What does that mean exactly?"

"There's going to be a Memorial Party for Buddy, at his house. Mr. Grillo will understand. Rochelle, his wife, sent the chauffeur down. Summoned me to help."

"So what's Grillo to do about all of this?"

"I want to know if he needs an invitation."

"I think you can take the answer as yes. When's this to be?"

"Tomorrow night."

"Short notice."

"People will come for Buddy," Ellen said. "He was very much loved."

"Lucky man," Tesla remarked. "So if Grillo wants you he can contact you up at Vance's house?"

"No. He mustn't call there. Tell him to leave a message with next door. Mr. Fulmer. He'll be looking after Philip."

"Fulmer. Right. I got that."

There was little else to say. Tesla accepted a picture from the invalid to take back to Grillo, along with the best wishes of mother and son, then set out on the homeward journey, inventing stories as she went.

NINE

William?"

It was Spilmont on the line, finally. The children were no longer laughing in the background. Evening had fallen, and with the sun gone the lawn-sprinkler's water would be more chilly than pleasurable.

"I haven't much time," he said. "I've wasted enough this afternoon as it is."

"What?" said William. He'd spent the afternoon in a frenzy of anticipation. "Tell me."

"I went up there to Wild Cherry Glade, just as soon as you left."

"And?"

"And nothing, guy. Big fat zero. The place was deserted and I looked like an asshole, going in ready for Christ knows what. Guess that's what you planned, right?"

"No, Oscar. You've got it wrong."

"Only once, guy. Once I can take a joke, OK? I'm not going to have anyone say I haven't got a sense of humor."

"It wasn't a joke."

"You really had me going for a moment there, you know? You should be writing books not selling real estate."

"The whole place was empty? There wasn't a trace of anything? Did you look in the pool?"

"Give me a break!" Spilmont said. "Yeah, it was empty. Pool; house; garage. All empty."

"Then they skipped. They got away before you arrived. Only I don't see how. Tommy-Ray said the Jaff didn't like—"

"*Enough!*" said Spilmont. "I've got too many wackoes on the block without the likes of you. Straighten up, will you? And don't try this on any of the other guys, Witt. They're warned, see? Like I say: once is enough!"

Without signing off Spilmont terminated the call, leaving William to listen to the disconnected tone for fully half a minute before he let the receiver slip from his grasp.

"Who'd have thought?" the Jaff said, stroking his newest charge. "There's fear in the unlikeliest places."

"I want to hold it," said Tommy-Ray.

"Consider it yours," the Jaff said, allowing the youth to claim the terata from his arms. "What belongs to you belongs to me."

"It doesn't look much like Spilmont."

"Oh but it does," said the Jaff. "There was never a truer portrait of the man. This is his root. His core. A man's fear is what makes him what he is."

"Is that right?"

"What's walking out there tonight, calling itself Spilmont, is just the husk. The residue."

He wandered to the window as he spoke, and drew the drapes aside. The terata that had been fawning over him when William came visiting dogged his heels. He shooed them away. They retreated respectfully only to creep back into his shadow when he returned from them.

"The sun's almost gone," he said. "We should get going. Fletcher is already in the Grove."

"Yes?"

"Oh yes. He appeared in the middle of the afternoon."

"How do you know?"

"It's impossible to hate someone as much as I hate Fletcher without knowing his whereabouts."

"So do we go kill him?"

"When we've got enough assassins," the Jaff said. "I don't want any mistakes, like Mr. Witt."

"I'll fetch Jo-Beth first."

"Why bother?" said the Jaff. "We don't need her."

Tommy-Ray threw Spilmont's terata to the ground. "*I* need her," he said.

"It's purely Platonic, of course."

"What does that mean?"

"It's irony, Tommy-Ray. What I mean to say is: you want her body."

Tommy-Ray chewed on this a moment. Then said:

"Maybe."

"Be honest."

"I don't know what I want," came the reply, "but I sure as shit know what I *don't* want. I don't want that fucker Katz touching her. She's *family*, right? You told me that was important."

The Jaff nodded. "You're very persuasive," he said.

"So, we go fetch her?" Tommy-Ray said.

"If it's that important," his father replied. "Yes, we'll go and fetch her."

Seeing Palomo Grove for the first time Fletcher had come close to despair. He had passed through towns like this aplenty in his months of warfare with the Jaff; planned communities that had every facility but the facility to feel; places that gave every impression of life but in truth had little or none. Twice, cornered in such vacuums, he'd come close to being annihilated by his enemy. Though beyond superstition he nevertheless found himself wondering if the third time would prove fatal.

The Jaff had already established his bridgehead here, of that Fletcher had no doubt. It would not be difficult to find here the weak and unprotected souls he liked to batten upon. But for Fletcher, whose hallucigenia were born of rich and pungent dream lives, the town, withered by comfort and complacency, offered little hope of sustenance. He'd have had more luck in a ghetto or a madhouse, where life was lived close to the edge, than in this well-watered wasteland. But he had no choice. Without a human agent to point the way he was obliged to go among these people like a dog, sniffing for some hint of a dreamer. He found a few down at the Mall, but he was given short shrift when he attempted to engage them in conversation. Though he did his best to keep up some pretence of normality it was a long time since he'd been human. The people he approached stared at him strangely, as though there was some part of his performance he'd overlooked and they were able to see through to the Nunciate beneath. Seeing, they retreated. There were one or two who lingered in his vicinity. An old woman who stood a little way off from him and simply smiled whenever he looked her way; two children who gave up looking in the pet shop window to come and stare at him, until their mother called them to her side. The pickings were as thin as Fletcher had feared. Had the Jaff been able to choose their final battlefield personally he could not have chosen better. If the war between them was to finish in Palomo Grove—and in his gut Fletcher sensed that one of them would perish here—the Jaff would surely be the victor.

As evening came, and the Mall emptied, he too left it, wandering through the empty streets. There were no pedestrians. Not so much as a dog-walker. He knew why. The human sphere, willfully insensitive as it was, couldn't entirely block out the presence of supernatural forces in its midst. The inhabitants of the Grove, though they could not have put words to their anxiety, knew their town was haunted tonight, and were taking refuge beside their televisions. Fletcher could see the screens glimmering in home after home, the sound of each set turned up abnormally loud, as if to block any songs the sirens abroad tonight might sing. Rocked in the arms of game-show hosts and soap-opera queens, the little minds of the Grove were lulled into innocent sleep, leaving the creature that might have kept them from extinction locked out on the street, and alone.

TEN

I

Watching from the corner of the street as dusk deepened into night, Howie saw a man he would later know to be the Pastor appear at the McGuire house, announce himself through the closed door, and—after a pause for the unlocking of locks and unbolting of bolts—be received into the sanctuary. Another such diversion would not present itself tonight, he suspected. If there was to be any opportunity to slip past the guardian mother and reach Jo-Beth this was it. He crossed the street, checking first that nobody was coming in either direction. He needn't have feared. The street was uncommonly quiet. It was from the houses the din came: televisions turned up so loud he'd been able to distinguish nine channels playing while he'd waited; hummed along to theme tunes, laughed with pay-off lines. Unwitnessed, therefore, he slipped to the side of the house, clambered over the gate, and started down the passage to the backyard. As he did so the light in the kitchen was turned on. He backed away from the window. It wasn't Mrs. McGuire who'd entered however, but Jo-Beth, dutifully preparing some supper for her mother's guest. He watched her, mesmerized. Going about this commonplace activity in a plain, dark dress, lit by a neon strip, she was still the most extraordinary sight he'd ever seen. When she came close to the window, with tomatoes to rinse at the sink, he stepped out of hiding. She caught his movement, and looked up. His finger was already at his lips to hush her. She waved him away—panic on her face. He obeyed not an instant too soon, as her mother appeared at the kitchen door. There was a short exchange between them, which Howie didn't catch, then Mrs. McGuire returned to the lounge. Jo-Beth glanced over her shoulder to check that her mother had gone, then crossed to the back door, and gingerly unbolted it. She refused to open it sufficiently to give him access however. Instead she put her face to the gap and whispered:

"You shouldn't be here."

"Well I am," he said. "And you're glad I am."

"No I'm not."

"You should be. I've got news. Great news. Come outside."

"I can't do that," she whispered. "Keep your voice down."

"We have to talk. It's life or death. No . . . it's more than life or death."

"What have you done to yourself?" she said. "Look at your hand."

His attempt to clean the wound had been perfunctory at best, squeamish as he was about picking pieces of bark from the flesh.

"This is all part of it," he said. "If you won't come out, let me in."

"I can't."

"*Please.* Let me in."

Was it his wound or his words that made her relent? Either way, she opened the door. He went to put his arms around her but she shook her head with such a look of terror on her face he backed off.

"Go upstairs," she said, not even whispering now but mouthing the word.

"Where?" he returned.

"Second door on the left," she said, obliged to raise her volume a little for these instructions. "My room. Pink door. Wait until I take the food through."

He wanted so much to kiss her. But instead he let her go about her preparations. With a glance in his direction, she headed through to the lounge. Howie heard an expression of welcome from the visitor, which he took as his cue to slip from the kitchen. There was a moment of danger when—visible at the lounge door—he hesitated before finding the stairs. Then he was away up them, hoping the exchange below would conceal the sound of his footfalls. It seemed they did. There was no change in the rhythm of the dialogue. He reached the pink door and took refuge behind it without incident.

Jo-Beth's bedroom! He'd not dared hope he'd be standing there, among these marshmallow colors, looking at the place where she slept and at the towel she used for showering and at her underwear. When she finally came up the stairs and entered behind him he felt like a thief interrupted in the act of stealing. She caught his embarrassment off him, a flushing sickness that left them avoiding each other's eyes.

"It's a mess," she said softly.

"It's OK," he said. "You weren't expecting me."

"No." She didn't move to hug him. She didn't even smile. "Momma would go mad if she knew you were here. All the time—when she was saying there were terrible things in the Grove—she was right. One of them came here last night, Howie. Came for me and Tommy-Ray."

"The Jaff?"

"You know about him?"

"Something came for me too. Not so much came as *called*. Fletcher his name is. He says he's my father."

"Do you believe him?"

"Yes," Howie said. "I believe him."

Jo-Beth's eyes were filling up. "Don't cry," he said. "Don't you see what all this means? We're not brother and sister. What's between us isn't wrong."

"It's us being together that *caused* all this," she said. "Don't you understand that? If we hadn't met—"

"But we did."

"If we hadn't met they'd never have come from wherever they came from."

"Isn't it better we know the truth about them—about *ourselves?* I don't give a fuck for their damn war. And I won't let it pull us apart."

He reached for her, and took hold of her right hand with his unwounded left. She didn't resist, but let his gentle pressure draw her closer. "We have to leave Palomo Grove," he said. "And leave together. Go somewhere they can't find us."

"What about Momma? Tommy-Ray's lost, Howie. She said so herself. That only leaves me to look after her."

"And what use are you if the Jaff gets to you?" Howie argued. "If we leave now, our fathers won't have anything to fight over."

"It's not just about us," Jo-Beth reminded him.

"No, you're right," he conceded, remembering what he'd learned from Fletcher. "It's about this place called Quid-dity." His hold on her hand tightened. "We went there, you and me. Or almost went. I want to finish that trip—"

"I don't understand."

"You will. When we go we'll go knowing what kind of journey it is. It'll be like a waking dream." It occurred to him as he spoke that not once had he stumbled or stammered. "We're supposed to hate each other, you know? That was their plan—Fletcher and the Jaff—to have us continue their war. Only we're not going to."

For the first time, she smiled:

"No, we're not," she said.

"Promise?"

"Promise."

"I love you, Jo-Beth."

"Howie—"

"Too late to stop me. I said it."

She kissed him suddenly, a small sweet stab which he sucked against his mouth before she could deny him, opening the seal of her lips with his tongue, which at that instant would have opened a safe had the taste of her mouth been locked up there. She pressed to him with a force which matched his own, their teeth touching, their tongues playing tag.

Her left hand, which had wrapped around him, now found his tender right and drew it towards her. He could feel the softness of her breast, despite the demure dress and his numbed fingers. He started to fumble with the buttons at her neck, undoing enough to slide his hand inside so that his flesh met hers. She smiled against his lips, and her hand, having guided him to where he'd be most good, went to the front of his jeans. The hard-on he'd begun to sport upon sight of her bed had gone west, bested by nerves. But her touch, and her kisses, which were one indistinguishable blur of mouth on mouth now, raised him again.

"I want to be naked," he said.

She took her lips off his.

"With them downstairs?" she said.

"They're occupied, aren't they?"

"They talk for hours."

"We'll need hours," he whispered.

"Do you have any kind of . . . protection?"

"We don't have to do everything. I just want that we can at least touch each other properly. Skin to skin."

She looked unpersuaded when she stepped back from him, but her actions belied her expression, as she proceeded to unbutton her dress. He started to strip off his jacket and T-shirt; then began the difficult task of unbuttoning his belt with one hand virtually useless. She came to his aid, doing the job for him.

"It's stifling in here," he said. "Can I open a window?"

"Momma locked them all. In case the Devil got in."

"He did," Howie quipped.

She looked up at him, her dress now open, her breasts bare.

"Don't say that," she said. Instinctively her hands went to cover her nakedness.

"You don't think I'm the Devil," he said. Then: ". . . do you?"

"I don't know if anything that feels this . . . this . . ."

"Say it."

". . . this *forbidden* . . . can be good for my soul," she replied with perfect seriousness.

"You'll see," he said, moving towards her. "I promise you. You'll see."

———

"I think I should speak to Jo-Beth," Pastor John said. He'd got past the point of humoring the McGuire woman once she started talking about the beast that had raped her all those years ago, and how it had come back to claim her son. Pontificating on abstractions was one thing (it drew female devotees to him in droves) but when the talk took a turn for the lunatic he beat a diplomatic retreat. Clearly Mrs. McGuire was verging on a mental breakdown. He needed a chaperone, or she might end up inventing all manner of overheated nonsense. It had happened before. He wouldn't be the first man of God to fall victim to a woman of a certain age.

"I don't want Jo-Beth to think about this any more than she has already," came the reply. "The creature that made her in me—"

"Her father was a man, Mrs. McGuire."

"I know that," she said, well aware of the condescension in his voice. "But people are flesh *and* spirit."

"Of course."

"The man made her flesh. But who made her spirit?"

"God in Heaven," he replied, grateful for this return to safer terrain. "And He made her flesh too, through the man you chose. *Be ye therefore perfect, even as your Father which is in Heaven is perfect.*"

"It wasn't God," Joyce replied. "I know it wasn't. The Jaff's nothing like God. You should see him. You'd know."

"If he exists then he's human, Mrs. McGuire. And I believe I should talk with Jo-Beth about his visit. If indeed he was here."

"He was here!" she said, her agitation increasing.

He stood up to detach the madwoman's hand from his sleeve.

"I'm sure Jo-Beth will have some valuable insights . . ." he said, taking a step back. "Why don't I fetch her?"

"You don't believe me," Joyce said. She was close to shouting now; and to tears.

"I do! But really . . . allow me a moment with Jo-Beth. Is she upstairs? I believe she is. *Jo-Beth! Are you there? Jo-Beth?*"

"What does he want?" she said, breaking their kiss.

"Ignore him," said Howie.

"Suppose he comes looking for me?"

She sat up, and swung her feet over the edge of the bed, listening for the sound of the Pastor's step on the stairs. Howie put his face against her back, reaching beneath her arm—his hand damming a trickle of sweat—and gently touching her breast. She made a small, almost agonized, sigh.

"We mustn't . . ." she murmured.

"He wouldn't come in."

"I hear him."

"No."

"I do," she hissed.

Again, the call from below:

"Jo-Beth! I'd like a word with you. So would your mother."

"I've got to get dressed," she said. She reached down to pick up her clothes. A pleasantly perverse thought passed through Howie's mind as he watched her: that he'd like it if in her haste she put *his* underwear on instead of her own, and vice versa. To push his cock into a space sanctified by her cunt, perfumed by it, dampened by it, would keep him the way he was—too hard for comfort—until the Crack of Doom.

And wouldn't she look sexy, with her slit just out of sight behind the slit of his briefs? Next time, he promised himself. There'd be no hesitation from now on. She'd allowed the desperado into her bed. Though they'd done no more than put their bodies side by side, that invitation had changed everything between them. Frustrating as it was to see her dress again so soon after their undressing, the fact of their having been naked together would be souvenir enough.

He plucked his jeans and T-shirt up, and began to put them on, watching her watching him as he clothed the machine.

He caught that thought, and modified it. The bone and muscle he occupied was no machine. It was a body, and it was frail. His hand hurt; his hard-on hurt; his heart hurt, or at least some heaviness in his chest gave him the impression of heart-ache. He was too tender to be a machine; and too much loved.

She stopped what she was doing for a moment, and glanced towards the window.

"Did you hear that?" she said.

"No. What?"

"Somebody calling."

"The Pastor?"

She shook her head, realizing that the voice she'd heard (was hearing still) was not outside the house or the room but in her head.

"The Jaff," she said.

Parched by protestations, Pastor John went to the sink, picked up a tumbler, ran the tap-water until it chilled, filled the glass and drank. It was almost ten. Time to bring this visit to an end, with or without seeing the daughter. He'd had enough talk of the darkness in humanity's soul to last a week. Pouring away the dregs of his water, he looked up and caught sight of his reflection in the glass. As his gaze lingered in self-appraisal and approval, something in the night outside moved. He put the tumbler in the sink. It rolled back and forth on its rim.

"Pastor?"

Joyce McGuire had appeared behind him.

"It's all right," he said, not certain which of them he hoped to soothe. The woman had got to him with her half-witted fantasies. He returned his gaze to the window.

"I thought I saw somebody in your yard," he said. "But there's nothing—"

There! There! A pale, blurred bulk, moving towards the house.

"No it's not," he said.

"Not what?"

"Not all right," he replied, taking a step back from the sink. "It's not all right at all."

"He's come back," Joyce said.

The last reply in all the world he wanted to give was yes, so he kept his peace, just stepping back from the window another foot, another two feet, shaking his head in denial. It saw his defiance. He saw it see. Eager to undo his hope it came out of the shadows suddenly, and made its presence plain.

"Lord God Almighty," he said. *"What is this?"*

Behind him he heard the McGuire woman start to pray. Nothing manufactured (who could write a prayer in anticipation of *this?*) but an outpouring of entreaties.

"Jesus help us! Lord, help us! Keep us from Satan! Keep us from the unrighteous!"

"*Listen!*" Jo-Beth said. "It's Momma."

"I hear."

"Something's wrong!"

As she crossed the room Howie overtook her, putting his back to the door.

"She's only praying."

"Never like that."

"Kiss me."

"*Howie?*"

"If she's praying, she's occupied. If she's occupied she can wait. I can't. I don't have any prayers, Jo-Beth. I've only got you." This flow of words astonished him, even as they came. "Kiss me, Jo-Beth."

As she leaned to do so a window downstairs shattered, and Momma's guest unleashed a yell that had Jo-Beth pushing Howie aside, hauling open the door.

"Momma!" she yelled. "Momma!"

Sometimes a man was wrong. Born into ignorance, it was inevitable. But to perish for that ignorance, and brutally, seemed so unfair. Nursing his bloodied face, and half a dozen such complaints, Pastor John crawled across the kitchen to take refuge as far from the broken window—and what had broken it—as his trembling limbs could carry him. How was it possible he'd come to such desperate straits as this? His life was not entirely blameless, but his sins were far from large, and he'd paid his dues to the Lord. He'd visited the Fatherless and Widows in their affliction, the way the Gospels instructed, he'd done his level best to keep himself unspotted from the world. And still the demons came. He heard them, though he had his eyes closed. Their myriad legs were making a din as they clambered over the sink and the dishes piled beside it. He heard their wet bodies flopping on to the tiles as their tide overflowed on to the floor, and their passage across the kitchen, urged on by the figure he'd glimpsed outside (The Jaff! The Jaff!), who'd been wearing them from head to toe, like a bee-keeper too much in love with his swarm.

The McGuire woman had ceased her prayers. Perhaps she was dead; their first victim. And perhaps that would be enough for them, and they'd pass him over. That was a prayer worth finding words for. *Please Lord,* he muttered, trying to make himself as small as possible. *Please Lord, make them blind to me, deaf to me, and only you hear my supplications and keep me in your forgiving eye. World without End—*

His requests were interrupted by a violent beating on the back door, and, rising above it, the voice of Tommy-Ray, the prodigal.

"Momma? Can you hear me? Momma? Let me in, will you? Let me in, and I swear I'll stop them coming. I swear I will. Only let me in."

Pastor John heard a sob from the McGuire woman by way of response, which became, without warning, a howl. Alive she was; and in a fury.

"How dare you!" she shrieked. *"How dare you!"*

Such was her din, he opened his eyes. The flow of demons from the window had stopped. That is, it had stopped advancing, though there was still motion across the pale stream. Antennae weaving, limbs readying themselves for new instructions, eyes bristling on stalks. There was nothing among them that resembled anything he knew; and yet he knew them. He didn't dare ask himself how, or from where.

"Open the door, Momma," Tommy-Ray said again. "I have to see Jo-Beth."

"Leave us alone."

"I have to see her and you're not going to stop me," Tommy-Ray raged. His demand was followed by the sound of splintering wood as he kicked at the door. Both the bolts and the lock were unseated. There was a moment's hiatus. Then he gently pushed the door open. His eyes had a vile sheen about them; a sheen Pastor John had seen in the eyes of people about to die. Some interior light informed them. He'd taken it as beatific until now. He couldn't make that error again.

Tommy-Ray's glance flitted first to his mother, who was standing at the kitchen door, barring it, then to her guest.

"Company, Momma?" he said.

Pastor John shook.

"You've got a hold on her," Tommy-Ray said to him. "She listens to you. Tell her to give me Jo-Beth, will you? Make it easier on all of us."

The Pastor looked round at Joyce McGuire:

"Do it," he said, plainly. "Do it or we're all dead."

"See, Momma?" came Tommy-Ray's response. "Advice from the holy man. He knows when he's beat. Call her down, Momma, or I'm going to get mad, and when I get mad so do Poppa's friends. *Call her!*"

"No need."

Tommy-Ray grinned at the sound of his sister's voice, the combination of gleaming eyes and ravishing smile chilling enough to teach ice a trick or two.

"There you are," he said.

She was standing in the doorway, behind her mother.

"Are you ready to leave?" he asked her politely, for all the world like a boy inviting his girl out on a first date.

"You have to promise to leave Momma alone," Jo-Beth said.

"I will," Tommy-Ray replied, his tone that of a man wronged by accusation. "I don't want to hurt Momma. You know that."

"If you leave her alone . . . I'll come with you."

Halfway down the stairs Howie heard Jo-Beth striking this bargain, and mouthed a silent *no*. He couldn't see what horrors Tommy-Ray had brought with him but he could hear them, like the sound his head heard in nightmares: phlegm-sounds, panting-sounds. He didn't give his imagination room enough to put pictures to the text; he'd see the truth for himself all too soon. Instead he took another step down the stairs, turning his wits to the problem of stopping Tommy-Ray in the theft of his sister. His concentration was such he failed to interpret the sounds emerging from the kitchen. By the time he'd reached the bottom stair he'd got himself a plan, however. It was simple enough. To cause as much chaos as he possibly could, and hope that under its cover Jo-Beth and her mother could escape to safety. If in running wild he managed to deliver

Tommy-Ray a blow, that would be the cherry on the cake; a satisfying cherry.

That thought and intention in mind he took a deep breath, and rounded the corner.

Jo-Beth was not there. Nor was Tommy-Ray; or the horrors he'd come here with. The door was open to the night, and slumped in front of it, face to the threshold, was Momma, her arms outstretched as though her last conscious act had been to reach out after her children. Howie went to her, across tiles that were gummy beneath his bare feet.

"Is she dead?" a gravel voice enquired. Howie turned. Pastor John had wedged himself between the wall and the refrigerator, as far from sight as he could get his overfed ass.

"No, she's not," Howie said, gently turning Mrs. McGuire over. "Much thanks to you."

"What could I do?"

"You tell me. I thought you had tricks of the trade." He moved towards the door.

"Don't go after them, boy," the Pastor said, "stay here with me."

"They took Jo-Beth."

"The way I hear it she was halfway theirs anyhow. The Devil's children, her and Tommy-Ray."

Do you think I'm the Devil? Howie had asked her, half an hour ago. Now it was she damned to hell; and from the mouth of her own minister, no less. Did that mean they were both tainted then? Or was it not a question of sin and innocence; darkness and light? Did they somehow stand *between* the extremes, in a place reserved for lovers?

These thoughts came and went in a flash, but they were sufficient to fuel his motion through the door to meet whatever lay in the night outside.

"Kill 'em all!" he heard the God-fearer yell after him. "There's not a clean soul among them! *Kill 'em all!*"

The sentiment enraged Howie, but he could think of no adequate riposte. In lieu of wit he yelled:

"*Fuck you,*" back through the door, and headed out in search of Jo-Beth.

II

There was sufficient light spilling from the kitchen for him to grasp the general geography of the yard. He could see a bank of trees bordering its perimeter, and an unkempt lawn between the trees and where he stood. As inside, so out here: there was no sign of brother, sister or the force that had set its sights on both. Knowing that he had no hope of surprising the enemy, given that he was stepping out of a well-lit interior with a hollered curse on his lips, he advanced calling Jo-Beth's name at the top of his voice in the hope that she might find breath to answer. There was no reply forthcoming. Just a chorus of barking dogs, roused by his shouts. Go ahead and bark, he thought. Get your masters moving. This was no time for them to be sitting watching game shows. There was another show out here in the night. Mysteries were walking; the earth was opening, spitting out wonders. It was a Great and Secret Show and it was playing tonight on the streets of Palomo Grove.

The same wind that carried the sound of the dogs moved the trees. Their sibilance distracted Howie from the sound of the army until he was a little way from the house. Then he heard the chorus of mutterings and cluckings behind him. He turned on his heel. The wall around the door through which he'd just stepped was a solid mass of living creatures. The roof, which sloped from two stories to one above the kitchen, was similarly occupied. Larger forms roamed there, shambling back and forth across the slates, muttering in their throats. They were too high to catch the light; just silhouettes against a sky which showed no stars. Neither Jo-Beth nor Tommy-Ray were among them. There was not a single outline in that clan that approximated the human.

Howie was on the point of turning away from the sight when he heard Tommy-Ray's voice behind him.

"Bet you never saw nothing like that, Katz," he said.

"You know I never did," said Howie, the politeness of his reply shaped by the knife point he felt pricking the small of his back.

"Why don't you turn round, real slow," said Tommy-Ray. "The Jaff wants a word with you."

"More than one," came a second voice.

It was low—scarcely louder than the wind in the trees—but every syllable was exquisitely, musically shaped.

"My son here thinks we should kill you, Katz. He says he can smell his sister on you. God knows I'm not sure brothers should know what their sisters smell like in the first place, but I suppose I'm old-fashioned. This is too late in the millennium to be fretting about incest. Doubtless you have a view on that."

Howie had turned, and could see the Jaff standing several yards behind Tommy-Ray. After all that Fletcher had said about the man, he'd expected a warlord. But there was nothing massively impressive about his father's enemy. He had the appearance of a patrician run part way to dereliction. An undisciplined beard grown over strong, persuasive features; the stance of someone barely concealing great weariness. Clinging to his chest was one of the terata; a wiry, skinned thing more distressing by far than the Jaff himself.

"You were saying, Katz?"

"I wasn't saying anything."

"About how woefully unnatural Tommy-Ray's passion for his sister is. Or are you of the opinion that we're *all* unnatural? You. Me. Them. I'd suppose we'd all of us have gone to the flames in Salem. Anyhow . . . he's very keen to do you mischief. Talks about castration a good deal."

Upon cue Tommy-Ray dropped his knife blade a few inches, from Howie's belly to his groin.

"Tell him," said the Jaff. "About how you'd like to cut him up."

Tommy-Ray grinned. "Let me just do it," he said.

"See?" said the Jaff. "It's taking all my parental skills to hold him in check. So here's what I'm going to do, Katz. I'm going to let you have a head start. I'm going to set you free and see if Fletcher's stock is the equal of my own. You never knew your father before the Nuncio. Better hope he was a runner, eh?" Tommy-Ray's grin became a laugh; the knife point turned against the weave of Howie's jeans. "And just to keep you entertained—"

At this, Tommy-Ray took hold of Howie and spun him round, hauling his captive's T-shirt from his jeans and slitting it from hem to neck, exposing Howie's back. There was a moment's delay while the night air cooled his sweaty skin. Then something touched his back. Tommy-Ray's fingers, licked and wet, spreading to right and left of Howie's spine, following the line of his ribs. Howie shuddered, and arched his back to avoid the contact. As he did so the touches multiplied 'til there were too many to be fingers; a dozen or more on each side, gripping the muscle so hard his skin broke.

Howie glanced over his shoulder, in time to see a white, many-jointed limb, pencil-thin and barbed, pressing its point into his flesh. He cried out, and wrenched himself round, his revulsion outweighing his fear of Tommy-Ray's knife. The Jaff was watching him. His arms were empty. The thing that he'd been nursing was now on Howie's back. He felt its cold abdomen against his vertebrae; its mouthparts sucked at his nape.

"*Get it off me!*" he said to the Jaff. "*Get it the fuck off me!*"

Tommy-Ray applauded the sight of Howie, spinning around like a dog with a flea on its tail.

"Go, man, go!" he whooped.

"I wouldn't try that if I were you," the Jaff said.

Before Howie could wonder why, he got his answer. The creature bit down hard on his neck. He yelled out, falling to his knees. The expression of pain brought a chorus of clicks and mutters from the roof and kitchen wall. Agonized, Howie turned back towards the Jaff. The patrician had let his face slip; the fetus-headed thing behind was vast and gleaming. He had only an instant to glimpse it before the sound of Jo-Beth's sobs took his gaze to the trees, where she was in Tommy-Ray's grip. That glimpse too (her wet eyes, her open mouth) was horribly brief. Then the ache at his neck made him close his eyes, and when he opened them again she, and Tommy, and their unborn father were gone.

He got to his feet. There was a wave of motion going through the Jaff's army. Those lowest on the wall were dropping to the ground, followed by those higher up, the process ascending at such a rate the battalions were soon three or four deep on the lawn. Some struggled free of the crush and began towards Howie by whatever means of propulsion they possessed. The larger creatures were skipping down the roof to join the pursuit. With what little lead the Jaff had offered eroded with every second he delayed, Howie ran pell-mell for the open street.

Fletcher felt the boy's terror and revulsion all too clearly; but he labored to put it from his mind. Howie had rejected his father to go in search of the Jaff's wretched offspring, blinded no doubt by mere appearance. If he was suffering the consequence of such willfulness then that was his burden, and let him carry it alone. If he survived, perhaps he'd be the wiser. If not, then his life, whose purpose he'd flown in the face of the moment he'd turned his back on his creator, would end in as wretched a fashion as Fletcher's, and there'd be justice in that.

Hard thoughts, but Fletcher did his best to keep them in focus, summoning up the image of his son's reflection every time he felt the boy's pain. It was not enough, however. Try as he might to expunge Howie's terrors, they demanded a hearing, and he had no choice, at the last, but to let them in. In a sense they completed this night of despair, and had to be embraced. He and his child were interlocking pieces in a pattern of defeat and failure.

He called to the boy:

Howardhowardhowardhow—

the same call he'd put out after first rising from the rock.

Howardhowardhowardhow—

He sent the message out rhythmically, like a cliff-top beacon. Hoping that his son was not too weak to hear, he turned his attention back to the end-game. With the Jaff's victory looming, he had one final gambit available to him, a hand he didn't want to tempt himself with, knowing how strong his desire for transformation was. It had been a torment to him all these years, being morally bound to stay on this level of being in the hope of defeating the evil he'd helped create, when an hour didn't pass without his thoughts turning to escape. He wanted so much to be free of this world and its nonsenses; to unhitch himself from this anatomy and aspire, as Schiller had said of all art, to the condition of music. Could it be that the time was now ripe to give in to that instinct, and in the last moments of his life as Fletcher hope to snatch a fragment of victory from near inevitable defeat? If so, he had to plan well, both the method of self-dispatch and its arena. There could be no repeat performance for the tribe who occupied Palomo Grove. If he, their rejected shaman, died unnoticed then more than a few hundred souls would be forfeit.

He had tried not to think too hard of the consequences of the Jaff's triumph, knowing that the sense of responsibility might well over-whelm him. But now, as the final confrontation approached, he'd bullied himself into facing it. If the Jaff secured the Art, and through it gained free access to Quiddity, what would it mean?

For one, a being not purified by the rigors of self-denial would have power over a place kept from all but the purged and the perfect. Fletcher did not entirely understand what Quiddity was (perhaps no human could), but he was certain the Jaff, who'd used the Nuncio to cheat his way out of his limitations, would wreak havoc there. The dream-sea and its island (*islands* perhaps; he'd heard Jaff once say there were archipelagos) were visited by humanity at three vital times, in innocence, extremis, and love. On the shores of Ephemeris they mingled briefly with absolutes; saw sights and heard stories that would keep them from insanity in the face of being alive. There, briefly, was pattern and purpose; there was a glimpse of continuity; there was the Show, the Great and Secret Show, which rhyme and ritual were created to be keep-sakes of. If that island were to become the Jaff's playground, the damage would be incalculable. What was secret would become commonplace; what was holy, desanctified; and a species kept from lunacy by its dream journeys there would be left unhealed.

There was another fear in Fletcher, less easily thought through because less coherent. It centered on the tale the Jaff had first presented him with, when he'd appeared in Washington with his offer of funds to pursue the riddle of the Nuncio. There had been, he'd said, a man called Kissoon: a shaman who'd known about the Art and its powers, whom the Jaff had finally found in a place that he'd claimed was a loop of time. Fletcher had listened to the account not really believing much of it, but subsequent events had spiralled to such fantastical heights the idea of Kissoon's Loop seemed small beer now. What part the shaman, with his attempt to have the Jaff murder him, played in the grand scheme, Fletcher couldn't know, but his instinct told him it was by no means finished with. Kissoon had been the last surviving member of the Shoal; an order of elevated human beings who had guarded the Art from the likes of the Jaff since *Homo sapiens* began to dream. Why then had he allowed a man like Jaff, who must have stunk of ambition from the outset, access to his Loop? Why indeed had he been in hiding there at all? And what had happened to the other members of the Shoal?

It was too late now to pursue answers to these questions; but he wanted to put them into somebody else's head besides his own. He would make one last attempt to bridge the gap between himself and his own. If Howard were not the recipient of these observations then they'd go to nothing when he, Fletcher, made his exit.

Which brought him back to the grim business ahead; its method and its setting. It had to be a piece of theater; a spectacular last act that would coax the people of Palomo Grove away from their television screens and into the streets, wide-eyed. After some weighing up of alternatives he chose one, and, still calling his son to him, started towards the site of his final liberation.

Howie had heard Fletcher's call as he fled before the Jaff's army, but the waves of panic that kept breaking over him kept him from fixing their place of origin. He ran blindly, the terata on his heels. It was only when he felt he'd gained sufficient lead to take a breath that his confounded senses heard his name called clearly enough for him to change his route, and follow the summons. When he went, he went with a speed in his heels he'd not believed himself capable of; and even though his lungs labored he squeezed from them sufficient breath for a few words in answer to Fletcher.

"I hear you," he said as he ran, "I hear you. *Father* . . . I hear you."

ELEVEN

I

Tesla had told it right. A lousy nurse she was; but a very capable bully. The moment Grillo woke and found her back in his room she told him plainly that suffering in an alien bed was the act of a martyr and became him all too well. If he wanted to avoid cliché he should allow her to take him back to L.A. and deposit his sickly frame where he could be reassured by the scent of his own unwashed laundry.

"I don't want to go," he protested.

"What's the use of staying here, besides costing Abernethy a heap of money?"

"That's a start."

"Don't be petty, Grillo."

"I'm sick. I'm allowed to be petty. Besides, this is where the story is."

"You can write it better at home than lying here in a pool of sweat feeling sorry for yourself."

"Maybe you're right."

"Oh . . . is the great man conceding something?"

"I'll go back for twenty-four hours. Get my shit together."

"You know you look about thirteen," Tesla said, mellowing her tone. "I never saw you like this before. It's kind of sexy. I like you vulnerable."

"Now she tells me."

"Old news, old news. There was a time I'd have given my right arm for you—"

"Now?"

"The most I'll do is take you home."

The Grove could have been a set for a post-holocaust movie, Tesla thought as she drove Grillo out towards the freeway: the streets were deserted in every direction. Despite all that Grillo had told her about what he'd seen or suspected was going on here, she was leaving without getting so much as a glimpse.

Hold that thought. Forty yards ahead of the car a young man stumbled around the corner and raced across the road. At the opposite sidewalk his legs gave out beneath him. He fell, and seemed to have some difficulty getting up again. The distance was too great and the light too dim for her to grasp much of his condition but he was evidently hurt. There was something misshapen about his body; hunched or swollen. She drove on towards him. At her side, Grillo, whom she'd instructed to doze until they reached L.A., opened his eyes.

"Are we there already?"

"That guy—" she said, nodding in the hunchback's direction. "Look at him. He looks even sicker than you do."

From the corner of her eye she saw Grillo sit bolt up-right, and peer through the windshield.

"There's something on his back," he muttered.

"I can't see."

She brought the car to a halt a little way from where the youth was still struggling to get to his feet; and still failing. Grillo was right, she saw. He was indeed wearing something. "It's a backpack," she said.

"No way, Tesla," Grillo said. He reached for the door handle. "It's alive. Whatever it is, it's alive."

"Stay here," she told him.

"Are you kidding?"

As he pushed the door open—that effort alone enough to set his head spinning—he caught sight of Tesla rummaging in the glove compartment.

"What've you lost?"

"When Yvonne was killed—" she said, grunting as she dug through the detritus "—I swore I'd never leave home unarmed again."

"What are you saying?"

She pulled a gun out of hiding. "And I never have."

"Do you know how to use that?"

"Wish I didn't," she said, and got out of the car. Grillo went to follow. As he did so the car began to roll backwards down the mild incline of the street. He pitched himself across the seat to the handbrake, an action violent enough to spin his head around. When he started to haul himself up again it was almost like tripping: total disorientation.

A few yards from where Grillo was clutching the car door, waiting for his high to pass, Tesla was almost at the boy's side. He was still attempting to get to his feet. She told him to hold on, help was coming, but all she got in reply was a panic-stricken look. He had reason. Grillo had been right. What she'd taken to be a backpack was indeed *alive*. It was an animal of some kind (or of many kinds). It glistered as it battened upon him.

"What the fuck is that?" she said.

This time he did reply; a warning wrapped in moans.

"Get . . . away . . ." she heard him say, ". . . they're . . . coming after me . . ."

She glanced back at Grillo, who was still clinging to the car door, his teeth chattering. No help to be had there, and the boy's situation seemed to be worsening. With every twitch of the parasite's limbs—there were so many limbs; and joints; and eyes—his face knotted up.

". . . Get away . . ." he growled at her, ". . . please . . . in God's name . . . they're coming."

He'd turned giddily to squint behind him. She followed the line of his agonized gaze, down the street from which he'd pelted. There she saw his pursuers. Seeing, she wished she'd taken his advice before she'd locked eyes with him, and all hope of playing the Pharisee was denied her. His plight was hers now. She couldn't turn her back on him. Her eyes—tutored in the real—tried to reject the lesson they saw coming down the street, but they couldn't. No use trying to deny the horror. It was there in all its absurdity: a pale, muttering tide creeping towards them.

"Grillo!" she yelled. "Get in the car!"

The pale army heard her, and picked up its speed.

"The car, Grillo, get in the fucking car!"

She saw him fumble for the door, barely in control of his responses. Some of the smaller beasts at the head of the tide were already scuttling towards the vehicle at speed, leaving their larger brethren to come after the boy. There were enough, more than enough, to take all three of them apart joint by joint, and the car too. Despite their multiplicity (no two alike, it seemed) there was the same blank-eyed, relentless intention in every one. They were destroyers.

She leaned down and took hold of the boy's arm, avoiding the racheting limbs of the parasite as best she could. Its hold on him was too intimate to be undone, she saw. Any attempt to separate them would only invite reprisals.

"Get up," she told him. "We can make it."

"You go," he murmured. He was utterly wasted.

"No," she said, "We *both* go. No heroics. We both go."

She glanced back at the car. Grillo was in the act of slamming the door as the army's foot-runners came at the car, hopping up on to the roof and hood. One, the size of a baboon, began to throw its body against the windshield repeatedly. The others tore at the door handle and worked their barbs between the windows and their frames.

"It's me they want," the boy said.

"If we go, they follow?" Tesla said.

He nodded. Hauling him to his feet, and turning his right arm (the hand badly injured, she saw) over her shoulder, she fired one shot into the approaching mass—which hit one of the larger beasts but didn't slow it a beat—then turned her back on it and began to haul them both away.

He had directions to give.

"Down the Hill," he said.

"Why?"

"The Mall . . ."

Again: "Why?"

"My father . . . is there."

She didn't argue. She just hoped father, whoever he was, had some help to offer, because if they succeeded in outrunning the army they were going to be in no fit state to defend themselves at the end of the race.

As she turned the next corner, the boy offering muttered instructions, she heard the car's windshield shatter.

A short distance from the drama just played out, the Jaff and Tommy-Ray, with Jo-Beth in tow, watched Grillo fumbling for the ignition, succeeding—after some effort—in getting the car started, and driving off, throwing from the hood the terata that had shattered the windshield.

"Bastard," said Tommy-Ray.

"It doesn't matter," the Jaff said. "There's plenty more where he came from. You wait 'til the party tomorrow. Such pickings."

The creature was not quite dead; it let out a thin whine of complaint.

"What do we do with it?" Tommy-Ray wondered.

"Leave it there."

"Some roadkill," came the boy's reply. "People are going to notice."

"It won't survive the night," the Jaff replied. "By the time the scavengers have got to it nobody'll know what the hell it was."

"What the fuck's going to eat *that*?" Tommy-Ray asked.

"Anything hungry enough," came the Jaff's reply. "And there's always something hungry enough. Isn't that right, Jo-Beth?" The girl said nothing. She'd given up weeping and talking. All she did was watch her brother with pitiful confusion on her face.

"Where's Katz going?" the Jaff wondered aloud.

"Down to the Mall," Tommy-Ray informed him.

"Fletcher's calling him."

"Yeah?"

"Just as I hoped. Wherever the son ends up, that's where we'll find the father."

"Unless the terata get him first."

"They won't. They have their instructions."

"What about the woman with him?"

"Wasn't that too perfect? What a Samaritan. She's going to die, of course, but what a great way to go, full of how big-fucking-hearted you are."

The remark elicited a response from the girl.

"Isn't there anything touches you?" she said.

The Jaff studied her. "Too much," he said. "Too much touches me. The look on your face. The look on his." He glanced at Tommy-Ray, who grinned, then back at Jo-Beth. "All I want to do is see clearly. Past the feelings, to the *reasons*."

"And this is how? Killing Howie? Destroying the Grove?"

"Tommy-Ray learned to understand, after his fashion. You can do the same if you'll give me time to explain. It's a long story. But trust me when I say that Fletcher's our enemy, and his son our enemy too. They'd kill me if they could—"

"Not Howie."

"Oh yes. He's his father's son even if he doesn't know it. There's a prize to be won soon, Jo-Beth. It's called the Art. And when I have it, I'll share it—"

"I don't want anything from you."

"I'll show you an island—"

"No."

"—and a shore—"

He reached to her, stroking her cheek. Against her better judgment his words soothed her. It was not the fetus-head she saw in front of her, but a face that had seen hardship; had been plowed by it, and perhaps had wisdom planted.

"Later," he said. "We'll have plenty of time to talk. On that island, the day never ends."

II

W hy don't they overtake us?" Tesla said to Howie.
    Twice the pursuing forces had seemed certain to overtake and overwhelm them, and twice their ranks had slowed at the very moment they were able to realize their ambition. The suspicion was growing on her that the chase was being choreographed. If so, she fretted, by whom? And what was their intention?

The boy—he'd muttered his name, Howie, several streets back—was heavier by the yard. The last quarter mile to the Mall stretched before her like a Marine assault course. Where was Grillo when she needed him? Lost in the maze of crescents and cul-de-sacs which made this town such a trial to traverse, or a victim of the creatures that had assaulted the car?

The answer was neither. Trusting that Tesla's wit would keep her ahead of the horde long enough for him to muster help, he drove like a wild man, first to a public telephone, then on to the address he found in it. Though his limbs felt like lead, and his teeth still chattered, his mental processes seemed to him quite clear, though he knew—from the months after the debacle, which he'd spent in a more or less constant alcoholic stupor—that such clarity could be self-deception. How many screeds had he written under the influence, which had seemed lucidity in ink but read like *Finnegans Wake* once he was sober? Perhaps that was the case now, and he was wasting valuable time when he should have been knocking on the first door he found and rousing help. His instinct told him he'd get none. The appearance of an unshaven individual talking monsters would earn a quick dismissal on any doorstep but that of Hotchkiss.

The man was at home, and awake.

"Grillo? Jesus, man, what the hell's wrong with you?"

Hotchkiss had no right to boast; he looked as used up as Grillo felt. He had a beer in his hand and several of its brothers in his eyes.

"Just come with me," Grillo said, "I'll explain as we go."

"Where?"

"Have you got guns?"

"I've got a handgun, yeah."

"Get it."

"Wait, I need—"

"No talk," Grillo said. "I don't know which way they've gone, and we—"

"Listen," Hotchkiss said.

"What?"

"Alarms. I hear alarms."

They'd begun to ring in the supermarket the moment Fletcher began to smash the windows. They rang in Marvin's Food and Drug, just as loudly, and in the pet store—the din here swelled by the animals woken from their sleep. He encouraged their chorus. The sooner the Grove shook off its lethargy the better, and he knew no surer way of stirring it than assaulting its commercial heart. The summons begun, he raided two of the six stores for props. The drama he had planned would need perfect timing if he was to touch the minds of those who came to watch. If he failed, at least he would not see the consequences of that failure. He'd had too much grief in his life, and too few friends to help him bear it. Of them all he'd perhaps been closest to Raul. Where was he now? Dead, most likely, his ghost haunting the ruins of the Misión de Santa Catrina.

Picturing the place, Fletcher stopped in his tracks. *What about the Nuncio?* Was it possible the remains of the Great Work, as Jaffe had liked to call it, was still there on the cliff-top? If so, and some innocent ever stumbled upon it, the whole sorry story might repeat itself. The self-invited martyrdom he was presently orchestrating would be rendered worthless. That was another task to charge Howard with, before they were parted forever.

Alarms seldom rang for long in the Grove; and certainly never so many at the same time. Their cacophony floated through the town from the wooded perimeter of Deerdell to the widow Vance's house, on the top of the Hill. Though it was too early for the adults of the

Grove to be asleep, most of them—whether touched by the Jaff or not—were feeling oddly dislocated. They talked with their partners in whispers, when they spoke at all; they stood in doorways or in the middle of their dining rooms having forgotten why they'd first risen from the comfort of their armchairs. If asked, many might have stumbled over their own names.

But the alarms commanded their attention, confirming what their animal instincts had known from daybreak: that things were not good tonight; not normal, not rational. The only place of safety was behind doors locked and locked again.

Not everyone was so passive however. Some drew blinds aside to see if anyone in the neighborhood was on the street; others got as far as going to the front door (husbands or wives calling them back, telling them there was no need to step outside; that there was nothing to see that couldn't be seen on the television). It only took one individual to venture out, however, before others followed.

"Clever," said the Jaff.

"What's he up to?" Tommy-Ray wanted to know. "Why the noise?"

"He wants people to see the terata," the Jaff said. "Maybe he's hoping they'll rise up in revolution against us. He's tried this before."

"When?"

"On our travels across America. There was no revolution then and there won't be now. People don't have the faith; don't have the dreams. And he needs both. This is sheer desperation. He's defeated and he knows it." He turned to JoBeth. "You'll be pleased to know I'm calling the hounds off Katz's heels. We know where Fletcher is now. And where he is his son's going to be."

"They stopped following us," Tesla said.

The horde had indeed halted.

"What the hell does that mean?"

Her burden didn't reply. He could barely raise his head. But when he did it was towards the supermarket, which was one of several stores in the Mall whose windows had been smashed.

"We're going shopping?" she said.

He grunted.

"Whatever you say."

Inside the store, Fletcher raised his head from his labors. The boy was within sight of him. He was not alone. A woman bore him up, half-carrying him across the lot towards the litter of shattered glass. Fletcher left off his preparations and went to the window.

"Howard?" he called.

It was Tesla who looked up; Howie didn't waste valuable energy in the attempt. The man she saw emerging from the store didn't look like a vandal. Nor did he look anything like the boy's father; but then she'd never been very good with family resemblances. He was a tall, sallow individual, who to judge by his ragged gait was in as wretched a condition as his offspring. His clothes were drenched, she saw. Her stinging sinuses identified the fluid as gasoline. He left a trail of it as he walked. She suddenly feared the chase had taken them into the grasp of a lunatic.

"Keep away," she said.

"I have to speak with Howard, before the Jaff arrives."

"The who?"

"You led him here. He and his army."

"It couldn't be helped. Howie's real sick. This thing on his back—"

"Let me see—"

"No naked flames," Tesla warned, "or I'm out of here."

"I understand," said the man, raising his palms like a magician to prove them empty of tricks. Tesla nodded, and let him approach.

"Lay him down," the man instructed.

She did so, her muscles buzzing with gratitude. No sooner was Howie on the ground than his father took a two-handed grip of the parasite. It immediately began to thrash wildly, its limbs tightening around its victim. Barely conscious, Howie began to gasp for breath.

"It's killing him!" Tesla yelled.

"Take hold of its head!"

"*What?*"

"You heard me! Its head. Just take hold!"

She glanced at the man, then at the beast, then at Howie. Three beats. On the fourth she took hold of the beast. Its mouthparts were fixed on

Howie's neck, but it loosed them long enough to chew on her hand. In that moment the gasoline man pulled. Body and beast separated.

"*Let go!*" the man yelled.

She needed no persuasion, pulling her hands free despite the sacrifice of flesh to its maw. Howie's father threw it backwards, into the market, where it struck a pyramid of cans, and was buried.

Tesla studied her hand. The palm was punctured in the center. She was not the only one interested in the wound.

"You have a journey to undertake," the man said.

"What is this, palm-reading?"

"I wanted the boy to go for me, but I see now . . . you came instead."

"Hey, I've done all I can do, guy," Tesla said.

"My name's Fletcher, and I beg you, don't desert me now. This wound reminds me of the first cut the Nuncio gave me—" He showed her his palm, which did indeed bear a scar, for all the world as though someone had driven a nail through it. "I have a great deal to tell you. Howie resisted my telling him. You won't. I know you won't. You're part of the story. You were born to be here, now, with me."

"I don't understand any of this."

"Analyze tomorrow. *Do*, now. Help me. We have very little time."

"I want to warn you," Grillo said as he drove Hotchkiss down towards the Mall, "what we saw coming out of the ground was just the beginning. There's creatures in the Grove tonight like nothing I ever saw before."

He slowed as two citizens crossed the path of the car, heading on foot to the source of the summons. They weren't alone. There were others, converging on the Mall as though heading to a Carnival.

"Tell them to go back," Grillo said, leaning out of his side of the car and yelling a warning. Neither his calls nor those of Hotchkiss were attended to. "If they see what I've seen," Grillo said, "there's going to be such panic."

"Might do them some good," Hotchkiss said, bitterly. "All those years they thought I was crazy, because I closed the caves. Because I talked about Carolyn's death as *murder*—"

"I don't follow."

"My daughter, Carolyn . . ."

"What about her?"

"Another time, Grillo. When you've got time for tears."

They'd reached the Mall's parking lot. Maybe thirty or forty Grovers were already gathered there, some wandering around examining the damage that had been visited on several of the stores, others simply standing and listening to the alarms as if to celestial music. Grillo and Hotchkiss got out of the car, and started across the lot towards the supermarket.

"I smell gasoline," Grillo said.

Hotchkiss concurred. "We should get these people out of here," he said. Raising his voice and his gun he instigated some primitive crowd control. His attempts drew the attention of a small, bald man.

"Hotchkiss, are you in charge?"

"Not if *you* want to be, Marvin."

"Where's Spilmont? There should be somebody in authority. My windows have all been smashed."

"I'm sure the police are on their way," Hotchkiss said.

"Pure vandalism," Marvin went on. "Kids up from L.A., joy-riding."

"I don't think so," said Grillo. The smell of gasoline was making his head spin.

"And who the hell are you?" Marvin demanded, his shouts shrill.

Before Grillo could respond somebody else joined the hollering match.

"There's somebody in there!"

Grillo looked towards the market. His stinging eyes verified the claim. There were indeed figures moving in the murk of the store. He began to walk through the shards towards the window, as one of the figures came clear.

"Tesla?"

She heard him; looked up; shouted.

"Stay away, Grillo!"

"What's going on?"

"Just stay away."

He ignored her advice, climbing in through the hole in the shattered pane. The boy she'd gone to save lay face down and naked to the waist on the tiles. Behind him, a man Grillo knew and didn't know. That is, a face to which he could put no name, but a presence which he instinctively recognized. It took him moments only to work from where. This was one of the escapees from the fissure.

"Hotchkiss," he yelled. "Get in here!"

"Enough's enough," Tesla said. "Don't bring anyone near us."

"*Us?*" said Grillo. "Since when was it us?"

"His name's Fletcher," Tesla said, as if in reply to the first question in Grillo's head. "The boy is Howard Katz." To the third question: "They're father and son." And the fourth? "It's all going to blow, Grillo. And I'm going to stay till it does."

Hotchkiss was at Grillo's side. "Holy shit," he breathed.

"The caves, right?"

"Right."

"Can we take the boy?" Grillo said.

Tesla nodded. "But be quick," she said. "Or it's over for us all." Her gaze had left Grillo's face and was directed out to the lot, or to the night beyond it. Somebody was expected at this party. The other wraith, surely.

Grillo and Hotchkiss took hold of the boy, and hauled him to his feet.

"Wait." Fletcher approached the trio, the smell of gasoline intensifying with his proximity. There was more than fumes off the man, however. Something akin to a mild electric shock passed through Grillo as the man reached to his son, and contact was made through all three systems. His mind momentarily soared, all bodily frailty forgotten, into a space where dreams hung like midnight stars. It was gone all too suddenly, almost brutally, as Fletcher dropped his hand from his son's face. Grillo looked towards Hotchkiss. By the expression on his face he too had shared the brief splendor. His eyes had filled with tears.

"What's going to happen?" Grillo said, looking back at Tesla.

"Fletcher is leaving."

"Why? Where?"

"Nowhere and everywhere," Tesla said.

"How do you know?"

"*Because I told her,*" came Fletcher's response. "*Quiddity must be preserved.*"

He looked at Grillo and the faintest murmur of a smile was on his face.

"*Take my son, gentlemen,*" he said. "*Keep him out of the line of fire.*"

"What?"

"Just go, Grillo," Tesla said. "Whatever happens from here on it's the way he wants it to be."

They took Howie out through the window as instructed, Hotchkiss stepping ahead to receive the boy's body, which was as limp as a fresh cadaver. As Grillo relinquished the boy's weight he heard Tesla speak behind him.

She simply said:

"The Jaff!"

The other escapee, Fletcher's enemy, was standing at the perimeter of the parking lot. The crowd, which had swelled to five or six times its earlier size, had parted, without being overtly requested to do so, leaving a corridor between the enemies. The Jaff had not come alone. Behind him were two Californian perfects Grillo could not name. Hotchkiss could.

"Jo-Beth and Tommy-Ray," he said.

At the name of one, or both, Howie raised his head.

"Where?" he murmured, but his eyes found them before there was time for a reply. "Let me go," he said, struggling to push Hotchkiss off. "They'll kill her if we don't stop them. Don't you see, they'll kill her."

"There's more than your girlfriend at stake," Tesla said, leaving Grillo once again wondering how she'd got to know so much so quickly. Her source, Fletcher, now stepped out of the market, and walked past them all—Tesla, Grillo, Howie and Hotchkiss—to stand at the other end of the human corridor to the Jaff.

It was the Jaff who spoke first:

"*What is all this about?*" he demanded. "*Your antics have woken half the town.*"

"The half you haven't poisoned," Fletcher returned.

"Now don't talk yourself into the grave. Beg a little. Tell me you'll give your balls if I let you live."

"That was never much to me."

"Your balls?"

"Living."

"You had ambition," the Jaff said, starting to walk towards Fletcher very slowly. *"Don't deny it."*

"Not like yours."

"True. I had scope."

"You must not have the Art."

The Jaff raised his hand and rubbed thumb and forefinger together, as though preparing to count money.

"Too late. I feel it in my fingers already," he said.

"All right," Fletcher replied. *"If you want me to beg, I'll beg. Quiddity must be preserved. I beg you not to touch it."*

"You don't get it, do you?" the Jaff said. He had come to a halt some distance from Fletcher. Now the youth came, bringing his sister.

"My flesh," the Jaff said, indicating his children, *"will do anything for me. Isn't that right, Tommy-Ray?"*

The boy grinned.

"Anything."

Intent on the exchange between the two men, Tesla had not noticed Howie slipping free of Hotchkiss until he turned to her and whispered:

"Gun."

She'd brought the weapon out of the market with her. Reluctantly she passed it into Howie's wounded hand.

"He's going to kill her," Howie murmured.

"That's his daughter," Tesla whispered in reply.

"You think he cares?"

Looking back, she saw the boy's point. Whatever changes Fletcher's Great Work (the Nuncio, he'd called it) had wrought in the Jaff they'd taken the man over the brink of sanity. Though she'd had all too short a time drinking down the visions Fletcher had shared with her, and had only a tenuous grasp of the complexities of the Art, Quiddity, Cosm and Metacosm, she knew enough to be sure that such power in this entity's hands would be power for immeasurable evil.

"*You lost, Fletcher,*" the Jaff said. "*You and your child don't have what it takes to be . . . modern.*" He smiled. "*These two, on the other hand, are at the cutting edge. Everything is experiment. Right?*"

Tommy-Ray had his hand on Jo-Beth's shoulder; now it moved down to her breast. Somebody in the crowd began to speak out at this, but was hushed as the Jaff looked in their direction. Jo-Beth pulled away from her brother, but Tommy-Ray was not about to relinquish her. He pulled her back towards him, inclining his head towards hers.

A shot stopped the kiss, the bullet plowing the asphalt at Tommy-Ray's feet.

"Let go of her," Howie said. His voice was not strong, but it carried.

Tommy-Ray did as he was instructed, looking at Howie with mild puzzlement on his face. He slid his knife from his back pocket. The imminence of bloodshed was not lost on the crowd. Some backed away, especially those with children. Most stayed.

Behind Fletcher, Grillo leaned over and whispered to Hotchkiss.

"Could you take him out from here?"

"The kid?"

"No. The Jaff."

"Don't bother to try," Tesla murmured. "It won't stop him."

"What will?"

"Christ knows."

"Going to shoot me down in cold blood in front of all these nice people?" Tommy-Ray said to Howie. "Go on, I dare you. Blow me away. I'm not afraid. I like death and death likes me. Pull the trigger, Katz. If you've got the balls."

As he spoke he slowly walked towards Howie, who was barely keeping himself upright. But he kept the gun pointed at Tommy-Ray.

It was the Jaff who brought the impasse to an end, seizing hold of Jo-Beth. His grip brought a cry. Howie looked towards her, and Tommy-Ray charged him, knife raised. It took only a push from Tommy-Ray to throw Howie down. The gun flew from his hand. Tommy-Ray kicked Howie hard between the legs then threw himself upon his victim.

"Don't kill him!" the Jaff commanded.

He let Jo-Beth go, and advanced towards Fletcher. From the fingers in which he'd claimed he could already feel the Art quickening beads of power oozed like ectoplasm, bursting in the air. He had reached the fighters, and seemed about to intervene, but instead simply cast a glance down at them, as at two brawling dogs, then stepped past them to continue his advance upon Fletcher.

"We'd better back off," Tesla murmured to Grillo and Hotchkiss. "It's out of our hands now."

Proof of that came seconds later, as Fletcher reached into his pocket, and pulled out a book of matches, marked *Marvin's Food and Drug*. What was about to happen could not have been lost on any of the spectators. They'd smelled the gasoline. They knew its source. Now here were the matches. An immolation was imminent. But there were no further retreats. Though none of them comprehended much, if any, of the exchange between the protagonists there were few among the crowd who didn't know in their guts that they were witnessing events of consequence. How could they look away, when for the first time they had a chance of peeking at the gods?

Fletcher opened the book; pulled a match from it. He was in the act of striking when fresh darts of power broke from the Jaff's hand and flew at Fletcher. They struck his fingers like bullets, their violence carrying match and matchbook out of Fletcher's hands.

"Don't waste your time with tricks," the Jaff said. *"You know fire's not going to do me any harm. Nor you, unless you want it to. And if you want extinction then all you have to do is ask."*

This time he took his poison to Fletcher rather than letting it fly from his hand. He approached his enemy, and touched him. A shudder went through Fletcher. With agonizing slowness he turned his head far enough around to be able to see Tesla. In his eyes she saw so much vulnerability; he'd opened himself up to perform whatever endgame he had in mind, and the Jaff's malice had direct access to his essence. The appeal in his expression was unambiguous. A message of chaos was spreading through his system from the Jaff's touch. The only way he sought to be saved from it was death.

She had no matches, but she had Hotchkiss's gun. Without a word she snatched it from his hand. Her motion drew the Jaff's glance, and for a chilling moment she met his mad eyes—saw a phantom head swelling around them; another Jaff in hiding behind the first.

Then she aimed the gun at the ground behind Fletcher, and fired. There was no spark, as she'd hoped there'd be. She aimed again, emptying her head of all thoughts but the will for ignition. She'd made fires before. On the page, to catch the mind. Now one for the flesh.

She exhaled slowly through her mouth, the way she did when she first sat down at her typewriter in the morning, and pulled the trigger.

It seemed she saw the fire coming before it actually ignited. Like a bright storm; the spark the lightning that ran before. The air around Fletcher turned yellow. Then it sprang into flame.

The heat was sudden, and intense. She dropped the gun and ran to where she could better see what followed. Fletcher caught her gaze through the blistering conflagration, and there was a sweetness in his expression that she'd carry through the adventures the future had planned for her as a reminder of how little she understood the workings of the world. That a man might enjoy to burn; might profit by it, might come to fruition in fire, that was a lesson no schoolmarm had come close to teaching. But here was the fact, made true by her own hand.

Beyond the fire she saw the Jaff stepping away with a shrug of ridicule. The fire had caught his fingers, where they'd touched Fletcher. It blew them out, like five candles. Behind him, Howie and Tommy-Ray were backing off before the heat, their hatred postponed. These sights held her only a beat, however, before she returned to the spectacle of the burning Fletcher. Even in that brief time his status had changed. The fire, which raged around him like a pillar, was not consuming him but *transforming*, the process throwing out flashes of bright matter.

The Jaff's response to these lights—which was to retreat like a rabid dog before thrown water—gave her a clue to their nature. They were to Fletcher what the beads that had snatched the matches were to the Jaff: some essential power released. The Jaff hated them. Their brightness made the face behind his face come clear. The sight of it, and of the miraculous change in Fletcher, drew her closer to the fire than was safe. She could smell her hair singeing. But she was too intrigued to be driven back. This was her doing, after all. She was the creator. Like the first ape to nurture a flame, and so transform the tribe.

That, she understood, was Fletcher's hope: the transformation of the tribe. This was not simply spectacle. The burning motes coming off Fletcher's body had their progenitor's intention in them. They went out from the column like bright seeds, weaving through the air in search of fertile ground. The Grovers were that ground, and the fireflies found them waiting. What struck her as miraculous was that nobody fled. Perhaps the previous violence had frightened off the weakhearted. The rest were game for the magic, some actually breaking rank and walking to greet the lights, like communicants to an altar rail. Children went first, snatching at the motes, proving them innocent of harm. The light broke against their open hands, or against their welcoming faces, the fire echoed momentarily in their eyes. The parents of these adventurers were next to be touched. Some, having been struck, called back to their spouses: "It's OK. It doesn't hurt. It's just . . . light!"

It was more than that, Tesla knew. It was Fletcher. And in giving himself away in this fashion his physical self was gradually deteriorating. Already his chest, hands and groin had all but disappeared, his head and neck attached to his shoulders and his shoulders to his lower torso by strands of dusty matter that were prey to every whim of the flames. As she watched they too broke, and went to become light. Watching, a childhood hymn tripped into her head. Her mind sang *Jesus wants me for a sunbeam*. An old song for a new age.

The opening act of that age was already coming to a conclusion. Fletcher's self was almost used up, his face eaten away at the eyes and the mouth, the skull fragmenting, his brain melted to brightness and being blown from its pan like a dandelion head in an August wind.

With its going the pieces of Fletcher that remained simply vanished in the fire. Bereft of fuel, the flame went out. There was no dwindling; no ashes; not even smoke. One moment brightness, heat and wonders. The next, nothing.

She had been watching Fletcher too closely to count how many of the witnesses had been touched by his light. Many, certainly. Possibly all. Perhaps it was their sheer numbers that prevented the Jaff from any attempt at reprisal. He had an army waiting in the night, after all. But he chose not to summon it. Instead, with the minimum of show, he left. Tommy-Ray went with him. Jo-Beth did not. Howie had positioned himself beside her during Fletcher's dissolution, gun in hand. All Tommy-Ray could do was offer a few barely coherent threats, then follow in his father's footsteps.

That, in essence, was the Shaman Fletcher's last performance. There would be repercussions of course, but not until the recipients of his light had slept on their gift for a few hours. There were some more immediate consequences. For Grillo and Hotchkiss the satisfaction of knowing their senses hadn't deceived them at the caves; for Jo-Beth and Howie, reunion after events that had brought them close to death; and for Tesla, the knowledge that with Fletcher's going a great weight of responsibility had passed to her.

It was the Grove itself, however, which had borne the brunt of the night's magic. Its streets had seen horrors. Its citizens had been touched by spirits.

Soon, war.

PART FIVE

SLAVES AND LOVERS

ONE

I

Any alcoholic would have recognized the behavior of the Grove the following morning. It was that of a man who'd been on a bender the night before and had to get up early the day after and pretend that nothing untoward had happened. He'd stand under a cold shower for a few minutes to shock his system into wakefulness, breakfast on Alka-Seltzer and black coffee, then step out into the day with a gait more purposeful than usual, and the permafrost smile of an actress who'd just lost an Oscar. There were more hellos and how-are-yous? that morning, more neighbors waving cheerily to each other as they backed out their cars, more radios playing weather reports (sun! sun! sun!) through windows thrown wide to prove that there were no secrets in *this* house. To a stranger, coming to the Grove that morning for the first time, it would have seemed as though the town were auditioning for Perfectsville, USA. The general air of enforced bonhomie would have curdled his stomach.

Down at the Mall, where the evidence of a Dionysian night could scarcely be ignored, the talk was of anything but the truth. Hell's Angels had ridden in from L.A., one story went, their sole purpose to wreak havoc. The explanation gained credibility with repetition.

Some claimed to have heard the bikes. A few even decided to have seen them, embroidering the collective fiction knowing nobody would raise a doubting voice. By mid-morning the glass had been entirely swept away, and boards nailed up over the smashed panes. By noon, fresh windows had been ordered. By two, they were in. Not since the days of the League of Virgins had the Grove been so single-minded in its pursuit of equilibrium; nor so hypocritical. For behind closed doors, in bathrooms and bedrooms and dens, it was a different story entirely. Here the smiles dropped, and the intent gait gave way to nervous pacing, and weeping, and the swallowing of pills searched for with the passion of gold-diggers. Here people confessed to themselves—not even to their partners or their dogs—that something was awry today and would never be quite right again. Here people tried to remember tales they'd been told as children—the old, fanciful stories adulthood had all but shamed from their memories—in the hope of countering their present fears. Some tried to drink away their anxiety. Some took to eating. Some contemplated the priesthood.

It was, all in all, a damn strange day.

Less strange, perhaps, for those who had hard facts to juggle, however much those facts flew in the face of what yesterday would have passed for reality. For these few, blessed now with the certain knowledge that there were monsters and divinities loosed in the Grove, the question was not: is it true? Rather: what does it mean?

For William Witt, the answer was a shrug of surrender. He had no way to comprehend the horrors he'd been terrorized by at the house in Wild Cherry Glade. His subsequent conversation with Spilmont, dismissing his story as fabrication, had made him paranoid. Either there was a conspiracy afoot to keep the Jaff's machinations secret, or else he, William Witt, was losing his mind. Nor were these memories mutually exclusive, which was doubly chilling. In the face of such bitter blasts he'd kept himself locked up at home, with the exception of his brief trip down to the Mall the previous night. He'd been a late attender, and today he remembered very little of it, but he did recall getting home and the night of video Babylon that followed. Usually he was quite sparing with his porno sessions, preferring to select one or two films to view rather than pig out on a dozen. But last night's viewing had turned into a binge. When the Robinsons next door were taking their kids off to the playground the following morning he was still sitting in front of the television, the blinds drawn, the beer cans a small city at his feet, watching and watching. He had his collection organized with the precision of a master librarian, referenced and cross-referenced. He knew the stars of these sweaty epics by all their aliases; he knew their breast and cock sizes; their early histories; their specialities. He had the narratives, crude as they were, by heart; his favorite scenes memorized down to each grunt and spurt.

But today the parade did not arouse him. He went from film to film like an addict among pillaged peddlers, looking for a fix no one could supply, until the videos were piled high around his television. Two-ways, three-ways, oral, anal, golden showers, bondage, discipline, lesbian scenes, dildo scenes, rape and romance scenes—he went through them all but none provided the release he needed. His search became a kind of pursuit of himself. What will rouse me will *be* me, was his half-finished thought.

It was a desperate situation. This was the first time in his life— excluding events with the League—that voyeurism had failed to excite. The first time he wanted the performers sharing his reality as he shared theirs. He'd always been happy to turn them off when he'd shot his wad; even been faintly contemptuous of their charms once their hold on him had been mopped up. Now he mourned them, like lovers he'd lost without ever knowing them properly, whose every orifice he'd sight of, but whose intimacy was denied him.

Yet, some time after dawn, his spirits as low as he'd known them, the strangest thought occurred: that perhaps he *could* bring them to him; by the sheer heat of his desire foment them into being. Dreams could be made real. Artists did it all the time, and didn't everyone have a little art in them? It was that thought, barely formed, that kept him watching the screen, through *The Last Lays of Pompeii* and *Born to Be Made* and *Secrets of a Women's Prison*; films he knew as well as his own history, but which, unlike his history, might yet live in the present tense.

———

He was not the only Grover visited by such thoughts, though none were as fixated on the erotic as William. The same idea—that some precious, essential person, or persons, might be called up from the mind and made a boon companion—occurred to every member of the crowd that had gathered in the Mall the evening before. Soap-opera stars, game-show hosts, dead or lost relations, divorced spouses, missing children, comic-book characters: there were as many names as there were minds to summon them.

For some, like William Witt, the face of their desire gathered momentum at such speed (fuelled in several cases by obsession, in others by longing or envy) that by dawn the following day there were already clots in corners of their rooms where the air had thickened in preparation for the miracle.

In the bedroom of Shuna Melkin, who was the daughter of Chris-tine and Larry Melkin, a fabled rock princess—dead of an overdose several years past but Shuna Melkin's sole and obsessive idol, was mak-ing herself known with croonings so subtle it could have passed for the breeze in the eaves but that Shuna knew the tune.

In Ossie Larton's loft there were scratchings he knew with an inward smile were the birth pangs of the werewolf he'd kept secret company with since he'd first known that such creatures were imagin-able. His name was Eugene, this werewolf, which—at the tender age of six, when Ossie had first created his companion—had seemed an appropriate name for a man who grew fur under the full moon.

For Karen Conroy the three leads of her favorite movie, *Love Knows Your Name*, a little-seen romance she'd wept through six days running during a long-past trip to Paris, could be sensed as a delicate European perfume in the lounge.

And so on, and so forth.

By noon that day there wasn't any one of the crowd who hadn't had an intimation—many of which were dismissed or ignored of course—that they had unexpected visitors. The population of Palomo Grove, which had swelled by a hundred horrors at the Jaff's summons, was about to swell again.

II

Y ou've already admitted you don't really understand what happened last night—"

"It's not a question of admitting anything, Grillo."

"OK. Let's not get mad at each other. Why do we always end up shouting?"

"We're not shouting."

"OK. We're not shouting. All I'm saying is, please consider the possibility that this errand he's sending you on—"

"*Errand?*"

"*Now* you're shouting. I'm just saying, *think* a minute. This could be the last trip you ever make."

"Possibility accepted."

"So let me come with you. You've never been south of Tijuana."

"Neither have you."

"It's rough—"

"Listen, I've pitched art movies to men perplexed by *Dumbo*. I know rough. If you want to do something really useful, stay here and get well."

"I'm well already. I never felt better."

"I need you here, Grillo. *Watching*. It's not over, by a long way."

"What am I supposed to be watching for?" Grillo asked, conceding the argument by no longer pursuing it.

"You've always had an eye for the hidden agenda. When the Jaff makes his move, however quietly, you'll know it. By the way, did you see Ellen last night? She was in the crowd, with her kid. You might start by seeing how *she* feels the morning after . . ."

It wasn't that Grillo's fears for her safety weren't legitimate, nor indeed that she wouldn't have taken pleasure in his company on the journey ahead. But for reasons she could find no gentle way of stating, and so didn't state at all, his presence would be an intrusion she had no right to risk, either for his good or for the good of the task ahead. It had been one

of Fletcher's last acts to choose her to go to the Mission; he'd even indi-
cated that it had somehow been preordained. Not so long ago she'd have
dismissed such mysticism; but after last night she was obliged to be more
open-minded. The world of mysteries she'd made light of in her spook
and spaceship screenplays was not to be so easily mocked. It had come
looking for her, found her, and pitched her—cynicism and all—among
its heavens and its hells. The latter in the shape of the Jaff's army, the former's presence in Fletcher's transformation: flesh to light.

Charged with being the dead man's agent on earth she felt a curious relaxation, despite the jeopardy that lay ahead. She no longer had
to keep her cynicism polished; no longer had to divide her imaginings
from moment to moment into the real (solid, sensible) and the fanciful (vaporous, valueless). If *(when)* she got back to her typewriter she'd
begin these tongue-in-cheek screenplays over from the top, telling
them with faith in the tale, not because every fantasy was absolutely
true but because no reality ever was.

Mid-morning she left the Grove, choosing a route that took her out
of the town past the Mall, where the status quo was well on its way to
being restored. With speed she'd be over the border by nightfall; and
at the Misión de Santa Catrina, or—if Fletcher's hope was well
founded—on the empty ground where it had stood, before dawn.

On his father's instructions Tommy-Ray had crept back to the Mall
the previous night, long after the crowd had dispersed. The police had
arrived by that point but he had no difficulty in achieving his purpose,
which was the retrieval of the terata which he had attached with his
own hands to Katz's flesh. The Jaff had other reasons for wanting the
creature back than keeping it from being found by the police. It was
not dead, and once returned to the hands of its creator it regurgitated
all it had seen and heard, the Jaff laying his hands on the beast like a
faith-healer and drawing the report from the terata's system.

When he'd heard what he needed to hear, he killed the messenger.

"Well now . . ." he said to Tommy-Ray, ". . . it seems you'll have the
journey I told you about sooner than I planned."

"What about Jo-Beth? That bastard Katz has got her."

"*We wasted effort last night trying to persuade her to join our family. She rejected us. We'll waste no more time. Let her take her chance in the maelstrom.*"

"But . . ."

"*No more on this,*" the Jaff said. "*Your obsession with her really is ludicrous. And don't sulk! You've been indulged for too long. You think that smile of yours can get you whatever you want. Well it won't get you her.*"

"You're wrong. And I'll prove it."

"*Not now you won't. You've got some travelling to do.*"

"First, Jo-Beth," Tommy-Ray said, and made to move away from his father. But the Jaff's hand was on his shoulder before he'd moved more than a step. His touch made Tommy-Ray yelp.

"*Shut the fuck up!*"

"You're hurting me!"

"*I meant to!*"

"No . . . I mean *really* hurting. Stop it."

"*You're the one death loves, right, son?*"

Tommy-Ray could feel his legs start to give out beneath him. He began to leak from dick, nose and eyes.

"*I don't think you're half the man you say you are,*" the Jaff told him. "*Not half.*"

"I'm sorry . . . don't hurt me any more, please . . ."

"*I don't think men sniff after their sisters all the time. They find other women. And they don't talk about death like it was easy stuff then snivel if they start to hurt a little.*"

"OK! OK! I get the point! Just stop, will you? *Stop!*"

The Jaff released him. He fell to the ground.

"*It's been a bad night for us both,*" his father said. "*We've both had something taken from us . . . you, your sister . . . me, the satisfaction of destroying Fletcher. But there are fine times ahead. Trust me.*"

He reached down to pick Tommy-Ray up. The boy flinched, seeing the fingers at his shoulder. But this time the contact proved benign; even soothing.

"*There's a place I want you to go for me,*" the Jaff said. "*It's called the Misión de Santa Catrina . . .*"

TWO

Howie hadn't realized until Fletcher had gone out of his life just how many questions he had left unanswered; problems only his father might have helped him solve. They didn't vex him through the night. He slept too soundly. It was only the next morning that he began to regret his refusal to learn from Fletcher. The only solution available to Jo-Beth and himself was to try to piece the story in which they clearly played such a vital role together from clues, and from the testimony of Jo-Beth's mother.

The previous night's invasion had brought about a change in Joyce McGuire. After years of attempting to hold the evil that had entered her house at bay, her failure, in the end, to do so had somehow freed her. The worst had happened: what more was there to fear? She had seen her personal hell created in front of her, and survived. God's agency—in the form of the Pastor—had been valueless. It had been Howie who had gone out in search of her daughter, and finally—both of them ragged, and bloodied—brought her back. She'd welcomed him into the house; even insisted he stay the night. The following morning she went about the house with the air of a woman who had been told a tumor in her body was benign, and she could expect a few more years of life.

When, in the early afternoon, all three of them sat down to talk, it took a little time to persuade her to unburden herself of the past, but the stories came, one by one. Sometimes, especially when she talked about Arleen, Carolyn and Trudi, she cried as she talked, but as the events she was describing became more tragic she told them more and more dispassionately. On occasion she'd go back to offer details she'd missed, or to praise somebody who'd helped her through the difficult years, when she was bringing up Jo-Beth and Tommy-Ray alone knowing she was talked about as the hussy who'd survived.

"The number of times I thought about leaving the Grove," she said. "Like Trudi."

"I don't think it saved her any pain," Howie said. "She was always unhappy."

"I remember her a different way. Always in love with somebody or other."

"Do you know . . . who she was in love with before she had me?"

"Are you asking me do I know who your father is?"

"Yes."

"I have a good idea. Your middle name was his first. Ralph Contreras. He was a gardener at the Lutheran Church. He used to watch us when we came home from school. Every day. Your mother was very pretty, you know. Not in a movie-star kind of way, like Arleen, but with dark eyes . . . you've got her eyes . . . a sort of liquid look in them. I think she was always the one Ralph loved. Not that he said very much. He had a terrible stammer."

Howie smiled at this.

"Then it *was* him. I inherited that."

"I don't hear it."

"I know, it's strange. It's gone. It's almost like meeting Fletcher took it out of me. Tell me, does Ralph still live in the Grove?"

"No. He left before you were even born. He probably thought there'd be a lynch-mob out after him. Your mother was a middle-class white girl, and he . . ."

She stopped, seeing the look on Howie's face.

"He?" Howie said.

"—was Hispanic."

Howie nodded. "You learn something new every day, right?" he said, playing lightly what clearly went deep.

"Anyway, that's why he left," Joyce went on. "If your mother had ever named him I'm sure he'd have been accused of rape. Which it wasn't. We were *driven*, all of us, by whatever the Devil had put inside us."

"It wasn't the Devil, Momma," Jo-Beth said.

"So you say," she replied, with a sigh. The energy suddenly seemed to go out of her, as the old vocabulary took its toll. "And maybe you're right. But I'm too old to change the way I think."

"Too old?" said Howie. "What are you talking about? What you did last night was extraordinary."

Joyce reached across and touched Howie's cheek. "You must leave me to believe what I believe. It's only words, Howard. The Jaff to you. The Devil to me."

"So what does that make Tommy-Ray and me, Momma?" Jo-Beth said. "The Jaff made us."

"I've wondered about that often," Joyce said. "When you were very young I used to watch you both all the time, waiting for the bad in you to show. It has in Tommy-Ray. His maker's taken him. Maybe my prayers have saved you, Jo-Beth. You went to church with me. You studied. You trusted in the Lord."

"So you think Tommy-Ray's lost?" Jo-Beth asked.

Momma didn't answer for a moment, though not, it was clear when the answer came, because she felt ambiguous on the subject.

"Yes," she said finally. "He's gone."

"I don't believe that," Jo-Beth said.

"Even after what he was up to last night?" Howie put in.

"He doesn't know what he's doing. The Jaff's controlling him, Howie. I know him better than a brother—"

"Meaning?"

"He's my twin. I feel what he feels."

"There's evil in him," Momma said.

"Then there's evil in me too," Jo-Beth replied. She stood up.

"Three days ago you loved him. Now you say he's gone. You've let the Jaff have him. I won't give up on him that way." So saying, she left the room.

"Maybe she's right," Joyce said softly.

"Tommy-Ray can be saved?" Howie said.

"No. Maybe the Devil's in her too."

Howie found Jo-Beth in the yard, face up to the sky, eyes closed. She glanced around at him.

"You think Momma's right," she said. "Tommy-Ray's beyond help."

"No, I don't. Not if you believe we can get to him. Bring him back."

"Don't just say that to please me, Howie. If you're not on my side in this I want you to tell me."

He put his hand on her shoulder. "Listen," he said, "if I'd believed what your mother said then I wouldn't have come back, would I? This is *me* remember? Mister Persistence. If you think we can break the Jaff's hold on Tommy-Ray then we'll damn well do it. Just don't ask me to like him."

She turned round fully, brushing her hair, which the breeze had caught, from her face.

"I never thought I'd be standing in your momma's backyard with my arms around you," Howie said.

"Miracles happen."

"No they don't," he said. "They're *made*. You're one, and I'm one, and the sun's one, and the three of us being out here together is the biggest of the lot."

THREE

Grillo's first call, after Tesla's departure, was to Abernethy. Whether to tell or not to tell was only one of the dilemmas with which he was presented. Now more than ever the real problem was *how*. He'd never had the instincts of a novelist. In his writing he'd sought a style that set the facts out as plainly as possible. No fancy footwork; no flights of vocabulary. His mentor in this was not a journalist at all but Jonathan Swift, author of *Gulliver's Travels*, a man so concerned to communicate his satire with clarity that he'd reputedly read his works aloud to his servants to be certain his style did not confound his substance. Grillo kept that story as a touchstone. All of which was fine when reporting on the homeless in Los Angeles, or on the drug problem. The facts were plain enough.

But this story—from the caves to Fletcher's immolation—posed a knottier problem. How could he report what he'd seen last night without also reporting how it had *felt*?

He kept his exchange with Abernethy oblique. It was useless to try to pretend nothing at all had happened in the Grove the night before. Reports of the vandalism—though not a major story—had already been carried on all the local newscasts. Abernethy was on to it.

"Were you there, Grillo?"

"Afterwards. Only afterwards. I heard the alarms and—"

"And?"

"There's not much to report. There were some windows broken."

"Hell's Angels on the rampage."

"Is that what you heard?"

"Is that what I heard? You're supposed to be the fucking reporter, Grillo, not me. What do you need? Drugs? Drink? A visit from the fucking Mude?"

"That's Muse."

"Mude, Muse; who the fuck cares? Just get me a story the people want to read. There must have been injuries—"

"I don't think so."

"Then invent some."

"I do have something . . ."

"What? *What?*"

"A story nobody's reported yet, I'll bet."

"It better be good, Grillo. Your job's on the fucking line here."

"There's going to be a shindig up at Vance's house. To celebrate his passing."

"OK. So you get inside the place. I want the works on him and his friends. The man was a no-good. No-goods have no-good friends. I want names and details."

"Sometimes you sound like you saw too many movies, Abernethy."

"Meaning what?"

"Skip it."

The image lingered, long after Grillo had put down the phone, of Abernethy sitting up nights rehearsing lines from newspaper epics, refining his performance as a hard-pressed, hard-bitten editor. He wasn't the only one, Grillo thought. Everyone had a movie playing somewhere at the back of their heads in which they were the name above the title. Ellen was the wronged woman, with terrible secrets to keep. Tesla was the wild woman of West Hollywood, loose in a world she never made. Which line of thought invited the obvious question: what was he? Cub reporter on a hit scoop? Man of integrity, dogged by crimes against a corrupt system? Neither part suited him the way they might have done when he'd first arrived, hot foot from his hovel, to report the Buddy Vance story. Events had somehow marginalized him. Others, Tesla in particular, had taken the starring roles.

As he checked his appearance in the mirror he mused on what it meant to be a star without a firmament. Free to take up another profession perhaps? Rocket scientist; juggler; lover. How about lover? How about the lover of Ellen Nguyen? That had a nice ring.

She was a long time coming to the door, and when she arrived it seemed she took several seconds to even recognize Grillo. Just as he was about to prompt her a smile surfaced, and she said:

"Please . . . come in. Are you recovered from the flu?"

"A little shaky."

"I think maybe I'm catching it too . . ." she said as she closed the door. "I woke feeling . . . I don't know . . ."

The curtains were still drawn. The place looked even smaller than Grillo remembered it.

"You'd like coffee," she said.

"Sure. Thanks."

She disappeared through to the kitchen, leaving Grillo abandoned in the middle of a room in which every article of furniture was piled high with magazines, or toys, or unsorted washing. Only as he moved to clear a space for himself did he realize he had an audience. Philip was standing at the head of the passage that led to his bedroom. His outing to the Mall the evening before had been premature. He still looked frail.

"Hi," Grillo said. "How you doin'?"

Surprisingly, the boy smiled; a lavish, open smile.

"Did you see?" he said.

"See what?"

"At the Mall," Philip went on. "You *did* see. I know you did. The beautiful lights."

"Yes, I saw them."

"I told the Balloon Man all about it. That's how I know I wasn't dreaming."

He crossed to Grillo, still smiling.

"I got your drawing," Grillo said. "Thank you."

"Don't need them now," Philip said.

"Why's that?"

"Philip?" Ellen had returned with coffee. "Don't bother Mr. Grillo."

"It's no bother," Grillo said. He returned his gaze to Philip. "Maybe we can talk about Balloon Man later," he said.

"Maybe," the boy replied, as though this would be entirely dependent upon Grillo's good behavior. "I'm going now," he announced to his mother.

"Sure, sweetie."

"Shall I tell him hello?" Philip asked Grillo.

"Please," Grillo replied, not certain of what the boy meant, "I'd like that."

Satisfied, Philip made his way back to his bedroom.

Ellen was busying herself clearing a place for them to sit. With her back to Grillo she bent to her work. The plain kimono-style dressing gown she wore clung. Her buttocks were heavy for a woman of her height. When she turned back the sash of the gown had loosened. The folds fell away at her breastbone. Her skin was dark, and smooth. She caught his appreciation as she handed him his coffee, but made no attempt to tie the gown more tightly. The gap tempted Grillo's eye every time she moved.

"I'm glad you came around," she said once they were seated. "I was concerned when your friend—"

"Tesla."

"Tesla. When Tesla told me you were ill. I felt responsible." She took a sip of coffee. She made a sharp backward motion when it touched her tongue. "Hot," she said.

"Philip was telling me you were down at the Mall last night."

"So were you," she replied. "Do you know if anybody was hurt? All that broken glass."

"Only Fletcher," Grillo replied.

"I don't believe I know him."

"The man who burned up."

"Somebody got burned?" she said. "Oh God, that's horrible."

"Surely you saw it."

"No," she replied. "We just saw the glass."

"And the lights. Philip was talking about the lights."

"Yes," she said, plainly puzzled. "He said the same to me. You know I don't remember any of that. Is it important?"

"What's important is that you're both well," he said, using the platitude to cover his confusion.

"Oh we're fine," she said, looking directly at him, her face suddenly cleansed of its bafflement. "I'm tired, but I'm fine."

She reached across to put the coffee cup down and this time the robe fell open enough for Grillo to catch sight of her breasts. He didn't have the slightest doubt that she knew exactly what she was doing.

"Have you heard any more from the house?" he asked, taking undeniable satisfaction from talking business while thinking sex.

"I'm supposed to go up there," Ellen said.

"When is the party?"

"Tomorrow. It's short notice, but I think a lot of Buddy's friends were expecting some kind of farewell celebration."

"I'd like to get in on the party."

"You want to report?"

"Of course. It's going to be quite a gathering, right?"

"I think so."

"But that's just part of it. We both know there's something extraordinary happening in the Grove. Last night, it wasn't simply the Mall . . ."

He trailed off, seeing that her expression, upon mention of the previous evening, had once again become distracted. Was this self-induced amnesia, or part of the natural process of Fletcher's magic? The former, he suspected. Philip, less resistant to changes in the status quo, had no such memory problems. When Grillo turned the conversation back to the party her attention was once more upon him.

"Do you think you could get me in?" he asked.

"You'll have to be careful. Rochelle knows what you look like."

"Can't you invite me officially? As press?"

She shook her head. "There won't *be* any press," she explained. "It's a strictly private gathering. Not all of Buddy's associates are gluttons for publicity. Some of them had too much of it too soon. Some of them would prefer never to have it. He mixed with a lot of men . . . what did he call them? . . . heavy-duty players. I think, Mafia probably."

"All the more reason I should be there," Grillo said.

"Well, I'll do what I can, especially after you getting sick on my account. I guess if there's sufficient guests you could melt into the crowd . . ."

"I'd appreciate the help."

"More coffee?"

"No, thanks." He glanced at his watch, though didn't register the time.

"You're not going to go," she said. It was not a question, but a statement. The same was true of his response.

"No. Not if you'd prefer I stay."

Without another word she reached and touched his breastbone through his shirt.

"I'd prefer you stay," she said.

He instinctively looked towards Philip's room.

"Don't worry," she said. "He'll play for hours." She looped her finger between the buttons of Grillo's shirt. "Come to bed with me," she said.

She got up and led the way through to her bedroom. By contrast with the clutter outside, the room was spartan. She crossed to the window and half closed the blinds, which lent the whole room a parchment tint, then sat down on the bed and looked up at him. He leaned down and kissed her face, slipping his hand inside her robe and lightly rubbing her breast. She pressed his hand to her, insisting on severer treatment. Then she pulled him down on top of her. Their comparative heights meant his chin rested on the top of her head, but she turned this to erotic advantage, pulling his shirt open and licking at his chest, her tongue leaving wet trails from nipple to nipple. All the while her hold on his hand didn't relax for an instant. Her nails dug into his skin with painful force. He fought her, dragging his hand away to reach for the sash of her robe but her hand was there before him. He rolled off her, and was about to sit up to undress, but she took hold of his shirt, this grip as fierce as its predecessor, and kept him at her side, her face at his shoulder, while she untied the loose knot of the sash one-handed, then threw the robe open. She was naked underneath. Doubly naked in fact. Her groin was completely shaved.

Now she turned her face away, and closed her eyes. One hand still gripping his shirt, the other limp at her side she seemed to be offering her body to him as a plate to be dined from. He put his hand on her stomach, running his palm down towards her cunt, pressing hard on skin that looked and felt almost burnished.

Without opening her eyes she murmured:

"Anything you want."

The invitation momentarily flummoxed him. He was used to this being a contract between partners, but here was this woman waving such niceties away, offering him total command of her body. It made him uneasy. As an adolescent her passivity would have seemed unbearably erotic. Now it shocked his liberal sensibilities. He said her name, hoping for some sign from her, but she ignored him. It wasn't until he once again sat up to pull off his shirt that she opened her eyes and said:

"No. Like this, Grillo. Like this."

The expression both on her face and in her voice was like rage, and it unearthed in him a hunger to respond in kind. He rolled on top of her, taking her head in his hands and pushing his tongue into her mouth. Her body pressed up from the mattress, rubbing so hard against him he was sure there was as much pain as pleasure in it for her.

In the room they'd vacated the coffee cups trembled as though the mildest quake were underway. Dust crept across the table, disturbed by the motion of an almost invisible something which slid its wasted shoulders from the gloomiest corner of the room and drifted rather than walked towards the bedroom door. Its form, though rudimentary, was still too recognizable to be dismissed as mere shadow, yet there was too little of it to deserve the name ghost. Whatever it had been, or was to become, even in its present condition it had purpose. Drawn by the woman who was presently dreaming it into being, it approached the bedroom. There—denied access—it mourned against the door, awaiting instructions.

Philip emerged from his sanctum and wandered through to the kitchen in search of food. He opened the cookie jar, dug for chocolate chip, and headed back the way he'd come, a cookie in his left hand for himself, and three in his right for his companion whose first words had been:

"I'm hungry."

Grillo raised his head from Ellen's wet face. She opened her eyes.

"What is it?" she said.

"There's somebody outside the door."

She raised her head from the bed and bit on his chin. It hurt, and he winced.

"Don't do that," he said.

She bit harder.

"*Ellen . . .*"

"So bite back," she said. He didn't have time to curb his bemused look. Catching it, she said: "I mean it, Grillo," and hooked her finger into his mouth, the ball of her hand locked against his chin. "Open," she said. "I want you to hurt me. Don't be afraid. It's what I want. I'm not fragile. I'm not going to break."

He shook her hold off.

"Do it," she said. "*Please,* do it."

"You want that?"

"How many times, Grillo? *Yes.*"

Her dislodged hand had gone to the back of his head. He let her draw his face back down to hers and began to nibble at her lips and then her neck, testing her resistance. There was none. Instead, moans that became louder the harder he bit. Her response drowned all misgivings. He began to work down her neck to her breasts, her moans becoming steadily louder, his name breathed between, urging him on.

Her skin began to redden, not just with bite-marks, but with arousal. Sweat broke out on her suddenly. He put his hand down between her legs, his other hand holding her arms above her head. Her cunt was wet, and took his fingers readily. He'd begun to pant with the exertion of holding her down, his shirt sticky on his back. Uncomfortable as he was, the scenario aroused him: her body utterly vulnerable, his closed up behind zipper and buttons. His cock hurt, hard at the wrong angle, but the ache only made him harder, hardness and ache feeding on each other as he fed on her, and on her insistence that he hurt her better, open her wider. Her cunt was hot around his straight fingers, her breasts covered with the twin crescents his teeth had left. Her nipples stood like arrow-heads. He sucked them in; chewed on them. Her moans became sobbing cries, her legs convulsing beneath him, almost throwing them both off the bed. When he relaxed his hold for an instant her hand took his and drove his fingers still deeper into her.

"*Don't stop,*" she said.

He took up the rhythm she'd set, and doubled it, which had her pushing her hips against his hand to have his fingers inside her to the knuckles. His sweat dropped off his face on to hers as he watched her. Eyes clenched closed she raised her head and licked his forehead and around his mouth, leaving him unkissed but gummy with her saliva.

At last, he felt her entire body stiffen, and she arrested the motion of his hand, her breath coming short and shallow. Then her grip on him—which had drawn blood—relaxed. Her head dropped back. She was suddenly as limp as she'd been when she'd first lain down and exposed herself to him. He rolled off her, his heartbeat playing squash against the walls of his chest and skull.

They lay for a time out of time. He could not have said whether it was seconds or minutes. It was she who made the first move, sitting up and pulling her robe around her. The movement made him open his eyes.

She was tying the sash, pulling the front of her robe together almost primly. He watched her start towards the door.

"Wait," he said. This was unfinished business.

"Next time," she replied.

"What?"

"You heard," came the response. It had the tone of a command. "Next time."

He got up from the bed, aware that his arousal probably seemed ridiculous to her now, but infuriated by her lack of reciprocity. She watched his approach with a half-smile on her face.

"That's just the start," she said to him. She rubbed at the places on her neck where he'd bitten her.

"And what am I supposed to do?" Grillo asked.

She opened the door. Cooler air brushed against his face.

"Lick your fingers," she said.

Only now did he remember the sound he'd heard, and half-expected to see Philip retreating from his spyhole. But there was only the air, drying the spittle on his face to a fine, taut mask.

"Coffee?" she said. She didn't wait for an answer, but headed to the kitchen. Grillo stood and watched her go. His body, weakened by his sickness, had begun to respond to the adrenaline pumped around it. His extremities trembled, as though from the marrow outwards.

He listened to the sound of the coffee-making: water running, cups being rinsed. Without thinking he put his fingers, which smelled strongly of her sex, to his nose and lips.

FOUR

Jokemeister Lamar got out of the limo at the front of Buddy Vance's house and tried to wipe the smile off his face. It was difficult for him at the best of times, but now—at the worst, with his old partner dead and so many harsh words never healed between them—it was virtually impossible. For every action there was a reaction, and Lamar's reaction to death was a grin.

He'd read once about the origins of the smile. Some anthropologist had theorized that it was a sophisticated form of the ape's response to those unwanted in the tribe: the weak or unstable. In essence it said: *You're a liability. Get out of here!* From that exiling leer had evolved laughter, which was the baring of teeth to a professional idiot. It too announced contempt, at root. It too proclaimed the object of mirth a liability: one to be kept at bay with grimaces.

Lamar didn't know how the theory stood up to analysis, but he'd been in comedy long enough to believe it plausible. Like Buddy he'd made a fortune acting the fool. The essential difference, in his opinion (and that of many of their mutual friends), was that Buddy had *been* a fool. Which wasn't to say he didn't mourn the man; he did. For fourteen years they'd been lords of all they'd convulsed, a shared success which left Lamar feeling the poorer for his ex-partner's death despite the breach that had opened between them.

That breach had meant Lamar had met the sumptuous Rochelle once only, and that by accident, at a charity dinner in which he and his wife Tammy had been seated at an adjacent table to Buddy and his bride of the year. That description was one he'd used—to gales of laughter—on several talk shows. At the dinner he'd taken the opportunity of putting one over on Buddy by insinuating himself with Rochelle while the groom was emptying his bladder of champagne. It had been a brief meeting—Lamar had returned to his table as soon as he saw that Buddy had seen him—but must have made some impression because Rochelle had called personally to invite him up to Coney Eye for the party. He had persuaded Tammy that she'd be bored by the shindig and arrived a day early to have some time with the widow.

"You look wonderful," he told her as he stepped over Buddy's threshold.

"It could be worse," she said, a reply which didn't mean that much until, an hour later, she told him that the party thrown in Buddy's honor had been suggested by the man himself.

"You mean he knew he was going to die?" Lamar said.

"No. I mean he came back to me."

Had he been drinking he might well have done the old choking and spraying routine, but he was glad he hadn't when he realized she was deadly serious.

"You mean . . . his *spirit?*" he said.

"I suppose that's the word. I don't really know. I don't have any religion, so I don't quite know how to explain it."

"You're wearing a crucifix," Lamar observed.

"It belonged to my mother. I never put it on before."

"Why now? Are you afraid of something?"

She sipped at the vodka she'd poured. It was early for cocktails, but she needed its comfort.

"Maybe, a little," she said.

"Where's Buddy now?" Lamar asked, impressed by his ability to keep a straight face. "I mean . . . is he in the house?"

"I don't know. He came to me in the middle of the night, said he wanted this party throwing, then he left."

"As soon as the check arrived, right?"

"This isn't a joke."

"I'm sorry. You're right of course."

"He said he wanted everyone to come to the house and celebrate."

"I'll drink to that," Lamar said, raising his glass. "Wherever you are, Buddy. *Skol.*"

Toast over, he excused himself to go to the bathroom. Interesting woman, he thought as he went. Nuts of course, and—rumor had it—addicted to every chemical high to be had, but he was no saint himself. Ensconced in the black marble bathroom, leered down upon by a row of ghost-ride masks, he set up a few lines of cocaine and snorted himself high, his thoughts turning back to the beauty below. He'd have her; that was the long and short of it. Preferably in Buddy's bed, with Buddy's towels to wipe himself off afterwards.

Leaving his smirking reflection he stepped back on to the landing. Which *was* Buddy's bedroom? he wondered. Did it have mirrors on the ceiling, like the whore-house in Tucson they'd patronized together once upon a time, and Buddy had said, as he put that damn snake of a dick of his away: one day, Jimmy, I want a bedroom like this?

Lamar opened half a dozen doors before he found the master bedroom. It, like all the other rooms, was decorated with carnivalia. There was no mirror on the ceiling. But the bed was large. Big enough for three, which had always been Buddy's favored number. As he was about to return downstairs Lamar heard water running in the en suite bathroom.

"Rochelle, is that you?"

The light was not on inside, however. Obviously a tap had simply been left to run. Lamar pushed the door open.

From inside, Buddy spoke:

"No light, please."

Without the coke in his system Lamar would have been out of the house before the ghost spoke again, but the drug pumped him up long enough for Buddy to reassure his partner that there was nothing to be afraid of.

"She said you were here," Lamar breathed.

"You didn't believe her?"

"No."

"Who are you?"

"What do you mean: who am I? It's Jimmy. Jimmy Lamar."

"Of course. Come in. We should have words."

"No . . . I'll stay out here."

"I can't hear you too well."

"Turn off the water."

"I need it to piss."

"You piss?"

"Only when I drink."

"You drink?"

"Do you blame me, with her down there and me unable to touch her?"

"Yeah. That's too bad."

"You'll have to do it for me, Jimmy."

"Do what?"

"Touch her. You're not gay are you?"

"You know better than that."

"Of course."

"The number of women we had together."

"We were friends."

"The best. And I must say you're real sweet, letting me have Rochelle."

"She's yours. And in return—"

"What?"

"Be my friend again."

"Buddy. I missed you."

"I missed *you*, Jimmy."

"You were right," he said when he got downstairs. "Buddy *is* here."

"You saw him."

"No, but he spoke to me. He wants us to be friends. Him and me. And you and me. Close friends."

"Then we will be."

"For Buddy."

"For Buddy."

Upstairs, the Jaff turned this new and unexpected element in the game over, and judged it good. He had intended to pass himself off as Buddy—a trick all too easy, given that he'd drunk down the man's thoughts—to Rochelle only. In that form he'd come visiting two nights before, and found her drunk in her bed. It had been easy to coax her into believing he was her husband's spirit; the only difficult part had been preventing himself from claiming marital rights. Now, with the partner under the same delusion, he had two agents in the house to assist him when the guests arrived.

After the events of the previous night he was glad he'd had the foresight to organize the party. Fletcher's machinations had caught him off-guard. In that act of self-destruction his enemy had contrived to put a sliver of his hallucigenia-producing soul into a hundred, maybe two hundred minds. Even now the recipients were dreaming up their personal divinities; and making them solid. They would not, on past evidence, be particularly barbaric; certainly not the equals of his terata. Nor, without their instigator alive to fuel them, would they linger long on this plane of being. But they could still do his well-laid plans much mischief. He might well need the creatures he could summon from the hearts of Hollywood to prevent Fletcher's last testament from interfering.

Soon, the journey that had begun the first time he'd heard of the Art—so long ago he couldn't even remember from whom—would end with his entering Quiddity. After so many years of preparation it would be like coming home. He'd be a thief in Heaven, and therefore King of Heaven, given that he'd be the only presence there qualified to steal the throne. He would own the dreamlife of the world; be all things to all men, and never be judged.

There were two days left, then. The first, the twenty-four hours it would take him to realize that ambition.

The second, the day of the Art, when he would reach the place where dawn and dusk, noon and night, occurred at the same perpetual moment.

Thereafter, there was only forever.

FIVE

I

For Tesla, leaving Palomo Grove was like waking from sleep in which some dream-tutor had instructed her that all life was dreaming. There would be no simple division from now on between sense and nonsense; no arrogant assumption that this experience was real and this one not. Maybe she was living in a movie, she thought as she drove. Come to think of it that wasn't a bad idea for a screenplay: the story of a woman who discovered that human history was just one vast family saga, written by that underrated team Gene and Chance, and watched by angels, aliens and folks in Pittsburgh who had tuned in by accident and were hooked. Maybe she'd write that story, once this adventure was over.

Except that it would never be over; not now. That was one of the consequences of seeing the world this way. For better or worse she would spend the rest of her life anticipating the next miracle; and while she waited, inventing it in her fiction, so as to prick herself and her audience into vigilance.

The drive was easy, at least as far as Tijuana, and left room for such musings. Once she had crossed the border, however, she had to consult the map she'd bought, and was obliged to postpone any further plottings or prophecies. She had committed Fletcher's instructions to memory like an acceptance speech, and they—with help from the map—proved good. Never having travelled the peninsula before she was surprised to find it so deserted. This was not an environment in which man and his works had much hope of sustained existence, which led to the expectation that the Mission ruins, when she reached them, would most likely have been eroded, or swept away into the Pacific, whose murmur grew in volume as her route took her closer to the coast.

She could not have been more wrong in that expectation. As she rounded the bend of the hill Fletcher had directed her to, it was immediately apparent that the Misión de Santa Catrina was very much intact. The sight made her innards churn. A few minutes' drive, and she'd be standing before the site at which an epic story—of which she knew only the tiniest part—had begun. For a Christian, perhaps Bethlehem would have aroused the same excitement. Or Golgotha.

It was not a place of skulls, she found. Quite the reverse. Though the fabric of the Mission had not been rebuilt—its blasted rubble was still spread over a substantial area—somebody had clearly preserved it from further dissolution. The reason for that preservation only became apparent once she'd parked the car, some way off from the building, and approached on foot across the dusty ground. The Mission, built for holy purpose, deserted, then turned to an endeavor its architects would surely have deemed heretical, was once again sanctified.

The closer she approached the jigsaw walls, the more evidence she found before her. First, the flowers, laid in rough bunches and wreaths among the scattered stones, their colors brilliant in the clear sea air.

Second, and more poignant, the small bundles of domestic items—a loaf, a jug, a door handle—that had been bound up with scraps of scrawled-upon paper and laid among the blossoms in such profusion she could scarcely take a step without treading on something. The sun was slipping away now, but its deepening gold only served to enhance the sense that this was a haunted place. She negotiated the rubble as quietly as she could, for fear of disturbing its occupants, human or otherwise. If there were miraculous beings in Ventura County (walking the streets, no less, unabashed) how much more likely that here, on this lonely headland, there should be wonder-workers?

Who they might be, and what shape (if any) they took, she didn't even concern herself to try to guess. But if the number of gifts and supplications laid underfoot testified to anything it was that prayers were answered here.

The bundles and the messages left outside the Mission were affecting enough, but those inside were more moving still. She stepped through a gap in one of the walls into a silent crowd of portraits: dozens of photographs and sketches of men, women and children fixed to the stone along with a fragment of clothing, or a shoe; even spectacles. What she'd wandered through outside had been gifts. These, she guessed, were items for some bloodhound god to sniff. They belonged to missing souls, brought here in the hope that the powers would usher the lost back on to a familiar road and so bring them home.

Standing in the gilded light, surveying this collection, she felt like an intruder. Religious displays had seldom if ever moved her. The sentiments were so smug in their certainty, the images so rhetorical. But this display of simple faith touched a nerve she'd thought numbed by cant. She recalled the way she'd felt the first time she'd returned home for Christmas after a self-imposed exile from the family bosom of five years. It had been as claustrophobic as she'd anticipated, but at midnight on Christmas Eve, walking on Fifth Avenue, a forgotten feeling had sucked all the breath from her, and brought her to tears in an instant: *that once she had believed.* That belief had come from inside, out. Not taught, not bullied, just there. The first tears that had come were gratitude for the bliss of knowing belief again; their sisters, sadness that it passed as quickly as it had come, like a spirit moving through her and away.

This time, it didn't go. This time it deepened in her, as the sun deepened in color, sinking towards the sea.

The sound of somebody moving, deep in the ruins, broke her reverie. Startled, she let her quickened pulse slow a little before asking:

"Who's there?"

There was no reply. Cautiously she ventured past the wall of lost faces and through a lintel-less door into a second chamber. It had two windows, like eyes in the brick, through which the setting sun delivered two ruddy beams. She had nothing except instinct to support the feeling, but she didn't doubt that this was the temple's most sacred place. Though it had no roof, and its eastern wall was grievously damaged, the place seemed charged, as though forces had accrued in it over a period of years. Its function, when Fletcher had occupied the Mission, had evidently been that of laboratory. There were benches overturned on every side, the equipment that had toppled from them apparently left where it had fallen. Neither offerings nor portraits had been allowed to disrupt this sense of a place *preserved*. Though sand had gathered around the fallen furniture, and seedlings sprouted here and there, the chamber was as it had been: testament to a miracle; or to its passing.

The protector of the sanctum stood in the corner furthest from Tesla, beyond the shafts from the window. She could make out little about him. Only that he was either masked or had features as broadly formed as those of a mask. Nothing she'd experienced here so far led her to fear for her safety. Though she was alone, she felt no anxiety. This was a sanctuary not a place of violence. Besides, she came on the business of the deity that had once worked in this very chamber. She had to speak with his authority.

"My name's Tesla," she said. "I was sent here by Doctor Richard Fletcher."

She saw the man in the corner respond to the name with a slow upward motion of the head; then heard him sigh.

"Fletcher?" he said.

"Yes," Tesla replied. "Do you know who he is?"

The answer was another question delivered with a heavily Hispanic accent: "Do I know *you?*"

"I told you," Tesla said. "He sent me here. I've come to do what he himself asked me to do."

The man stepped away from the wall, far enough for his features to touch the beams.

"Could he not come himself?" he said.

It took Tesla a few moments to muster a reply. The sight of the man's heavy brow and lumpen nose had thrown her thoughts into a spin. Quite simply she'd never seen in the flesh a face so ugly.

"Fletcher isn't alive any more," she replied after a moment, her thoughts half on repugnance, half on how instinctively she'd avoided using the word dead.

The wretched features in front of her became sorrowful, something in their plasticity almost making a caricature of that emotion.

"I was here when he left," the man said. "I've been waiting for him to . . . come back."

She knew who he was as soon as he proffered this information. Fletcher had told her there might be a living remnant of the Great Work left.

"Raul?" she said.

The deep-set eyes grew wide. They showed no whites. "You *do* know him," he said, and took another quicker step into the light, which carved his features so cruelly she could barely look at him. She'd countless times seen creatures on the screen more studiedly vile than this—and the night before been bloodied by a beast of nightmare design—but the confusion of signals from this hybrid distressed her more than anything she'd set eyes on. It was so close to being human, yet her innards were not deceived. The response taught her something, though she wasn't quite certain what. She put the lesson aside for more urgent stuff.

"I've come to destroy whatever remains of the Nuncio," she said.

"Why?"

"Because Fletcher wants it that way. His enemies are still in the world, even though he isn't. He fears for the consequences if they come here and find the experiment."

"But I've waited . . ." Raul said.

"It's good that you did. It's good you guarded the place."

"I haven't moved. All these years. I've stayed where my father made me."

"How have you survived?"

Raul looked away from Tesla, squinting into the sun, which was almost gone from sight.

"The people look after me," he said. "They don't understand what happened here, but they know I was a part of it. The Gods were on this hill, once. That's what they believe. Let me show you."

He turned and led Tesla out of the laboratory. Beyond the door was another, barer chamber; this with a single window. The walls had been painted, she saw; murals whose naive rendering merely emphasized the passion with which they were felt.

"This is the story of that night," Raul said, "as they believe it happened."

There was no more light here than in the room they'd exited, but the murk lent mystery to the images.

"Here's the Mission as it was," Raul said, indicating an almost emblematic picture of the cliff upon which they were standing. "And there's my father."

Fletcher stood in front of the hill, face white and wild against its darkness, his eyes twin moons. Strange forms sprang from his ears and mouth, and hung around his head like satellites.

"What are those?" Tesla enquired.

"His ideas," came Raul's reply. "I painted those."

"What kind of ideas look like that?"

"Things from the sea," came the reply. "Everything comes from the sea. Fletcher told me that. At the beginning, the sea. At the end, the sea. And between—"

"Quiddity," said Tesla.

"What?"

"He didn't tell you about Quiddity?"

"No."

"Where humans go to dream?"

"I'm not human," Raul gently reminded her. "I'm his experiment."

"Surely that's what made you human," Tesla said. "Isn't that what the Nuncio does?"

"I don't know," Raul said simply. "Whatever it did to me, I don't thank it for. I was happier . . . being an ape. If I'd stayed an ape I'd be dead by now."

"Don't talk that way," Tesla said. "Fletcher wouldn't want to hear you full of regrets."

"Fletcher left me," Raul reminded her. "He taught me enough to know what I could never be, then he left me."

"He had his reasons. I've seen his enemy, the Jaff. The man has to be stopped."

"There—" said Raul, pointing to a place further along the wall. "There's Jaffe."

The portrait was able enough. Tesla recognized the devouring stare, the swollen head. Had Raul actually seen Jaffe in his evolved condition or was this portrait of man as monstrous babe an instinctive response? She had no opportunity to enquire. Raul was coaxing her away again.

"I'm thirsty," he said. "We can look at the rest later."

"It'll be too dark."

"No. They'll come up and light candles when the sun goes. Come and talk with me for a while. Tell me how my father died."

II

It took Tommy-Ray longer to reach the Misión de Santa Catrina than the woman he was racing against because of an incident along the route which, though minor, showed him a place in himself he would later come to know very well. In a small town south of Ensenada, stopping in the early evening to get something for his parched throat, he found himself in a bar that offered—for a mere ten bucks— access to an entertainment undreamed of in Palomo Grove. It was too tasty an offer to refuse. He put his money down, bought a beer, and was allowed entrance to a smoke-filled space which could only have been twice the size of his bedroom. There was an audience of maybe ten men, sprawled on creaking chairs. They were watching a woman having sex with a large black dog. He found nothing about the scene arousing. Neither, apparently, did the rest of the audience; at least not in the sexual sense. They leaned forward to watch the display with an excitement he didn't understand until the beer began to work on his wearied system, tunnelling his vision until the woman's face mesmerized him. She might once have been pretty, but her face, like her body, was wasted now, her arms showing plain proof of the addiction that had brought her so low. She teased the hound with the expertise of one who'd done this countless times before, then went on all fours before it. It sniffed, then lazily put itself to the task. Only once it had mounted her did Tommy-Ray realize what claim her expression had upon him, and, presumably, upon the others. She looked like somebody already dead. The thought was a door in his head opening on to a stinking yellow place; a wallowing place. He'd seen this look before, not just on the faces of girls in the skin mags, but on celebrities trapped by cameras. Sex-zombies, star-zombies; dead folks passing for living. When he plugged back into the scene in front of him the dog had found its rhythm, and was making at the girl with doggy lust, foam dripping from its mouth on her back; and this time—thinking of the girl as dead—it *was* sexy. The more excited the animal became the more excited he became and the more dead the woman looked to him, feeling the dog's dick in her and his eyes on her, until it became a race between him and the dog as to which was going to finish first.

The dog won, working itself up into a stabbing frenzy then stopping suddenly. On cue one of the men sitting in the front row stepped up and separated the pair, the animal instantly uninterested. Her partner led away, the woman was left center stage to gather up a scattering of clothes she'd presumably shed before Tommy-Ray had entered. She then exited through the same side door where the dog and its pimp had gone, her face the same slack mask it had been from the outset. There was apparently another part of the show to follow, because nobody vacated their seats. But Tommy-Ray had seen all he needed to see. He made his way back towards the door, pushing through a soft-bodied knot of newcomers, and out into the dusky bar.

It was only much later, when he was almost at the Mission, that he realized his pockets had been picked. There was no time to go back, he knew; nor indeed any purpose. The thief could have been any of the men who'd crowded his path as he'd left. Besides, it had been worth the lost dollars. He had found a new definition of death. Not even new. Simply his first and only.

The sun had long set by the time he drove up the hill towards the Mission, but as he began the ascent a distinct sense of *déjà vu* crept over him. Was he seeing the place with the Jaff's eyes? Whether or not, the recognition proved useful. Knowing that Fletcher's agent had undoubtedly arrived ahead of him he decided to leave the car a little way down the hill and climb the rest of the way on foot so as not to alert her to his coming. Dark though it was, he didn't travel blind. His feet knew the way even though his memory didn't.

He'd come prepared for violence, should the occasion demand. The Jaff had provided him with a gun—courtesy of one of the many victims the Jaff had relieved of their terata—and the idea of using it was undoubtedly appealing. Now, after a climb which had made his chest ache, he was within sight of the Mission. The moon had risen behind him, the color of a shark's underbelly. It lit the ruined walls, and the skin of his arms and hands, with its sickly light, making him long for a mirror in which to study his face. Surely he'd be able to see the bones beneath the meat; the skull gleaming the way his teeth gleamed when he smiled. After all, wasn't that what a smile said? Hello world, this is the way I'll look when the wet parts are rotted.

His head tender with such thoughts, he trod through the withering blossoms to the Mission.

III

Raul's hut was fifty yards beyond the main building, a primitive structure in which two occupants were a crowd. He depended, he explained to Tesla, entirely on the generosity of the local people, who supplied him with food and clothing in return for his being caretaker of the Mission. Despite the poverty of his means he had been at pains to elevate the hut from a hovel. There were signs everywhere of a delicate sensibility at work. The squat candles on the table were seated in a ring of stones chosen for their smoothness; the blanket on the simple cot had been decorated with the feathers of seabirds.

"I have one vice only," Raul said, once he'd set Tesla down in the single chair. "I have it from my father."

"What's that?"

"I smoke cigarettes. One a day. You'll share with me."

"I used to smoke," Tesla began, "but I don't any longer."

"Tonight you will," Raul said, leaving no room for dissension. "We'll smoke to toast my father."

He brought a hand-rolled cigarette from a small tin, along with matches. She watched his face as he went about the business of lighting it up. All that she'd found unnerving about him at first sight remained unnerving. His features were neither simian nor human, but the unhappiest of marriages between the two. And yet in every other respect—his speech, his manners, the way he was even now holding the cigarette between his long, dark fingers—he was so very civilized. The kind of man, indeed, mother might have wished her to marry, had he not been an ape.

"Fletcher hasn't gone, you know," he said to her, handing the cigarette across. She took it reluctantly, not particularly eager to put to her lips what had been between his. But he watched her, candle light flickering in his eyes, until she obliged, smiling with pleasure at her sharing with him. "He became something else, I'm sure," he went on. "Something other."

"I'll toast that," she said, taking another drag. Only now did it occur to her that perhaps the tobacco they smoked down here was a little more potent than in L.A.

"What's in this?" she said.

"Good stuff," he replied. "You like it?"

"They bring you dope as well?"

"They grow it themselves," Raul said in a matter-of-fact way.

"Good for them," she said, and claimed a third hit before handing it back to him. It was indeed strong stuff. Her mouth was already half way through a sentence her mind had no idea of how to finish before she knew she was even speaking.

". . . this is the night I tell my kids about . . . except that I won't have any kids . . . well, my grandchildren then . . . I'll tell them when I sat with a man who used to be a monkey . . . you don't mind me telling you that do you? Only it's my first time . . . and we sat and we talked about his friend . . . and my friend . . . who used to be a man . . ."

"And when you tell them," Raul said, "what will you say about yourself?"

"About myself?"

"Where will *you* fit into the pattern? What are *you* going to become?"

She mused on this. "Do I have to become anything?" she asked eventually.

Raul passed the remnants of the cigarette back to her. "Everything is becoming. Sitting here, we're becoming."

"What?"

"Older. Closer to death."

"Oh shit. I don't want to be closer to death."

"No choice," Raul said simply. Tesla shook her head. It kept moving, long after the motion had ceased.

"I want to understand," she said finally.

"Anything in particular?"

She mused a little more, running through all the possible options, and came up with one.

"Everything?" she said.

He laughed, and his laughter sounded like bells to her. Good trick, she was about to tell him, until she realized that he was up and at the door.

"Somebody's at the Mission," she heard him say.

". . . come to light the candles," she suggested, her head seeming to precede her body in pursuit of him.

"No," he said to her as he stepped out into the darkness. "They don't step where the bells are . . ."

She had been staring into the candle flame as she'd mulled over

Raul's questions, and its image was imprinted on the darkness she now stumbled through, a will o' the wisp that might have led her over the cliff-edge had she not followed his voice. As they approached the walls he told her to stay where she was but she ignored him and followed anyway. The candlelighters had indeed come visiting; their handiwork threw its glamour through from the room of portraits. Though the contents of Raul's cigarette had put space between her thoughts they were cogent enough to fear that she'd idled too long, and that her purpose here was now in jeopardy. Why hadn't she just found the Nuncio immediately and pitched it into the ocean as Fletcher had directed? Her irritation with herself made her bold. In the murk of the mural room she managed to overtake Raul and so step through into the candlelit laboratory first.

It was not candles that had been lit here, nor was the visitor a supplicant.

In the middle of the chamber a small, smoky fire had been lit, and a man—with his back at present turned to her—was ferreting through the tangle of equipment with his bare hands. She had not expected to recognize him when he looked in her direction, which was, on reflection, foolish. In the last few days she'd come to know most of the actors in this piece, if not by name then at least by sight. This one she knew by both. Tommy-Ray McGuire. He turned full face. In the perfect symmetry of his features a little ball of lunacy—the Jaff's inheritance—bounded back and forth, glittering.

"Hi!" he said; a bland, casual greeting. "I wondered where you were. The Jaff said you'd be here."

"Don't touch the Nuncio," she told him. "It's dangerous."

"That's what I'm hoping," he said with a grin.

There was something in his hand, she saw. Catching her glance he proffered it. "Yeah, I got it," he said. The vial was indeed as Fletcher had described it.

"Throw it away," she advised, attempting to be cool.

"Was that what you were going to do?" he asked.

"Yes. I swear, *yes*. It's lethal."

She saw his eyes flit from her face to Raul, whose breath she heard behind and a little to the side of her. Tommy-Ray looked in no way concerned at being out-numbered. Indeed she wondered if there was any threat to life or limb that would dislodge the smug satisfaction from his face. The Nuncio, perhaps? God Almighty, what possibilities would it find waiting in his barbaric heart, to praise and magnify?

Again she said: "Destroy it, Tommy-Ray, before it destroys you."

"No way," he said. "The Jaff's got plans for it."

"And what about you, when you've finished working for him? He doesn't care about you."

"He's my father and he loves me," Tommy-Ray replied, with a certainty that would have been touching in a sane soul.

She began to move towards him, talking as she went. "Just listen to me for a few moments, will you . . . ?"

He pocketed the Nuncio, and reached into his other pocket as he did so. He brought out a gun.

"What did you call the stuff?" he asked, pointing the weapon at her.

"Nuncio," she said, slowing her advance but still approaching steadily.

"No. Something else. You called it something else."

"Lethal."

He grinned. "Yeah," he said, slurring the word. "Lethal. That means it kills you, right?"

"Right."

"I like that."

"No, Tommy . . ."

"Don't tell me what I like," he said. "I said I like lethal and I mean it."

She suddenly realized she'd entirely miscalculated this scene. If she'd written it, he'd have held her at gunpoint till he made his escape. But he had his own scenario.

"I'm the Death-Boy," he said, and pulled the trigger.

SIX

I

U nnerved by the episode at Ellen's house, Grillo had taken refuge in writing, a discipline he felt more in need of the deeper this pool of ambiguities became. At first it was easy. He struck out for the dry ground of fact, and stated it in prose Swift would have been proud of. Later he could extract from this account the sections to be sent through to Abernethy. For now his duty was to set down as much as he could remember.

Mid-way through the process, he got a call from Hotchkiss, who suggested that they might have an hour drinking and talking together. The Grove had only two bars, he explained, Starky's, in Deerdell, being the less tame of the two and consequently the preferable. An hour after the conversation, with the bulk of the previous night's events securely laid on paper, Grillo left the hotel and met with Hotchkiss.

Starky's was practically empty. In one corner an old man sat quietly singing to himself, and there were two kids at the bar who looked too young to be drinking; otherwise they had the place to themselves. Even so, Hotchkiss barely raised his voice above a whisper throughout the entire conversation.

"You don't know much about me," he said at the outset. "I realized that last night. It's time you knew."

He didn't need any further encouragement to tell. His account was offered without emotion, as though the burden of feeling were so heavy it had long ago squeezed the tears from him. Grillo was glad of the fact. If the teller could be dispassionate then it freed him to be the same, probing between the lines of Hotchkiss's account for details the man had passed over. He spoke of Carolyn's part in the story first, of course, not praising or damning his daughter, merely describing her and the tragedy that had taken her from him. Then he threw the net of his story wider, and drew in others, first giving a thumbnail portrait of Trudi Katz, Joyce McGuire and Arleen Farrell, then relating how each of them had fared. Grillo was busily filling in details for himself as Hotchkiss spoke: creating a family tree whose roots went where Hotchkiss's account so often returned: underground.

"That's where the answers are," he said more than once. "I believe Fletcher and the Jaff, *who*ever they are, *what*ever they are, were responsible for what happened to my Carolyn. And to the other girls."

"They were in the caves all this time?"

"We saw them escape didn't we?" Hotchkiss said. "So yes, I think they waited down there all these years." He swallowed a mouthful of Scotch. "After last night at the Mall I just stayed up, trying to work it all out. Trying to make sense of it all."

"And?"

"I've decided to go down into the caves."

"What the hell for?"

"All those years, locked away, they must have been doing *something*. Maybe they left clues. Maybe we can find a way to destroy them down there."

"Fletcher's already gone," Grillo reminded him.

"Has he?" Hotchkiss said. "I don't know any more. Things linger, Grillo. They seem to disappear, but they linger, just out of sight. In the mind. In the ground. You climb down a little way and you're in the past. Every step another thousand years."

"My memory doesn't go back that far," Grillo quipped.

"But it does," Hotchkiss said, in deadly earnest. "It goes back to being a speck in the sea. That's what haunts us." He raised his hand. "Looks solid, doesn't it?" he said. "But it's mostly water." He seemed to be struggling for another thought, but it wouldn't come.

"The creatures the Jaff made look like they've been dug up," Grillo said. "You think that's what you're going to find down there?"

Hotchkiss's response was the thought he'd been unable to shape a moment earlier. "When she died," he said. "Carolyn I mean . . . when Carolyn died I had dreams of her just dissolving in front of me. Not rotting. Dissolving. Like the sea took her back."

"Do you still have those dreams?"

"Nope. I never dream now."

"Everybody dreams."

"Then I don't allow myself to remember them," Hotchkiss said.

"So . . . are you with me?"

"With you on what?"

"The descent."

"You really want to do it? I thought it was virtually impossible to get down there."

"So, we die trying," Hotchkiss said.

"I've got a story to write."

"Let me tell you, my friend," Hotchkiss said. "That's where the story *is*. The only story. Right beneath our feet."

"I should warn you . . . I'm claustrophobic."

"We'll soon sweat that out of you," Hotchkiss replied, with a smile Grillo thought might have been a jot more reassuring.

II

Though Howie had valiantly fought off sleep through most of the afternoon, by early evening he could barely keep his eyes open. When he told Jo-Beth he wanted to return to the hotel Momma intervened, telling him she'd feel much comforted if he remained in the house. She made up the spare room (he'd spent the previous night on the sofa) and he retired to it. His body had taken a considerable beating in the last few days. His hand was still badly bruised, and his back, though the punctures inflicted by the terata were not deep, still ached. None of which kept him from sleep for more than a few moments.

Jo-Beth prepared food for Momma—salad for Momma, as ever—and herself, going through the familiar domestic processes as though nothing in the world had changed since a week ago, and for short spaces of time, involved in her labors, forgetting the horrors. Then a look on her mother's face, or the sight of the shiny new lock on the back door, brought the memories back. She could no longer put them into any kind of order: there was just humiliation and pain upon further humiliation and further pain. Leering through it all the Jaff; near to her, *too* near to her, coming so close on occasion to persuading her to his vision the way he'd persuaded Tommy-Ray. Of all her fears the one that distressed her the most was that she might actually have been capable of joining the enemy. When he'd explained to her how he wanted reasons rather than feelings, she'd understood. Even been moved to sympathy. And that teasing talk of the Art, and the island he wanted to show her . . .

"Jo-Beth?"

"Momma?"

"Are you all right?"

"Yes. Of course. Yes."

"What were you thinking of? The expression on your face . . ."

"Just . . . about last night."

"You should put it out of your head."

"Maybe I'll drive over to see Lois; talk with her for a while? Would you mind?"

"No. I'll be fine here. Howard's with me."

"Then I'll go."

Of all her friends in the Grove none represented the normality from which her life had departed as perfectly as Lois. For all her moral strictures she had a strong and simple faith in what was good. In essence, she wanted the world a peaceful place, where children raised in love could in their turn raise children. She knew evil too. It was any force mounted against that vision. The terrorist, the anarchist, the lunatic. Now Jo-Beth knew that such human forces had allies on a more rarefied plane of being. One of those was her father. It was never more important that she sought the company of those whose definition of good was unshakable.

She heard noise and laughter from Lois's house as she got out of the car; which was welcome after the hours of fear and unease she'd spent. She knocked on the door. The raucousness continued unabated. It sounded to be quite a crowd.

"*Lois?*" she called, but such was the level of hilarity from within both calls and knocks went unheard, so she rapped on the window, again calling. The drapes were drawn aside and Lois's quizzical face appeared, mouthing Jo-Beth's name. The room behind her was full of people. She was at the door ten seconds later, with an expression on her face so unusual Jo-Beth almost failed to recognize her: a smile of welcome. Behind her every light in the house seemed to be burning; a dazzling wash of light that spilled on to the step.

"Surprise," said Lois.

"Yes, I just thought I'd call round. But you've . . . got company."

"Sort of," Lois replied. "It's a little difficult just at the moment."

She cast a glance back into the house. It seemed to be a costume party she was flinging. A man dressed in a full cowboy outfit sauntered up the stairs, spurs glinting, past another in full military garb. Crossing the hall, arm in arm with a woman in black, was a guest who'd come as a surgeon, of all things, his face masked. That Lois should have planned such a jamboree without mentioning it to Jo-Beth was odd enough; Lord knows they had spare time enough at the store to chat. But that she was throwing it at all—staid, reliable Lois—was doubly odd.

"I don't suppose it matters," Lois was saying. "You're a friend after all. You should be a part of it, right?"

A part of *what* was the question on Jo-Beth's lips, but she had no time to ask it before she was drawn inside by Lois, who took her arm with proprietorial force, and the door was shut hard behind her.

"Isn't it wonderful?" Lois said. She was positively glowing. "Have you had the people come to see you?"

"People."

"The Visitors."

Jo-Beth merely nodded, which was sufficient to set Lois bubbling in a new direction. "Next door, the Kritzlers had Visitors from *Masquerade*—you know, that series about the sisters?"

"The TV show?"

"Of course the TV show. And my Mel . . . well, you know how much he loves the old westerns . . ."

None of this made much, if any, sense but Jo-Beth let Lois race on, for fear that asking a question out of turn might mark her as uninitiated, and she'd be denied any further confessions.

"Me? I'm the luckiest one," Lois burbled. "So, so lucky. All the people from *Day by Day* came over. The whole family. Alan, Virginia, Benny, Jayne. They even brought Morgan. Imagine."

"Where did they come *from*, Lois?"

"They just appeared in the kitchen," came the answer. "And of course they've been telling me all the gossip about the family—"

Only the store obsessed Lois as much as *Day by Day*, the story of America's favorite family. She would regularly sit and tell Jo-Beth every detail of the previous night's episode as though it were part of her own life. Now it seemed the delusion had taken hold of her. She was talking about the Pattersons as though they were actually guests in her house.

"They're every bit as sweet as I knew they'd be," she was saying, "though I didn't think they'd mix with the people from *Masquerade*. You know, with the Pattersons being so *ordinary*; that's what I love about them. They're so . . . ."

"Lois. Stop this."

"What's wrong?" she said.

"You tell me."

"Nothing's wrong. Everything's wonderful. The Visitors are here and I couldn't be happier."

She smiled at a man in a pale blue jacket who waved a welcome.

"That's Todd, from *The Last Laugh*—" she said.

Late-night satire was no more to Jo-Beth's taste than *Day by Day* but the man did look vaguely familiar. As did the girl he'd been showing card-tricks to; and the man who was clearly competing with him for her affections, who might have passed—even at this range—for the host of Momma's favorite game show, *Hideaway*.

"What's going on here?" Jo-Beth said. "Is it a look-alike party or something?"

Lois's smile, which had been a permanent fixture since her greeting Jo-Beth at the door, slipped a little.

"You don't believe me," she said.

"Believe you?"

"About the Pattersons."

"No. Of course not."

"But they came, Jo-Beth," she said, now, suddenly, in deadly earnest. "I suppose I'd always wanted to meet them, and they *came*." She took hold of Jo-Beth's hand, her smile igniting again. "You'll see," she said. "And don't worry, you'll have somebody come to you if you want them badly enough. It's happening all over town. Not just TV people. People from billboards and magazines. Beautiful people; wonderful people. There's no need to be frightened. They belong to us." She drew a little closer. "I never really understood that, until last night. Only they need us just as much, don't they? Maybe more. So they won't do us any harm . . ."

She pushed open the door from which much of the laughter was coming. Jo-Beth followed Lois in. The lights that had first dazzled her in the hallway were brighter here, though there was no source apparent. It was as if the people in the room came already lit, their hair gleaming, their eyes and teeth the same. Mel was standing at the mantelpiece, portly, bald and proud, surveying a room filled with famous faces.

Just as Lois had promised, the stars had come to Palomo Grove. The Patterson family—Alan and Virginia, Benny and Jayne—even their mutt, Morgan—were holding court in the center of the room, with several other characters from the series—Mrs. Kline from next door, the bane of Virginia's life; the Haywards, who owned the corner store—also in attendance. Alan Patterson was engaged in an animated discussion with Hester D'Arcy, much abused heroine of *Masquerade*. Her oversexed sister, who had poisoned half the family to gain control of incalculable wealth, was in the corner making eyes at a man from an ad for briefs, who'd come as he was best known: almost naked.

"Everybody!" Lois said, raising her voice above the hubbub. "Everybody please, I want you all to meet a friend of mine. One of my very best friends—"

The familiar faces all turned to look, like the covers of a dozen *TV Guides* all staring Jo-Beth's way. She wanted to get out of this insanity before it touched her, but Lois had a firm grip of her hand. Besides, this was part of the whole insanity. If she was to understand it she had to stay put.

"—this is Jo-Beth McGuire," Lois said.

Everybody smiled; even the cowboy.

"You look as though you need a drink," Mel said, when Lois had taken Jo-Beth on one complete circuit of the room.

"I don't drink liquor, Mr. Knapp."

"Doesn't mean you don't look as though you need it," came the reply. "I think we've all got to change our ways after tonight, don't you? Or maybe last night." He glanced over at Lois, whose laughter was rising in peals. "I've never seen her so happy," he said. "And that makes me happy."

"But do you know where all these people come from?" Jo-Beth said.

Mel shrugged. "Your guess is as good as mine. Come through, will you? *I* need a drink if you don't. Lois has always denied herself these little pleasures. I always said: God isn't looking. And if He is, He doesn't care."

They pressed their way through the guests to the hallway. Numbers of people had gathered there to escape the crush in the lounge, among them several church members: Maeline Mallett; Al Grigsby; Ruby Sheppherd. They smiled at Jo-Beth, no sign on their faces that they found this gathering untoward. Had they perhaps brought Visitors of their own?

"Did you go down to the Mall last night?" Jo-Beth asked Mel as she watched him pour her orange juice.

"I did indeed," he said.

"And Maeline? And Lois? And the Kritzlers?"

"I think so. I forget who was there exactly, but yes, I'm sure most of them . . . are you sure you wouldn't like something *in* the juice?"

"Maybe I will," she said vaguely, her mind putting the pieces of this mystery together.

"Good for you," said Mel. "The Lord isn't looking, and even if He is . . ."

". . . He doesn't care."

She took the drink.

"That's right. He doesn't care."

She sipped it; then gulped.

"What's in it?" she said.

"Vodka."

"Is the world going mad, Mr. Knapp?"

"I think it is," came the reply. "What's more, I like it that way."

Howie woke at a little after ten, not because he was sufficiently rested but because he'd rolled over in sleep and trapped his wounded hand under his body. Pain soon slapped him conscious. He sat up and studied his throbbing knuckles in the moonlight. The cuts had opened again. He dressed and went to the bathroom to wash them of blood, then went in search of a bandage. Jo-Beth's mother provided one, along with the expertise to bind his hand properly, plus the information that Jo-Beth had gone to Lois Knapp's house.

"She's late now," Momma said.

"It's not ten-thirty yet."

"Even so."

"You want me to go look for her?"

"Would you? You can take Tommy-Ray's car."

"Is it far?"

"No."

"Then I think I'll walk."

The warmth of the night and his being out in it without hounds on his heels put him in mind of his first night here in the Grove: seeing Jo-Beth in Butrick's Steak House; speaking with her; falling, in a matter of seconds, in love. The calamities that had come upon the Grove since were a direct result of that meeting. But significant as his feelings for Jo-Beth were, he couldn't quite bring himself to believe they'd brought such vast consequence. Was it possible that beyond the enmity between the Jaff and Fletcher—beyond Quiddity and the struggle for its possession—lay an even vaster plot? He'd always vexed himself with such imponderables; like trying to imagine infinity, or what it would feel like to touch the sun. The pleasure lay not in a solution, but in the stretch it took to tackle the question. The difference, in this case, lay with his place in the problem. Suns and infinities vexed far greater minds than his. But what he felt for Jo-Beth vexed only him, and if—as some buried instinct in him (Fletcher's echo, perhaps?) suggested—the fact of their meeting was a tiny but vital part of some massive tale, then he could not leave the thinking to those greater minds. The responsibility, at least in part, devolved upon him; upon them both. How much he wished it didn't. How much he longed to have time to court Jo-Beth like any small-town suitor. To lay plans for the future without the weight of an inexplicable past pressing upon them. But that couldn't be, any more than a written thing could be unwritten, or a wished-for thing unwished.

If he'd wanted any more concrete proof of that, none could have been had but the scene that awaited him beyond the door of Lois Knapp's house.

"There's someone here to see you, Jo-Beth."

She turned and met the same expression that must have been on her face when, two hours and more before, she'd stepped into the lounge.

"Howie," she said.

"What's going on here?"

"A party."

"Yeah, I can see that. But all these actors. Where'd they come from? They can't all live in the Grove."

"They're not actors," she said. "They're people from the TV. And a few movies too. Not many, but—"

"Wait, wait."

He moved closer to her. "Are these Lois's friends?" he said.

"They sure are," she said.

"This town just keeps on going, doesn't it? Just when you think you've got it fixed in your head—"

"But they're not *actors*, Howie."

"You just said they were."

"No. I said they were people from TV. See the Patterson family, over there? They even have that dog with them."

"Morgan," Howie said. "My mother used to watch that show."

The dog, a lovable mongrel in a long tradition of lovable mongrels, heard his name called and scooted over, followed by Benny, the youngest of the Patterson children.

"Hi," the kid said. "I'm Benny."

"I'm Howie. This is—"

"Jo-Beth. Yeah, we met. You want to come outside and play ball with me, Howie? I'm bored."

"It's dark out there."

"No it isn't," Benny said. He directed Howie's gaze towards the patio doors. They were open. The night beyond was, as Benny had said, far from dark. It was as if the odd radiance that permeated the house, about which he'd had no time to speak with Jo-Beth, had seeped out into the yard.

"See?" Benny said.

"I see."

"So come on, huh?"

"In a minute."

"Promise?"

"I promise. By the way, what's your real name?"

The kid looked puzzled. "Benny," he said. "Always was." He and the mutt headed off for the bright night.

Before Howie could put the countless questions in his head into askable order he felt a friendly pat on the back and a rotund voice enquired:

"Something to drink?"

Howie raised his bandaged hand in apology for the absence of a handshake.

"Good to have you here anyhow. Jo-Beth was telling me about you. I'm Mel, by the way. Lois's husband. You met Lois already, I gather."

"That's right."

"I don't know where she got to. I think one of those cowboys is having his way with her." He raised his glass. "To which I say, better him than me." He faked a look of shame. "What am I saying? I should have the bastard out in the street. Gun him down, eh?" He grinned. "That's the New West for you, right? Can't be fucking bothered. You want another vodka, Jo-Beth? You're going to have something, Howie?"

"Why not?"

"Funny, isn't it?" Mel said. "It's only when these damn dreams come in you realize who you are. Me . . . I'm a coward. And I don't love her." He turned from them. "Never did love her," he said as he reeled away. "Bitch. Fucking bitch."

Howie watched him enveloped by the crowd, then looked back at Jo-Beth. Very slowly he said:

"I don't have the slightest clue what's happening. Do you?"

"Yes."

"Tell me. Words of one syllable."

"This is because of last night. What your father did."

"The fire?"

"Or what came from it. All these people . . ." She smiled, surveying them, ". . . Lois, Mel, Ruby over there . . . all of them were at the Mall last night. Whatever came from your father—"

"Keep your voice down, will you? They're staring at us."

"I'm not talking loud, Howie," she said. "Don't be so paranoid."

"I tell you they're staring."

He could feel the intensity of their gazes: faces he'd only ever seen in glossy magazines, or on the television screen, staring at him with strange, almost troubled, looks.

"So let them stare," she said. "They don't mean any harm."

"How do you know that?"

"I've been here all evening. It's just like a normal party—"

"You're slurring your words."

"So why shouldn't I have a little fun once in a while?"

"I'm not saying you shouldn't. I'm just saying you're in no state to judge whether they're dangerous or not."

"What are you trying to do, Howie?" she said. "Keep all these people to yourself?"

"No. No, of course not."

"I don't want to be a part of the Jaff—"

"*Jo-Beth.*"

"He may be my father. Doesn't mean I like it that way."

The room had fallen entirely silent at the mention of the Jaff. Now everyone in the room—cowboys, soap-opera stars, sitcom folks, beauties and all—were looking their way.

"Oh shit," said Howie, softly. "You shouldn't have said that." He scanned the faces surrounding them. "That was a mistake. She didn't mean it. She's not . . . she doesn't belong . . . what I mean is, we're together. She and me. We're together, see? My father was Fletcher, and hers . . . hers *wasn't.*" It was like being in sinking sand. The more he struggled, the deeper he sank.

One of the cowboys spoke first. He had eyes the press would call ice-blue.

"You're Fletcher's son?"

"Yes . . . I am."

"So you know what we're to do."

Howie suddenly understood the significance of the stares he'd been garnering since he'd entered. These creatures—*hallucigenia,* Fletcher had called them—*knew* him; or at least thought they did. Now he'd identified himself, and the need in their faces couldn't have been plainer.

"Tell us what to do," one of the women said.

"We're here for Fletcher," said another.

"Fletcher's gone," said Howie.

"Then for you. You're his son. What are we here to do?"

"Do you want the child of the Jaff destroyed?" said the cowboy, turning his blue eyes on Jo-Beth.

"Jesus Christ, no!"

He reached out to take hold of Jo-Beth's arm but she'd already retreated from him, slow steps towards the door. "Come back," he said. "They're not going to hurt you."

From the look on her face his words were scant comfort in such company.

"Jo-Beth . . ." he said, ". . . I'm not going to let them hurt you."

He started towards her, but his father's creatures weren't about to let their only hope for guidance go. Before he could reach her he felt a hand snatch at his shirt, and then another and another, until he was entirely surrounded by pleading, adoring faces.

"*I can't help you,*" he yelled. "*Let me alone!*"

From the corner of his eye he saw Jo-Beth, running scared to the door, opening it and slipping away. He called after her, but the din of pleas had risen around him until his every syllable was drowned out. He started to push harder through the crowd. Dreams they might be, but they were solid enough; and warm; and, it seemed, frightened. They needed a leader, and they'd elected him. It was not a role he was prepared to accept, especially not if it separated him from Jo-Beth.

"Get the fuck out of my way!" he demanded, clawing his way through the back-lit, glossy faces. Their fervor didn't diminish, but grew in proportion to his resistance. It was only by ducking down and tunnelling his way through his admirers that he got free of them. They followed him out into the hallway. The front door stood open. He sprinted for it like a star besieged by fans, and was out into the night before they caught up with him. Some instinct kept them from coming after him into the open, though one or two, Benny and the dog Morgan leading, followed, the boy's shout—"Come back and see us some time soon!"—pursuing him like a threat down the street.

SEVEN

I

The bullet struck Tesla in the side, like a blow from a heavyweight champ. She was thrown backwards, the sight of Tommy-Ray's grinning face replaced with the stars through the open roof. They got bigger in moments, swelling like bright sores, edging out the clean darkness.

What happened next was beyond her powers of comprehension. She heard a commotion, and a shot, followed by shrieks from the women Raul had told her would be gathering about this time. But she couldn't find the will to be much interested in what was happening on earth. The ugly spectacle above her claimed all her attention: a sick and brimming sky about to drown her in tainted light.

Is this death? she wondered. If so, it was overrated. There was a story to be had there, she began to think. About a woman who—

The thought went the way of consciousness: out.

The second shot she'd heard had been fired at Raul, who'd come at Tesla's assassin at speed, leaping over the fire. The bullet missed him, but he threw himself aside to avoid another, giving Tommy-Ray time to dart out of the door he'd entered through, into a crowd of women which he

parted with a third shot aimed over their veiled heads. They put up a
clamor and fled, hauling their children after them. Nuncio in hand, he
headed off down the hill to where he'd left the car. A backward glance
confirmed that the woman's companion—whose misbegotten features
and weird turn of speed had taken him aback—was not giving chase.

Raul put his hand to Tesla's cheek. She was feverish, but alive. He
took off his shirt and clamped the bundle to her wound, laying her
limp hand upon it to keep it in place. Then he went out into the darkness and called the women out of hiding. He knew all of them by
name. They in turn knew and trusted him. They came when called.
"Look after Tesla," he instructed them. Then he went after the
Death-Boy and his prize.

Tommy-Ray was within sight of the car, or rather its ghost-form in
the moonlight, when his foot slid from beneath him. In his effort to
keep hold of gun and vial, both went from his hands. He fell heavily,
face down in sharp dirt. Stones stabbed his cheek, chin, arms and
hands. As he got to his feet blood began to run.
"My face!" he said, hoping to God he'd not damaged his looks.
There was more bad news to come. He could hear the sound of the
Ugly Fuck following down the hill.
"Want to die, do you?" he grunted to his, pursuer. "No problem.
We can supply. No problem."
He scrabbled for the gun but it had skidded some distance from
him. The vial was there beneath his hand, however. He picked it up.
Even as he did so he realized it was no longer passive. It was warm in
his bloodied palm. There was motion behind the glass. He grasped it
more tightly, to be certain it didn't slip from him again. It responded
instantly, the fluid glowing between his fingers.
Many years had passed since the rest of the Nuncio had worked its
work upon Fletcher and Jaffe. This, the remnants, had been buried,
out of sight, amid stones too revered to be turned. It had grown cold;
forgetful of its message. But it remembered now. Tommy-Ray's enthusiasm woke old ambition.

He saw it push against the walls of the vial, bright as a knife, as a gun-flash. Then it broke its cage, and came at him, between his fingers—spread now against its attack—up towards his already wounded face.

Its touch seemed light enough—a spatter of warmth, like a jism when he jerked off, hitting his eye and the corner of his mouth. But it flipped him over on to his back—the stones bringing blood to his elbows, ass and spine. He tried to yell but no sound came. He tried to open his eyes, so as to see where he was lying, but he couldn't do that either. Jesus! He couldn't even breathe. His hands, touched by the Nuncio as it leapt, were clamped to his face, blocking eyes, nose and mouth. It was like being screwed down in a coffin made for someone two sizes smaller than he. Again, he cried out against the gag of his palm, but it was a lost cause. Somewhere at the back of his head a voice said:

"Let go. This is what you want. To be the Death-Boy, you first have to know Death. Feel it. Understand it. *Suffer* it."

In this, as in perhaps no other lesson in his short life, he was a good pupil. He stopped resisting the panic, and went with it, riding it like a wave at Zuma, towards the darkness of some unmapped shore. The Nuncio went with him. He felt it make new stuff of him with every sweating second, prancing on the points of his stiffened hair, beating a rhythm, death's rhythm, between the throbs of his heart.

Suddenly, it was full of him; or he of it; or both. His hands came off his face like suckers, and he breathed again.

After half a dozen gasps he sat up and looked down at his palms. They were bloody, both from his cut face and from their own injuries, but the stains faded before a more insistent reality. Granted a grave-dweller's sight, he saw his own flesh corrupting before his eyes. The skin darkened and swelled with gases, then broke open, the lesions spilling pus and water. Seeing, he grinned, and felt the grin spreading up from the corners of his mouth to his ears as his face split. It wasn't just the bone of his smile he was showing; the rods of his arms, wrists and fingers were appearing now, as decay uncovered them. Beneath his shirt, his heart and lungs sank into sewerage and drained away; his balls were washed with them; his withered dick the same.

And still the grin grew wider, until all the muscle had gone from his face and he was smiling the Death-Boy's smile, wide as any smile could get.

The vision didn't linger. Once given, it was gone, and he was left kneeling on the sharp stones, staring down at his bloody palms.

"I'm the Death-Boy," he said, and stood up, turning to face the lucky fuck who'd be the first to see him transfigured.

The man had stopped in his tracks, a few yards off.

"Look at me," Tommy-Ray said. "I'm the Death-Boy."

The poor shit just stared, not understanding. Tommy-Ray laughed. All desire to kill the man had gone out of him. He wanted this witness alive, to testify in days to come. To say: I was there, and it was awesome, seeing Tommy-Ray McGuire die and rise again.

He took a moment to look at the remains of the Nuncio-fragments of the vial and a few spots of spilled fluid on the stones. There was not enough to gather up and take back to the Jaff. But he was bringing something better now. Himself, changed; cleansed of fear, cleansed of flesh. Without looking back at the witness, he about-faced and left him to his confusion.

Though the glory of corruption had left him now, a subtle aftersight remained—which he didn't comprehend until a piece of stone underfoot caught his eye. He bent to pick it up; a pretty thing for Jo-Beth, maybe. Once in his hand he realized it was not stone at all, but a bird's skull, fractured and dirty. To his eyes, it gleamed.

Death shines, he thought. When I see it, it shines.

Pocketing the skull he sauntered back to the car and reversed down the hill until the road offered space enough for him to turn. Then he was away at a speed that would have been suicidal on such bends and in such darkness had suicide not been one of his many playthings now.

Raul put his fingers to one of the splashes of Nuncio. It rose in beads to meet his hand, winding into the spirals of his fingerprints, then climbing up through the marrow of hand, wrist and forearm, before petering out at his elbow. He felt, or imagined he felt, some subtle reconfiguration in his muscle, as though his hand, which had never quite lost its simian proportions, was being coaxed a little closer to the human. He let the sensation delay him only a moment; Tesla's condition concerned him more than his own.

It was as he went to make his way back up the hill that it occurred to him that the drops of Nuncio left in the ground might somehow help heal the woman. If she didn't have comfort of some kind soon she'd surely die. What was there to lose in letting the Great Work do what it could?

With that thought in mind he started back towards the Mission, knowing that were he to attempt to touch the broken vial it would be he who received its benefit. Tesla would have to be carried down the road to where these precious drops were scattered.

The women had set their candles all around Tesla. She looked like a corpse already. He was swift with his instructions. They wrapped her up and helped him carry her down the road a little way. She wasn't heavy. He took her head and shoulders and two of the women supported her lower half, a third held the bundled shirt, now thoroughly soaked, to the bullet hole.

It was a slow process, stumbling in the darkness, but having been twice touched by the Nuncio, Raul had no difficulty finding the spot again. Like called to like. Warning the women to keep feet and fingers clear of the spilled fluid he took Tesla's weight entirely into his own arms and laid her down, her head haloed by splashes of the Nuncio. The remains of the vial itself still contained the bulk of the fluid; at most, a teaspoonful. With great gentleness, he turned her head towards the vial. At her proximity the fluid inside had begun a firefly dance—

—the poison brightness that had rained on Tesla as she fell before Tommy-Ray's bullet had solidified in seconds: become a gray, featureless place where she lay now without any sense of how she'd come to be there. She couldn't remember the Mission, Raul, or Tommy-Ray. Even her own name was beyond her. It was all outside the wall, where she couldn't go. Perhaps would never go again. She had no feelings either way about this. With no memory, she had nothing to mourn.

But now something began to scratch at the wall from the other side. She heard it humming to itself as it worked, like a lover digging at the stone of her cell, determined to reach her. She listened, and waited, no longer quite so forgetful, nor so indifferent to escape. Her name came back to her first, heard in the hum from outside. Then a memory of the pain the bullet had brought with it, and the grinning face of Tommy-Ray, and Raul, and the Mission, and—

Nuncio.

That was the power she'd come looking for, and now in its turn it was looking for her, eroding the walls of limbo. Her exchanges with Fletcher about its transforming talents had been all too brief, but she understood its basic function well enough. It ran with whatever baton it was passed; a race against entropy towards some conclusion not even its client/victim could guess, much less its subject. Was she ready for such a proving touch? It had made a swollen evil of Jaffe, and a bewildered saint of Fletcher.

What might it make of her?

At the last possible moment Raul doubted the wisdom of this medicine, and reached to take Tesla out of the way of the Nuncio's touch, but it was already leaping from the shattered vial towards her face. She inhaled it like a liquid breath. Around her head the other drops flew towards her scalp and neck.

She gasped, her whole body responding with tremors to the entry of the messenger. Then, just as suddenly, every jitter in her joints and nerves ceased.

Raul murmured:

"Don't die. Don't die."

He was about to put his mouth to hers in one last snatch at preserving her when he saw the motion behind her closed lids. Her eyes were roving back and forth wildly, scanning some sight only she could see.

"Alive . . ." he murmured.

Behind him, the women—who'd witnessed this entire scene without comprehending any of it—began to pray and wail, either out of gratitude or of fear of what they'd seen. He didn't know. But he added his own muttered prayers, no more certain of his reasons than of theirs.

II

The walls went suddenly. Like a dam first breached in a tiny place, then broken from side to side by the flood behind it.

She had expected the world she'd left to be waiting when the walls were rubble. She was wrong. There was no sign of the Mission, nor of Raul. Instead there was laid before her a desert lit by a sun which had yet to reach its full ferocity, and crossed by a gusting wind which picked her up the instant the walls fell, and carried her over the ground. Her velocity was terrifying, but she had no way to slow herself, or indeed change direction, because she possessed neither limbs nor body. She was *thought* here; pure, in a pure place.

Then, ahead, a sight that gave the lie to that. There was sign of human occupancy on the horizon; a town set in the middle of this nowhere. Her speed didn't slow as she approached. This, apparently, was not her destination, if indeed she had one. It occurred to her that perhaps she could simply travel and travel. That this state of being was simply one of motion; a journey without purpose or conclusion. She had time, as she passed through the Main Street, to register that though the town was solidly constructed stores and houses arrayed to either side—it was also completely characterless. That is, unpeopled, and unparticularized. There were no signs on the stores or at the cross-streets; no mark of human presence whatsoever. Even as she registered this weirdness she was at the other side of the town, and once more speeding over sun-scorched ground. The sight of the town, however brief, had given weight to her suspicion that she was utterly alone here. Not only was her journey to be endless, but unaccompanied too. This was Hell, she thought; or a good working definition of same.

She began to wonder how long it would be before her mind took refuge from this horror in insanity. A day? A week? Were there even such distinctions here? Did the sun set, and rise again? She strained to turn her sight skyward, but the sun was behind her, and having no body she neither threw a shadow by which to read its position nor possessed the power to turn and see it for herself.

There was something else to see, however, more curious than the town: a single tower or pylon, built of steel, standing in the middle of the desert, with wires tethering it as though it might at any moment float away. Again she was at it and past in seconds. Again, it gave her no comfort. But once beyond it a new sensation crept over her: that she, and the clouds and the sand beneath her were all *fleeing* from something. Had some entity been lurking in that blank town, just out of sight, and now, aroused by a human presence here, was coming after her? She couldn't turn, she couldn't hear, she couldn't even feel its footsteps in the earth as it approached. But it would come. If not now, then soon. It was relentless, inevitable. And the first moment she saw it would be her last.

Then, refuge! A fair distance away yet, but growing in size as she speeded towards it, what appeared to be a small stone hut, its walls painted white. Her sickening pace slowed. The ride apparently had a destination after all: this hovel.

Her sight was fixed upon the place, looking for signs of occupancy, but her peripheral vision nevertheless caught sight of a movement way off to the right of the hut. Though slowing, her speed was still considerable, and her inability to scan the scene prevented her catching more than a glimpse of the figure. But it was human; female; clothed in rags: that much she *did* grasp. Even if the hut turned out to be as empty as the town, she had the comfort—albeit slight—that some other soul wandered these wastes. She looked hard for the woman again, but she'd come and gone. And there was more urgent business: the fact that the hut was almost upon her, or her upon it, and her speed was still sufficient to demolish hovel and visitor on impact. She readied herself, reflecting that a death by dashing would be preferable to the unending journey she'd feared.

And then, she was at a dead stop; and at the door. From two hundred miles an hour to zero in half a heartbeat.

The door was closed, but she sensed something over her shoulder (bodiless though she was, it was impossible not to think of *over* and *behind*) which reached into her field of vision. It was serpentine, the thickness of her wrist, and so dark that even in bright sunlight she could make out no detail of its anatomy. It had no patterning; no head; no eyes; no mouth; no digits. It had strength however. Enough to push the door open. Then it withdrew, leaving her undecided as to whether she'd seen the whole beast, or merely one of its limbs.

The hut was not large; one glance and she'd taken it in. The walls unadorned stone, the floor bare earth. There was no bed, nor any furniture. Only a small fire, burning in the middle of the floor, its smoke given an escape route through a hole in the middle of the roof but instead choosing to stay and dirty the air between her and the hut's sole occupant.

He looked as old as the stone of this hovel's walls, naked and grimy, his paper skin stretched to splitting point over bird's bones. He'd singed off his beard patchily, leaving clumps of gray hairs in places. She wondered he had the wit to do that. The expression on his face suggested a mind in an advanced state of catatonia.

But no sooner had she entered than he looked up at her, seeing her despite the fact that she had no substance. He cleared his throat, splitting the phlegm into the fire.

"Close the door," he said.

"You can see me?" she replied. "And hear me?"

"Of course," he replied. "Now close the door."

"How do I do that?" she wanted to know. "I've got . . . no hands. Nothing."

"You can do it," he replied. "Just imagine yourself."

"Huh?"

"Oh for fuck's sake how difficult can it be? You've looked at yourself often enough. Picture what you look like. Make yourself real. Go on. Do it for me." His tone veered between that of bully and wheedler. "You have to close the door . . ."

"I'm trying."

"Not hard enough," came the reply.

She paused a moment before daring the next question.

"I'm dead, aren't I?" she said.

"Dead? No."

"No?"

"The Nuncio preserved you. You're alive and kicking, but your body's still back at the Mission. I want it here. We've got business to do."

The good news, that she was still alive, albeit separated flesh from spirit, fuelled her. She thought hard of the body she'd almost lost, the body she'd grown into over a period of thirty-two years. It was by no means perfect, but at least it was all hers. No silicone; no nips and tucks. She liked her hands and her fine-boned wrists, her squinty breasts with the left nipple twice the size of the right, her cunt, her ass. Most of all she liked her face, with its quirks and laugh-lines.

To imagine it was the trick. To picture its essentials, and so bring it into this other place where her spirit had come. The old man was aiding her in the process, she guessed. His gaze, though still on the door, was directed inward. The sinews of his neck stood out like harp strings; his lipless mouth twitched.

His energies helped. She felt herself losing her lightness, becoming substantial here, like a soup thickening in the heat of her imagining. There was a moment of doubt, when she almost regretted losing the ease of being thought, but then she remembered her face smiling back at her when she stepped from the shower in the morning. It was a fine feeling, maturing in that flesh, learning to enjoy it for its own sake. The simple pleasure of a good belch, or better yet a solid fart: the kind that had Butch blaming himself. Teaching her tongue to distinguish between vodkas; her eyes to appreciate Matisse. There were more gains than losses in bringing her body to her mind.

"Almost," she heard him say.

"I feel it."

"A little more. *Conjure*."

She looked down at the ground, aware that she had the freedom to do so. Her feet were there, standing on the threshold, naked. So, solidifying in front of her eyes, was the rest of her body. She was stark naked.

"Now . . ." said the man at the fire. "Close the door."

She turned and did so, her nakedness embarrassing her not at all, particularly after the effort she'd used bringing her body here. She worked out at the gym three times a week. She knew her belly was trim and her ass tight. Besides, her host was unconcerned, both with his own nudity and, it seemed, with giving her more than a cursory glance. If there'd ever been lechery in those eyes it had long ago dried up.

"So," he said. "I'm Kissoon. You're Tesla. Sit. Talk with me."

"I've got a lot of questions," she told him.

"I'd be surprised if you hadn't."

"I can ask?"

"Ask. But first, sit."

She squatted down on the opposite side of the fire to him. The floor was warm; the air too. Within thirty seconds her pores had begun to ooze. It was pleasant.

"First—" she said "—how did I get here? And where am I?"

"New Mexico is where you are," Kissoon replied. "And the how of it? Well, that's a more difficult question, but what it comes down to is this: I've been watching you—you and several others—waiting for a chance to bring someone here. Your near-death, and the Nuncio, helped erode your resistance to the journey. Indeed you had little choice."

"How much do you know about what's happening in the Grove?" she asked him.

He made dry sounds with his mouth, as though trying to summon saliva. When he finally replied it was with a weary tone.

"Oh God in Heaven, too much," he said, "I know too much."

"The Art, Quiddity . . . all that?"

"Yes," he said, with the same dispirited air. "All that. It was me began it, fool that I am. The creature you know as the Jaff once sat where you're sitting now. He was just a man then. Randolph Jaffe, impressive in his way—he had to have been to have got here in the first place—but still just a man."

"Did he come the way I came?" she asked. "I mean, was he near death?"

"No. He just had a greater hunger for the Art than most who went after it. He wasn't put off by the smoke screens, and the shams, and all the tricks that throw most people off the scent. He kept looking, until he found me."

Kissoon regarded Tesla with eyes narrowed, as if he might sharpen his sight that way, and get inside her skull.

"What to tell," he said. "Always the same problem: what to tell."

"You sound like Grillo," she remarked. "Have you spied on him?"

"Once or twice, when he crossed the path," Kissoon said. "But he's not important. You are. You're very important."

"How do you figure that?"

"You're here, for one. Nobody's been here since Randolph, and look what consequences that brought. This is no normal place, Tesla. I'm sure you've already guessed that. This is a Loop—a time out of time—which I made for myself."

"Out of time?" she said. "I don't understand."

"Where to begin," he said. "That's the other question, isn't it? First, what to tell. Then, where to begin . . . Well. You know about the Art. About Quiddity. Do you also know about the Shoal?"

She shook her head.

"It is, or *was*, one of the oldest orders in world religion. A tiny sect—seventeen of us at any one time—who had one dogma, the Art, one heaven, Quiddity, and one purpose, to keep both *pure*. This is its sign," he said, picking a small object up from the ground in front of him and tossing it across to her. At first glance she thought it was a crucifix. It was a cross, and at its center was a man, spreadeagled. But a closer perusal gave the lie to that. On each of the four arms of the symbol other forms were inscribed, which seemed to be corruptions of, or developments from, the central figure.

"You believe me?" he said.

"I believe you."

She threw the symbol back over to his side of the fire.

"Quiddity must be preserved, at any cost. No doubt you understood this from Fletcher?"

"He said that, yes. Was he one of the Shoal?"

Kissoon looked disdainful. "No, he'd never have made the grade. He was just an employee. The Jaff hired him to provide a chemical ride: a short-cut to the Art, and Quiddity."

"That was the Nuncio?"

"It was."

"Did it do the job?"

"It might have done, if Fletcher hadn't been touched with it himself."

"That was why they fought," she said.

"Yes," Kissoon replied. "Of course. But you know this. Fletcher must have told you."

"We didn't have much time. He explained bits and pieces. A lot of it was vague."

"He was no genius. Finding the Nuncio was more luck than talent."

"You met him?"

"I told you, nobody's been here since Jaffe. I'm alone."

"No you're not," Tesla said. "There was somebody outside—"

"The Lix, you mean? The serpent that opened the door? Just a little creation of mine. A doodle. Though I have enjoyed breeding them . . ."

"No. Not that," she said. "There was a woman, in the desert. I saw her."

"Oh really?" Kissoon said, a subtle shadow seeming to cross his face. "A woman?" He made a little smile. "Well, forgive me," he said. "I do *dream* still, once in a while. And there was a time when I could conjure whatever I desired by dreaming it. She was naked?"

"I don't think so."

"Beautiful?"

"I didn't get that close."

"Oh. A pity. But best for you. You're vulnerable here and I wouldn't want you hurt by a possessive mistress." His voice had lightened, become almost artificially casual.

"If you see her again, keep your distance," he advised. "On no account approach her."

"I won't."

"I hope she finds her way here. Not that I could do much now. The carcass . . ." He looked down at his withered body, ". . . has seen better days. But I could look. I like to look. Even at you, if you don't mind me saying."

"What do you mean, *even?*" Tesla said.

Kissoon laughed, low and dry. "Yes, I'm sorry. I meant it as a compliment. All these years alone. I've lost my social graces."

"You could go back, surely," she said. "You brought me here. Isn't there a two-way traffic?"

"Yes and no," he said.

"Meaning?"

"Meaning, I could, but I can't."

"Why?"

"I'm the last of the Shoal," he said. "The last living preserver of Quiddity. The rest have been murdered, and all attempts to replace them brought to nothing. Do you blame me for keeping out of sight? For watching from a safe distance? If I die without somehow reestablishing the tradition of the Shoal, Quiddity will be left unguarded, and I think you understand enough to know how cataclysmic that could be. The only possible way I can get out into the world and begin that vital work is in another shape. Another . . . body."

"Who are the murderers? Do you know?"

Again, that subtle shadow.

"I have my suspicions," he replied.

"But you're not telling."

"The history of the Shoal's littered with attempts on its integrity. It's got enemies human; sub; in; ab. If I started to explain we'd never be finished."

"Is any of this written down?"

"You mean, can you research it? No. But you can read between the lines of other histories, and you'll find the Shoal everywhere. It's the secret behind all other secrets. Entire religions were seeded and nurtured to distract attention from it, to direct spiritual seekers *away* from the Shoal, the Art and what the Art opened onto. It wasn't difficult.

People are easily thrown off track if the right scent is laid down. Promises of Revelation, Resurrection of the Body, that sort of thing—"

"Are you saying—"

"Don't interrupt," Kissoon said. "Please. I'm getting into my rhythm here."

"I'm sorry," Tesla said.

It's almost like a pitch, she thought. Like he's trying to *sell* me this whole extraordinary story.

"So. As I was saying . . . you can find the Shoal every where, if you know how to look. And some people did. There were several men and women down the years, like Jaffe, who managed to look through the shams and the smoke screens, and just kept on digging up the clues, breaking the codes, and the codes within the codes, until they got close to the Art. Then of course, the Shoal would be obliged to step in and act as we thought fit on a case-by-case basis. Some of these seekers, Gurdjieff, Melville, Emily Dickinson; an interesting cross-section, we simply initiated into a most sacred and secret adepthood, to train them to take over in our stead when death depleted our numbers. Others we judged unfit."

"What did you do with them?"

"Used our skills to blank all memory of their discovery from their heads. Which often proved fatal of course. You can't take a man's search for meaning away one day and expect him to survive it, especially if he's come close to finding an answer. It's my suspicion one of our rejects had remembered himself, or herself—"

"And murdered the Shoal."

"It seems the likeliest theory. It has to be somebody who knows about the Shoal and its workings. Which brings me to Randolph Jaffe."

"It's hard for me to think of him as *Randolph*," Tesla said. "Even as human."

"Believe me, he is. He's also the greatest error of judgment I ever made. I told him too much."

"More than you're telling me?"

"The situation's desperate now," Kissoon said. "If I don't tell you,

and get help from you, we're all lost. But with Jaffe . . . it was my stupidity. I wanted someone to share my loneliness with, and I chose
badly. Had the others been alive they would have stepped in, stopped
me making such a crass decision. They would have seen the corruption in him. I didn't. I was pleased he'd found me. I wanted the company. Wanted somebody to help me carry the burden of the Art. What
I created was a worse burden. Someone with the power to get access to
Quiddity but without the least spiritual refinement."

"He's got an army too."

"I know."

"Where do they come from?"

"The same place everything originates. The mind."

"Everything?"

"You're asking questions again."

"I can't help it."

"Yes, everything. The world and all its works; its makings and
unmakings; gods, lice and cuttlefish. All from the mind."

"I don't believe you."

"Why assume I care?"

"The mind can't create everything."

"I didn't say the *human* mind."

"Ah."

"If you listened more closely you wouldn't ask so many questions."

"But you want me to understand, or you wouldn't be spending all
this time."

"Time out of time. But yes . . . yes, I want you to understand. Given
the sacrifice you'll have to make it's important you know why."

"What sacrifice?"

"I told you: I can't get out of this place in my body. I'll be found,
and murdered, like the others . . ."

She shuddered, despite the warmth.

"I don't think I follow," she said.

"Yes you do."

"You want me to get you out somehow? Carry your thoughts."

"Near enough."

"Can't I simply act *for* you?" she said. "Be your agent? I'm good out there."

"I'm sure you are."

"You brief me, I'll do what it takes."

Kissoon shook his head. "There's so much you don't know," he said. "So vast a picture, I haven't even tried to unveil. I doubt your imagination could cope with it."

"Try me," she said.

"Are you sure?"

"I'm sure."

"Well, the issue here isn't simply the Jaff. He may taint Quiddity, but it'll survive."

"So what's the big problem?" Tesla said. "You give me all this shit about needing *sacrifice*. What for? If Quiddity can look after itself, *what for?*"

"Will you not simply trust me?"

She looked hard at him. The fire had sunk low but her eyes were by now well used to the amber gloom. Part of her wanted very much to put her trust in someone. But she'd spent most of her adult life learning the danger of that. Men, agents, studio executives, so many of them had asked her for her trust in the past, and she'd given it, and been fucked over. It was too late to learn a new way now. She was cynical to the marrow. If she ever stopped being that she'd stop being Tesla, and she liked being Tesla. It therefore followed—as night, day—that cynicism suited her too.

So she said:

"No. I'm sorry. I can't trust you. Don't take it personally. I'd be the same whoever you were. I want to know the bottom line."

"What does that mean?"

"I want the truth. Or I don't give you anything."

"Are you so sure you can refuse?" Kissoon said.

She half turned her face from him, glancing back, tightlipped, the way her favorite heroines did, with a look of accusation.

"That was a threat," she said.

"You could construe it that way," he observed.

"Well, fuck you—"

He shrugged. His passivity—the almost lazy way he regarded her—inflamed her further.

"I don't have to sit and listen to this, you know!"

"No?"

"No! You're hiding something from me."

"Now you're being ridiculous."

"I don't think so."

She stood up. His eyes didn't follow her face, but lingered at groin height. She was suddenly uncomfortable being naked in his presence. She wanted the clothes that were presumably still back at the Mission, stale and bloody as they'd be. If she was to get back there, she'd better start walking. She turned to the door.

Behind her, Kissoon said:

"Wait, Tesla. Please wait. The error's mine. I concede; the error's mine. Come back, will you?"

His tone was placating, but she read a less benign undertow. He's riled, she thought; for all his spiritual poise, he's pissed. It was a lesson in the facilities of dialogue to hear the bristle beneath the purr. She turned back to hear more, no longer certain that she could get the truth from this man. She only had to be threatened once to doubt.

"Go on," she said.

"You won't sit?"

"That's right," she said. She had to pretend she wasn't afraid, though suddenly she was; had to think of her skin as fashion enough. Stand, and be defiantly naked. "I won't sit."

"Then I'll try to explain as quickly as I can," he said. He'd effectively smoothed out every ambiguity in his manner. He was considerate; even humble.

"Even I, you must understand, don't have all the facts at my disposal," he said. "But I have enough, I hope, to convince you of the danger we're in."

"Who's *we*?"

"The inhabitants of the Cosm."

"Again?"

"Fletcher didn't explain this to you?"

"No."

He sighed.

"Think of Quiddity as a sea," he said.

"I'm thinking . . ."

"On one side of that sea is the reality we inhabit. A continent of being, if you like, the perimeters of which are sleep and death."

"So far, so good."

"Now . . . suppose there's another continent, on the other side of the sea."

"Another reality."

"Yes. As vast and complex as our own. As full of energies and species and appetites. But dominated, as the Cosm is, by one species in particular, with strange appetites."

"I don't like the sound of this."

"You wanted the truth."

"I'm not saying I believe you."

"That other place is the Metacosm. That species is the Iad Uroboros. They exist."

"And the appetites?" she said, not certain she really wanted to know.

"For *purity*. For *singularity*. For *madness*."

"Some hunger."

"You were right when you accused me of not telling the truth. I told a part of it only. The Shoal *did* stand guard at the shores of Quiddity to prevent the Art from being misused by human ambition; but it also stood to *watch* the sea . . ."

"For an invasion?"

"That's what we feared. Maybe even expected. It wasn't simply our paranoia. The profoundest dreams of evil are those in which we scent the Iad across Quiddity. The deepest terrors, the foulest imaginings that haunt human heads are the echoes of *their* echoes. I am giving you more reason to be afraid, Tesla, than you could hear from any other lips. I'm telling you what only the strongest psyches can bear."

"Is there any good news?" Tesla said.

"Who ever promised that? Who ever said there'd be *good* news?"

"Jesus," she replied. "And Buddha. Mohammed."

"Fragments of stories, massaged into cults by the Shoal. Distractions."

"I can't believe that."

"Why not? Are you a Christian?"

"No."

"Buddhist? Muslim? Hindu?"

"No. No. No."

"But you insist on believing the good news anyway," Kissoon said. "Convenient."

She felt she'd been struck, very hard, across the face, by a teacher who'd been three or four steps ahead of her throughout the entire argument, leading her steadily and stealthily to a place where she could not help but mouth absurdities. And absurd it was, to cling to hopes for Heaven when she poured piss on every religion that passed beneath her window. But she reeled not because Kissoon had scored a solid debating point. She'd taken her lumps in countless arguments, and come back to give worse. What made her sick to her stomach was that her defense against so much else he'd said was forfeit at the same moment. If even a part of what he'd told her was true, and the world she lived in—the Cosm—was in jeopardy, then what right did she have to value her little life over his desperate need for assistance? Even assuming she could find her way out of this time out of time she couldn't return to the world without wondering every moment if in leaving him she'd lost the Cosm's one chance for survival. She had to stay; had to give herself over to him, not because she entirely believed him, but because she couldn't risk being wrong.

"Don't be afraid," she heard him say. "The situation's no worse than it was five minutes ago, when you were quite the debater. You just know the truth now."

"Not much comfort," she said.

"No," he replied softly. "I do see that. And you must see that this burden has been hard to carry alone, and that without assistance my back'll break."

"I understand," she said.

She'd stepped away from the fire, and was standing against the wall of the hut, both for its support and for its coolness against her spine. Leaning there, she stared at the ground, aware that Kissoon had started to stand up. She didn't look at him, but she heard his grunts. And then his request.

"I need to occupy your body," he said. "Which means, I'm afraid, that you must vacate it."

The fire had dwindled to almost nothing, but its smoke was thickening. It pressed the top of her skull, making it impossible for her to raise her head and look at him even if she'd wanted to. She started to tremble. First her knees, then her fingers. Kissoon continued to talk as he approached. She heard his soft shuffling.

"This won't hurt," he said. "If you just stand still, and keep your eyes on the ground—"

A slow thought came: was he making the smoke heavy, by some means, in order to stop her looking at him?

"It'll be over quickly—"

He sounds like an anesthetist, she thought. The trembling intensified. The smoke pressed more heavily upon her the closer he came. She was certain now that this was indeed his doing. He didn't want her looking up at him. Why? Was he coming at her with knives, to scoop out her brain so he could slip in behind her eyes?

Resisting curiosity had never been one of her stronger points. The closer he came the more she wanted to push against the weight of smoke, and look directly at him. But it was difficult. Her body was weak, as though her blood had gone to dishwater. The smoke was like a lead hat; its brim too tight around her brow. The harder she pushed, the heavier it became.

He really doesn't want me to look, she thought, that thought feeding her passion to do so. She braced herself against the wall. He was within two yards of her now. She could smell him; his sweat was bitter and stale. Push, she told herself, push! It's only smoke. He's making you think you're being crushed, but it's only smoke.

"Relax," he murmured; the anesthetist again.

Instead she put one last surge of effort into raising her head. The lead hat dug into her temples; her skull creaked beneath the weight of the crown. But her head moved, trembling as she fought the weight. Once begun, the motion became easier. She lifted her chin an inch, then another two, raising her eyes at the same moment until she was looking straight at him.

Standing, he was crooked in every place but one, each joint and juncture a little askew, shoulder on neck, hand on arm; thigh on hip, a zig-zag with a single straight line prodding from his groin. She stared, appalled.

"What the fuck's that for?" she said.

"Couldn't help myself," he said. "I'm sorry."

"Oh yeah?"

"When I said I want your body, I don't mean that way."

"Where have I heard that before?"

"Believe me," he said. "It's just my flesh responding to yours. Automatic. Be flattered."

She might have laughed, in different circumstances. Had she been able to open the door and walk away, for instance, instead of being lost out of time, with a beast on the threshold and a desert beyond. Every time she thought she had a grasp of what was going on here she lost it again. The man was one surprise after another, and none of them pleasant.

He reached towards her, his pupils vast, crowding out the whites. She thought of Raul; of how there was beauty in his gaze, despite his hybrid's face. There was no beauty here; nothing even vaguely readable. No appetite; no anger. If there was feeling at all, it was eclipsed.

"I can't do this," she said.

"You must. Give up the body. I have to have the body or the Iad wins. You want that?"

"No!"

"Then stop resisting. Your spirit'll be safe in Trinity."

"*Where?*"

Momentarily he let something show in his eyes, a spark of fury — self-directed, she thought.

"*Trinity?*" she said, throwing the question out to delay his touching and claiming her. "*What's Trinity?*"

As she asked this question several things happened simultaneously, their speed defying her power to divide one from the other, but central to them all the fact that his hold on the situation slipped as she asked him about Trinity. First she felt the smoke dissolving above her, its weight no longer bearing her down. Taking her chance while it was still available she reached for the handle of the door. Her eyes were still on him however, and in the same instant as her release she saw him transfigured. It was a glimpse, no more, but so powerful as to be unforgettable. He appeared with his upper body covered in blood, splashes of it reaching as far as his face. He knew she saw, because his hands went up to cover the stains, but his hands and arms were also running with blood. Was it his? Before she could look to find a wound he had control of the vision once again, but like a juggler attempting to hold too many balls in the air catching one meant losing another. The blood vanished, and he appeared before her unscathed again, only to unleash some other secret his will had kept in check.

It was far more cataclysmic than the blood splashes: its shock wave striking the door behind her. Too powerful for the Lix, even if they were massed, it was a force Kissoon was clearly in terror of. His eyes went from her to the door itself, his hands dropping to his sides and all expression gone from his face. She sensed that every particle of his energies was being put to a single purpose: the stilling of whatever raged on the threshold. This too had its consequence, as the hold he'd had upon her—bringing her here, and keeping her—finally and comprehensively slipped. She felt the reality she'd left catch hold of her spine, and pull. She didn't even attempt to resist. It was as inevitable a claim as gravity.

The last glimpse she had of Kissoon he was once more blood-stained, and standing, his face still drained of expression in front of the door. Then it threw itself open.

There was a moment when she was certain whatever had beaten against the door would be waiting on the step to devour her, and

Kissoon too. She thought she even glimpsed its brightness—so bright, so blindingly bright—flood Kissoon's features. But his will got the better of it at the last moment, and its glare diminished at the very moment the world she'd left claimed her and hauled her through the door.

She was flung back the way she'd come, at ten times the speed of her arrival, so fast she wasn't even able to interpret the sights she was passing—the steel tower, the town—until she was miles beyond them.

She wasn't alone this time, however. There was somebody near to her, calling her name.

"Tesla? Tesla! Tesla!"

She knew the voice. It was Raul.

"I hear you," she muttered, aware that through the blur of speed another, darker reality was vaguely visible. There were points of light in it—candle flames perhaps—and faces.

"Tesla!"

"Almost there," she gasped. "Almost there. Almost there."

Now the desert was being subsumed; the darkness took precedence. She opened her eyes wide to see Raul more clearly. There was a wide smile on his face as he went down on his haunches to greet her.

"You came back," he said.

The desert had gone. It was all night now. Stones beneath her, stars above; and, as she guessed, candles, being carried by a ring of astonished women.

Beneath her, between body and ground, were the clothes she'd slipped from when she'd called her body to her, recreating it in Kissoon's Loop. She reached up to touch Raul's face, as much as to be certain she was indeed back in the solid world as for the contact. His cheeks were wet.

"You've been working hard," she said, thinking it was sweat. Then she realized her error. Not sweat at all; tears.

"Oh, poor Raul," she said, and sat up to embrace him. "Did I disappear completely?"

He pressed himself to her. "First like fog," he said. "Then . . . just gone."

"Why are we here?" she said. "I was in the Mission when he shot me."

Thinking of the shot, she looked down at where the bullet had struck. There was no wound; not even blood.

"The Nuncio," she said. "It healed me."

The fact was not lost on the women. Seeing the unmarked skin they muttered prayers, and backed away.

"No . . ." she murmured, still looking down at her body. "It wasn't the Nuncio. This is the body I *imagined*."

"Imagined?" said Raul.

"Conjured," she replied, scarcely even aware of Raul's confusion because she had a puzzle of her own. Her left nipple, twice the size of its neighbor, was now on the right. She kept staring at them, shaking her head. It wasn't the kind of thing she'd make a mistake about. Somehow, on the journey to the Loop, or back, she'd been flipped. She brought her legs up for study. Several scratches—Butch's work— that had adorned one shin now marked the other.

"I can't figure it," she said to Raul.

Not even understanding the question he was hard-pressed to reply, so simply shrugged.

"Never mind," she said, and started to get dressed.

Only then did she ask what had happened to the Nuncio.

"Did I get it all?" she said.

"No. The Death-Boy got it."

"Tommy-Ray? Oh Jesus. So now the Jaff has a son and a half."

"But you were touched too," Raul said. "So was I. It got into my hand. Climbed up to the elbow."

"So it's us against them."

Raul shook his head. "I can't be of use to you," he said.

"You can and you must," she said. "There's so many questions we have to have answered. I can't do it on my own. You must come with me."

His reluctance was perfectly apparent without his voicing it.

"I know you're afraid. But please, Raul. You brought me back from the dead—"

"Not me."

"You helped. You wouldn't want that wasted, would you?"

She could hear something of Kissoon's persuasions in her own, and didn't much like the sound. But then she'd never experienced a steeper learning curve in her life than in the time she'd spent with Kissoon. He'd made his mark without so much as laying a finger on her. But if she'd been asked whether he was a liar or a prophet, a savior or a lunatic, she couldn't have said. Perhaps that ambiguity was the steepest part of the curve, though what lesson she'd gained from it she couldn't say.

Her thoughts went back to Raul, and his reluctance. There was no time for involved argument. "You simply have to come," she told him. "There's no getting out of it."

"But the Mission—"

"—is *empty*, Raul. The only treasure it had was the Nuncio, and that's gone."

"It had memories," he said softly, the tense of his reply signalling his acceptance.

"There'll be other memories. Better times to remember," she said. "Now . . . if you've got people to say goodbye to, say it, because we're rolling—"

He nodded, and began to address the women in Spanish. Tesla had a smattering of the language; enough to confirm that he was indeed making his farewells. Leaving him to it, she headed up the hill towards the car.

As she walked the solution to the puzzle of the flipped body appeared in her head, without the problem being consciously turned. In Kissoon's hut she'd imagined herself the way she most often *saw* herself: in a mirror. How many times in her thirty odd years had she looked at her own reflection, building up a portrait in which right was left, and vice versa?

She'd come back from the Loop a different woman, literally; a woman who'd only ever existed as an image in glass. Now that image was flesh and blood, and walking the world. Behind its face the mind remained the same, she hoped, albeit touched by the Nuncio, and by knowing Kissoon. Not, in sum, negligible influences.

What with one thing and another she was a whole new story. No better time to tell herself to the world than the present.

Tomorrow might never come.

PART SIX

In Secrets, Most Revealed

ONE

Tommy-Ray had been in the driver's seat of a car since his six-teenth birthday. Wheels had signalled freedom from Momma, the Pastor, the Grove and all they stood for. Now he was heading back to the very place a few years ago he couldn't have escaped from fast enough, his foot on the accelerator every mile of the way. He wanted to walk the Grove again with the news his body carried, wanted to go back to his father, who'd taught him so much. Until the Jaff the best life had offered was an off-shore wind and a west swell at Topanga; him on a crest knowing the girls were all watching him from the beach. But he'd always known those high times couldn't last forever. New heroes came along, summer after summer. He'd been one of them, supplanting surfers no more than a couple of years older, who weren't quite as lithe. Boy-men like himself who'd been the cream of the swell the season before, suddenly old news. He wasn't stupid. He knew it was only a matter of time before he joined their ranks.

But now, he had a purpose in his belly and brain he'd never had before. He'd discovered ways to think and behave the airheads at Topanga never even guessed existed. Much of that he had to thank the Jaff for. But even his father, for all his wild advice, hadn't prepared him for what had happened at the Mission. He was a *myth* now. Death at the wheel of a Chevy, racing for home. He knew music that would have people dancing till they dropped. And when they dropped, and went to meat, he knew all about that too. He'd seen the spectacle at work on his own flesh. It gave him a boner remembering.

But the night's fun had only just started. Less than a hundred miles north of the Mission his route took him through a small village on the fringes of which lay a cemetery. The moon was still high. Its brightness gleamed on the tombs, washing the color from the flowers that were laid here and there. He stopped the car, to get a better look. After all, this was his territory from now on. It was home.

If he'd needed any further proof that what had happened at the Mission was not the invention of a crazyman, he got it when he pushed open the gate and wandered in. There was no wind to stir the grass, which grew to knee height in several places, where tombs had been left untended. But there was movement there nevertheless. He advanced a few more paces, and saw human figures rising into view from a dozen places. They were dead. Had their appearance not testified to the fact the luminescence of their bodies—which were as bright as the bone shard he'd found beside the car—would have marked them as part of his clan.

They knew who had come to visit them. Their eyes, or in the case of the ancients among them, their *sockets*, were set on him as they moved to do him homage. None even glanced at the ground as they came, though it was uneven. They knew this turf too well, familiar with the spots where badly built tombs had toppled, or a casket been pushed back up to the surface by some motion in the earth. Their progress was, however, slow. He was in no hurry. He sat himself down on the grave which contained, the stone recorded, seven children and their mother, and watched the ghosts come his way. The closer they came the more of their condition he saw. It wasn't pretty. A wind blew out of them, twisting them out of true. Their faces were either too wide or too long, their eyes bulging, their mouths blown open, cheeks flopping. Their ugliness put Tommy-Ray in mind of a film he'd seen of pilots enduring G-force, the difference being that these were not volunteers. They suffered against their will.

He was not disturbed in the least by their distortions; nor by the holes in their wretched bodies, or their slashed and severed limbs. It was nothing he hadn't seen in comic books by the age of six; or on a ghost-train ride. The horrors were everywhere, if you wanted to look. On bubble-gum cards, and Saturday morning cartoons, or in the stores on T-shirts and album covers. He smiled to think of that. There were outposts of his empire everywhere. No place was untouched by the Death-Boy's finger.

The speediest of these, his first devotees, was a man who looked to have died young, and recently. He wore a pair of jeans two sizes too big for him, and a muscle shirt adorned with a hand presenting the fuck sign to the world. He also wore a hat, which he took off when he came within a few yards of Tommy-Ray. The head beneath had been practically shaved, exposing several long cuts to view. The fatal wounds, presumably. There was no blood out of them now; just a whine of the wind that blew through the man's gut.

A little distance from Tommy-Ray he stopped.

"Do you speak?" the Death-Boy asked him.

The man opened his mouth, which was already wide, a little wider, and proceeded to make a reply as best he could, by working it up from his throat. Watching him, Tommy-Ray remembered a performer he'd seen on a late show, who'd swallowed and then regurgitated live gold-fish. Though it was several years ago the sight had struck a chord in Tommy-Ray's imagination. The spectacle of a man able to reverse his system by practice, vomiting up what he'd held in his throat—not in the stomach surely; no fish, however scaly, could survive in acid—had been worth the queasiness he'd felt while watching. Now the Fuck-You-Man was giving a similar performance, only with words instead of fishes. They came at last, but dry as his innards.

"Yes," he said, "I speak."

"Do you know who I am?" Tommy-Ray asked.

The man made a moan.

"Yes or no?"

"No."

"I'm the Death-Boy, and you're the Fuck-You-Man. How 'bout that? Don't we make a pair?"

"You're here for us," the dead man said.

"What do you mean?"

"We're not buried. Not blessed."

"Don't look at me for help," Tommy-Ray said. "I'm burying nobody. I came to look because this is my kind of place now. I'm going to be King of the Dead."

"Yes?"

"Depend on it."

Another of the lost souls—a wide hipped woman—had approached, and puked up some words of her own.

"You . . ." she said, ". . . are *shining*."

"Yeah?" said Tommy-Ray. "Doesn't surprise me. You're bright too. Real bright."

"We belong together," the woman said.

"All of us," said a third cadaver.

"Now you're getting the picture."

"Save us," said the woman.

"I already told the Fuck-You-Man," Tommy-Ray said, "I'm burying nobody."

"We'll follow you," the woman said.

"Follow?" Tommy-Ray replied, a shudder of excitement running down his spine at the idea of returning to the Grove with such a congregation in tow. Maybe there were other places he could visit along the way, and swell the numbers as he went.

"I like the idea," he said. "But how?"

"You lead. We'll follow," came the response.

Tommy-Ray stood up. "Why not?" he said, and started back towards the car. Even as he went he found himself thinking: this is going to be the end of me . . .

And thinking, didn't care.

Once at the wheel he looked back towards the cemetery. A wind had blown up from somewhere, and in it he saw the company that he'd chosen to keep seem to *dissolve*, their bodies coming undone as though they were made of sand, and being blown apart. Specks of their dust blew in his face. He squinted against it, unwilling to look away from the spectacle. Though their bodies were disappearing he could still hear their howls. They were like the wind, or *were* the wind, making their presence known. With their dissolution complete he turned from the blast, and put his foot on the accelerator. The car leapt forward, kicking up another spurt of dust to join the pursuing dervishes.

He had been right about there being more places along the route to gather ghosts. *I'll always be right from now on,* he thought. *Death's never wrong; never, ever wrong.* He found another cemetery within an hour's drive of the first, with a dust dervish of half-dissolved souls running back and forth along its front wall like a dog on a leash, impatiently awaiting the arrival of its master. Word of his coming had gone before him apparently. They were waiting, these souls, ready to join the throng. He didn't even have to slow the car. At his approach the dust storm came to meet him, momentarily smothering the vehicle before rising to join the souls behind. Tommy-Ray just drove straight on.

Towards dawn his unhappy band found yet more adherents. There had been a collision at a crossroads, earlier in the night. There was broken glass scattered across the road; blood; and one of the two cars—now barely recognizable as such—overturned at the side of the road. He slowed to look, not expecting there to be any haunters here, but even as he did so he heard the now familiar whining wind and saw two wretched forms, a man and a woman, appear from the darkness. They'd not yet got the trick of their condition. The wind that blew through them, or out of them, threatened with every faltering step they took to throw them over on to their broken heads. But newly dead as they were, they sensed their Lord in Tommy-Ray, and came obediently. He smiled to see them; their fresh wounds (glass in their faces, in their eyes) excited him.

There was no exchange of words. As they drew closer they seemed to take a signal from their comrades in death behind Tommy-Ray's car, allowing their bodies to erode completely, and join the wind.

His legion swelled, Tommy-Ray drove on.

There were other such meetings along the way; they seemed to multiply the further north he drove, as though word of his approach went through the earth, from buried thing to buried thing, graveyard whispers, so that there were dusty phantoms waiting all along the way. By no means all of them had come to join the party. Some had apparently come simply to stare at the passing parade. There was fear on their faces when they looked at Tommy-Ray. He'd become the Terror in the ghost-train now, and they were the chilled punters. There were hierarchies even among the dead it seemed, and he was too elevated a company for many of them to keep; his ambition too great, his appetite too depraved. They preferred quiet rot to such adventure.

It was early morning by the time he reached the nameless hick-town in which he'd lost his wallet, but the daylight did not reveal the host in the dust storm that followed him. To any who chose to look — and few did, in such a blinding wind — a cloud of dirty air came in the car's wake; that was the sum of it.

He had other business here than the collecting of lost souls — though he didn't doubt for a moment that in such a wretched place life was quickly and violently over, and many bodies never laid to sanctified rest. No, his business here was revenge upon the pocket-picker. Or if not upon him, at least upon the den where it had happened. He found the place easily. The front door wasn't locked, as he'd expected at such an early hour. Nor, once he stepped inside, did he find the bar empty. Last night's drinkers were still scattered around the place, in various stages of collapse. One lay face down on the floor, vomit spattered around him. Another two were sprawled at tables. Behind the bar itself was a man Tommy-Ray vaguely remembered as the doorman who'd taken his money for the backroom show. A lump of a man, with a face that looked to have been bruised so many times it'd never lose the stain.

"Looking for someone?" he demanded to know.

Tommy-Ray ignored him, crossing to the door that let on the arena where he'd seen the woman and the dog performing. It was open. The space beyond was empty, the players gone home to their beds and their kennels. The barman was a yard from him when he turned back into the bar.

"I asked a fucking question," he said.

Tommy-Ray was a little taken aback by the man's blindness. Did he not recognize the fact that he was speaking to a transformed creature? Had his perception been so dulled by years of drinking and dog-shows he couldn't see the Death-Boy when he came visiting? More fool him.

"Get out of my way," Tommy-Ray said.

Instead, the man took hold of the front of Tommy-Ray's shirt. "You been here before," he said.

"Yeah."

"Left something behind, did you?"

He pulled Tommy-Ray closer, till they were practically nose to nose. He had a sick man's breath.

"I'd let go if I were you," Tommy-Ray warned.

The man looked amused at this. "You're looking to get your fucking balls ripped off," he said. "Or do you want to join the show?" His eyes widened at this notion. "Is that what you came looking for? An audition?"

"I told you . . ." Tommy-Ray began.

"I don't give a fuck what you told me. I'm doing the talking now. Hear me?" He put one vast hand over Tommy-Ray's mouth. "So . . . do you want to show me something or not?"

The image of what he'd seen in the room behind him came back into Tommy-Ray's head as he stared up at his assaulter: the woman, glassy-eyed; the dog, glassy-eyed. He'd seen death here, in life. He opened his mouth against the man's palm, and pressed his tongue against the stale skin.

The man grinned.

"Yeah?" he said.

He dropped his hand from Tommy-Ray's face. "You got something to show?" he said again.

"*Here* . . ." Tommy-Ray murmured.

"What?"

"*Come in . . . come in . . .*"

"What are you talking about?"

"Not talking to you. *Here. Come . . . in . . . here.*" His gaze went from the man's face to the door.

"Don't give me shit, kid," the man responded. "You're on your own."

"*Come in!*" Tommy-Ray yelled.

"Shut the fuck up!"

"*Come in!*"

His din maddened the man. He hit Tommy-Ray across the face, so hard the blow knocked the boy out of his grip to the floor. Tommy-Ray didn't get up. He simply stared at the door, and made his invitation one more time.

"*Please come in,*" he said, more quietly.

Was it because he *asked* this time instead of demanded, that the legion obeyed? Or simply that they'd been mustering themselves, and were only now ready to come to his aid? Either way, they began to rattle the closed doors. The barman grunted and turned. Even to his bleary eyes it must have been perfectly apparent that it was no natural wind that was pushing to come in. It pressed too rhythmically; it beat its fist too heavily. And its howls, oh its howls were nothing like the howls of any storm he'd heard before. He turned back to Tommy-Ray.

"What the fuck's out there?" he said.

Tommy-Ray just lay where he'd been thrown and smiled up at the man, that legendary smile, that forgive-me-my-trespasses smile, that would never be the same again now that he was the Death-Boy.

Die, that smile now said, *die while I watch you. Die slowly. Die quickly. I don't care. It's all the same to the Death-Boy.*

As the smile spread the doors opened, shards of the lock, and splinters of wood, thrown across the bar before the invading wind. Out in the sunlight the spirits in this storm had not been visible; but they made themselves so now, congealing their dust in front of the witnesses' eyes. One of the men slumped on the table roused himself in time to see three figures forming from the head down in front of him, their torsos trailing like innards of dust. He backed off against the wall, where they threw themselves upon him. Tommy-Ray heard his screech but didn't see what kind of death they gave him. His eyes were on the spirits that were coming at the bartender.

Their faces were all appetite, he saw; as though travelling together in that caravan had given them time to simplify themselves. They were no longer as distinct from each other as they'd been; perhaps their dust had mingled in the storm, and each had become a little like the other. Unparticularized, they were more terrible than they'd been at the cemetery wall. He shuddered at the sight, the remnants of the man he'd been in fear of them, the Death-Boy in bliss. These were soldiers in his army: eyes vast, mouths vaster, dust and want in one howling legion.

The bartender started to pray out loud, but he wasn't putting his faith in prayer alone. He reached down to his side and picked Tommy-Ray up one-handed, hauling him close. Then, with his hostage taken, he opened the door to the sex arena and backed through it. Tommy-Ray heard him repeating something as they went, the hook of the prayer perhaps? *Santo Dios! Santo Dios!* But neither words nor hostage slowed the advance of the wind and its dusty freight. They came after him, throwing the door wide.

Tommy-Ray saw their mouths grow huger still, and then the blur of faces was upon them both. He lost sight of what happened next. The dust filled his eyes before he had an opportunity to close them. But he felt the bartender's grip slide from him, and the next moment a rush of wet heat. The howling in the wind instantly rose in volume to a keening that he tried to stop his ears against, but it came anyway, boring into the bone of his head like a hundred drills.

When he opened his eyes he was red. Chest, arms, legs, hands: all red. The bartender, the source of the color, had been dragged on to the stage where the night before Tommy had seen the woman and the dog. His head was in one corner, upended; his arms, hands locked in supplication, in another; the rest of him lay center stage, the neck still pumping.

Tommy-Ray tried not to be sickened (he was the Death-Boy, after all) but this was too much. And yet, he told himself, what had he expected when he'd invited them over the threshold? This was not a circus he had in tow. It was not sane; it was not civilized.

Shaking, sickened and chastened, he got to his feet and hauled himself back out into the bar. His legion's labors here were as cataclysmic as those he'd turned his back upon. All three of the bar's occupants had been brutally slaughtered. Giving the scene only the most casual perusal, he crossed through the destruction to the door.

Events inside the bar had inevitably attracted an audience outside, even at such an early hour. But the velocity of the wind—in which his ghost army was once more dissolved—kept all but the most adventurous, youths and children, from approaching the scene, and even they were cowed by the suspicion that the air howling around them was not entirely empty.

They watched the blond, blood-spattered boy emerge from the bar and cross to his car, but made no attempt to apprehend him. Their scrutiny made Tommy-Ray take note of his gait. Instead of slouching he walked more upright. When they remembered the Death-Boy, he thought, let them remember someone *terrible*.

As he drove he began to believe he'd left the legion behind; that they'd found the game of murder more exciting than follow the leader and were going on to slaughter the rest of the town. He didn't much mind the desertion. Indeed he was in part thankful for it. The revelations that had seemed so welcome the previous night had lost some of their glamour.

He was sticky and stinking with another man's blood; he was bruised from the bartender's handling of him. Naively enough he'd believed that the touch of the Nuncio had made him immortal. What was the use of being the Death-Boy, after all, if death could still master you? In learning the error of his ways he'd come closer to losing his life than he cared to think too hard about. As to his saviors, his *legion*— he'd been equally naive in his belief that he had control of them.

They were not the shambling, fawning refugees he'd taken them for the previous night. Or if they had been, their being together had changed their nature. Now they were lethal, and would probably have slipped from his control sooner or later anyhow. He was better off without them.

He stopped to wipe the blood from his face before crossing the border, turned his bloodied shirt inside out to conceal the worst of the stains, then drove on. As he reached the border itself he saw the dust cloud in the mirror, and knew his relief at losing his legion had been premature. Whatever slaughter had detained them they'd done with it. He put his foot down, hoping against hope to lose them, but they had the scent of him, and followed like a pack of loyal but lethal dogs, closing on the car till they were once more swirling behind him.

Once over the border the cloud picked up its pace, so that instead of following, it surrounded the car to left and right. There was more purpose in the maneuver than mere intimacy. Spirits hauled the windows and rattled at the passenger door, finally pulling it open. Tommy-Ray reached to drag it closed again. As he did so the bartender's head, much battered by being carried by the storm, was pitched out of the dust on to the seat beside him. Then the door was slammed, and the cloud once more took its dutiful place as his train.

His instinct was to stop and throw the trophy out on to the street, but he knew that to do so would confirm his weakness in his legion's estimation. They'd not brought him the head simply to humor him, though that might be their pretense. There was a warning here; even a threat. *Don't try to cheat or betray them*, the dusty, bloody ball announced from its gaping mouth, *or you and I'll be brothers.*

He took the silent message to heart. Though he was still ostensibly the leader, the dynamic changed thereafter. Every few miles the cloud would once more pick up its pace and merge one way or another, pointing him towards more of their number; many waiting in the unlikeliest of places: squalid street corners and minor intersections (often at intersections); once in the lot of a motel; once outside a boarded-up gas station, where a man, a woman and a child all waited, as though they'd known this transport would be coming along.

As the numbers swelled, so did the scale of the storm that carried them, until its passage was sufficient to cause minor damage along the highway, driving cars off the road, and blowing down signs. It even made the news bulletin. Tommy-Ray heard the report as he drove. It was described as a freak wind, which had blown up off the ocean and was proceeding north towards Los Angeles County.

He wondered, as he listened, if anyone in Palomo Grove would hear the report. The Jaff maybe; or Jo-Beth. He hoped so. He hoped they heard, and understood what was coming their way. The town had seen some strange sights since his father's return from the rock, but nothing, surely, the equal of the wind he had in tow, or the living dust that danced on its back.

TWO

It was hunger that drove William out from his home on Saturday
morning. He went reluctantly, like a man at an orgy suddenly
aware that his bladder had to be emptied, and exiting with many a
backward glance. But hunger, like the need to piss, couldn't be
ignored forever, and William had exhausted what few supplies his
refrigerator had contained very quickly. Working as he did at the Mall
he'd never stocked up on food, but taken a quarter of an hour every
day to wander around the supermarket and pick up whatever got him
salivating. But he'd not been shopping now for two days, and if he
wasn't to starve to death in the lap of the tasty but inedible luxuries
gathered behind the drawn blinds of his home he had to fetch himself
something to eat. This was easier said than done. His mind was so
wholly obsessed by the company he was keeping that the simple problem of making himself presentable for a public appearance and going
down to the Mall became a major challenge.

Until recently, his life had been so very organized. The week's shirts
were always washed and pressed on a Sunday, laid out on his dresser
with the five bow ties selected from his hundred and eleven to com-
plement the shade of the shirt; his kitchen could have been shot for an

ad campaign, its surfaces always pristine; the sink smelled of lemon; the washing machine of his flower-scented fabric conditioner; his toilet bowl of pine.

But Babylon had taken control of his house. He'd last seen his best suit being worn by the notorious bisexual Marcella St. John, while she straddled one of her girlfriends. His bow ties had been purloined for a competition to see which of three erections could wear the most, a tournament won by Moses "The Hose" Jasper, who'd ended up sporting seventeen.

Rather than try and tidy up, or claim any of these belongings back, William decided to let the celebrants have their way. He rummaged in his bottom drawer and found a sweatshirt and jeans he'd not worn for several years, put them on, and wandered down to the Mall.

At about the time he was doing so Jo-Beth was waking with the worst hangover of her life. The worst, because the first.

Her memories of the previous night's events were uncertain. She remembered going to Lois's house, of course, and the guests, and Howie arriving, but how all of this had ended up she couldn't be sure. She got up feeling giddy and sick, and went to the bathroom. Momma, hearing her moving about, came upstairs and was waiting for her when she emerged.

"Are you all right?" she asked.

"No," Jo-Beth freely admitted. "I feel terrible."

"You were drinking last night."

"Yes," she said. There was no purpose in denial.

"Where did you go?"

"To see Lois."

"There'd be no liquor in Lois's house," Momma said.

"There was last night. And a lot more besides."

"Don't lie to me, Jo-Beth."

"I'm not lying."

"Lois would never have that poison in the house."

"I think you should hear her tell it herself," Jo-Beth said, defying Momma's accusing looks. "I think we should both go down to the store and speak to her."

"I'm not leaving the house," Momma told her flatly.

"You went out into the yard the night before last. Today you can get in the car."

She spoke as she'd never spoken to Momma before, with a kind of rage in her tone which was in part response to Momma's calling her a liar, and in part against herself for not being able to think her way through the blur of the previous night. What had happened between Howie and herself? Had they argued? She thought so. They'd certainly parted on the street . . . but why? It was another reason to speak to Lois.

"I mean what I say, Momma," she said. "We're both of us going to go down to the Mall."

"No, I can't . . ." Momma said. "Really I can't. I feel so sick today."

"No you don't."

"Yes. My stomach . . ."

"*No*, Momma! Enough of that! You can't pretend to be sick for the rest of your life, just because you're afraid. *I'm* afraid too, Momma."

"It's good you're afraid."

"No it's not. It's what the Jaff wants. What he feeds on. The fear inside. I know that because I've seen it working and it's horrible."

"We can pray. Prayer—"

"—won't do us any good any longer. It didn't help the Pastor. It won't help us." She was raising her voice, which in turn made her head spin, but she knew this had to be said now before full sobriety returned, and with it, fear of offending.

"You always said it was dangerous outside," she went on, not liking to hurt Momma the way she surely was, but unable to stem the flow of feeling. "Well it *is* dangerous. Even more than you thought. But *inside*, Momma—" she jabbed at her chest, meaning her heart, meaning Howie and Tommy-Ray and the terror that she'd lost them both "—*inside*, it's worse. Even worse. To have things . . . *dreams* . . . just for a while . . . then have them taken away before you can get a hold of them properly."

"You're not making any sense, Jo-Beth," Momma said.

"Lois'll tell you," she replied. "I'm going to take you down to see Lois, and then you'll believe."

———

Howie sat at the window and let the sun dry the sweat on his skin. Its smell was as familiar to him as his own face in the mirror, more familiar, perhaps, because his face kept changing and the smell of sweat didn't. He needed the comfort of such familiarity now, with nothing certain in all the world but that nothing was certain. He could find no way through the tangle of feelings in his gut. What had seemed simple the day before, when he'd stood in the sun at the back of the house and kissed Jo-Beth, was no longer simple. Fletcher might be dead but he'd left a legacy here in the Grove, a legacy of dream-creatures which viewed him as some substitute for their lost creator. He couldn't be that. Even if they didn't share Fletcher's view of Jo-Beth, which after last night's confrontation they surely did, he still couldn't fulfill their expectations. He'd come here a desperado and become, albeit fleetingly, a lover. Now they wanted to make a general of him; wanted marching orders and battle plans. He could supply neither. Nor would Fletcher have been able to offer such direction. The army he'd created would have to elect a leader from its own ranks, or disperse.

He'd rehearsed these arguments so often now he almost believed them; or rather, had almost convinced himself he wasn't a coward for *wanting* to believe them. But the trick hadn't worked. He came back and back to the same stark fact: that once, in the woods, Fletcher had warned him to make a choice between Jo-Beth and his destiny, and he'd flown in the face of that advice. The consequences of his desertion, whether direct or indirect was immaterial now, had been Fletcher's public death, a last, desperate attempt to seize some hope for the future. Now here was he, the unprodigal son, willfully turning his back on the product of that sacrifice.

And yet; and yet; always, and yet. If he sided with Fletcher's army then he became part of the war he and Jo-Beth had studiously attempted to remain untouched by. She would become one of the enemy, simply by birth.

What he wanted more than anything, ever in his life—more than the pubic hair he'd tried to will into growing at age eleven, more than the motorcycle he'd stolen at fourteen, more than his mother back from death for two minutes just so he could tell her how sorry he was for all the times he'd made her cry; more, at this moment, than Jo-Beth—was *certainty*. Just to be told which way was the right way, which act was the right act, and have the comfort that even if it turned out not to be the way or the act it was not his responsibility. But there was nobody to tell him. He had to think this out for himself. Sit in the sun and let the sweat dry on his skin, and work it out for himself.

The Mall was not as busy as it usually was on a Saturday morning, but William nevertheless met half a dozen people he knew on his way to the supermarket. One was his assistant Valerie.

"Are you all right?" she wanted to know. "I've been calling your house. You never answer."

"I've been ill," he said.

"I didn't bother to open the office yesterday. What with all the trouble the night before. It was a real mess. Roger went down, you know, when the alarms started?"

"Roger?"

She stared at him. "Yes, Roger."

"Oh yes," William said, not knowing whether this was Valerie's husband, brother or dog, and not much caring.

"He's been ill too," she said.

"I think you should take a few days off," William suggested.

"That *would* be nice. A lot of people are going away at the moment, have you noticed? Just taking off. We won't lose much business."

He made some polite remark about how she should treat herself to a rest, and parted from her.

The muzak in the market reminded him of what he'd left at home: it sounded so much like the soundtracks of some of his early movies, a wash of nondescript melodies bearing no relation to the scenes they accompanied. The memory hurried him up and down the long aisles, filling his basket more by instinct than planning. He didn't bother to cater for his guests. They only fed on each other.

He wasn't the only shopper in the store ignoring practical purchases (household cleaners, detergents and the like) in favor of quick-fix items and junk foods. Distracted as he was he noticed others doing just as he was doing, indiscriminately filling up their carts and baskets with trash, as though new reassurances had supplanted the rituals of cooking and eating. He saw on the purchasers' faces (faces he'd known by name once, but could only half remember now) the same secretive look he'd known had been on his own face all his life. They were going about their shopping pretending there was nothing different about this particular Saturday, but everything was different now. They all had secrets; or almost all. And those that didn't were either leaving town, like Valerie, or pretending not to notice, which was, in its way, another secret.

As he reached the checkout, adding two fistfuls of Hershey bars to his basketload, he saw a face he hadn't set eyes on in many a long year: Joyce McGuire. She came in with her daughter, Jo-Beth, arm-in-arm. If he had ever seen them together it must have been before Jo-Beth grew to be a woman. Now, side by side, the similarities in their faces was enough to take his breath away. He stared, unable to prevent himself from remembering the day at the lake and the way Joyce had looked as she'd stripped down. Did the daughter look that way now, beneath her loose clothes, he wondered; small dark nipples, long, tanned thighs?

He realized suddenly that he was not the only customer looking towards the McGuire women; practically everyone was doing the same. Nor could he doubt that similar thoughts were in every head: that here, in the flesh, was one of the first clues to the apocalypse that was stealing up over the Grove. Eighteen years ago Joyce McGuire had given birth in circumstances that had then seemed merely scandalous. Now she stepped back into the public eye at the very time the most ludicrous rumors surrounding the League of Virgins seemed to be being proved true. There *were* presences walking the Grove (or lurking beneath it) which had power over lesser beings. Their influence had made flesh children in the body of Joyce McGuire. Was it perhaps that same influence that had made his dreams? They too were flesh from mind.

He looked back at Joyce, and understood something about himself he'd never grasped before: that he and the woman (beholder and beheld) were forever and intimately associated. The realization lasted a moment only: it was too difficult to grasp for any longer. But it made him put down his basket and press his way past the line waiting at the checkout, then walk straight towards Joyce McGuire. She saw him coming, and a look of fear crossed her face. He smiled at her. She tried to back away but her daughter had hold of her hand.

"It's all right, Momma," he heard her say.

"Yes—" he said, extending his own hand to Joyce. "Yes, it is. Really it is. I'm . . . so pleased to see you."

The sincere emotion, simply stated, seemed to mellow her anxiety; the frown softened. She even began to smile.

"William Witt," he said, putting his hand in hers. "You probably don't remember me, but . . ."

"I remember you," she said.

"I'm glad."

"See, Momma?" Jo-Beth said. "This isn't so bad."

"I haven't seen you in the Grove for such a long time," William said.

"I've been . . . unwell," Joyce said.

"And now?"

She declined to answer at first. Then she said:

"I think I'm getting better."

"That's good to hear."

As he spoke the sound of sobbing came to them from one of the aisles. Jo-Beth noticed it more than any of the other customers: a strange tension between her mother and Mr. Witt (whom she'd seen most every morning of her working life, but never dressed in so disheveled a fashion) had claimed their attention utterly, and everyone else in the line seemed to be making a studied attempt *not* to notice. She let go of Momma's arm and went to investigate, tracing the sound of the weeping from aisle to aisle until she found its source. Ruth Gilford, who was the receptionist at the offices of Momma's doctor, and was familiar to Jo-Beth, was standing in front of a selection of cereals, a box of one brand in her left hand and of another in her right, tears pouring down her cheeks. The cart at her side was heaped high with more boxes of cereal, as though she'd simply taken one of each as she'd wheeled her way along the aisle. "Mrs. Gilford?" Jo-Beth ventured.

The woman didn't stop sobbing, but tried to speak through her tears, which resulted in a watery and at times incoherent monologue. ". . . don't know what he wants . . ." she seemed to be saying. ". . . after all this time . . . don't know what he wants . . ."

"Can I help?" Jo-Beth said. "Do you want me to take you home?"

The word *home* made Ruth look around at Jo-Beth, attempting to focus on her through the tears.

". . . I don't know what he wants . . ." she said again.

"Who?" Jo-Beth said.

". . . all these years . . . and he's got something hiding from me . . ."

"Your husband?"

". . . I said nothing, but I knew . . . I always knew . . . he loved somebody else . . . and now he's got her in the house . . ."

The tears redoubled. Jo-Beth went to her, and very gently claimed the packets of cereal from her hands, putting them back on the shelves. With her talismans gone, Ruth Gilford took fierce hold of Jo-Beth.

". . . help me . . ." she said.

"Of course."

"I don't want to go home. He's got somebody there."

"All right. Not if you don't want to."

She started to coax the woman away from the cereal display. Once out of their influence, her anguish diminished somewhat.

"You're Jo-Beth, aren't you?" she managed.

"That's right."

"Will you take me to my car . . . I don't think I can get there on my own."

"We're going, you'll be fine," Jo-Beth reassured her, moving to Ruth's right-hand side so as to protect her from the gaze of those waiting in line if they chose to stare. She doubted they would. Ruth Gilford's collapse was too tender a sight for them to look straight at; it would remind them all too forcibly of what secrets they themselves were barely holding in check.

Momma was at the door, with William Witt. Jo-Beth decided to forsake introductions, which Ruth was in no state to respond to anyway, and just tell Momma she'd meet her at the bookstore, which had still been closed when they'd arrived. For the first time in her life, Lois was late opening up. But it was Momma who took the initiative.

"Mr. Witt will bring me home, Jo-Beth," she said. "Don't worry about me."

Jo-Beth glanced at Witt, who had the look of a man almost mesmerized.

"Are you sure?" she said. It had never occurred to her before but perhaps the ever unctuous Mr. Witt was the type Momma had been warning her about all these years. The deep, silent type whose secrets were always the most depraved. But Momma was insistent; almost casual in the way she waved Jo-Beth off.

Crazy, Jo-Beth thought as she escorted Ruth to the car, the whole world's gone crazy. People changing at a moment's notice, as though the way they'd been all these years was just a pretense: Momma sick, Mr. Witt neat, Ruth Gilford in charge. Were they just reinventing themselves, or was this the way they'd always been?

As they got to the car Ruth Gilford was taken over by another, even more desperate, bout of crying, and tried to return to the supermarket, insistent that she couldn't go back home without cereal. Jo-Beth gently persuaded her otherwise, and volunteered to drive home with her, an invitation which was gratefully accepted.

Jo-Beth's thoughts returned to Momma as she drove Ruth home, but they were literally overtaken, as a convoy of four black stretch limos purred past and turned up the Hill, their presence so utterly alien they might just have driven in from another dimension.

Visitors, she thought. As if there weren't enough.

THREE

S o it begins," said the Jaff.
He was standing at the highest window of Coney Eye, looking down upon the driveway. It was a little before noon, and the limos gliding up the driveway announced the first of the party guests. He would have liked to have Tommy-Ray at his side at this juncture, but the boy had not yet returned from his trip to the Mission. No matter. Lamar had proved a more than able substitute. There had been one uncomfortable moment, when the Jaff had finally put off the mask of being Buddy Vance and presented his true face to the comedian, but it hadn't taken long to bring the man around. In some regard he was more preferable company to Tommy-Ray; more sensual, more cynical. What was more he had a thorough knowledge of the guests who would soon be gathering in Buddy Vance's memory; a more thorough knowledge, indeed, than the widow Rochelle. She had sunk deeper and deeper into a drug-induced stupor since the previous evening; a condition which Lamar had taken sexual advantage of, much to the Jaff's amusement. Once upon a time (so long ago) he might have done the same, of course. No, not might, *would*. Rochelle Vance was undoubtedly beautiful, and her addiction, informed as it was by a constant

undercurrent of rage, made her even more attractive. But these were affairs of the flesh, and for another life. There were more urgent pursuits: namely, the power to be garnered from the guests who were even now gathering below. Lamar had run down the list with him, offering some savage observation or other on practically every one. Corrupt lawyers, addicted actors, reformed whores, pimps, priapists, hitmen, white men with black souls, hot men with cold, ass-kissers, coke-sniffers, the wretched high, the more wretched low, egotists, onanists and hedonists to a man. Where better to find the kind of forces he needed to keep him from harm when the Art opened? He would find fears in these addicted, bewildered, inflated souls of a kind he'd never have found in the mere bourgeois. From them he'd raise terata the like of which the world had never seen. Then he'd be ready. Fletcher was dead, and his army, if it had indeed manifested itself, was keeping its head low.

There was nothing left between the Jaff and Quiddity.

As he stood at the window and watched the victims disembark, greeting one another with rhinestone smiles and pinched kisses, his thoughts went—of all places—to that dead-letter room in Omaha, Nebraska, where, so many lives ago, he'd first had a hint of America's secret self. He remembered Homer, who'd opened the door to that treasure house, and later died against it, his life stabbed out by the blunt-bladed knife the Jaff still carried in his jacket pocket. Death had meant something then. Been an experience to go in dread of. It wasn't until he'd stepped into the Loop that he'd realized how irrelevant such fears were, when time could be suspended, even by a minor charlatan like Kissoon. Presumably the shaman was still secure in his refuge, as far from his spiritual creditors, or the lynch-mob, as it was possible to get. Lingering in the Loop, planning the getting of power. Or holding it at bay.

That last notion occurred to him now for the first time, like a long-postponed solution to a puzzle he hadn't even known he'd been gnawing at. Kissoon had been holding the moment because if he once let it slip he'd unleash his own death . . .

"Well . . ." he murmured.

Lamar was behind him. "Well, what?"

"Just musing," the Jaff said. He turned from the window. "Is the widow already downstairs?"

"I'm trying to rouse her."

"Who's greeting the guests?"

"Nobody."

"Go to it."

"I thought you wanted me here."

"Later. Once they've all arrived you can bring them up one by one."

"As you wish."

"One question."

"Only one?"

"Why aren't you afraid of me?"

Lamar narrowed his already narrow eyes. Then said:

"I've still got my sense of the ridiculous."

Without waiting for any riposte from the Jaff he opened the door and headed about his duties as host. The Jaff turned back to the window. Another limo was at the gates, this one white, its driver showing his passengers' invitations to the guards.

"One by one," the Jaff murmured to himself. "One by wretched one."

Grillo's invitation to the party at Coney Eye had been delivered by hand mid-morning, its courier Ellen Nguyen. Her manner was friendly but brisk; there was no trace of the intimacy that had flowered between them the previous afternoon. He invited her into his hotel room but she insisted that there was no time:

"I'm needed up at the house," she said. "Rochelle seems to be completely out of it. I don't think you need give a second thought to being recognized. But you will need the invitation. Fill in whatever name you want to invent. There'll be a lot of security so don't lose it. This is one party you won't be able to talk your way into."

"Where will you be?"

"I don't even think I'll be there."

"I thought you said you were going up there now."

"Just for the preparations. As soon as the party starts, I'm out. I don't want to mix with those people. Parasites, all of them. None of them really loved Buddy. It's just a show."

"Well I'll tell it like I see it."

"Do that," she said, turning to go.

"Could we just talk a moment?" Grillo said.

"About what? I haven't got much time."

"About you and me," Grillo said. "About what happened yesterday."

She looked at him without focusing her gaze. "What happened, happened," she said. "We were both there. What's to say?"

"Well for one: how about trying it again?"

Again, the unfixed look.

"I don't think so," she said.

"You didn't give me a chance—" he said.

"Oh no," she replied, eager to correct any error he was about to make. "You were fine . . . but things have changed."

"Since yesterday?"

"Yes," she said. "I can't quite tell you how . . ." She let the sentence hang, then took another thought up. "We're both adults. We know how these things work."

He was about to say that no, he didn't know how this or any other thing worked any longer, but that after this conversation his self-esteem was enfeebled enough without beating it to its knees with further confessions.

"Be careful at the party," she said as she once more turned to go.

He couldn't keep himself from saying, "Thanks for that at least."

She returned him a small, enigmatic smile, and left.

FOUR

The trip back to the Grove had been lengthy for Tommy-Ray, but it was lengthier still for Tesla and Raul, though for less metaphysical reasons. For one, Tesla's car was not so hot, and it had taken quite a beating on the way down; it was now much the worse for wear. For another, though she had been raised from near death by the touch of the Nuncio, it had left her with side-effects the full extent of which she didn't really grasp until they were over the border. Though she was driving a solid car along a solid highway her grasp of that solidity was not as good as it had been. She felt a pull on her from other places and other states of mind. She'd driven high on drugs and drink in the past but what she was experiencing now was a wilder ride altogether, as though her brain had summoned up from memory fragments of every trip she'd ever taken, every hallucinogen, every tranquilizer, and was running her through the lot, giving her mind a shot of each. One moment she knew she was whooping like a wild thing (she could hear herself, like another voice), the next she was floating in ether with the high-way dissolving in front of her, the next her thoughts were filthier than the New York subway, and it was all she could do to stop herself putting an end to the whole damn farce of living with one turn of the

CLIVE BARKER

wheel. Through it all, two facts. One, that of Raul sitting beside her, gripping the dashboard with white-knuckled hands, his fear pungent. The other, the place that she'd visited in her Nunciate dream, Kissoon's Loop. Though it was not as real as the car she was travelling in, and the smell of Raul, it was no less insistent. She carried its memory with her every mile they covered. Trinity, he'd called it, and it, or Kissoon himself, wanted her back. She felt its pull, almost like a physical claim upon her. She resisted it, though not entirely willingly. Though she'd been glad to be delivered back into life, what she'd seen and heard in her time in Trinity made her curious to return; even anxious. The more she resisted the more exhausted she became, until by the time they reached the outskirts of L.A. she was like someone deprived of sleep: with waking dreams threatening to erupt at any moment into the texture of reality.

"We're going to have to stop for a while," she told Raul, aware that she was slurring as she spoke. "Or I'm going to end up killing us both."

"You want to sleep?"

"I don't know," she said, afraid that to sleep would invite as many problems as it would solve. "At least rest. Get some coffee inside me, and put my mind in order."

"Here?" said Raul.

"Here what?"

"We stop here?"

"No," she said. "We'll go back to my apartment. It's half an hour from here. That's if we fly—"

You already are, baby, her mind said, and you'll probably never stop. You're a resurrected woman. What do you expect? That life should simply fumble on as though nothing had happened? Forget it. Things'll never be the same again.

But West Hollywood hadn't changed; still Boy's Town prettified: the bars, the style stores where she bought her jewelry. She took a left off Santa Monica on to North Huntley Drive, where she'd lived for the five years she'd been in L.A. It was almost noon now, and the smog was burning off the city. She parked the car in the garage below the building, and took Raul up to Apartment V. The windows of her downstairs neighbor, a sour, repressed little man with whom she'd exchanged no more than three sentences in half a decade, and two of those invective, were open, and he doubtless saw her passing. She estimated it would take him twenty minutes at the most to inform the block that Miss Lonelyhearts, as she'd heard he called her, was back in town — looking like shit, and accompanied by Quasimodo. So be it. She had other things to worry about, like how to align her key with the lock, a trick which repeatedly defeated her confounded senses. Raul came to the rescue, taking the key from her trembling fingers and letting them both in. The apartment, as usual, was a disaster area. She left the door wide and opened the windows to let in some less stale air, then played her messages. Her agent had called twice, both times to report that there was no further news on the castaway screenplay; Saralyn had called, asking if she knew where Grillo was. Following Saralyn, Tesla's mother: her contribution more a litany of sins than a message — crimes committed by the world in general, and her father in particular. Finally there was a message from Mickey de Falco, who made spare bucks providing orgasmic grunts for fuck films, and needed a partner for a gig. In the background, a barking dog. "And as soon as you're back," he said in signing off, "come and get this fucking dog before it eats me outta house and home." She caught Raul watching her as she listened to the calls, his bemusement unconcealed.

"My peer group," she said when Mickey had said his farewells. "Aren't they a gas? Look, I'm going to have a little nap. It's obvious where everything is, right? Refrigerator; TV; toilet. Wake me in an hour, yeah?"

"An hour."

"I'd like tea, but we don't have the time." She stared at him, staring at her. "Am I making any sense?"

"Yes . . ." he replied doubtfully.

"Slurring my words?"

"Yes."

"Thought so. OK. The apartment's yours. Don't answer the phone. See you in an hour."

She stumbled through to the bathroom without waiting for further confirmation, stripped down completely, contemplated a shower, settled for a splash of cold water on her face, breasts and arms, then went through to the bedroom. The room was hot, but she knew better than to open the window. When her immediate neighbor Ron woke, which was around now, he would start to play opera. It was either the heat of the room or *Lucia di Lammermoor.* She chose to sweat.

Left to his own devices Raul found a selection of edibles in the refrigerator, took them to the open window, sat down, and shook. He could not remember being so afraid, back since the day Fletcher's madness had begun. Now, as then, the rules of the world had suddenly changed without warning, and he no longer knew what his purpose was to be. In his heart of hearts he'd given up hoping to see Fletcher again. The shrine he'd kept at the Mission, which had been a beacon at the start, had become a memorial. He'd expected to die there, alone, humored to the last as a half-wit, which in many ways he was. He could scarcely write, except to scrawl his own name. He couldn't read. Most of the objects in the woman's room were a total mystery to him. He was lost.

A cry from the next room stirred him from self-pity.

"Tesla?" he called.

There was no coherent reply: only further muted cries. He got up and followed the sound. The door to her bedroom was closed. He hesitated, hand on handle, nervous of entering without invitation. Then another round of cries reached him. He pushed the door open.

He'd never in his life seen a woman so exposed. The sight of Tesla sprawled on the bed transfixed him. Her arms were at her sides, gripping the sheet, her head rolled from side to side. But there was a fogginess about her body that reminded him of what had happened on the road below the Mission. She was moving away from him again. Back towards the Loop. Her shouts had become moans now. They were not of pleasure. She was going unwillingly.

He called her name again, very loudly. She suddenly sat bolt upright, eyes wide and staring at him.

"*Jesus!*" she said. She was panting, as though she'd just run a race. "*Jesus. Jesus. Jesus.*"

"You were shouting . . ." he said, trying to begin to explain his presence in the room.

Only now did she seem to realize their situation: her nakedness, his
embarrassed fascination. She reached for a sheet and started to haul it
over her, but her intention was distracted by what she'd just experienced.

"I was there," she said.

"I know."

"Trinity. Kissoon's Loop."

As they'd driven back up the coast she'd done her best to explain to
him the vision she'd had while the Nuncio had been healing her, both
as a way to fix its details in her head and to keep a recurrence at bay by
coaxing the memories out of the sealed cell of her inner life and into
shared experience. She painted a repulsive picture of Kissoon.

"You saw him?" Raul said.

"I didn't get to the hut," she replied. "But he wants me there. I can
feel him *pulling.*" She put her hand on her stomach. "I can feel him
now, Raul."

"I'm here," he said. "I won't let you go."

"I know, and I'm glad."

She reached out. "Take hold of my hand, huh?" He tentatively
approached the bed. *"Please,"* she said. He did so. "I saw that town
again," she went on. "It seems so real, except there's nobody there,
nobody at all. It's . . . it's like a stage . . . like something's going to be
performed there."

"Performed."

"This is making no sense, I know, but I'm just telling you what I
feel. Something terrible's going to happen there, Raul. The worst
thing imaginable."

"You don't know what?"

"Or maybe it already happened?" she said. "Maybe that's why
there's nobody in the town. No. No. That's not it. It's not over, it's just
about to happen."

She tried to make sense of her confusions the best way she knew. If
she were setting a scene in that town, for a movie, what would it be? A

gun-fight on Main Street? The citizens locked up behind their doors while the White Hats and the Black Hats shot it out? Possibly. Or a town vacated as some stomping behemoth appeared on the horizon? The classic fifties monster scenario: a creature woken by nuclear tests—

"That's closer," she said.

"What is?"

"Maybe it's a dinosaur movie. Or a giant tarantula. I don't know. That's definitely closer. Christ, this is frustrating! I know something about this place, Raul, and I can't quite get hold of it."

From next door, the strains of Donizetti's masterpiece. She knew it so well now she could have sung along with it had she had the voice.

"I'm going to make some coffee," she said. "Wake myself up. Will you go and ask Ron for some milk?"

"Yes. Of course."

"Just tell him you're a friend of mine."

Raul got up off the bed, detaching his hand from hers.

"Ron's apartment's number four," she called after him, then went through to the bathroom and took her postponed shower, still vexed by the problem of the town. By the time she'd sluiced herself down and found a clean T-shirt and jeans Raul was back in the apartment, and the telephone was ringing. From the other end, opera and Ron.

"Where did you find him?" he wanted to know. "And does he have a brother?"

"Is it impossible to have a private life around here?" she said.

"You shouldn't have *paraded* him, girl," Ron replied. "What is he, a truck driver? Marines? He's so *broad*."

"That he is."

"If he gets bored just send him back over."

"He'll be flattered," Tesla said, and put the phone down. "You've got yourself an admirer," she told Raul. "Ron thinks you're very sexy."

Raul's look was less perplexed than she'd anticipated. It made her ask: "Are there gay apes, do you suppose?"

"Gay?"

"Homosexual. Men who like other men in bed."

"Is Ron?"

"Is Ron?" She laughed. "Yes, Ron is. It's that kind of neighborhood. That's why I like it."

She started to measure out the coffee into the cups. As she heard the granules slide from the spoon she felt the vision beginning in on her again.

She dropped the spoon. Turned to Raul. He was a long way from her, across a room that seemed to be filling with dust.

"Raul?" she said.

"What's wrong?" she saw him say. Saw rather than heard; the volume had been turned down to zero in the world she was slipping from. Panic set in. She reached out for Raul with both hands.

"*Don't let me go—*" she yelled at him. "*—I don't want to go! I don't—*"

Then the dust came between them, eroding him. Her hands missed his in the storm and instead of falling into his solid embrace she was pitched back into the desert, moving at speed across by now familiar terrain. The same baked earth she'd travelled twice before.

Her apartment had disappeared completely. She was back in the Loop, heading through the town. Above her, the sky was delicately tinted, as it had been the first time she'd travelled here. The sun was still close to the horizon. She could see it clearly, unlike that first time. More than see, stare at, without having to look away. She could even make out details. Solar flares leaping from its rim like arms of fire. A cluster of sun-spots marking its burning face. When she looked back to earth she was approaching the town.

With the first flush of panic over she began to take control of her circumstances, reminding herself sharply that this was the third time she'd been here, and she should be able to grasp the trick of it by now. She willed her pace to slow, and found that indeed she *was* slowing, giving her more time to study the town as she came to its fringes. Her instinct, seeing it for the first time, had been that it was somehow fake. That instinct was now confirmed. The boards of the houses were not weather-beaten, nor even painted. There were no curtains at the windows; no key-holes in the doors. And beyond those doors and windows?

She told her floating system to veer towards one of the houses, and peered through the window. The roof of the house had been improperly finished; sunlight darted between the cracks and illuminated the interior. It was empty. There was no furniture, nor any other sign of human habitation. There was not even any division of the interior into *rooms*. The building was a complete sham. And if this one, then the next too presumably. She moved along the row to confirm the suspicion. It was also completely deserted.

As she drew away from the second window she felt the pull she'd experienced back in the other world: Kissoon was trying to bring her to him. She hoped now that Raul made no attempt to wake her, if indeed her body was still present in the world she'd left. Though she had a fear of this place, and a profound suspicion of the man who'd called her here, her curiosity laid stronger claim upon her. The mysteries of Palomo Grove had been bizarre enough, but nothing in Fletcher's hurried transfer of information about the Jaff, the Art and Quiddity went far towards explaining this place. The answers lay with Kissoon, she'd not the slightest doubt of that. If she could dig between the lines of his conversation, oblique as it was, she might have a hope of understanding. And with her newfound confidence in this condition she felt easier at the thought of returning to the hut. If he threatened her, or got a hard-on, she'd simply leave. It was within her power. Anything was within her power, if she wanted it badly enough. If she could look at the sun and not be blinded, she could certainly deal with Kissoon's fumbling claims on her body.

She started on through the town, aware that she was now *walking*, or had at least decided to present herself with that illusion. Once she'd imagined herself here, as she'd done the first time, the process of bringing her flesh with her was automatic. She couldn't feel the ground beneath her feet, nor did the act of walking take the least effort, but she had carried with her from the other world that idea of how to advance, and was using it here whether it was necessary or not. Probably not. Probably a thought was all that was required to whisk her around. But the more of the reality she knew best that she imported into this place, she reasoned, the more control she had over it. She would operate here by the rules she'd assumed were universal, until recently. Then, if they changed, she'd know it was not her doing. The more she thought this through the more solid she felt. Her shadow deepened beneath her; she began to feel the ground hot beneath her feet.

Reassuring as it was to have natural senses here, Kissoon clearly did not approve. She felt his pull on her strengthen, like he'd put his hand into her stomach and was tugging.

"All right . . ." she murmured ". . . I'm coming. But in *my* time, not in yours."

There was more than weight and shadow in the condition she was learning; there was smell and sound. Both of these brought surprises; both unwelcome. To her nostrils a sickening smell, one she knew without doubt to be that of putrefying meat. Was there a dead animal somewhere on the street? She could see nothing. But sound gave her a second clue. Her ears, sharper than they'd ever been, caught the seething of insect life. She listened closely to discover its direction, and guessing it, crossed the street to another of the houses. It was as featureless as those whose windows she'd peered through, but this one was not empty. The strengthening stench and the sound that came with it confirmed that instinct. There was something dead behind that banal facade. Many things, she began to suspect. The smell was getting to be overpowering; it made her innards churn. But she had to see what secret this town concealed.

Halfway across the street she felt another tug on her stomach. She resisted it, but Kissoon wasn't quite so ready to let her off the hook this time. He pulled again, harder, and she found herself moved down the street against her will. One moment she was approaching the House of the Stench, the next she was twenty yards from where she'd been.

"*I want to see,*" she said through gritted teeth, hoping that Kissoon could hear her.

Even if he couldn't he pulled again. This time she was ready for the tug and actively fought against it, demanding that her body move back towards the House.

"You're not going to stop me," she said.

In reply, he pulled once more, and despite her best efforts hauled her even further from her target.

"Fuck you!" she yelled out loud, furious at his intervention.

He used her anger against her. As she burned energy in her outburst he pulled yet again, and this time succeeded in moving her almost all the way down the street to the other end of the town. There was nothing she could do to resist him. He was quite simply stronger than her, and the more furious she became the more his grip strengthened, until she was moving at some speed away from the town, prey to his summons the way she'd been the first time she'd come into the Loop.

She knew her anger was weakening her resistance, and calmly instructed herself to control it as the desert speeded by.

"Calm yourself, woman," she told herself. "He's just a bully. Nothing more. Nothing less. Chill out."

Her advice to herself worked. She felt self-determination beginning to swell in her again. She didn't allow herself the luxury of satisfaction. She simply exercised the power she'd claimed back to show herself once more. Kissoon didn't relinquish his claim, of course; she felt his fist in her gut pulling as hard as ever. It hurt. But she resisted, and went on resisting, until she had almost come to a dead stop.

He'd succeeded in one of his ambitions at least, however. The town was a speck on the horizon behind her. The trek back to it was presently beyond her. She was not certain, even if she began it, that she could resist his tugging for such a distance.

Again, she offered herself some silent advice: this time to stand still for a few moments and take stock of her situation. She'd lost the fight in the town, there was no two ways about that. But she'd gained a few sticky questions to ask Kissoon when she was finally face to face with him. One, what the source of the stench actually was, and two, why he was so afraid of her seeing it. But given the strength he clearly possessed, even at this distance, she knew she had to be careful. The greatest mistake she could make in these circumstances was to assume any government she had over herself was permanent. Her presence here was at Kissoon's behest, and whatever he'd told her about being a prisoner here himself he knew more about its rules than she did. She was prey every moment to his power, the limits of which she could only guess. She had to proceed with greater caution, or risk losing what little authority she had over her condition.

Turning her back on the town she began to move in the direction of the hut. The solidity she'd earned in the town had not been taken from her, but when she moved it was with a lightness of step utterly unlike anything she'd experienced hitherto. A moonwalk of a type: her strides long and easy, her speed impossible even for the fastest of sprinters. Sensing her approach Kissoon no longer hauled on her gut, though he maintained a presence there, as if to remind her of the strength he could use should he turn his will to it.

Ahead now she saw the second of the landmarks here: the tower. The wind whined in its tethering wires. Again she slowed her pace, so as to study the structure better. There was very little to see. It stood perhaps a hundred feet high, was made of steel, and had atop it a simple wood platform covered on three of its sides by sheets of corrugated iron. Its function defied her. As a viewing platform it seemed singularly useless, given that there was so little to view. Nor did it seem to be serving any technical purpose. Besides the corrugated iron up top— and some parcel hanging between—there was no sign of aerials or monitoring apparatus. She thought of Buñuel, of all people, and of her favorite of his films, *Simon del Desierto*, a satiric vision of St. Simon tempted by the Devil as he sat in penitence on the top of a pillar in the middle of nowhere. Perhaps the tower had been built for a similarly masochist saint. If so, he'd gone to dust, or Godhood.

There was nothing more to be seen here, she decided, and moved on past the tower, leaving it to its whining, enigmatic life. She could not yet see Kissoon's hut, but she knew it couldn't be far. There was no dust storm on the horizon to keep it from sight; the scene before her— the desert floor and the sky above—was exactly as she remembered it from her last trip here. The fact momentarily struck her as strange: that nothing whatsoever seemed to have changed. Maybe nothing ever changed here, she thought. Maybe it was forever, this place. Or like a movie, re-run and re-run, until the sprocket holes snapped or the picture burned up in the gate.

She'd no sooner imagined constancy than a rogue element she'd almost forgotten came into view. The woman.

Last time, with Kissoon drawing her to the hut, she'd had no chance to make contact with this other player on the desert stage. Indeed Kissoon had attempted to convince her that the woman had been a mirage; a projection of his erotic musings, and to be avoided. But now, with the woman close enough to call to, Tesla thought the explanation a likelier fantasy than the woman. However perverse Kissoon was, and she didn't doubt he'd had his moments, the figure before her was no masturbatory aid. True, she was close to naked, the shreds of clothing wrapped around her body pitifully inadequate. True, she had a face luminous with intelligence. But her long hair looked to have been torn out in several places, the blood dried to a dirty brown on her brow and cheeks. Her body was thin, and badly bruised, scratches on her thighs and arms only partially healed. There was a more profound wound, Tesla suspected, beneath the scraps of what might have once been a white dress. It was glued to the middle of her body, and she hugged herself there, almost bent double with pain. She was no pin-up; nor a mirage. She existed in the same plane of being as Tesla, and suffered here.

As she'd suspected Kissoon was aware that his warning had been ignored, and had begun to tug on Tesla once more. This time she was completely prepared for it. Instead of raging against his claim on her she stood quite still, preserving her calm. His mind-fingers fought for purchase, then began to slip through her innards. He snatched at them again; slipped again, and snatched. She didn't respond in any way, but simply kept her place, her eyes fixed on the woman all the time.

She'd stood upright, and was no longer holding her belly, but let her hands hang by her sides. Very slowly, Tesla began to walk towards her, preserving as best she could the calm that was denying Kissoon his hold. The woman made no move either to advance or retreat. With every step Tesla took she got a better impression of her. She was fifty, maybe, her eyes, though sunk in their sockets, the liveliest part of her; the rest was fatigue. Around her neck she wore a chain on which hung a simple cross. It was all that remained of the life she might once have had before she'd become lost in this wilderness.

Suddenly, she opened her mouth, a look of anguish crossing her face. She started to speak, but either her vocal cords weren't strong enough or her lungs large enough for the words to cover the space between them.

"Wait," Tesla told her, concerned the woman not exhaust what little energy she had. "Let me get closer."

If she understood, the woman ignored the instruction, and began to speak again, repeating something over and over.

"I can't hear you," Tesla shouted back, aware that her distress at the woman's distress was giving Kissoon a handle on her. "Wait, will you?" she said, picking up speed.

As she did so she realized that the look on the woman's face was not anguish at all, but fear. That her eyes were no longer looking at Tesla, but at something else. And that the word she was repeating was "Lix! Lix!"

In horror, she turned, to see the desert floor behind her alive with Lix: a dozen on first glance, twice that on second. They were all exactly the same, like snakes from which every distinguishing mark had been struck, reducing them to ten-foot lengths of writhing muscle, coming at her at full speed. She had thought the one she'd glimpsed previously, pulling open the door, mouthless. She'd been wrong. They had mouths, all right, black holes lined with black teeth, opened wide. She was readying herself for their attack when she realized (too late) they'd been summoned as a distraction. Kissoon clutched her gut and pulled. The desert slid away beneath her, the Lix dividing as she was hauled through their throng.

Ahead, the hut. She was at its threshold in seconds, the door opening on cue.

"Come on in," Kissoon said. "It's been too long."

Left behind in Tesla's apartment, Raul could only wait. He had no doubt of where she'd gone, or who'd claimed her, but without a means of access, he was helpless. Which wasn't to say he didn't *sense* her. His system had been touched by the Nuncio twice, and it knew she was not that far from him.

When, in the car, Tesla had attempted to describe what her trip into the Loop had felt like, he'd badly wanted to articulate something he'd come to understand in the years he'd spent at the Mission. His vocabulary was not equal to the task, however. It still wasn't. But the feelings had borne strongly upon the way he now sensed Tesla.

She was in a different place, but place was just another kind of being, and all states could, if the means were found, speak with every other state. Ape with man, man with moon. It was nothing to do with technologies. It was about the indivisibility of the world. Just as Fletcher had made the Nuncio from a soup of disciplines, not caring where science became magic, or logic nonsense; just as Tesla moved between realities like a dreaming fog, in defiance of established law; just as he had moved from the apparently simian to the apparently human, and never known where one became the other, or if it ever did, so he knew he might reach now, if only he had the wit or the words, which he didn't, through to the place where Tesla was. It was very close, as were all spaces at all times; parts of the same landscape of mind. But he could shape none of this into action. It was beyond him, as yet.

All he could do was *know*, and wait, which in its way was more painful than believing himself forsaken.

"You're a fuckhead and a liar," she said when she'd closed the door.

The fire was burning brightly. There was very little smoke. Kissoon sat on its far side, staring up at her, his eyes brighter than she remembered. There was excitement in them.

"You wanted to come back," he said to her. "Don't deny it. I felt it in you. You could have resisted while you were out there in the Cosm but you really didn't want to. Tell me I'm a liar about that. I dare you."

"No," she said. "I admit it. I'm curious."

"Good."

"But that doesn't give you the right to just drag me here."

"How else was I to show you the way?" he asked her lightly.

"*Show me the way?*" she said, knowing he was infuriating her deliberately but unable to get the sensation of helplessness out of her head. She hated nothing more vehemently than to be out of control, and his hold of her made her mad as hell.

"I'm not stupid," she said. "And I'm not a toy you can just pull on when it suits you."

"I don't mean to treat you as either," Kissoon said. "Please, can't we make peace? We're on the same side after all?"

"Are we?"

"You can't doubt that."

"Can't I?"

"After all I told you," Kissoon said. "The secrets I shared with you."

"Seems to me there's a few you're not willing to share."

"Oh?" Kissoon said, his gaze moving from her to the flames.

"The town, for instance."

"What about it?"

"I wanted to see what was in the house, but no, you just hauled me away."

Kissoon sighed. "I don't deny it," he said. "If I hadn't, you wouldn't be here."

"I don't follow."

"Don't you sense the atmosphere there? I can't believe you don't. The sheer *dread*."

Now it was she who expelled breath, softly, between her teeth.

"Yes," she said. "I felt something."

"The Iad Uroboros has its agents everywhere," Kissoon said. "I believe one of them is in hiding in that town. I don't know what form it takes, and I don't want to know. But it would be fatal to look, I suspect. Anyway, I'm not about to risk it, and you shouldn't either, however *curious* you are."

It was difficult to argue with this point of view when it so closely approximated her own feelings. Only minutes ago, back in her apartment, she'd told Raul she sensed something about to happen in that empty Main Street. Now Kissoon was confirming her suspicion.

"I suppose I have to thank you then," she said reluctantly.

"Don't bother," Kissoon replied. "I didn't save you for your sake, I saved you for more important duties." He took a moment to dig at the core of the fire with a blackened stick. It blazed higher, and the hut was illuminated more brightly than ever. "I'm sorry," he went on, "if I frightened you when you were last here. I say if. I know I did and I can't apologize enough." He didn't look at her through this speech, which had a rehearsed quality to it. But coming from a man she suspected had a major ego, it was doubly welcome. "I was . . . *moved*, shall we say . . . by your physical presence in a way I hadn't quite taken account of, and you were right to be suspicious of my motives." He put one hand between his legs and took his penis between forefinger and thumb. "I'm chastened now," he said. "As you can see."

She looked. He was quite limp.

"Apology accepted," she said.

"So now, we can get back to business I hope."

"I'm not going to give my body to you, Kissoon," she said flatly. "If that's what you mean by business, no deal."

Kissoon nodded. "I can't say I blame you. Apologies sometimes aren't enough. But you *must* understand the gravity of this. Even now, up in Palomo Grove, the Jaff is preparing to use the Art. I can stop him. But not from here."

"Teach me then."

"There isn't time."

"I'm a quick learner."

Kissoon looked up at her, his face sharp.

"That really is a monstrous arrogance," he said. "You step into the middle of a tragedy that's been moving towards its final act for centuries and think you can just change its course with a few words. This isn't Hollywood. This is the real world."

His cold fury subdued her; but not much.

"All right, so I get feisty once in a while. Shoot me for it. I've told you I'll help but I won't do any of this body-swapping shit."

"Maybe, then . . ."

"What?"

". . . you can find someone who *is* willing to give themselves over to me."

"That's a tough call. What am I supposed to tell them?"

"You're persuasive," he said.

She thought back to the world she'd stepped out of. The apartment building had twenty-one occupants. Could she persuade Ron, or Edgar, or one of her friends, Mickey de Falco perhaps, to step back into the Loop with her? She doubted it. It was only when her seeking centered on Raul that she glimpsed a little hope. Might *he* dare what she wouldn't?

"Maybe I can help," she said.

"Quickly?"

"Yes. Quickly. If you can get me back to my apartment."

"Easily done."

"I'm not promising anything, mind you."

"I understand."

"And I want something from you in return."

"What's that?"

"The woman I tried to speak to; the one you said was a sex-aid?"

"I wondered when you'd get to her."

"She's hurt."

"Don't believe it."

"I saw for myself."

"It's an Iad trick!" Kissoon said. "She's been wandering around out there for a while now, trying to get me to open the door to her. Sometimes she pretends she's hurt, sometimes she's all purrs, like a sex-kitten. Rubs herself against the door." He shuddered. "I hear her, rubbing herself, begging me to let her in. It's just another trick."

As with almost every statement Kissoon made Tesla found herself not knowing whether to believe or disbelieve. On her last visit he'd told her he thought the woman was most likely a dream-mistress. Now he was saying she was an Iad agent. One but not both.

"I want to speak to her myself," she said. "Make up my own mind. She doesn't look that dangerous."

"You don't know," Kissoon warned. "Appearances lie. I keep her at bay with the Lix out of fear of what she might do."

She contemplated asking what he could possibly fear about a

woman so clearly in pain, then decided it was a question for a less desperate hour.

"I'll go back then," she said.

"You understand the urgency."

"You don't have to keep telling me," Tesla said. "Yes, I understand. But like I said you're asking a lot. People get attached to their bodies. Joke."

"If all goes well, and I can stop the Art being used, then the supplier gets his flesh back intact. If I fail it's the end of the world anyway, so what will it matter?"

"Nice," Tesla said.

"I try."

She turned back to the door.

"Go quickly," he said. "And don't get distracted—"

The door opened without her touching it.

"You're still a condescending fucker, Kissoon—" was Tesla's parting remark. Then she'd stepped out into the same early morning light.

Off to the left of the hut a cloud-shadow seemed to be moving over the desert floor. She studied it a moment, and saw that the sun-beaten ground was covered with Lix, a small sea of them. Sensing her gaze they stopped moving, and raised their heads towards her. Hadn't Kissoon said that he'd made these creatures?

"Go, will you?" she heard him say. "There isn't much time."

Had she acted upon his instructions immediately she'd have missed the sight of the woman appearing beyond the Lix. She didn't, so she didn't. And the sight of her, despite the warnings Kissoon had issued, held her on the step. If this was indeed one of the Iad Uroboros' agents, as Kissoon had claimed, it was a brilliant conceit to present herself in such a vulnerable guise. Try as she might she couldn't quite believe a villainy as vast or indeed as ambitious as the Iad would present itself in so wretched a manner. Wasn't evil too full of itself, even in its machinations, to come so undressed? She couldn't ignore her instinct, which told her unequivocally that in this at least Kissoon was wrong. The woman was no agent. She was a human being in pain. Tesla could turn her back on many appeals, but never on that.

Ignoring a further entreaty from the man in the but behind her, she took a step towards the woman. The Lix were alive to her approach. They began to seethe as she stepped towards them, raising their heads like cobras. The sight quickened her approach rather than slowing it. If this was Kissoon's instruction, and it surely was, then their keeping her from the woman only further reinforced her suspicion that she was being misled. He was trying to keep them apart; *why?* Because this wretched, anguished woman was dangerous? No! Every fiber of Tesla's being refused that interpretation. He wanted to keep them apart because of something that might pass between them; something that might be said or done that would throw him into doubt.

The Lix had new instructions it seemed. To harm Tesla would be to keep the messenger from her purpose; so they instead turned their heads towards the woman. She saw their intention, and fear came over her face. It occurred to Tesla that she was familiar with their malice; that maybe she'd dared them before in an attempt to get to Kissoon, or one of his visitors. She certainly seemed versed in how best to confuse them, running back and forth quickly so that they tied their nest in knots trying to decide which way to lunge.

Tesla added her own contribution to the defense by yelling at them as she picked up her pace, suddenly certain that they dared not harm her as long as Kissoon was so desperate to be out of his prison, and she his only hope.

"*Get away from her!*" she yelled at them. "*Leave her alone, fuck-heads!*"

But they had their target fixed, and weren't about to be deflected from it by shouts. As Tesla came within a few yards of them they started after their quarry.

"*Run!*" Tesla yelled.

The woman heeded the advice, but too late. The speediest from the nest was at her heels; then climbing her body to wind itself around her. There was a vile elegance to its motion, whipping around the woman's torso and pulling her to the ground. The Lix that followed were quickly upon her. By the time Tesla got within a few yards of the woman she was all but indistinguishable from her attackers. They'd virtually mummified her. Still she fought them, tearing at their bodies as they closed ranks around her.

Tesla didn't waste time with further words. She simply tore at the Lix with her bare hands, first attempting to free the woman's face for fear they smothered her, then, that done, pulling her arms free. Though they were many, they weren't particularly strong. Several simply broke apart as she hauled on them, yellow-white blood oozing from them over her hands, and spraying up in her face. She let disgust fuel her, fighting their every twisting trick, pulling and pulling at them until she was sticky with fluids. The woman they'd come so close to killing had taken fire from her rescuer, and was struggling free of her assassins' grip.

Sensing that victory was available, albeit snatched, Tesla readied herself for escape. She could not go alone, she knew. The woman had to come with her, back to the apartment in North Huntley Drive, or she'd be prey to further attacks, and after such an assault she'd have little power to resist them. Kissoon had taught her to imagine her way *into* the Loop. Could she now do the same in the opposite direction, not only for herself but on the woman's behalf? If not they'd both fall to the Lix, who seemed to be appearing from all sides now, as though an alarm call had been sent out from their maker. Putting their approach out of her mind as best she could, Tesla pictured herself and the woman in front of her out of this place and into another. Not any other. Into West Hollywood. North Huntley Drive. Her apartment. You do this, she told herself. If Kissoon can do it, you can.

She heard the woman cry out—the first sound she'd actually made. There was a disturbance in the scene around them, but not the instant transfer from Kissoon's Loop to West Hollywood she'd hoped for; and the Lix were massing around them in greater and yet greater numbers.

"Again," Tesla told herself. "Do it again."

She focused on the woman in front of her, who was still tearing pieces of the Lix from around her body, and pulling them from her hair. It was this mirage she had to focus on. The other passenger, herself, was easily imagined.

"Go!" she said. "Please God, go!"

This time the images in her head jelled; she not only saw herself and the woman clearly, she saw them in flight, the world around them dissolving and reconfiguring like a jigsaw blown to pieces and remade as another puzzle.

She knew the scene. It was the very spot she'd left from. The coffee was still spilled across the floor; the sun was pouring in through the window; Raul was standing in the middle of the room, waiting for her return. She knew by the look on his face that she'd succeeded in bringing the woman through with her. What she hadn't realized until she looked was that she'd brought the whole image, including the Lix that had been battening upon her. Though they were separated from Kissoon their unnatural life was no less fevered here than in the Loop. The woman dropped them to the floor of the apartment where they continued to writhe, their shit-smelling blood oozing on the floor. But they were only pieces: heads, tails, mid-sections. And already the violence of their motion was slowing. Rather than waste time stomping them out Tesla called Raul to her, and together they carried the woman through to the bedroom and laid her down.

She'd fought hard, and was the worst for it. The wounds on her body had reopened. But she seemed not so much in pain as simply exhausted.

"Watch over her," Tesla told Raul, "I'm going to get some water to clean her up."

"What happened?" he wanted to know.

"I almost sold your soul to a fuckhead and a liar," Tesla said. "But don't worry. I just bought it back."

FIVE

A week previous, the arrival in Palomo Grove of so many of the brightest stars in Hollywood's firmament would have brought the inhabitants of the town out on to the streets in significant numbers, but today there was barely a witness on the sidewalks to watch them appear. The limos eased their way up the Hill unnoticed, their passengers either getting high or fixing their make-up behind smoked-glass windows; the older ones wondering how long it would be before people gathered to pay hypocritical tribute to them the way they were to Buddy Vance, the younger assuming a cure for death would have been found by the time mortality threatened. There were few among the gathering assembly who had truly loved Buddy. Many had envied him; some had lusted after him; nearly all had taken some pleasure in his fall from grace. But love came infrequently in company such as this. It was a flaw in armor they could ill afford to shed.

The passengers in the limos were aware of the absence of admirers. Even though many of them had no desire to be recognized it offended their tender egos being greeted with such indifference. They quickly turned the insult to good purpose. In car after car the same subject arose: why the dead man had chosen to hide himself away in a God-forsaken shithole like Palomo Grove. He'd had secrets; that was why. But what? His drink problem? Everybody knew about that. Drugs? Who cared? Women? He'd been the first to boast about his dick and its doings. No, there must have been some other dirt that drove him to this hell-hole. Theories flowed like vitriol as the mourners turned over the possibilities, breaking off from their bitchery to step out of their cars and offer their condolences to the widow at the threshold of Coney Eye, only to pick it up again as soon as they stepped inside.

Buddy's collection of Carnivalia caused considerable comment, dividing its audience down the middle. Many considered it a perfect encapsulation of the dead man: vulgar, opportunist and now, out of its context, useless. Others declared it a revelation, a side of the deceased they'd never known existed. One or two approached Rochelle to see if any of the pieces were available for sale. She told them that nobody yet knew to whom the Will would ascribe them, but that if they came to her she'd happily give them away.

Jokemeister Lamar went among the celebrants with a smile plastered from ear to ear. In all the years since his parting from Buddy he'd never dared believe he'd be where he now was, lording himself over Buddy's court. He made no attempt to disguise his pleasure. What was the use? Life was too short. Better take pleasure where there was pleasure to be taken, before it was snatched away. The thought of the Jaff only two floors above added an extra glitter to his smile. He didn't know what the man's full intentions were, but it was entertaining to think of these people as fodder. He held all of them in contempt, having seen them or their like perform acts of moral acrobatics that would have shamed a Pope, all for the achieving of profit, position or profile. Sometimes all three. He'd come to view with disgust the self-obsession of his tribe, the ambition that drove so many of them to bring down their betters, and smother the little good in themselves. He'd never let that contempt show, however. He had to work among them. It was better to conceal his feelings. Buddy (poor Buddy) had never been able to achieve such detachment. With a little too much drink in his system he'd railed loud and long against fools he refused to suffer. It was this indiscretion, above all others, that had been his downfall. In a town where words were cheap, talk could be expensive. They'd forgive embezzlement, addiction, molestation of minors, rape and even, on occasion, murder. But Buddy had called them *fools*. They'd never forgiven him that.

Lamar worked the room, kissing the beauties, acknowledging the studs, shaking the hands of the hirers and firers of both. He imagined Buddy's revulsion at this ritual. Time and time again during their years together he'd had to coax Buddy out of a party just like this one because he couldn't keep his insults to himself. Time and time again he'd failed.

"You're looking good, Lam."

The overnourished face in front of him was Sam Sagansky, one of Hollywood's most successful power-brokers. At his side stood a big-breasted waif, one in a long line of big-breasted waifs Sam had raised to glitterdom then parted from in public dramas that had left the women's careers destroyed and his reputation as a ladykiller enhanced.

"What does it feel like?" Sagansky wanted to know, "being at his funeral?"

"It's not exactly that, Sam."

"Still, he's dead, and you're not. Don't tell me it doesn't make you feel good."

"I guess so."

"We're survivors, Lam. We've got a right to scratch our balls and laugh. Life's good."

"Yeah," Lamar said, "I suppose it is."

"We're all winners here, eh, honey?" He turned to his wife, who displayed her dental work. "Don't know any better feeling than that."

"I'll catch you later, Sam."

"Are there going to be fireworks?" the waif wondered.

Lamar thought of the Jaff, waiting upstairs, and smiled.

Once round the room, then he headed up to see his master.

"Quite a crowd," the Jaff said.

"You approve?"

"Wholly."

"I wanted a word before things got too . . . busy."

"About what?"

"Rochelle."

"Ah."

"I know you're planning something heavy-duty, and believe me I couldn't be happier. If you wipe them all off the face of the fucking earth you'll be doing the world a favor."

"I'm sorry to disappoint you," said the Jaff. "They won't all be joining the great Power Breakfast in the sky. I may take a few liberties with them but I'm not interested in death. That's more my son's area of endeavor."

"I just want to be certain Rochelle can be kept out of it."

"I won't lay a finger on her," the Jaff replied. "There? Does that satisfy you?"

"It does, yes. Thanks."

"So. Shall we begin?"

"What are you planning?"

"I just want you to bring the guests up to see me, one by one. Let them get a little liquor in their systems first, then . . . show them the house."

"Men or women?"

"Bring the men first," the Jaff said, wandering back over to the window. "They're more pliable. Is it my imagination or is it getting dark?"

"Just clouding over."

"Rain?"

"I doubt it."

"Pity. Ah, more guests at the gate. You'd better go down and welcome them in."

SIX

It was an empty gesture, Howie knew, to go back to the woods on the edge of Deerdell. There could be no repetition of the meeting he'd had there. Fletcher had gone, and with him, so much clarification. But he went back anyway, vaguely hoping that returning to the place he'd met his father would spark some memory, however vestigial, which would help him dig through to the truth.

The sun was veiled with a hazy layer of cloud, but it was as hot beneath the trees as it had been on the other two occasions he'd come here. Hotter perhaps; certainly clammier. Though he'd intended to make directly for the place where he'd met Fletcher his route became as wandering as his thoughts. He didn't try to correct it. He'd made his gesture of respect, coming here; figuratively tipped his hat to his mother's memory, and to the man who'd reluctantly fathered him.

But chance, or some sense he was not even aware of, brought him back on to his intended course, and without even realizing it at first he stepped from the trees into the circle of clear ground where, eighteen years before, his life had been conjured. That was the right word. Not conceived; *conjured*. Fletcher had been a magician, of a kind. That was the only word Howie had been able to find to describe him. And

he, Howie, had been a trick. Except that instead of applause and bou-
quets all they'd got—Howie, his mother and the magician—was misery and pain. He'd wasted valuable years in failing to come here
sooner, and learning this essential fact about himself: that he was no
desperado at all. Just a rabbit pulled from a hat, held up by the ears,
and *squirming*.

He wandered towards the cave entrance, which was still fenced off
and marked with police notices warning adventurers away. Standing at
the barricade he peered down into the gaping hole in the ground.
Somewhere down there in the dark his father had waited and waited,
holding on to his enemy like death itself. Now there was only the
comedian down there, and from what he'd gathered the corpse would
never be recovered.

He looked up, and his whole system somersaulted. He wasn't alone.
On the far side of the grave stood Jo-Beth.

He stared, convinced that she was going to disappear. She couldn't
be here; not after last night. But his eyes kept seeing her.

They were too far apart for him to ask what she was doing here
without raising his voice, which he didn't want to do. He wanted to
hold the spell. And besides, did he really need an answer? She was
here because he was here because she was here; and so on.

It was she who moved first, her hand going up to the button of the
dark dress she wore, and undoing it. The expression on her face didn't
seem to change, but he couldn't be certain he wasn't missing nuances.
He'd taken off his spectacles when he'd stepped among the trees, and
short of digging for them in his shirt pocket he could only watch, and
wait, and hope the moment would come for them to approach each
other. Meanwhile, she had unbuttoned the top of her dress, and now
she slipped the buckle of the belt. Still he resisted making any
approach, though it was barely within his power to control himself.
She was letting the belt of her dress drop now, and, crossing her arms,
took the hem in her hands to pull it up over her head. He didn't dare
breathe, for fear he miss an instant of this ritual. She was wearing
white underwear, but her breasts, when they came into view, were
bare.

She had made him hard. He moved a little to adjust his position, which motion she took as her cue, dropping the dress to the ground and moving towards him. One step was enough. He started to walk towards her in his turn, each keeping close to their barricade. He shrugged off his jacket as he walked, and dropped it behind him.

As they came within a few feet of each other she said:

"I knew you'd be here. I don't know how. I was driving up from the Mall with Ruth—"

"Who?"

"That doesn't matter now. I just wanted to say I'm sorry."

"About what?"

"Last night. I didn't trust you and I should have."

She put her hand to his face.

"Do you forgive me?"

"Nothing to forgive," he said.

"I want to make love to you."

"Yes," he said, as though she hadn't needed to tell him, which was true.

It was easy. After all that had happened to separate them, it was easy. They were like magnets. However or whoever pulled them apart they were bound to come back together, like this; they couldn't help themselves. Didn't want to.

She started to pull his shirt from his trousers. He helped her, hauling it over his head. There were two seconds of darkness while it covered his face, in which her image, face, breasts and underwear, was as sharp in his head as a scene lit by lightning. Then she was there again, unbuckling his belt. He heeled off his shoes, then performed a monopodal dance to pull his socks off. Finally, he let his trousers drop and stepped out of them.

"I was afraid," she said.

"Not now. You're not afraid now."

"No."

"I'm not the Devil. I'm not Fletcher's. I'm yours."

"I love you."

She put her palms on his chest, and ran them outwards, as if smoothing pillows. He put his arms around her and pulled her towards him.

His dick was doing push-ups in his shorts. He placated it by kissing her, moving his hands down her back to the band of her panties, then sliding beneath. Her kisses were moving from his nose to chin, he licking at her lips when her mouth crossed his. She pressed her body against him.

"Here," she said softly.

"Yes?"

"Yes. Why not? No one to see us. I want to, Howie."

He smiled. She stepped away from him, going down on her knees in front of him and pulling his shorts down far enough that his dick sprang into view. She took hold of it gently, then suddenly harder, using her hold to bring him down to ground level. He knelt in front of her. She still didn't relinquish her hold, but rubbed him until he put his hand over hers and coaxed her fingers away.

"Not good?" she said.

"Too good," he breathed. "I don't want to shoot."

"Shoot?"

"Come. Spurt. Lose it."

"I want you to lose it," she said, lying down in front of him. His dick was now solid against his belly. "I want you to lose it in me."

He leaned over and put his hands on her hips, then began to pull her panties down. The hair around her slit was a darker blonde than her hair, but not much. He put his face to her, and licked between the lips. Her body tensed beneath him, then relaxed.

He ran his tongue up from her cunt to her navel, from her navel to her breasts, from her breasts to her face, until he was lying on top of her.

"I love you," he said, and entered her.

SEVEN

It was only as she was washing the bloodstains from the woman's neck that Tesla came to look more closely at the cross around her neck. She recognized it instantly, as a companion to the medallion Kissoon had shown her. The same central figure, spreadeagled; the same four lines of variations on the human spreading from it.

"Shoal," she said.

The woman opened her eyes. There was no period of coming-to. One moment she was to all intents and purposes asleep. The next her eyes were wide and alert. They were dark gray.

"Where am I?" she said.

"My name's Tesla. You're in my apartment."

"In the Cosm?" the woman said. Her voice was frail; eroded by heat, wind and fatigue.

"Yes," Tesla said. "We're out of the Loop. Kissoon can't get us here."

This she knew was not altogether true. The shaman had twice reached Tesla in this very apartment. Once in her sleep; once while coffee-making. There was nothing, presumably, to stop him doing the same again. But she'd felt no touch from him, nothing at all. Perhaps he was too concerned that she get about her labors on his behalf to interfere. Perhaps he had other plans. Who knew?

"What's your name?" she asked.

"Mary Muralles," she said.

"You're one of the Shoal," Tesla said.

Mary's eyes flickered towards Raul, who was at the door.

"Don't worry," Tesla said. "If you can trust me you can certainly trust him. If you won't trust either of us then we're all lost. So tell me . . ."

"Yes. I'm one of the Shoal."

"Kissoon told me he was the last."

"He and I."

"The rest were murdered, like he said?"

She nodded. Again her gaze went to Raul.

"I told you," Tesla began.

"Something strange about him," Mary said. "He's not *human*."

"Don't worry, I know," Tesla said.

"Iad?"

"Ape," she said. She turned to Raul. "Don't mind me telling her do you?"

Raul said and did nothing by way of response.

"How?" Mary wanted to know.

"It's quite a story. I thought maybe you'd know more about it than me. Fletcher? A guy called Jaffe; or the Jaff? No?"

"No."

"So . . . we've both got things to learn."

Back in the wastes of the Loop, Kissoon sat in his hut and called for help. The Muralles woman had escaped. Her wounds were surely profound, but she'd survived worse. He had to reach her, which meant stretching his influence into real time. He'd done it before of course. He'd brought Tesla to him that way. Before her, there'd been a few others who'd strayed along the *Jornada del muerto*. Randolph Jaffe had been one such wanderer, whom he'd been able to guide into the Loop. It wasn't so difficult. But the influence he wished to exercise now was not upon a human mind, it was upon creatures who had no mind, nor in any legitimate sense were even alive.

He pictured the Lix now, lying inert on a tile floor. They'd been forgotten. Good. They weren't particularly subtle beasts. To work their
mischief best they needed the victims distracted. That, at the moment,
they surely were. If he was quick he could still silence the witness.

His call had been answered. Help was coming, in crawling hundreds, under the door. Beetles, ants, scorpions. He unlocked his
crossed legs and drew his feet up to his body, to give them free access
to his genitals. Years ago he'd been able to achieve erection and ejacu-
lation by will alone, but age, and the Loop, had taken its toll. He
needed help now, and given that the laws of this suit explicitly forbade
the conjuror to touch himself a little artificial aid was required. They
knew their business, crawling up over him, the motion of their limbs,
and their bites and stings, arousing him. This was the way he'd made
the Lix, ejaculating on to his own excrement. Seminal suits had always
been his favorite kind.

Now, as they worked on him, he let his thoughts return to the Lix
on the tiles, allowing the rolls of sensation climbing his thronged per-
ineum and balls to push his intention out towards the place where
they lay.

A little life was all they needed, to bring a little death . . .

Mary Muralles had asked to be told Tesla's story before she told her
own, and for all her quiet voice she spoke like a woman whose requests
were seldom denied. This one certainly wasn't. Tesla was happy to tell
her story, or rather *the* story (so little of it was hers), as best she could,
hoping that Mary would be able to throw some light on its more
puzzling details. She held her silence however, until Tesla had
finished, which—by the time she'd told what she knew about Fletcher,
the Jaff, the children of both, the Nuncio and Kissoon—was close to
half an hour. It might have been much longer but that she'd had practice in the craft of concision preparing plot summaries for studios.
She'd practiced with Shakespeare (the tragedies were easy, the come-
dies a bitch) until she'd had the trick of it down pat. But this story was
not so easily pigeon-holed. When she started to tell the tale it spilled
out in all directions. It was a love story and an origin of species. It was

about insanity, apathy and a lost ape. When it was tragic, as in Vance's death, it was also farcical. When its settings were most mundane, as at the Mall, its substance was often visionary. She could find no way to tell all this neatly. It refused. Every time she thought she had a clear line to a point something would intersect.

If she said, "It's all connected . . ." once in her telling she said it a dozen times, though she didn't always know (in fact seldom) how or why.

Perhaps Mary could furnish the connections.

"I'm about done," Tesla said. "It's your turn."

The other woman took a moment to gather her strength. Then she said:

"You've certainly got a good grasp of recent events, but you want to know what happened to shape those events. Of course. They're a mystery to you. But I have to say much of it's a mystery to me too. I can't answer all the problems. There's a lot I don't know. If your account proves anything, it's that there's a good deal *neither* of us knows. But I can tell you some facts straight off. First, and simplest: it was Kissoon who murdered the rest of the Shoal."

"Kissoon? Are you kidding me?"

"I was one of them, remember?" Mary said. "He'd been conspiring against us for years."

"Conspiring with whom?"

"At a guess? The Iad Uroboros. Or their representatives in the Cosm. With the Shoal dead, he might have intended to use the Art, and let the Iad through."

"Shit! So what he told me about the Iad, and Quiddity . . . all of that's true?"

"Oh yes. He only tells lies when he needs to. He told you the truth. That's part of his brilliance—"

"I don't see what's so brilliant about hiding in a hut—" Tesla said, then: "Wait a minute. This doesn't figure. If he's responsible for the deaths of the Shoal, what's he got to fear? Why's he hiding at all?"

"He isn't *hiding*. He's trapped there. Trinity's his prison. The only way he can get out—"

"Is by finding another body to get out *in*."

"Exactly."

"Me."

"Or Randolph Jaffe before you."

"But neither of us fell for it."

"And he doesn't get many visitors. It takes a very extraordinary set of circumstances to bring anyone within sighting distance of the Loop. He created it to hide his crime. Now *it* hides *him*. Once in a while somebody like the Jaff—driven half insane—gets to the point where Kissoon can take control, and guide him in. Or you, with the Nuncio in your system. But otherwise, he's alone."

"Why's he trapped?"

"I trapped him. He thought I was dead. Had my body brought into the Loop with the others. But I rose. Confronted him. Angered him to the point where he attacked me, putting *my* blood on *his* hands."

"And chest," Tesla said, remembering the glimpse she'd had of Kissoon's blood-spattered body, when she'd first escaped him.

"The conditions of the looping suit are explicit. Blood may not be spilled inside the Loop, or the conjuror becomes its prisoner."

"What do you mean by *suit*?"

"Petition. Maneuver. Trick."

"Trick? You call making a loop in time a *trick*?"

"It's an ancient suit," Mary said. "A time out of time. You'll find accounts of it everywhere. But there are laws pertaining to all conditions of matter, and I made him break one. He became his own victim."

"And you were trapped there too?"

"Not strictly. But I wanted him dead, and I knew nobody in the Cosm who could do it. Not with the rest of the Shoal murdered. I had to stay and hope to kill him."

"Then you'd have shed blood too."

"Better that, and be trapped, than he go on living. He'd killed fifteen great men and women. Pure, good souls. Just had them slaughtered. Tortured some of them, for the pleasure of it. Not personally of course. He'd had agents. But he'd masterminded the whole thing. Arranged that we be separated from each other, so that he could dispatch us one by one. Then had our bodies taken back in time to Trinity, where he knew no trace would remain."

"Where are they?"

"In the town. What's left of them."

"My God," Tesla remembered the House of the Stench, and shuddered, "I almost got to see them for myself."

"Kissoon prevented you of course."

"Not forcibly. It was more a matter of *persuasion*. He's very convincing."

"Certainly. He had us all fooled for years. The Shoal is—I mean *was*—the most difficult society to join in the world. There are means, incredibly elaborate, to test and purify possible members before they even realize the society exists. Some-how Kissoon faked his way through those procedures. Or else the Iad somehow tainted him once he was a member, which is possible."

"Is as little known about the Iad as he said?"

"Scarcely any information emerges from the Metacosm. It's a sealed condition of being. What we know about the Iad can be summed up in a few words. They are many; their definition of life is not that of you humans—indeed may be its antithesis; and they want the Cosm."

"What do you mean, *you* humans?" Tesla said. "You're as human as I am."

"Yes and no," Mary replied. "I certainly was once as you are. But the processes of purification change your nature. If I'd been human I couldn't have survived in Trinity for twenty odd years, with scorpions to eat and mud to drink. I'd be dead, the way Kissoon intended."

"How come you survived the murder attempt and the others didn't?"

"Luck. Instinct. Sheer refusal to let that bastard win. It isn't just Quiddity that's at stake, though that's valuable enough. It's the Cosm. If the Iad break through nothing on this plane of being will survive intact. I believe—" She stopped talking suddenly, and sat up in bed.

"What is it?" Tesla said.

"I heard something. Next door."

"Grand opera," Tesla said. *Lucia di Lammermoor* still trailed through.

"No," Mary said. "Something else."

Raul was already off in search of the sound's source before Tesla asked him. She turned her attention back to Mary.

"There's still some stuff I haven't got straight," she said. "A lot of stuff. Like, why Kissoon went to the trouble of taking the bodies into the Loop. Why didn't he destroy them out here in the normal world? And why did you let him take you?"

"I was wounded; almost dead. Near enough for him and his assassins to think I *was* dead. It was only when they were tossing me on a pile of bodies I came to my senses."

"So what happened to his assassins?"

"Knowing Kissoon he probably let them die in the Loop, trying to find their way out. That sort of thing would amuse him."

"So for twenty odd years the only human beings in the Loop—or *near* human—were you and Kissoon."

"Me half mad. And him all the way."

"And those fucking Lix, whatever *they* are."

"His shit and semen is what they are," Mary said. "His turds, got fat and frisky."

"Jesus."

"They're trapped there the way he is," Mary said, with some satisfaction. "At Zero, if Zero can be—"

Raul's yell from the next room stopped her in mid-thought. Tesla was up and through into the kitchen in seconds, to find him wrestling with one of Kissoon's shit-creatures. Her assumption, that they'd been dying when they were brought through from the Loop, could not have been farther off the mark. If anything the beast in his hands looked stronger than those she and Mary had fought, despite being only the head-end. Its mouth was wide and closing on Raul's face. It had already struck there twice at least. There was blood pouring from a wound in the center of his forehead. She crossed to him and took hold of it with both hands, more disgusted by its feel and smell than ever now she knew its origins. Even with four hands to keep it from doing further damage it was not about to be subdued. It had the strength of three of its earlier incarnations. She knew it was only a matter of time before it wore them both down, and got to Raul's face again. This time it wouldn't be just his frown it bit off.

"I'm going to let go," Tesla said, "and get a knife. OK?"

"Be quick about it."

"You betcha. On a count of three, right? Get ready to take the whole thing."

"I'm ready."

"One . . . two . . . *three!*"

She let go on three, and ran through to the sink. There were piles of unwashed dishes beside it. She rummaged amongst the chaos looking for a suitable weapon, the dishes sliding in every direction, several of them smashing as they fell to the floor. But the avalanche uncovered steel; one of a set of kitchen knives her mother had given her two Christmases ago. She picked it up. Its handle was sticky with last week's lasagna and the mold it had sprouted since, but it felt good in her hand.

As she turned back to go to Raul's aid it struck her that there had been more than one of the Lix pieces brought through from the Loop—five or six at least, she thought—and that only one was visible. The others had gone from the floor. She had not time to concern herself any further. Raul cried out. She rushed to his aid, stabbing at the body of the Lix with the knife. The beast responded instantly to the attack, snapping its head around, black needle-teeth bared. She aimed a stab at its face, opening a wound in its jaw, from which the dirty yellow muck that she'd taken for blood 'til minutes ago spat in fat spurts. Its gyrations became a frenzy, which Raul was only barely able to control.

"Count of three—" she said to him.

"What this time?"

"Throw it!"

"It can move quickly."

"I'll stop it," she said. "Just do as I say! On three! One . . . two . . . three!"

He did as instructed. The Lix flew across the room and hit the floor.

As it struggled to get itself ready to attack again Tesla raised the knife and brought it down in one two-handed stab that transfixed the creature. Mother had good taste in knives. The blade sliced into the creature and buried itself in the floor, effectively nailing it down, while its life-fluids continued to leak from the wounds.

"Got you, you fucker!" she said, then turned to Raul. The attack had left him shaking, and the blood was still flowing copiously from his face.

"Better wash those wounds," Tesla told him. "You don't know what kind of poison's in those things."

He nodded, and headed through to the bathroom, while she returned her gaze to the death-throes of the Lix. Just as she recaptured the thought she'd had as she'd emerged with the knife (where were the rest of them?) she heard Raul say:

". . . Tesla."

and she knew where they'd gone.

He was standing at the door of her bedroom. It was clear from the expression of horror on his face what he was looking at. But it still brought a sob of revulsion from her to see what Kissoon's beasts had done to the woman she'd left lying on her bed. They were still busy with their murder. Six of them in all, like the one that had attacked Raul, stronger than those they'd encountered in the Loop. Mary's resistance had profited her not at all. While Tesla had been busy digging for a blade to protect Raul—an attack mounted as a distraction—they'd crawled on her and wound themselves around her neck and head. She'd struggled fiercely, her fight throwing her half off the bed, where her body, a racked bag of bones, still lay. One of the Lix unravelled itself from around her face. It had crushed her features beyond recognition.

She was suddenly aware of Raul, still shuddering at her shoulder.

"Nothing to be done," she said. "You should go wash."

He nodded grimly, and left her side. The Lix were running down, their motions becoming sluggish. Presumably Kissoon had better things to do with his energies than waste them pressing his agents to further mischief. She closed the door on the sight, sickened to her stom-

ach, and went back through to check under the furniture that there
were no others lurking around. The creature she'd nailed to the floor
was now completely dead; or at least inert. She stepped past it and went
to find another weapon before checking the rest of the apartment.

In the bathroom Raul let the bloodied water run from the sink, and
peered at the hurt the Lix had done him. It was superficial. But some
of its poison *had* got into his system, as Tesla had warned. His whole
body seemed to be shaking from the inside out, and the arm that had
been touched by the Nuncio was throbbing as though he'd just
plunged it into boiling water. He looked down. The arm was insub-
stantial in front of him, the sink behind it showing through more solid
flesh and bone. Panicking, he looked back up at his reflection. That
too was growing hazy, the bathroom wall blurring, and some other
image—harsh and bright—demanding to be seen behind it.

He opened his mouth to cry for Tesla's help but before he could do
so his image disappeared from the mirror entirely; and so—a moment
of utter dislocation later—did the mirror itself. The glare grew blinding around him, and something took hold of his Nunciate arm. He
remembered Tesla describing Kissoon's grip on her gut. Now that
same mind took his hand, and pulled.

As the last trace of Tesla's apartment gave way to an endless, burning horizon, he threw his untainted arm out to where the sink had
been. He seemed to connect with something in the world he'd left,
but he couldn't be sure.

Then all hope was gone, and he was in Kissoon's Loop.

Tesla heard something drop in the bathroom.

"Raul?" she said.

There was no answer.

"Raul? Are you all right?"

Fearing the worst she went quickly, knife in hand. The door was
closed but not locked.

"Are you there?" she said. When she received no reply a third time
she opened the door. A bloody towel had been dropped on the floor,

or fallen, carrying a number of toiletry items with it: the noise she'd heard. But Raul was not there.

"Shit!"

She turned off the faucet, which was still gushing, and about-faced, calling his name again, then going through the apartment, dreading with every turn she was going to find him prey to the same horror that had claimed Mary. But there was no sign of him; nor of any further Lix. Finally, steeling herself for the sight on the sheets, she opened her bedroom door. He was not there either.

Standing at the door brought back to Tesla the look of horror on his face when he'd seen Mary's corpse. Had that simply been too much for him? She shut off the sight of the body on the bed and went to the front door. It was ajar, the way she'd left it when they'd first come in. Leaving it that way she started down the stairs and along the side of the building, calling after him as she went, the certainty growing in her that he'd simply decided he could stand no more of this madness and had taken to the streets of West Hollywood. If he had he was exchanging one madness for another, but that was his choice and she couldn't be responsible for the consequences.

He wasn't in the street when she reached it. In the porch of the house opposite two young men were sitting enjoying the last light of the afternoon. She knew the names of neither, but she crossed to them and said:

"Have you seen a man?" which raised eyebrows and smiles from both.

"Recently?" one of them said.

"Just now. Ran out of the building opposite?"

"We just came out here," said the other. "Sorry."

"What'd he do?" the first said, looking at the knife in Tesla's hand. "Too much or not enough?"

"Not enough," Tesla said.

"Fuck him," came the reply. "There's plenty more."

"Not like him," she replied. "Trust me. Not like him. Thanks anyhow."

"What did he look like?" came the question as she recrossed the street.

A little vengeful part of Tesla, one she wasn't much proud of but which always came to the fore when someone did the dirty on her like this, replied: "Like a fucking monkey," in a voice that must have been heard halfway down Santa Monica and Melrose. "He looked like a fucking monkey."

So, Tesla babe, what now?

She poured herself a Tequila, sat herself down, and reviewed the overall picture. Raul gone; Kissoon in league with the Iad; Mary Muralles dead in the bedroom. Not a lot to take comfort from. She poured herself a second Tequila, not unaware that drunkenness, like sleep, might put her closer to Kissoon than she'd strictly like to be, but needing the burn of it in her throat and belly.

There was no purpose in staying in the apartment. The real action was back in Palomo Grove.

She put a call through to Grillo. He was not at the hotel. She asked the hotel operator to put her through to the front desk and enquired there if anyone knew where he was. Nobody did. He'd gone out in the middle of the afternoon she was told. It was now four-twenty-five. They estimated he'd been gone an hour at least. To the party on the Hill she guessed.

With nothing to detain her at North Huntley Drive but mourning her sudden loss of allies, her best move now, she decided, was to go find Grillo, before circumstance took him from her too.

EIGHT

Grillo hadn't come to the Grove with garb appropriate for the gathering up at Coney Eye, but this being California, where sneakers and jeans were formal dress, he thought he wouldn't be conspicuous in his casual gear. That was the first of the afternoon's many errors. Even the guards at the front gate were wearing tuxedos and black ties. But he had the invitation, on which he'd inscribed a false name (Jon Swift), and it was not questioned.

This was not the first time he'd slipped into a gathering under an assumed identity. Back in his days as an investigative reporter (as opposed to his present role as muckraker) he'd attended a neo-Nazis' revival meeting in Detroit as a distant relation of Goebbels, several faith-healing sessions by a defrocked priest whose scam he'd later uncovered in a series of pieces that had earned him a Pulitzer nomination, and, most memorably, a gathering of sado-masochists, his account of which had been smothered by the senator he'd seen chained up eating dog food. In those various companies he'd felt like a just man in dangerous company, going in search of truth: Philip Marlowe with a pen. Here he simply felt nauseous. A beggar sickened at the feast. From Ellen's account of the party he'd expected to see famous faces; what he hadn't anticipated was the strange authority they'd had over him, quite out of proportion to their skills. Gathered under Buddy Vance's roof were dozens of the most well-known faces in the world; legends, idols, style-makers. Around them, faces he couldn't have put names to but he recognized from copies of *Variety* and *Hollywood Reporter*. The potentates of the industry—agents, lawyers and studio executives. Tesla, in her frequent railings against the New Hollywood, saved the sourest venom for these, the business-school types who'd superseded the old-style studio bosses, Warner, Selznick, Goldwyn and their clan, to rule the dream factories with their demographics and their calculators. These were the men and women who chose next year's deities, and put their names on audiences' lips around the world. It didn't always work of course. The public was fickle, sometimes positively perverse, deciding to deify an unknown against all expectation. But the system was prepared for such anomalies. The rank outsider would be drawn into the pantheon at startling speed, and everyone would claim how they'd known all along the man was a star.

There were several such stars among this gathering, young actors who could not have known Buddy Vance personally but were presumably here because this was the Party of the Week; the place to be seen, and the company to be seen in.

He caught sight of Rochelle across the room, but she was engaged in being flattered—a whole gamut of admirers gathered around her, feeding on her beauty. She didn't look Grillo's way. Even if she had he doubted she would have recognized him. She had the distracted, dreamy air of one high on something other than admiration. Besides which, experience had taught him that his face was interchangeable with many others. There was a blandness about him which he'd put down to being so much a mongrel. Swedish, Russian, Lithuanian, Jewish and English trails could be found in his blood. They effectively cancelled each other out. He was everything and nothing. In such circumstances as these it gave him a strange confidence. He could pass himself off as any number of characters and not be called on it unless he made a major *faux pas*, and even then he could usually extricate himself.

Accepting a glass of champagne from one of the waiters he mingled with the crowd, mentally noting the names of faces he recognized;

and the names of the company they kept. Though nobody in the room, other than Rochelle, had the slightest idea who he was he garnered nods from almost everyone whose eyes he met, and even a wave or two from individuals who were presumably scoring points among their circle as to how many of this dazzling congregation they were acquainted with. He fuelled the fiction, nodding when he was nodded at, waving when he was waved at, so that by the time he'd crossed the room his credentials were firmly established: he was one of the boys. This in turn led to an approach by a woman in her late fifties, who buttonholed him with a glance and a sharp:

"So who are you?"

He hadn't prepared a detailed alter-ego, as he had with the neo-Nazis and the faith-healer, so he simply said:

"Swift. Jonathan."

She nodded, almost as though she knew.

"I'm Evelyn Quayle," she said. "Please call me Eve. Everyone does."

"Eve it is."

"What do people call you?"

"Swift," he said.

"Fine," she said. "Would you catch that waiter and get me a fresh glass of champagne? They move so damn fast."

It was not the last she drank. She knew a great deal about the company they were keeping, which she furnished in greater detail the more glasses of champagne and compliments Grillo provided, one of the latter quite genuine. He'd guessed Eve to be in her mid-fifties. In fact she admitted to seventy-one.

"You don't look anything like that."

"Control, my dear," she said. "I have every vice, but none to excess. Would you reach for another of those glasses before they slip by?"

She was the perfect gossip: beneficent in her bitchery. There was scarcely a man or woman in the room she couldn't supply some dirt about. The anorexic in scarlet, for instance, was the twin sister of Annie Kristol, darling of the celebrity game shows. She was wasting away at a rate that would prove fatal, Eve opined, within three months. By contrast, Merv Turner, one of the recently sacked board of Universal, had put on so much weight since exiting the Black Tower his wife refused to have sex with him. As for Liza Andreatta, poor child, she'd been hospitalized for three weeks after the birth of her second child having been persuaded by her therapist that in nature the mother always ate the placenta. She'd eaten her own and been so traumatized she'd almost orphaned her child before it had seen its mother's face.

"Madness," she said, smiling from ear to ear, "isn't it?"

Grillo had to agree.

"A wonderful madness," she went on. "I've been part of it all my life and it's as wild now as it ever was. I'm getting rather warm; shall we step outside for a while?"

"Sure."

She took Grillo's arm. "You listen well," she said as they stepped out into the garden. "Which is unusual in this kind of company."

"Really?" said Grillo.

"What are you: a writer?"

"Yes," he said, relieved not to have to lie to the woman. He liked her. "It's not much of a trade."

"None of us have much of a trade," she said. "Let's be honest. We're not finding a cure for cancer. We're *indulging*, sweetheart. Just indulging."

She drew Grillo across to the locomotive facade which stood out in the garden. "Will you look at this? So ugly, don't you think?"

"I don't know. They've got a certain appeal."

"My first husband collected American Abstract Expressionists. Pollock, Rothko. Chilly stuff. I divorced him."

"Because of the painting?"

"Because of the collecting, the relentless collecting. It's a sickness, Swift. I said to him towards the end—Ethan, I don't want to be just another of your possessions. *They* go or *I* go. He chose the stuff that didn't talk back at him. He was that kind of man. Cultured, but stupid."

Grillo smiled.

"You're laughing at me," she chided.

"Absolutely not. I'm enchanted."

She sparkled at the compliment. "You don't know anybody here, do you?" she remarked suddenly.

The observation left him flummoxed.

"You're a gatecrasher. I watched you when you first came in, eyeing the hostess in case she set eyes on you. I thought—at last!—someone who knows *nobody* and wants to, and me who knows *everybody* and wishes she didn't. A marriage made in heaven. What's your real name?"

"I told you—"

"Don't insult me," she said.

"My name's Grillo."

"Grillo."

"Nathan Grillo. But please . . . just Grillo. I'm a journalist."

"Oh how boring. I thought you were maybe an angel, come down to judge us. You know . . . like Sodom and Gomorrah. Christ knows, we deserve it."

"You don't like these people much," he said.

"Oh my dear I'd rather be here than Idaho, but only for the weather. The conversation's shit." She pressed close to him. "Don't look now but we've got company."

A short, balding and faintly familiar man was approaching.

"What's his name?" Grillo whispered.

"Paul Lamar. He was Buddy's partner."

"Comedian?"

"So his agent'd claim. Have you seen any of his films?"

"No."

"There's more laughs in *Mein Kampf*."

Grillo was still attempting to suppress his guffaws when Lamar presented himself to Eve.

"You look wonderful," he said. "As ever." He turned to Grillo. "And who's your friend?" he asked.

Eve glanced at Grillo with a tiny smile on her face. "My guilty secret," she said.

Lamar turned his spotlight smile on Grillo. "I'm sorry, I didn't catch your name."

"Secrets shouldn't have names," Eve said. "It spoils their charm."

"I'm suitably slapped down," Lamar said. "Allow me to correct the error and give you a tour of the house."

"I don't think I can manage the stairs, sweetheart," Eve said.

"But this was Buddy's palace. He was very proud of it."

"Never proud enough to invite me," she returned.

"It was a retreat," Lamar said. "That's why he lavished so much attention on it. You should come and look, if only for him. Both of you."

"Why not?" said Grillo.

Evelyn sighed. "Such curiosity," she said. "Well . . . lead on."

Lamar did so, taking them back into the lounge, where the tempo of the gathering had subtly altered. With drinks imbibed and the buffet scavenged the guests were settling into a quieter mode, eased on by a small band offering languid versions of the standards. A few people were dancing. Conversation was no longer raucous, but subdued. Deals were being done; plots being laid.

Grillo found the atmosphere unnerving, and so, clearly, did Evelyn. She took his arm as they ran the gauntlet of whispers and followed Lamar out the other side to the stairs. The front door was closed. Two of the guards from the gate stood with their backs to it, hands fisted in front of their crotches. Despite the drifting melody of show-tunes all celebration had gone out of the place. What remained was paranoia.

Lamar was already a dozen steps up the flight.

"Come along, Evelyn . . ." he said, beckoning to her. "It's not steep."

"It is at my age."

"You don't look a day over—"

"Don't sweet-talk me," she said. "I'll come in my own good time."

With Grillo at her side she started to climb the stairs, her age evidencing itself for the first time. There were a few guests at the top of the flight, Grillo saw, empty glasses in hand. None of them were speaking, even in whispers. The suspicion grew on him that all was far from well here; an instinct confirmed when he glanced back down the stairs. Rochelle was standing at the bottom, looking up. She stared straight at him. He, certain he'd been recognized and was about to have his bluff called, stared back. But she said nothing. She looked at him until he looked away. When he glanced back down to the hallway she'd gone.

"There's something wrong here," he murmured in Eve's ear. "I don't think we should do this."

"Darling, I'm halfway up," she replied loudly, and tugged on his arm. "Don't desert me now."

Grillo glanced up at Lamar, to find the comedian's eyes were on him just as Rochelle's had been. *They know,* he thought. *They know and they're saying nothing.*

Again he tried to dissuade Eve. "Can't we go later?" he said.

She was not about to be turned. "I'm going with or without you," she said, and carried on climbing.

"This is the first landing," Lamar announced when they got there. Besides the curious, silent guests there was not much to see, given that Eve had already stated her aversion to Vance's art collection. She knew several of the loiterers by name, and said hello. They acknowledged her, but only distractedly. There was something about their languor that put Grillo in mind of addicts who'd just found a fix. Eve was not one to be so lightly treated.

"Sagansky," she said to one of their number. He had the looks of a matinee idol gone to seed. Beside him, a woman who seemed to have all trace of animation drained from her. "What are you doing up here?"

Sagansky looked up at her. "Sssh . . . ," he said.

"Did somebody die?" Eve said. "Besides Buddy."

"Sad," Sagansky said.

"Happens to us all," was Eve's unsentimental response. "You too. See if it doesn't. Have you had the grand tour of the house?"

Sagansky nodded. "Lamar . . ." he said, his eyes swivelling in the comedian's direction and overshooting their target, then coming back to settle on him, "Lamar showed us around."

"It better be worth it," Eve said.

"It is," was Sagansky's response. "Really . . . it is. Especially the upper rooms."

"Ah yes," Lamar said. "Why don't we just go straight up there?"

Grillo's paranoia hadn't been mellowed an iota by encountering Sagansky and wife. Something deeply weird was going on here.

"I think we've seen enough," Grillo said to Lamar.

"Oh, I'm sorry," the comedian replied. "I was forgetting about Eve. Poor Eve. It must be all too much for you."

His condescension, beautifully pitched, created precisely the effect he intended.

"Don't be ridiculous," she snorted. "I may be getting on, but I'm not senile. Take us up!"

Lamar shrugged. "Are you sure?"

"Sure I'm sure."

"Well, if you insist . . ." he said, and led on, past the loiterers, to the bottom of the next flight of stairs. Grillo followed. As he passed Sagansky he heard the man muttering snatches of his previous exchange with Eve. Dead fish floating around in the back of his head.

". . . it is . . . really, it is . . . especially the upper rooms . . ."

Eve was already a little way up the flight, determined she could match Lamar step for step.

Grillo called after her, "Eve. Don't go any further."

She ignored him.

"*Eve?*" he said again.

This time she glanced round.

"Are you coming, Grillo?" she said.

If Lamar realized that she'd let slip the name of her secret he didn't register anything. He simply led her to the top of the stairs and round a corner, out of sight.

More than once in his career Grillo had avoided a beating up by taking notice of the very danger signals he'd been getting since they'd started the climb. But he wasn't about to see Eve's ego undo her. In the space of an hour he'd become fond of the lady. Cursing himself and her in equal measure, he followed where she and her seducer had gone.

Outside, a minor fracas was occurring at the gate. It had begun with a wind that had blown up out of nowhere, running up through the trees that overhung the Hill like a tide. It was dry and dusty, and drove several late-arriving guests back into their limos to fix their streaming mascara.

Emerging from the gusts was a car; in the car a filthy young man who casually demanded entry to the house.

The guards kept their cool. They'd dealt with countless gatecrashers like this in their time; kids with more balls than brains who just wanted to get a glimpse of the high life.

"No invitation, son," one of them told the boy.

The gatecrasher got out of his car. There was blood on him; not his own. And in his eyes a rabid look that had the guards' hands moving towards the weapons beneath their jackets.

"I have to see my father," the boy said.

"Is he a guest?" the guard wanted to know. It was not impossible this was some rich kid from Bel-Air, head fucked with drugs, come looking for Papa.

"Yeah, he's a guest," said Tommy-Ray.

"What's his name?" the guard asked. "Give me the list, Clark."

"He's not on any of your lists," Tommy-Ray said. "He lives here."

"You've got the wrong house, son," Clark told him, having to raise his voice over the roar of wind in the trees, which continued unabated. "This is Buddy Vance's house. Unless you're one of his bastards!" He grinned at a third man, who didn't return the smile. His gaze was on the trees themselves, or on the air stirring them up. He narrowed his eyes, as if he could almost see something in the dust-dirtied sky.

"You're going to regret this, nigger," the kid was telling the first guard. "I'm coming back, and I'm telling you—you're the first to go." He stabbed a finger at Clark. "You hear me? He's the first. You come right after."

He got back into the car, and backed up, then turned around and headed down the Hill. By some unnerving coincidence, the wind seemed to go with him, back down into Palomo Grove.

"Fucking strange," the sky-watcher said, as the last of the motion in the trees died away.

"Go up to the house," the first guard told Clark. "Just check everything's OK up there . . ."

"Why shouldn't it be?"

"Just fucking do it, will you?" the man replied, still staring down the Hill after the boy and the wind.

"Keep your tits on," Clark replied, and did as ordered.

With the wind gone, the two remaining guards were aware of just how quiet it was. No sound from the town below. No sound from the house above. And them in a silent alley-way of trees.

"Ever been under fire, Rab?" the sky-watcher asked.

"Nope. Have you?"

"Sure," came the reply. He snorted dust into the hand-kerchief his wife Marci had pressed for the top pocket of his tux. Then, sniffing, he surveyed the sky.

"Between attacks . . ." he said.

"Yeah?"

"It feels just like this."

Tommy-Ray, the Jaff thought, turning from his business momentarily, and going to the window. He'd been distracted by his work, and hadn't realized his son was near until he was driving away down the Hill. He tried to send a call out to the youth, but the message was not received. The thoughts the Jaff had found it easy to manipulate on previous occasions were not so simple any longer. Something had changed; something of great significance which the Jaff couldn't interpret. The boy's mind was no longer an open book. What signals he did receive were confounding. There was a fear in the boy he'd never felt before; and a *chill*, a profound chill.

It was no use trying to make sense of the signals; not with so much else to occupy him. The boy would come back. In fact that was the only clear message he was receiving: that Tommy-Ray intended to return.

Meanwhile there were more urgent demands upon the Jaff's time. The afternoon had proved profitable. In a matter of two hours his ambition for this gathering had been realized. It had produced allies possessed of a profound purity undreamed of among the Grovers' terata. The egos that had yielded them had resisted his persuasions at first. That was to be expected. Several of them, thinking they were about to be murdered, had produced their wallets and attempted to bribe their way out of the upper room. Two of the women had bared their silicone breasts and offered their bodies rather than die; one of the men had attempted a similar bargain. But their narcissism had crumbled like a sugar wall, their threats, negotiations, pleas and performances been silenced as soon as they started to sweat out their fears. He'd sent them all back to the party, milked and passive.

The assembly that now lined the walls was purer for its fresh recruits, a message of entropy passing from one terata to another, their multiplicity devolving in the shadows to something more ancient; darker, simpler. They'd become unparticularized. He could no longer ascribe to any of them the names of their creators. Gunther Rothbery, Christine Seapard, Laurie Doyle, Martine Nesbitt: where were they now? Become a common clay.

He had as large a legion as he could hold sway over; many more and his army would become unruly. Indeed perhaps it had already become so. Yet he continued to put off the moment when he finally let his hands do what they had been created, and re-created, to do: use the Art. It was twenty years since that life-shattering day when he'd found the symbol of the Shoal, lost in transit in the wilds of Nebraska. He'd never returned. Even during his war with Fletcher the trail of battle had never led him back to Omaha. He doubted there'd be anybody left he knew. Disease and despair would have taken a good half of them. Age, the other half. He, of course, had remained untouched by such forces. The passage of years had no authority over him. Only the Nuncio had that, and there was no way back from such alteration. He had to go forward, to see realized the ambition which had been laid in him that day, and the days following. He'd flown from the banality of his life into strange territories, and seldom looked back. But today, as the parade of famous faces had appeared before him in the upper room, and wept and shuddered and bared their breasts then their souls for him, he couldn't help but glance back to the man he'd been, who would never have dared hope to keep such celebrated company. When he did, he found something in himself he'd hidden, almost successfully, all these years. The very thing he was sweating from his victims: fear.

Though he'd changed out of all recognition a little part of him was still and would always be Randolph Jaffe, and that part whispered in his ear, and said: *this is dangerous. You don't know what you're taking on. This could kill you.*

After so many years it came as a shock to hear the old voice in his head, but it was also strangely reassuring. Nor could he entirely ignore it, because what it warned was true: he didn't know what lay beyond the using of the Art. Nobody really did. He'd heard all the stories; he'd studied all the metaphors. But they were only stories, only metaphors. Quiddity was not literally a sea; the Ephemeris was not literally an island. These were a materialist's way of describing a *state of mind*. Perhaps *the* State of Mind. And now he stood minutes from opening the door to that condition, in almost complete ignorance of its true nature.

It might lead to lunacy, hell and death as easily as to heaven and life everlasting. He had no way of knowing, but to use the Art.

Why use it at all? the man he'd been thirty years before whispered in him. *Why not just enjoy the power you've got? It's more than you ever dreamed of, isn't it? Women coming in here offering their bodies to you. Men falling down on their knees with snot running from their noses begging for mercy. What more do you want? What more could anybody want?*

Reasons, was the answer. Some meaning behind the tits and the tears; some glimpse of a larger picture.

You've got all there is, the old voice said. *This is as good as it gets. There is no more.*

There was a light tapping on the door: Lamar's code.

"Wait," he murmured, trying to hold on to the argument he'd been running in his head.

Outside the door, Eve tapped Lamar on the shoulder:

"Who's up here?" she said.

The comedian offered a small smile.

"Somebody you should meet," he said.

"A friend of Buddy's?" she said.

"Very much so."

"Who?"

"You don't know him."

"So why bother meeting him?" Grillo said. He took hold of Eve's arm. Suspicion had given way to certainty now. There was a rank smell up here, and the sound of more than one presence on the other side of the door.

The invitation to enter came. Lamar turned the doorhandle, and opened up.

"Come along, Eve," he said.

She pulled her arm from Grillo's grip and allowed Lamar to escort her up a step into the room.

"It's dark," Grillo heard her say.

"Eve," he said, pushing past Lamar and reaching through the door after her. As she'd said, it was indeed dark. Evening had come over the Hill, and what little light fell through the far window scarcely etched the interior. But Eve's figure was visible in front of him. Again, he took hold of her arm.

"Enough," he said, and started to turn towards the door. As he did so Lamar's fist met the middle of his face, a solid, unexpected blow. His hand slipped from Eve's arm; he fell to his knees, smelling his own blood in his nose. Behind him, the comedian slammed the door.

"What's happening?" he heard Eve say. "Lamar! What's going on?"

"Nothing to worry about," the man murmured.

Grillo raised his head, causing a hot gush of blood to run from his nose. He put his hand to his face to stem it, and looked around the room. In the brief moment he'd had to glimpse the interior he'd thought it piled with furniture. He'd been wrong. This was living stuff.

"Lam . . ." Eve said again, all bravado gone from her voice now. "Lamar . . . who's up here?"

"Jaffe . . ." a soft voice said. "Randolph Jaffe."

"Shall I put on the light?" Lamar said.

"No," came the answer from the shadows. "No, don't. Not yet."

Despite his buzzing head Grillo recognized the voice and the name. Randolph Jaffe: the Jaff. Which fact gave him the identity of the forms that lurked in the darkest corners of his huge room. It was lavish with the beasts he'd made.

Eve had seen them too.

"My God . . ." she murmured. "My God, my God, what's going on?"

"Friends of friends," Lamar said.

"Don't hurt her," Grillo demanded.

"I'm not a murderer," the voice of Randolph Jaffe said. "Everyone who came in here has walked out alive. I just want a little part of you . . ."

His voice didn't carry the same weight of confidence it had when

Grillo had heard him at the Mall. He'd spent much of his professional life listening to people talk; looking for signs of the life beneath the life. How had Tesla put it? Something about having an eye for the hidden agenda. There was certainly subtext to the Jaff's voice now. An ambiguity that had not been there before. Did it offer some hope of escape? Or at least a stay of execution.

"I remember you," Grillo said. He had to draw the man out: make subtext text. Make him tell his doubts. "I saw you catch fire."

"No . . ." said the voice in the darkness, ". . . that wasn't me . . ."

"My mistake. Then who . . . may I ask . . . ?"

"No you may not," Lamar said behind him. "Which of them do you want first?" he asked the Jaff.

The inquiry was ignored. Instead the man said: "Who am I? Strange you should ask." His tone was almost dreamy.

"Please," Eve murmured. "I can't breathe up here."

"Hush," Lamar said. He had moved to take hold of her. In the shadows, the Jaff shifted in his seat like a man who couldn't find a comfortable way to be.

"Nobody knows . . ." he began, ". . . just how terrible it is."

"What is?" Grillo said.

"I have the Art," the Jaff replied. "I have the Art. So I have to use it. It'd be a waste not to, after all this *waiting*, all this *change*."

He's shitting himself, Grillo thought. He's close to the edge and he's terrified of slipping over. Into what, he didn't know, but it was surely an exploitable condition. He decided to stay on the floor, where he offered no physical threat to the other man. Very softly he said:

"The Art. What *is* that?"

If the Jaff's next words were intended as an answer they were oblique.

"Everybody's lost, you know. I use that. Use the fear in them."

"Not you?" Grillo said.

"Not me?"

"Lost."

"I used to think I found the Art . . . but maybe the Art found me."

"That's good."

"Is it?" he said. "I don't know what it's going to do—"

So *that's* it, Grillo thought. He's got his prize and now he's afraid of unwrapping it.

"It could destroy us all."

"That's not what you said," Lamar muttered. "You said we'd have dreams. All the dreams America ever dreamt; that the *world* ever dreamt."

"Maybe," said the Jaff.

Lamar let go of Eve and took a step towards his master.

"But now you're saying we could *die?*" he said. "I don't want to die. I want Rochelle. I want the house. I've got a future. I'm not giving that up."

"Don't try and slip the leash," the Jaff said. For the first time since these exchanges had begun Grillo heard an echo of the man he'd seen at the Mall. Lamar's resistance was winning the old spirit back. Grillo cursed him for his rebellion. It bore one useful fruit only: it allowed Eve to step back towards the door. Grillo kept his place on the ground. Any attempt to join her would only draw attention to them both, and prevent any chance of escape for either. If she could get out she could raise the alarm.

Lamar's complaints, meanwhile, had multiplied.

"Why did you lie to me?" he said. "I should have known from the beginning you weren't going to do me any good. Well, fuck you—"

Silently, Grillo egged him on. The deepening dusk had kept pace with his eyes' attempt to pierce it, and he could see no more of his captor than he'd been able to see when he first came in, but he saw the figure stand. The motion caused consternation in the shadows, as the beasts hidden there responded to their creator's discomfiture.

"How dare you?" the Jaff said.

"You told me we were safe," Lamar said.

Grillo heard the door creak behind him. Though he wanted to turn he resisted the temptation.

"Safe, you said!"

"It's not that simple!" the Jaff said.

"I'm out of here!" Lamar replied, and turned to the door. It was too dark for Grillo to see the expression on his face, but a spill of light from behind him, and the sound of Eve's footsteps as she fled the room, was evidence enough. Grillo stood up as Lamar, cursing, crossed to the door. He was woozy from the blow, and reeled as he stood, but got to the door a pace before Lamar. They collided, their joint weights toppling against the door and slamming it again. There was a moment of confusion, almost farcical, in which they each fought for the handle of the door. Then something intervened, looming behind the comedian. It was pale in the darkness; gray against black. Lamar made a small noise in his throat as the creature took hold of him from behind. He reached out towards Grillo, who slipped from beneath his fingers, back towards the middle of the room. He couldn't work out how the terata was battening upon Lamar, and he was glad of the fact. The man's flailing limbs and guttural sounds were enough. He saw the comedian's bulk slump against the door, then slide down it, his body increasingly eclipsed by the terata. Then both were still.

"Dead?" Grillo breathed.

"Yes," said the Jaff. "He called me a liar."

"I'll remember that."

"You should."

The Jaff made a motion in the darkness, which Grillo failed to make sense of. But it had consequences that made a great deal plain. Beads of light broke from the man's fingers, illuminating his face, which was wasted, his body, which was clothed as it had been at the Mall, but seemed to spill darkness, and the room itself, with terata, no longer the complex beasts they'd been but barbed shadows, lining every wall.

"Well, Grillo . . . ," the Jaff said, ". . . it seems I must do it."

NINE

After love, sleep. They hadn't planned it that way, but neither Jo-Beth nor Howie had slept more than a handful of uninterrupted hours since they'd met, and the ground they'd made love on was soft enough to tempt them. Even when the sun slipped behind the trees, they didn't waken. When finally Jo-Beth opened her eyes it wasn't the chill: the night was balmy. Cicadas made music in the grass around them. There was a gentle motion in the leaves. But beneath these reassuring sights and sounds was a strange, unfixable glow between the trees.

She rocked Howie out of sleep as gently as possible. He opened his eyes reluctantly, until they focused on his waker's face.

"Hi," he said. Then: "We overslept, huh? What time is—"

"There's somebody here, Howie," she whispered.

"Where?"

"I just see lights. They're all around us. Look!"

"My glasses," he whispered. "They're in my shirt."

"I'll get them."

She moved away from him in search of the clothes he'd dropped. He squinted at the scene. The police barricades, and the cave beyond:

the abyss where Buddy Vance was still lying. It had seemed so natural to make love here in the full light of day. Now it seemed perverse. There was a dead man lying down there somewhere, in the same darkness where their fathers had waited all those years.

"Here," she said.

Her voice startled him. "It's OK," she murmured. He dug his glasses from the pocket of his shirt and hooked them on. There were indeed lights in between the trees, but their source was undefined.

Jo-Beth not only had some luck with his shirt, but with the rest of their clothes. She started to put on her underwear. Even now, with his heart thumping hard for quite another reason, the sight of her aroused him. She caught his look, and kissed him.

"I don't see anyone," he said, still keeping his voice low.

"Maybe I was wrong," she said, "I just thought I heard somebody."

"Ghosts," he said, then regretted inviting the thought into his head. He began to pull on his shorts. As he did he caught a movement between the trees. "Oh shit," he murmured.

"I see," she said. He looked towards her. She was looking in the opposite direction. Following her gaze he saw motion there too, in the shadows of the canopy. And another movement. And another.

"They're on all sides," he said, pulling on his shirt and reaching for his jeans. "Whatever they are they've got us surrounded."

He stood up, pins and needles in his legs, his thoughts turning desperately to how he might arm himself. Could he trash one of the barricades perhaps, and find a weapon in the wreckage? He glanced at Jo-Beth, who'd almost finished dressing, then back at the trees.

From beneath the canopy a diminutive figure emerged, trailing a phantom light. Suddenly it all came clear. The figure was that of Benny Patterson, whom Howie had last seen in the street outside Lois Knapp's house, calling after him. There was no sunny smile on his face now. Indeed his face was somehow blurred, his features like a picture taken by a palsied photographer. The light he'd brought from his TV appearances came with him, however. That was the radiance that haunted the trees.

"Howie," he said.

His voice, like his face, had lost its individuality. He was holding on to being Benny, but only just.

"What do you want?" Howie asked.

"We've been looking for you."

"Don't go near him," Jo-Beth said. "It's one of the dreams."

"I know," Howie said. "They don't mean us any harm. Do you, Benny?"

"Of course not."

"So show yourselves," Howie said, addressing the whole ring of trees. "I want to see you."

They did as they were instructed, stepping from the corner of the trees on every side. All of them, like Benny, had undergone a change since he'd seen them at the Knapp house, their honed and polished personalities smudged, their dazzling smiles dimmed. They looked more like each other than not, smeared forms of light who held on to the remains of identities only tenuously. The imaginations of the Grovers had conceived them, and shaped them, but once gone from their creator's company they slid towards a plainer condition: that of the light that had emanated from Fletcher's body as he'd died at the Mall. This was his army, his hallucigenia, and Howie didn't need to ask them what they'd come here searching for. Him. He was the rabbit from Fletcher's hat; the conjuror's purest creation. He'd fled before their demands the previous night, but they'd sought him out nevertheless, determined to have him as their leader.

"I know what you want from me," he said. "But I can't supply it. This isn't my war."

He surveyed the assembly as he spoke, distinguishing faces he'd seen at the Knapp house, despite their decay into light. Cowboys, surgeons, soap-opera queens and game-show hosts. Besides these there were many he hadn't seen at Lois's party. One form of light that had been a werewolf; several that might have been comic-book heroes; several more, four in fact, who had been incarnations of Jesus, two bleeding light from brow, side, hands and feet; another dozen who looked as though they'd stepped from an X-rated movie, their bodies wet with come and sweat. There was a balloon man, colored scarlet; and

Tarzan; and Krazy Kat. And mingled with these identifiable deities, others who'd been private imaginings, called, he guessed, from the wish-list of those Fletcher's light had touched. Lost spouses, whose passing no other lover could replace; a face seen on a street whom their dreamers had never had the nerve to approach. All of them, real or unreal, bland or Technicolored, *touchstones*. The true stuff of worship. There was something undeniably moving about their existence. But he and Jo-Beth had been passionate in their desire to stay apart from this war; to preserve what was between them from taint or harm. That ambition hadn't changed.

Before he could reiterate the point one of the number he couldn't name, a woman in early middle age, stepped out of the ranks to speak.

"Your father's spirit's in all of us," she said. "If you turn your back on us, you turn your back on him."

"It's not as simple as that," he told her. "I've got other people to consider." He extended his hand to Jo-Beth, who rose to stand beside him. "You know who this is. Jo-Beth McGuire. Daughter of the Jaff. Fletcher's enemy, and therefore, if I understand you right, *your* enemy. But let me tell you . . . she's the first person I ever met in my life . . . I can really say I love. I put her before everything. You. Fletcher. This damn war."

Now a third voice rose from the ranks.

"It was my error—"

Howie looked round to see the blue-eyed cowboy, Mel Knapp's creation, moving forward. "My error thinking you wanted her killed. I regret it. If you don't wish harm done to her—"

"*Don't wish harm?* My God, she's worth ten of Fletcher! Value her as *I* value her or you can all go to Hell."

There was a resounding silence.

"Nobody's arguing," Benny said.

"I hear."

"So you'll lead us?"

"Oh Jesus."

"The Jaff's on the Hill," the woman said. "About to use the Art."

"How do you know?"

"We're Fletcher's spirit," the cowboy said. "We know the Jaff's purpose."

"And you know how to stop him?"

"No," the woman returned. "But we have to try. Quiddity must be preserved."

"And you think I can help? I'm no tactician."

"We're decaying," Benny said. Even in the brief time since he'd appeared his facial features had become more smudged. "Getting . . . dreamy. We need someone to keep us to our purpose."

"He's right," said the woman. "We're not here long. Many of us won't make it through to morning. We have to do what we can. Quickly."

Howie sighed. He'd let Jo-Beth's hand slip from his when she'd stood up. He took it again.

"What do I do?" he asked her. "Help me."

"You do what feels right."

"What feels right . . ."

"You said to me once, you wished you'd known Fletcher better. Maybe—"

"What? Say it."

"I don't like the idea of us going up against the Jaff with these . . . dreams as an army . . . but maybe doing as your father would have done is the only way to be true to him. And . . . be *free* from him."

He looked at her with fresh understanding. She had a grasp of his deepest confusions, and could see a way through the maze to a clear place, where Fletcher and the Jaff would have no hold on either of them. But payment had to be made first. She'd paid: losing her family for him. It was his turn now.

"All right," he said to the assembly. "We'll go up the Hill."

Jo-Beth squeezed his hand.

"Good," she said.

"You want to come?"

"I have to."

"I wanted so much for us to be out of this."

"We will be," she said. "And if we don't escape it . . . if something happens to one or both of us . . . we've had our time."

"Don't say that."

"It's more than your momma had, or mine," she reminded him. "More than most people here. Howie, I love you."

He put his arms around her, and hugged her to him, glad that Fletcher's spirit, albeit in a hundred different shapes, was there to see.

I suppose I'm ready to die, he thought. Or as ready as I'll ever be.

TEN

E ve had left the room at the top of the stairs breathless and terrified. She'd glimpsed Grillo getting up and crossing to the door
and Lamar intercepting him. Then the door was slammed in her face.
She waited long enough to hear the Jokemeister's death-cough, then
she hurried down the flight to raise the alarm.

Though darkness had now descended upon the house there were
more lights burning outside than in: colored floods illuminating
the various exhibits she and Grillo had wandered among earlier. The
wash of mingled colors, scarlet, green, yellow, blue and violet, lit
her way to the landing where she and Lamar had encountered Sam
Sagansky. He was still there, with his wife. They seemed not to have
moved at all, except to cast their eyes towards the ceiling.

"Sam!" Eve said, hurrying to him. "Sam!" Panic, and the speed of
her descent, had made her breathless. Her description of the horrors
she'd seen in the room above came in a series of gasps and non
sequiturs.

". . . You have to stop him . . . you never saw anything . . . terrible
things . . . Sam, look at me . . . Sam, look! . . ."

Sam didn't oblige. His whole posture was one of complete passivity.

"For Christ's sake, Sam, what are you *no?*"

Giving up on him she turned and sought help elsewhere among the loiterers. There were perhaps twenty guests gathered around. None of them had moved since she'd appeared, either to help or hinder her. None, now she looked at them, was even looking in her direction. Like Sagansky and his wife they all had their eyes turned ceilingward, as if in expectation. Panic hadn't taken Eve's wits from her. She needed no more than a scanning of this crowd to realize that they'd be of no use to her. They knew perfectly well what was going on a floor above them: that was why they turned their eyes up like dogs awaiting judgment. The Jaff had them on a leash.

She started down to the ground floor, clinging to the banister, her pace slowing as breathlessness and stiff joints took their toll. The band had finished playing but somebody was still at the piano, which comforted her. Rather than waste energy shouting from the stairs she waited until she was at the bottom to buttonhole somebody. The front door was open. Rochelle was standing on the step. A party of half a dozen, Merv Turner and his wife, Gilbert Kind and his girlfriend of the moment, plus two women she didn't recognize, were making their farewells. Turner saw her coming, and a look of distaste came over his fat face. He returned his gaze to Rochelle, speeding up his departure speech.

". . . so sad," Eve caught him saying. "But very moving. Thank you *so* much for sharing this with us."

"Yes—" his wife began, but was cut off before she could offer platitudes of her own by Turner, who, glancing back at Eve, hurried away into the open air.

"Merv—" his wife said, clearly irritated.

"No time!" Turner replied. "It's been *wonderful*, Rochelle. Hurry up, Gil. The limos are waiting. We're going on ahead."

"No, wait," said the girlfriend. "Oh, shit, Gilbert, he's going without us."

"Please excuse us," Kind said to Rochelle.

"Wait!" Eve called after him. "Gilbert, *wait!*"

Her call was too loud to be ignored, though to judge by the look on Kind's face when he turned back to her he'd have preferred it that way.

He put a less than radiant smile over his feelings and opened his arms, not in welcome but in a shrug.

"Isn't it always the way?" he called to her. "We didn't get to talk, Eve. So sorry. So sorry. Next time." He took hold of the girlfriend's arm. "We'll call you," he said. "Won't we, hon?" He blew her a kiss. "You look wonderful!" he said, and hurried after Turner.

The two women followed, not even concerning themselves to make their goodbyes to Rochelle. She didn't seem to care. If common sense hadn't already told Eve that Rochelle was in league with the monster on the upper floor, she saw evidence of it now. As soon as the guests had gone from the door she rolled her eyes up in an all too recognizable fashion, her muscles relaxing so that she lay against the door jamb as though barely able to stand upright. No help to be had there, Eve thought, and headed through to the lounge.

Again, the only illumination came from outside the house, the garish colors of the Carnivalia. The light was bright enough for Eve to see that in the half hour she'd been detained by Lamar the party had wound down almost to a dead stop. Fully half of the guests had gone, sensing perhaps the change that had come over the gathering as more and more people had been touched by the evil on the upper floor. Another group was in the act of departing as she got to the door, bustle and loud talk covering their anxiety. She knew none of them, but wasn't about to let that stop her. She took hold of a young man's arm.

"You've got to help me," she said.

She knew the face from the billboards on Sunset. The boy was Rick Lobo. His prettiness had made him a sudden star, though his love scenes looked like lesbianism.

"What's wrong?" he said.

"There's something upstairs," she said. "It's got a friend of mine—"

The face was only capable of a smile and a sultry pout; with those responses inappropriate, all it could do was look blankly back at her.

"Please come," she said.

"She's drunk," somebody in Lobo's party said, not caring to conceal the accusation.

Eve looked the way of the speaker. The whole pack of brats was young. None of them over twenty-five. And most, she guessed, well high. But untouched by the Jaff.

"I'm not drunk," Eve said. "Please listen—"

"Come on, Rick," a girl in the party said.

"Do you want to come with us?" Lobo asked.

"Rick!" the girl said.

"No. I want you to come upstairs—"

The girl laughed. "But you do," she said. "Come on, Ricky."

"I have to go. Sorry," Lobo said. "You should go too. This party's a bummer."

The boy's incomprehension was solid as a brick wall, but Eve wasn't about to let go.

"Trust me," she said. "I'm not drunk. There's something horrible happening here." She threw a glance towards the rest of them. "You all feel it," she said, feeling like a cut-rate Cassandra but knowing no other way to put it. "There's something going on here—"

"Yeah," said the girl. "There is. We're leaving."

Her words had touched a nerve in Lobo, however.

"You should come with us," he said, "it's getting weird in here."

"She doesn't want to go," said a voice on the stairs. Sam Sagansky made the descent. "I'll look after her, Ricky, don't you worry."

Lobo was clearly happy to be relieved of the responsibility. He let Eve's arm go.

"Mr. Sagansky'll look after you," he said.

"No—" Eve insisted, but the group was already heading towards the door, the same anxiety fuelling their hurried exit as had fuelled that of the Turner party. Eve saw Rochelle lift herself up from her languor to accept the proffered thanks. Any attempt to follow after them was blocked by Sam. All Eve could do was seek some help in the room behind her.

The pickings looked slim. Of the remaining thirty or so guests most seemed beyond helping themselves, never mind her. The pianist was providing a soporific medley of songs for dancing in the dark, and four couples were doing just that, draped about each other as they shuffled around on the same spot. The rest of the room's occupants seemed to be drugged or drunk or touched with the Jaff's torpor, some sitting, many lying on the furniture, barely aware of their surroundings. The anorexic Belinda Kristol was among them, her wasted frame no possible use in this jeopardy. On the sofa beside her, his head in her lap, was the son of Buddy's agent, equally wasted.

Eve glanced back towards the door. Sagansky was following her. She scanned the room in desperation, looking for the best hope of a bad hand and decided upon the pianist. She wove between the dancers, her panic getting the better of her again.

"Stop playing," she said when she reached him.

"Want something different?" he said, looking around at her. His gaze was blurred by drink but at least his eyes didn't roll up.

"Yeah, something loud. Really loud," she said. "And fast. Let's get the party going, shall we?"

"Little late for that," he said.

"What's your name?"

"Doug Frankl."

"OK, Doug. You keep playing . . ." She looked back towards Sagansky, who was standing beyond the dancers, watching her. ". . . I need your help, Doug."

"And I need a drink," he slurred. "Any chance of getting one for me?"

"In a moment. First, you see that man on the other side of the room?"

"Yeah, I know him. Everyone knows him. He's a fuckhead."

"He just tried to assault me."

"He did?" Doug said, frowning up at Eve. "That's disgusting."

"And my partner . . . Mr. Grillo . . . is at the top of the house . . ."

"That's really disgusting," Doug said again. "You're old enough to be his mother."

"Thanks, Doug."

"That's really disgusting."

Eve leaned in towards her unlikely knight. "*I need your help,*" she whispered. "*And I need it now.*"

"Got to keep playing," Doug said.

"You can come back and play when we've got a drink for you and Mr. Grillo for me."

"I really need a drink."

"You do. I can see that. And you deserve one. Playing like this. You deserve a drink."

"I do. I really do."

She reached over, put her hands around Frankl's wrists, and lifted his hands from the keys. He didn't protest. Though the music stopped the dancers continued to shuffle.

"Get up, Doug," she whispered.

He struggled to his feet, kicking over the piano stool as he did so.

"Which way for the drinks?" he said. He was further gone than she'd thought. His playing must have been on remote control because he could barely take a step ahead of him. But he was company at least. She took his arm, hoping Sagansky would interpret Doug as the supporting strength rather than the other way about. "This way," she murmured to him, and led them both around the perimeter of the dance floor towards the door. From the corner of her eye she saw Sagansky moving in their direction, and attempted to pick up their pace, but he came between them and the door.

"No more music, Doug?" he said.

The pianist tried hard to focus on Sagansky's face.

"Who the fuck are you?" he said.

"It's Sam," Eve told him.

"Get the music going, Doug. I want to dance with Eve."

Sagansky reached to claim Eve, but Frankl had ideas of his own.

"I know what you think," he said to Sagansky. "I heard the things you say and you know what? I don't give a fuck. If I want to suck cock, I'll fucking suck cock and if you won't employ me Fox will! So fuck you!"

A small thrill of hope touched Eve. There was a psychodrama here she hadn't counted on. Sagansky was notoriously homophobic. He'd obviously offended Doug somewhere down the line.

"I want the lady," Sagansky said.

"Well you're not going to have her," came the response, Doug pushing Sagansky's arm away. "She's got better things to do."

Sagansky wasn't about to give up so easily. He reached for Eve a second time, was slapped away, and instead put his hands on Doug, dragging the man from Eve's grip.

Eve took her chance while it was offered, slipping away towards the door. Behind her she heard both men's voices raised in rage, and glanced back to see that they were scattering the dancers as they staggered around each other, fists flailing. Sagansky landed the first blow, sending Frankl reeling back against the piano. The glasses he'd lined up there went west, smashing noisily. He came after Eve with a lunge.

"You're wanted," he said, snatching her. She stepped back to avoid him, her legs giving out as she did so. Before she hit the floor two arms were there to catch her, and she heard Lobo say: "You should come with us."

She tried to protest, but her mouth wouldn't make the words between gasps. She was half-carried to the door, trying to explain that she couldn't go, couldn't leave Grillo, but unable to make her point clear. She saw Rochelle's face swim past her, then the night air was cold on her face, its shock merely worsening her disorientation.

"Help her . . . help her . . ." she heard Lobo saying, and before she knew it she was inside his limo, stretched out on the fake fur seat. He followed her in.

"Grillo—" she managed to say as the door was slammed. Her pursuer was at the step, but the limo was already moving off, down towards the gate.

"Weirdest fucking party I ever went to," Lobo said. "Let's get the fuck out of here."

Sorry, Grillo, she thought as she passed out. Be well.

At the gate Clark waved Lobo's limo off, and turned to look back at the house.

"How many more to go?" he asked Rab.

"Another forty maybe," Rab replied, scanning the list. "We won't be here all night."

The cars that were waiting for the remaining guests had no room to park on the Hill, so were in the Grove below, circling, awaiting radio orders to come back up and collect their passengers. It was a routine they were well used to, its boredom usually broken by a stream of banter between cars. But tonight there was no gossip about the sex-lives of the passengers, or horny talk about what the drivers were going to do when the job was finished. Most of the time the airwaves were silent, as if the drivers didn't want to advertise their locations. When it was broken, it was by someone making a would-be casual remark about the town.

"Deadwood Gulch," one of them called it. "It's like a fucking cemetery."

It was Rab who silenced the man. "If you've got nothing worth saying, don't say it," he remarked.

"What's your problem?" the man said. "Getting spooked?"

The reply was interrupted by a call from another car.

"You there, Clark?"

"Yeah. Who is this?"

"*Are you there?*"

Contact was bad, and worsening, the voice from the car breaking up into static.

"There's a fucking dust storm blowing up down here—" the driver was saying. "I don't know if you can hear me, but it's just come out of nowhere."

"Tell him to get out of there," Rab said. "Clark! Tell him!"

"I hear you! Driver? *Back off! Back off!*"

"Can anybody hear me?" the man yelled, the message almost drowned out by a spiralling howl of wind.

"Driver! Get the fuck out of there!"

"Can anybody—"

In place of the question the sound of the car coming to grief, the driver's voice cut off in the din of wreckage.

"*Shit!*" Clark said. "Any of you out there know who that was? Or *where* he was?"

There was silence from the other cars. Even if any of them knew, nobody was volunteering to go help. Rab stared through the trees lining the road, down towards the town.

"That's it," he said. "Enough of this shit. I'm out of here."

"There's only us left," Clark reminded him.

"If you've got any sense you'll get out too," Rab said, pulling on his tie to unknot it. "I don't know what's going on here, but let the rich folks sort it out."

"We're on duty."

"I just came off!" Rab said. "I ain't being paid enough to take this shit! Catch!" He tossed his radio to Clark. It spat white noise. "Hear that?" he said. "Chaos. That's what's coming."

In the town below Tommy-Ray slowed his car to get a look at the wrecked limo. The ghosts had simply picked it up, and thrown it over. Now they were dragging the driver from his seat. If he wasn't already primed to be one of their number they were quick to put that right, their violence reducing his uniform to tatters and the body beneath it the same.

He'd led the ghost-train away from the Hill to give himself space to plot his way into the house. He didn't want a repeat of the humiliation at the bar, with the guards bruising him then all hell breaking loose. When his father saw him in his new incarnation as the Death-Boy, he wanted to be in control. But that hope was fading fast. The longer he delayed his return the more unruly they became. They'd already demolished the Lutheran Prince of Peace Church, proving, as if any proof were needed, that stone was as ripe for undoing as flesh. A part of him, the part that hated Palomo Grove to its foundations, wanted to let them rampage. Let them level the whole town. But if he gave in to that urge he knew he'd lose power over them completely. Besides, somewhere in the Grove was the one human being he wanted to preserve from harm: Jo-Beth. Once loosed the storm would make no distinctions. Her life would be forfeit, along with every other.

Knowing he had only a short time left before their impatience got the better of them, and they destroyed the Grove anyway, he drove to his mother's house. If Jo-Beth was in town, she'd be here; and if worst came to worst he'd snatch her, and take her back up to the Jaff, who would know how best to subdue the storm.

———

Momma's house, like most of the houses in the street, indeed in the Grove, was in darkness. He parked and got out of the car. The storm, no longer content to tag along behind, came to meet him, buffeting him.

"Back off," he told the gaping faces that flew in front of him. "You'll get what you want. Everything you want. But you leave this house, and everyone in it, *alone*. Understand me?"

They sensed the force of his feelings. He heard their laughter, mocking such pitiful sensibilities. But he was still the Death-Boy. They owed him a dwindling devotion. The storm receded down the street a little way, and waited.

He slammed the car door and went up to the house, glancing back down the street to be certain his army was not going to cheat him. It stayed at bay. He knocked at the door.

"Momma?" he shouted. "It's Tommy-Ray, Momma. I got my key but I'm not coming in 'less you ask me. Can you hear me, Momma? Nothing to be afraid of. I'm not going to hurt you." He heard a sound on the other side of the door. "Is that you, Momma? Please answer me."

"What do you want?"

"Just let me see you, please. Let me see you."

The door was unbolted, and opened. Momma was dressed in black, her hair unbraided. "I was praying," she said.

"For me?" said Tommy-Ray.

Momma didn't answer.

"You weren't, were you?" he said.

"You shouldn't have come back, Tommy-Ray."

"This is home," he said. The sight of her hurt him more than he'd thought possible. After the revelations of the trip to the Mission (the dog and the woman), then events at the Mission and the horrors of his return trip, he'd thought himself beyond what he was feeling now: a choking sorrow.

"I want to come in," he said, knowing even as he said it that there was no way back. The family bosom had never been a place he'd much wanted to lay his head. Jo-Beth's had. It was her his thoughts went to now. "Where is she?" he said.

"Who?"

"Jo-Beth?"

"She's not here," Momma replied.

"Where then?"

"I don't know where."

"Don't tell me lies. *Jo-Beth!*" he started yelling. *"Jo-Beth!"*

"Even if she were—"

Tommy-Ray didn't let her finish. He pushed past her and stepped over the threshold. "Jo-Beth! It's Tommy-Ray! I need you, Jo-Beth! I need you, baby!"

It didn't matter any longer if he called her baby, told her he wanted to kiss her and lick her cunt: that was OK. It was love, and love was the only defense he had, or anyone had, against the dust and the wind and all that howled in it: he needed her more than ever. Ignoring Momma's shouts he started through the house from room to room in search of her. Each had a scent of its own, and with the scent a sum of memories—things he'd said, done or felt in this place or that—which flooded over him as he stood in the doorways.

Jo-Beth wasn't downstairs, so he headed up, throwing each door open along the landing: first Jo-Beth's, then Momma's. Finally, his own. His room was as he'd left it. The bed unmade, the wardrobe open, his towel on the floor. Standing at the door he realized he was looking at the belongings of a boy who was as good as dead. The Tommy-Ray who'd lain in that bed, sweated, jerked off, slept and dreamed of Zuma and Topanga, had gone forever. The grime on the towel and the hairs on the pillow were the last of him. He wouldn't be remembered well.

Tears started to run down his cheeks. How had it happened that half a week ago he'd been alive and going about his business and now be so changed he did not belong here, nor could ever belong here again? What had he wanted so badly it had taken him from himself? Nothing that he'd got. It was useless being the Death-Boy: only fear and shining bones. And knowing his father: what use was that? The Jaff had treated him well at the beginning, but it had been a trick to make a slave of him. Only Jo-Beth loved him. Jo-Beth had come after him, tried to heal him, tried to tell him what he hadn't wanted to hear. Only she could make things good again. Make sense of him. Save him.

"*Where is she?*"? he demanded.

Momma was at the bottom of the stairs. Her hands were clasped in front of her as she looked up at him. More prayers. Always prayers.

"*Where is she, Momma? I have to see her.*"

"She's not yours," Momma said.

"*Katz!*" Tommy-Ray yelled, starting down towards her. "*Katz has got her!*"

"Jesus said . . . I am the resurrection, and the life . . ."

"Tell me where they are or I won't be responsible—"

"He that believeth in me . . ."

"*Momma!*"

". . . though he were dead . . ."

She'd left the front door open, and dust had begun to blow over the threshold, insignificant amounts at first, but growing. He knew what it signalled. The ghost-train was getting up steam. Momma looked towards the door, and the gusty darkness beyond. She seemed to grasp that fatal business was at hand. Her eyes, when they settled on her son again, were filling up with tears.

"Why did it have to be this way?" she said softly.

"I didn't mean it to be."

"You were so beautiful, son. I thought sometimes that'd save you."

"I'm still beautiful," he said.

She shook her head. The tears, dislodged from the rims of her eyes, ran down her cheeks. He looked back towards the door, which the wind had begun to throw back and forth.

"Stay out," he told it.

"What's out there?" Momma said. "Is it your father?"

"You don't want to know," he told her.

He hurried down the stairs to try to close the door, but the wind was gathering strength, gusting into the house. The lamps started to swing. Ornaments flew from their places along the shelves. As he got to the bottom of the flight windows shattered at the front of the house and back.

"*Stay out!*" he yelled again, but the phantoms had waited long enough. The door flew off its hinges, thrown down the length of the hallway to smash against the mirror. The ghosts came howling after. Momma screamed at the sight of them, their faces drawn and hungry, smears of need in the storm. Gaping sockets, gaping maws. Hearing the Christian woman scream, they turned their venom in her direction. Tommy-Ray yelled a warning to her but dusty fingers tore the words to nonsense, then flew past him to Momma's throat. He reached back towards her but the storm had hold of him, and threw him round towards the door. The ghosts were still flying in. He was pitched through their speeding faces, against the tide, and across the threshold. Behind him he heard Momma let out another shriek, as with one shattering every window left unbroken in the house burst outwards. Glass showered around him. He fled the rain, but didn't escape unscathed.

It was little harm, however, compared with the damage the house and its occupant were sustaining. When he stumbled to the safety of the sidewalk and looked back he saw the storm weaving in and out of every window and door like a demented ghost-ride. The structure was not the equal of the assault. Cracks were gaping in the walls, the ground at the front of the house opening up as the riders got into the basement and wreaked havoc there. He looked towards the car, half-fearing they'd destroyed that in their impatience. But it was still intact. He fled towards it as the house began to growl, its roof thrown up in surrender, its walls bowing out. Even if Momma had been alive to call after him, she could not have been heard over the din, nor seen in the confusion.

He got into the car, sobbing. There were words on his lips he didn't even realize he was saying until he began to drive:

". . . I am the resurrection and the life . . ."

In the rear-view mirror he saw the house give up entirely, as the vortex in its guts threw it outwards. Bricks, slate, beams and dirt burst in all directions.

"... he that believeth in me ... *my God, Momma, Momma* ... he that believeth in me ..."

Brick shards flew against the back window, shattering it, and fell on the roof in rattling percussion. He put his foot down and drove, half blind with tears of sorrow and terror. He'd tried to outrun them once, and failed. Still he hoped he might succeed a second time, racing through the town by the most circuitous route he knew, praying he'd confound them. The streets were not entirely empty. He passed two limos, both black stretches, cruising the streets like sharks. And then, on the edge of Oakwood, staggering into the middle of the street, someone he knew. Loath as he was to stop, he needed the comfort of a familiar face more than he'd ever needed anything, even if it *was* William Witt. He slowed.

"Witt?"

William took a little time to recognize him. When he did Tommy-Ray expected him to retreat. Their last meeting, up at the house on Wild Cherry Glade, had ended with Tommy-Ray in the pool, wrestling Martine Nesbitt's terata, and Witt running for his sanity. But the intervening period had taken as much toll on William as it had on Tommy-Ray. He looked like a hobo, unshaven, clothes stained and in disarray, a stare of complete despair on his face.

"Where are they?" was his first question.

"Who?" Tommy-Ray wanted to know.

William reached through the window and stroked Tommy-Ray's face. His palm was clammy. His breath smelt of bourbon.

"Have you got them?" he asked.

"Who?" Tommy-Ray wanted to know.

"My ... visitors," William said. "My ... dreams."

"Sorry," Tommy-Ray said. "You want a ride?"

"Where are you going?"

"Getting the fuck out of here," Tommy-Ray said.

"Yeah. I want a ride."

Witt got in. As he slammed the door Tommy-Ray saw a familiar sight in the mirror. The storm was following. He looked across at William.

"It's no good," he said.

"What isn't?" Witt asked, his eyes barely focusing on Tommy-Ray.

"They're going to come after me wherever I go. There's no stopping them. They'll come and come."

William glanced over his shoulder at the wall of dust advancing down the street towards the car.

"Is that your father?" he said. "Is he in there somewhere?"

"No."

"What is, then?"

"Something worse."

"Your momma—" Witt said "—I talked with her. She said he was the Devil."

"I wish it were the Devil," Tommy-Ray said. "You can cheat the Devil."

The storm was gaining on the car.

"I have to go back up the Hill," Tommy-Ray said, as much to himself as Witt.

He swung the wheel round and started in the direction of Windbluff.

"Is that where the dreams are?" Witt said.

"That's where everything is," Tommy-Ray replied, unaware of how much truth he spoke.

ELEVEN

T he party's over," the Jaff said to Grillo. "Time we went down."
      Little had been said between them since Eve's panicked departure. The man had simply sat back down in the seat from which he'd risen to deal with Lamar's mutiny, and waited there while raised voices drifted from below, limos drove up to the front door, took their passengers and left, and—finally—the music stopped. Grillo had made no attempt to slip away. For one, Lamar's slumped body blocked the door, and by the time he'd attempted to move it the terata, indistinct as they now were, would surely have claimed him. For another, and more significantly, he'd come by chance into the company of the *first cause*, the entity responsible for the mysteries he'd been encountering in Palomo Grove since he'd arrived. Here, slumped before him, was the man who'd shaped the horrors, and by extension therefore comprehended the visions that were loose in the town. To attempt to leave would be a dereliction of duty. Diverting as his short run as Ellen Nguyen's lover had been, he had only one role to play in all of this. He was a reporter; a conduit between the known world and the unknown. If he turned his back on the Jaff he committed a crime worse than any he knew: he failed to be a witness.

Whatever else the man was (insane; lethal; monstrous) he was not what so many of the people Grillo interviewed or investigated in his professional life had proved: a fake. Grillo had only to look around the room at the creatures the Jaff had spawned, or caused to be spawned, to know that he was in the company of a power with the capacity to change the world. He dared not turn his back on such a power. He would go with it wherever it went, and hope to understand its workings better.

The Jaff stood up.

"Make no attempt to intervene," he said to Grillo.

"I won't," Grillo told him. "But let me come with you."

The Jaff looked at him for the first time since Eve's escape. It was too dark for Grillo to see the eyes turned upon him, but he felt them, sharp as needles, probing him.

"Move the body," the Jaff instructed.

Grillo said: "Sure," and moved to the door. He'd needed no further reminder of the Jaff's strength, but picking up Lamar's corpse offered it to him anyhow. The body was wet and hot. His hands, when he dumped it down again, were sticky with the comedian's blood. The feel and smell made Grillo nauseous.

"Just remember . . ." the Jaff said.

"I know," Grillo replied. "Don't intervene."

"So. Open the door."

Grillo did so. He hadn't been aware of how fetid the room had become until a wave of cool, clean air swept in and over his face.

"Lead on," the Jaff said.

Grillo stepped out on to the landing. The house was completely silent, but it was not empty. At the bottom of the first flight of stairs he saw a small crowd of Rochelle's guests waiting. Their eyes all turned up towards the door. There was no sound nor movement from any of them. Grillo recognized many of their faces; they'd been waiting here when he and Eve had been ascending. Now the awaited moment had come. He began down the stairs towards them, the thought shaping in his head that the Jaff had sent him down to be torn apart by these worshippers. But he moved through their eye line, and out, without their gazes following him. It was the organ-grinder they were here to see, not the monkey.

From the room above emerged the sound of mass movement: the terata were coming. Reaching the bottom of the flight Grillo turned and looked back the way he'd come. The first of the creatures was emerging through the doorway. He'd seen that they were changed, but he'd not been prepared for the degree of change. Their busy foulness had been purged. They'd become plainer, most of their features veiled by the darkness they emitted.

Following the first few came the Jaff. Events since the final confrontation with Fletcher had taken their toll on him. He looked used up, almost skeletal. He started his descent, passing through pools of color from the lights outside the house, their vividness flooding his pallid features. Tonight the movie was *The Masque of the Red Death*, Grillo thought; and *The Jaff* was the name above the title.

The supporting cast of terata followed, pushing their bodies through the door and shambling down the stairs in pursuit of their maker.

Grillo glanced around at the silent assembly. They still had their fawning eyes upon the Jaff. He headed on, down the second flight. There was a second assembly waiting at the bottom, Rochelle among them. The sight of her extraordinary beauty momentarily reminded Grillo of his first encounter with her, descending the stairs just as the Jaff was now doing. Seeing her had been a revelation. She had seemed inviolate in that beauty. He'd learned differently. First from Ellen, with her account of Rochelle's past profession and present addiction, and now with the evidence of his own eyes, seeing the woman as lost to the depravities of the Jaff as any of his victims. Beauty was no defense. Most likely there *was* no defense. He reached the bottom of the stairs and waited for the Jaff to finish his descent, his legions trailing after. In the short time since his appearance at the top of the flight a change had come over him, subtle but unnerving. His face, which had betrayed tremors of apprehension, was now as blank as that of his congregation, his muscles so completely drained of tone his descent was a barely controlled walking fall. All the forces of his power had gone to his left hand, the hand which—back at the Mall—had bled the motes of power which had almost destroyed Fletcher. It was doing the same now, beads of bright corruption dripping from it like sweat as it hung by his side. They couldn't be the power itself, Grillo presumed, only its by-product, because the Jaff was making no attempt to prevent their breaking into small dark blooms on the stairs.

The hand was charging itself, draining power from every other part of its owner (perhaps, who knew? from the assembly itself); stoking its strength in preparation for the labors ahead. Grillo tried to study the Jaff's face for some sign of what he was feeling, but his eyes kept being drawn back and back to the hand, as though all lines of force led to it, all the other elements in the scene rendered irrelevant.

The Jaff moved through into the lounge. Grillo followed. The shadow legion remained on the stairs.

The lounge was still occupied, mostly by recumbent guests. Some were like disciples, their eyes fixed on the Jaff. Some were simply unconscious, sprawled on the furniture, undone by excess. On the floor lay Sam Sagansky, his shirt and face bloody. A little way from him, his hand still grasping Sagansky's jacket, lay another man. Grillo had no idea what had started the fracas between them but it had ended in a knockout.

"Turn on the lights," the Jaff told Grillo. His voice was as expressionless as his face had become. "Turn them full on. No mystery now. I want to see *clearly*."

Grillo located the switches in the gloom, and flipped them all on. Any theatricality in the scene was abruptly banished. The light brought growls of complaint from one or two of the slumberers, who threw their arms across their faces to shut it out. The man clasping Sagansky opened his eyes, and moaned, but didn't move, sensing his jeopardy. Grillo's gaze went back to the Jaff's hand. The beads of power had stopped dropping from it now. It had ripened. It was ready.

"No use delaying . . ." he heard the Jaff say, and saw him raise his left arm to eye level, his hand open. Then he walked to the far wall and laid his palm upon it.

Then, hand still pressed against solid reality, he began to make a fist.

Down at the gates Clark saw the lights go on in the house, and breathed a sigh of relief. That could only signal an end to the party. He put a general call out to the circling drivers (those that had not taken fright, and gone) instructing them to make their way back up the Hill. Their passengers would be emerging soon.

Coming off the freeway at the Palomo Grove exit, with four miles to cover to the outskirts of the town, a shudder ran through Tesla. The kind her mother had said meant someone was walking over your grave. Tonight, she knew better. The news was worse than that.

I'm missing the main event, she realized. It's begun without me. She felt something change around her, something vast, as though the flat-earthists had been right all along and the whole world had suddenly tipped a few degrees, everything on it sliding towards one end. She didn't flatter herself for an instant she was the only one sensitive enough to be experiencing this. Perhaps she had a perspective that allowed her to confess the feeling, but she didn't doubt that across the country at this moment, most likely across the world, people were waking in a cold sweat, or thinking of their loved ones and fearing for them. Children crying without quite knowing why. Old people believing their last moment was upon them.

She heard the din of a collision on the freeway she'd just left, followed by another and another, as cars—their drivers distracted by a moment of terror—piled up. Horns began to blare in the night.

The world's round, she told herself, like the wheel I'm holding. *I can't fall off. I can't fall off.* Gripping that thought and the wheel with equal desperation, she drove on towards the town.

Watching for the returning cars, Clark saw lights coming up the Hill. Their advance was too slow to be headlamps, however. Curious, he left his post and started down the incline a little way. He got maybe twenty yards before the bend in the road revealed the source of the light. It was human. A mob of fifty, maybe more, climbing towards the summit, their bodies and faces blurred, but all glowing in the dark like Halloween masks. At the head of the group were two kids who looked to be normal enough. But given the gang they had in tow he doubted that. The boy looked up the Hill towards him. Clark backed away, turning around to put some distance between him and the mob.

Rab had been right. He should have gone a lot earlier, and left this damn town to its own devices. He'd been hired to keep gatecrashers out of the party, not to stop whirlwinds and walking torches. Enough was enough.

He threw his radio down, and clambered over the fence opposite the house. On the other side the shrubbery was thick, and the ground fell off steeply, but he slid away through the darkness not caring if he reached the other side of the Hill in tatters, simply wanting to be as far from the house when the mob reached the gate as he could get.

Grillo had seen sights in the last few days that had slapped the breath out of him, but he'd found a way to slot them into his world-view. But in front of him now was a sight so utterly beyond his comprehension all he could do was say *no* to it.

Not once, a dozen times.

"No . . . no . . ." and so on, "*no.*"

But denial didn't work. The sight refused to pack its bag and leave. It stayed. Demanded to be seen.

The Jaff's fingers had entered the solid wall, and clutched it. Now he took a step back, and a second step, pulling the substance of reality towards him as though it were made of sun-softened candy. The carnival pictures hanging on the wall began to twist out of true; the intersection of wall and ceiling and wall and floor eased in towards the Artist's fist, losing their rigor.

It was as if the whole room were projected on a cinema screen and the Jaff had simply snatched hold of the fabric, dragging it towards him. The projected image, which moments before had seemed so life-like, was revealed for the sham it was.

It's a movie, Grillo thought. *The whole fucking world's a movie.*

And the Art was the calling of that bluff. A snatching away of the sheet, the shroud, the screen.

He wasn't the only one reeling before this revelation. Several of Buddy Vance's mourners, shaken from their stupor, had opened their eyes to see a sight their worst bad trips had never proffered.

Even the Jaff seemed to be shocked by the ease of the task. A tremor was running through his body, which had never looked so frail, so vulnerable, so *human*, as now. Whatever trials he'd undergone to anneal his spirit for this moment, they were not enough. Nothing could be enough. This was an art in defiance of the condition of flesh. All the profoundest certainties of being were forfeit in the face of it. From somewhere behind the screen, Grillo heard a rising sound, which filled his skull like the thud of his heart. It summoned the terata. He glanced around to see them coming through the door to lend their maker aid in whatever was imminent. They were uninterested in Grillo; he knew he could leave at any moment and not be challenged. But he could not turn his back on this, however it wrenched his gut. Whatever played behind the screen of the world was about to be seen, and his eyes wouldn't be coaxed from the sight. If he fled now, what would he do? Run to the gate and watch from a safe distance? There *was* no safe distance, knowing what he now knew. He'd spend the rest of his life touching the solid world and knowing that had he the Art at his fingertips, it would melt.

Not everyone was so fatalistic. Many of those conscious enough were attempting to make for the door. But the disease of malleability that had infected the walls had spread across half the floor. It became glutinous beneath the escapees, pitching as the Jaff pulled, two-handed now, at the matter of the room.

Grillo sought out some solid place in the shifting environment, but could only find a chair, which was as prone to the new vagaries of physics as any other item in the room. It slipped from his grasp, and he fell to his knees, the impact re-starting the flow of the blood from his nose. He let it run.

Looking up, he saw that the Jaff had pulled so hard on the far end of the room that it was distorted out of all recognition. The brilliance of the lights in the yard outside were dimmed, had gone, smeared into a featureless sweep so taut it could not be long before it broke. The sound from the other side had not grown any louder, but became, in a matter of seconds, almost inevitable, as though it had always been there, just out of hearing range.

The Jaff pulled another handful of the room's stuff into his grasp, and in doing so pressed the screen beyond endurance. It didn't tear in one place but in several. The room tipped again. Grillo clung to the heaving floor as bodies rolled past him. In the chaos he glimpsed the Jaff, who seemed at this last moment to be regretting all he'd done, struggling with the raw substance of reality he'd gathered up as if attempting to throw it away. Either his fists wouldn't obey him and release it or else it had its own momentum now and was opening itself without his aid, because a look of wild terror crossed his face, and he screamed a summons to his legions. They started towards him, their anatomies finding some purchase in this shifting chaos. Grillo was pressed to the ground as they clambered over him. No sooner had they begun their advance, however, than something brought them to a halt. Grasping the hides to right and left of him, no longer afraid of them with so much worse on view, Grillo hauled himself upright, or as near upright as was possible, and looked back towards the door. That end of the room was still more or less intact. Only a subtle twisting of the architecture gave any clue to what was happening behind him. He could see through into the hall, and beyond to the front door. It was open. In it stood Fletcher's son.

There were calls greater than that of makers and masters, Howie understood. There was the call of a thing to its opposite, to its natural enemy. That was what fuelled the terata now, as they turned back towards the door, leaving whatever chaos was unleashed inside the house to the Jaff's control.

"They're coming!" he yelled to Fletcher's army, backing off as the tide of terata approached the door. Jo-Beth, who'd stepped inside with him, lingered on the threshold. He took hold of her arm and pulled her away.

"It's too late," she said. "You see what he's doing? My God! You see?"

Lost cause or not, the dream-creatures were ready to face the terata, pouncing as soon as the flood emerged from the house. Climbing the Hill Howie had expected the fight ahead to be somehow *refined*; a battle of wills or wits. But the violence that erupted all around him now was purely physical. All they had was their bodies to pitch into the battle, and they put themselves to the task with a ferocity he'd not have guessed the melancholy souls gathered at the woods—much less the civil folk they'd been at the Knapp house—capable of. There was no distinction between children and heroes. They were barely recognizable now, as the last traces of the people they'd been dreamt into being faded in the face of an equally plain enemy. It was essential stuff now. Fletcher's love of light against the Jaff's passion for the dark. Beneath both was a single intention, which unified them. The destruction of the other.

He'd done as they requested, he thought; he'd led them up the Hill, calling the stragglers when they forgot themselves, and began to dissolve. With several, those less coherently conjured in the first place, perhaps, he'd lost. Their bodies had dispersed before he could get them within scenting distance of their enemy. For the rest, the sight of the terata was stimulus enough. They'd fight until torn apart.

Grievous damage was already being done on both sides. Fragments of sleek darkness torn from the bodies of the terata; washes of light breaking from the dream-army when they were opened up. There was no sign of pain among the warriors. No blood from the wounds. They endured assault after assault, fighting on having sustained damage that would have incapacitated anything remotely alive. Only when more than half their substance had been torn from them did they unravel, and disperse. Even then the air they dissolved into wasn't empty. It buzzed and shook as though the war was continuing on a sub-atomic level, negative and positive energies fighting to impasse, or the extinction of both.

The latter, most likely, if the forces warring in front of the house were any model. Equally matched, they were simply eradicating each other, countering harm with harm, their numbers dwindling.

The battle had spread down to the gate by the time Tesla reached the top of the Hill, and was spilling out on to the road. Forms that might once have been recognizable but were now abstractions, smears of darkness, smears of light, tearing at each other. She stopped the car, and started up towards the house. Two combatants emerged from the trees that lined the driveway, and fell to the ground a few yards ahead, their limbs locked around—and it seemed *through*—each other. She looked on, appalled. Was this what the Art had released? How they escaped from Quiddity?

"*Tesla!*"

She looked up. Howie was in sight. His explanation was quick and breathless.

"It's started," he said. "The Jaff's using the Art."

"Where?"

"In the house."

"And these?" she said.

"The last defense," he replied. "We were too late."

What now, babe? she thought. You don't have any way of stopping this. The world's on a tilt and everything's sliding.

"We should all get the hell out of here," she told Howie.

"You think?"

"What else can we do?"

She looked up towards the house. Grillo had told her it was a folly, but she hadn't expected architecture as wild as this. The angles all subtly off, no upright that wasn't askew by a few degrees. Then she understood. It wasn't some post-modernist joke. It was something *inside* the house, pulling it out of shape.

"My God," she said. "Grillo's still in there."

Even as she spoke the facade bent a little more. In the face of such strangeness the remnants of the battle all around her were of little consequence. Just two tribes tearing at each other like rabid dogs. Men's stuff. She skirted it, ignored.

"Where are you going?" Howie said.

"Inside."

"It's mayhem."

"And it isn't out here? I've got a friend in there."

"I'll come with you," he said.

"Is Jo-Beth here?"

"She was."

"Find her. I'll find Grillo and we'll both get the fuck out of here."

Without waiting for a reply she headed on towards the door.

The third force loose in the Grove tonight was halfway up the Hill when Witt realized that however profound his grief at losing his dreams, tonight he didn't want to die. He started to struggle with the door handle, fully ready to pitch himself out, but the dust storm on their tail dissuaded him. He looked across at Tommy-Ray. The boy's face had never sung out intelligence, but its slackness now was shocking. He looked almost moronic. Spittle ran from his lower lip, his face was glossy with sweat. But he managed a name as he drove.

"Jo-Beth," he said.

She didn't hear *that* call, but she heard another. From inside the house a cry, put out mind to mind, from the man who'd made her. It was not directed at her, she guessed. He didn't know she was even near. But she caught it: an expression of terror which she couldn't ignore. She crossed through the matter-thickened air to the front door, the uprights of which were blowing in.

The scene was worse inside. The whole interior had lost its solidity, and was being drawn inexorably to some central point. It wasn't difficult to find that point. The whole softening world was moving in its direction.

The Jaff was there of course, at the core. In front of him a hole in the very substance of reality, which was exercising this claim on living and non-living alike. What was on the other side of the hole she couldn't see, but she could guess. *Quiddity*; the dream-sea; and on it an island both Howie and her father had told her about, where time and space were laughable laws, and spirits walked.

But if that was the case—he'd succeeded in his ambition, used the Art to gain access to the miracle—why was he so *afraid*? Why was he trying to retreat from the sight, tearing at his own hands with his teeth to make them let go the matter his fingers had penetrated?

All her reason said: go back. Go back while you can. The pull of whatever lay beyond the hole already had a hold of her. She could resist it for a short time, but that window was getting smaller. What she couldn't resist, however, was the hunger that brought her into the house in the first place. *She wanted to see her father's pain.* Not a sweet, daughterly desire, but he was not the sweetest of fathers. He'd caused her pain, and Howie too. He'd corrupted Tommy-Ray out of all recognition. He'd broken Momma's heart and life. Now she wanted to see him suffer, and she couldn't take her eyes off the sight. His self-mutilation was increasingly manic. He spat out pieces of his fingers, shaking his head back and forth in an attempt to deny whatever he saw beyond the hole the Art had made.

She heard a voice behind her say her name, and looked around to see a woman whom she'd never met, but Howie had described, beckoning her back to the safety of the threshold. She ignored the summons. She wanted to see the Jaff undo himself completely; or be dragged away and destroyed by his own mischief. She hadn't realized until this moment how much she hated him. How much cleaner she'd feel when he was gone out of the world.

Tesla's voice had found other ears besides Jo-Beth's. Clinging to the ground a couple of yards behind the Jaff, on the eroding island of solidity around the Artist, Grillo heard Tesla call, and turned—against the call of Quiddity—to look her way. His face felt fat with blood, as the hole pulled his fluids up through his body. His head pounded as if ready to burst. The tears were being sucked from his eyes, his eyelashes plucked out. His nose poured two bloody streams, which ran straight from his face towards the hole.

He'd already seen most of the room snatched away into Quiddity. Rochelle had been one of the first to go, relinquishing what little hold her addicted body had on the solid world. Sagansky and his punched-out opponent had gone. The party-goers had followed, despite their attempts to get to the door. The pictures had been stripped from the walls, then the plaster cladding from the wood underneath; now the wood itself was giving up and bending to the call. Grillo would have joined them, walls, guests and all, had it not been for the fact that the Jaff's shadow offered a tenuous solidity in this chaotic sea.

No, not *sea*. That was what he'd glimpsed on the other side of the hole, and it shamed every other image of the world.

Quiddity was the essential sea; the first, the fathomless. He'd given up all hope of escaping its summons. He'd come too close to its shore to turn away. Its undertow had already hauled most of the room away. It would soon take him.

But seeing Tesla he suddenly dared hope he might survive to tell the tale. If he was to have the least chance he'd have to be quick. What little cover the Jaff afforded was being eroded by the moment. Seeing Tesla reach for him, he reached back in her direction. The distance was too great. She couldn't stretch any further into the room without losing her hold on the relative solidity beyond the door.

She gave up the attempt, and stepped away from the opening.

Don't desert me now, he thought. Don't give me hope and then desert me.

He should have known better. She'd simply withdrawn in order to pull her belt from the loops of her trousers, then she was back at the door, letting Quiddity's pull unroll the belt and put it within his grasp.

He snatched hold.

Outside on the battlefield, Howie had found the remains of the light that had been Benny Patterson. It had almost lost all trace of the boy it had been, but there was enough left for Howie to recognize. He went down on his knees beside it, thinking it was nonsense to mourn the passing of something so transitory, then correcting that thought with another. That he too was transitory, and no more certain of his purpose than this dream, Benny Patterson, had been.

He put his hand to the boy's face, but it was already dissolving, and blew away like bright pollen beneath his fingers. Distressed, he looked up to see Tommy-Ray at the gate of Coney, starting up towards the house. Behind him, lingering at the gate, was a man Howie didn't know. And behind them both, a wall of moaning dust that followed Tommy-Ray in a swirling cloud.

His thoughts went from Benny Patterson to Jo-Beth. Where was she? In the confusion of the last few minutes he'd neglected her. He didn't doubt she was Tommy-Ray's target.

He stood up, and moved to intercept his enemy, who was as changed from the tanned, gleaming hero he'd first met in the Mall as it was possible to get. Blood-spattered now, eyes sunk in their sockets, he threw back his head and yelled:

"*Father!*"

The dust on his heels flew at Howie as he came within striking distance of Tommy-Ray. Whatever haunted it, hate-bloated faces, with mouths like tunnels, swatted him aside, and moved in to better business, uninterested in his little life. He fell to the ground, covering his head until they'd passed over him. When they had, he got to his feet. Tommy-Ray, and the cloud that had followed him, had disappeared inside.

He heard Tommy-Ray's voice raised above the din of the Art.

"*Jo-Beth!*" he bellowed.

She was inside the house, he realized. Why she'd gone there was beyond him, but he had to get to her before Tommy-Ray, or the bastard would take her.

As he raced to the front door, he saw the last of the dust storm snatched by a force inside, and dragged out of sight.

The power that had taken it was visible the moment he stepped over the threshold; he saw the last, chaotic trails of the cloud being pulled into a maelstrom which was claiming the entire house. In front of it, his hands barely recognizable, stood the Jaff. Howie got only a glimpse of the scene before Tesla yelled for his attention.

"Help me! Howie? *Howie?* For Christ's sake help me!"

She was clinging to the inner door, its geometry gone to hell, her other hand holding on to somebody who was about to be claimed by the maelstrom. He was with her in three strides, a hail of crap flying past him (the step which he'd just crossed), and seized her hand. As he did so he recognized the figure standing a yard beyond Tesla, and closer to the maw the Jaff had opened. Jo-Beth!

His recognition came as a cry. She turned in his direction, half-blinded by the assault of debris. As their eyes met he saw Tommy-Ray move towards her. The machine had taken a beating of late but it still had power. He pulled on Tesla, dragging her and the man she'd been struggling to save out of the most chaotic zone into the hall. It was the moment Tommy-Ray needed to reach Jo-Beth, flinging himself at her with sufficient force to throw her off her feet.

He saw the terror in her eyes as she lost her balance. Saw Tommy-Ray's arms close around her, in the tightest of embraces. Then the Quiddity claimed them both, sweeping them across the room past their father, and away, into the mystery.

Howie let out a howl.

Behind him Tesla was yelling his name. He ignored the call. His eyes on the place where Jo-Beth had gone he took a step towards the door. The power egged him on. He took another step, vaguely aware that Tesla was yelling for him to stop, to turn back before it was too late.

Didn't she know it had been too late the moment after he'd seen Jo-Beth? Everything had been lost, way back then.

A third step, and the whirlwind snatched him up. The room turned over and over. He saw his father's enemy for an instant, gaping, followed by the hole, gaping wider still.

Then he was gone, where his beautiful Jo-Beth had gone, into Quiddity.

"Grillo?"

"Yeah?"

"Can you stand up?"

"I think so."

He'd tried twice, and failed, and Tesla had no strength left to pick him up and carry him down to the gate.

"Give me a moment," he said. Not for the first time his eyes went back to the house they'd barely escaped from.

"There's nothing to see, Grillo," she said.

That wasn't true, by any means. The facade was like something from *Caligari*, the door sucked in, the windows going the same way. And inside, who knew?

As they stumbled down to the car a figure emerged from the chaos and stumbled out into the moonlight. It was the Jaff. The fact that he'd stood on Quiddity's shore and resisted its waves was testament to his power, but that resistance had taken its toll. His hands were reduced to gnawed flesh, the remains of the left hanging from the bones of his wrist in strips. His face was as brutally devoured, not by teeth but by what he'd seen. Blank-eyed and broken, he staggered down to the gate. Wisps of darkness, the last of the terata, followed him.

Tesla badly wanted to ask Grillo what glimpse he'd had of Quiddity, but this wasn't the moment. It was enough to know that he was alive to tell. Flesh in a world where flesh was forfeit every moment. Alive, when life ended with each exhalation and began again with every snatched breath.

In the trough between, there was such *jeopardy*. And now, as never before. She didn't doubt that the worst had come to pass, and that somewhere on Quiddity's furthest shore the lad Uroboros were sharpening their envy and starting across the dream-sea.

PART SEVEN

SOULS AT ZERO

ONE

Presidents, messiahs, shamans, popes, saints and lunatics had attempted—over the passage of a millennium—to buy, murder, drug and flagellate themselves into Quiddity. Almost to a one, they'd failed. The dream-sea had been more or less preserved, its existence an exquisite rumor, never proved, and all the more potent for that. The dominant species of the Cosm had kept what little sanity it possessed by visiting the sea in sleep, three times in a life span, and leaving it, always wanting more. That hunger had fuelled it. Made it ache; made it rage. Made it do good in the hope, often unconscious, of being granted more regular access. Made it do evil out of the idiot suspicion that it was conspired against by its enemies, who knew the secret but weren't telling. Made it create gods. Made it destroy gods.

The few who'd taken the journey that Howie, Jo-Beth, Tommy-Ray and twenty-two guests from Buddy Vance's house were taking now had not been accidental travellers. They'd been chosen, for Quiddity's purposes, and gone (for the most part) prepared.

Howie, on the other hand, was no more prepared for this than any stick of furniture hauled into the throat of the schism. He was pitched first through loops of energy and then into what appeared to be the middle of a thunderhead, lightning setting brief, bright fires all around him. Any trace of sound from the house had disappeared the moment he'd entered the throat. So had the pieces of trash that had flown in along with him. Helpless to steer or orient himself, all he could do was tumble through the cloud, the lightning becoming less frequent and more brilliant, the passages of darkness between steadily more profound, until he wondered if perhaps his eyes were closing, and the darkness—along with the falling sensation that accompanied it—was in his head. If so, he was happy with its embrace, his thoughts now also in free-fall, fixing momentarily on images which appeared out of the darkness, seeming to be completely solid though he was almost certain they were in his mind's eye.

He conjured Jo-Beth's face over and over again, always glancing back at him over her shoulder. He recited words of love to her; simple words that he hoped she heard. If she did they didn't bring her any closer. He wasn't surprised. Tommy-Ray was dissolved in the same thought-shot cloud that he and Jo-Beth were falling through, and twin brothers had claims on their sisters that went back to the womb. They'd floated together in that first sea, after all, their minds and cords intertwining. Howie envied Tommy-Ray nothing in all the world—not his beauty, his smile, nothing—except that time of intimacy he'd shared with Jo-Beth, before sex, before hunger, before breath even. He could only hope that he'd be with her at the end of her life the way Tommy-Ray had been at the beginning, when age took sex, appetite and, finally, breath away.

Then her face, and the envy, were gone, and new thoughts came to fill his head, or snapshots of same. No people now, only places, appearing and vanishing again as though his mind was sifting through them looking for one in particular. It found what it was searching for. A blurred blue night, which flew into solidity all around him. The falling sensation ceased in a heartbeat. He was solid in a solid place, running on echoing boards, a fresh cold wind blowing in his face. At his back he heard Lem and Richie calling his name. He ran on, looking over his shoulder as he did so. The glance solved the mystery of where he was. Behind him was the Chicago skyline, its lights brilliant against the night, which meant that the wind on his face was coming off Lake Michigan. He was running along a pier, though he didn't know which, with the Lake slopping around its struts. It was the only body of water he'd ever been familiar with. It influenced the city's weather, and its humidity; it made the air smell a different way in Chicago than any other place; it bred thunderstorms and threw them against the shore. Indeed the Lake was so constant, so inevitable, that he seldom thought about it. When he did it was as a place where people who had money took their boats, and those who'd lost it drowned themselves.

Now, however, as he ran on down the length of the pier, Lem's calls fading behind him, the thought of the Lake waiting at the end moved him as never before. He was small; it was vast. He was full of contradictions; it simply embraced everything, making no judgments on sailors or suicides.

He picked up his pace, barely feeling the pressure of his soles on the boards, the sense growing in him that however real this scene felt it was another of his mind's inventions, shaped from fragments of memory to ease him through what would otherwise have driven him mad: a stepping stone between the dreaming wakefulness of the life he'd left and whatever paradox lay ahead. The closer he got to the end of the pier the more certain he became that this was the case. His step, already light, became lighter still, his strides longer and longer. Time softened, and extended. He had a chance to wonder if the dream-sea truly existed, at least in the way that Palomo Grove existed, or whether the pier he'd created jutted into pure *thought*.

If so, there were many minds meeting there; tens of thousands of lights moving in the waters ahead, some breaking surface like fireworks, others diving deep. Howie had found some incandescence of his own, he realized. Nothing to boast about, but there was a distinct glow in his skin, like a faint echo of an echo of Fletcher's light.

The barrier at the end of the pier was a few feet from him. Beyond it, the waters of what he'd now ceased to think of as the Lake. This was Quiddity, and in moments it would be closing over his head. He wasn't afraid. Quite the reverse. He couldn't get to the barrier quickly

enough, throwing himself at it rather than waste time with steps. If any
further proof had been required that none of this was real he had it on
impact, the barrier flying into laughing splinters as he touched it. He
flew too. A falling flight into the dream-sea.

The element he plunged into was unlike water in that it neither
soaked nor chilled him. But he floated in it nevertheless, his body rising through brilliant bubbles to the surface without any effort on his
part. He had no fear of drowning. Only the profoundest sense of gratitude that he was here, where he belonged.

He looked back over his shoulder (so many backward glances) at
the pier. It had served its purpose, making a game of what might have
been a terror. Now it was flying into pieces, like the barrier.

He watched it go, happily. He was free of the Cosm, and floating in
Quiddity.

Jo-Beth and Tommy-Ray had gone into the schism together, but
their minds had found different ways to picture the journey and the
plunge.

The horror Jo-Beth had felt as she'd been snatched had been wiped
from her head in the thunder cloud. She forgot the chaos, and felt
calm. It was no longer Tommy-Ray who gripped her arm, but
Momma, in earlier years, when she'd still been able to face the world.
They were walking in a soothing twilight, with grass underfoot.
Momma was singing. If it was a hymn, she'd forgotten the words. She
was making up nonsense to fill the lines, which seemed to have the
rhythm of their step. Every now and then Jo-Beth would say something she'd learned at school, so Momma would know what a good
student she was. All the lessons were about water. About there being
tides everywhere, even in tears, about how the sea was where life had
begun, and how bodies were made more of water than any other element. The counterpoint of fact and song went on a long, easy while,
but she sensed subtle changes in the air. The wind became gustier,
and she smelled the sea. She put her face up to it, forgetting her
lessons. Momma's hymn had grown softer. If they were still holding
hands, Jo-Beth couldn't feel it. She kept walking, not looking back.

The ground wasn't grassy any longer, but bare, and somewhere up ahead it fell away into the sea, where there seemed to be countless boats bobbing, with candles lit on their prows and masts.

The ground went suddenly. There was no fear, even as she fell. Only the certainty that she'd left Momma behind.

Tommy-Ray found himself at Topanga, either at dawn or dusk, he wasn't sure which. Though the sun was no longer in the sky he wasn't alone here. He heard girls in the murk, laughing, and talking in breathy whispers. The sand beneath his bare feet was warm where they'd been lying, and sticky with suntan oil. He couldn't see the surf, but he knew which way to run. He started in the direction of the water, knowing that the girls were watching him. They always did. He didn't acknowledge their stares. When he was out there on the crests, really moving, he'd maybe flash them a smile. Then on the way back up the beach he'd let one of them get lucky.

Now, as the waves came in sight ahead of him, he realized that things weren't right here. Not only was the beach gloomy, and the sea dark, but there seemed to be bodies lolling in the surf, and, worse still, phosphorescence in their flesh. He slowed his pace, but knew he couldn't stop and turn around. He didn't want anyone on the beach, particularly the girls, to think he was afraid. He was, however; horribly. Some radioactive shit was in the sea. The surfers had fallen from their boards, poisoned, and were being washed up by the very crests they'd gone to ride. He could see them clearly now, their skin silvery in places and black in others, their hair like blond haloes. Their girls were with them, dead as the surfers in the tainted foam.

He had no choice but to join them, he knew. The shame of turning away and climbing back up the beach was worse than dying. They'd all be legends after this. Him, and the dead riders, carried off by the same tide. Steeling himself, he stepped into the sea, which instantly became deep, as though the beach had simply fallen away under his feet. The poison was already burning up his system; he could see his body getting brighter. He stared to hyperventilate, each breath more painful than the one before.

Something brushed his side. He turned, thinking it would be

another dead surfer, but it was Jo-Beth. She said his name. He couldn't find any words to answer with. As much as he wanted not to show his fear he couldn't help it. He was pissing now in the sea; his teeth were chattering.

"Help me," he said. "Jo-Beth. You're the only one who can help me. I'm dying."

She looked at his chattering face.

"If you're dying, we both are," she said.

"How did I get here? And why are you here? You don't like the beach."

"This isn't the beach," she said. She took hold of his arms, their motion making them bob like buoys. "This is Quiddity, Tommy-Ray. Remember? We're on the other side of the hole. You pulled us through."

She saw memory flooding his face as he spoke.

"Oh my God . . . oh Jesus God . . ." he said.

"You remember?"

"Yes. Jesus, yes." The chattering turned into sobs, as he pulled them close together, wrapping his arms around her. She didn't resist. There was little purpose in being vengeful, when they were both in such jeopardy.

"Hush," she said, letting him bury his hot, stricken face against her shoulder. "Hush. There's nothing we can do."

Nothing needed to be done. Quiddity had him, and he would float, and float, and perhaps—eventually—catch up with Jo-Beth and Tommy-Ray. Meanwhile, he liked being lost in this immensity. It made his fears—his whole life, in fact—seem inconsequential. He lay on his back and looked up at the sky. It was not, as he'd first thought, a night sky. There were no stars, either fixed or falling. No clouds, hiding a moon. In fact it seemed completely featureless at first, but as the seconds passed—or minutes; or hours; he neither knew nor much cared— he realized the subtlest waves of color were hundreds of miles across, moving over it. The Aurora Borealis seemed small stuff beside this show, in which, at intervals, he thought he saw forms swooping and climbing, like flocks of half-mile manta-rays, feeding in the stratosphere. He hoped they'd come down a little way, so he could see them more clearly, but perhaps, he mused, they had no more clarity to show. Not everything was available to the eye. Some sights defeated focus, and capture, and analysis. Like all he felt for Jo-Beth, for instance. That was every bit as strange and difficult to fix as the colors above his head, or the forms that made play there. Seeing them was as much a matter of feeling as of retina. The sixth sense was sympathy.

Content with his lot, he gently flipped himself over in the ether and experimented with swimming in it. The basic strokes worked well enough, though it was difficult to be certain he was making much progress with nothing to relate his motion to. The lights in the sea all around him—fellow passengers like himself, he supposed, though they seemed not to have form as he did—were too indistinct to be used as markers. Were they dreaming souls, perhaps? Infants, lovers and the dying, all travelling in Quiddity's waters as they slept, to be soothed and rocked, touched by a calm that would carry them, as the tide carried them, through the tempest they'd wake to? A life to be lived, or lost; love they'd go in fear of staling or disappearing after this epiphany. He put his face beneath the surface. Many of the lightforms were far below him, some so deep they were no larger than stars. Not all of them were moving in the same direction as he. Some, like the half-mile mantas above, were in groups, *shoals*, rising and falling. Others went side by side. The lovers, he assumed, though presumably not all the dreamers here, who were sleeping beside the lover of their lives, had that feeling reciprocated. Perhaps very few. Which thought led him back to the time he and Jo-Beth had travelled here; and to her present whereabouts. He had to be careful the calm didn't stupefy him; make him forgetful of her. He raised his face from the sea.

In doing so he avoided, by moments, a collision. Yards from him, its appearance shocking in the middle of such tranquility, was a fragment of garishly colored wreckage from the Vance house. And a few yards beyond that, more distressing still, a piece of flotsam far too ugly to belong here, yet not recognizably of the Cosm. It stood four or more feet above the water-line, and hung as far or further below; a gnarled, waxy island floating like pale dung in this pure sea. He reached out and took hold of the wreckage ahead of him, throwing himself on to it and kicking. His action carried him closer to the enigma.

It was alive. Not simply occupied by something living, but entirely made of living matter. He heard the thump of two heartbeats from it. Its surface had the unmistakable sheen of skin, or some derivative of same. But what it actually *was* didn't become apparent until he was almost brushing against it. Only then did he see the thin figures—two of the party guests—clutching each other with looks of fury on their faces. He hadn't been privileged to keep the company of Sam Sagansky, or hear the nimble fingers of Doug Frankl on the keyboards. All he saw were two enemies, locked not only together but at the heart of an island that seemed to have sprung out of them. From their backs, like huge hunches. From their limbs, like further limbs that put up no defense against their enemy but fused with his flesh. The structure was still sprouting further nodules, the beginning of new growth, bursting along the limbs, each variation referring not to the root form—an arm, a spine—but to its immediate predecessor, so that each successive variation became less human, and less fleshy. The image was more fascinating than distressing, the focus of the combatants upon each other suggesting they felt no pain at this process. Watching the structure grow and spread Howie vaguely comprehended that this was the birth of solid ground. Perhaps the fighters would die and decay eventually, but the structure itself was not so corruptible. Already the perimeters of the island, and its heights, resembled coral rather than flesh, tough and encrusted. When the fighters died they'd become fossils buried in the heart of an island they themselves had created. The island itself would float on.

He let go of the raft of wreckage and kicked on, past the island. Flotsam and jetsam littered the surface of the sea now: furniture, clumps of plaster, lighting fixtures. He swam past the head and neck of a carousel horse, its painted eye glaring backwards as if horrified by its dismemberment. But there was no sign of island-making amid this litter. Quiddity didn't create, it seemed, from things without minds, though he wondered if its genius would respond—given time—to the evidence of the minds that had made these artifacts. Could Quiddity grow from the head of a wooden horse some island named for the horse's maker? Anything was possible.

Never a truer word said or thought.

Anything was possible.

They weren't alone here, Jo-Beth knew. It was not much comfort, but it was some. Every now and then she'd hear somebody calling out, their voices distressed on occasion, but just as often ecstatic, like a congregation half in terror, half in awe, spread across the surface of Quiddity. She didn't answer any of the calls. For one thing, she'd seen forms floating past, always at some distance, that suggested people didn't stay human here. They grew freakish. She had enough problems dealing with Tommy-Ray (who was the second reason she didn't reply to the calls) without inviting more bad news. He demanded her constant attention; speaking to her as they floated, his voice drained of all emotion. He had a good deal to say, between the apologies and the sobs. Some of it she already knew. About how good he'd felt when their father had returned, and how betrayed when she'd rejected them both. But there was a lot more, and some of it broke her heart. He told her first about the trip to the Mission, his story mostly fragments but suddenly becoming stream-of-consciousness descriptions of the horrors he'd witnessed and performed. She might have been tempted to disbelieve the worst of it—the murders, the visions of his own decay— but for his lucidity. She'd never in her life heard him so articulate as when he told her how it felt to be the Death-Boy.

"Remember Andy?" he said at one point. "He had a tattoo . . . it was a skull . . . on his chest, above his heart?"

"I remember," she said.

"He used to say one day he'd go out on the crests at Topanga—one last ride—and never come back. Used to say he loved Death. But he didn't Jo-Beth . . ."

"No."

"He was a coward. He made a lot of noise but he was a coward. I'm not, am I? I'm no momma's boy . . ."

He started to sob again, more violently than ever. She tried to hush him but this time none of her soothing worked.

"Momma . . ." she heard him saying, "Momma . . ."

"What about Momma?" she said.

"It wasn't my fault."

"What wasn't?"

"I only went looking for you. It wasn't my fault."

"I said *what wasn't?*" Jo-Beth demanded, pushing him off her a little way. "Tommy-Ray, *answer me.* Did you hurt her?"

He looked like a chided child, she thought. Any pretense to machismo had been stripped from him. He was a raw, snotty child. Pathetic and dangerous: the inevitable combination.

"You hurt her," she said.

"I don't want to be the Death-Boy," he protested. "I don't want to kill anybody—"

"Kill?" she said.

He looked straight at her, as though his direct look might convince her of his innocence. "It wasn't me. It was the dead people. I went looking for you, and they followed me. I couldn't shake them off. I tried, Jo-Beth, I really tried."

"My God!" she said, thrusting him out of her arms.

Her action wasn't that violent, but it churned Quiddity's element out of all proportion to the size of her motion. She was vaguely aware that her repugnance was the cause of this; that Quiddity was matching her mental agitation with its own.

"It wouldn't have happened if you'd stayed with me," he protested. "You should have stayed, Jo-Beth."

She kicked away from him, her feelings making Quiddity boil.

"*Bastard!*" she yelled at him. "*You killed her! You killed her!*"

"You're my sister," he said. "You're the only one who can save me!"

He reached for her, his face a mess of sorrow, but all she could see in his features was Momma's murderer. He could protest his innocence to the end of the world (if they weren't beyond that already), she'd never forgive him. If he saw her revulsion he chose to ignore it. He began grappling with her, his hands clutching her face, then her breasts.

"Don't leave me!" he started to shout. "I won't let you leave me!"

How many times had she made excuses for him, because they'd been twin eggs in the same tube? Seen his corruption, and still extended a forgiving hand? She'd even coaxed Howie into putting his disgust at Tommy-Ray aside, for her sake. Enough was enough. This man might be her brother, her twin, but he was guilty of matricide. Momma had survived the Jaff, Pastor John and Palomo Grove, only to be killed in her own house, by her own son. His crime was beyond forgiveness.

He reached for her again, but this time she was ready. She hit him across the face, once, then once again, as hard as she could muster. Shock at the blows made him give up his hold on her for a moment and she started away from him, kicking the churning sea up in his face. He threw his arms in front of him to shield himself and she was gone out of his reach, vaguely aware that her body was not so sleek as it had been, but not taking time to discover why. All that was important now was to be as far from him as she could be; to keep him from touching her ever again; *ever*. She struck out strongly, ignoring his sobs. This time she didn't look behind her, at least until his din had faded. Then she slowed her pace, and glanced back. He wasn't in sight. Grief filled her up—agonized her—but a more immediate horror was upon her before the full consequences of Momma's death could touch her. Her limbs felt heavy as she pulled them from the ether. Tears half blinding her she raised her hands in front of her face. Through the blur she saw that her fingers were encrusted, as though she'd dipped her hands in oil and oatmeal; her arms were misshapen with some similar filth.

She started to sob, knowing all too clearly what this horror signified. Quiddity was at work on her. Somehow it was making her fury *solid*. The sea had made her flesh a fertile mud. Forms were springing from it as ugly as the rage which inspired them.

Her sobs became a yell. She'd almost forgotten what it was like to unleash a shout like this, tamed as she'd been by so many years being Momma's domesticated daughter, smiling for the Grove on Monday mornings. Now Momma was dead, and the Grove was probably in ruins. And Monday? What was Monday? Just a name arbitrarily attached to a day and a night in the long history of days and nights which were the life of the world. They meant nothing now: days, nights, names, towns or dead mothers. All that made sense to her was Howie. He was all she had left.

She tried to picture him, desperate to hold on to something in this insanity. His image slipped from her at first—all she could see was Tommy-Ray's wretched face—but she persevered, conjuring him by particulars. His spectacles, his pale skin, his odd gait. His eyes, full of love. His face, flushed with blood the way it was when he spoke with passion, which was often. His blood and love, in one hot thought.

"Save me," she sobbed, hoping against hope that Quiddity's strange waters carried her despair to him. "Save me, or it's over."

TWO

A bernethy?"
It was an hour before dawn in Palomo Grove, and Grillo had quite a report to file.

"I'm surprised you're still in the land of the living," Abernethy growled.

"Disappointed?"

"You're an asshole, Grillo. I don't hear from you for days then you call up at six o'clock in the fucking morning."

"I've got a story, Abernethy."

"I'm listening."

"I'm going to tell it the way it happened. But I don't think you're going to print it."

"Let me be the judge of that. Spit it out."

"Piece begins. Last night in the quiet residential town of Palomo Grove, Ventura County, a community set in the secure hills of the Simi Valley, our reality, known to those who juggle such concepts as the Cosm, was torn open by a power that proved to this reporter that all life is a movie—"

"*What the fuck?*"

"Shut up, Abernethy. I'm only going to tell you this once. Where was I? Oh yeah . . . a movie. This force, wielded by one Randolph Jaffe, broke the confines of what most of our species believed to be the only and absolute reality, and opened a door to another state of being: a sea called Quiddity—"

"Is this a resignation letter, Grillo?"

"You wanted the story nobody else would dare print, right?" Grillo said. "The real dirt. This is it. This is the great revelation."

"It's ridiculous."

"Maybe that's the way all earth-shattering news sounds. Have you thought of that? What would you have done if I'd tried to file a report on the Resurrection? Crucified man rolls away the stone. Would you have printed that?"

"That's different," Abernethy said. "That happened."

"So did this. I swear to God. And if you want proof, you're going to get it real soon."

"Proof? From where?"

"Just listen," Grillo said, and picked up his report again. "This revelation about the fragile state of our being took place in the midst of one of the most glamorous gatherings in recent movie and TV history, when about two hundred guests—Hollywood's movers and shakers— assembled at the hill-top house of Buddy Vance, who died here in Palomo Grove earlier in the week. His death, under circumstances both tragic and mysterious, began a series of events which climaxed last night with a number of the guests at his memorial party being snatched out of the world as we know it. There are no details yet as to the complete list of victims; though Vance's widow Rochelle was certainly among them. Nor is there any way of knowing their fate. They may be dead. They may simply exist in another state of being which only the most foolhardy of adventurers would dare enter. To all intents and purposes they have simply vanished off the face of the earth."

He expected Abernethy to interrupt at this juncture, but there was silence from the other end of the line. So profound a silence, indeed, that Grillo said:

"Are you still there, Abernethy?"

"You're nuts, Grillo."

"So put the phone down on me. Can't do it, can you? See, there's a real paradox here. I hate your fucking guts but I think you're just about the only man with the balls to print this. And the world's got to know."

"You *are* nuts."

"You watch the news through the day. You'll see . . . there's a lot of famous people missing this morning. Studio executives, movie stars, agents—"

"Where are you?"

"Why?"

"Let me make some calls, then get back to you."

"What for?"

"See if there's any rumors flying. Just give me five minutes. That's all I'm asking. I'm not saying I believe you. I don't. But it's one fuck of a story."

"It's the truth, Abernethy. And I want to warn people. They have to know."

"Like I said, give me five minutes. Are you at the same number?"

"Yeah. But you may not get through. The place is practically deserted."

"I'll get through," Abernethy said, and put down the phone.

Grillo looked across at Tesla.

"I did it," he said.

"I still don't think it's wise, telling people."

"Don't start again," Grillo said. "This is the story I was born to tell, Tesla."

"It's been a secret for so long."

"Yeah, for people like your friend Kissoon."

"He's not my friend."

"Isn't he?"

"For Christ's sake, Grillo, you heard what he did—"

"So why do you talk about him with this sneaking envy in your voice, huh?"

She looked at him like he'd just slapped her.

"Call me a liar?" he said.

She shook her head.

"What's the appeal?"

"I don't know. You're the one who just kept watching the Jaff do his stuff. No attempt to stop him. What was the appeal of *that?*"

"I wouldn't have had a chance against him, you know that."

"You didn't try."

"Don't change the subject. I'm right, aren't I?"

Tesla had crossed to the window. Coney Eye was screened by trees. There was no telling from here whether the damage was spreading.

"Do you think they're alive?" she said. "Howie, and the others?"

"I don't know."

"You got to look into Quiddity, right?"

"I got a glimpse," Grillo said.

"And?"

"It was like one of our telephone calls. Cut off short. All I got to see was a cloud. There was no sign of Quiddity itself."

"And no Iad."

"No Iad. Maybe they don't exist."

"You wish."

"You're sure of your sources?"

"Couldn't be more sure."

"I love it," Grillo remarked somewhat bitterly. "I dig around for days and all I get is a fucking peek. But *you*—you plug straight in."

"Is this what this is about?" Tesla said. "You getting a *story?*"

"Yeah. Maybe it is. And telling it. Making people understand what's going on in Happy Valley. But seems to me you don't really want that. You'd be happier if we kept this among the chosen few. You, Kissoon, the fucking Jaff—"

"OK, you want to report the end of the world? You do it, Orson. Listeners across America are just waiting to panic. Meanwhile, I've got problems—"

"You smug bitch."

"*I'm* smug! *I'm* smug! Listen to Mister Hotshot Tell Them The Truth Or Die Trying Grillo! Has it occurred to you that if Abernethy publishes what's going on up here we're going to have a major tourist industry in twelve hours? Freeways blocked in both directions? And won't that be nice for whatever's coming out of the throat, huh? Feeding time!"

"Shit."

"Didn't think of that, did you? And while we're talking turkey, you—"

The telephone silenced her in mid-accusation. Grillo picked it up.

"Nathan?"

"Abernethy."

Grillo looked across at Tesla, who was standing with her back to the window glaring at him.

"I'm going to need a lot more than two paragraphs."

"What convinced you?"

"You were right. A lot of people didn't come home from the party."

"Has it made the news this morning?"

"Nope. So you've got an edge. Of course your explanation about where they've gone's crap. Biggest fiction I ever heard. But it's a great front page."

"I'll get back to you with the rest."

"An hour."

"An hour."

He put the phone down.

"All right," he said, looking at Tesla. "So suppose I hold off giving him the full story till noon? What can we do in that time?"

"I don't know," Tesla admitted. "Maybe find the Jaff."

"And what the hell can he do?"

"Not *do* much. But *undo* plenty."

Grillo stood up and went through to the bathroom, turning on the faucet and splashing cold water on his face.

"You think the hole can be closed?" he said, wandering back in, water dripping from his face.

"I told you, I don't know. Maybe. I don't have any other answers, Grillo."

"And what happens to the people inside? The McGuire twins. Katz. The rest."

"They're probably dead already," she sighed. "We can't help them."

"Easily said."

"Well you seemed ready enough to fling yourself in a few hours ago, so maybe you should go in after them. I'll get you a piece of string, to hold on to."

"All right," Grillo said, "I haven't forgotten you saved my life, and I'm grateful."

"Jeez, I've made some errors in my time . . ."

"Look, I'm sorry. I'm coming at this all wrong. I know I am. I should be planning some plan. Being a hero. But see . . . I'm not. The only response I've got to all this is the same old Grillo. I can't change. I see something, I want the world to know."

"It will," Tesla said quickly. "It will."

"But you . . . *you*'ve changed."

She nodded. "You got that right," she said. "I was thinking, when you were telling Abernethy he wouldn't have printed the Resurrection story: that's *me*. I'm resurrected. And you know what freaks me? I'm not freaked. I'm cool. I'm fine. I go walking around in a fucking time loop, and it's like . . ."

"What?"

". . . it's like I was born for this, Grillo. Like I could be . . . oh shit, I don't know."

"Say it. Whatever's on your mind, say it."

"You know what a shaman is?"

"Sure," said Grillo. "Medicine-man. Witch-doctor."

"More than that," she said. "He's a mind-healer. Gets inside the collective psyche and explains it. Stirs it around. I think all the major performers in this—Kissoon, the Jaff, Fletcher—they're shamans. And Quiddity . . . is America's dream-space. The world's maybe. I've seen these men fucking it up, Grillo. All on their own trips. Even Fletcher couldn't get his shit together."

"So maybe what's needed is a change of shaman," Grillo said.

"Yeah. Why not?" Tesla replied. "I can't do any worse than they have."

"That's why you want to keep it to yourself."

"That's one of the reasons, sure. I can *do* this, Grillo. I'm weird enough, and most of these shamans, you know, were a little off in some way. Cross-dressers; gender-fuckers. All things to all men. Animal, vegetable and mineral. I want to be that. I've always wanted . . . ," she trailed off. ". . . you know what I've always wanted."

"Not till now."

"Well now you do."

"You don't look very happy about it."

"I've done the resurrection scene. That's one of those scenes shamans have to do. Die and rise again. But I keep thinking . . . it's not finished. I've got more to prove."

"You think you have to die again?"

"I hope not. Once was enough."

"It usually is," Grillo said.

His remark brought a smile to her lips, unbidden.

"What's funny?" he said.

"That. You. Me. Things don't get any weirder than this, do they?"

"That's a fair bet."

"What time is it?"

"About six."

"The sun'll be up soon. I'm thinking I should go out to look for the Jaff, before the light drives him into hiding."

"That's if he's not left the Grove."

"I don't think he's capable," she said. "The circle's closing. Getting tighter and tighter. Coney Eye's suddenly the center of the known universe."

"And the unknown."

"I don't know whether it *is* so unknown," Tesla said. "I think Quiddity's maybe more like home than we think."

The day was on its way by the time they stepped out of the hotel, the darkness giving way to an uneasy no-man's land between moonset and sunrise. As they crossed the hotel lot a wretched, grimy individual stepped out of the murk, his face ashen.

"I have to speak with you," he said. "You're Grillo, right?"

"Yeah. And you?"

"My name's Witt. I used to have offices in the Mall. And friends here at the hotel. They told me about you."

"What do you want?" Tesla said.

"I was up at Coney Eye," he said. "When you came out. I wanted to speak to you then but I was hiding . . . I couldn't move myself." He glanced down at the front of his trousers, which were damp.

"What's going on up there?"

"I suggest you get out of the Grove as quickly as possible," Tesla advised. "There's worse on the way."

"There's no Grove to leave," Witt replied. "The Grove's gone. Finished. People have left on vacations and I don't think they're going to come back. But I'm not leaving. I've got nowhere to go. Besides—" he looked close to tears as he spoke "—this is my town. If it's going to get swallowed up somehow, then I want to be here when it goes. Even if the Jaff—"

"Wait!" said Tesla. "What do you know about the Jaff?"

"I . . . met him. Tommy-Ray McGuire's his son, you know that?" Tesla nodded. "Well, McGuire introduced me to the Jaff."

"Here in the Grove?"

"Sure."

"Where?"

"In Cherry Tree Glade."

"Then that's where we start," said Tesla. "Can you take us there?"

"Of course."

"You think he'll have just gone back there?" Grillo said.

"You saw his condition," Tesla replied. "I think he'll go looking for someplace *familiar*, where he feels reasonably safe."

"Makes sense," said Grillo.

"If it does," said Witt, "it's the first thing tonight that has."

Dawn showed them what William Witt had already described: a town practically deserted, its occupants fled. A pack of domestic dogs roved the streets, having either been turned loose or escaped from owners whose minds were on the business of panicked departure. In the space of a day or two they'd become a small scavenging band. Witt recognized the dogs. Mrs. Duffin's poodles were in the pack; so were two dachshunds belonging to Blaze Hebbard, the pups of the pups of the pups of dogs owned by a Grover who'd died when Witt was a boy, one Edgar Lott. Died and left his money to be used to put up a memorial to the League of Virgins.

Besides the dogs there were other, perhaps more distressing signs of hurried exits. Garage doors left open; toys dropped on the front path or in the driveway as sleepy children were put into cars in the middle of the night.

"Everybody knew," Witt said as they drove. "They knew all along but nobody said anything. That's why most of them just slipped away in the middle of the night. They thought they were the only ones who were losing their minds. They *all* thought they were the only ones."

"You worked here, you said."

"Yeah," Witt told Grillo, "real estate."

"Looks like business may be booming tomorrow. Plenty of properties for sale."

"And who's going to buy?" Witt said. "This is going to be cursed ground."

"It's not the Grove's fault that all this happened," Tesla put in. "It's an accident."

"It is?"

"Of course. Fletcher and the Jaff ended up here because they ran out of power, not because the Grove was somehow *chosen.*"

"I still think it'll be cursed ground," Witt began, breaking off to instruct Grillo: "This next turning's Cherry Tree Glade. And Mrs. Lloyd's house is the fourth or fifth on the right."

From the outside at least it looked unoccupied. When they broke in, that was confirmed. The Jaff hadn't been in the house since he'd taunted Witt in the upper room.

"It was worth a try," Tesla said. "I guess we just have to keep looking. The town's not that big. We just go from street to street till we get a sniff of him. Anybody got any better ideas?" She looked at Grillo, whose gaze and concentration were elsewhere. "What is it?" she said.

"Huh?"

"Somebody left water running," Witt said, following the direction of Grillo's gaze.

Water was indeed running out from under the front door of a house opposite the Lloyd house, a steady stream which made its way down the incline of the driveway, across the sidewalk and into the gutter.

"What's so interesting?" Tesla said.

"I just realized . . ." Grillo said.

"What?"

He kept staring at the water, disappearing down the sewer. "I think I know where he's gone."

He turned and looked at Tesla.

"A familiar place, you said. The place he knows best in the Grove isn't above ground, it's *below*."

Tesla's face brightened. "The caves. Yeah. That makes perfect sense."

They got back into the car, and with Witt directing them by the fastest route, drove back through the town—in defiance of red lights and one-way streets—towards Deerdell.

"It's not going to be long before the police start to arrive," Grillo remarked. "Looking for lost movie stars."

"I should go up to the house and warn them away," Tesla said.

"You can't be in two places at one time," Grillo said. "Unless that's another talent I don't know about."

"Ha fucking ha."

"They'll have to find out the hard way. We've got more urgent stuff to do."

"True," Tesla conceded.

"If the Jaff *is* in the caves," Witt said, "how do we get down to him? I don't think he's just going to appear if we holler."

"You know a man called Hotchkiss?" Grillo said.

"Of course. Carolyn's father?"

"Yeah."

"We can get help from him. I betcha he's still in town. He can get us down there. Whether he can get us back up again's another problem, but he seemed confident enough a couple of days back. He tried to get me to go into the caves with him."

"Why?"

"He's obsessed with things *buried* under the Grove."

"I don't follow."

"I'm not sure I do. Let him explain it."

They'd reached the woods. There was no sound of a dawn chorus, however ragged. They stepped in among the trees, the silence oppressive.

"He's been here," Tesla said.

Nobody needed to ask how she knew. Even without the benefit of senses sharpened by the Nuncio it was clear the atmosphere in the woods was charged with anticipation. The birds hadn't left, they were just scared to sing.

It was Witt who led the way through to the clearing, his sense of direction that of a man who knew exactly where he was headed.

"You come here often?" Grillo said, half joking.

"Almost never," Witt replied.

"Stop," Tesla suddenly whispered.

The clearing was just ahead, visible through the trees. She nodded towards it.

"Look there," she said.

A yard or two beyond the police barricade, turning over and over in the grass, was proof positive that the Jaff had indeed taken refuge here. One of the terata, too weak and wounded to cover the last few yards to the safety of the caves, was living out its last moments, its dissolution giving off a sickly luminescence.

"It's not going to do us any harm," Grillo said, about to step into view.

Tesla took hold of his arm. "It can maybe alert the Jaff," she said. "We don't know what kind of contact he has with those things. We don't need to go any further. We know he's there."

"True."

"Let's *go* find Hotchkiss."

They began to retrace their steps.

"Do you know where he lives?" Grillo asked Witt, once they were a good distance from the clearing.

"I know where everybody lives," Witt said. "Or lived."

The sight of the caves seemed to have shaken him, fuelling Grillo's suspicion that despite the claim that he seldom ventured there it was some kind of place of pilgrimage.

"Take Tesla to Hotchkiss," Grillo said. "I'll meet you both there."

"Where are you going?" Tesla wanted to know.

"I want to be sure Ellen left the Grove."

"She's a sensible lady," came the reply, "I'm sure she has."

"I'm going to check anyhow," Grillo said, not about to be dissuaded.

He left them at the car, and started off in the direction of the Nguyen house, leaving Tesla to summon Witt from staring at the woods. When Grillo turned the corner she still hadn't succeeded. He was gazing towards the trees as though the clearing was calling him back into some shared past, and it was all he could do to keep himself from obeying the summons.

THREE

I t wasn't Howie that came to help Jo-Beth in her solitary terror, but the tide, which picked her up and carried her—her eyes often closed (and when they were open, blurred with tears)—towards the place she'd glimpsed all too briefly when she and Howie had swum in Quiddity together: the Ephemeris. There was the beginnings of a disturbance in the element that bore her up, but she was as ignorant of that as she was of the proximity of the island. Others were not. Had she been more aware of her surroundings she'd have seen a subtle but undeniable agitation pass among the souls swimming in Quiddity's ether. Their motion was no longer so steady. Some—perhaps those more sensitive to the rumor the ether was carrying—stopped advancing and hung in the darkness like drowned stars. Others took themselves deeper, hoping to avoid the cataclysm that was being whispered. Still others, these very few as yet, went out altogether, waking in their beds in the Cosm grateful to be out of danger. For most, however, the message was too hushed to be heard; or if it was heard the pleasure of being in Quiddity outweighed the anxiety. They rose and fell, rose and fell, their route more often than not taking them where Jo-Beth was going: to the island on the dream-sea.

_____

Ephemeris.

The name had echoed in Howie's head since he'd first heard it spoken, by Fletcher.

What's on Ephemeris? he'd asked, imagining some paradise island. His father's reply hadn't been particularly illuminating. *The Great and Secret Show,* he'd said, an answer which begged a dozen more questions. Now, as the island came into view ahead of him, he wished he'd pursued his questions with more persistence. Even from a distance it was quite clear his picturing of the place had been spectacularly short of the mark. Just as Quiddity wasn't in any conventional sense a sea, so Ephemeris demanded a redefinition of the word island. For one, it was not a single land-mass but many, perhaps hundreds, joined by arches of rock, the whole archipelago resembling a vast, floating cathedral, the bridges like buttresses, the islands towers which mounted in scale as they approached the central island, from which solid pillars of smoke rose to meet the sky. The similarity was too strong to be coincidence. This image was surely the subconscious inspiration of architects the world over. Cathedral builders, tower raisers, even—who knew?—children playing with building blocks, had this dream place somewhere at the back of their minds, and paid homage as best they could. But their masterworks could only be approximations, compromises with gravity and the limitations of their medium. Nor could they ever aspire to a work so massive. The Ephemeris was many miles across, Howie guessed, and there was no portion of it that had not been touched by genius. If it was a natural phenomenon (and who knew what *natural* was, in a place of mind?) then it was nature in a frenzy of invention. It made solid matter play games only cloud or light would be capable of in the world he'd left behind. Made towers as fine as reeds on which globes the size of houses balanced; made sheer cliff faces fluted like shells and canyon walls that seemed to billow like curtains at a window; made spiral hills; made boulders like breasts, and dogs, and the sweepings from some vast table. So many likenesses, but none he could be certain were intended. A fragment in which he'd seen a face was part of another likeness the glance after, each interpretation subject to change at a moment's notice. Perhaps they were all true, all intended. Perhaps none were, and this game of resemblances was, like the creation of the pier when he'd first approached Quiddity, his mind's way of taming the immensity. If so, there was one sight it failed to master: the island at the center of the archipelago, which rose straight out of Quiddity, sheer, the smoke that gouted from countless fissures on its walls rising with the same verticality. Its pinnacle was completely concealed by the smoke, but whatever mystery lay behind it was nectar to the spirit-lights, who rose to it unburdened by flesh and blood, not entering the smoke but grazing its blossom. He wondered if it was fear that kept them from moving into the smoke, or if it was a more solid barrier than it seemed. Perhaps when he got closer, he'd discover the answer. Eager to be there as quickly as possible, he aided the tide with strokes of his own, so that within ten or fifteen minutes of first seeing the Ephemeris he was hauling himself up on to its beach. It was dark, though not as dark as Quiddity, and harsh beneath his palms, not sand but encrustations, like coral. Was it possible, he suddenly wondered, that the archipelago had been created the way the island he'd seen floating among the flotsam from the Vance house had been created, formed around the presence of human beings in Quiddity? If so, how long ago must they have come into the dream-sea, to have grown so massive?

He started along the course of the beach, choosing left over right because whenever he was faced with two roads about which he knew equally little he always chose the left. He kept close to the edge of the sea, in the hope that he'd find Jo-Beth on the beach, brought by the same current that had caught him. Once out of the soothing waters, his body no longer borne up and caressed, anxieties the sea had lulled from him took hold. The first, that he might search the archipelago for days, weeks even, and never find Jo-Beth. Second, that even if he did, there was still Tommy-Ray to contend with. Nor was Tommy-Ray alone; he'd come to the Vance house with phantoms. Three—and this was the least of his worries, in a sense, but it became steadily more important—that something was changing in Quiddity. He no longer cared what words were most appropriate for this reality: whether it was another dimension or a state of mind was not relevant. They were probably one and the same anyhow. What did matter was the *holiness* of this place. He didn't doubt for a moment that all that he'd gleaned about Quiddity and the Ephemeris was true. This was the place in which all his species that knew of glory got their glimpses. A constant place; a place of comfort, where the body was forgotten (except for trespassers like himself) and the dreaming soul knew flight, and mystery. But there were subtle signs—some so subtle he couldn't have pinpointed them—that the dream place was not secure. The small waves splashing up on the beach, their surf bluish, were not as rhythmical as they'd been when he first stepped out of the sea. The motion of the lights in Quiddity seemed similarly changed, as though something was happening in the system that was distressing it. He doubted that the simple intrusion of flesh and blood from the Cosm was responsible. Quiddity was vast, and had ways of dealing with those who resisted the calm of its waters: he'd seen that process at work. No, whatever was souring the tranquillity had to be more significant than the presence of himself, or any of the invaders from the other side.

He began to come across evidence of that trespass, washed up on the shore. A door frame, pieces of smashed furniture, cushions, and, inevitably, fragments of Vance's collection. A short distance beyond this pitiful litter, around a bend in the beach, he found hope that the tide had brought Jo-Beth here: another survivor. She was standing at the very edge of Quiddity, gazing out over the sea. If she heard him approaching she didn't look his way. Her posture (hands limp at her sides, shoulders slumped) and the steadiness of her stare suggested someone mesmerized. Loath as he was to break her trance, if that was how she'd chosen to deal with the shock of dislocation, he had no choice:

"Excuse me," he said, knowing his politeness was pathetic in such circumstances, "are you the only one here?"

She looked around at him and he got a second surprise. He'd seen this face dozens of times, smiling out from the TV screen, extolling the virtues of shampoo. He didn't know her name. She was simply the Silksheen Woman. She frowned at him, as though she was having difficulty focusing on his face. He tried the question again, rephrased.

"Are there any other survivors?" he said. "From the house?"

"Yes," she said.

"Where are they?"

"Just keep on walking."

"Thank you."

"This isn't happening, is it?" she said.

"I'm afraid it is," he said.

"What happened to the world? Did they drop the bomb?"

"No."

"What then?"

"It's back there somewhere," he said. "Back over Quiddity. Over the sea."

"Oh," she said, though it was clear she hadn't quite grasped this information. "Do you have any coke?" she said. "Or pills? Anything?"

"Sorry."

She returned her gaze to Quiddity, leaving him to follow her instructions and make his way along the beach. The agitation in the waves was increasing with every step he took. Either that or he was simply becoming more sensitive to it. Perhaps the latter, because he was noticing other signs besides that of the wave-rhythm. In the air around his head a restlessness, as though conversations between invisibles were being conducted just out of hearing range. In the sky, the waves of color were breaking up into patches, like herring-bone cloud, their tranquil progressions replaced by the same agitation that had tainted Quiddity. Lights still passed overhead, moving towards the smoke tower, but there were fewer and fewer of them. The dreamers were definitely waking.

Ahead, the beach was partially blocked by a rock formation of chain-link boulders, between which he had to climb before continuing his search. The Silksheen Woman had offered good directions however. A little way beyond the boulders, around another sweep in the beach, he found several more survivors, both men and women. None seemed to have been able to climb more than a few yards from the sea. One of them was still lying with his feet in the waves, his body sprawled as though dead. Nobody went to help him. The same languor that kept the Silksheen Woman staring out over Quiddity had affected many of them, but several were inert for a different reason. They'd hauled themselves from Quiddity *changed* by floating in its waters. Their bodies were encrusted and misshapen, as though the same process that had turned the warring guests into an island was underway in them too. He could only guess what quality, or its absence, marked these people out from the rest. Why had he, and perhaps half the dozen here, crossed the same distance in the same element as these sufferers and stepped out of Quiddity unchanged? Had the victims entered the sea hot with emotion, and Quiddity battened on it, whereas he'd drifted much as the dreamers did, his life left behind in another place, and with it all ambition, obsession; all feeling indeed, but the quiescence Quiddity induced? It had even lulled from him his desire to find Jo-Beth, but not for long. That was his only thought now. He went among the survivors looking for her, but he was disappointed. She wasn't among this number, nor was Tommy-Ray.

"Are there any others?" he asked a heavily set man slumped by the shore.

"Others?"

"You know . . . like us."

There was the same puzzled and distracted air about this man as there'd been about the Silksheen Woman. He seemed to be laboring to put the words he'd heard together.

"*Us*," Howie said. "From the house."

There was no answer forthcoming. The man just kept on staring, his gaze glassy. Howie gave up and searched for a more useful source of information, electing the one man among the survivors who wasn't looking out over Quiddity. Instead he was standing high up on the beach, staring up at the smoke tower at the core of the archipelago. The journey here hadn't left him unmarked. There were signs of Quiddity's work on his neck and face, and running down his spine. He'd taken off his shirt and bound it around his left hand. Howie approached him.

No excuse me this time, just the plain statement:

"I'm looking for a girl. She's blonde. About eighteen. Have you seen her?"

"What's up there?" the man replied. "I want to go. I want to see."

Howie tried again. "I'm looking—"

"I heard you."

"Have you seen her?"

"No."

"Do you know if there are any more survivors?"

The reply was the same deadpan syllable. It got Howie raging.

"What the fuck's wrong with everybody?" he said.

The man looked at him. His face was pock-marked and far from handsome, but he had a lop-sided smile that Quiddity's handiwork couldn't spoil.

"Don't get mad," he said. "It's not worth it."

"*She's* worth it."

"Why? We're all dead anyhow."

"Not necessarily. We got in, we can get out."

"What, you mean *swim?* Fuck that, man. I'm not going back in that fucking soup. I'd prefer to die. Somewhere up there."

He looked back towards the mountain. "There's something up there. Something wonderful. I know it."

"Maybe."

"You want to come with me?"

"Climb, you mean? You'll never make it."

"Not all the way, maybe, but I can get closer. Get a sniff of it."

His appetite for the mystery of the tower was welcome when everyone else was so lethargic, and Howie was loath to part company with him. But wherever Jo-Beth was, it wasn't on the mountain.

"Just come some of the way," the guy said. "You'll get a better view up there. Maybe spot your lady-friend."

That was no bad idea, especially when they had so little time. The unrest in the air was more palpable with every minute that passed.

"Why not?" Howie said.

"I've been looking for the easiest route. Seems to me we're best going back along the beach aways. By the way, who are you? I'm Garrett Byrne. Two R's. No u. Just in case you get to write the obit. You are?"

"Howie Katz."

"I'd shake your hand only mine isn't fit for shaking." He raised the shirt-swathed limb. "I don't know what happened out there but I'll never draft another contract. Maybe I'm glad, you know? It was a fucking dumb business anyhow."

"What was?"

"Entertainment lawyer. You know the joke? What have you got if you've got three entertainment lawyers up to their necks in shit?"

"What?"

"Not enough shit."

Byrne laughed out loud at this.

"Want to see?" he said, unwrapping his hand. It was scarcely recognizable as such. The fingers and thumb had fused and swollen.

"You know what?" he said. "I think it's trying to turn itself into a dick. All those years fucking people with this, just taking them up the ass, and it's finally got the message. It's a dick, don't you think? No, don't tell me. Let's just climb."

Tommy-Ray felt the dream-sea working upon him as he floated, but he didn't waste effort looking to see what changes it was making. He just let the fury that was fuelling those changes come.

Perhaps it was that—the anger and the snot—that brought the phantoms back. He became aware of them as a memory first, his mind picturing their pursuit of him down the empty highways of the Baja, their cloud like tin cans tied to a dog's tail. No sooner thought than *felt*. A cold wind blew on his face, which was the only part of him showing out of the sea. He knew what was coming. Smelled the tombs, and the dust in the tombs. It wasn't until the sea around him started to churn, however, that he opened his eyes and saw the cloud circling above him. It was not the great storm it had been in the Grove; the destroyer of churches and mommas. It was a mad runty spiral of dirt. But the sea knew it belonged to him, and it began new work on his body. He felt his limbs getting heavier. His face itched furiously. He wanted to say: this isn't my legion. Don't blame me for what they feel. But what was the use of denying it? He was the Death-Boy, now and always. Quiddity knew it, and worked its work accordingly. There were no lies here. No pretenses. He watched as the spirits descended towards the surface of the sea, their circle centering on him. The fury in Quiddity's ether intensified. He was spun like a top, his motion screwing him down. He tried to throw his arms up over his head, but they were leaden, and the sea simply closed over his head. His mouth was open. Quiddity flooded his throat; his system. In the confusion one simple knowledge—carried by Quiddity, now swallowed in its bitter whole—touched him. That there was an evil coming he had never known the likes of; that no one had ever known the likes of. He felt it in his chest first, then in his stomach and bowels. Finally, in his head, like a blossoming night. It was called *Iad*, this night, and the chill it brought had no equal on any planet in the system; even those so far from the sun they could bear no life. None owned a darkness this deep, this murderous.

He rose to the surface again. The phantoms had gone, not *away*, but into him, subsumed into his transforming anatomy as part of Quiddity's work. He was suddenly, perversely, glad of it. There would be no salvation in the night that was coming, except for those who were its allies. Better he should be a death among many deaths, then, when he might have a hope of being passed over in the holocaust.

He took a breath, and expelled it in laughter, putting his remade hands, heavy as they were, up to his face. It had finally taken on the shape of his soul.

Howie and Byrne climbed for several minutes, but however high they got the best view was always above them: the spectacle of the smoke tower. The closer they got the more Byrne's obsession with the sight touched Howie. He began wondering, as he had when the tide had first brought him within sighting distance of the Ephemeris, what great unknown was hiding up there, so powerful it drew the sleepers of the world to its threshold. Byrne was by no means agile, given that he had only one hand available. He repeatedly slipped. But there was no murmur of complaint from him, though with every fall the number of cuts and scrapes on his bare body multiplied. Eyes fixed on the highest reaches of the mountain he pushed on, not seeming to give a damn what damage he did himself as long as he closed the gap between himself and the mystery. Howie found it easy enough to keep up with him, but had to halt every few minutes to survey the scene below from a new vantage point. There was no sign of Jo-Beth along any visible stretch of shore, and he now began to question the wisdom of his coming with Byrne. The journey was increasingly perilous, as the formations they were ascending became steeper, and the bridges they crossed narrower. Beneath the bridges it was a straight fall, usually on to rock. Sometimes, however, there was a glint of Quiddity at the bottom of these chasms, its waters as frenzied as they were beyond the shore.

There were fewer and fewer spirits in the air, but as they crossed an arch no broader than a plank a flight of them passed directly overhead and Howie saw that within each of the lights was a single sinuous line, like a bright snake. Genesis couldn't have been more misguided, or misguiding, he thought, to picture the serpent crushed beneath a human heel. The soul was that serpent, and it could fly.

The sight brought him to a halt, and a decision.

"I'm not going any further," he said.

Byrne looked back at him. "Why not?"

"I've got as good a view of the shore-line as I'm going to get."

The view was by no means comprehensive, but climbing higher wasn't going to improve it significantly. Besides, the figures on the beach below were now so small they were barely recognizable. Another few minutes' ascent and he'd not know Jo-Beth from any other survivor.

"Don't you want to see what's up there?" Byrne said.

"Yes, of course," Howie replied. "But another time." He knew the response was ridiculous. There'd be no other time this side of his death-bed.

"I'll leave you then," Byrne said. He didn't waste breath with a goodbye, fond or otherwise. Instead he turned back to the business of the climb. His body was running with blood and sweat, and he was stumbling now with every second step he took, but Howie knew it was a vain course trying to call him back. Vain, and presumptuous. What-ever kind of life he'd lived—and it sounded to have been lacking char-ity—Byrne was seizing his last chance to be touched by the holy. Maybe death was the inevitable consequence of such pursuit.

Howie returned his gaze to the scene below. He followed the line of the beach, looking for the least sign of movement. To his left lay the stretch of shore they'd climbed from. He could still see the party of survivors, at the margin of the sea, as mesmerized as ever. To their right, the solitary figure of the Silksheen Woman, the waves that broke against the shore—their boom carried to his ears—large enough to threaten her with acquisition. Beyond her again, the beach upon which he'd first found himself.

It wasn't empty. His heart did double time. There was somebody stumbling along the shore, keeping well away from the encroaching sea. Her hair shone, even at this distance. It could only be Jo-Beth. With the recognition came fear for her. It looked as though every step she took was an agony.

He immediately started down the way they'd come, the rock marked in several places by splashes of Byrne's blood. At one such spot, after ten minutes of descent, he looked back to see if he could spot the man, but the heights were dark and, as far as he could see, empty. The last remaining souls had gone from the smoke tower; and with them much of the light. There was no sign of Byrne.

When he turned back, there was. The man was standing two or three yards lower down the slope. The multitude of wounds he'd col-lected on his way up were nothing beside his newest. It ran from the side of his head to his hip, and had opened him up to his innards.

"I fell," he said simply.

"All the way down here?" Howie said, marvelling at the fact that the man was even standing.

"No. I came down of my own accord."

"How?"

"It was easy," Byrne replied. "I'm *larvae* now."

"What?"

"Ghost. Spirit. I thought maybe you'd seen me fall."

"No."

"It was a long drop, but it ended well. I don't think anybody ever died on the Ephemeris before. That makes me one of one. I can make my own rules. Play it any way I like. And I thought I should come help Howie—" His obsessive heat had been replaced by a calm authority. "You have to be quick," he said. "I understand a lot of things suddenly, and the news isn't good."

"Something's happening, isn't it?"

"The Iad," Byrne said. "They're starting across Quiddity." Terms that he hadn't known minutes before were now commonplace from his lips.

"What are Iad?" Howie asked.

"Evil beyond words," Byrne said, "so I won't even try."

"Going to the Cosm?"

"Yes. Maybe you can get there ahead of them."

"How?"

"Trust to the sea. It wants what you want."

"Which is?"

"You, *out*," Byrne said. "So go. And quickly."

"I hear."

Byrne stood aside to let Howie pass. As he did so he took hold of Howie's arm with his good hand.

"You should know—" he said.

"What?"

"What's on the mountain. It's *wonderful*."

"Worth dying for?"

"A hundred times."

He let go of Howie.

"I'm glad."

"If Quiddity survives," Byrne said. "If *you* survive this, look for me. I'm going to be wanting words with you."

"I will," Howie replied, and began down the slope as fast as he was able, his descent veering between the ungainly and the suicidal. He started to yell Jo-Beth's name as soon as he came within what he guessed was hailing distance, but his call went unheeded. The blonde head didn't look up from its study. Perhaps the sound of the waves was drowning him out. He reached beach level in a scrambling, sweaty daze and began to race towards her.

"*Jo-Beth!* It's me! *Jo-Beth!*"

This time she did hear, and she looked up. Even with several yards between them he could see clearly the reason for her stumbling. Horrified, he slowed his pace, barely aware he was doing so. Quiddity had been at work on her. The face he'd fallen in love with at Butrick's Steak House, the face from the sight of which he dated his life, was a mass of spiky growths that spread down her neck and disfigured her arms. There was a moment, one he'd never quite forgive himself for, in which he wished she wouldn't know him, and he'd be able to walk on past her. But she did; and the voice that came from behind the mask was the same that had told him she loved him.

Now it said: "Howie . . . help me . . ."

He opened his arms and let her come into them. Her body was feverish, racked with shudders.

"I thought I'd never see you again," she said, her hands over her face.

"I wouldn't have left you."

"At least we can die together now."

"Where's Tommy-Ray?"

"He's gone," she said.

"We've got to do the same," Howie said. "Get off the island as quickly as possible. Something terrible's coming."

She dared to look up at him, her eyes as clear and blue as they'd ever been, staring out at him like the gleam of treasure in muck. The sight made him hold her tighter, as if to prove to her (and to himself) that he'd mastered the horror. He hadn't. It was her beauty that had first taken his breath away. Now that was gone. He had to look beyond its absence to the Jo-Beth he'd later come to love. That was going to be hard.

He looked away from her, towards the sea. The waves were thunderous.

"We have to go back into Quiddity," he said.

"We can't!" she said. "I can't!"

"*We've* got no choice. It's the only way back."

"It did this to me," she said. "It changed me!"

"If we don't go now," Howie said, "we never go. It's as simple as that. We stay here and we die here."

"Maybe that's for the best," she said.

"How can that be?" Howie said. "How's dying for the best?"

"The sea'll kill us anyway. It'll twist us up."

"Not if we trust it. Give ourselves over to it."

He remembered, briefly, his journey here, floating on his back, watching the lights. If he thought the return trip would be so mellow he was kidding himself. Quiddity was no longer a tranquil sea of souls. But what other choice did they have?

"We can stay," Jo-Beth said again. "We can die here, together. Even if we got back—" she started to sob again, "—even if we got back I couldn't live like this."

"Stop crying," he told her. "And stop talking about dying. We're going to get back to the Grove. Both of us. If not for our sakes, then to warn people."

"About what?"

"There's something coming across Quiddity. An invasion. Heading home. That's why the sea's going wild."

The commotion in the sky above them was every bit as violent. There was no sign, either in sea or sky, of the spirit-lights. However precious these moments on the Ephemeris were, every last dreamer had forsaken the journey, and woken. He envied them the ease of that passage. Just to be able to snap out of this horror and find yourself back in your own bed. Sweaty, maybe; scared, certainly. But home. Sweet and easy. Not so for the trespassers like themselves, flesh and blood in a place of spirit. Nor, now he thought of it, for the others here. He owed them a warning, though he suspected his words would be ignored.

"Come with me," he said.

He took hold of Jo-Beth's hand and they headed back along the beach to where the rest of the survivors were gathered. Very little had changed, though the man who'd been lying in the waves had now gone, dragged away, Howie presumed, by the violence of the sea. Apparently nobody had gone to his aid. They were standing or sitting as before, their lazy gazes still on Quiddity. Howie went to the nearest of them, a man not much older than himself, with a face born for its present vacuity.

"You have to get out of here," he said. "We all have to."

The urgency in his voice did something to rouse the man from his torpor, but not much. He managed a wary "Yeah?" but did nothing.

"You'll die if you stay," Howie told him, then raised his voice above the waves to address them all. *"You'll die!"* he said. "You have to go into Quiddity, and let it take you back."

"Where?" said the young man.

"What do you mean, where?"

"Back *where?*"

"To the Grove. The place you came from. Don't you remember?"

There was no answer forthcoming from any of them. Maybe the only way to get an exodus going was to start it, Howie reasoned.

"It's now or never," he said to Jo-Beth.

There was still resistance, both in her expression and in her body. He had to take firm hold of her hand and lead her down towards the waves.

"Trust me," he said.

She didn't answer him, but nor did she fight to stay on the beach. A distressing docility had come over her, its only virtue, he thought, that maybe Quiddity would leave her alone this time. He was not so sure it would treat him with such indifference. He was by no means as detached from high emotion as he'd been on the outward journey. There were all kinds of feelings running rife in him, any or all of which Quiddity might want to make play with. Fear for their lives ranked highest, of course. Close after, the confusion of repugnance at Jo-Beth's condition and his guilt at that repugnance. But the message in the air was urgent enough to keep him moving down the beach in spite of such anxieties. It was almost a physical sensation now, which reminded him of some other time in his life, and of course of some other place; a memory he couldn't quite grasp. It didn't matter. The message was unambiguous. Whatever the Iad were, they brought pain: relentless, unendurable. A holocaust in which every property of death would be explored and celebrated but the virtue of cessation, which would be postponed until the Cosm was a single human sob for release. Somewhere he'd known a hint of this before, in a little corner of Chicago. Perhaps his mind was doing him service, refusing to remember where.

The waves were a yard ahead, rising in slow ares and booming as they broke.

"This is it," he said to Jo-Beth.

Her only response—one he was mightily grateful for—was to tighten her hold on his hand, and together they stepped back into the transforming sea.

FOUR

The door of the Nguyen house was answered to Grillo, not by Ellen, but by her son.

"Is your mom in?" he asked.

The boy still looked far from well, though he was no longer dressed for bed, but in grubby jeans and a grubbier T-shirt.

"I thought you'd gone away," he said to Grillo.

"Why?"

"Everybody else has."

"That's right."

"You want to come in?"

"I'd like to see your mom."

"She's busy," Philip said, but opened the door anyway. The house was even more of a shambles than it had been before, the remains of several *ad hoc* meals spread around. The creations of a child gourmet, Grillo guessed: hot dogs and ice cream.

"Where *is* your mom?" Grillo asked Philip.

He pointed in the direction of the bedroom, picked up a plate of half-devoured food, and wandered away.

"Wait," Grillo said. "Is she ill?"

"Nope," said the boy. He looked as though he hadn't slept a full eight hours in weeks, Grillo thought. "She doesn't come out any more," he went on. "Except at night."

He waited for Grillo to answer with a nod, then headed to his room, having supplied all the information he felt obliged to offer. Grillo heard the boy's door close, leaving him to ponder the problem alone. Recent events hadn't given him much time for erotic day-dreams, but the hours he'd spent here, in the very room where Ellen had holed herself up, exercised a strong hold on his mind and groin. Despite the hour of the morning, his general fatigue, and the despera-tion of circumstances in the Grove, a part of him wanted to conclude the business left unfinished last time: to make proper love to Ellen just once before he took the trip underground.

He crossed to Ellen's door, and knocked on it. The only sound from inside was a moan.

"It's me," he said. "Grillo. Can I come in?"

Without waiting for a reply he turned the handle. The door was not locked—it opened half an inch—but something prevented it from opening further. He pushed a little harder, and harder still. A chair, wedged under the handle on the far side, slid noisily to the floor. Grillo opened the door.

At first he thought she was alone in the room. Sick, and alone. She lay on an unmade bed in her dressing gown, which was untied, and spread open. Beneath, she was naked. Only very slowly did she turn her face in his direction, and when she did—her eyes gleaming in the stale murk—it took her several seconds to rouse any reply to his appearance.

"Is it really you?" she said.

"Of course. Yes. Who else—?"

She sat up a little way on the bed, and pulled the bottom of the gown across her body. She hadn't shaved since he'd been here, he saw. Indeed he doubted she had been out of the room very much. It smelled of prolonged occupation.

"You shouldn't . . . see," she said.

"I've seen you naked before," he murmured. "I wanted to see again."

"I don't mean *me*," she replied.

He didn't understand her remark until her eyes fell away from him and went to the furthest corner of the room. His gaze went with hers. At their destination, deep in the shadows, was a chair. In the chair was what he'd taken, on entering the room, to be a heap of clothes. It was not. The paleness wasn't linen but bare skin, the folds those of a man sitting naked in the chair, his body bent almost double, so that his forehead rested on his clasped hands. They were tied together at the wrists. The cord that bound them went on down to his ankles, which it also bound together.

"This," Ellen said softly, "is Buddy."

At the sound of his name the man raised his head. Grillo hadn't seen more than the last remnants of Fletcher's army, but it had been enough to recognize the look they'd had when their half-life began to run out. He saw that look now. This was not the real Buddy Vance, but a figment of Ellen's imagination, something her desires had summoned and shaped. The face was still very much intact: perhaps she'd imagined that with more precision than the rest of his anatomy. It was deeply lined—almost plowed—but undeniably charismatic. When he sat completely upright the second most detailed part of him came into view. Tesla's gossip had, as ever, been reliable. The hallucigenia was hung like a donkey. Grillo stared, only to be shaken from his envy when the man spoke.

"Who are you to come in here?" he said.

The fact that this artifact had sufficient self-will to speak shocked him.

"Hush," Ellen told him.

The man looked across at her, struggling against his bonds.

"He wanted to leave last night," she told Grillo. "I don't know why." Grillo did, but said nothing.

"I wouldn't let him, of course. He likes to be kept this way. We used to play this game a lot."

"Who is this?" Vance said.

"Grillo," Ellen replied. "I told you about Grillo." She pulled herself up on the bed, until her back was against the wall, her arms resting on her raised knees. She was presenting her cunt to Vance's gaze. He ogled it, gratefully, while she continued to speak. "I told you about Grillo," she said. "We made love, didn't we, Grillo?"

"Why?" Vance said. "Why are you punishing me?"

"Tell him, Grillo," Ellen said. "He wants to know."

"Yes," Vance said, his tone suddenly tentative. "Tell me. Please tell me."

Grillo didn't know whether to throw up or laugh. He thought the last scene he'd played out in this room had been perverse enough, but this was something else again. A dream of a dead man in bondage, begging to be castigated with a report of sex with his mistress.

"Tell him," Ellen said again.

The strange undertow in her demand gave Grillo voice.

"This isn't the real Vance," he said, taking pleasure in the idea of stripping her of this dream. But she was there ahead of him.

"I know that," she said, letting her head loll as she regarded her prisoner. "He's out of my mind." She kept staring at him. "And so am I."

"No," Grillo said.

"He's dead," she replied softly. "He's dead but he's still here. I know he isn't real but he's here. So I must be mad."

"No, Ellen . . . this is just because of what happened at the Mall. You remember? The burning man? You're not the only one."

She nodded, her eyes half closing.

"Philip . . ." she said.

"What about him?"

"He had dreams too."

Grillo thought of the boy's face again. The pinched look; the loss in his eyes.

"So if you know this . . . *man* isn't real, why the games?" he said.

She let her eyes close completely.

"I don't know . . ." she began, ". . . what's real or not any more." *There* was a sentiment that struck a chord, Grillo thought. "When he appeared I knew he wasn't here the way he *used* to be here. But maybe that doesn't matter."

Grillo listened, not wanting to break Ellen's train of thought. He'd seen so much that confounded him of late—miracles and mysteries—

and in his ambition to be a witness to these sights he'd held himself at
a distance. Paradoxically, that made the telling of the story a problem.
And it was *his* problem too. He was eternally the observer, keeping
feelings at bay for fear they touched him too deeply and so drowned
out his hard-earned disinterestedness. Was that why what had happened on this bed held such sway over his imagination? To be disconnected from the essential act; become a function of somebody else's
desire, somebody else's heat and intention? Did he envy that more
than Buddy Vance's twelve inches?

"He was a great lover, Grillo," Ellen was saying. "Especially when
he's burning up, because somebody else is where he wants to be.
Rochelle didn't like to play that game."

"Didn't see the joke," Vance said, his eyes still on what was out of
sight to Grillo. "She never—"

"My God!" Grillo said, suddenly realizing. "He was *here*, wasn't he?
He was here when you and I . . ." The thought took the words away.
All he could manage was ". . . outside the door."

"I didn't know at the time," Ellen said softly. "It wasn't planned that
way."

"Christ!" Grillo said. "It was all a performance for him. You set me
up. You set me up to get your fantasy heated up."

"Maybe . . . I had a suspicion," she conceded. "Why are you so
angry?"

"Isn't it obvious?"

"No, it isn't," she said, her tone all reason. "You don't love me. You
don't even know me, or you wouldn't be so shocked. You just wanted
something from me, and you got it."

Her account was accurate; and hurt. It made Grillo mean.

"You know this *thing's* not here forever," he said, jabbing his thumb
at Ellen's prisoner; or more correctly, at the truncheon.

"I know," she said, her tone betraying some little sadness at this fact.
"But none of us *are*, right? Even you."

Grillo stared at her, willing her to look around at him; see his pain.
But she only had eyes for the fabrication. He gave up on the possibility, and delivered the message he'd come here with.

"I advise you to leave the Grove," he said. "Take Philip and leave."

"Why's that?" she said.

"Just trust me. There's a good chance the Grove won't even be standing tomorrow."

Now she deigned to look around at him.

"I understand," she said. "Close the door, will you, when you leave?"

"Grillo." It was Tesla who opened the door to Hotchkiss's house. "You meet some damn weird people."

He'd never thought of Hotchkiss as weird. A man in mourning, yes. An occasional drunkard; who wasn't? But he wasn't prepared for the level of the man's obsession.

At the back of the house was a room given over entirely to the subject of the Grove and the ground it was built on. Geological maps covered the walls, along with photographs, taken over a period of years, and neatly dated, of cracks in the streets and sidewalks. Tacked up alongside were newspaper cuttings. Their single subject: earthquakes.

The obsessive himself sat unshaven in the midst of this information with a cup of coffee in his hand and a look of weary satisfaction on his face.

"Didn't I say?" were his first words to Grillo. "Didn't I tell you? The real story's beneath our feet. Always was."

"You want to do it?" Grillo asked him.

"What? The climb? Sure." He shrugged. "What the fuck? It'll kill us all, but what the fuck? The question is: do *you* want to do it?"

"Not much," Grillo said. "But I've got a vested interest. I want the whole story."

"Hotchkiss has got an extra angle you don't know about," Tesla said.

"What's that?"

"Any more coffee?" Hotchkiss asked Witt. "I need to sober up."

Witt dutifully went off to get refills.

"Never liked that man," Hotchkiss remarked.

"What was he, the town flasher?" Tesla said.

"Shit, no. He was Mr. Clean. Everything I used to despise about the Grove."

"He's coming back," Grillo said.

"So what?" Hotchkiss went on, as Witt stepped into the room. "He knows. Don't you, William?"

"Know what?" Witt said.

"What a shithead you were."

Witt took the insult without a flicker.

"Never much liked me, right?"

"Right."

"And I never much liked you," Witt replied. "For what it's worth."

Hotchkiss smiled. "Glad we got that sorted out," he said.

"I want to know about this *angle*," Grillo said.

"Simple really," Hotchkiss said. "I got a call in the middle of the night, from New York. A guy I hired when my wife left, to find her. Or try at least. His name's D'Amour. He specializes—I guess—in supernatural stuff."

"Why'd you hire him?"

"My wife got involved with some very peculiar people after our daughter's death. She never really accepted that Carolyn was gone from us. She tried contacting her through spiritualists. Eventually joined a spiritualist church. Then she ran off."

"Why look for her in New York?" Grillo asked.

"She was born there. It seemed the likeliest place for her to go."

"And did D'Amour find her?"

"No. But he dug up a whole bunch of stuff about the church she'd joined. I mean . . . this guy knew what he was doing."

"So why did he call you?"

"He's coming to that," said Tesla.

"I don't know who D'Amour's contacts are, but the call was a *warning.*"

"About what?"

"About what's happening here in the Grove."

"He knew?"

"Oh he knew all right."

"I think that maybe I should talk to him," Tesla said. "What time's it in New York?"

"Just after noon," said Witt.

"You two make whatever arrangements you need to make about the climb," she said. "Where's D'Amour's number?"

"Here," Hotchkiss said, passing a pad over to Tesla. She pulled off the top sheet, with the digits and the name (Harry M. D'Amour, Hotchkiss had written) scrawled on it, and left the men to their deliberations. There was a phone in the kitchen. She sat down, and dialled the eleven numbers. It rang at the other end. An answering machine picked up.

"There's nobody here to take your call at the moment. Please leave a message after the beep."

She started to do so. "This is a friend of Jim Hotchkiss, in Palomo Grove. My name's—"

A voice broke into her message.

"Hotchkiss has friends?" it said.

"Is this Harry D'Amour?"

"Yeah. Who's this?"

"Tesla Bombeck. And yeah, he *does* have friends."

"Every day you learn something. What can I do for you?"

"I'm calling from Palomo Grove. Hotchkiss says you know what's going on here."

"I've got some idea, yeah."

"How?"

"I've got friends," D'Amour said. "People plugged in. They've been saying for months something was going to break out on the West Coast, so nobody's that surprised. Saying a lot of prayers, but not surprised. What about you? Are you one of the few?"

"You mean psychic? No."

"So what have you got to do with all this?"

"It's a long story."

"So cut to the chase," said D'Amour. "That's a movie expression."

"I know," Tesla said. "I work in movies."

"Oh yeah. What as?"

"I write them."

"You written anything I'd know? I see a lot of movies. Keeps my mind off my work."

"Maybe we'll meet sometime," Tesla said. "Talk about movies. Meanwhile, I need your take on a few things."

"Like what?"

"Well, for one: have you ever heard of the *Iad Uroboros?*"

There was a long, long-distance silence.

"D'Amour? Are you still there? *D'Amour?*"

"Harry," he said.

"Harry. So . . . have you heard of them or not?"

"As it happens, yes."

"Who from?"

"Does it matter?"

"As it happens, yes," Tesla returned. "There's sources and sources. You know that. People you trust and those you don't."

"I work with a woman called Norma Paine," D'Amour said. "She's one of the people I was talking about before. She's plugged in."

"What does she know about the Iad?"

"First," D'Amour said. "Around dawn something happened on the East Coast, in dreamland. Do you know why?"

"I've got a good idea."

"Norma keeps talking about a place called Oddity."

"Quiddity," Tesla corrected him.

"So you *do* know."

"No need for the trick questions. Yes, I know. And I need to hear what she has to say about the Iad."

"That they're the things about to break out. She's not sure where. She gets mixed messages."

"Do they have any weaknesses?" Tesla said.

"Not from what I hear."

"Just how much do you know about them? I mean, what will an Iad invasion be like? Are they going to bring an army through from Quiddity? Are we going to see machines, bombs, *what?* Shouldn't somebody be trying to tell the Pentagon?"

"The Pentagon already knows," D'Amour said.

"It does?"

"We're not the only people who've heard of the Iad, lady. People all over the world have got images of it built into their culture. They're the *enemy.*"

"You mean like the Devil? Is that what's coming through? Satan?"

"I doubt it. I think we Christians have always been a little naive," D'Amour said. "I've met demons, and they never look the way you think they're going to look."

"Are you kidding me? Demons? In the flesh? In New York?"

"Listen, it doesn't sound any more sane to me than it does to you, lady—"

"My name's Tesla."

"Every time I finish one of these damn investigations I end up thinking: maybe that didn't happen. Till the next time. Then it's the same damn-fool process. You deny the possibility till it tries to bite off your face."

Tesla thought of the sights she'd seen in the last few days: the terata, Fletcher's death, the Loop, and Kissoon in the Loop; the Lix, seething on her own bed; finally, the Vance house, and the schism it contained. She couldn't deny any of that. She'd seen those sights, in hard focus. Almost been killed by them. D'Amour's talk of demons came as a shock only because the vocabulary was so archaic. She didn't believe in the Devil or Hell. The idea of demons in New York was therefore fundamentally absurd. But suppose what he called *demons* were the products of corrupt men of power like Kissoon? Things like the Lix, made of shit, semen and babies' hearts? She'd believe in them *then,* wouldn't she?

"So," she said. "If *you* know, and the Pentagon knows, why's there nobody here in the Grove now, to stop the lad appearing? We're holding the fort with four guns, D'Amour—"

"Nobody knew where the breakout would happen. I'm sure there's a file on the Grove somewhere, as a place where things weren't quite *natural.* But that's a long, long list."

"So we can expect help soon?"

"I'd guess so. But in my experience it usually comes too late."

"What about you?"

"What about me?"

"Any chance of help?"

"I've got problems here," D'Amour said. "There's all hell breaking loose. There've been a hundred and fifty cases of double suicides in Manhattan alone in the last eight hours."

"Lovers?"

"Lovers. Sleeping together for the first time. Dreaming of the Ephemeris, and getting a nightmare instead."

"*Jesus.*"

"Maybe they did the right thing," D'Amour said. "At least they're out of it."

"What's that supposed to mean?"

"I think what those poor bastards saw for themselves we all *guess*, right?"

She remembered the lurching pain she'd felt as she'd come off the freeway the night before. The world tipping towards a maw.

"Yeah," she said. "We guess it."

"We're going to see a lot of folks responding to that in the next few days. Our minds are very finely balanced. Doesn't take much to push them over the edge. I'm in a city full of people ready to fall. I have to be here."

"And if the cavalry doesn't turn up?" Tesla said.

"Then somebody giving the orders in the Pentagon is a disbeliever—and there's plenty of those—or he's working for the Iad."

"They've got agents?"

"Oh yes. Not many, but enough. People have been *worshipping* the Iad, by other names. For them this is the Second Coming."

"There was a first?"

"That's another story, but yes, apparently there was."

"When?"

"There's no reliable accounts, if that's what you're asking. Nobody knows what the Iad look like. I think we should just pray they're the size of mice."

"I don't pray," Tesla replied.

"You should," D'Amour replied. "Now that you know how much is out there besides us, it makes sense. Look, I've got to go. I wish I could be more use."

"I wish you could."

"But the way I hear it, you're not completely alone."

"I've got Hotchkiss, and a couple of—"

"No. I mean, Norma says there's a savior out there."

Tesla kept her laughter to herself.

"I don't see any savior," she replied. "What should I be looking for?"

"She's not sure. Sometimes she says it's a man, sometimes a woman. Sometimes not even human."

"Well that makes for easy identification."

"Whoever it is, he, she or it may just swing the balance."

"And if they don't?"

"Move out of California. Quick."

Now she did laugh, out loud. "Thanks a bunch," she said.

"Stay happy," D'Amour replied. "As my father used to say, you shouldn't have joined if you couldn't take a joke."

"Joined what?"

"The race," D'Amour said, and put down the phone. The line buzzed. She listened to the noise, and distant conversations laced through it. Grillo appeared at the door.

"This is looking more and more like a suicide trip," he announced. "We don't have the proper equipment, and we don't have any map of the system we're going into."

"Why not?"

"They don't exist. Apparently the whole town's built on ground which keeps shifting."

"Do you have any alternatives?" Tesla said. "The Jaff's the only man—" She stopped for a moment.

"What?" Grillo said.

"I don't suppose he's really a man, is he?" she said.

"I don't follow."

"D'Amour said there was a savior in the vicinity. Someone not human. That has to be the Jaff, right? Nobody else fits the description."

"I don't see him as much of a savior," Grillo said.

"Then we'll have to persuade him," came the answer. "If it crucifies him."

FIVE

The police had arrived in the Grove by the time Tesla, Witt, Hotchkiss, and Grillo left the house to start the descent. Lights were flashing at the top of the Hill; and ambulance sirens wailing. Despite all this din and activity there was no sign of any of the town's occupants, though presumably some of them were still in residence. They were either holed up with their deteriorating dreams, as Ellen Nguyen had been, or locked away, mourning their passing. The Grove was effectively a ghost-town. When the siren wails wound down there was a hush through the four villages more profound than any midnight. The sun beat down on empty sidewalks, empty yards, empty driveways. There were no children playing on the swings; no sound of televisions, radios, lawn-mowers, food-mixers, air conditioners. The lights still flipped colors at the intersections, but—excepting patrolcars and ambulances, whose drivers ignored them anyway—nobody was on the roads. Even the packs of dogs they'd seen in the gloom before dawn had gone about business that didn't bring them into the open. The sight of the brilliant sun, shining upon the empty town, had spooked even them.

Hotchkiss had made a list of items they were going to need if they were to have a hope of making the proposed descent: ropes, torches and a few articles of clothing. So the Mall was first stop on the journey. Of the quartet it was William who was most distressed by the place when they got there. Every day of his working life he'd seen the Mall bustling, from early morning to early evening. Now there was nobody. The new glass in the store-fronts that had been damaged by Fletcher gleamed, the products stacked in the windows beckoned, but there were neither buyers nor sellers. The doors were all locked; the stores silent.

There was one exception: the pet store. Unlike every other business in the Mall it was open for business as usual, its door wide, its products yapping, squawking and making a general hullabaloo. While Hotchkiss and Grillo went to pillage their way through the shopping list, Witt took Tesla into the pet store. Ted Elizando was at work refilling the drip-feed water bottles along the rows of kittens' cages. He didn't look surprised to see customers. He didn't express anything in fact. Not even recognition of William, though from their first exchange Tesla gathered they knew each other.

"All alone this morning, Ted?" Witt said.

The man nodded. He hadn't shaved in two or three days; nor showered. "I . . . didn't want to get up, really . . . but I had to. For the animals."

"Of course."

"They'd die if I didn't look after them," Ted went on, with the slow, studied speech of one who was trying hard to keep his thoughts coherent. As he spoke he opened up the cage beside him and brought one of the kittens out from a nest of newspaper strips. It lay along his arm, head in the crook. He stroked it. The animal enjoyed the attention, arching its back to meet each slow motion of his hand.

"I don't think there's anybody left in town to buy them," William said.

Ted stared at the kitten.

"What am I going to do?" he asked softly. "I can't feed them forever, can I?" His voice dropped in volume with every word, until he was barely whispering. "What's happened to everyone?" he said. "Where did they go? Where did everyone go?"

"Away, Ted," William said. "Out of town. And I don't think they're going to be coming back."

"You think I should go too?" Ted said.

"I think maybe you should," William replied.

The man looked devastated.

"What will the animals do?" he said.

For the first time—witnessing Ted Elizando's misery—Tesla was struck by the scale of the Grove's tragedy. When she'd first wandered through its streets, message-carrying for Grillo, she'd plotted its fictional overthrow. The bomb-in-asuitcase scenario, with apathetic Grovers throwing the prophet out just as the big bang came. That narrative had not been wide of the mark. The explosion had been slow and subtle rather than quick and hard, but it had come nevertheless. It had cleared the streets, leaving only a few—like Ted—to wander in the ruins, picking up whatever shreds of furry life remained. Her scenario had been a sort of imagined revenge upon the cosy, smug existence of the town. But in retrospect she'd been as smug as the Grove, as certain of her moral superiority as it had been of its invulnerability. There was real pain here. Real loss. The people who'd lived in the Grove, and fled it, had not been cardboard cut-outs. They'd had lives and loves, families, pets; they'd made their homes here thinking they'd found a place in the sun where they'd be safe. She had no right to judge them.

She couldn't bear to go on looking at Ted, who stroked the kitten with such tenderness, as though it was all he had of sanity. She left Witt to talk with him and went out into the brightness of the lot, walking around the corner of the block to see if she could locate Coney Eye among the trees. She studied the top of the Hill until she made out the row of shaggy palms that led up to the driveway. Just visible between them was the brightly colored facade of Buddy Vance's dream house. It was small comfort, but at least the fabric of the building was still standing. She'd feared the hole inside would simply keep getting bigger, unknitting reality until it consumed the house. She dared not hope it had simply closed up—her gut knew that not to be the case. But as long as it had stabilized that was something. If they could move quickly, and locate the Jaff, perhaps some way of undoing the damage he'd done could be found.

"See anything?" Grillo asked her. He was coming around the corner with Hotchkiss, both weighed down with booty: loops of rope, torches, batteries, a selection of sweaters.

"It'll be cold down there," Hotchkiss explained when she queried them. "Damn cold. And probably wet."

"We get a choice," Grillo said with forced good humor. "Drown, freeze or fall."

"I like options," she said, wondering if dying a second time would be as distasteful as the first. *Don't even think about it,* she told herself. *There's no second resurrection for you.*

"We're ready," Hotchkiss said. "Or as ready as we'll ever be. Where's Witt?"

"He's at the pet store," she told him. "I'll go get him."

She headed back around the corner to find that Witt had left the store and was gazing through another window.

"Seen something?" she asked.

"These are my offices," he said. "Or were. I used to work *there*." He pointed a finger to the glass. "At the desk with the plant."

"Dead plant," she observed.

"It's all dead," Witt said, with a kind of vehemence.

"Don't be so defeatist," she told him, and hurried him back to the car, which Hotchkiss and Grillo had already finished loading up with equipment.

As they drove Hotchkiss laid his concerns out, plain and simple:

"I already told Grillo," he said, "that this is a completely suicidal thing for us all to be doing. Especially you," he said, catching Tesla's eye in the mirror. He didn't expand on that observation, but passed straight on to practicalities. "We haven't got any of the necessary equipment. The stuff we found in the stores is for domestic use; it won't save our lives in a crisis. And we're untrained. All of us. I've made a few climbs myself, but a long time ago. I'm really just a theoretician. And this is no easy system. There's good reason why Vance's corpse wasn't brought up. Men died down there—"

"That wasn't because of the caves," Tesla said. "It was the Jaff."

"But they didn't go back in," Hotchkiss pointed out. "God knows, nobody wanted to leave a man down there without a decent burial, but enough was enough."

"You were ready to take me down," Grillo reminded him. "Just a few days ago."

"That was you and me," Hotchkiss said.

"Meaning that you didn't have a woman along?" Tesla said. "Well let's be real clear about this. Going underground when it looks like half the world's caving in isn't my idea of fun, but I'm as good as any man at anything that doesn't need a dick. I'm no more of a liability than Grillo. Sorry, Grillo, but it's true. We'll get down there, safely. The problem isn't the caves, it's what's hiding in them. And I've got a better chance with the Jaff than any of you. I've met Kissoon; I've heard the same lies the Jaff was told. I've got half a clue as to why he became what he became. If we're to have any chance of persuading him to help us, I've got to do the persuading."

There was no response from Hotchkiss. He kept his silence, at least until they'd parked the car and were unloading the gear. Only then did he take up his instructions again. This time there were no overt references to Tesla.

"I propose to take the lead," he said. "With Witt following. You next, Miss Bombeck. Grillo can bring up the rear."

String o'pearls, Tesla thought, and me in the middle, presumably because Hotchkiss lacked faith in her muscle power. She didn't argue. He was leading this expedition, which she didn't doubt was every bit as foolhardy as he'd stated, and attempting to undermine his authority when they were about to make the descent was lousy politics.

"We've got torches," he went on, "two each. One for us to pocket, the other to tie around our necks. We couldn't find much in the way of protective headgear; we'll just have to make do with knitted hats. We've got gloves, some boots, two sweaters and two pairs of socks for everyone. Let's get to it."

They carried the gear through the trees to the clearing, and there kitted up. The woods were as silent now as they'd been in the early morning. The sun that beat so strongly on their backs, bringing them out into sweat as soon as they put on the extra layers of clothing, could not coax a single bird to song. Once dressed, they roped themselves together, about ten feet apart. Hotchkiss the theoretician knew his knots, and made play with the fact, tying them, particularly Tesla's, with a theatrical casualness. Grillo was the last to be added to the chain. He was sweating more heavily than anyone else, and the veins at his temples were almost as fat as the rope round his waist.

"Are you OK?" Tesla asked him as Hotchkiss sat on the edge of the fissure and swung his feet into the hole.

"I'm fine," Grillo replied.

"Never a great liar," she replied.

Hotchkiss had one last instruction.

"When we're down there," he said, "let's keep the chatter to the minimum, huh? We've got to preserve our energy. Remember, getting down's only half the trip."

"It's always faster on the way home," Tesla said.

Hotchkiss gave her a disparaging look, and began the descent.

The first few feet were relatively easy, but the privations began no more than ten feet down, when, maneuvering themselves through a space that only just allowed access, the sunlight disappeared so suddenly and so totally it was as if it had never existed. Their torches were feeble substitutes.

"We'll wait here a moment," Hotchkiss called back up. "Let's get our eyes accustomed to the dark."

Tesla could hear Grillo breathing hard behind her; almost panting.

"Grillo," she murmured.

"I'm OK. I'm OK."

It was easily said, but it was very far from the way he felt. The symptoms were familiar from previous attacks: in elevators stuck between floors, or a crowded subway. His heart was working up a sweat in his chest, and it felt like a wire was tightening around his throat. But these were just externalizations. The real fear was of a panic that would rise to such an unbearable pitch that his sanity would simply switch off like a lamp, and darkness become a continuum, outside and in. He had a regime of remedies—pills, deep breathing; in extremis, prayer—none of which were the least use to him now. All he could do was endure. He said the word to himself. Tesla heard.

"Did you say enjoy?" she said. "Some pleasure trip."

"Keep it quiet back there," Hotchkiss hollered from the front. "We're going to move off again."

They continued, in a silence broken only by grunts, and a single call from Hotchkiss warning that progress ahead was going to get steeper. What had been a zig-zag descent, squeezing between rocks thrown up by the rush of water when the Nunciates had escaped, now became a straight climb down a shaft whose bottom was untouched by their torchbeams. It was deadly cold, and they were glad of the layers of clothing Hotchkiss had demanded they wear, though their bulk impeded easy movement. The rock beneath their gloves was wet in places, and twice sprays of water, hitting a shelf on the opposite side of the shaft, caught them.

The sum of discomforts left Tesla wondering what bizarre imperative drove men (surely they were all men: women wouldn't be so perverse) to pursue this as recreation. Was it, as Hotchkiss had said when she and Witt had first got to his house, that all the great secrets were *underground?* If so, she was keeping good company. Three men who could not have had stronger reasons for wanting to see those secrets and maybe haul one of them up into the light. Grillo, with his passion to tell the whole story to the world. Hotchkiss, still haunted by the memory of his daughter, who'd died because of events here. And Witt, who'd known the Grove to its length and breadth, but never to its depth, and was getting here a fundamental vision of the town he'd loved like a wife. There was another call from Hotchkiss, this one more welcome.

"There's a ledge down here," he said. "We can rest up a while." One by one they climbed down to join him. The ledge was wet, and narrow, only just affording space to accommodate them all. They perched there in silence. Grillo pulled a pack of cigarettes from his back pocket, and lit up.

"Thought you'd given up," Tesla remarked.

"So did I," he said. He passed the cigarette over to her. She took a lungful, savoring it, then passed it back to Grillo.

"Do we have any idea of how far down we have to go?" Witt asked.

Hotchkiss shook his head.

"But there is a bottom down there somewhere."

"Can't even say that."

Witt went down on his haunches and scrabbled around on the ledge.

"What are you looking for?" Tesla said.

He stood up again with the answer. A piece of rock the size of a tennis ball, which he tossed out into the darkness. There was silence for several seconds, then the sound of it striking the rock face below, shattering, and its pieces rattling away in all directions. It took a long time for the echoes to die, making it near impossible to tell anything about the distance below them.

"Good try," Grillo said. "It works in the movies."

"Wait up," Tesla said, "I hear water."

In the silence that followed her claim was verified. Water was running close by.

"Is that below us, or behind one of those walls?" Witt said. "I can't make it out."

"Could be both," Hotchkiss said. "There's two things that can stop us getting all the way down. A simple blockage, and water. If the system becomes flooded there's no way we can go on."

"Let's not get pessimistic," Tesla said. "Let's just go on."

"We already seem to have been here hours," Witt remarked.

"Time's different down here," Hotchkiss said. "We don't have the usual signals. Sun passing overhead."

"I don't tell the time by the sun."

"Your body does."

Grillo started to light up his second cigarette, but Hotchkiss said: "No time," and started to ease himself over the lip of the shelf. The drop was by no means straight down. Had it been, their lack of experience and equipment would have thrown them down the shaft after a few feet of the descent. But it was steep enough, and got steadily steeper, some stretches offering cracks and handholds that made for relatively easy progress, other stretches sheer, slippery and treacherous. These they descended almost inch by inch, Hotchkiss signalling to Witt where the best opportunities lay, Witt passing the message on to Tesla, and so on to Grillo. They kept such comments terse: breath and concentration were now at a premium.

They were just reaching the end of one such stretch when Hotchkiss called a halt.

"What is it?" Tesla said, looking down at him. The answer was one grim word.

"Vance," he said.

She heard Witt say *oh Jesus* in the darkness.

"We're at the bottom then," Grillo said.

"No," came the reply, "just another ledge."

"Shit."

"Is there a way around it?" Tesla called.

"Give me time," Hotchkiss snapped back, his voice betraying the shock he felt.

There was what seemed to be several minutes (but was probably less than one) during which they clung to whatever handhold they had while Hotchkiss surveyed the routes available to them. With one selected, he called them to begin the descent afresh.

The lack of light the torches offered had been galling, but now they offered too much. As the other three climbed past the ledge it was impossible not to look its way. There, sprawled on the glistening rock, was a bundle of dead meat. The man's head had cracked on the rock like a dropped egg. His limbs were bent back on themselves every which way, the bones surely broken from joint to joint. One hand was laid on the nape of his neck, palm up. The other was just in front of his face, its fingers a little open, as though he was playing hide and seek.

The sight was a reminder, if one were needed, of what a single slip on the descent might result in. They proceeded even more cautiously thereafter.

The sound of rushing water had diminished for a while but now it began afresh. This time it wasn't muted by the rock wall. It was clearly below them. They continued down towards it, taking time every ten feet or so for Hotchkiss to survey the darkness below them. He had nothing to report until the fourth such halt, when he called back over the din of water that there was good news and bad. The good, that the shaft ended here. The bad, that it was flooded.

"Is there no solid ground down there?" Tesla wanted to know.

"Not much," Hotchkiss replied. "And none of it looks reliable."

"We can't just climb straight back up," Tesla returned.

"No?" came the reply.

"No," she insisted. "We've come all this way."

"He's not down here," Hotchkiss yelled back.

"I want to see that for myself."

He didn't reply, though she pictured him cursing her in the darkness. After a few moments, however, he began the descent again. The din of the water became so loud any further conversation was out of the question, until they were finally gathered at the bottom, and could stand close to each other.

Hotchkiss had reported right. The small platform at the bottom of the shaft was no more than a collection of detritus, which the torrent was rapidly carrying away.

"This is recent," Hotchkiss said. As if to lend force to the observation the wall through which the flood broke crumbled a little more as he spoke, the force of water bearing a sizeable portion of it off into the roaring darkness. The water beat itself against the bank upon which they were standing with renewed gusto.

"If we're not out of here quick," yelled Witt over the din of the flood, "we're going to get washed away."

"I think we should begin back up," Hotchkiss agreed. "We've got a long climb ahead of us. We're all cold and tired."

"Wait!" Tesla protested.

"He's not here!" replied Witt.

"I don't believe that."

"What do you propose, Miss Bombeck?" Hotchkiss yelled.

"Well we can start by giving the *Bombeck* shit a rest, OK? Isn't it possible this stream's going to trickle out eventually?"

"Maybe. After a few hours. Meanwhile we'll freeze to death while we wait. And even if it stops—"

"Yes?"

"Even if it stops we haven't got any clue which direction the Jaff went." Hotchkiss played his torch-beam around the shaft. It was only just strong enough to strike the four walls, but it was clear there were several tunnels leading off from this spot. "Want to make a guess?" Hotchkiss hollered.

The prospect of failure rose up and took a good long look at Tesla. She ignored it as best she could, but it was tough. She'd been too hopeful, thinking the Jaff would be simply sitting—like a frog in a well—waiting for them. He could have taken any one of the tunnels on the other side of the torrent. Some were probably cul-de-sacs; others led off to dry caverns. But even if they could walk on water (and she was out of practice) which would they choose? She put on her torch in order to scan the tunnels herself, but her fingers were numb with cold, and as she fumbled to turn the torch on it slid from her grasp, hitting the rock and rolling towards the water. She reached down to keep from losing it, and almost lost her balance with it, her foot—perched on the eroding edge of the platform—sliding across the wet rock. Grillo reached for her, snatching hold of her belt, and pulling her upright. The torch went into the water. She watched it go, then turned to thank him, but the look of alarm on his face diverted her eyes to the ground beneath her and her thanks to a shout of alarm. Even that never came, as the flood had its way with their little beach of rocks, finding a keystone that, once washed away, brought the capitulation of the rest.

She saw Hotchkiss fling himself at the shaft wall to find a purchase before the water took them. But he wasn't quick enough. The ground went from under him, under them all, and they were pitched into the brutally cold water. It was as violent as it was cold, seizing them in an instant and carrying them away, throwing them back and forth in a dark blur of hard water and harder rock.

Tesla managed to grab hold of somebody's arm in the torrent, Grillo's she thought. She managed to hold on for fully two seconds— no mean achievement—then a curve in the passage threw the torrent into fresh fits, and they were pulled apart. There was a passage of total confusion, the water a frenzy, then—suddenly—it became still, as it broke out into a wide, shallow place, its speed slowing sufficiently for Tesla to lay her arms out to either side of her and steady herself. There was no light whatsoever, but she felt the weight of the other bodies on the rope, and heard Grillo gasping behind her.

"Still alive?" she said.

"Just."

"Witt? Hotchkiss? You there?"

There was a moan from Witt, and from Hotchkiss an answering holler.

"I dreamed this . . ." she heard Witt say. "I dreamed I swam."

She didn't want to think about what it might mean for them all if Witt had dreamed of swimming—of Quiddity—but the thought was there anyhow. Three times to the dreamsea: at birth, in love, and on death's door.

"I dreamed this . . ." he said again, more softly now.

Before she could hush his prophecies she realized the speed of the water had picked up again, and there was a growing roar from the darkness ahead.

"Oh shit," she said.

"What?" Grillo yelled.

The water was really moving now, the din louder and louder.

"Waterfall," she said.

There was a tug on the rope, and a yell from Hotchkiss, not of warning but of horror. She had time to think *pretend it's Disneyland* then the tug became a hard pull and her black world tipped. The water encased her, a straitjacket of ice which pressed breath and consciousness out of her. When she came to Hotchkiss was hauling her face clear of the water. The cataract they'd ridden down was roaring beside them, its fury turning the water white. It didn't register that she could see, not until Grillo surfaced beside them, spluttering, and said:

"Light!"

"Where's Witt?" Hotchkiss gasped. *"Where's Witt?"*

They scanned the surface of the pool they'd been delivered into. There was no sign of him. There was, however, solid ground. They swam for it as best they could; ragged, desperate strokes which brought them to dry rock. Hotchkiss was first out, and dragged her out after him. The rope between them had snapped somewhere on the ride. Her body was a numb, shuddering weight, and she could barely move it.

"Anything broken?" Hotchkiss said.

"I don't know," she said.

"We're done for now," Grillo murmured. "Jesus, we're in the bowels of the fucking earth."

"There's light coming from somewhere," Tesla gasped. She mustered what scraps of muscle-power she had to raise her head from the rock and look for the source of the light. The motion told her things weren't well with her. There was a spasm in her neck, which ran down to her shoulder. She yelped.

"Hurt?" Hotchkiss said.

She sat up gingerly. "All over," she said. Pain was getting through numbness in a dozen places: head, neck, arms, belly. To judge by the way Hotchkiss moaned as he began to stand up, he had the same problem. Grillo was simply staring at the water that had claimed Witt, his teeth chattering.

"It's behind us," Hotchkiss said.

"What is?"

"The light. It's coming from behind us."

She turned, the aches in her side becoming short stabbing pains. She tried to keep her complaints to herself, but Hotchkiss caught her intake of breath.

"Can you walk?" he said.

"Can you?" she returned.

"Competition?" he said.

"Yeah."

She made a small sideways glance at him. There was blood coming from the region of his right ear, and he was nursing his left arm with his right.

"You look like shit," she said.

"So do you."

"Grillo? Are you coming?"

There was no reply; only chattering teeth.

"Grillo?" she said.

He had turned his eyes from the water and was looking up at the roof of the cavern.

"It's on top of us," she heard him murmur. "All that earth. On top of us."

"It's not going to fall," Tesla said. "We're going to get out."

"No we're not. We're fucking buried alive! We're buried alive!"

He was suddenly on his feet, and the chattering had become ringing sobs. "Get me out of here! Get me out of here!"

"Shut up, Grillo," Hotchkiss said, but Tesla knew no words were going to stop the panic running its course. She let him sob, and started towards the crack in the wall through which the light was coming.

It's the Jaff, she thought as she went. It can't be daylight, so it must be the Jaff. She'd planned what she was going to say to him, but the persuasions had been sluiced out of her head. All she could do was wing it. Confront the man and hope her tongue would do the rest.

Behind her, she heard Grillo's sobs stop, and Hotchkiss say:

"That's Witt."

She looked around. Witt's body had come to the surface of the pool, and was lying face down in the water, some way from the shore. She didn't stare, but turned back towards the crack and headed on, her pace painfully slow. She had a distinct sense of being *drawn* to the light, that sense stronger the closer she got, as though her cells, touched by the Nuncio, sensed the proximity of someone similarly touched. It gave her weary body the necessary momentum to cross to the crack. She leaned against the stone, and peered in. The cavern beyond was smaller than the one she was leaving. In the middle was what on first viewing she took to be a fire, but it was only a distant relation. The light it gave off was cold, and its flickering was far from steady. There was no sign of its maker.

She stepped inside, announcing her presence to be certain he didn't misread her approach and attack.

"Anyone here?" she said. "I want to speak with . . . with *Randolph Jaffe*."

She chose to call him by that name in the hope of appealing to the man he'd been rather than the Artist he'd aspired to being. It worked. From a fissure in the furthest corner of the chamber a voice as fatigued as her own emerged.

"Who are you?"

"Tesla Bombeck."

She started towards the fire, using it as an excuse to enter. "Don't mind do you?" she said, stripping off her sodden gloves and extending her palms to the joyless flames.

"There's no heat," Jaffe said. "It's not a real fire."

"So I see," she said. The fuel looked to be rotted matter of some kind. Terata. The smoky glow which she'd taken for flame was the last vestiges of their decay.

"Looks like we're on our own," she said.

"No," he said. "*I'm* on my own. You've brought people."

"Yes. I have. You know one of them. Nathan Grillo?"

The name brought Jaffe out of hiding.

Twice she'd seen insanity in his eyes. Once at the Mall, pointed out by Howie. The second time when he'd stumbled out of the Vance house, leaving the schism he'd opened roaring behind him. Now she saw it a third time, but intensified.

"Grillo is here?" he said.

"Yes."

"Why?"

"Why what?"

"Why are you here?"

"To find you," she explained. "We need . . . we need your help."

The lunatic eyes swivelled in Tesla's direction. There was, she thought, some vague other form hovering around him, like a shadow thrown through smoke. A head swollen to grotesque proportions. She tried not to think too hard about what it was, or what its appearance signified. There was only one issue here: getting this madman to unburden himself of his secrets. Best perhaps that she volunteered one of her own first.

"We've got something in common," she said. "Quite a few things in fact, but one in particular."

"The Nuncio," he said. "Fletcher sent you for it, and you couldn't resist it."

"That's true," she said, preferring to agree with him rather than argue and lose his attention. "But that's not the important thing."

"What is?"

"*Kissoon,*" she said.

His eyes flickered.

"*He* sent you," he said.

Shit, she thought, that's blown it.

"No," she said quickly. "Absolutely not."

"What does he want from me?"

"Nothing. I'm not his go-between. He got me into the Loop for the same reason he got you in, all those years ago. You remember that?"

"Oh yes," he said, his voice totally devoid of color. "Difficult to forget."

"But do you know why he wanted you in the Loop?"

"He needed an acolyte."

"No. He needed a *body.*"

"Oh yes. He wanted that too."

"He's a prisoner there, Jaffe. The only way he could ever get out was by stealing a body."

"Why are you telling me this?" he said. "Haven't we got better things to do, before the end?"

"The end?"

"Of the world," he said. He put his back against the wall and allowed gravity to take him down on to his haunches. "That's what's going to happen, isn't it?"

"What makes you think that?"

Jaffe raised his hands in front of his face. They hadn't healed at all. The flesh had been bitten off down to the bone in several places. Two fingers and the thumb of his right hand had gone entirely.

"I get glimpses," he said, "of things Tommy-Ray is seeing. There's something *coming* . . ."

"Can you see *what?*" she asked him, eager for any clue, however small, as to the Iad's nature. Did they come bearing baubles or bombs?

"No. Just a terrible night. An everlasting night. I don't want to see it."

"You have to look," Tesla said. "Isn't that what Artists are supposed to do? To look and keep looking, even when the thing you're looking at is too much to bear. You're an Artist, Randolph—"

"No. I'm not."

"You opened the schism didn't you?" she said. "I'm not saying I agree with your methods, I don't, but you did what nobody else *dared* do. Maybe could ever do."

"Kissoon planned it all this way," Jaffe said. "I see that now. He made me his acolyte even though I didn't know it. He used me."

"I don't think so," Tesla said. "I don't think even he could have plotted something so byzantine. How could he know you and Fletcher would discover the Nuncio? No. What happened to you wasn't planned . . . you were your own agent in this, not Kissoon's. The power's yours. And so's the responsibility."

She let her argument rest there for a little while, as much because she was exhausted as for any other reason. Jaffe didn't follow through. He just stared at the pseudofire, which would soon be guttering out, and then at his hands. It was only after a minute of this that he said:

"You came down here to tell me that?"

"Yes. Don't tell me I came on a fool's errand."

"What do you want me to do?"

"Help us."

"There's no help to be had."

"You opened the hole, you can close it."

"I'm not going near that house."

"I thought you wanted Quiddity," Tesla said. "I thought being there was your great ambition."

"I was wrong."

"You got all that way, just to discover you were *wrong?* What changed your mind?"

"You won't understand."

"Try me."

He looked back towards the fire. "That was the last of them," he said. "When the light goes, we're all in the dark."

"There must be other ways out of here."

"There are."

"Then we'll take one of them. But first . . . *first* . . . tell me why you changed your mind."

He took a lazy moment to contemplate his answer, or whether he was going to give it at all.

Then he said:

"When I first began looking for the Art, all the clues were about crossroads. Not all. But many. Yes, many. The ones that made any sense to me. And so I kept looking for a crossroads. I thought that was where I'd find the answer. Then Kissoon drew me into his Loop, and I thought, here he is, the last of the Shoal, in a hut in the middle of nowhere. No crossroads. I must have been wrong. And all that's happened since: at the Mission, in the Grove . . . none of it happened at a crossroads. I was being *literal,* you see. I've always been so damn literal. Physical. Actual. Fletcher thought of air and sky, and I thought of power and bone. He made dreams from people's heads, I made stuff from their guts and sweat. Always thinking the obvious. And all the time . . ." his voice was thickening with feeling; hatred in it, self-directed, ". . . all the time I didn't *see*. Until I used the Art, and realized what the crossroads were—"

"What?"

He put the less injured of his hands to his shirt, fumbling inside it. There was a medallion around his neck, on a fine chain. He pulled, hard. The chain broke, and he tossed the symbol over to Tesla. She knew before she caught it what it was going to be. She'd played this scene once before, with Kissoon. But that time she'd not been ready to understand what she understood now, holding the Shoal's sign in her hand.

"The crossroads," she said. "This is its symbol."

"I don't know what symbols are any longer," he replied. "It's all one."

"But this *stands* for something," she said, looking again at the forms inscribed on the arm of the cross.

"To *understand* it is to *have* it," Jaffe said. "At the moment of comprehension it's no longer a symbol."

"Then . . . make me understand," Tesla said. "Because I look at this and it's still just a cross. I mean, it's beautiful an' all, but it doesn't mean a whole lot. There's this guy in the center, looks like he's being crucified, 'cept there's no nails. And then all these creatures."

"Doesn't it make *any* sense?"

"Maybe if I wasn't so tired."

"Guess."

"I'm not in the mood for guessing games."

A sly look came over Jaffe's face. "You want me to come with you—help you stop whatever's coming through Quiddity—but you haven't got any grasp of what's going on. If you did have, you'd understand what you've got in your hand."

She realized what he was proposing before he said it.

"So if I can work it out, you'll come?"

"Yeah. Maybe."

"Give me a few minutes," she said, looking down at the Shoal symbol with fresh eyes.

"A few?" he said. "What's a few? *Five* maybe. Let's say *five*. My offer's good for five minutes."

She turned the medallion over in her hand, suddenly self-conscious.

"Don't stare at me," she said.

"I like to stare."

"You're distracting me."

"You don't have to stay," he replied.

She took him at his word, and got up, her legs unsteady, returning to the crack she'd entered through.

"Don't lose it," he said, his tone almost satiric. "It's the only one I've got."

Hotchkiss was a yard beyond the entrance.

"You heard?" she said to him.

He nodded. She opened her palm and let him look at the medallion. The sole light source, the decaying terata, was fitful, but her eyes

were well accustomed to it by now. She could read the expression of
befuddlement on Hotchkiss's face. There'd be no revelations from that
source.

She claimed the medallion from his fingers and looked over to
Grillo, who hadn't moved.

"He's fallen apart," Hotchkiss said. "Claustrophobia."

She went to him anyway. He wasn't staring at the ceiling any
longer, nor at the body in the water. His eyes were closed. His teeth
were chattering.

"Grillo."

He chattered on.

"*Grillo.* It's Tesla. I need your help."

He shook his head; a small, violent motion.

"I have to know what this means."

He didn't even open his eyes to find out what she was talking about.

"Thanks a bunch, Grillo," she said.

On your own, babe. No help to be had. Hotchkiss doesn't get it,
Grillo won't; and Witt's dead in the water. Her eyes went to the body,
momentarily. Face down, arms spread. Poor bastard. She'd not known
him at all, but he'd seemed decent enough.

She turned away, opened her palm, and looked at the medallion
again, her concentration completely fucked by the fact that the seconds were ticking by.

What did it mean?

The figure in the center was human. The forms that spread from it
were not. Were they familiars, maybe? Or the central figure's children? That made more sense. There was a creature between the
spread legs like a stylized ape; beneath that something reptilian;
beneath that—

Shit! They weren't children, they were *ancestors*. It was devolution.
Man at the center, ape below; lizard, fish and protoplasm (an eye, or a
single cell) below that. *The past is below us,* Hotchkiss had said once.
Maybe he'd been right.

Assuming that to be the correct solution, what did it imply about
the designs on the other three arms? Above the figure's head some-

thing seemed to be dancing, its head huge. Above that the same form, only simplified; and again above that, a simplification, which reached its conclusion as another eye (or single cell) which echoed the shape below. In the light of the first interpretation this wasn't so difficult to understand. Below were images of life leading up to man; above, surely, *beyond* man, the species elevated to a perfect spiritual state.

Two out of four.

How long did she have?

Don't think about the time, she told herself, just solve the problem.

Reading from right to left across the medallion, the sequence was by no means as easy as south to north. At the extreme left was another circle, with something like a cloud in it. Beside it, closer to the figure's outstretched arm, a square, divided into four; closer still what looked to be lightning; then a splash of some kind (blood from the hand?); then the hand itself. On the other side a series of even less comprehensible symbols. What might have been another spurt from the figure's left hand; then a wave, perhaps, or snakes (was she committing Jaffe's sin here? being too literal?); then what could only be described as a scrawl, as though some sign had been scratched out, and finally the fourth and final circle, which was a hole, bored in the medallion. From solid to insolid. From a circle with a cloud to an empty space. What the hell did it mean? Was it day and night? No. Known and unknown, maybe? That made better sense. *Hurry, Tesla, hurry.* So what was round, and cloudy, and *known?*

Round, and cloudy. The world. And known. *Yes.* The world; the *Cosm!* which implied that the empty space on the other arm, the *un*-known, was the Metacosm! Which left the figure in the middle: the crux of the whole design.

She started back towards the cave, where Jaffe was waiting for her, knowing there could only be seconds left.

"I've got it!" she shouted through to him, "I've got it!" It wasn't quite true, but the rest would have to be instinct.

The fire inside the cave was very low, but there was a horrible brightness in Jaffe's eyes.

"I know what it is," she said.

"You do?"

"It's evolution on one axis, from a single cell to Godhood."

She knew by the look on his face that she'd got that part right at least.

"*Go on,*" he said. "What's the other axis?"

"It's the Cosm and the Metacosm. It's what we know and what we don't know."

"*Very good,*" he said. "Very good. And in the middle?"

"Us. Human beings."

His smile spread. "*No,*" he said.

"No?"

"That's an old mistake, isn't it? It's not as simple as that."

"But it's a human being, right there!" she said.

"You still see the symbol."

"Shit. I hate this! You're so damn smug. Help me!"

"Time's up!"

"I'm close! I'm really close, aren't I?"

"You see how it is? You can't work it out. Even with a little help from your friends."

"I didn't get any help. Hotchkiss can't do it. Grillo's lost his mind. And Witt's—"

Witt's lying in the water, she thought. But didn't say that, because the image had suddenly struck her with revelatory force. He was lying sprawled in the water with his arms spread out and his hands open.

"My God," she said. "It's Quiddity. It's our dreams. It's not flesh and blood at the crossroads, it's the *mind.*"

Jaffe's smile disappeared, and the light in his eyes got brighter; a paradoxical brightness that didn't illuminate but took light from the rest of the chamber, into itself.

"It is, isn't it?" she said. "Quiddity's the center of everything. It's the *crossroads.*"

He didn't answer her. He didn't need to. She knew without the least doubt that she'd got it right. The figure was *floating,* in Quiddity, arms spread out as he, she, or it dreamed in the dream-sea. And somehow that dreaming was the place where everything originated: the first cause.

"No wonder," she said.

He spoke now as if from the grave.

"No wonder what?"

"No wonder you couldn't do it," she replied. "When you realized what you faced in Quiddity. No wonder."

"You may regret this knowledge," he said.

"I never regretted knowing anything in my life."

"You'll change your mind," he said. "I guarantee it."

She allowed him his sour grapes. But a deal was a deal, and she was ready to insist upon it.

"You said you'd come with us."

"I know I did."

"You will, won't you?"

"It's useless," he said.

"Don't try and get out of it. I know what's at stake here just as much as you do."

"And what do you propose we do about it?"

"We go back to the Vance house and we try and close the schism."

"How?"

"Maybe we have to take some advice from an expert."

"There are none."

"There's Kissoon," she said. "He owes us one. In fact he owes us several. But first, we have to get out of here."

Jaffe looked at her for a long time, as though he wasn't yet certain whether to acquiesce or not.

"If you don't do this," she said, "you'll end up here in the dark where you spent how long . . . twenty years? The Iad will break through and you'll be here, underground, knowing the planet's been taken. Maybe they'll never find you. You don't eat, do you? You're beyond eating. You can survive, perhaps a hundred years, a thousand years. But you'll be alone. Just you and the dark and certain knowledge of what you did. Does that sound tasty enough for you? Personally, I'd prefer to die trying to stop them getting through—"

"You're not very persuasive," he said. "I can see right through you. You're a talkative bitch, but the world's full of them. Think you're clever. You're not. You don't know the first thing about what's coming. But *me?* I can see, I've got that fucking son of mine's eyes. He's moving towards the Metacosm, and I can feel what's up ahead. Can't see it. Don't want to. But I feel it. And let me tell you, we don't have a fucking chance."

"Is this some last-ditch effort to stay put?"

"No. I'll come. Just to watch the look on your face when you fail, I'll come."

"Then let's do it," she said. "You know a way out of here?"

"I can find one."

"Good."

"But first—"

"Yes?"

He extended his less broken hand.

"My medallion."

Before they could begin the climb she had to coax Grillo from his catatonia. He was still sitting beside the water when she emerged from her conversation with Jaffe, his eyes closed tight.

"We're getting out of here," she said to him softly. "Grillo, do you hear me? We're getting out of here."

"Dead," he said.

"No," she told him. "We're going to be all right." She put her arm through his, the pains in her side stabbing her with every movement she made. "Get up, Grillo. I'm cold and it's going to get dark soon." Pitch black, in fact; the luminescence from the decaying terata was dimming fast. "There's sun up there, Grillo. It's warm. It's light."

Her words made him open his eyes.

"Witt's dead," he said.

The waves from the cataract had pushed the corpse to the shore.

"We're not going to join him," Tesla said. "We're going to live, Grillo. So get the fuck up."

"We . . . can't . . . swim *up* . . ." he said, looking at the cataract.

"There's other ways out," Tesla said. "Easier ways. But we have to be quick."

She looked across the chamber to where Jaffe was surveying the cracks in the walls, looking, she presumed, for the best exit. He was in no better shape than the rest of them, and a strenuous climb was going to be out of the question. She saw him call Hotchkiss over, and put him to work digging out rubble. He then moved on to survey other holes. It crossed Tesla's mind that the man didn't have any more clue how to get out of here than they did, but she distracted herself from that anxiety by returning to the business of getting Grillo to his feet. It took some more coaxing, but she succeeded. He stood up, his legs almost buckling beneath him until he rubbed some life back into them.

"Good," she said. "Good. Now let's go."

She allowed herself one last glance at Witt's body, hoping that wherever he was, it was a good place. If everybody got their own Heaven she knew where Witt would be now. In a celestial Palomo Grove: a small, safe town in a small, safe valley, where the sun always shone and the realty business was good. She silently wished him well, and turned her back on his remains, wondering as she did so if perhaps he'd known all along that he was going to die today, and was happier to be part of the foundation of the Grove than wasted in smoke from a crematorium.

Hotchkiss had been called away from his rubble-cleaning at one crack to the same duties on another, fuelling Tesla's unwelcome suspicion that Jaffe didn't know his way out of here. She went to Hotchkiss's aid, bullying Grillo out of his lethargy to do the same. The air from the hole smelled stale. There was no breath of anything fresh from above. But then perhaps they were too deep for that.

The work was hard, and harder still in the gathering darkness. Never in her life had she felt so close to complete collapse. There was no sensation in her hands whatsoever: her face was numb; her body sluggish. She was sure most corpses were warmer. But an age ago, somewhere in the sun, she'd told Hotchkiss she was as able as any man, and she was determined to make that claim good. She drove herself hard, pulling at the rocks with the same gusto as he did. But it was Grillo who did the bulk of the work, his eagerness undoubtedly fuelled by desperation. He cleared the largest of the rocks with a strength she'd not have thought him capable of.

"So," she said to Jaffe. "Do we go?"

"Yes."

"This is the way out?"

"It's as good as any," he said, and took the lead.

There began a trek that was in its way more terrifying than the descent. For one, they had only a single torch between them, which Hotchkiss, who followed after Jaffe, carried. It was pitifully inadequate, its light more like a beam for Tesla and Grillo to follow than a means to illuminate the path. They stumbled, and fell, and stumbled again, the numbness welcome in a way, postponing as it did any knowledge of what harm they were doing themselves.

The first part of the route didn't even take them up, it merely wound through several small compartments, the sound of water roaring in the rock around them. They passed along one tunnel that had clearly been a recent water-course. The mud was thigh-deep; and dripped from the ceiling on to their heads, for which, a little while on, they were duly grateful, when the passage narrowed to the point where had they not been slick with the stuff they'd. have been hard pressed to squeeze through. Beyond this point they began to climb, the gradient gentle at first, then steepening. Now, though the sound of water diminished, there was a new threat in the walls: the grinding of earth on earth. Nobody said anything. They were too exhausted to waste breath on the obvious, that the ground that the Grove was built upon was in revolt. The sounds got louder the higher they climbed, and several times dust fell from the tunnel roof, spattering them in the darkness.

It was Hotchkiss who felt the breeze first.

"Fresh air," he said.

"Of course," said Jaffe.

Tesla looked back towards Grillo. Her senses were so whacked out she wasn't sure of them any longer.

"You feel it?" she said to him.

"I think so," he said, his voice barely audible.

The promise speeded their advance, though it was tougher going all the time, the tunnels actually shaking at several points, such was the violence of the motion in the ground around them. But there was more than a hint of clean air to coax them on now; there was the faintest suspicion of light somewhere above them, which became more of a certainty by and by, until they could actually see the rock they were climbing up, Jaffe hauling himself one-handed, with a strange, almost floating ease, as though his body weighed next to nothing. The others scrambled after, barely able to keep up with him despite the adrenaline that had begun to pump through their weary systems. The light was strengthening, and it was that which led them on, its glare making them squint. It continued to get brighter, and brighter still. They climbed to it with fervor now, all caution in their hand and footholds forgotten.

Tesla's thoughts were a ragged bundle of non sequiturs, more like daydreams than conscious thought. Her mind was too exhausted to organize itself. But time and again it visited the five minutes she'd had to solve the problem of the medallion. Quite why she only grasped as the sky finally came in sight: that this ascent from the darkness was like a climb out of the past; out of death, too. From the coldblooded thing to the warmblooded. From the blind and immediate to the far-sighted. Vaguely she thought: this is why men go underground. To remember why they live in the sun.

At the very last, with the brightness from above overwhelming, Jaffe stood back and let Hotchkiss overtake him.

"Changing your mind?" Tesla said.

There was more than doubt on his face, however.

"What's to be afraid of?" she asked him.

"The sun," he said.

"Are you two moving?" Grillo said.

"In a moment," Tesla told him. "You go on."

He pressed past them both, scrabbling up the remaining feet to the surface. Hotchkiss was already there. She heard him laughing to himself. Postponing the pleasure of joining him was hard but they hadn't come this far to leave their prize behind.

"I hate the sun," Jaffe said.

"Why?"

"It hates me."

"You mean it hurts? Are you some kind of vampire?"

Jaffe squinted up at the light.

"It was Fletcher who loved the sky."

"Well maybe you should learn something from him."

"It's too late."

"No it isn't. You've done some shit stuff in your time, but you've got a chance to make good. There's worse coming than you. Think about that."

He didn't respond.

"Look," she went on, "the sun doesn't care what you did. It shines on everyone, good and bad. I wish it didn't but it does."

He nodded.

"Did I ever tell you . . ." he said, ". . . about Omaha?"

"Don't try and put it off, Jaffe. We're going up."

"I'll die," he said.

"Then all your troubles will be over, won't they?" she said. *"Come on!"*

He stared hard at her, the gleam she'd seen in his eyes when they'd been in the cave entirely gone. Indeed there was nothing about him that signalled any supernatural capacity. He was completely unremarkable: a gray, wretched husk of a man, whom she wouldn't have given a second glance to on the street, except perhaps to wonder what trauma had brought him so low. They'd spent a lot of time, effort (and Witt's life) getting him out of the earth. He didn't look like much of a reward for that. Head bowed against the glare, he climbed on up the last few feet and into the sun. She followed, the brightness becoming dizzying, almost nauseating. She closed her eyes against it, until the sound of laughter made her open them.

It was more than relief that had Hotchkiss and Grillo chuckling to themselves. The route home had brought them out in the middle of the parking lot of the Terrace Motel.

"Welcome to Palomo Grove," the sign read. *"The Prosperous Haven."*

SIX

As Carolyn Hotchkiss had liked to remind her three best friends all those years ago, the earth's crust was thin, and the Grove had been built along a flaw in that crust, which would one day crack and drop the town into an abyss. In the two decades since she'd silenced her own prophecies with pills, the technology for predicting that moment had advanced by leaps and bounds. Hairline cracks could be mapped, their activity closely monitored. In the event of the big one the warnings would hopefully come fast enough to save the lives of millions, not only in San Francisco and Los Angeles, but in smaller communities like the Grove. None of these monitors and mapmakers, however, could have predicted the suddenness of events up at Coney Eye, or the scale of their consequences. The skewing of the interior of the Vance house had sent a subtle but persuasive message into the Hill, and out through the caves and tunnels below the town, urging a system that had been murmuring for years to roll over and shout. Though the most spectacular consequences of that mutiny occurred on the lower reaches of the Hill, where the ground opened up as though the big one was indeed underway, tipping one of the Crescents into a fissure two hundred yards long and twenty wide, every village sustained damage.

The destruction didn't die down after the first shock-wave, as might have been expected with a conventional quake. It escalated, the message of anarchy spreading, minor subsidence becoming significant enough to devour houses, garages, sidewalks and stores. In Deerdell, the streets closest to the woods were the first to suffer damage, the few residents remaining warned of the coming destruction by a mass exodus of animals, who made their escape before the trees began to try to uproot themselves and follow. Failing, they fell. The houses followed soon after, street on street toppling like dominoes. Stillbrook and Laureltree sustained equally comprehensive damage, but without due warning or any discernible pattern. Crevasses opened suddenly in the middle of streets and back yards. Pools drained of water in a matter of seconds; driveways turned into models of the Grand Canyon. But whether arbitrary or systematic, sudden or signalled, in the end it came down to the same thing from village to village. The Grove was being swallowed up by the ground it had been built upon.

There were deaths, of course; many. But for the most part they went unnoticed, being those of people who'd stayed locked up alone in their houses for several days, nursing suspicions about the world they dared not take out into the light. Nobody missed them because nobody knew who'd left town and who'd stayed. The Grovers' show of solidarity, after that first night at the Mall, had been strictly cosmetic. There'd been no emergency community meetings called; no sharing of mutually held fears. As things got steadily worse families had simply sloped away, often by night, still more often without saying anything to the neighbors. The loners who'd remained were buried under the rubble of the roofs without anybody even knowing they'd been there in the first place. By the time the authorities became aware of how widespread the damage was, many of the streets were no-go areas, and finding the victims was a task for another day, when the more urgent issue of what had happened (and was still happening) in the Buddy Vance residence was not so pressing.

It had been apparent to the first investigators—seasoned patrolmen who'd thought they'd seen everything—that some power had been released in Coney Eye that wasn't going to be easily defined. An hour and a half after the first car reached Coney Eye, and the patrolman reported to his superiors the condition of the house, several FBI men were on the scene, and two professors—a physicist and a geologist—were on their way from L.A. The house was entered, and the phenomenon in its interior, which defied all easy explanation, judged to be potentially lethal. What was perfectly clear, among countless uncertainties, was the fact that the Grovers had somehow been aware of some fundamental disruption occurring (or about to occur) in their midst. They'd started to desert their town hours or perhaps days before. Why none of them had chosen to alert anyone beyond the perimeters of the Grove to the danger there was just one of countless mysteries the site presented.

Had the investigators known where to look they'd have had their answers from any one of the individuals who'd dragged themselves up out of the ground in front of the Terrace Motel. They'd probably have dismissed those answers as lunacy, but even Tesla—who'd been passionately determined that Grillo not tell his story—would have told it freely now, had she had the strength. The warmth of the sun, indeed the sight of it, had revived her somewhat, but it had also dried the mud and blood on her face and body, and sealed in the deep chill in her marrow. Jaffe had been the first to seek the shadows of the motel. After only a few minutes, she followed. The motel had been deserted by guests and staff alike, and with good reason. The fissure in the lot was one of many, the largest of which spread through the front door of the building, its cracks climbing its facade like earth-born lightning. Inside there were ample signs of how hurried a departure the last occupants had made, luggage and personal items scattered up and down the stairs, the doors that hadn't been unseated by the tremors thrown wide. She wandered along the row of rooms till she found some abandoned clothes, ran herself a shower, the water as hot as she could stand, stripped and stepped in. The warmth made her dreamy, and it was all she could do to drag herself out of its bliss and dry herself. There were mirrors, unfortunately. Her bruised, aching body was a pitiful sight. She covered it as quickly as possible, with items that neither fitted nor

matched, which pleased her—Hobo had always been her preferred aesthetic. While dressing she availed herself of cold coffee, left in the
room. It was three-twenty when she emerged: almost seven hours since
the four of them had driven to Deerdell to make the descent.

Grillo and Hotchkiss were in the office. They'd brewed hot coffee.
They'd also washed, though not as thoroughly as she, instead scrub-
bing masks of clean skin out of the surrounding muck. They'd also
stripped off their sodden sweaters and found jackets to wear. Both were
smoking.

"We got it all," Grillo said, his manner that of a man profoundly
embarrassed, and determined to brave it out. "Coffee. Cigarettes.
Stale doughnuts. All we're missing's serious drugs."

"Where's Jaffe?" Tesla wanted to know.

"Don't know," Grillo said.

"What do you mean, you don't know?" Tesla said. "For Christ's
sake, Grillo, we shouldn't let him out of our sight."

"He came this far, didn't he?" Grillo replied. "He's not going to
walk away now."

"Maybe," Tesla conceded. She poured herself coffee. "Is there any
sugar?"

"No, but there's pastries and cheesecake. Stale but edible. Somebody had a sweet tooth. You want?"

"I want," Tesla said. She sipped the coffee. "I suppose you're right—"

"About the sweet tooth?"

"About Jaffe."

"He doesn't give a fuck for us," Hotchkiss said. "Makes me sick to
look at him."

"Well, you've got reason," Grillo said.

"Damn right," said Hotchkiss. He gave Tesla a sideways glance.
"When this is done with," he said, "I want him to myself. OK? We've
got scores to settle."

He didn't wait for a reply. Taking his coffee he headed back out into
the sun.

"What was that about?" Tesla said.

"Carolyn," Grillo said.

"Of course."

"He blames Jaffe for what happened to her. And he's right."

"He must be going through hell."

"I don't think the trip's anything new to him," Grillo said.

"I suppose not." She emptied her mug of coffee. "That's wired me for a while," she said. "I'm going to find Jaffe."

"Before you do—"

"Yeah?"

"I just want to say . . . what happened to me down there . . . I'm sorry I wasn't more use. I've always had this thing about being buried alive."

"Sounds reasonable to me," Tesla said.

"I want to make it up to you. Want to help any way I can. Just say the word. I know you've got a take on all of this. I haven't."

"Not really."

"You persuaded Jaffe to come with us. How'd you do that?"

"He had a puzzle. I solved it."

"You make it sound real simple."

"Thing is, I think maybe the whole thing's simple. What we're facing's so big, Grillo, we just have to go on instinct."

"Yours was always better than mine. I like facts."

"They're simple too," she said. "There's a hole, and something coming through it from the other side which people like you and me don't even have the capacity to imagine. If we don't close the hole, we're fucked."

"And the Jaff knows how?"

"How what?"

"To close the hole."

Tesla stared at him.

"At a guess?" she said. "No."

She found him, of all places, on the roof, which was literally the last place in the motel she'd chosen to look. Surprisingly, he was engaged in the last activity she'd have expected from him. He was staring at the sun.

"I thought maybe you'd left us to our own devices," she said.

"You were right," he replied, not looking at her. "It shines on everyone, good and bad. But it doesn't make me warm. I've forgotten what it was like to feel warm or cold. Or hungry. Or full. I miss that so much."

The sour self-confidence he'd evidenced in the caves had entirely drained from him. He was almost cowed.

"Maybe you'll get that back," she said. "The human stuff, I mean. Undo what the Nuncio did."

"I'd like that," he said. "I'd like to be Randolph Jaffe of Omaha, Nebraska. Turn the clock back and not go into that room."

"What room?"

"The Dead Letters Room at the Post Office," he said, "where all this began. I should tell you about that."

"I'd like to hear. But first—"

"I know. I know. The house. The schism."

Now he did look at her; or rather, beyond her, at the Hill.

"We have to go up there sooner or later," she reminded him. "I'd prefer we do it now, while it's light, and I've got some energy left."

"And when we get there?"

"We hope for inspiration."

"That has to come from somewhere," he said. "And we've neither of us got gods, have we? That's what I've traded on all these years, people being godless. That's us now."

She remembered what D'Amour had said when she'd told him she didn't pray. Something about praying making sense once you knew how much there was out there.

"I'm coming round to being a believer," she said. "Slowly."

"A believer in *what?*"

"In higher forces," she said, with a faintly embarrassed shrug. "The Shoal had their aspirations, why shouldn't I?"

"Did they?" he said. "Were they guarding the Art because Quiddity had to be preserved? I don't think so. They were just afraid of what might break out. They were watch dogs."

"Maybe their duties elevated them."

"Into what? Saints? Didn't do much for Kisson, did it? All he worshipped was himself. And the Iad."

That was a grim thought. What more perfect counterpoint to D'Amour's talk of faith in mysteries than Kissoon's revelation that all religions were masks for the Shoal; ways to keep the hoi-polloi distracted from the secret of secrets.

"I keep getting glimpses," Jaffe said, "of where Tommy-Ray is."

"What's it like?"

"Darker and darker," Jaffe replied. "He was moving for a long while, but now he's stopped. Maybe the tide's changed. There's something coming, I think, out of the darkness. Or maybe it *is* the darkness, I don't know. But it's getting closer."

"The moment he sees anything," Tesla said, "let me know. I want details."

"I don't want to look, with his eyes or mine."

"You may not have any choice. He's your son."

"He's failed me over and over. I don't owe him anything. He's got his phantoms."

"Perfect family unit," Tesla said. "Father, Son and—"

"—Holy Ghost," Jaffe said.

"That's right," she replied, another echo coming back to her from the past. "*Trinity.*"

"What about it?"

"That was what Kissoon was so afraid of."

"The Trinity?"

"Yeah. When he brought me into the Loop the first time, he dropped the name. It was an error, I think. When I challenged him on it he was so damn flustered he let me go."

"I never took Kissoon for a Christian," Jaffe remarked.

"Me neither. Maybe he meant some other god. Or *gods*. Some force the Shoal could invoke. Where's the medallion?"

"In my pocket. You'll have to get it for yourself. My hands are very weak."

He took them from his pockets. In the guttering light of the cave their mutilation had been sickening, but here in bright sunlight they were more disgusting still, the flesh blackened and dewy, the bone beneath crumbling.

"I'm coming apart," he said. "Fletcher used fire. I used my teeth. Both of us suicides. It's just that his was faster."

She reached into his pocket and took the medallion out.

"You don't seem to mind," she said.

"What about?"

"Falling apart."

"No, I don't," he admitted. "I'd like to die, the way I would have done if I'd stayed in Omaha and just got old. I don't want to live forever. What's the use of going on and on if you can't make sense of anything?"

The rush of pleasure she'd experienced solving the medallion's enigmas came back to her as she studied it. But there was nothing in the design, even when examined in daylight, which could be interpreted as a Trinity. There were quartets, certainly. Four arms, four circles. But no trios.

"This is no use," she said. "We could waste days trying to work it out."

"Work what out?" said Grillo, emerging into the sunlight.

"The Trinity," she said. "Have you any idea what that means?"

"Father, Son and—"

"Besides the obvious."

"Then *no*, I don't. Why?"

"Just a little hope I had."

"How many Trinities can there be?" he said. "It shouldn't be that hard to find out."

"Where from? Abernethy?"

"I could start with him," Grillo said. "He's a God-fearing man. Or at least he claims to be. Is it that important?"

"At this stage everything's important," she said.

"I'll get on to it," he replied, "if the phone lines are still working. You just want to know—"

"Anything about the Trinity. *Anything*."

"Hard facts, that's what I like," he said. "Hard facts."

He headed off down the stairs. As he did so Tesla heard Jaffe mutter: "Look away, Tommy. Just look away—"

He'd closed his eyes. Now he began to shake.

"Can you see them?" she said to him.

"It's so dark."

"*Can you see them?*"

"I can see something moving. Something huge. So *huge*. Why don't you *move*, boy? Get away before they see you. *Move!*"

His eyes suddenly sprang open.

"Enough!" he said.

"Have you lost him?" Tesla said.

"I told you: *enough!*"

"He's not dead?"

"No, he's . . . he's riding the waves."

"Surfing on Quiddity?" she said.

"Doing his damnedest."

"And the Iad?"

"Are behind him. I was right, the tide has changed. They're coming."

"Describe what you saw," she said.

"I told you. They're vast."

"That's all?"

"Like mountains, moving. Mountains covered in locusts, or fleas. Big and small. I don't know. None of it makes much sense."

"Well we just have to close the schism as quickly as we can. Mountains I can take. But let's keep the fleas out, huh?"

Hotchkiss was at the front door when they got down there. Grillo had already spoken to him about the Trinity, and he had a better idea than asking Abernethy.

"There's a book store in the Mall," he said. "Do you want me to go look up Trinities there?"

"It can't hurt," Tesla said. "If the Trinity scared Kissoon, maybe it'll scare his paymasters. Where's Grillo?"

"Out looking for a car. He'll take you up the Hill. That's where you're both going?" He glanced in Jaffe's direction, repugnance on his face.

"That's where we're going," Tesla said. "And that's where we'll stay. So you know where to find us."

"Right to the end?" Hotchkiss said, not taking his eyes off Jaffe.

"Right to the end."

Grillo had found and hot-wired a car that had been left in the motel lot.

"Where'd you learn to do that?" she asked him as they drove up towards the Hill. The Jaff sat slumped on the back seat, his eyes closed.

"I did a piece, way back in my investigative phase—"

"On car thieves?"

"That's right. I picked up a few tricks of the trade, and I've never forgotten them. I'm a mine of useless information. Always something new out of Grillo."

"But nothing about Trinity?"

"You keep coming back to that."

"Desperation," she said. "We haven't got much else to hold on to."

"Maybe it's something to do with what D'Amour said, about the Savior."

"A last-minute intervention from on high?" Tesla said. "I'm not going to hold my breath waiting."

"Shit."

"Problem?"

"Up ahead."

A crevasse had opened up at the intersection they were approaching. It was across both street and sidewalk. There was no way past it up the Hill.

"We'll have to try another way," Grillo said. He put the car into reverse, backed up, and took a cross-street for three blocks. There was evidence of the Grove's growing instability on every side. Lampposts and trees felled, sidewalks buckled, water running from fractured pipes.

"It's all going to blow," Tesla said.

"Ain't that the truth."

The next street he tried gave them clear access to the Hill, and they headed up. As they began the ascent Tesla caught sight of a second car, coming off the feed road from the freeway. It wasn't a police car, unless the local cops had taken up driving Volkswagens and painting them fluorescent yellow.

"Foolhardy," she said.

"What is?"

"Somebody coming back into town."

"Probably a salvage operation," Grillo said. "People taking *what* they can, *while* they can."

"Yep."

The color of the car, so garishly inappropriate, lingered with her for a little while. She wasn't sure why; perhaps because it was so very West Hollywood, and she doubted she'd ever see her apartment in North Huntley Drive again.

"Looks like we've got a welcome committee," Grillo said.

"Perfect movie moment," Tesla said. "Step on it, driver."

"Lousy dialogue."

"Just drive."

Grillo swerved to avoid collision with the patrol car, put his foot on the accelerator, and was past the vehicle before its driver had a chance to block him.

"There'll be more at the top," he said.

Tesla looked back at the car they'd left behind. There was no attempt to give chase. Its driver would simply be alerting the rest of the unit.

"Do whatever you've got to do," Tesla told Grillo.

"Meaning what?"

"Meaning trash 'em if they get in our way. We've got no time to make nice."

"The house is going to be crawling with cops," he warned.

"I doubt it," she said. "I think they'll be keeping their distance."

She was right. As they came in sight of Coney Eye it was apparent that the patrolmen had decided this whole mess was beyond them. The cars were parked well down from the gate, the men themselves standing a good way behind their vehicles. Most were just staring up at the house, but there was a contingent of four officers waiting at a barricade that had been set up, blocking the Hill.

"You want me to drive straight through?" Grillo said.

"Damn right!"

He put his foot down. Two of the quartet ahead went for their guns; the other two threw themselves aside. Grillo rammed the barricade at speed. The wood splintered and broke, a piece shattering the windshield. He thought he heard a shot in the confusion but as he was still driving, assumed it hadn't killed him. The car struck one of the patrol vehicles a glancing blow, its back end slewing around and striking another, before Grillo regained control and headed it for the open gates of Buddy Vance's house. Engine revved, they roared up the driveway.

"Nobody's following," Tesla said.

"I don't fucking blame them," Grillo replied. As they reached the bend in the driveway he put on the brakes. "This is near enough," he said. "Jesus. *Will you look at that?*"

"I'm looking."

The facade of the house resembled a cake that had been left out all night in a heavy rain, the whole thing softened and thrown out of whack. There were no straight lines in the door frames, no right angles in the windows—even those at the very top of the house. The power Jaffe had unleashed here had sucked everything towards its maw, distorting the bricks, the tiles, the panes of glass; the whole house *tending* towards the schism. When Tesla and Grillo had staggered out through the doorway the place had been a maelstrom, but the hole, once opened, seemed to be pacified. There was no sign of further violence. There was no doubting the proximity of the schism, however. When they stepped from the car they felt its energies in the air. It made the hair on the back of their necks stand up straight, and their guts shudder. It was as quiet as the eye of a hurricane. A tremulous calm just begging to be broken.

Tesla glanced through the car window at their passenger. Jaffe, sensing her scrutiny, opened his eyes. The fear in him was perfectly plain. However much skill he'd had at concealing his feelings in the past—and she suspected he'd had much—he was beyond such pretenses now.

"Do you want to come see?" she said.

He didn't leap at the offer, so she left him where he was. She had a duty to perform before they actually ventured inside, and she could give him time to work up his courage while she performed it. She headed back the way they'd come, until she emerged from behind the line of palms that bordered the driveway. The cops had followed as far as the gate, but no further. It occurred to her that it wasn't simply fear that kept them from following, but orders from their superiors. She didn't dare hope the cavalry would be rolling up the Hill in the next few minutes, but perhaps they were mustering, and these footsoldiers had been instructed to keep their distance until the full force arrived. They were certainly nervous. She emerged with her hands up, to face a row of levelled muzzles.

"This property's off-limits," somebody shouted from below. "Come back down with your hands in the air. All of you."

"I'm afraid I can't do that," Tesla replied. "Just *keep* it off-limits, will you? We've got business here. Who's in charge?" she asked, feeling like a visitor from space, asking to be taken to their leader.

A man in a well-cut suit stepped into view from behind one of the vehicles. He was not, she guessed, a policeman. More likely FBI.

"I'm in charge," he said.

"Are you getting back-up?" she asked.

"Who are you?" he demanded to know.

"*Are you getting back-up?*" she said again. "You're going to need more than a few patrol cars, believe me. There's going to be a major invasion starting from this house."

"What are you talking about?"

"Just get the Hill surrounded. And seal the Grove. We're not going to get a second chance."

"I'm only going to ask one more time—" the leader began, but she cut him off short, slipping out of sight before he could finish his demands.

"You're good at that," Grillo said.

"You know what practice makes," she said.

"They could have shot you," Grillo observed.

"But they didn't," she said, returning to the car and opening the door. "Shall we?" she said to Jaffe. He ignored her invitation at first. "The sooner we start the sooner we finish," she said. Sighing, he got out. "I want you to stay here," she told Grillo. "If any of them make a move, holler."

"You just don't want me inside," he said.

"That too."

"Do you have any clue what you're going to do in there?"

"We're going to make like a couple of critics," Tesla said. "We're going to fuck the Art."

Hotchkiss had been an avid reader in his younger days, but Carolyn's death had killed his taste for fiction. Why bother to read thrillers written by men who'd never heard gunfire? They were all lies. Not just the novels. These books, too, he thought, as he dug through the shelves in the Mormon Book Store. Volumes of stuff about revelation and God's work on earth. There were a few that listed Trinity in their index, but the reference was always in passing, and illuminated nothing. The only satisfaction he got from the search was the pleasure of throwing the place into disarray, tossing the books aside. Their pat certitudes disgusted him. If he'd had the time he might have set a match to the lot.

As he moved deeper into the shop he saw a bright yellow Volkswagen turn into the lot. Two men stepped out. They couldn't have looked more unalike. One was dressed in a dusty ragbag of ill-fitting garments, and had—even from a distance—a face ugly enough to make a mother weep. His companion was a tanned Adonis by comparison, dressed in peacock casuals. Neither, Hotchkiss judged, knew where they were, nor the danger they were in being here. They looked around at the empty lot in bewilderment. Hotchkiss went to the door.

"You guys should get out of here," he called across to them.

The peacock looked in his direction.

"This *is* Palomo Grove?"

"Yeah."

"What happened? Was there a 'quake?"

"It's coming," Hotchkiss said. "Listen, just do yourselves a favor. Get the fuck out of here."

The ugly one spoke now, his face looking more misshapen the closer he got.

"Tesla Bombeck," he said.

"What about her?" Hotchkiss said.

"I have to see her. My name's Raul."

"She's up the Hill," Hotchkiss said. He'd heard Tesla mention the name *Raul* when speaking to Grillo; he didn't recall in what context.

"I've come to help her," Raul said.

"And you?" Hotchkiss asked the Adonis.

"Ron," came the reply. "I'm just the chauffeur," he shrugged. "Hey, if you want me out of here I'm happy to go."

"It's up to you," Hotchkiss said, returning into the store. "It's not safe here. That's all I'm saying."

"I hear you," Ron said.

Raul had lost interest in the conversation, and was scanning the stores. He seemed to be sniffing as he did so.

"What do you want me to do?" Ron called over to him.

The man looked back at his friend.

"Go home," he said.

"You don't want me to take you up to find Tesla?" Ron replied.

"I'll find her myself."

"It's a long walk, man."

Raul cast a glance in Hotchkiss's direction. "We'll work something out," he said.

Hotchkiss didn't volunteer for duty, but went back to his search, paying only half an ear's attention to the conversation that continued in the lot.

"Are you sure you don't want us to go find Tesla? I thought this was urgent?"

"It was. It *is*. I just . . . need to spend a little time here first."

"I can wait. I don't mind."

"I told you, no."

"You don't want me to take you back? I thought maybe we could hang out tonight. You know, go to a few bars . . ."

"Another time, maybe."

"Tomorrow?"

"Just another time."

"I get it. This is thanks but no thanks, right?"

"If you say so."

"You're fucking weird, man. First you come on to me. Now you don't want to know. Well, fuck you. I can get my dick sucked plenty of places."

Hotchkiss glanced round to see the Adonis stalking back to his car. The other man was already out of sight. Pleased to have the distraction over with he went back to searching the shelves. The section of books on Motherhood didn't look too promising, but he began to make his way through it anyhow. It was, as he'd anticipated, all pap and platitudes. There was nothing in the pages that made reference, even obliquely, to any Trinity. Only talk of motherhood as a divine calling, woman in partnership with God, bringing new life into the world, her greatest and most noble task. And for the offspring, trite advice. *"Children, obey your parents in the Lord: for this is right."*

He dutifully went through every title, throwing the volumes aside when they proved useless, until he'd exhausted the shelves. There were only two sections remaining to be searched. Neither of them seemed too promising. He stood up and stretched, looking out towards the sun-beaten lot. A sickening sense of foreboding was churning in his guts. The sun was shining, but for how long?

Beyond the lot—a long way beyond—he caught sight of the yellow Beetle, making its way out of the Grove towards the freeway. He didn't envy the Adonis his liberty. He had no wish to get in a car and drive. As places to die went, the Grove was as good as any: comfortable, familiar, empty. If he died screaming, nobody would hear his cowardice. If he died silently, nobody would mourn him. Let the Adonis go. He presumably had his life to live, somewhere. And it would be brief. If they failed in their endeavors here in the Grove—and the night beyond this world broke through—it would be *very* brief. If they succeeded (small hope) it would still be brief.

And always better in the ending than the beginning, the interval between being what it was.

If the exterior of Coney Eye had been the eye of a hurricane, the interior was a glint in that eye. A sharper stillness, which made Tesla alive to every tic in her cheek and temple, every small raggedness in her breath. With Jaffe following in after her she crossed the hallway towards the lounge where he'd committed his crime against nature. The evidence of that crime was everywhere around them, but cold now, the distortions set like so much melted wax.

She stepped through into the room itself. The schism was still in place: the entire environment pulled towards a hole no more than six feet across. It was quiescent. There was no visible sign that it was trying to make itself any wider. If and when the lad reached the threshold of the Cosm, they'd have to step over it one by one, unless, with this lesion begun, they could simply hack it open till it gaped.

"It doesn't look too dangerous," she said to Jaffe. "We've got a chance if we move quickly."

"I don't know how to seal it."

"*Try*. You knew how to open it."

"That was instinct."

"And what do your instincts tell you now?"

"That I haven't got the power left in me," he said. He raised his broken hands. "I ate it up and spat it out."

"It was all in your hands?"

"I think so."

She remembered the night at the Mall: the Jaff passing poison into Fletcher's system from fingers which seemed to be sweating potency. Now those same hands were decaying wreckage. And yet she couldn't bring herself to believe power was a matter of anatomy. Kissoon had been no demigod, but his scrawny body was a reservoir of the direst suits. *Will* was the key to authority, and Jaffe seemed to have none left.

"So you can't do it," she said simply.

"No."

"Then maybe I can."

He narrowed his eyes. "I doubt that," he said, with the faintest trace of condescension in his tone. She pretended not to have noticed.

"I can try," she said. "The Nuncio got into me too, remember? You're not the only God in the squad."

This remark bore the fruit it had been planted to produce.

"*You?*" he said. "You've not a hope in hell." He looked down at his hands, then back up at the schism. "I'm the one who opened it. I'm the only one who ever dared do that. And I'm the only one who can seal it up again."

He walked past her towards the schism, that same lightness in his step as she'd noticed when they were climbing out of the caves. It allowed him to negotiate the uneven floor with relative ease. It was only when he came within a yard or two of the hole that his pace slowed. Then he stopped completely.

"What is it?" she said.

"Come look for yourself."

She started across the room towards him. It wasn't simply the visible world that was twisted and dragged towards the hole, she realized; so was the invisible. The air, and the minute particles of dust and dirt it carried, was hauled out of true. Space itself was knotted up, its convolutions pliable enough to be pressed through but only with the greatest difficulty. The effect got stronger the closer to the hole she went. Her body, already bruised and battered within an inch of its Lazarite life, was barely equal to the challenge. But she persevered. And step by step she achieved her goal, coming close enough to the hole to see down its throat. The sight was not easy to take. The world she'd assumed all her life to be complete and comprehensible was here undone utterly. It was a distress she'd not felt since childhood when somebody (she'd forgotten who) had taught her the trick of looking at infinity by putting two mirrors face to face, each staring into the other's reflection. She'd been twelve, thirteen at most, and completely spooked by the idea of this emptiness echoing emptiness, back and forth, back and forth, until they reached the limits of light. For years after she'd remembered that moment, confronted with a physical representation of something her mind revolted at. Here was the same process. The schism, defying her every idea about the way the world was. Reality as a comparative science.

She looked into its maw. Nothing that she saw was certain. If it was cloud, then it was cloud half turned to rain. If it was rain, then it was rain on the verge of combusting, and becoming a falling fire. And beyond the cloud, and rain, and fire, another place entirely, as ambiguous as the confusion of elements that half hid it: a sea that became a sky with no horizon to divide or define them. *Quiddity.*

She was seized by a fierce, barely controllable desire to *be* there, to climb through the schism and taste the mystery beyond. How many thousands of seekers, glimpsing in fever dreams and drug dreams the possibility of being where she now stood, had woken wanting to die rather than live another hour, knowing they could never have that access? Woken, mourned, and still gone on living, hoping, in the agonized, heroic way her species hoped, that miracles were possible; that the epiphanies of music and love were more than self-deception, were clues to a greater condition, where hope was rewarded with keys and kisses, and doors opened to the everlasting.

Quiddity was that everlasting. It was the ether in which *being* had been raised, as humanity had been raised from the soup of a simpler sea. The thought of Quiddity tainted by the lad was suddenly more distressing to her than the fact of their imminent invasion. The phrase she'd first heard from Kissoon revisited her. *Quiddity must be preserved.* As Mary Muralles had said, Kissoon only told lies when he needed to. That was no small part of his genius: to hold to the truth as long as it served his purpose. And Quiddity *did* need to be preserved. Without dreams, life was nothing. Perhaps it would not even have come into being.

"I suppose I must try," Jaffe said, and took one more step towards the maw, bringing himself within touching range of it. His hands, which had seemed completely devoid of strength a minute before, had a lick of power about them, all the more visible because it oozed from such wounded flesh. He raised them towards the schism. That it sensed his presence and purpose became apparent before he'd even made contact. A spasm passed out from its lips, running up through the room it had hauled into itself. The frozen distortions shuddered, softening once again.

"It's wise to us," Jaffe said.

"We've still got to try," Tesla replied. The floor beneath their feet was suddenly jittery; pieces of plaster dropped from the walls and ceiling. Inside the maw the clouds of fiery rain bloomed towards the Cosm.

Jaffe laid his hands on the softening intersection, but the schism was having no truck with undoers. It threw a second spasm off, its violence sufficient to throw Jaffe back into Tesla's arms.

"No good!" he said. "No good!"

Worse than no good. If they'd needed evidence of the Iad's approach they had it now, as the cloud darkened, its motion unmistakable. As Jaffe had guessed, the tide had changed. The throat of the schism was not concerned with swallowing, but with vomiting up whatever was choking it. To do so, it started to open.

With that motion the beginning of the end began.

SEVEN

T he book in Hotchkiss's hands was called *Preparing for Armageddon*, and it was a manual instructing faithful brethren on how to do just that, a step-by-step guide to surviving the imminent Apocalypse. There were chapters on Livestock, on Water and Grain, on Clothing and Bedding, Fuel, Heat and Light. There was a five-page check-list entitled *Commonly Stored Foods* that ran the gamut from Molasses to Venison jerky. And as if to whip up fear in any procrastinators who might be tempted to put off their preparations, the book interspersed these lists with photographs of calamities that had occurred across America. Most of them were natural phenomena. Forest fires raging, unchecked and uncheckable; hurricanes laying towns flat in their passage. There were several pages given over to a flood in Salt Lake City in May of 1983, accompanied by pictures of Utahans building walls of sandbags to contain the water. But the image that loomed largest amid this catalogue of final acts was the mushroom cloud. There were several photographs of that cloud, underneath one of which Hotchkiss found the simple legend:

The first atom-bomb was detonated at 0530 hours July 16, 1945, at a location named Trinity by the bomb's creator, Robert Oppenheimer. With that detonation, Mankind's last age began.

There was no further explanation. The purpose of the book was not to explain the atomic bomb and its construction, but to offer guidance on how the members of the Church of Jesus Christ of Latter-day Saints might survive it. No matter. He didn't need details. All he needed was that one word, *Trinity*, in some other context than Father, Son and Holy Ghost. Here it was. The Three-in-One reduced to a single place—a single event, indeed. This was the Trinity that superseded all others. In the imagination of the twentieth century the mushroom cloud loomed larger than God.

He stood up, *Preparing for Armageddon* in his hand, and crossed through the chaos of discarded books to the front of the store. Awaiting him outside was a sight that stopped him in his tracks. There were dozens of animals running free in the lot. Puppies rolling around, mice running for cover with kittens on their tails; lizards basking on the hot asphalt. He looked along the row of store-fronts. A parrot flew out through the open door of Ted Elizando's store. Hotchkiss didn't know Ted at all, but he knew the stories about the man. As a source of gossip himself he'd always attended closely to what was said about others. Elizando had lost his mind, his wife and his baby. Now he was losing his little ark in the Mall as well; setting it free.

The task of getting the information on Trinity to Tesla Bombeck was more important than offering words of comfort or warning to Elizando, even if he'd had any words to offer. The man clearly knew what danger he was in or he wouldn't have been releasing his stock. And as to comfort: what words were there to offer? Decision made, Hotchkiss started across the lot to his car, only to be stopped again, not by a sight this time but by a sound: a short, anguished human cry. Its source was the pet store.

He was at the open door in ten seconds. Inside there were more animals underfoot, but no sign of their liberator. He called the man's name.

"Elizando? Are you OK?"

There was no answer, and it occurred to Hotchkiss that the man had killed himself. Set the animals free then slit his wrists. He picked up his speed, weaving through the displays, the perches and the cages. Halfway down the store he saw Elizando's body slumped on the far side of a sizeable cage. The occupants, a small flock of canaries, were panicked, fluttering back and forth, feathers dashed from their wings against the wire.

Hotchkiss dropped the book and went to Ted's aid.

"What have you done?" he said as he approached. "Jesus, man, what have you done?"

As he got closer to the body he realized his error. This was no suicide. The wounds on his face—which was pressed against the wire—were not self-inflicted. They were traumatic; cobs of flesh torn out of his cheek and neck. The blood had spilled through the mesh and covered the bottom of the canaries' cage, but it had ceased to pump with any gusto. He'd been dead for several minutes.

Hotchkiss stood up, very slowly. If it hadn't been Elizando's cry he'd heard, what had it been? He took a step towards the book to reclaim it, but as he stooped to pick it up a motion between the cages distracted him. What seemed to be a black snake was gliding across the floor just beyond Elizando's corpse. It moved quickly, its clear intention to come between him and the exit. Had he not had to pick up the book he might have outrun it, but by the time he had *Preparing for Armageddon* in his hand it was at the door. Now that it was in full sight several facts became clear. That this was no escapee from the store (no household in the Grove would have given it a home). That it bore as much resemblance to a Moray eel as it did to a snake, but even that likeness was vague: it was, in truth, like nothing he'd seen before. And finally, that it had left smears of blood on the tiles to mark its advance; and that the interior of its mouth was also wet with blood. This was Elizando's killer. He retreated in front of it, evoking the name of the Savior he'd long ago forsaken:

"Jesus."

The word brought laughter from somewhere at the back of the store. He turned. The door to Ted's office was wide open. Though the room beyond had no windows, and the lights weren't on, he could make out the figure of a man sitting cross-legged on the floor. He could even make a guess at his identity: the misshapen features of Tesla Bombeck's friend Raul were unmistakable, even in the gloom. He was naked. It was that fact—his nakedness, and therefore his vulnerability—that tempted Hotchkiss into taking a step towards the open door. Given the choice between fighting the snake or its charmer— and they were surely in league—he chose the charmer. A naked man, squatting, was not much threat.

"What the fuck's going on here?" Hotchkiss demanded as he approached.

The man grinned in the murk. His smile was wet and wide.

"I'm making Lix," he replied.

"Lix?"

"Behind you."

Hotchkiss didn't need to turn around to know his exit was still blocked. He had no choice but to stand his ground, even though he was increasingly appalled by the sight in front of him. Not only was the man naked, but his body, from the middle of his chest to the middle of his thigh, was swarming with bugs, the store's supply of lizard food and fish food, here assuaging another appetite. Their motion had him hard, his crooked member the focus of their endeavors. But there was a sight as repulsive or worse on the ground in front of him: a small heap of animal excrement, droppings gathered from the cages, in the midst of which a creature was nesting. No, not nesting, being *born*, swelling and unknotting itself in front of Hotchkiss. It raised its head from the shit, and he saw it was another of what this monster-maker had called Lix.

Nor was it the only one. Glistening forms uncoiled in the corners of the little room, all lengths of featureless muscle, malice in their every squirming motion. Two emerged from behind their maker. Another was climbing up the counter to the right of Hotchkiss, and wriggling towards him. In order to avoid it, he took a backward step, and realized too late that the maneuver had put him within reach of another of the beasts. It was at his leg in two beats, ascending it in three. He dropped *Armageddon* a second time and reached down to strike at the thing, but its gaping mouth struck first, the twin motions throwing him off balance. He staggered back against a shelf of cages, his flailing arms bringing several of them down. A second snatch, this time at the shelf itself, was just as fruitless. Built only to bear kittens and their cages, it gave way beneath his weight, and he fell to the ground, the shelf and its load coming down after him. Had it not been for the cages he might have been slaughtered on the spot, but they delayed the Lix converging on him from front door and back. He was granted ten seconds' reprieve while they tried to worm their way between the cages, during which he managed to roll over and prepare to get to his feet, but the creature fixed to his leg brought such hope to an end, its jaws sinking into the flesh of his hip. The pain took his sight for a moment, and when it returned the other beasts had found their way to him. He felt one of them at the back of his neck; another wrapped itself around his torso. He started to yell for help, before the breath was squeezed out of him.

"There's only me," came the reply.

He gazed up at the man called Raul who was no longer squatting in ordure, but standing over him—still hard, still swarming—one of the Lix draped around his neck. He had the first two fingers of his hand in its open mouth, stroking the back of its throat.

"You're not Raul," Hotchkiss gasped.

"No."

"Who . . . ?"

The last word he heard before the Lix wound around his chest tightened its knot, was the answer to that question. A name, made up of two gentle syllables. *Kiss* and *soon.* It was these words he thought of at the last, like a prophecy. Kiss; soon. Carolyn, waiting on the other side of death, lips ready to press to his cheek. It made his last moments bearable, after all the horrors.

"I think what we've got here is a lost cause," Tesla said to Grillo as she emerged from the house.

She was shaking from head to foot, hour upon hour of exertion and hurt taking its toll. She longed to sleep, but she had a terror that if she did she'd have the dream Witt had had the night before: the visit to Quiddity that meant dying was very close. Maybe it was, but she didn't want to know about it.

Grillo took hold of her arm, but she waved him away.

"You can't hold me up any more than I can hold you—"

"What's happening in there?"

"The hole's started to open again. It's like a dam's going to burst."

"Shit."

The entire house was creaking now; the palms lining the driveway were shaking down dead fronds as they rocked, the driveway cracking as though it was sledge-hammered from below.

"I should warn the cops," Grillo said. "Tell them what's coming."

"I think we lost this one, Grillo. Do you know what happened to Hotchkiss?"

"No."

"I hope he gets out before they come through."

"He won't."

"He should. No town's worth dying for."

"I think it's time I made my call, don't you?"

"What call?" she said.

"To Abernethy? Break the bad news."

Tesla made a small sigh. "Yeah, why don't you? The Last Scoop."

"I'll be back," he said. "Don't think you're getting out of here alone, you're not. We're going together."

"I'm not leaving."

He got into the car not really aware until he tried to align his hand with the ignition key just how violent the shaking in the ground had become. When he finally succeeded in getting the car started, and backed it down the driveway to the gate, he found any warning to the cops was redundant. The bulk of them had withdrawn a good distance down the Hill, leaving a single vehicle just outside the gates, with two men posted as observers. They paid little notice to Grillo. Their twin concerns—one professional, one personal—were watching the house, and preparing for a rapid retreat if the fissures spread in their direction. Grillo drove on past them, and down the Hill. There was a half-hearted attempt by one of the officers lower down the slope to halt him, but he simply drove on by, heading to the Mall. There he'd hope to find a public telephone in which to make his call to Abernethy. There too he'd find Hotchkiss, and warn him, if he didn't already know, that the game was up. As he negotiated the rat maze of streets blocked or plowed up or turned into chasms, he experimented with headlines for this last report. *The End of the World Is Nigh* was so commonplace. He didn't want to be just another in a long line of prophets promising the Apocalypse, even if this time (finally) it was true. As he turned into the Mall, just before his eyes alighted on the animal jamboree going on there, he had an inspiration. It was Buddy Vance's collection that brought it to mind. Though he suspected he'd have a hard time selling the idea to Abernethy he knew there was no more appropriate headline for this story than *The Ride Is Over*. The species had enjoyed its adventure, but it was coming to an end.

He stopped the car at the entrance to the lot, and stepped out to survey the bizarre spectacle of animal playtime. A smile came to his lips, despite himself. What bliss they knew, knowing nothing: playing in the sun without the least suspicion of how short their span was. He crossed the lot to the book store but Hotchkiss wasn't there. The stock was scattered over the floor, evidence of a search that had presumably ended in failure. He headed along to the pet store, in hope of finding some human company, and a phone. There was a din of birds from inside: the store's last captives. If he had time he'd set them free himself. No reason why they shouldn't get a glimpse of the sun.

"Anyone home?" he said, putting his head around the door.

A gecko ran out between his legs. He watched it go, the same inquiry on his tongue. It went unsaid. The gecko had run through blood on its way out the door; blood smeared and spattered everywhere he looked. He saw Elizando's body first, then the companion corpse, half buried beneath cages.

"Hotchkiss?" he said.

He began to haul the cages off the body. There was more than a smell of blood in the air, there was the stench of shit too. It came off on his hands, but he kept up his labors until he'd seen enough of

Hotchkiss to be certain he was dead. Uncovering his head confirmed that fact. The skull had been crushed to smithereens, shards of bone sticking up like broken crockery from the mush of his mind and senses. No animal housed in a store this size could have committed such violence; nor was it easy to see what weapon might have caused it. He didn't linger to ponder the problem, not with the very real possibility that those responsible were still in the vicinity. He scanned the floor, looking for some weapon. A leash, a studded collar, anything to ward off the slaughter. His search took him to a book, dropped on the floor a little way from Hotchkiss's body.

He read the title aloud:

"*Preparing for Armageddon?*"

Then he picked it up, flipping through it quickly. It seemed to be a manual on how to survive the Apocalypse. These were words of wisdom from Mormon Brethren to members of the Church, telling them that all would be well; that they had God's living oracles, the First Presidency and the Council of the Twelve Apostles to watch over them and advise them. All they needed to do was take of that advice, spiritual and practical, and whatever the future brought could be survived.

"*If ye are prepared, ye need not fear*" was the hope—no, *certainty*—of these pages. "*Be pure in heart, love many, be just, and stand in holy places. Maintain a year's supply.*"

He flipped on through it. Why had Hotchkiss selected this book? Hurricanes, forest fires and floods? What did they have to do with Trinity?

And then there it was: a grainy photograph of a mushroom cloud, and the words beneath, identifying the place where it had been detonated.

Trinity, New Mexico.

He read no further. Book in hand he ran out into the lot, animals scattering in front of him, and got into the car. His call to Abernethy would have to wait. How the simple fact that Trinity was the birthplace of the bomb fitted into this story he didn't know, but perhaps Tesla would. And even if she didn't he'd have the satisfaction of bringing her the news. It was absurd, he knew, to be so suddenly *pleased* with himself, as though this information made some difference to things. The world was going to end *(The Ride Is Over)* yet having this small piece of the puzzle in his hands was enough to momentarily put the terror of that fact aside. He knew no greater pleasure than to be a bringer of news, a messenger, a *Nuncio*. It was the closest he'd ever got to understanding the word *happy*.

Even in the short time—no more than four or five minutes—that he'd spent at the Mall the Grove's stability had deteriorated further. Two streets that had been accessible on his way down from the Hill now no longer were. One had virtually disappeared entirely—the earth had simply opened up and guzzled it—the other was strewn with wreckage from two toppled houses. He found a third route that was still passable, and began up the Hill, the tremors in the ground becoming so violent that on occasion he could barely control the car. A few observers had appeared on the scene during his absence, in three unmarked helicopters, the largest of which was hovering directly over the Vance house, its passengers attempting to make, no doubt, an assessment of the situation. They must have guessed by now that this was no natural phenomenon. Perhaps they even knew the root cause. D'Amour had told Tesla the existence of the Iad was known to the highest of the high. If so, there should have been firepower ranged around the house hours before, instead of a few frightened cops. Had they not believed the evidence in their hands, the generals and the politicians? Were they too pragmatic to think that their empire could be put in jeopardy by something that belonged on the other side of dreams? He couldn't blame them. He wouldn't have lent that notion a moment's credibility seventy-two hours ago. He'd have judged it a nonsense: like the talk of God's living oracles in the book on the seat beside him, an overheated fantasy. If the observers stayed where they were, directly over the schism, they'd have a chance to change their minds. Seeing was believing. And see they would.

The gates of Coney Eye had been toppled; so had its perimeter wall. He left the car in front of the pile of rubble, and clutching the book climbed towards the house, upon the face of which something he took to be a cloud-shadow seemed to sit. The ructions had opened up the fissures in the driveway and he had to tread with care, his concentration befuddled by a distressing quality in the atmosphere around the house. The closer he got to the door the darker the shadow seemed to get. Though the sun was still beating down on the back of his head, and on Coney Eye's cake-in-the-rain facade, the whole scene was grimy, as though a layer of dirty varnish had been painted over everything. It made his head ache to see it; his sinuses pricked, his ears popped. More distressing than these minor discomforts was a palpable sense of dread that grew stronger in him with every step he took. His head started to fill up with sickening images, culled from his years in the newsrooms of a dozen papers, looking at photographs no editor, however squalid, would have put to the press. There were automobile wrecks, of course, and plane crashes—bodies in pieces that would never be reassembled. Inevitably, there were murder scenes. But it wasn't these that headed this assault. It was pictures of innocents, and the harm done to them. Babies and children, beaten, maimed, dumped out with the trash; the sick and the old brutalized; the retarded humiliated. So many cruelties, all filling up his head.

"*The Iad*," he heard Tesla say, and swung his eyes around in the direction of her voice. The air between them was thick, her face grainy, as though reproduced. Not real. None of it real. Pictures on a screen.

"It's the Iad coming," she said. "That's what you're feeling. You should get away from here. There's no use in your staying—"

"No," he said, "I've got . . . a message."

He was having difficulty holding on to that thought. The innocents kept appearing, one after the other, bearing every kind of wound.

"What message?" she said.

"Trinity."

"What about it?"

She was shouting, he realized, but still her voice was barely audible.

"You said Trinity, Grillo."

"Yes?"

"What about it?"

So many eyes, looking at him. He couldn't think past them; past their hurt and their powerlessness.

"Grillo!"

He focused his attention as best he could on the woman shouting his name in a whisper.

"Trinity," she said again.

The book in his hand had the answer to her question, he knew, though the eyes, and grief in the eyes, kept on distracting him. Trinity. What was Trinity? He raised the book and gave it to her, but as she took it from him he remembered.

"The bomb," he said.

"What?"

"Trinity is where they exploded the first atomic bomb."

He saw a look of comprehension cross her face.

"You understand?" he said.

"Yes. Jesus! *Yes!"*

She didn't bother to open the book he'd brought, she just told him to get away, back towards the road. He listened as best he could but he knew there was another piece of information he needed to convey. Something almost as vital as Trinity; and as much about death. Try as he might he couldn't bring it to mind.

"Go on back," she told him again. "Out of this filth."

He nodded, knowing he was useless to her, and stumbled away through the dirty air, the sunlight brightening the further he got from the house, the images of the dead innocents no longer dominating his thoughts. As he turned the corner of the driveway, and came in sight of the Hill again, he remembered the information he'd failed to convey. *Hotchkiss was dead*; murdered; head crushed. Somebody or something had committed that murder, and they were still loose in the Grove. He had to go back and tell her; warn her. He waited a moment, to let the images the Iad's proximity had induced clear from his cortex. They didn't go entirely; he knew that the instant he went back towards the house they'd return with fresh intensity. The poisoned air that had brought them on was spreading, and had already caught up with him again. Before it befuddled him afresh he pulled out a pen he'd brought from the motel in case he'd needed to take notes. He'd brought a paper too, from the receptionist's desk, but the parade of cruelties was coming at him again and he feared losing the thought while finding the pad, so he simply scrawled the word on the back of his hand.

"Hotchk—" was as much as he could manage. Then his fingers lost the power to write, and his mind the power to hold anything but grief for dead innocents and the thought that he had to see Tesla again. Message and messenger one flesh, he turned about and stumbled back into the Iad's cloud of influence. But when he reached the place where the woman who shouted in whispers had been, she'd gone closer still to the source of these cruelties, where he doubted his sanity could survive to follow.

So much suddenly made sense to Tesla, not least the atmosphere of anticipation she'd always felt in the Loop, particularly when passing through the town. She'd seen films of the bomb's detonation, and of the destruction of the town, on documentaries about Oppenheimer. The houses and stores she'd puzzled over had been built to be blasted to ash, so that the bomb's creators could observe their baby's wrath at work. No wonder she'd tried to set a dinosaur movie there. Her dramatic instinct had been on the button. This *was* a town waiting for doomsday. It was just the monster she'd got wrong. What better place for Kissoon to hide the evidence of his crime? When the flash came the bodies would be utterly consumed. She could well imagine what perverse pleasure he'd have taken in plotting such an elaborate creation, knowing that the cloud that destroyed the Shoal was one of the most indelible images of the century.

But he'd been outplotted. Mary Muralles had trapped him in the Loop, and until he could find a new body to leave in he was its prisoner, his will perpetually holding the moment of detonation at bay. He'd lived like a man with his finger on a crack in a dam, knowing that the moment he neglected his duty the dam would burst and overwhelm him. No wonder the word Trinity had thrown his thoughts into confusion. It was the name of his terror.

Was there a way to use this knowledge against the Iad? An outlandish possibility occurred to her as she returned into the house, but she'd need Jaffe's assistance.

It was hard to hold on to any coherent thought process in the cesspool that was spilling from the schism, but she'd fought off influences before, from movie producers and shamans, and she was able to hold the worst of it at bay. It was getting stronger, however, the closer the Iad came to the threshold. She tried not to contemplate the extent of their corruption if this, the merest rumor of their approach, could so profoundly affect the psyche. Not in all her attempts to imagine the nature of that invasion had she considered the possibility that their weapon would be madness. But perhaps it was. Though she was able to ward off this assault of vileness for a time she knew she'd capitulate to it sooner or later. No human mind could keep it at bay forever, and would have no choice, drawing in such horrors, but to take refuge in insanity. The Iad Uroboros would rule a planet of lunatics.

Jaffe was already well on his way to mental collapse, of course. She found him standing at the door of the room where he'd practiced the Art. The space behind him had been entirely commandeered by the schism. Looking through the door she truly understood for the first time why Quiddity was called a sea. Waves of dark energy were beating against the shore of the Cosm, their surf spilling through the schism. Beyond it she saw another motion, which she was only able to glimpse briefly. Jaffe had talked about mountains that moved; and fleas. But Tesla's mind fixed upon another image to characterize the invaders. They were giants. The living terrors of her earliest nightmares. Often, in those childhood encounters, they'd had the faces of her parents, a fact her analyst had made much of. But these were giants of a different order. If they had faces at all, which she doubted, they were impossible to assimilate as such. One thing she was certain of: caring parents they weren't.

"Do you see?" Jaffe said.

"Oh yes," she said.

He asked the question again, his voice lighter than she'd ever heard it.

"Do you see, Poppa?"

"*Poppa?*" she said.

"I'm not afraid, Poppa," the voice out of the Jaff went on. "They won't hurt me. I'm the Death-Boy."

Now she understood. Jaffe wasn't simply seeing with Tommy-Ray's eyes, he was speaking with the boy's voice. She'd lost the father to the son.

"Jaffe!" she said. "Listen to me. I need your help! *Jaffe?*" He made no reply. Avoiding sight of the schism as best she could she went to him and took hold of his tattered shirt, hauling him towards the front door. "*Randolph!*" she said. "You've got to speak to me."

The man grinned. It wasn't an expression that had ever belonged on that face. It was the grin of a Californian prince, wide and toothy. She let him go.

"A lot of good you'll do me," she said.

She couldn't afford the time to try to coax him back from the adventure he was sharing with Tommy-Ray. She'd have to do what she was planning alone. It was a notion simple in the conceiving and, she guessed, damn difficult—if not impossible—in the execution. But she had no alternative. She was not a great shaman. She couldn't seal the schism. But she might *move* it. She'd proved twice before that she had the power to pass in and out of the Loop. To dissolve herself—and others—in thought, and remove them to Trinity. Could she also jump dead matter? Wood, and plaster? A piece of a house, for instance? *This* part of *this* house, for instance? Could she dissolve the slice of the Cosm she and the schism occupied, and remove it to Point Zero, where a force was ticking that might fell the giants before they spread their madness?

There was no answer to the questions this side of attempting the suit. If she failed, the answer was no. Simple as that. She'd have a few moments the wiser for her failure before wisdom, failure and her aspirations to shamanhood became academic.

Tommy-Ray had started to speak again, his monologue now deteriorated to a ragged babble.

". . . up like Andy . . ." he was saying, ". . . only higher . . . see me, Poppa? . . . up like Andy . . . I can see the shore! I can see the shore!"

That at least did make sense. He was within sighting distance of the Cosm, which meant the Iad were almost as close.

"... Death-Boy ..." he started to say again, "... I'm the Death-Boy ..."

"Can't you tune him out?" she said to Jaffe, knowing her words were falling on deaf ears.

"Whoo-ee!" the kid was shouting. "Here we come! Here—we—*come!*"

She didn't look back towards the schism to see if the giants were visible, though she was sorely tempted. The moment would come when she'd have to look it in the eye but she wasn't yet ready; wasn't calm, wasn't *girded*. She took another step back to the front door, and seized firm hold of the door jamb. It felt so damn solid. Her common sense protested at the idea of being able to think such solidity into another place and time. She told her common sense to go get fucked. It and the madness that was spewing from the schism were not opposites. Reason could be cruel; logic could be lunacy. There was another state of mind that put aside such naive dichotomies; that made power from being *in between* conditions.

All things to all men.

She remembered suddenly what D'Amour had said, about there being a savior rumored. She'd thought he'd meant Jaffe, but she'd been looking too far afield. *She* was that savior. Tesla Bombeck, the wild woman of West Hollywood, reversed and resurrected.

The realization gave her new faith; and with the faith, a simple grasp of how she might make the suit work. She didn't try to block out Tommy-Ray's idiot whoops, or the sight of Jaffe limp and defeated, or the whole nonsense of the solid becoming thought and thought moving the solid. It was all a part of her, even the doubt. Perhaps especially that. She didn't need to deny the confusions and contradictions to be powerful; she needed to embrace them. Devour them with the mouth of her mind, chew them up, swallow them. They were all devourable. The solid and insolid, this world and that, all edible and moveable feasts. Now she knew that, nothing could keep her from the table.

She looked at the schism, dead on.

"Not even you," she said, and began to eat.

As Grillo had got within two steps of the front door the innocents had come back to claim him, their assault more pitiless than ever, this close to the schism. He lost the power to move forward or back, as brutalities rose around him. He seemed to be treading on small, bloody bodies. They turned their sobbing faces up to him, but he knew there was no help for them. Not now. The shadow that was moving across Quiddity brought with it an end to mercy. Nor would its reign ever end. It would never be judged; never be brought to account.

Somebody moved past him towards the door, a form barely visible in an air thick with suffering. Grillo tried hard to grasp a solid sight of the man, but garnered only the briefest glimpse of a thuggish face, heavy-boned and lanternjawed. Then the stranger went into the house. A movement on the ground around his feet took his glance from door to floor. The children's faces were still visible, but now the horror had a new twist. Black snakes, as thick as his arm, were crawling over the children as they followed the man inside. Appalled, he took a step forward in the vain hope of stamping one or all of them out. The step took him closer to the edge of insanity, which paradoxically lent force to his crusade. He took a second step, and a third, trying to put his heel on the heads of these black beasts. The fourth step took him over the threshold of the house, and into another madness entirely.

"Raul?"

Of all people, Raul.

Just as she'd got a grip on the task before her he stepped through the door, his appearance here so shocking she might have put it down to some mental aberrance, had she not been certain of her mind's workings now as she'd never been certain in her life before. This was no hallucination. He was here in the flesh, her name on his lips and a look of welcome on his face.

"What are you doing here?" she said, feeling her grasp of the suit slipping from her.

"I came for you," was his reply. On its heels, and on his, came grim comprehension of what he meant by that. There were Lix slithering over the doorstep into the house.

"What have you done?" she said.

"I told you," he replied. "I came for you. We all did."

She took a step away from him, but with the schism occupying half the house and the Lix guarding the door, the only route of escape available to her was up the stairs. At best that promised a temporary reprieve. She'd be trapped up there, waiting for them to find her in their own good time, except that they wouldn't need to bother. In minutes, the Iad would be in the Cosm. After which, death might very well be desirable. She had to stay put, Lix or no Lix. Her business was here, and it had to be done quickly.

"Keep away from me," she said to Raul. "I don't know why you're here, but just *keep your distance!*"

"I came to see the arrival," Raul replied. "We can wait here together if you like."

Raul's shirt was unbuttoned, and around his neck she caught sight of a familiar object: the Shoal medallion. With the sight came a suspicion: that this wasn't Raul at all. His manner wasn't that of the frightened Nunciate she'd met at the Misión de Santa Catrina. There was somebody else behind his semi-simian face: the man who'd first shown her the Shoal's enigmatic sigil.

"*Kissoon,*" she said.

"Now you've spoiled my surprise," he replied.

"What have you done to Raul?"

"Unhoused him. Occupied the body. It wasn't difficult. He'd got a lot of Nuncio in him. That made him available. I pulled him into the Loop, the same way I did with you. Only he didn't have the wits to resist me the way you or Randolph resisted. He gave in quickly enough."

"You murdered him."

"Oh no," Kissoon said lightly. "His spirit's alive and kicking. Keeping my flesh from the fire till I go back for it. I'll reoccupy it once it's out of the Loop. I certainly don't want to stay in *this*. It's repulsive."

He came at her suddenly, agile as only Raul could be, leaping to catch hold of her arm. She yelled at the force of his grip. He smiled at her again, closing on her in two quick steps, his face inches from hers in a heartbeat.

"*Gotcha*," he said.

She looked past him to the door, where Grillo was standing, staring into the schism, against which Quiddity's waves were breaking with mounting frequency and ferocity. She yelled his name, but he didn't respond. Sweat ran down his face; saliva dribbled from his slack jaw. Wherever he was out wandering, he wasn't home.

Had she been able to sit in Grillo's skull she'd have understood his fascination. Once over the threshold the innocents had disappeared from his mind's eye, superseded by a sharper distress. His eyes were drawn to the surf, and in it he saw horrors. Closest to the shore were two bodies, thrown towards the Cosm then dragged back by an undertow which threatened to drown them. He knew them, though their faces were much changed. One was Jo-Beth McGuire. The other was Howie Katz. Further out in the waves he thought he glimpsed a third figure, pale against the dark sky. This one he didn't know. There appeared to be no flesh left on his face to recognize. He was a death's-head, riding the surf.

It was further out still, however, where the real horror began. Forms massive and rotting, the air around them dense with activity, as though flies the size of birds were feeding on their foulness. The Iad Uroboros. Even now, mesmerized, his mind (inspired by Swift) looked for words to describe the sight, but the vocabulary was impoverished when it came to evil. Depravity, iniquity, godlessness: what were those simple conditions in the face of such unredeemable essences? Hobbies and entertainments. Palate cleansers between viler courses. He almost envied those closer to the abominations the comprehension that might come with proximity—

Tossed in the tumult of the waves, Howie could have told him a thing or two. As the Iad had closed on them, he'd remembered where he'd sensed this horror before: in the Chicago slaughterhouse where he'd worked two years previous. It was memories of that month that filled his head. The slaughterhouse in summer, blood congealing in the gutters, the animals emptying their bladders and bowels at the sound of the deaths that went before them. Life turned to meat with a single shot. He tried to look beyond these loathsome images to

Jo-Beth, with whom he'd come so far, on a tide which had conspired to keep them together, but couldn't get them to the shore fast enough to save them from the slaughterers at their backs. The sight of her, which might have sweetened these last despairing moments, was denied him. All he could see was the cattle beaten on to the ramps, and the shit and blood being hosed away, and kicking carcasses being hooked up by one broken leg and sent down the line for disembowelment. The same horror filling his head forever and forever.

The place beyond the surf was as invisible to him as Jo-Beth, so he had no idea of how far—or indeed how *near*—they were to its shores. Had he had the power of sight he'd have seen Jo-Beth's father, stricken, and speaking with Tommy-Ray's voice:

"... *here we come!* ... *here we come* ..."

—and Grillo staring out at the Iad; and Tesla, on the verge of losing her life to a man she called—

"*Kissoon!* For pity's sake! Look at them! *Look!*"

Kissoon glanced towards the schism, and the freight being brought by the tide.

"I see them," he said.

"You think they give a fuck about you? If they come through you're dead like all of us!"

"No," he said. "They're bringing a new world, and I've earned my place in it. A high place. You know how many years I've waited for this? Planned for it? Murdered for it? They'll reward me."

"Signed a contract did you? Got it in writing?"

"I'm their liberator. I made this possible. You should have joined the team back in the Loop. Lent me your body for a while. I'd have protected you. But no. You had your own ambitions. Like *him*." He looked at Jaffe. "Him the same. Had to have a piece of the pie. You both choked on it." Knowing Tesla couldn't leave now, when there was nowhere to leave *to*, he let her go and took a step towards Jaffe. "He got closer than you did, but then he had the *balls*."

Tommy-Ray's whoops of exhilaration were no longer issuing from Jaffe. There was only a low moan, which might have been the father, or the son, or a combination of both.

"You should *see*," Kissoon said to the tormented face. "Jaffe. Look at me. *I want you to see!*"

Tesla looked back towards the schism. How many waves were there left to break before the Iad reached the shore? A dozen? Half that number?

Kissoon's irritation with Jaffe was growing. He began to shake the man. "*Look at me, damn you!*"

Tesla let him rage. It granted her a moment's grace; a moment in which she might just begin the process of removal to the Loop afresh.

"Wake up and see me, fucker. It's Kissoon. I got out! *I got out!*"

She let his haranguings become part of the scene she was picturing. Nothing could be excluded. Jaffe, Grillo, the doorway out to Cosm, and of course the doorway to Quiddity, all of it had to be devoured. Even she, the devourer, had to be part of this removal. Chewed up and spat into another time.

Kissoon's shouts suddenly stopped.

"What are you doing?" he said, turning to look at her. His stolen features, not used to expressing rage, were knotted up in a grotesque fashion. She didn't let the sight distract her. That too was part of the scene to be swallowed. She was equal to it.

"*Don't you dare!*" Kissoon said. "*Hear me?*"

She heard, and ate.

"I'm warning you," he said, moving back in her direction. "*Don't you dare!*"

Somewhere in the recesses of Randolph Jaffe's memory those three words, and the tone of their delivery, started an echo. He'd been in a hut once, with the man who'd delivered them in just that fashion. He remembered the hut's stale heat, and the smell of his own sweat. He remembered the scrawny old man squatting beyond the fire. And most of all he remembered the exchange now delivered into his head out of the past:

"*Don't you dare.*"

"*Red rag to a bull, saying dare to me. I've seen stuff . . . done stuff . . .*"

Prompted by the words, he remembered a motion. His hand going down to the pocket of his jacket, to find a bluntbladed knife that was waiting there. A knife with an appetite for opening up sealed and secret things. Like letters; like skulls.

He heard the words again—

"*Don't you dare.*"

—and opened his sight to the scene in front of him. His arm, a parody of the strong limb he'd once owned—went down to his pocket. All these years he'd never let the knife out of his possession. It was still blunt. It was still hungry. His withered digits closed around the handle. His eyes focused on the head of the man who'd spoken from his memories. It was an easy target.

Tesla saw the motion of Jaffe's head from the corner of her eye; saw him push himself away from the wall and start to raise his right arm up from the vicinity of his pocket. She didn't see what was in it, not until the last possible moment, by which time Kissoon's fingers were tight around her neck, and the Lix around her shins. She'd not let his assault stop the removal. It too became part of the picture she was devouring. And now Jaffe. And his raised hand. And the knife she finally saw glinting in his raised hand. Raised, and falling, driving into the back of Kissoon's neck.

The shaman screamed, his hands dropping from her throat and going around the back of his head to protect himself. She liked his cry. It was the pain of her enemy, and her power seemed to rise on its arc, the task she'd undertaken suddenly easier than it had ever been, as though part of Kissoon's strength was passing to her in the sound. She felt the space they occupied in her mind's mouth, and chewed on it. The house shuddered as a significant piece of it was wrenched away and removed into the closed moments of the Loop.

Instantly, light.

The light of the Loop's perpetual dawn, pouring in through the door. With it the same wind that had blown on her face whenever she'd been here. It blew through the hallway, and took a portion of the Iad's taint with it, off across the wasteland. With its passing she saw the glazed look leaving Grillo's face. He grabbed hold of the door jamb, squinting against the light and shaking his head like a dog maddened with fleas.

With their maker wounded, the Lix had left off their attack, but she didn't hope they'd leave her be for long. Before he could redirect them she made for the door, pausing only to push Grillo ahead of her.

"What in God's name have you done?" he said as they stepped out on to bleached desert earth.

She hurried him away from the relocated rooms, which without a structure around them to spread the load of Quiddity's breakers were already coming apart at every corner.

"You want the good news or the bad?" she said.

"The good."

"This is the Loop. I brought part of the house through—"

Now she'd done it she could barely believe she'd succeeded.

"I did," she said, as though Grillo had contradicted her. "Fuck me, I *did!*"

"Including the Iad?" Grillo said.

"The schism and whatever's on the other side came too."

"So what's the bad news?"

"This is Trinity, remember? Point Zero?"

"Oh Jesus."

"And that—" she pointed to the steel tower, which was no more than a quarter of a mile from where they stood, "—is the bomb."

"So when does it blow? Have we got time—"

"I don't know," she said. "Maybe it won't detonate as long as Kissoon's alive. He's held that moment, all these years."

"Is there any way out?"

"Yes."

"Which direction? Let's do it."

"Don't waste time wishing, Grillo. We're not getting out of here alive."

"You can *think* us out. You thought us in."

"No. I'm staying. I have to see it to the end."

"This *is* the end," he said, pointing back towards the fragment of the house. "Look."

The walls were toppling in clouds of plaster dust, as Quiddity's waves were thrown against them. "How much more *end* do you want? Let's get the fuck out of here."

Tesla looked for some sign of either Kissoon or Jaffe in the confusion, but the ether of the dream-sea was spilling out in all directions, too thick now to be dispersed by the wind. They were in it somewhere, but out of sight.

"Tesla? Are you listening to me?"

"The bomb won't go till Kissoon's dead," she said. "He's holding the moment—"

"So you said."

"If you want to run for the exit, you might make it. It's in that direction." She pointed beyond the cloud through the town and out the other side. "You'd better get going."

"You think I'm a coward."

"Did I say that?"

A wave of ether curled towards them.

"If you're going to go, *go*," she said, her gaze fixed on the rubble of Coney Eye's lounge and hall. Above it, just visible through Quiddity's spillage, was the schism, hanging in the air. It doubled in size in the space between blinks, tearing itself open. She readied herself for the sight of the giants. But it was human forms she saw first, two of them, thrown up and out on to this arid shore.

"Howie?" she said.

It was. And beside him, Jo-Beth. Something had happened to them, she saw. Their faces and bodies were a mass of growths, as though their tissue had sprouted some vile blossom. She braved the next wave of ether to go back to them, shouting their names as she went. It was Jo-Beth who looked up first. Leading Howie by the hand she sought Tesla out in the turmoil.

"This way," Tesla said. "You have to get away from the hole—"

The tainted ether was inducing nightmares. They itched to be seen. But Jo-Beth seemed able to think her way through them to a simple question.

"Where are we?"

There was no simple answer.

"Grillo will tell you," she said. "Later. *Grillo?*"

He was there, already getting that same distracted look she'd seen in his eyes at the door of Coney Eye.

"Children," he said. "Why's it always children?"

"I don't know what you're talking about," she told him. "Listen to me, Grillo."

"I'm . . . listening," he said.

"You wanted to get out. I told you the way, remember?"

"Through the town."

"Through the town."

"Out the other side."

"Right."

"Take Howie and Jo-Beth with you. Maybe you can still outrun it."

"Outrun what?" Howie said, only raising his head with difficulty. It was weighed down with monstrous growths.

"The Iad or the bomb," Tesla told him. "Take your pick. Can you run?"

"We can try," Jo-Beth said. She looked at Howie. "We can try."

"Then go to it. All of you."

"I still . . . don't see . . ." Grillo began, his voice betraying the Iad's influence.

"Why I have to stay?"

"Yes."

"It's simple," she said. "This is the final trial. All things to all men, remember?"

"Damn stupid," he said, holding her gaze, as though the sight of her helped him keep the insanity at bay.

"Damn right," she said.

"So many things . . ." he said.

"What?"

"I haven't said to you."

"You didn't need to. And I hope neither did I."

"You were right."

"Except one. Something I should have told you."

"What?"

"I should have said—" she began; then grinned a wide, almost ecstatic grin that she didn't need to fake because it came from some contented place in her; and with it terminated her sentence as she'd terminated so many telephone calls between them and turned away, heading off into the next wave out of the schism, where she knew he couldn't follow.

Somebody was coming her way; another swimmer in the dream-sea, thrown up on the beach.

Tommy-Ray, the Death-Boy. The changes wrought in Jo-Beth and Howie had been profound, but they were kindness itself compared with what he'd sustained. His hair was still Malibu gold, and his face still bore the grin which had once charmed Palomo Grove to its knees. But his teeth were not the only gleam about him. Quiddity had bleached his flesh so that it resembled bone. His brows and cheeks had swollen up, his eyes sunk. He looked like a living skull. He wiped a thread of saliva from his chin with the back of his hand, the pinpoints of his gaze directed past Tesla to where his sister stood.

"Jo-Beth . . ." he said, moving through the wash of dark air. Tesla saw Jo-Beth look back towards him, then take a step away from Howie as though she was ready to part from him. Though she had urgent business to finish Tesla could not help but watch, as Tommy-Ray moved to claim his sister. The love that had ignited between Howie and Jo-Beth had begun this whole story, or at least its most recent chapter. Was it possible that Quiddity had undone that love?

She had the answer a beat later, as Jo-Beth took a second step from Howie's side, till they were at arm's length, her right hand still holding his left. With a thrill of comprehension Tesla saw what Jo-Beth was displaying to her brother. She and Howie Katz were not simply holding hands. *They were joined.* Quiddity had fused them, their interlocked fingers became a knot of forms that bound them together.

There was no need for words. Tommy-Ray let out a shout of disgust, and stopped in his tracks. Tesla could not see the expression on his face. Most probably there was none. Skulls could only grin and grimace; opposites collided in one expression. She saw Jo-Beth's look, however, even through the intervening murk. There was a little pity in it. But only a little. The rest was dispassion.

Tesla saw Grillo speak, words to summon the lovers away. They went immediately; all three. Tommy-Ray didn't move to follow.

"Death-Boy?" she said.

He looked around at her. The skull was still capable of tears. They welled on the curve of his sockets.

"How far are they behind you?" she asked him. "The Iad?"

"Iad?" he said.

"The giants."

"There are no giants. Just darkness."

"How far?"

"Very close."

When she looked back towards the schism she understood what he meant by darkness. Clots of it were emerging, carried out on the waves like gobs of tar the size of boats, then rising up into the air above the desert. They had some kind of life, propelling themselves with rhythmic motions that ran down through the dozens of limbs arrayed along their flanks. Filaments of matter as dark as their bodies trailed beneath them, like coils of decaying gut. This was not, she knew, the Iad itself; but they couldn't be far behind.

She glanced away from the sight towards the steel tower, and the platform on top of it. The bomb was her species' ultimate idiocy, but it might justify its existence if it was quick in its detonation. There was no flicker from the platform, however. The bomb hung in its cradle like a bandaged baby, refusing to wake.

Kissoon was still alive; still holding the moment. She started back towards the rubble in the hope of finding him, and in the vainer hope of stopping his life with her own hands. As she approached she realized the clots had purpose in their upward movement. They were assembling themselves in layers, their filaments knotting so as to create a vast curtain. It was already thirty feet in the air, and each wave that broke brought more clots, their number rising exponentially as the schism widened.

She searched the maelstrom for a sign of Kissoon, and found both him and Jaffe on the far side of the rubble that had been the rooms. They were standing face to face, hands at each other's throats, the knife still in Jaffe's fist but held from further work by Kissoon. It had been busy. What had once been Raul's body was covered in stab wounds, from which blood was freely running. The cuts seemed not to have impaired Kissoon's strength. Even as she came in sight of them the shaman tore at Jaffe's throat. Pieces of his flesh came away. Kissoon went back for more instantly, opening the wound further. She directed him from his assault with a cry.

"*Kissoon!*"

The shaman glanced her way.

"Too late," he said. "The Iad's almost here."

She took what comfort she could from that *almost*.

"You both lost," he said, taking a back-handed swipe at Jaffe which threw the man off him to the ground. The frail, bony body didn't land heavily; it had too little weight. But it rolled some distance, the knife going from Jaffe's hand. Kissoon offered his opponent a contemptuous glance, then laughed.

"Poor bitch," he said to Tesla. "What did you expect? A reprieve? A blinding flash to wipe them all away? Forget it. It can't happen. The moment's held."

He started towards her as he talked, his approach slower than it might otherwise have been had he not sustained so many wounds.

"You wanted revelation," he said. "And now you've got it. It's almost here. I think you should show your devotion to it. That's only right. Let it see your flesh."

He raised his hands, which were bloody, the way they'd been in the hut when she first heard the word Trinity, and glimpsed him daubed with Mary Muralles's blood.

"The breasts," he said. "Show it the breasts."

A long way behind him, Tesla saw Jaffe getting to his feet. Kissoon failed to notice the motion. His eyes were all for Tesla.

"I think I should bare them for you," he said. "Allow me to do you that *kindness.*"

She didn't retreat; didn't put up any resistance. Instead she dropped all expression from her face, knowing how much he liked the pliant. His bloody hands were repulsive, the hard-on pressing against the soaked fabric of his trousers more disgusting still, but she succeeded in concealing her repugnance.

"Good girl," he said. "Good girl."

He put his hands on her breasts.

"What say we fuck for the millennium?" he said.

She couldn't quite discipline the shudder that ran through her at the touch and the thought.

"Don't like it?" he said, suddenly suspicious. His eyes flickered off to his left as he understood the conspiracy. There was a glint of fear in them. He started to turn. Jaffe was two yards from him, and closing, the knife raised above his head, the glint on its blade an echo of the glint in Kissoon's eyes. Two lights that belonged together.

"Don't—" Kissoon began, but the knife dared to descend before he could forbid it, sliding into his wide right eye. Kissoon didn't scream this time, but expelled his breath as a long moan. Jaffe pulled the knife out and stabbed again, the second stab as accurate as the first, puncturing the left eye. He drove the blade in to the hilt, and pulled it out. Kissoon flailed, his moan becoming sobs as he fell to his knees. With both his fists wrapped around the knife Jaffe delivered a third blow to the top of the shaman's skull, then went on stabbing, the force of the blows opening wound after wound.

Kissoon's sobs stopped as suddenly as they'd begun. His hands, which had been scrabbling at his head to ward off further cuts, fell to his sides. His body stayed upright for two beats. Then he fell forward.

A spasm of pleasure ran through Tesla that was indistinguishable from the highest pleasure. She wanted the bomb to detonate at that moment, matching its completion with her own. Kissoon was dead and it would not be bad to die now, knowing the Iad would be swept away in the same moment.

"Go on," she said to the bomb, trying to sustain the bliss she felt until the flesh was burned off her bones. "Go on, will you? Go on."

But there was no explosion. She felt the rush of pleasure start to drain from her, and the realization appear in its place that she'd missed some vital element in all of this. Surely with Kissoon dead the event he'd sweated all those years to hold at bay had to come? Now; on delay. But there was nothing. The steel tower still stood.

"What have I missed?" she asked herself. "What in God's name have I missed?"

She looked towards Jaffe, who was still staring down at Kissoon's corpse.

"Synchronicity," he said.

"What?"

"I killed him."

"It doesn't seem to have answered the problem."

"What problem?"

"This is Point Zero. There's a bomb, just waiting to detonate. He was holding that moment at bay."

"Who was?"

"*Kissoon!* Isn't it obvious?"

No, babe—she told herself—it's not. Of course it's not. The thought was suddenly clear in her head that Kissoon had left the Loop in Raul's body intending to come back to claim his own. Once out in the Cosm he hadn't been able to hold the moment. Somebody else must have done it for him. That somebody, or rather, that some-*spirit*, was still doing it.

"Where are you going?" Jaffe wanted to know as she started in the direction of the wastes beyond the tower. Could she even find the hut? He followed after her, still asking questions.

"How did you get us here?"

"Ate it up and spat it out."

"Like my hands?"

"No, not like your hands. Not at all."

The sun was steadily being blocked out by the mesh of clots, the light only breaking through in patches.

"Where are you going?" he said again.

"The hut. Kissoon's hut."

"Why?"

"Just come with me. I need help."

A cry in the gloom slowed progress a moment.

"*Poppa?*"

She looked round to see Tommy-Ray stepping out of shadow into a patch of light. The sun was strangely kind to him, its brilliance bleaching out the worst details of his transformed state.

"Poppa?"

Jaffe stopped following Tesla.

"Come on," she urged him, but she already knew she'd once more lost him to Tommy-Ray. The first time it had been to his thoughts. This time it was to his presence.

The Death-Boy started to stumble towards his father.

"Help me, Poppa," he said.

The man opened his arms, saying nothing, nor needing to. Tommy-Ray fell into them, clutching at Jaffe in return.

Tesla offered him one last chance to assist her.

"Are you coming or not?"

The answer was simple:

"*Not*," he said.

She didn't bother to waste breath on the issue. The boy had a prior claim; a primal claim. She watched their embrace tighten, as though they were squeezing the breath from each other, then she again set her sights on the tower and began to run.

Though she forbade herself a backward glance, as she came to the tower—her lungs already aching, and still a bruising distance to go before she found the hut—she looked. Father and son had not moved. They stood in a patch of brightness, wrapped around each other, with the clots still assembling behind them. From this distance their construction resembled the work of a monumental and funereal lace-maker. She studied the curtain a moment, her mind racing through interpretations and finding a solution to its existence both preposterous and plausible: that this was a veil behind which the Iad Uroboros were going to rise. Indeed there seemed to be motion behind its folds already; a greater darkness, assembling.

She took her gaze from the sight, glanced up briefly at the tower and its lethal load, then started off again in the direction of the hut.

The trip in the opposite direction, through the town towards the perimeter of the Loop, was no easier than Tesla's. They'd all been on too many journeys: into the earth, into the sea, to islands, caves and to the limits of their sanity. This last trip demanded energies they scarcely had to give. With every other step their bodies threatened to give out, the hard desert floor looking comfortable by contrast with the agony of advancing. But the oldest fear known to man drove them on: that of the pursuing beast. It had neither claws nor fangs, of course, but it was all the more lethal for that. A beast of fire. It was only when they reached the town that they slowed their pace long enough to exchange a few gasping words.

"How much farther?" Jo-Beth wanted to know.

"Just on the other side of the town."

Howie was staring back at the Iad curtain, which had now mounted a hundred feet and more.

"Do you think they see us?" he said.

"Who?" said Grillo. "The Iad? If they do they don't seem to be following."

"That isn't them," Jo-Beth said. "That's just their veil."

"So we've still got a chance," Howie said.

"Let's take it," said Grillo, and set the pace down the Main Street.

It wasn't chance. Tesla's mind, befuddled as it was, had the route across the desert to the hut inscribed deep into it. As she trotted (running was beyond her) it was the conversation she'd had with Grillo back at the motel that she went over in her mind, the exchange in which she'd confessed to him the extent of her spiritual ambition. If she died here in the Loop—and that was virtually inevitable—she knew she'd come to understand more about the workings of the world in the days since she'd arrived in Palomo Grove than in all the years previous. She'd had adventures beyond her body. She'd encountered incarnations of good and evil, and learned something of her condition because she resembled neither. If she was gone from this life soon, either at the instant of detonation, or at the Iad's arrival, she had no complaint at that.

But there were so many souls who had not yet made their peace with extinction, nor should have to. Infants, children, lovers. Peaceable people the planet over, whose lives were still in the making and enriching, who, if she failed now, would wake up tomorrow with any chance to taste the same adventures in spirit she'd had denied them. Slaves of the

Iad. What justice was there in that? Before coming to the Grove she'd
have given the twentieth century's answer to that question. There was no
justice because justice was a human construct and had no place in a system of matter. But mind was in matter, always. That was the revelation
of Quiddity. The sea was the crossroads, and from it all possibilities
sprang. Before everything, Quiddity. Before life, the dream of life.
Before the thing solid, the solid thing dreamt. And mind, dreaming or
awake, knew justice, which was therefore as natural as matter, its
absence in any exchange deserving of more than a fatalistic shrug. It
merited a howl of outrage; and a passionate pursuit of *why*. If she wished
to live beyond the impending holocaust it was to shout that shout. To
find out what crime her species had committed against the universal
mind that it should now be tottering on execution. That was worth living to know.

The hut was in sight. Behind her the suspicion she'd had, that the Iad
were rising behind the veil of clots, was confirmed. The giants of her
childhood nightmares were emerging from the schism, and would soon
draw that veil away. When they did they'd surely see her, and come in a
few thunderous strides to stamp her out. But they didn't hurry. Their vast
limbs took time to draw up from Quiddity; their heads (the size of houses,
every window blazing) were immense, and needed the full machinery of
their anatomies before they could be raised. When she began again
towards the hut the glimpse she'd had of the emergents began to resolve
itself in her mind's eye, her wits making coherence of their titanic mystery.

The door of the hut was closed, of course. But it wasn't locked. She
pulled it open.

Kissoon was waiting for her. The shock of the sight of him took her
breath away, and she was about to retreat out into the sun until she
realized that the body propped up against the far wall was vacated by
spirit, its system ticking on to preserve it from mortification. There was
nobody behind the glazed eyes. The door slammed closed, and without wasting any more time she named the only spirit here that could
possibly be holding the moment in Kissoon's stead.

"Raul?"

The weary air in the hut whined with his unseen presence.

"Raul? For God's sake, I know you're here. I know you're afraid. But if you can hear me, show me somehow, will you?"

The whine intensified. She had the sense that he was circling the hut, like a fly trapped in a jar.

"Raul, you've got to let go. Trust me and *let go.*"

The whine was beginning to hurt her.

"I don't know what he did to you to make you give up your body, but I know it wasn't your fault. He tricked you. He lied to you. He did the same to me. Do you understand? You're not to blame."

The air began to settle somewhat. She took a deep breath and began her persuasions again, remembering how she'd first bullied him into coming with her, back at the Mission.

"If it's anybody's fault, it's mine," she said. "Forgive me, Raul. We've both of us come to the end. But if it's any comfort, so's Kissoon. He's dead. He won't be coming back. Your body . . . won't be coming back. It's destroyed. There was no other way of killing him."

The hurt of the whine had been replaced by another, deeper ache: that of knowing how much his spirit must be suffering, dislocated and frightened, unable to let go of the moment. Kissoon's victim, as they'd both been. In some ways, so much alike. Nunciates both, learning to climb out of their limitations. Strange bedfellows, but bedfellows nevertheless. Which thought inspired another.

She spoke it.

"Can two minds occupy the same body?" she said. "If you're afraid . . . *come into me.*"

She let that notion hang in the silence, not pressing him for fear his panic would escalate. She waited beside the cold ashes of the fire, knowing every second he remained unpersuaded gave the Iad another foothold, but devoid of further arguments or invitations. She'd offered him more than she'd offered anyone in her life: total possession of her body. If he didn't accept she had no more persuasions.

After a few, breathless seconds something seemed to brush the nape of her neck, like lover's fingers, the stroke suddenly becoming a needle point.

"Is this you?" she said.

In the beat it took her to ask the question it became self-directed, as his spirit entered her head.

There was no dialogue, nor any need for dialogue. They were twin ghosts in the same machine, and in the instant of his entering entirely conversant with each other. She read from his memories the method by which Kissoon had claimed him, pulling him through to the Loop from the bathroom in North Huntley Drive, using his confusion to subdue him. He'd been easy meat. Weighed down by leaden smoke, mesmerized into performing one duty and one alone, the holding of the moment, then wrenched from his body to do that duty in a blind round of terror that had not ceased until she'd opened the door. She had no more need to instruct him in their next act they had to perform together than he'd had to tell her his story. He shared her comprehension.

She went back to the door, and opened it.

The Iad's curtain was huge enough now that its shadow touched the hut. There were still some shafts of sun breaking through, but none near the threshold upon which Tesla stood. Here there was darkness. She looked towards the veil, seeing the Iad assembled behind it. Their silhouettes were the size of thunderheads, their limbs like whips plaited to beat mountains with.

Now, she thought. *Or never. Let the moment go.*

Let—it—go.

She felt Raul do just that, his will releasing its hold and shedding the burden Kissoon had laid upon him. A wave seemed to move from them towards the tower above which the Iad loomed. After years of suspension, time was unfettered. Five-thirty on the sixteenth of July was moments away, and so was the event that marked that innocent instant as the beginning of Mankind's Last Madness.

Her thoughts went to Grillo, and to Jo-Beth and Howie, urging them on through the exit and into the safety of the Cosm, but her urgings were interrupted as a brightness began in the heart of the shadow. She couldn't see the tower, but she saw the shock spring from the platform, the ball of fire becoming visible and a second flash appearing the instant after, the brightest light she'd ever seen, from yellow to white in a blink—

We can do no more, she thought, as the fire began to swell obscenely.
I could be home.

She pictured herself—woman, man and ape in one bruised body—
standing on the step of the hut, the light of the bomb blazing on her
face. Then she imagined that same face and body in another place.
She had only seconds to work with. But thought was fast.

Across the desert she saw the hosts of the lad drawing their veil of
clots aside, as the blazing cloud grew to eclipse them. Their faces were
like flowers the scale of mountains, and they kept opening, throat
upon throat upon throat. It was an awesome display, their hugeness
seeming to conceal labyrinths, which turned inside out as they uncovered themselves. Tunnels becoming towers of flesh, if it was flesh they
had, and turning again, and turning, so that every part of them was in
constant transformation. If singularity was indeed their appetite, then
it was as salvation from this prodigious flux.

Mountains and fleas, Jaffe had said, and she saw now what he'd
meant by that. The lad was either a nation of leviathans, itching with
numberless parasites and opening their guts, over and over, in the vain
hope of shedding them, or the parasites themselves, so numerous they
imitated mountains. She would not know which, this side of life, or
Trinity. Before she could interpret the countless forms they took, the
explosion eclipsed them, burning their mystery out.

At the same moment Kissoon's Loop—its task fulfilled in a fashion its
creator could never have anticipated—disappeared. If the device on the
tower failed to consume them utterly they were undone nevertheless,
their madness and their appetite sealed up in a moment of lost time.

EIGHT

As Howie, Jo-Beth and Grillo had entered the confounding terrain at the perimeter of the Loop, the tiny time to either side of 5:30 A.M., July 16th, 1945, which Kissoon had created, commandeered and been captive of, a light had bloomed behind them. No, not bloomed. Mushrooms had no flowers. None of them looked back, but pushed their exhausted bodies to one last, superhuman effort, which carried them, the fire at their backs, into the safety of real time. They'd lain on the desert floor, unable to move, for a long while, only dragging themselves to their feet when the risk of being fricasseed where they lay became impossible to discount.

It was a long and difficult haul back to California. They found a highway after an hour of wandering, and after another hour a deserted garage along that highway. There Grillo left the lovers, knowing that hitching a ride with such freaks in tow would be impossible. He found a ride himself, after some considerable time, and in a small town bought a beaten-up truck with the entire contents of his wallet, including his credit cards, then headed back to the garage to pick Jo-Beth and Howie up and drive them back to Ventura County. They lay in the back of the truck in a deep sleep, their exhaustion so utter nothing woke them. They arrived back at the Grove just before dawn of the following day, but there was no possibility of access. The same authorities who'd been so slow, negligent, or—as was Grillo's suspicion—complicit in not defending the Grove against the forces erupting in its midst had now, with the eclipse of those forces, become obsessively cautious. The town was scaled off. Grillo didn't challenge the edict. He simply turned around before he came to the barricades, and headed along the highway until he found a place to park the truck and sleep. Their slumbers weren't interrupted. Some hours later, when he woke, he found the back seat empty. His every joint aching he got out, took a piss, then went to look for the lovers. He found them up an incline, sitting in the sun. The transformations that Quiddity had worked upon them both were already in retreat. Their hands were no longer fused, the bizarre forms that had remade their faces had burned away in the sunlight, until they were no more than marks on once flawless skin. With time they too would probably disappear. What he doubted would ever fade was the look in their eyes when they met his gaze: the stare of two people who had shared an experience nobody else in the world had shared, and had become, in that sharing, possessed by each other. More than a minute spent in their presence and he felt like an intruder. The three of them talked briefly of what was wisest to do now, and concluded that staying in the vicinity of the Grove was best. They made no mention of events in the Loop, or in Quiddity, though Grillo burned to ask what it had been like to float in the dream-sea. With rough plans laid, Grillo went back to the truck and waited for them to come down. They came after a few minutes, hand in hand.

There had been no paucity of witnesses to Tesla's relocation of a part of Coney Eye. Observers and photographers both parked on the Hill and hovering above it saw the facade grow smoky, become transparent and finally vanish entirely. With a portion of its structure summarily removed the entire house succumbed to gravity. Had there been only two or three witnesses, doubts might have been cast on the veracity of these accounts. It was only in the pages of the *National*

Enquirer and its fanciful ilk that solid wood and slate were whisked off into another plane of being. But there were twenty-two spectators in all. They each had their vocabularies to describe what they'd seen—some stark, some flowery—but the root facts remained a constant. A substantial part of Buddy Vance's museum to the true Art of America had been snatched into a different reality.

Some of the witnesses (those weariest among the number) even claimed to have caught a glimpse of that place. A white horizon and a bright sky; dust blowing around. Nevada, maybe; or Utah. Any one of a thousand wide open places. America had no shortage of those. The country was huge, and still full of emptiness. Places where a house could reappear and never be found; where mysteries could be happening every day of the week and nobody be any the wiser for it. For a few of the witnesses, seeing what they'd seen, it was the first time it had ever occurred to them that maybe a country could be *too* big, *too* full of open space. But it occurred now, and it haunted them.

One of those spaces, at least for the foreseeable future, would be the ground upon which Palomo Grove had been built.

The steady process of its destruction didn't end with Coney Eye's relocation into the Loop. Far from it. The earth had been waiting for a sign, and had got it. Cracks widened to fissures and fissures became chasms, overturning entire streets. The most affected of the villages were Windbluff and Deerdell, the latter virtually flattened by shock-waves from the vicinity of the wood, which disappeared in its entirety, leaving churned, smoking earth in its place. The Hill and its sumptuous properties were dealt as severe a blow; or several blows. It was not the houses immediately below the place where Coney Eye had stood that took the brunt of the destruction (though it would scarcely have mattered—their owners had been among the first to leave, vowing they'd not return). It was the Crescents. Emerson moved south two hundred yards, its houses concertinaed in the process. Whitman went west, the houses, by some quirk of geology, pushed and tipped into their own pools. The other three Crescents were simply laid flat, much of the debris finding its way down the Hill and damaging countless houses in its descent. All of which was academic. Nobody would be salvaging anything from their houses; the entire area was deemed unstable for six days, during which time fires raged unattended, destroying a large part of the property which the ground had not over-turned or swallowed. In this regard the unluckiest village was Still-brook, the sometime occupants of which might have eventually claimed some of their personal belongings from their houses had a fire not flared in a house on Fellowship Street on a night when the kind of wind that had once brought Grovers out into their yards to smell the ocean been blowing, the gusts driving the flames through the village with devastating speed. By morning half the village was ashes. By the evening of the same day, the other half.

It was that night, the night after Stillbrook burned, and six days after events on the Hill, that Grillo came back to the Grove. He had slept more than half of the intervening time, but he didn't feel that much better for the rest. Sleep was not the palliative it had been. He wasn't eased by it, soothed and comforted by it. When he closed his eyes his head played out scene after scene from the past. Most of the show was recent. Ellen Nguyen featured strongly, asking him over and over again to give up kisses and use his teeth; so did her son, sitting in bed surrounded by Balloon Men. There were guest appearances by Rochelle Vance, who did and said nothing, but offered her beauty to the parade: there was Good Man Fletcher, down at the Mall. There was the Jaff in the upper room at Coney Eye, sweating out power. And Witt alive. And Witt dead, face down in the water.

But starring in the story was Tesla, who'd played out her last trick on him, smiling and not saying goodbye even though she knew it was. They'd not been lovers; not even close. In a sense he'd never quite understood what he felt for her. Love certainly, but of a kind difficult to express; perhaps impossible. Which made mourning her equally problematic.

It was that sense of unfinished business between Tesla and himself which kept him from returning any of the calls Abernethy left on his answering machine back home, though God knows the story itched in him, and itched, and itched. She'd always expressed ambiguity about his making the truth public, even though she'd sanctioned his doing so at the end. But that had only been because she'd thought the issue academic, the world almost finished and little hope left for the saving of it. But the end hadn't come, and she'd died in the act of preservation. He felt honor-bound to keep his silence. Discreet as he was being, however, he couldn't keep from returning to the Grove to find out how its demise was progressing.

The town was still a no-go area when he arrived, police barricades surrounding it. They weren't difficult to bypass. The Grove's guardians had become lax in their duties in the days since it had been sealed off, given that very few people, whether sightseers, looters or residents, had been foolhardy enough to want to tread its turbulent streets. He slipped through the cordon with ease, and started his exploration of the town. The wind that had driven the fire through Still-brook the day before had dropped away completely. The smoke of that conflagration had now settled, its taste almost sweet in his mouth, like the smoke from a fire of good wood. It might have been elegiac under different circumstances, but he'd learned too much about the Grove and its tragedies to indulge such sentiments. It was impossible to view the destruction without regretting the Grove's passing. Its worst sin had been hypocrisy—going on its blithe, sunny way willfully concealing its secret self. That self had sweated out fears, and made dreams real for a while, and it had been those fears and dreams, not Jaffe and Fletcher, which had finally torn the Grove apart. The Nunciates had used the town for their arena, but they'd invented nothing in their war that the Grove had not already nurtured and fed in its heart.

He found himself wondering as he walked if perhaps there was some other way to tell the story of the Grove without flying in the face of Tesla's edict. If he forsook Swift, perhaps, and tried to find some poetic mode in which to couch all he'd experienced. It was a route he'd contemplated taking before, but now (as then) he knew without attempting it he'd fail. He'd come to the Grove a literalist, and nothing it had shown him would ever dissuade him from the cult of the reportable fact.

He made a circuit of the town, only avoiding areas where trespass would have amounted to suicide, making mental notes of the sights he saw even though he knew he couldn't *use* them. Then he slipped out again, unchallenged, and returned to L.A., and to more nights filled with replayed memories.

It wasn't the same for Jo-Beth and Howie. They'd had their dark night of the soul on Quiddity's tide, and the nights that followed, back in the Cosm, were dreamless. At least, they woke remembering nothing.

Howie tried to persuade Jo-Beth that they were best going back to Chicago, but she insisted that any such plans were premature. As long as the Grove remained a danger zone, and the bodies there were unrecovered, she wasn't going to leave the vicinity. She didn't doubt that Momma was dead. But until she was found and brought out of the Grove to be given a Christian burial any thought of a life for them both beyond this tragedy was not to be contemplated.

In the meanwhile, they had a lot of healing to do, which they did behind closed doors in a motel in Thousand Oaks, close enough to the Grove so that when it was deemed safe to return Jo-Beth would be among the first to do so. The marks that Quiddity had left upon them soon receded into memory, and they were left in a strange limbo. Everything was finished, but nothing new could begin. And, while they waited, a distance grew between them that neither encouraged or intended but neither could prevent. The love that had begun in Butrick's Steak House had instigated a series of cataclysms for which they knew they could not be held responsible, but which haunted them nevertheless. Guilt began to weigh on them as they waited in Thousand Oaks, its influence growing as they healed, and came to realize that unlike dozens, perhaps hundreds, of innocent Grovers they'd emerged physically unscathed.

On the seventh day after events in Kissoon's Loop the morning news informed them that search-parties were going into the town. The destruction of the Grove had been a big story, of course, theories being advanced from countless sources as to why the town had been singled out for such devastation when the rest of the Valley had survived with no more than a few tremors and some cracks in the freeway. There was no mention amid these reports of the phenomena witnessed at Coney Eye; governmental pressure had silenced all those who'd seen the impossible happen in front of their eyes.

The entry into the Grove was cautious at first, but by the end of the day a large number of survivors were back in the town, looking to salvage keepsakes and souvenirs from the wreckage. A few were lucky. Most weren't. For every Grover who came back to a once familiar street to find their house intact there were six who met a scene of total ruination. Everything gone; splintered, smashed or simply vanished into the ground. Of all the neighborhoods the one least damaged was paradoxically the least populated: the Mall and its immediate environs. The polished pine *Palomo Grove Shopping Center* sign at the entrance to the parking lot had slid into a hole, as had a fair portion of the lot itself, but the stores themselves were virtually undamaged, which meant, of course, that a murder investigation (never solved) got underway as soon as the bodies in the pet store were discovered. But corpses aside, had there been Grovers to shop the Mall could have opened for business that day without much more than a dusting off. Marvin Jr., of Marvin's Food and Drug, was the first to organize a removal of unspoiled stock. His brother had a store in Pasadena, and customers who couldn't give a damn where their bargains originated. He made no apology for the haste with which he got about his profiteering. Business was business, after all.

The other removal from the Grove, of course, and this a business of a grimmer sort, was that of bodies. Dogs and sound-sensitive equipment were brought in to establish whether anybody was left alive, the efforts of both drawing a blank. Then came the grisly task of retrieval. By no means every Grover who'd lost his life was found. When the final calculations were made, almost two weeks after the search began, forty-one of the town's members were unaccounted for. The earth had claimed them, then closed over their corpses. Or else the individuals in question had slipped away into the night, taking this opportunity to re-invent themselves and start afresh. One of the latter group, so rumor went, was William Witt, whose body was never recovered but whose house, upon investigation, was found to contain enough pornography to keep the Combat Zones of several cities supplied for months. He'd had a secret life, had William Witt, and the general suspicion was that he'd chosen to go and live it elsewhere.

When the identity of one of the two corpses in the pet store was revealed to be that of Jim Hotchkiss one or two of the astuter journalists noted that his had been a life dogged by tragedy. His daughter, they reminded their readers, had been one of the so-called League of Virgins, and in remarking on this the writers took a paragraph to comment on just how much grief the Grove had endured in its short life. Had it been doomed from the outset, the more fanciful commentators asked, built on cursed ground? There was some shred of solace in that thought. If not, if the Grove had simply been a victim of chance, then how many of the thousands of such communities across America were vulnerable to the same outrages?

On the second day of the search Joyce McGuire's body was found in the ruins of her house, which had sustained considerably worse damage than any of the surrounding property. It was taken for identification, as were the bulk of the bodies, to a makeshift mortuary in Thousand Oaks. That onerous duty fell to Jo-Beth, whose brother would be numbered among the missing forty-one. Identification made, arrangements were begun for her burial. The Church of Jesus Christ of Latter-day Saints looked after its own. Pastor John had survived the levelling (indeed he'd left the Grove the night of the Jaff's attack on the McGuire house and hadn't come back till the dust had settled) and it was he who organized Momma's funeral. Only once in that time did he and Howie cross paths, and Howie was quick to remind the Pastor of the night he'd blubbered beside the refrigerator. The Pastor insisted he remembered no such incident.

"Pity I haven't got a photo," Howie said. "To jog your memory. But I've got one up here." He pointed to his temples, upon which the last traces of Quiddity's reconfiguration of his flesh was fading. "Just in case I ever get tempted."

"Tempted to what?" the Pastor asked.

"To be a believer."

Momma McGuire was consigned into the embrace of her chosen God two days after that exchange. Howie didn't attend the ceremony, but was waiting for Jo-Beth when it was all over. They left for Chicago twenty-four hours later.

Their part in events was very far from over, however. The first sign that the adventure of Cosm and Quiddity had made them part of a very select band of players came half a week after they'd got to Chicago, with the arrival on their doorstep of a tall, handsome-gone-to-harrowed stranger, dressed too lightly for the weather, who introduced himself as D'Amour.

"I'd like to talk to you about what happened at Palomo Grove," he said to Howie.

"How did you find us?"

"It's my job, finding people," Harry explained. "You may have heard Tesla Bombeck mention me?"

"No, I don't think so."

"Well you can check with her."

"No I can't," Howie reminded him. "She's dead."

"So she is," D'Amour said. "So she is. My mistake."

"And even if you did know her there's nothing Jo-Beth and me have to say. We just want to forget about the Grove."

"There's not much chance of that," a voice from behind him observed. "Who is this, Howie?"

"He says he knew Tesla."

"D'Amour," the stranger said, "Harry D'Amour. I really would appreciate a few minutes of your time. Just a few. It's very important."

Howie glanced at Jo-Beth.

"Why not?" she said.

"It's damn cold out there," D'Amour observed as he stepped inside. "What happened to summer?"

"Things are bad all over," Jo-Beth said.

"You noticed," D'Amour replied.

"What are you two talking about?"

"The news," she said. "I've been watching it, you haven't."

"It's like a full moon every night," D'Amour said. "A lot of people are acting very strange. The suicide rate's doubled since the Grove Breakout. There's riots in asylums across the country. And I'd lay money we're only seeing a little part of the whole picture. There's a lot being kept under wraps."

"Who by?"

"The government. The church. Am I the first one to find you?"

"Yes," said Howie. "Why? Do you think there's going to be others?"

"For certain. You two are at the center of all this—"

"It wasn't our fault!" Howie protested.

"I'm not saying it was," D'Amour replied. "Please. I haven't come here to accuse you of anything. And I'm sure you deserve to be left in peace to get on with living. But it's not going to happen. That's the truth. You're too important. You've seen too much. Our people know it, and so do theirs."

"*Theirs?*" Jo-Beth said.

"The Iad's people. The infiltrators who kept the army at bay when it looked like the Iad were about to break out."

"How do you know so much about all this?" Howie wanted to know.

"I have to be a little careful about my sources just at the moment, but I hope I can reveal them to you eventually."

"You make it sound like we're in this with you," Howie said. "We're not. You're right, we do want to get on with living our lives, together. And we'll go wherever we have to—Europe, Australia, wherever—to do that."

"They'll find you," D'Amour said. "The Grove brought them too close to succeeding for them to give up now. They know they've got us spooked. Quiddity's tainted. Nobody's going to have many sweet dreams from now on. We're easy meat, and they know it. You might want to live ordinary lives but you can't. Not with fathers like yours."

It was Jo-Beth's turn to express shock at his words.

"What do you know about our fathers?" she said.

"They're not in Heaven, I know that," D'Amour said. "Sorry. Bad taste. Like I said, I've got my sources, and very soon I hope I can reveal them. In the meantime I need to understand what happened at the Grove better, so that we can learn by it."

"I should have done that," Howie said softly. "I had a chance to learn from Fletcher, but I never took it."

"You're Fletcher's son," D'Amour said. "His spirit's in you. It's just a question of listening to it."

"He was a genius," Howie told Harry. "I really believe that. I'm sure he was out of his mind on mescaline half the time, but he was still a genius."

"I want to hear," said D'Amour. "Do you want to tell me?"

Howie stared at him for a long moment. Then he sighed, and with a tone very like surprise said:

"Yes. I think I do."

Grillo was sitting in the 50's Café on Van Nuys Boulevard in Sherman Oaks, trying to remember what it was like to enjoy food, when somebody came and sat opposite him in the booth. It was the middle of the afternoon, and the café wasn't full. He raised his head to request some privacy but instead said:

"Tesla?"

She was dressed in quintessential Bombecksquerie: a flock of ceramic swans pinned to a midnight-blue blouse, a red bandanna, dark glasses. Her face was pale, but her lipstick, which clashed with the bandanna, was glitzy. Her eyeshadow, when she slipped her glasses down her nose, was the same shade of riot.

"Yes," she said.

"Yes what?"

"Yes *Tesla*."

"I thought you were dead."

"I've made that mistake. It's easily done."

"This isn't some illusion?" he said.

"Well the whole damn thing's that, isn't it? All a show. But us, are we any more illusory than you? No."

"Us?"

"I'll come to that in a minute. First you. How are things?"

"There's not much to tell. I went back to the Grove a couple of times, just to see who survived."

"Ellen Nguyen?"

"She wasn't found. Nor was Philip. I went through the rubble personally. God knows where she went."

"Want us to look for her? We've got *contacts* now. It hasn't been much fun, as far as homecomings go. I had a body to deal with, back at the apartment. And a lot of people asking difficult questions. But we've got some influence now, and I'm using it."

"What is this *we* business?"

"Are you going to eat that cheeseburger?"

"No."

"Good." She pulled the plate over to her side of the table. "You remember Raul?" she said.

"I never met the mind, only the body."

"Well you're meeting him now."

"I beg your pardon?"

"I found him, in the Loop. At least I found his spirit." She smiled, ketchup round her mouth. "It's difficult to make this sound *wholesome* . . . but he's inside me. Him, and the ape he used to be, and me, all in one body."

"Your dream come true," Grillo said. "All things to all men."

"Yes, I suppose so. I mean, *we* suppose so. I keep forgetting to include us all. Maybe it's best I don't try."

"You've got cheese on your chin."

"That's it, bring us down."

"Don't get me wrong. I'm glad to see you. But . . . I was just beginning to get used to the fact that you weren't around. Should I still call you Tesla?"

"Why not?"

"Well you're not, are you? You're more than that."

"Tesla's fine. A body's called by what it seems to be, right?"

"I suppose so," Grillo said. "Do I look like I'm freaked out by all this?"

"No. Are you?"

He shook his head. "Weird, but no. I'm cool."

"That's my Grillo."

"You mean *our* Grillo."

"No. I mean mine. You can fuck all the great beauties in Los Ange-les and I've still got you. I'm the great imponderable in your life."

"It's a plot."

"You don't like it?"

Grillo smiled. "It's not bad," he said.

"Don't be coy," she said. She took hold of his hand. "We've got some times ahead, and I need to know you're with me."

"You know I am."

"Good. Like I said, the ride's not over."

"Good. Where'd you get that from? That was my headline."

"Synchronicity," Tesla said. "Where was I? D'Amour thinks they'll try New York next. They've got footholds there. Had them for years. So I'm gathering half the team together, he's gathering the other half."

"What can I do?" Grillo said.

"How do you fancy Omaha, Nebraska?"

"Not much."

"That's where this last phase began, believe it or not. In the Omaha Post Office."

"You're kidding me."

"That's where the Jaff got his half-witted idea of the Art."

"What do you mean: half-witted?"

"He only got a piece of the thing, not the whole solution."

"I don't follow."

"Even Kissoon didn't know what the Art was. He had clues, but only clues. It's vast. It collapses time and place. It makes every-thing *one* again. *The past, the future and the dreaming moment between . . . one immortal day . . .*"

"Beautiful," Grillo said.

"Would Swift approve?"

"Fuck Swift."

"Somebody should have."

"So . . . *Omaha?*"

"That's where we start. That's where all the lost mail of America ends up, and it may have some clues for us. People know stuff, Grillo. Even without realizing it, they *know*. That's what makes us wonderful."

"And they write it down?"

"Yes. Then they send the letters out."

"And they end up in Omaha."

"Some of them. Pay for the cheeseburger. I'll be waiting outside."

He did, and she was.

"I should have eaten," he said. "I'm suddenly hungry."

D'Amour didn't leave until late in the evening, and when he did he left two exhausted storytellers behind him. He took copious notes, flipping the pages of his pad back and forth as he tried to make sense of the way fragments of information related to one another.

When Howie and Jo-Beth were talked out, he gave them his card with a New York address and number on it, scrawling another, private number on the back.

"Move as soon as you can," he advised. "Tell nobody where you're going. Nobody at all. And when you get there—wherever it is— change your names. Pretend you're married."

Jo-Beth laughed.

"Old-fashioned, but why not?" D'Amour said. "People don't gossip about married folks. And as soon as you've arrived, call me and tell me where I'll be able to find you. I'll be in contact from then on. I can't promise guardian angels, but there are forces that can watch out for you. I've got a friend called Norma I'd like you to meet. She's good at finding watchdogs."

"We can buy a dog for ourselves," Howie said.

"Not her kind you can't. Thank you for all you've told me. I have to get going. It's a long drive."

"You driving to New York?"

"I hate flying," he said. "I had a bad experience in the air one time, minus plane. Remind me to tell you about it. You should know the dirt on me now I know it about you."

He went to the door, and let himself out, leaving the small apartment reeking of European cigarettes.

"I need some fresh air," Howie said to Jo-Beth once he'd gone. "Want to walk with me?"

It was well past midnight, and the cold from which D'Amour had stepped five hours before had worsened, but it stirred them from their exhaustion. As their torpor lifted they talked.

"There was a lot you told D'Amour that I didn't know," Jo-Beth said.

"Like what?"

"The stuff that happened on the Ephemeris."

"You mean Byrne?"

"Yes. I wonder what he saw up there."

"He said he'd come back and tell me, if we all survived."

"I don't want secondhand reports. I'd like to see for myself."

"Go back to the Ephemeris?"

"Yes. As long as it was with you, I'd like that."

Perhaps inevitably, their route had brought them down to the Lake. The wind had teeth, but its breath was fresh.

"Aren't you afraid of what Quiddity could do to us," Howie said, "if we ever go back?"

"Not really. Not if we're together."

She took hold of his hand. They were both suddenly sweating, despite the cold, their innards churning the way they had the first time, when their eyes had met across Butrick's Steak House. A little age had passed since then, transforming them both.

"We're both desperadoes now," Howie murmured.

"I suppose we are," Jo-Beth said. "But it's all right. Nobody can separate us."

"I wish that was true."

"It *is* true. You know it is."

She raised her hand, which was still locked in his, between them.

"Remember this?" she said. "That's what Quiddity showed us. It joined us together."

The shudders in her body passed through her hand, through the sweat that ran between their palms, and into him.

"We have to be true to that."

"Marry me?" he said.

"Too late," she replied. "I already did."

They were at the Lake's edge now, but of course it wasn't Michigan they saw as they looked out into the night, it was Quiddity. It hurt, thinking of that place. The same kind of hurt that touched any living soul when a whisper of the dream-sea touched the edge of consciousness. But so much sharper for them, who couldn't dismiss the longing, but knew Quiddity was real; a place where love might found continents.

It would not be long before dawn, and at the first sign of the sun they'd have to go to sleep. But until the light came—until the real insisted upon their imaginations—they stood watching the darkness, waiting, half in hope and half in fear, for that other sea to rise from dreams and claim them from the shore.